PROPHECY:

WEB OF DECEIT

M. K. HUME

PROPHECY
BOOK THREE

WEB OF DECEIT

headline
review

First published in 2013 by HEADLINE REVIEW
An imprint of HEADLINE PUBLISHING GROUP

1

Cataloguing in Publication Data is available from the British Library

Hardback ISBN 978 0 7553 7150 1
Trade paperback ISBN 978 0 7553 7151 8

Typeset in Golden Cockerel by Avon DataSet Ltd,
Bidford-on-Avon, Warwickshire

Printed and bound in Great Britain by
Clays Ltd, St Ives plc

Headline's policy is to use papers that are natural, renewable and recyclable
products and made from wood grown in sustainable forests. The logging and
manufacturing processes are expected to conform to the environmental
regulations of the country of origin.

HEADLINE PUBLISHING GROUP
An Hachette UK Company
338 Euston Road
London NW1 3BH

www.headline.co.uk
www.hachette.co.uk

This book is dedicated to Doctor Maurice Heiner, a thoracic physician *par excellence* who achieved the impossible task of convincing my recalcitrant husband, Michael Hume, that if he did not give up smoking his tenure on life would be measured in months.

That he was successful is a measure of Maurice's professional ability and the personal qualities that Michael admires in all of his friends.

Michael has survived to continue his adventurous life for twenty-three years after coming under Maurice's care, twenty-three years of leaping (small) buildings at a single bound and only tripping on rare occasions. He hasn't touched a cigarette, not for fear of the Grim Reaper, but for the sole reason of not wanting to fail Maurice's confidence in him.

In many respects, Maurice is probably responsible for all of my books being written, for Michael is the renowned bully who frog-marched me into becoming a novelist. Without his 'pushy' manner and his unsurpassed ability as an editor, my writing career wouldn't have happened.

ACKNOWLEDGEMENTS

I know that most readers are so anxious to get into the nitty-gritty of their latest acquisition that they barely glance at the acknowledgements pages of a novel. But I hope you make an exception in this case because my advisers and helpers have made a major contribution towards bringing this novel to life. They made a deep impression on me, the book and the outcome I was seeking.

My editor, Clare Foss, is a veritable tiger: she is a dynamite stick and is the ideal editor for an author who lives in remote parts of the world. She is clever, supportive, quick-thinking and far-sighted, and I'm so glad that she brings my books to the public. I thank her.

Aslan Byrne and Emily Griffin are vital to the support I receive from Headline, and both gave me excellent moral and practical help in the production of this epic. Aslan is a Sales genius whose finger is firmly on the pulse, while Emily helped to smooth the way and, for a distant Australian, what more can I ask? My thanks go to you both. My thanks also go to the editors and artists whose labours and professionalism have brought my Merlin to life. I thank you, and I couldn't have completed this mammoth task without you.

Nancy Webber, *my* copy editor, is a genius, pure and simple. I always try to present a mistake-free manuscript, but Nancy finds every weakness, every redundancy and every error. Her wit, cleverness and deft touch will always make her a valuable asset for any publishing house. Thank you, Nancy.

Yet, it's the faces of the people I met when researching this work that still haunt me, friends who took in this wandering Australian and treated me kindly in strange historic places. Inga Hobbs, Ken Warner and Veryan Polglase of Glastonbury and the people of The Marketplace Inn were a joy to meet and a pleasure to befriend. I also thank you. Nancy Noble, Pat and Nick Taunton and Niel Owens of The Coachhouse Inn of Chester were also wonderful, and are people who are going to play a major part in a future project.

Thank you also to Julie and Peter Humphreys and Gwyllym of Carnavon who provided me with a whole new perspective on the Welsh People. Up and down the wild and strange places, I travelled and marvelled at their generosity of spirit. Again, I thank you, and I hope you like Myrddion's tests of strength. As my husband often says, the greatest export that ever came out of Wales were the Welsh people, both men and woman, who emigrated to foreign countries such as Canada and Australia and made our world such a wonderful place in which to live. Their courage heartens me.

M. K. Hume

DRAMATIS PERSONAE

Agricola	The Roman commander who conquered Britain during the first century AD. Among other atrocities attributed to him was the mass murder of the Druid population who had been driven from Britain to Mona Island off the coast of Wales.
Ambrosius	Also known as Ambrosius Aurelianus or Ambrosius Imperator, he was the son of Constantine III and the brother of Constans II and Uther Pendragon, all of whom were, at various times, High Kings of the Britons. According to the legend, Constans II was succeeded in turn by Vortigern, Ambrosius, Uther and Arthur.
Andrewina Ruadh	Also known as Bridei (Pict). As a young girl, Ruadh is captured by the Picts, marries Garnaid and bears his children. Later, she is captured by the Celts when King Talorc is defeated in a battle with the forces of Prince Luka of the Brigante. She becomes the concubine of King Ambrosius and, later, of Myrddion Merlinus. She is an essential character in the birth and rescue of the babe, Artorex, from the clutches of Uther Pendragon.
Annwynn	A female healer who resides in Segontium.

	She is the original master of Myrddion Merlinus.
Ardabur Aspar	Flavius Ardabur Aspar, Magister Militum of Constantinople, made a clandestine visit to Britain approximately 435AD. Shipwrecked and washed up on a remote beach outside of Segontium, he was rescued by Branwyn, a royal princess. He raped her and she became pregnant with Myrddion Merlinus.
Artorex/Artor:	The legitimate son of Uther Pendragon, High King of the Britons, and Ygerne, widow of Gorlois, the King of Cornwall.
Aude	Aude is one of the women who is recruited into Myrddion's household as a servant woman. She is placed in charge of the cleanliness of the house, bandages and medications used by the healers. She had previously been a prostitute.
Berwyn	A female gardener at the House of Healers. She is disfigured by a strawberry mark across her face.
Bors	The nephew and successor of King Gorlois of Cornwall.
Botha	A senior officer in the service of Uther Pendragon. He is oath-bound to the High King for life.
Bouddicca	The Iceni queen who led a revolt against the Romans in the region surrounding Londinium.
Brangaine	A camp follower whose husband died in the service of King Vortigern, she becomes an assistant to Myrddion Merlinus and travels to

	Constantinople with the party of healers. She adopts two children during the journey.
Branwyn	The daughter of Olwyn and Godric, and granddaughter of Melvig ap Melwy, king of the Deceangli Tribe. She is the mother of Myrddion Merlinus after suffering rape at the hands of Flavius Ardabur Aspar.
Bridie	Like Brangaine, she is one of Myrddion's assistants who travels to Constantinople. She marries Finn Truthteller and bears a child to him. Myrddion agrees to accompany Uther to Venta Belgarum if Bridie and Finn are permitted to return to Segontium.
Brychan	`Fat-Arse Brychan', as he is called, is a slovenly innkeeper at Tomen-y-Mur. Myrddion stays here when he visits his mother. He also uses this inn to meet with the ex-slave, Gruffydd, who is part of Myrddion's spy network.
Bryn ap Synnel	Father of Llanwith pen Bryn, later to become mentor to King Arthur.
Cadoc ap Cadwy	A warrior in Vortigern's service who comes from the Forest of Dean. He becomes Myrddion's assistant and accompanies the healer on the journey to Constantinople and later follows him to the court of King Ambrosius.
Cait	The serving girl at Brychan's inn at Tomen-y-Mur. She is Brychan's bastard daughter.
Carwen	A prostitute in Aquae Sulis who seduces Myrddion Merlinus.
Carys	Daughter of Calgacus Minor, the son of Calgacus Major, King of the Novantae Tribe.

Uther's concubine, she is murdered by the High King.

Cathan   Cathan is an infant found under a pile of dead bodies at the wall at Verulamium when the common folk who lived outside the town walls were slaughtered by the Saxons. Brangaine becomes the child's foster mother.

Catigern   The illegitimate second son of King Vortigern who is killed by Hengist in revenge for his brother's murder on the Night of the Long Knives.

Ceridwen   A Celtic enchantress. She possesses the Cauldron of Poetic Inspiration.

Cletus One Ear   Husband of Fillagh, and brother-in-law of Olwyn. He is a successful farmer, and lives with Fillagh on a farm near Caer Fyrddin. Along with his son, he becomes part of Myrddion's spy network.

Constans II   High King of the Britons and elder brother of Ambrosius and Uther. He was murdered by Vortigern and his throne was stolen.

Don   The Celtic goddess representing the Mother. Out of superstition, her name was rarely spoken aloud. She develops some of the characteristics of the Roman goddess as well.

Dyfri   A male servant at the House of Healers. He works in the scriptorium and is trained as a herb-master responsible for potions and herbs.

Fillagh   Aunt Fillagh is the younger sister of Myrddion's grandmother, Olwen. She assisted with his birth and gave sanctuary to

	Branwyn and Olwen in her home at Caer Fyrddin.
Finn (Truthteller)	Finn is Myrddion's apprentice who travels with the healer to Constantinople. He marries Bridie.
Fionnuala	Fionnuala is the wife of Gron, the owner of The Flower Maiden Inn, which is situated just within the walls of Verulamium. Myrddion's party breaks a journey here and they are trapped here during a Saxon raid.
Flavia	One of Myrddion's great loves who betrays him and becomes a concubine of his father, Flavius Ardabur Aspar.
Flavius Aetius	Aetius, the last great general of the Roman Empire, was murdered by the Emperor Valentinian. With a coalition force of 200,000 Visigoth, Frank and Roman warriors, he fought an army of twice that size under the command of Attila the Hun at the Battle of the Catalaunian Plains near Châlons. The battle took approximately one day, and he fought Attila's forces to a standstill in one of the world's greatest battles of all time.
Fortuna	The Roman goddess of chance or luck.
Gawayne	Son of King Lot and Queen Morgause, brother of Agravaine and Geraint.
Geoffrey	Geoffrey of Monmouth wrote a number of works including *The History of the Kings of Britain* and the Vita Merlini. His writings are influential in that they are believed to be copies of far earlier works that have been lost over time.

Goll	Goll is a humble shepherd who tends his sheep near Tomen-y-Mur. He gives information to Myrddion about his master, Maelgwr, who is Branwyn's husband.
Gorlois	The Boar of Cornwall who is the king of the Dumnonii tribe. He is married to Ygerne, and is the father of Morgan and Morgause.
Gron	Gron is the gloomy, pessimistic landlord of The Flower Maiden, an inn just within the walls of Verulamium.
Gruffydd	A Celtic warrior who is taken into captivity by the Saxons. A fluent Saxon speaker, he becomes central to Myrddion's spy network and later becomes an aide to Uther Pendragon and King Arthur.
Hengist	A Saxon aristocrat who serves under Vortigern as a mercenary for a number of years. He eventually rejoins the Saxons and becomes the Thane of the Kentish Saxons and, later, rules the lands to the north of the Wash.
Horsa	Horsa is the brother of Hengist. He was treacherously murdered by the Celts in an incident that resulted in the famed Night of the Long Knives. In the Saxon histories, he is linked in legend to the horse.
Hrothnar	A Saxon bully who holds the post of docks master in Dubris.
Leonates	Leonates is the king of the Dobunni Tribe. They are notable for their Roman, epicurean habits.
Llanwith pen Bryn	Son of Bryn ap Synnell. He becomes a mentor to King Arthur.

Lot	King of the Otadini tribe north of Hadrian's Wall. He is the husband of Morgause.
Lucius	The Bishop of Glastonbury.
Luka	Prince of the Brigante tribe. He becomes a mentor to King Arthur.
Madoc pen Madar	Ex-king of the Cantii tribe. He is the Seneschal in the court of Ambrosius.
Maelgwn	Elder brother of Maelgwr. He is the first husband of Branwyn.
Maelgwr	Brother of Maelgwn. He becomes Branwyn's second husband.
Magnus Maximus	The legendary Roman ruler of Britain. The grandfather of Ambrosius.
Maerwen (Grannie)	A widow who is employed by Myrddion to care for his mother, Branwyn, after she is saved from ill-treatment at the hands of his stepfather, Maelgwr.
Melvig ap Melwy	The king of the Deceangli Tribe. He is the father of Olwyn, grandfather of Branwyn and great-grandfather of Myrddion Merlinus.
Melvyn ap Melvig	He is the son of Melvig, and succeeds him on the throne.
Mithras	An obscure deity in Zoroastrianism. He represents the father figure and was adopted as the warrior god of the Roman soldiery.
Morgan	Eldest daughter of Gorlois and Ygerne, sister to Morgause and half-sister to Arthur, who becomes High King of the Britons.
Morgause	Daughter of Gorlois and Ygerne, sister to Morgan and half-sister to King Arthur. Husband of King Lot and mother of Agravaine, Gawaine and Geraint.

Muirne (Sea Bright)	Wise woman in Venta Belgarum who is an advisor to Uther Pendragon.
Myrddion Merlinus	Myrddion is the modern-day Merlin. He is named after the Sun, and his name means Lord of Light. He is often referred to in the legends as the Demon Seed.
Olwyn	Daughter of Melvig ap Melwy, husband of Eddius, mother of Branwyn and grandmother of Myrddion. She dies at the hands of King Vortigern.
Pascent	Real name is Vengis. He is the eldest son of King Vortigern and Rowena, a Saxon princess.
Paulus	The bishop of Venta Belgarum.
Praxiteles	Praxiteles is Myrddion's personal assistant. They met in Constantinople after the servant lost his trading empire through misadventure. He is a member of the Scipio family.
Pridenow	Father of Queen Ygerne of Cornwall.
Rhedyn	One of Myrddion's female assistants. She travels to Constantinople with Myrddion's party of healers.
Rowena	The second wife of King Vortigern. She is of Saxon descent and is the mother of Vengis and Katigern. She is poisoned by Uther Pendragon.
Seirian	A red-haired servant who is the lover of Maelgwr, the husband of Myrddion's mother, Branwyn.
Septimus	Septimus is the captain of a century hired by Uther Pendragon to fight at Verulamium.
Targo	A mercenary in Ambrosius's army at the

	Battle of Verulamium. He will later become the mentor of King Arthur.
Thorketil	The Saxon thane who wins a major battle at Verulamium. He is later defeated by an army led by Ambrosius and Uther Pendragon.
Ulfin	A warrior in Uther Pendragon's guard.
Uther Pendragon	The son of Constantine III and the brother of Constans II and Ambrosius Aurelianus, all of whom were to become High Kings of the Britons. Constans II was succeeded in turn by Vortigern, Ambrosius, Uther and Arthur. Uther, in company with Ambrosius, returned to Britain after many years in exile.
Vortigern	The High King of the northern Britons of Cymru some generations before the emergence of Ambrosius, Uther Pendragon and Arthur. He is remembered as the monarch who welcomed the Saxons to migrate into Britain to appease his Saxon queen, Rowena.
Vortimer	Son of King Vortigern and brother of Catigern. They are half-brothers of Vengis and Katigern.
Willa	An orphan child who travels with Myrddion to Constantinople. She was found as one of the few survivors of the battle of Tornai that was put to the sword by Attila the Hun.
Ygerne	Ygerne is the wife of Gorlois, the Boar of Cornwall. After his death, she marries Uther Pendragon. She is the natural mother of King Arthur.

Myrddion's chart of pre-Arthurian Roman Britain

PROLOGUE

Do not hide
that 'twas he was my heart's love,
Whatso'er I love beside.

Celtic poem

The wind was a live thing. It swirled through the conical stone huts that clung to the side of the cliff like neat, round limpets. It lifted the long grasses between the narrow paths and then twisted them into plaits of green, as if Tintagel were preparing for her bridegroom as she combed her long, turquoise and emerald hair. While she dreamed, the wind took Ygerne's own plaits and dragged them into long skeins that bared her fragile face and lit her eyes from within. Tintagel breathed gently below her feet; she felt the soft thrumming of its heart fluttering through the stones of the court overlooking the causeway. She sensed the surge of waves around Tintagel's heels and almost believed that her hands could sink into the rock and become one with the fabric of the fortress, which was both her home and her protection.

'I am the Queen of the Dumnonii,' she whispered aloud to remind herself of her title and her life, but her words were blown away by the winds running before the storm.

As the first raindrops pattered fatly onto the flagging, the sound of a hunting horn shivered up her spine with its raucous combination of threat and welcome. A horse's hooves could be heard clearly from far below. Because of their speed, Ygerne knew that no enemy sought to invade the causeway fortifications. Only the master, or one of his allies, would approach the castle with such haste and arrogance.

'The master comes,' a stout serving woman cried, and began to straighten Ygerne's plain unbleached skirts and the ornate scarf that covered her hair. 'The master is at the gates, my queen. Come away, and I'll comb that ragamuffin hair of yours.'

The servant clucked her tongue with affectionate irritation at the state of her mistress's locks, knotted into snarls by the fingers of the wind. Ygerne's cheeks were flushed from the cold air, and excitement gave them the high colour of a girl. Gorlois was at the gates: her heart lifted at the thought of her doting husband and his huge, beautiful brown eyes.

Herded into the fortress by her maidservants, Ygerne consented to be combed and polished, dressed and prodded, until her women were satisfied with her appearance. But Ygerne was careless of her beauty, being ignorant of the worth of a face of such delicacy of bone and shape that men ached to own her. She set little store by surface appearances, and possessed few traces of guile or vanity. If anything, she distrusted the quality and depth of her character and the strength of her personality; her superficial attractiveness was an accident of birth.

Then Gorlois was in the fortress and she could hear his iron-heeled boots striking the stones while his huge, generous nature filled the walls so that the castle rang and echoed with his laughter.

'Ah, my beloved wife, you are as beautiful as ever. My eyes have hungered to see you,' he shouted as he picked her up and swung her easily off her feet until she was dizzy and giggling.

'Gorlois, my lord – enough!' she laughed as her plaits began to unravel and curl all over again. 'My maid will be cross with me now, for she's only just straightened my hair.'

Gorlois held her close and breathed in the perfume of that knee-length hair and the shimmer of gold and russet in its nut-brown waves. He loved his wife's hair and could play with its long tresses for hours once the sharp pang of his physical need was satisfied. Ygerne always smelled of lavender and roses, although as a mere male the king had no idea how she managed to be so sweet and clean. He was content to languish in her arms and to luxuriate in her never-failing beauty.

'Put me down, Gorlois,' she whispered, tugging playfully on his greying beard. 'What will Ceri and Valmai think to see the master and mistress cavorting like newly promised lovers rather than an old married couple. I am nearly seven and thirty, so I am well past the age for such behaviour.'

'You will remain lovely forever and I have missed my wife during my absence,' Gorlois muttered into her soft white throat, his voice thickening with desire. He had ridden with Ambrosius, the High King of the Britons, throughout the spring and summer as they drove the barbarous Saxons back to Londinium, but he had yearned for his wife through every weary mile and in each ugly conflict as if she were the most potent and addictive of wines.

For all her protestations, the queen retained her extraordinary appeal despite the approach of old age. She was very tall for a woman, but any appearance of robustness was nullified by an extreme slenderness that suggested fragility. Her skin was remarkably thin and very white, so that the contours of her face held a blue tinge from the flood of blood through the surface veins. Her features were so symmetrical and cleanly sculpted that her appearance could easily have seemed bland, but her huge, lambent blue-grey eyes created an incandescence that seemed as frail as new grass and as crystalline as clean water. From her long, delicate fingers to her elegant, narrow feet, every aspect of Ygerne's appearance was pleasing to the eye.

'I have received word from King Lot, beloved,' Gorlois told her later, as they luxuriated in the king's great bed under a coverlet of bearskin. 'Morgause quickens with child once more.'

'Another? So soon? Our daughter will populate the north at this rate. Still, I do long to see her *bairns*, as her dull husband calls them.' Ygerne giggled like a girl into her husband's masculine shoulder, which still smelled faintly of horse. 'Why are Morgause's children given names that are so similar? Gawayne, Agravaine, Geraint . . . heavens! It's hard to remember them all, I swear. Still, I wish Morgan were settled, like her sister. She'll be four and twenty by the winter solstice and I swear she shows no inclination to wed. She'll drive me crazy with her passion for magic, and she fills her room with some very odd and ugly things. I fear for her, Gorlois. She dabbles with forces she doesn't understand.'

'And you *do* understand them, my lovely?' Gorlois asked lazily and nuzzled the palm of her hand. His luxuriant moustache tickled her skin and she giggled once more, but distractedly, and her lovely face was soon serious again.

'She doesn't know her own strength,' Ygerne whispered. 'She's too passionate and impatient to count the cost. She longs for power and will come to ruin if we don't check her. We've cosseted our girl overmuch.'

'That little spitfire should have been born a boy.' Gorlois grinned at his worried wife with a satiated man's indulgence. 'What a son she'd have made! But I'll not pine if she remains a child for a little longer. Like her mother's, Morgan's beauty is ageless.'

'Nothing lasts forever, husband. Not beauty and certainly not love. It's time that Morgan put away her childishness, else she'll perish from her own foolhardy nature. Dark magic will devour her whole.'

Gorlois ran his forefinger sleepily down the perfection of Ygerne's cheekbone. 'Any child of yours couldn't fail to be beautiful and good. Now, go to sleep, woman, for your old husband is weary.' Manlike, he rolled over and was soon snoring robustly.

For several hours, wakeful in the thick warm darkness, Ygerne watched as her husband slept with the intensity and abandon of a child. When his eyes began to move under his closed lids she knew that he dreamed, and when his body thrashed and struggled in their warm, dark nest she knew that he battled unseen enemies. So she watched over him as the windy, rain-drowned night wore away to be replaced by a newly woven dawn that was fresh, highly coloured and vivid. Only then did the eyes of the Dumnonii queen close in sleep.

And even in the thrall of her own dreams, she felt a compulsion to guard her beloved Gorlois, as if only the alertness of her pale eyes could protect him from some nameless horror. She could hear the monster coming as she slept, drawing ever closer to Tintagel on scaly talons, so that even in the safety of Gorlois's arms she knew that neither husband nor wife would ever sleep in perfect peace again.

Ygerne had not been the only soul who was awake during the long hours of darkness. In a narrow room, Morgan leaned on a wooden window ledge and stared out at the last of the storm. The darkness was impenetrable before the dawn, except when forked lightning sizzled and flashed into the sea. Morgan held her hand out into the darkness of the night and imagined that she could grasp that power and master it, until she was acknowledged as the most fearsome woman in the world.

She smiled and sucked raindrops off her fingers as if tasting the sweat of the gods.

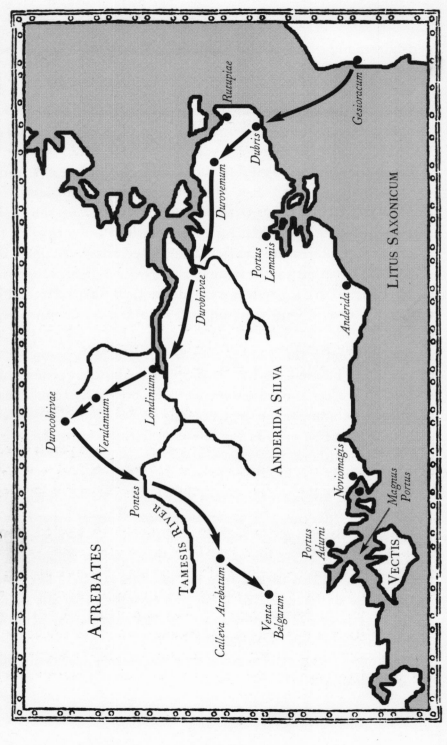

CHAPTER I

AN UNPROMISING WELCOME

Men are in the shout (of war); the ford is frozen over;
Cold the wave, variegated the bosom of the sea;
The eternal God give us counsel!

Black Book of Carmarthen

The most eagerly anticipated return to places of one's past is often a bitter disappointment, for nothing stays the same. And so it was with Dubris, when the travellers returned after their sea journey from Gesoriacum.

Spring had barely come when they set sail, so the healers wore thick cloaks to protect their chilled flesh after some years in warmer climes where even the coldest of winters lacked a true bite. But weather apart, Dubris had changed in the six years since their departure for the Middle Sea. The Saxons had arrived in a slow trickle of traders that had escalated into a flood of unchecked immigrants. Without having to strike a single blow, the Saxon stain had spread throughout the city and out into the surrounding countryside where it began to take root.

Myrddion had learned that the isles of Britain were not the entire world and that their towns were small, unimportant and bucolic when compared with the great cities of Rome, Ravenna or Constantinople. More tellingly, the healers had experienced the great ports of the Middle Sea, so that Dubris, which had seemed so large and bustling six years earlier, now seemed a minor centre of trade. This impression was not improved by a layer of grime, wood-smoke and neglect that reminded Myrddion of the port of Ostia. The warehouses and docks were in a similar state of dilapidation and the faces of the labourers had the same pinched tenseness as those of the inhabitants of the Italic port.

But there the similarities ended. Fish in huge wicker baskets added their own distinctive aroma to small docks of splintering wood that stretched out into the deeper waters. Piles of goods were stacked ready to be carried to the warehouses, while huge bales were being loaded onto vessels of all shapes, sizes and styles for the voyages to their ultimate destinations.

The faces were as mixed in race as those they had seen in Ostia, but without the exotic tints of Africa and the east. Myrddion even recognised some Franks on a large, disciplined vessel and reminded himself that these northerners had been crude barbarians fifty years earlier when they were scrabbling for land and power in Gaul.

'But the Franks are now civilised and so the world changes,' Cadoc snorted cynically at his master's comment. 'Eventually, the Saxons will be indistinguishable from us.'

The healers began the arduous task of disembarkation, moving their many barrels, bales, chests and packages into a neat pile on the dock. While they worked, Myrddion wondered at the ease with which the northern tribes had passed down through the land of the Franks and then crossed the narrow channel to Britain.

'At least our homeland still smells of the Britain we knew.' Cadoc spoke for them all. 'Woodsmoke and rain!'

'Aye. But this place makes me nervous. We're attracting far too much attention from the dockworkers, so I'd like to be gone as soon as possible.' Myrddion worried at his thumbnail with his teeth as he examined the melange of faces. 'Work your magic, Cadoc. Find us two wagons and sufficient horses for our needs. And make it as fast as you can, because my shoulder blades are starting to itch.'

'Too many sodding great Saxons – and all eyeing our baggage,' Cadoc whispered in agreement. 'I'll be back as soon as I complete my task, master.'

He disappeared into the crowd on the edges of the wharf.

In the bustle of the dock, Myrddion felt intimidated by the hostile stares that were fixed on the small party. He knew they presented an exotic and alien picture in their outlander clothing, but this wharf was part of home so he felt dislocated and disappointed. Uncharacteristically, he loosened his sword in its sheath, conscious that many covert glances had assessed every weapon of these newcomers.

'You can't leave your shit on my wharf, my fine young cockerel,' a raucous voice bellowed from behind him.

Myrddion spun swiftly and fell into a slight crouch, one hand on the pommel of his sword and the other gripping his tall staff. The women huddled together nervously and Finn handed his infant son to his wife, Bridie, in order to reach his own weapon if the need should arise. White-haired Praxiteles, the Greek servant who had accompanied them from Constantinople, merely grinned widely and waited.

'Who are you to accost my party and tell me where or what I may put on a wharf used for public access?' Myrddion's voice was as imperious and as careless as the tone that would have been adopted by Ardabur Aspar, his father, at the eastern emperor's court. Sometimes arrogance had it usefulness.

The man who confronted the small party looked, superficially, like any wharf rat grown powerful because of his added bulk and height. A large man, he was very wide in girth, almost fat, which was an unusual feature in a northerner. But, unlike Hengist and Horsa, whom Myrddion had admired, this man was filthy. His nails were black crescents on greasy, unwashed paws and it was impossible to determine the colour of his hair because it was so heavily thickened by bear grease and grime. His eyes were a muddy green and his face was very brown and weathered, with a ruddy hue under a generous coating of dirt.

When he spoke, he revealed yellowed fangs and several missing teeth, especially in the front of his mouth. Myrddion noted the ridged scar tissue on the man's knuckles and swiftly concluded that this thug loved to fight.

'I'm Hrothnar of Dubris, master of the docks, and you owe me a gold coin for landing.' The large man grinned as a small group of shifty dockworkers moved into position behind him. 'Pay up, my fine cockerel, and I'll guarantee your women will go untouched.'

Myrddion sneered back at the hulking brute with a contemptuous twitch of his lips. 'Is this the way that Dubris greets travellers, Hrothnar?' He smiled as he waited for the big man to make an aggressive movement against them. 'What law permits you to levy these ridiculous charges?'

'It's not a charge – it's a donation to the poor workers of the docks. And it's your choice if you pay or not, but three men won't stop us from taking what is ours to confiscate. What have you got that's so precious, I wonder.'

Myrddion continued to smile reasonably, but he felt his slow anger eating away at his common sense, and he bit his lip to mitigate his rising fury.

'Beware, Hrothnar of Dubris, for I have friends in high places.'

'You? You're a damned Celt! No matter how fine your clothes might be, you're nothing but a stinking, Rome-loving shit-eater like the rest of your cowardly tribe. What are you going to do that would stop us taking what we want from those packs of yours?'

'Little Willa began to cry at the raised voices, so Brangaine rummaged in a nearby pack and produced a small cake, drenched and sticky with honey. The lout barely spared the widow a glance, which was foolish, for Praxiteles saw her palm one of her master's scalpels in her right hand.

'I have served many kings. Among them were High King Vortigern of the Britons, King Merovech of the Frankish lands and King Theodosius of the Visigoths, and I am owed a debt of honour by your thane, Hengist, who carves a kingdom out of the northern lands of Britain. You would be foolish to presume that I, Myrddion Merlinus, or my companions, are harmless.'

Myrddion had difficulty framing the prideful words with their necessary disdain for lesser mortals, but if he read his adversary correctly, Hrothnar would only be dissuaded from violence if he feared personal repercussions. Unfortunately, greed was too powerful an incentive for the thug.

'Hengist is far away, and he grows old and weak in the north, Myrddion whoever-you-are. I've not heard of you, young cock. But you *will* hand over a gold coin, or I'll take everything you've got.'

'Not easily,' Finn said softly, and drew his sword. Praxiteles produced a stout club from beneath his cloak and Myrddion hefted his serpent staff.

'Oh, I'm so frightened!' Hrothnar scoffed, beginning to move forward with five of his thugs spread out behind him. He was swinging a leather tube filled with sand, a deadly and effective weapon in knowledgeable hands. The weighted sap hissed through the air as Hrothnar swung it with the proficiency of much practice.

But it never reached its target. The Saxon had chosen to attack Myrddion because he was the leader and seemed to be the weakest among the men in his party, but Myrddion had been under-estimated by many adversaries. The serpent staff, purchased at Marathon, was swung in a backhanded movement that caught the lout squarely on the side of his jaw. By luck rather than good management, the blow connected with sufficient force to fell Hrothnar like a slaughtered ox.

With their leader lying insensible on the ground, his followers continued to move forward threateningly in the belief that five men were more than enough to smother any opposition. Perhaps this assumption would have proved to be correct, but Brangaine sensed their distraction and leapt off the pile of baggage with a blood-curdling, tribal scream. She slashed at the foremost bully with the scalpel she had palmed and the razor-sharp tool caught him across the arm, slashing through cloth, skin and muscle as if it were slicing its way through butter.

As he stared foolishly at the sudden rush of blood that began to gush down his arm, the man was easily knocked unconscious by Praxiteles's club, while Finn advanced towards the four remaining thugs with eyes that were reddening with rage. As they saw the blood pouring from their felled accomplices, the louts wavered in their attack and then, confused by the speed at which their fortunes had been reversed, they turned and took to their heels, leaving Hrothnar and his bleeding companion to their fates.

Myrddion sighed and turned to Finn. 'See if you can find some-one in charge to arrest these two idiots. They obviously practise their trade on any newcomers who arrive at the docks.'

Wary of reprisals, he scrutinised the wooden wharves for further danger, but none of the sailors, traders or merchants showed the slightest interest in the small, bloody battle that had taken place. Here, wise men walked abroad with their eyes closed. 'It's obvious that there's no rule of law in Dubris. I'm beginning to wish we had wings to spirit us out of here.'

Finn returned, but without any person of authority. With an expressive shrug of his shoulders, he explained that various thanes controlled different sectors of the city, and these lords would need to know whom Hrothnar served and what his normal duties were before they could take any action against the two wounded captives. Hrothnar was a citizen of the city, and the party of healers had no standing in this new, lawless community.

'We are unlikely to see these scum placed into any sort of custody, so they feel safe to prey on strangers,' Finn explained. 'Dubris is much changed since we were last here, master, and the Celts have abandoned the town and its administration to the Saxon traders. To add to my frustration, I barely understood what anyone said. The languages spoken here are quite different from the Frankish tongues.'

'There are superficial differences, but I understood Hrothnar well enough, and heaven knows what race could lay claim to him.' Myrddion frowned with irritation. 'What are we supposed to do with these beauties?' He thought briefly, shrugged, and began to hunt for his satchel. 'Brangaine, do we have any clean water in our flasks?' he asked. Used to his eccentricities, she nodded. 'Good. Then find some clean cloth and we'll attend to their bumps and bruises.'

Now that Myrddion had decided on a course of action, he turned and spoke over his shoulder to Finn and Praxiteles. 'Keep an eye on our sleeping beauties while I stitch them up, although why we should repair them so the damned idiots can rob other respectable travellers is more than I can fathom.'

Grumbling like an old man, the healer cleansed and stitched two broken heads and one slashed forearm. He had barely finished when Hrothnar began to stir, his hands swatting ineffectually at the empty air. When he came to his senses, Myrddion dragged the wharf rat unceremoniously to his feet. The man was heavy and the stink of his body odour made the other flinch.

'I neglected to tell you that we are healers, Hrothnar, not that you'd have cared while you were robbing us. However, no matter how harmless our group of travellers might seem, we couldn't have journeyed through the strife and warfare we have seen in the land of the Franks without being able to protect ourselves. If I were you, Hrothnar, I'd consider another trade if you want to survive to make old bones. Or learn to see beyond superficial appearances.'

Hrothnar tried to focus his blurred vision while keeping his aching head perfectly still. His green eyes were puzzled and almost childlike. 'Why haven't you killed us? Why have you stitched my head? I could still turn on you before you have an opportunity to leave Dubris.'

Myrddion grinned ruefully, for Hrothnar was correct in his analysis. A party containing three women and two children, one of whom was a babe in arms, was vulnerable while travelling through narrow, dangerous streets.

'If you can understand the meaning of what I am about to explain, you may learn something that is of lasting value to you. As healers, we are duty bound by our oaths to our profession. Those who perform our trade swear to do no harm to others, even to persons who threaten our safety. I am obliged to repair the damage I have done to you, so you can have no reason to fear us. Nor will you suffer any ill effects from your attempts at extortion, although we have served in the armies of great and ruthless men. We have stood in blood to our ankles as we plied our craft, and we've learned from bitter experience the tricks that are needed to protect ourselves from armed enemies. Now, collect your friend and leave us in peace.'

Hrothnar stared blankly at Myrddion as he tried to puzzle out the underlying motives behind the healer's generosity. Harsh experience had taught him that strength and brutality filled his belly, rather than dispensing mercy or kindness. He knew that the healers could have cut their throats while they were unconscious, and he was certain that he would have removed any fallen opponents in just this fashion. So, in lawless Dubris, that the healers should allow their captives to depart seemed madness . . . unless there was a deeper purpose at work.

As if reading Hrothnar's mind, Myrddion replied by throwing the lout's leather purse, which had been dislodged from his belt when he fell, back at him. Hrothnar caught it awkwardly with one hand and hefted its weight. The coins were still in place.

'Why?' Hrothnar muttered thickly. 'To be blunt, you have us at your mercy. It would have been easy for you to keep my money and refuse to give it back to me, yet you've returned it in full. I don't understand you, Myrddion Merlinus.'

Puzzled, Finn also gaped at Myrddion in surprise. At the very least, Hrothnar's purse would have recompensed the healers for the inconvenience that the man had caused.

'If I kept your money, I'd also be a common thief,' Myrddion retorted grimly. 'Just like you.'

For the first time, Hrothnar replied with a cynical approximation of humour. 'No, you're not a thief like me, are you? But you are something odd and dangerous, so I'm beginning to wonder just what you are.'

'I know nothing about you, Hrothnar, or what has driven you to earn your bread by a brutal and vicious trade, but I've learned much about the world during my travels, especially of its cruelty and the hardships it places on the poor. Once again, Hrothnar, I hope you'll benefit from this experience and trouble us no more.'

Hrothnar remained silent, for the young healer puzzled and confused him. This young man was either a fool or very dangerous. In either case, Hrothnar wanted nothing more to do with the healer or his party. As he struggled to lift his companion, he bowed his head to replicate a respectful, obsequious nod. Silently, he hefted his unconscious confederate over one shoulder and turned to trudge away, while around him the bustle of the docks swirled and scuttled along as if nothing had happened.

Cadoc returned before noon with a lugubrious face and two wagons, one of which was driven by a bluff young Saxon whose accent was so broad that even Myrddion had difficulty understanding much that he said. The reason for Cadoc's dismay was immediately obvious.

Oxen!

A single, dun-coloured horse was tethered at the rear of the leading wagon, but the beasts between the traces were huge brown oxen with brass-tipped, sawn-down horns and dull eyes. Cadoc loathed oxen because they were slow, stupid and difficult to master. In emergencies, they had only one pace, regardless of how harshly whips were applied, and the time required to turn them could be fatal if the wagons were under attack. Even Myrddion, who was unbiased, disliked travelling behind a team of oxen as their broad hooves stirred up a fug of dust.

'Would you credit that horses seem to have vanished from Dubris? The best I could muster was this spavined creature from a Dumnonii trader who needed extra funds to return home. The Celts are deserting Dubris in hordes, but there's no lack of migrating northerners eager to take their places.'

'Aye, Cadoc, we've already established that the docks here are more dangerous than those of Ostia, and I thought that was bad,' Finn added. 'I've dreamed of home every step of the way from Constantinople, and now that we're here, home is stranger and more threatening than most of the outlandish places we've been to.'

'Let's get out of this foul place.' Myrddion sighed gustily. 'I can't believe that six years have wrought so many changes in Britain.

We've seen the movement of the tribes in Gaul and we know from first-hand experience what violence has filled the void created by the Roman retreat. Somehow, I never expected to find it here, in Britain, so we've missed astonishing changes during our wanderings.'

'Nothing much of benefit to the people has happened, master, and that's for certain,' Cadoc grunted as he climbed down from the primitive, poorly constructed wagon, which lacked even the refinement of leather covers. 'Look at this thing! Even the wheels are made of wood. Remember those metal rims on the wagons in Rome?'

'We're not in Rome now,' Finn snapped back unnecessarily.

'I have a strong desire to see broad skies and breathe clean air,' Myrddion muttered under his breath. 'Let's dust Dubris off our backs as soon as possible.'

With the economy of long practice, the healers packed the wagons. They were conscious of the hard, envious inspection of the watching dockworkers so, nervous of further interference by footpads and thieves, the men worked with dispatch. As they laboured, Praxiteles asked numerous questions about the size and quality of Britain's largest port, and the healers felt a certain embarrassment as they compared grubby little Dubris with the wonders of Constantinople.

Once they had loaded the wagons and climbed aboard, the crack of Cadoc's long whip urged the oxen into grudging movement. And so, with Praxiteles driving the other wagon and Myrddion riding the dun-coloured horse, the journey through Dubris began. The evidence of wide-sweeping and destructive change was all around them and Myrddion, with his new sophistication, told himself that this shift was the way of the world, as natural as rain or sunshine.

Nevertheless, these fresh scars on his homeland caused him pain. Even the smaller temples had been stripped of stone, while vandals had toppled whole columns in many buildings so that Myrddion could see the clever engineering that had pegged the sections together. Mute, and yet eloquent, naked plinths reminded him that gods of marble had once stood here and blessed the citizens of Dubris with peace and plenty.

'All things change,' Myrddion whispered aloud in a vain attempt at self-persuasion. 'To stay still is to rot and die.'

Then the forum hove into view and the entire party was silenced by its complete ruination. Even more poignant were the ragged children who played with shards of marble in the weak spring sunshine. Like young animals, they were tormenting a starving dog by tossing pieces of stone at it. The poor creature attempted to slink away through a forest of columns, but the children pursued it, screaming with excitement. Across the wide road, the roofless remains of the baths still sported slimy green water within the calidarium, where more ragged children were tossing stones into the scummed depths. Myrddion had bathed here only six years earlier, and now . . . ? Stone and wood had been dragged away by the immigrants to create makeshift structures on the edges of the city.

A brightly coloured object caught Myrddion's attention from the centre of a thick growth of thistles that were flourishing between slabs of cracked marble paving. Without thinking, he leapt from his horse and thrust aside the spiky foliage to retrieve a fragment of carved and painted marble. He raised it like a trophy and his companions were able to identify his discovery.

A carved marble hand, painted brick red to simulate tanned flesh, raised an index finger imperiously towards the sky. Miraculously, the fingers remained unbroken. A carved ring on the pointing finger had been painted blue and captured the light as if it were a true gem, rather than a mere simulacrum.

'Perhaps it came from a statue of a god? Or it might have been part of a dedication to an emperor or a noble senator. No matter, for it's now as dead as its owner, or the Roman Dubris we passed through on our way to Constantinople. There is no point in mourning the peaceful days that fled during our absence.'

Still, despite his rational acceptance of the natural and organic nature of change, Myrddion stroked the marble hand and asked Brangaine to care for it until he had time to examine it more closely. Equally reverently, Brangaine found a strip of waste cloth and wrapped the hand carefully, as if it belonged to a man who still lived and regretted the loss of his amputated flesh.

As the travellers passed through the city, hard-eyed men stared at them and recognised something Celt in their plaited forelocks and antique jewellery. But the healers had become hardened and strong from years of travelling, so they carried with them a faint aura of danger that silenced the sullen men and their tall, angular wives. Only the children were either courageous or careless enough to shout insults that followed the wagons through the streets.

'Smelly Celts! Cowardly dogs! Run away home to your smelly huts.'

'Where are your Roman friends now?' a blonde woman screamed from the steps of a small theatre, as she suckled a child at a brown-nippled breast. 'They've all scurried away, so you'd better hurry after them to the bastard Ambrosius.'

She shut her mouth eventually when Myrddion drew his huge Celtic sword and rested it across his saddle. With unerring accuracy, she spat at the feet of his horse. The healer stared straight ahead and ignored the woman and the pack of small boys and youths that ran after them.

'We'll soon need supplies, master,' Cadoc shouted back to his leader without turning his head. The ever-prudent servant was careful not to lift his eyes from the road while they were passing through enemy territory.

'Speak in Latin, Cadoc,' Myrddion replied sharply. 'There's no need to advertise that we have money.'

'Aye! But we still need supplies – and that soft spot between my shoulder blades is itching. These streets are full of hidden eyes.'

'We might stop on the outskirts if we can find a safe market place. But if we must travel night and day with only water to fill our bellies, then that's what we'll do. We're hated here, so I'll not pause willingly, even out of hunger.'

Praxiteles held his club easily across his knees while he plied the reins. Finn had also drawn his sword, and, armed and ready, the cavalcade passed through the hostile streets at a steady, lumbering pace. Eventually, night fell and the party was forced to halt. Even then, the men stood guard while the women slept, conscious that the night was full of menace and the rank stink of hatred.

'Welcome home to Britain!' Myrddion muttered ironically to Cadoc as he bedded down under the wagon. 'I'd rather sleep on the streets of Rome than in this cesspit.'

Cadoc discovered that he had little to say when he was profoundly troubled. His ebullience and humour had seeped away in the slow journey from the docks. But, like his master, he mourned the loss of so much he had loved.

Before first light, that hour when the sky faded to grey and the stars were extinguished, the healers were on the road and moving once more. The night had been cold with a memory of winter chill, so they huddled miserably in their cloaks and dreamed of hot food. Fog hung over the buildings of the town and loaned the pillaged ruins an illusion of wholeness, blurring the details of mud and sagging wooden door frames to create an illusion of beauty in simple shapes. Weedy courtyards and rank gardens were softened and clothed in glistening dew. The deserted streets echoed mysteriously, as if the stones remembered the marching, sandalled feet of the legions and the wild, fair singing of Celt warriors as they prepared for war. It was an hour when the ghosts of the past seemed to call to unwary travellers out of the mists, before the rising sun brought back the prosaic, ugly reality of Dubris under her new masters.

'We'll have left the city by the time the sun is up, and with luck we'll find suitable markets, master,' Bridie consoled Myrddion as he rode close to the wagon and smiled at the sleeping countenance of her small son.

'You've been very patient and brave, Bridie. Bearing a child on board a ship bound for Gaul is no small thing. But you'll soon return to our lands and you can present your son to Ceridwen. Then he will become a true Celt.'

Bridie stroked the small golden charm that hung round the neck of the sleeping infant, her eyes shining with the unconditional love that mothers feel for their children. 'I thank you for his bulla, my lord. The gold is so fine that you must have purchased it in Constantinople. It is a wonderful gift for my boy, and he will be forever marked by your favour.'

Myrddion blushed, for he had been afraid that Bridie would be offended by the Roman custom of gifting an infant with a tiny casket to hold an amulet. But Bridie had travelled far from Cymru and had learned to judge the hearts of men with instinctive accuracy.

'Your boy deserves a better future than following the fortunes of war from one cruel place to another.' Myrddion spoke regretfully as he watched Finn sleep on the heaped baggage in the wagon. Praxiteles was handling the reins and singing Greek songs in a soft and tuneful voice. 'I'd like you to persuade Finn to take my place in Segontium, Bridie. I expect I'll become a wandering healer, for these are so many souls suffering in the small hamlets and farms. But you and your babe deserve a snug little house of your own. My

21

mistress, Annwynn, who taught me so much in the years when I was her apprentice, is very old and needs a young back and a strong pair of hands to help her prepare her healing remedies. You will build a good life on Annwynn's farm and your son will grow tall and healthy.'

Bridie eyed Myrddion sharply under the fall of her plaits. 'Do you want to be rid of us, master? Are we an encumbrance?'

Myrddion jerked the rains in surprise and denial, until the stolid horse danced and bridled in protest. 'No, Bridie, not at all! My heart will be saddened when we part, but you and Finn must do what is right for the little one.'

Bridie sighed and nodded. 'You'll have your own children one day, master. Will you cease to roam then?'

'I'm certain I won't father children for many years to come,' Myrddion whispered, his lips twisted with bitter regret. 'So far, I've displayed poor judgement in my choice of women, as you are aware. Some men are born to be alone.'

'Oh, master,' Bridie whispered sadly, but Myrddion's horse had moved ahead and he didn't hear her. Then the moment of intimacy passed as her son woke and wailed for the breast.

As the sun began to light the horizon, the travellers drove into a market that was being set up on the outskirts of the city. The healers were thankful to see local farmers, as well as Saxons, hefting baskets of live birds, eggs packed in straw and panniers of new vegetables, alongside traders displaying their wares on coarse, blanket-covered tables which proclaimed their affluence. These goods were designed to tempt the crowds who would come once the day was more advanced, and included every tawdry bauble that could be bought cheaply in any of the Frankish ports, as well as ill-made trifles from as far away as Massilia. Bridie, Brangaine and Rhedyn descended from the wagons and fell on the fresh food with the avidity of desperate shoppers. They were far too experienced to waste even a copper on jewellery that would blacken almost immediately or pans that were so thin they would fall apart within a short period after purchase, and they haggled, cajoled and demanded the best possible deals with the confidence of women who had learned a smattering of six languages in all the market places of the Middle Sea. Within minutes of completing their business, their purchases were packed in the wagons and the party quit the markets to leave the poor huts on the outskirts of Dubris far behind them. The journey home had begun.

The air smelled clean now and gave off the rich aroma of newly turned earth, fresh growth, woodsmoke, and the wild flowers that flourished in drifts between tree roots. Suddenly, the smell of home was so strong that Myrddion felt his eyes prickle with tears and he was forced to turn his head to one side in case his friends should catch him weeping. He had left Britain in a spirit of mingled adventure, resentment and excitement, but he had learned that the land of his birth, no matter how backward it now seemed, was a part of his blood and bones.

'I swear I'll never leave again, no matter what our futures may bring. If Dubris is any example, then we'll have an inordinately busy time right here in Britain.'

But his companions didn't hear him. They'd not have argued anyway, for home was everything to them . . . and always had been. Myrddion had pursued his own dream to Constantinople, and they had followed him willingly, but they had never lost sight of their roots.

Never again, Myrddion thought. His fingers remembered the texture of Flavia's skin and the marvellous fineness of her hair; his lips recalled the taste of her honeyed mouth and her wicked tongue; his body continued to hunger for her. But she had chosen to become the concubine of his father, if only for a season, and Myrddion had vowed that he would never love a woman again.

Love and passion did little to assuage his terrible loneliness, and brought only pain in their wake.

From this time onwards, he determined that love of his homeland would be sufficient to sustain the needs of his solitary heart.

CHAPTER II

WHERE THE SOFT WINDS BLOW

Our world is lovely in different ways,
Hung with beauty and works of hands,
I saw a strange machine, made
For motion, slide against the sand,
Shrieking as it went. It walked swiftly
On its only foot, this odd-shaped monster,
Travelled in an open country without
Seeing, without arms, or hands,
With many ribs, and its mouth in its middle.

Anglo-Saxon riddle

All the healers felt dislocated. The road they travelled was long, broad and still well maintained, although hedges of hawthorn were beginning to encroach onto the carriageway. Beyond the hedges, or over the low walls of stones that had been ploughed out of the fields, farms proliferated across the flat and fertile land. But Myrddion also saw signs of neglect where fields remained unploughed and crops had not been planted in the late winter. Many of the simple stone crofts were obviously deserted, for doors gaped open and many thatched roofs had collapsed.

'It looks as though most farmers of the Cantii tribe have fled from the lands around Dubris,' Myrddion reported to Finn and Cadoc, after he had ridden off to explore a one-room cottage and cow byre just beyond the roadway. 'The croft has been stripped bare and all the livestock has gone. I saw no signs of violence, no bodies and no bones, so the farm must have been abandoned. The tribe is probably on the move into the west, taking everything of value with them.'

'I can't imagine deserting the home where the ashes of my ancestors have rested for hundreds of years,' Finn murmured, his eyes dark with empathy.

'This retreat will become commonplace for *all* the tribes of Britain if Ambrosius can't find a solution that will pin the Saxons down on the east coast,' Myrddion replied with morose fatality. 'I wager we'll meet many refugees on the road between here and Segontium.'

Yet, for all the despondency of the travellers, birds still sang sweetly in the thickets, wild flowers sweetened the dust from the roadway with drifts of perfume and the sky remained a clean-rinsed blue barred with white, scudding clouds.

The land is as it has always been, Myrddion thought. It's only we ants who crawl upon it who have changed. After we are dust, the land will continue.

Although they were travelling in easy stages for the comfort of the women and children, the party began to overtake slow-moving family groups trudging wearily towards Durovernum. The men and boys were afoot, herding their few cattle and sheep before them, while horses and oxen drew farm carts laden high with furniture, children and baskets of live fowl. Dogs scouted ahead on the orders of their masters. The faces of the women were drawn with loss and care, because they were venturing into the unknown and dooming their children to landlessness. Ashamed by their retreat, the farmers refused to look directly into the eyes of the chance-met strangers.

On several occasions before they reached Durovernum, the travellers stumbled over newly erected fortifications constructed by Saxons from massive tree trunks. Saxon farmers now tilled the soil and they shaded their sun-dazzled eyes with their hands as the healers' wagons passed. When they recognised Celtic faces, they spat into the newly ploughed furrows of black soil, causing Myrddion's stomach to tighten with concern.

But no lasting trouble came from these signs of enmity. On one occasion, tall warriors forced the healers to halt their oxen. Knowing they could never hope to outrun the troop of Saxons, Myrddion instructed his companions to keep their mouths shut while he negotiated with them. Then, with his heart in his mouth, he explained that they were healers who had just returned from Gaul, where they had served King Merovech during the wars against Attila the Hun. Shamelessly name-dropping, he claimed the protection of his friendship with Hengist, and because his Saxon was passable the ruling thane gave them free passage through his domain, provided they treated a number of minor ailments suffered by his men.

Gratefully, Myrddion complied, thanking their luck that this Saxon lordling was more interested in acquiring land than Celtic heads.

'Some of our farmers seem to be fighting back,' Myrddion commented in Celt as he lanced an infected wound in the thigh of a tall, red-haired warrior. 'This injury is a puncture wound and was probably caused by a hay fork or some similar farm implement.' As his scalpel found the deep-seated abscess, vile-smelling pus gushed out of the wound. 'Ah! Got it!'

He grimaced with satisfaction, for his patient had fainted. Swiftly, the healer cleaned up the discharge and began to swab out the wound with raw alcohol. The sudden stab of pain caused the warrior, barely twenty years of age, to come to his senses. The young man began to sweat profusely, so Myrddion called for honey in hot water to counteract the shock.

'Good for them,' Cadoc replied laconically as he struggled with a broken tooth in the mouth of an older Saxon who gripped his stool with white-knuckled hands, while he tried to suppress a moan of terror. For country dwellers, broken teeth were almost endurably painful and this stoic patient had suffered for some time. Cadoc noted cynically that the Saxon must have been a favourite of the gods, for no abscess had formed on the root of the tooth.

'Gently, Cadoc! Remember that we've vowed to avoid harming our patients.'

Cadoc grinned as he brandished the offending tooth in his pliers and then stooped to staunch the sudden rush of blood. 'Aye, master. At least this old fellow won't die of the brain disease, for the tooth cavity is quite clean.

Finn allowed himself a sour grin. 'I know I'm being uncharitable,' he snapped as he prepared herbal painkillers and drawing ointments to leave with the patients. 'But I can't see that it would hurt the Saxons to bathe a little more frequently. They smell worse than Cadoc's armpit.'

'Enough foolishness, Finn! Have you smelled our peasants from downwind in recent times? They're none too precious about bathing either. You've lived in the Roman way for far too long.'

'Since birth, master, and it's not hurt me,' Finn retorted. 'The Romans had a fondness for Dyfed and Gwent, and left their fortresses and their baths up and down the coast. And we sickened less for the sake of a little oil and clean water.'

As Myrddion knew that Finn was correct, he permitted the

conversation to lapse and moved on to a new patient sporting a painful bunion.

Eventually, with the grudging thanks of the local thane ringing in their ears and carrying a gift of several leather flagons of Saxon beer from the man with the broken tooth, the healers took to the road again. The whole party felt relieved when Durovernum hove into view.

At first the town seemed unchanged, although Saxons now made up over half of the population. Many Celt craftsmen had stayed in the old Roman settlement, because their skills were still needed and welcomed, even though outland masters now controlled their day-to-day lives. But a new crop of younger Saxon traders were burrowing deeply into the life of Durovernum. These newcomers were inclined to treat any travellers with suspicion, so the healers soon felt resentful, hostile eyes following their movements through the heart of the township.

Finn's eyes flashed with anger as they passed a simple Christian church that had been burned to the ground and stripped of any objects of value. Old death seemed to hang over the ruins and this taint, perhaps, accounted for the fact that the land hadn't been converted to another purpose. A young sapling and lush weeds grew out of the foundations, further cracking and lifting old slabs of stone that had served as flooring in the small, simple structure.

'To kill men and women who have dedicated themselves to the service of their gods is a very serious sin,' Cadoc whispered, his eyes narrowing with disgust. 'When I spoke to some of the warriors back at the fortress, I gathered that they save their greatest scorn for the priests and nuns of the Christian orders, for they believe them to follow a Roman religion. The Saxons still hold a passionate hatred for the Romans and all that they stood for.'

'I've been told they hate the Christian habit of refusing to fight back whenever a religious community is attacked,' Myrddion added. 'Perhaps, for all their protestations, the Saxons understand that it is wrong to kill defenceless men and women who are so pious that they pray and honour their god while they're being murdered.'

'Perhaps they just don't like anyone who isn't of their own kind,' Rhedyn hissed angrily from the wagon. 'Perhaps they like to kill, and that's the end of it.'

'Who knows?' Myrddion said quietly. 'I'm not convinced that the Saxon race is naturally wicked or that they are more violent than we are. Their motives are foreign to us, so perhaps they're just different. I wouldn't choose to hate them simply because I don't understand them.'

Rhedyn flushed, but she squared her rounded shoulders defiantly. 'Then I'll hate them enough for both of us, master. As far as I'm concerned, it will always be sinful to slay people who are harmless and innocent.'

'Aye. But few of us are truly without sin, Rhedyn.'

Agreeing to disagree, Rhedyn held her tongue, and the small party quit the city to set up camp beyond the walls of Durovernum.

Word of their trade had preceded them, so they were kept busy for the remainder of the day in the mundane practice of their craft. It was always so, for healers provided a small hedge against disaster, a bulwark when illness came calling or accident threatened to turn fragile human flesh into dust. Serious disease rarely came their way, for such patients lived or died quickly, but ambulatory sufferers were fast to seek out a cure when healers arrived in their town.

The treatment of non-fatal ailments served the purpose of providing Myrddion and his assistants with much-needed inform-ation about the political and social realities of this small corner of the world. Farmers and townsfolk loved to gossip, especially about the lives of the great ones, as long as there was no danger in it for them, so they talked and talked to distract themselves from the pain of broken teeth, rheumatic fingers and ingrown toenails, and the healers listened and remembered what they heard.

The Saxons spoke fearfully of Uther Pendragon, younger brother of Ambrosius, High King of the Britons, and said that his ferocity and ruthlessness matched the most brutal of the Saxon thanes. No cruelty seemed beyond him, so simple men speculated that the many years of exile, after his family's escape from the wrath of King Vortigern, had left a permanent, unhealed scar on his soul. The murder of his oldest brother, Constans, had created in him an unquenchable thirst for revenge on his mortal enemies – a group that was large and varied. Now, as the strong right arm of the High King, Uther led Ambrosius's warriors into unceasing battle against the Saxon forts and villages. He showed no mercy towards his enemies, and was renowned for treating women and children as harshly as fully grown warriors. As justification for this barbarity, he boasted openly that lice breed and even nits spread and grow as they infest healthy hair. In his opinion, it was far better to destroy all parasites, especially when they were still growing and unable to resist.

Myrddion remembered Uther's cold blue eyes and shuddered at such a callous metaphor, knowing from experience that men such as the prince were capable of almost any horror in pursuit of their ambitions. It was six years since he had treated a jagged wound on the warrior's arm, but the memory was still vivid enough to leave him in no doubt that, if he saw the need, Uther Pendragon would turn the whole land into a sterile desert.

On the other hand, Ambrosius was honoured for possessing a more reasoned approach to the wars he was forced to fight. When the High King led offensives against the Saxons, Angles or Jutes, he spared women and children and took orphans to be raised as slaves and servants. Ambrosius believed that small children, when they were removed from their families before they had become imbued with outland culture, could be trained to become useful Celts as they grew. His moderate approach was applauded by the Celts, but scorned as weakness by the Saxon traders. Wisely, Ambrosius forbade any Saxon merchants from straying onto his lands, having learned that infiltration via commerce was soon followed by an invasion that used the intelligence gained by the merchants.

Myrddion had never met Ambrosius, but he was impressed by what he heard of the High King's strategic planning and his analytical assessment of the political realities of life in Britain. He understood instinctively that Ambrosius was seeking to absorb the barbarians, rather than waiting to be gobbled up by the sheer weight of their encroaching numbers.

'Ambrosius is an astute ruler,' Myrddion told his fellow healers as they shared the information they had learned during their ministrations to the sick. 'May he live long, for his method of dealing with the Saxon menace is likely to work. If they can be harnessed to his throne as vassals, perhaps Celts and Saxons can live together amicably. We are not so very different, under the skin. Remember Captus, King Merovech's officer at Châlons? He was a perfect example of a man of common sense who had learned to deal fairly and reasonably with men of many races.'

Myrddion spun a pretty eating knife on his palm, the blade Captus had given him when they parted after the Battle of the Catalaunian Plain. The Frank officer had been amusing company and was fiercely devoted to his land but, like many of his race, he had discovered that the earth must be shared if it was to flourish. Captus recognised that constant warfare turns fertile acres into scorched desert.

'Aye, Ambrosius holds the fate of the west in his hands, so we must be thankful that the High King's common sense and Uther's brilliance as a warrior have kept the Saxons stalled at Londinium, although the brothers must be constantly vigilant.

Heaven help us if the heirs of Constans should ever perish.'

'Then I'll pray for them . . . hard,' Cadoc said ironically. 'I'll even pray for that bastard Uther. I've only seen him the once, but I know why superstitious folk whisper that his sire was a dragon. I could easily believe it, once I'd met the son of a bitch.'

'Master?' Brangaine called from the shadows. The flickering from the fire softened her harsh, middle-aged features and exposed the delicate bones under her weather-beaten complexion. Long acquaintance and familiarity can blind the keenest eyes. With a pang, Myrddion recognised that she must have been a lovely creature in her youth.

'Yes, Brangaine?'

'The others won't question you, believing that you would never willingly take us into danger, but I have Willa to consider and she's very frightened, so I must ask. In fact, she has been terrified ever since that thug tried to attack us on the docks. The poor child has odd dreams that haunt her and she's been fair demented from some kind of premonition since we've returned home. I don't know for sure what she sees or dreams about, but I'd like to tell her we're going somewhere safe and gentle just to set her mind at rest. She's nigh on eight now and she's growing like a weed, but maybe she saw things at Tournai that might have twisted her mind out of balance.'

Myrddion bit his lip guiltily, because he had scarcely spared a thought for the scarred child who travelled with them and had become the centre of Brangaine's universe. Now that he was forced to consider the matter, Willa had appeared very pale and remote of late.

'I'm sorry that I've been thoughtless about the little mite, Brangaine. She never complains, so I sometimes forget she is with us, but that's no excuse for my carelessness. You say she's been troubled? How?'

Now it was Brangaine's turn to be mortified at her forwardness in implying any fault in her master, a man who had always put the welfare of his dependants before his own health. She would have remained silent, but her love for Willa drove her to answer.

'Willa doesn't talk much to anyone, even when she's alone with me. It's almost as if she doesn't need to put her thoughts into words . . . or she doesn't trust anyone with whatever memories lie in her head. You've always been kind to her, master, but the poor little creature is very troubled. I've asked her about her worries over and over again, but up until yesterday she wouldn't tell me.'

Myrddion stifled his impatience at Brangaine's rambling, apologetic explanation. He waited, as did the rest of the party, their eyes softened by pity, interest or shame at their previous indifference to the child's concerns.

'Willa's not lacking in wit, Master Myrddion, for all she scarcely opens her mouth. She often knows exactly what I'm thinking before I say a word. And now she tells me she's scared of the dragon that will burn her up. She says you are taking us to a place where we will be captured, imprisoned and scorned. She seems to have waking dreams just like you do, master, but she doesn't fit and she doesn't forget what she sees in her dreams. She just knows things, and I'm frightened for her.'

'Not another soothsayer!' Cadoc exclaimed acidly, speaking without thinking. 'You're bad enough, master, and you fair give me the collywobbles when your eyes get that look about them.'

'Don't poke fun at Willa, Cadoc.' Finn cuffed his friend lightly. 'The Sight is no joke.'

Cadoc's frankness was sometimes inappropriate and hurtful, although the scarred healer would never deliberately wound anyone. But he was impelled to fill any silence with words, and these utterances were often too close to the truth for comfort.

'No, it's not,' Myrddion agreed. 'And I hope, for Willa's sake, that you're mistaken, Brangaine. But if Ceridwen has chosen the child to drink from her cauldron, then we cannot change what the goddess has decided.' He gazed down into Brangaine's eyes. 'It is possible that one of the Mother's priestesses might consent to tutor Willa so that she learns the obligations of her Sight and how to control it for the benefit of other people. Have no fears. I assume you are speaking of Uther Pendragon, but I'll not take the child into the dragon's jaws. We'd all be safer and happier if she never sees the prince.'

'Thank you, master,' Brangaine whispered, her lined face transformed by a wide, relieved grin. Her smile was only slightly marred by a missing canine that had been knocked out by a brutal husband, a man who regularly relieved his own fears of the future on her flesh until the day he perished in Vortigern's army near Tomen-y-mur.

'I, for one, am far happier avoiding the High King and his brother,' Cadoc added. 'And I'm sorry, Brangaine, for my unkind jokes. You know I don't know when to keep my mouth shut sometimes. But that's no excuse for hurting the feelings of a friend.'

Brangaine waved away Cadoc's apology, forgiving him, as always, for the sake of his huge, warm heart. The others murmured their relief and gratitude until Myrddion was forced to acknowledge how apprehensive they had been at the prospect of returning to the ambit of Ambrosius and his brother. Out of loyalty and love, these ordinary people had followed him into the paths of many dangerous and unpredictable men. They had forgiven him again and again for the injuries and the dangers they had experienced in helping him to achieve his ambitions. Bridie had paid a price in pain and permanent disfigurement when she had inadvertently crossed Rome's former *magister militum*, Flavius Aetius, at Myrddion's bidding, so the whole party of healers had cause to fear any future contact with men as unpredictable as Uther Pendragon and

Ambrosius Imperator. But love of Myrddion had kept them silent while he, high-handed and blind as he often was to the needs and fears of less clever people, had failed to see how deeply they had longed for a quiet life.

I'll try to be more considerate in the future, he promised himself silently. I've taken their loyalty for granted, while they've saved me from the consequences of my stupidity again and again.

Durobrivae passed under the wheels of the wagon, leaving impressions of the same ruin, hostility and threat in the healers' deepening dismay. The Saxons were quite at home now, and were deeply rooted in the British soil. Myrddion wondered if any Celts regretted their part in the defeat of Hengist and Horsa, brothers who would have shared the land with the original inhabitants because they had initially been invited in as immigrants. These new invaders were the sweepings of the north, and lacked most of Hengist's virtues. They were transforming each village and township into replicas of the places they had known in their distant homelands and were scouring away all signs of the culture that had existed before their arrival.

What, then, can we expect of Londinium when we arrive? Myrddion asked himself. He realised that thoughts of the great city preyed on the minds of the whole party, but no one was prepared to give voice to their feelings of apprehension.

Privately, Myrddion had already decided to skirt the central parts of the city entirely, though they would be forced to use a bridge to cross the Tamesis river and pass through the outskirts. With a pang of recognition, Myrddion conceded that he had already broken his promise that he would share his decisions with Cadoc and Finn. He sighed inwardly, for he understood that he, *alone*, had determined that it would be unkind to add to the women's nervousness.

I have patronised them as if they were children. How would I feel in their places?

But the habits of leadership are strong and Myrddion had been making decisions that affected the lives of other, older people since he was sixteen years old. He knew in his heart of hearts that he would find it difficult to change.

As on their previous visit, Londinium continued to spread outwards, but because the land was featureless and flat the city lacked the impact and visual beauty of Rome's seven hills. Nor did it enjoy the stunning clarity of light that glittered on the blue waters that surrounded Constantinople on three sides. The Tamesis was brown and fouled and, like the Tiber river, threatened anyone who drank its brackish waters with infection, disease or death, but the graceful bridges that spanned the Roman river loaned elegance to the Tiber's turgid depths. The many trees, frescoes and mosaics of Ravenna shouted aloud the pride of its citizens, but Londinium barely boasted a single tree, as the poor had hewed down every sapling to feed their winter fires.

The shell of one building caused Myrddion to dismount and explore the dusty ruins. He sighed as he picked up a set of rusted forceps from the remains of a bed. Now that he examined one of the long, narrow rooms that lay open to the sky, he could see the detritus of a hospital: barrels for water and scraps of rags left to moulder on the leaf-strewn ground. Everything of value had been pilfered long ago and only the forceps remained to remind the healer that Roman surgeons had laboured here by the banks of the Tamesis to drive death away from strong young warriors.

Wherever their eyes rested, the healers had noticed evidence of rapid social change and the havoc that had been deliberately wreaked on fine old buildings. Either their purpose had been swept away by the Saxon advance or the invaders had utterly rejected the religious beliefs that had given the original architects cause to raise one stone upon another. Christian churches, Roman temples, the forum, the baths, theatres built in the Greek style and even the hippodrome had been chopped up piecemeal. In their places stood halls, huts and barn-like storage sheds all constructed from timber. Open markets still flourished as they always had, but the goods for sale were either local or northern, as if the time-honoured commerce with the continent was now curtailed or, at the very least, much diminished.

Yet, for all its tawdriness and sprawling dirt, something lingered in the air of Londinium. Perhaps any place that has known the chariots of the Iceni, wicked and glowing in the sunlight, or the might of the Roman galleys, resplendent with red-dyed sails, coursing down the Tamesis to berth on an island in the flood, retains some sheen of past glories. Rome had never felt the hand of a master who was not Roman-born until she was as ancient as the Seven Hills themselves. Ravenna had been newly built and even Constantinople seemed set for generations of peace.

But Londinium had known many masters, receding back in time until it was a collection of rough huts on the edges of Tamesis's mud flats. Blood stained her streets, whether sod or stone, and every passing conqueror had left some part of his spirit in the city's soul. Londinium smelled of home, but Myrddion's prescience stirred and he knew the city also awaited greatness like a half-woven cloak of scarlet wool.

'Let's get out of here as fast as we can,' he ordered as he remounted his horse, and the uncomplaining oxen were forced to move at their fastest pace, the speed of a walking man, to escape the distrust and jealousy that gleamed in the eyes of the denizens of this place. Myrddion recognised the sheen of greed and resentment in the many eyes that assessed the value of the goods in the two wooden wagons. The threat from footpads was very real.

Eventually, the fading light forced the healers to call a halt when they arrived at a small farming community on the outskirts of Londinium. Six years earlier, they had paused at this same spot to ply their trade when they were travelling across Britain to Dubris, and Myrddion was reminded once again of his meeting with Uther Pendragon. In the intervening years the community had scarcely changed, for the huts had already carried the stamp of Saxon traders and gradual neglect. What was new was the hatred that shadowed every face, for small villages on the margins of Londinium regularly felt the sting of Uther's attacks. Saxon and Celt alike resented and feared the prince's ruthless tactics.

This time, the healers paused only long enough to eat and to replenish their water barrels from the communal well before repacking the cooking utensils and moving on. Myrddion gave Cadoc the rusted forceps to repair and the two assistants were appalled to learn that a Roman hospital, a miracle of modern healing, had been allowed to rot.

'Typical of Saxons!' Cadoc grunted. 'They spoil everything they touch.'

Myrddion shook his head sadly. 'No, I wish it were so, but it isn't. That building was looted and gutted long before the Saxons came, probably as soon as the galleys left their island harbour and headed out to the open sea for the last time. I have no doubt that our own people destroyed that hospital through greed, superstition or their hatred for the Romans.' Cadoc would have argued, but Myrddion cut him short. 'I hate what the Saxons have done to Londinium, but I refuse to be blinded by patriotism. We are just as venal as they are.'

The healers broke camp in unusual silence.

Before they left, Myrddion searched through his clothes chest until he found a cylinder filled to bursting with simple maps of Britain and the countryside. Opening the cylinder, he thanked the goddess for his habit of charting his movements during the time he had followed Vortigern's standard. He found his chart of the lands near Londinium and his tapered forefinger sought out the web of Roman roads that branched out from the hub of the city like spokes in a chariot wheel.

He rejected the road to Calleva Atrebatum, which ultimately branched towards Ambrosius's stronghold at Venta Belgarum. Common sense dictated that the High King would ensure the route to his capital was frequently patrolled, and Myrddion had no desire to come to his attention. Above this thoroughfare, he had sketched in an alternative route that wound towards the north and bypassed the old Roman fortresses. This roadway would lead them into higher country, but the Saxons would avoid it because the Catuvellauni and Dobunni tribes would surely prevent the invaders from gaining a single toehold on such an important communications route. At Verulamium, a town still perilously close to Londinium, a smaller, less travelled path led across the uplands to Corinium and, from this centre, to Glevum and onwards into Cymru.

'We must head north-west to join the Roman road to Verulamium,' Myrddion told Cadoc and Finn, who had taken the reins of the two wagons. 'Praxiteles, your task is to protect Finn and the women from any attack. I will support Cadoc in the lead wagon and, if we push on through the night, we'll reach Verulamium some time tomorrow.'

'Good!' Praxiteles spoke carefully in his halting Celt. 'I smell trouble all around us, master, worse than Italia or the Frankish kingdoms. There is no law here.'

The night was full of the sounds and smells of spring and should have been pleasant had the travellers not sensed a pall of danger that hung over the roads like an invisible spider's web. Every corner represented a possible threat and every dark coppice could have concealed watching eyes. Moonlight illuminated the roadway, but so much was hidden by the darkness among trees and ground cover that enemies could be all around without being seen. Within the wagons, the women slept lightly, but Myrddion could make out the gleam of Willa's eyes as she stared out at the dark trees that hemmed in the road, one girlish hand resting on her downy cheek.

He pulled his horse close to the side of the wagon.

'Sleep, little one,' he whispered, so as not to disturb Brangaine. 'Tomorrow will see us far along the road and safe from the clutches of the Saxons, Uther Pendragon and the High King.'

The child looked up at his tall, dark form with eyes shadowed with a maturity that was far beyond her years. Her hand fell and Myrddion noticed, irrelevantly, that it was the arm that had been scarred by fire.

'We aren't safe,' she whispered sadly. 'Not safe. He will come!'

The novelty of hearing Willa speak took Myrddion aback. The young healer could recall only a half a dozen instances when she had chosen to express her thoughts beyond a single word, and her vocal cords were rusty from disuse.

'I'll protect you, Willa, I promise. Go to sleep now so the night will pass quickly. Thieves and warriors rarely attack at night.'

The child lay down and nestled into the crook of Brangaine's arm. Feeling the sudden weight, even through the fog of dreams, Brangaine hugged the child closely to her breast and whimpered in her sleep. Willa's eyes seemed enormous in her small face as she looked up at her master.

'Please look after my mother, master. Promise me. There's no saving me, but she'll mourn for me and I'd not want her to be unhappy.'

Then, as Myrddion gasped like a gaffed fish dragged into the poisonous air, Willa closed her eyes. Within moments she was asleep, and Myrddion felt a deep spasm of pity as the child began to suck her thumb for comfort.

She can't know anything, Myrddion thought, but he felt an icy finger stir the hairs on the nape of his neck, for an owl suddenly screamed in a nearby thicket. Myrddion shivered in superstition, for the Mother was out hunting and all sensible men found shelter on such nights and barred the door against unseen malice.

The owl shrieked again and Willa stirred in her sleep. Myrddion's horse shied as he rode towards the stand of trees and the darkness was suddenly filled with rushing wings and long talons.

Verulamium appeared much as Myrddion had imagined it, although he had never visited its stone monuments, wooden towers and graceful marble forum. On the surface, the bustling streets and busy marketplace were untouched by either time or trouble. Only a sharp-eyed stranger would have noticed the absence of mature men and youths in the busy throngs of people on the streets of the town.

'Uther and Ambrosius have taken the able-bodied men away to fight their wars,' he said quietly to Cadoc, who nodded in reply. 'We must buy our supplies and leave as quickly as possible.'

'The women are wearied from their journey, Myrddion, and they must rest. Bridie won't complain, but she thinks she'll lose her milk if she has no opportunity to sleep comfortably. And if you haven't noticed, Finn, Praxiteles and I haven't slept for two nights and we're nearly spent. I don't know how you keep going: you've rested even less than we have, and we're exhausted. No matter how dangerous the road ahead might be, we'll be ineffective if we don't take the time to sleep in a real bed.'

Cadoc rarely complained, being a man who jested easily and understood the necessities of the road. If he counselled breaking their journey, Myrddion was obliged to consider the advice seriously.

On cue, Bridie's son began to wail thinly and Bridie eased her aching limbs into a more comfortable position before she bared one breast. Myrddion could see the furrows between her eyes and the pouches of violet skin around the sockets that spoke of exhaustion.

'Very well, friend, perhaps it's time to find us an inn. But it must be within the walls of Verulamium, for I'd not wish to be caught in the lower town if the Saxons should attack.'

Cadoc nodded in reply, and Myrddion caught the swift twitch of the scarred man's lips that spoke eloquently of his satisfaction . . . and his relief. 'Then I'll follow my nose and find a suitable inn,' he said, and set the oxen moving to a chorus of creaks and groans from the ill-made wagon.

The Flower Maiden was an inn with an auspicious name from Myrddion's perspective. Blodeuwedd, the Maid of Flowers and Owls, possessed the dual personality ascribed to so many of his people's deities, including Grannie Ceridwen, as his grandmother had called the goddess, who was reputed to be an ancestor. Myrddion had never put much credence in this kinship, but the Maid of Flowers and Owls had always captured his imagination. He felt they could dwell under her sign with some impunity, as if the gods were smiling on them.

The innkeeper, Gron, was a cadaverous man who had made a sensible choice when naming his inn, for his namesake had been Blodeuwedd's lover in the legends. This particular Gron lacked the grace, manners or beauty of the original, however, being in the habit of predicting ruination for the city at the slightest sign of political trouble. Myrddion decided that the man had a jaundiced eye and a pessimistic nature, neither of which traits made for success in his trade. Still, the inn was well sited near the city gates, the beer and wine were good and the food was excellent, courtesy of Gron's matronly wife Fionnuala, who was as merry as her husband was glum.

The rooms were also a surprise, for they were clean, plain and well ventilated. Despite the presence of an inn cat, a ginger male called Mouser who insisted on twining himself around Myrddion's legs and pushing himself on the healer's chest whenever he reclined on the straw-stuffed pallet, the party was very pleased with everything the Flower Maiden had to offer. After a filling meal of mutton stew and fresh vegetables, the party was made comfortable in the two rooms rented for the night and soon fell into the dreamless sleep of the seasoned traveller.

Gron had been eager to accept the healers' coin, judging by their dress and bright swords that they were men of substance. But long habits of complaint ran deeply in his nature, so he started to whine as soon as the guests had departed to their beds.

'I don't trust men with heavy purses and real swords who come from the Londinium road. How are we to know they're not Saxon spies?'

'Are you daft, man? When did Saxons wear their hair like Master Myrddion, or have such a crop of freckles as Master Cadoc? If you weren't such a curmudgeon, you'd admit we're lucky to have such distinguished guests.'

'Then it's to be hoped that their coin is good, Fionnuala, else we'll have been cheated. And none of that foreign shite either, for I want good British gold!'

'Ah, man, you'd complain if it rained silver and the rivers were made of gold because you missed the running water.' Then Fionnuala made her way to her own bed and was soon happily snoring.

Just before dawn, shouts and screams disturbed the inhabitants of the inn. Myrddion woke with an acrid, bitter taste in his mouth from smoke that was billowing into the room through the open shutters. A major fire fanned by the stiff morning breeze was obviously out of control in the town. Cadoc, shaken awake by his master, immediately leaned out of the second-storey window to ascertain the location of the fire, and reported that a red glow in the lightening sky indicated buildings near the southern gate were ablaze.

'You and Finn stay here with the women, Cadoc,' Myrddion decided. 'Praxiteles will come with me to find out what's amiss. Gods, but I'm glad we're within the walls, although we've seen before that fortifications aren't always proof of safety. I still remember Tournai.'

'How could we ever forget that place?' Cadoc asked unnecessarily. 'Willa came from that benighted town, but no one was left alive to tell us who she was. Off you go, then, and we'll stay here to protect the women and children. Don't forget your satchel.'

Cadoc's face had a determined set as he hunted up his sword, a weapon he hadn't used since he was a foot soldier in Vortigern's army. Placing himself outside their rooms, he prepared to defend the women with his life.

Trusting to the military skills of his companions to keep the women safe, Myrddion snatched up his satchel and followed Praxiteles into the street where the older men of the town were making for the walls. Many of these townsmen carried bows, while the young boys were armed with slingshots and other makeshift weapons that had been snatched from more mundane duties in their homes. One buxom, red-haired wench pushed past Myrddion with a nasty-looking garden hoe slung over one shoulder. Judging by the affronted, martial steeliness in her brown eyes, Myrddion decided that the attackers' heads would be cloven if she had any say in the matter.

Weaving through the jostling crowd, healer and servant followed the press of townsmen and women towards the southern fortifications. 'What's amiss?' Myrddion asked of a running youth, halting his progress with one hand.

The youth angrily tried to shake him off. 'The Saxons are burning the lower town outside the gates. They're slaughtering everything that lives down there – men, women, children and beasts, damn them all.'

'Then we'd best offer our help, Praxiteles. If the town is taken, then so are we.'

Pushing their way forward, the two men found themselves at the bottom of a flight of open wooden stairs. The wall was built of cyclopean blocks of irregular stone that had been raised to a level some three times the height of a fully grown man, but as they mounted the steps to climb to the ramparts the scene outside the town became visible in all its grisly carnage.

The Saxons had attacked during the pre-dawn light at a time when the denizens of the lower town were still asleep. Consequently, few of the traders were able to seek shelter inside the walls. The gates of Verulamium were closed and barred between dusk and dawn and the gatekeeper had refused to risk the township, or his own skin, by opening the smaller inner doors to save those souls trapped between Saxon weapons and the solid stone defences. With no hope of salvation, the innocent women and children of the lower town pounded on the gates until their fists bled, but were soon cut down by the tall Saxon warriors who continued to pillage the shops, inns and dwellings where the unprotected citizens resided. Once they were finished with a building, the Saxons set it afire, often with the inhabitants trapped inside.

Sickened, Myrddion turned away from the pile of dead flesh below him. Such needless brutality! The healer was familiar with the casual cruelties of war, the fate of non-combatants caught on battlefields and the lack of mercy extended to the wounded and the weak. But, regardless of the blood he had seen spilt in the past, he was still shocked whenever he saw women and children pointlessly slaughtered.

Then the time for reflection was over as the top rungs of a crude ladder thudded against the ramparts. Praxiteles and Myrdion acted without hesitation as they pushed on each of the vertical supports and sent the first Saxon on the ladder tumbling with it to the ground.

Myrddion heard the wicked hiss of stones released from slingshots and watched a huge Saxon collapse in a boneless heap as one of the smooth river stones struck him in the temple. Along the walls, boys took aim at Saxon heads while older men used bows to equally deadly effect. The more able-bodied women and younger men who had not been collected by Uther Pendragon's levy joined Myrddion and Praxiteles in casting down the crude rope-lashed siege ladders.

The Battle of Verulamium was short and bloody. Just when the sheer weight of Saxon numbers threatened to turn the tide against the town's defenders, foot soldiers in disciplined phalanxes trotted into the lower township, led by men on large horses who were armed with long, bright swords. Like a deadly killing machine, the new arrivals joined battle with the Saxons, who had no answer to the Celtic use of Roman military tactics. Step by step, the Celts advanced, and although they fought with great personal heroism, the Saxons were driven back until the city wall blocked any further retreat. Then, in vicious, dour, individual contests, the remaining Saxons were cut to pieces. No quarter was asked for – or given.

Above the straining, blood-spattered figures, Myrddion waited with his satchel containing his healer's equipment slung over his shoulder. Periodically, he patted the smooth old leather to reassure himself that his tools were safe and readily at hand. Knowing that his skills would soon be needed for friend and foe alike, he crisply ordered Praxiteles to return to the Flower Maiden with instructions to send Cadoc and Finn to him with all the equipment necessary to save whatever wounded survived in the stew of bodies that lay at the foot of the walls.

Finally, as the sun began to rise over the smoking ruins of the lower town, Myrddion could see the full horror of the attack in the merciless clarity of day. The bodies of dead and dying Saxon warriors lay over the corpses of the citizens who had been massacred against the city walls. Even this early in the day, ruddy shafts of sunlight reflected off bloodied blades and spear points as wounded barbarians were summarily executed. This exercise in cold-blooded slaughter might have been expedient for Ambrosius's commanders, but the stain on the Celtic standard shamed Myrddion.

The commander of Ambrosius's forces trotted his horse to the gates, driving the unwilling beast over the heaped bodies of the dead without compunction for either friend or foe, until he could use the pommel of his sword to batter at the wooden barricade and demand entrance. As the warrior removed his plumed helmet to wipe his sweating forehead with his mailed arm, Myrddion recognised the wildly curling, ruddy hair of Uther Pendragon, and his heart sank with dismay. Viewed from above and ignorant of Myrddion's careful scrutiny, Uther cut a reckless, brutal figure, and the healer remembered how frightened he had been when he'd treated Prince Uther's wound outside Londinium six years earlier.

The prince's arms were thick with clotting blood to the elbows, so that any watcher could imagine that he had sunk both hands and forearms into a river of gore. His sword was so filthy with mud, brain matter and drying blood that no light reflected off it. Blood spatter marked Uther's whole body, except for where his helmet had protected his face. A further band across his eyes and the bridge of his nose, which had been uncovered, was stippled with red, matting his golden eyebrows and staining the creases around his pale eyes. He looked like a bleeding gladiator or a monster out of legend whose sole purpose was to bring death to mankind.

Then, just as Myrddion began to turn away, Uther looked upward into the morning light and his hard blue eyes fell upon the healer, who was little more than a dark shape looking down on him. The prince's brows narrowed with perplexity for a moment as he searched through his memory for this shadowy face, outlined by the last of the fires, but then the machine-like brain recognised the healer and Ambrosius's brother raised his blade in an ironic salute.

As Myrddion flinched away in alarm, the gates were thrust open and Uther applied his spurs to his horse's flanks. The startled creature leapt forward into Verulamium.

Myrddion shuddered. As clearly as if it had been yesterday, he heard again the prince's mocking words as Myrddion finished dressing his wound, six years before: 'When you return from your journey to Constantinople, I would have one of the finest healers in the land as my personal physician.' If Uther remembers me, he'll have me ordered to Venta Belgarum with no hope of refusal. I've travelled thousands of miles to avoid having a master, only to be betrayed by fate once I arrive home.

But Myrddion did not complain aloud. Men such as Uther Pendragon purchase sharp ears and eyes everywhere, so any criticism would certainly be repeated to the High King's brother. The reckoning that followed would be bloody and swift.

And so Uther's force secured Verulamium, and as his warriors executed the last of the Saxon wounded, the crows and ravens began to mass in the nearby woods. The birds were hungry, but like all scavengers they were prepared to wait. When armed men set the dawn ablaze, the meat-eaters knew that they would soon dine well.

THE FAMILY TREE OF UTHER PENDRAGON

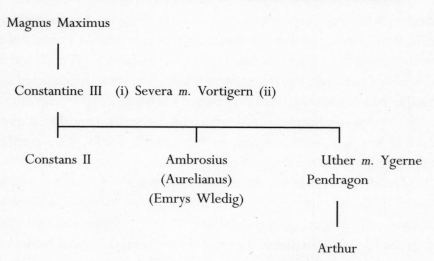

Magnus Maximus

Constantine III (i) Severa *m.* Vortigern (ii)

Constans II   Ambrosius   Uther *m.* Ygerne
                     (Aurelianus)   Pendragon
                     (Emrys Wledig)

                                            Arthur

THE FAMILY TREE OF KING GORLOIS OF CORNWALL

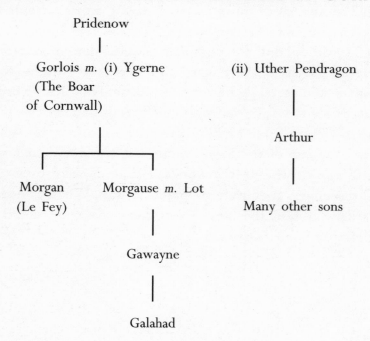

Pridenow

Gorlois *m.* (i) Ygerne   (ii) Uther Pendragon
(The Boar
of Cornwall)
                                        Arthur

Morgan   Morgause *m.* Lot
(Le Fey)
                                        Many other sons

            Gawayne

            Galahad

The information above is culled from Geoffrey of Monmouth's work,
The History of the Kings of Britain. Other historical sources include Wace,
Layamon, Gildas, Nennius and John Rhys.

CHAPTER III

AN UNWILLING SERVANT

Three things always threaten a man;
Sickness or age or the shock of quick death
Will snatch the soul from the strongest warrior
Thus has he need, who treasures his name,
The praise of his people after his parting,
To daunt the devil before his departing,
Do well on earth and worthily conquer.

From a very old English poem, *The Soul's Voyage*

'Shite!' Myrddion swore crudely while Cadoc and Finn stared at him askance. 'I know Uther Pendragon saw me. I know it! I saw his eyes try to place me in his memory. Damn and shite!'

'Perhaps you need to rejoin the women, master. Surely he won't search too hard for you if he can't find you among the wounded.' Cadoc wasn't convinced by his own argument, whatever platitudes his mouth might utter.

Myrddion wasn't convinced either, knowing full well that Uther Pendragon had a mind that was wholly focused on achieving his personal ends and fanatically fixed on the destruction of his enemies. By Uther's reasoning, Myrddion would serve to keep his warriors alive and fighting: ergo, Myrddion must be forced to accede to Pendragon's wishes.

'Finn, listen to me. Have you and Bridie discussed what I said to her? If Uther Pendragon decides to demand my services, I'll try to ensure that you are free to continue on to Segontium. If Annwynn is still alive, she will take your family into her household and give you a good life in exchange for your skills. But if she has already passed to the shades in our absence, you should seek out Eddius, my grandmother's husband. He will ensure that you and yours are kept safe.'

The healers had reached the gate and found the bodies stacked three high as Uther's warriors stripped the dead of any wealth they possessed. A crude cart drawn by a complaining mule was brought as close to the carnage as possible and, once naked, the enemy dead were flung unceremoniously into its depths like so much rubbish.

'I'll not leave you with that bastard, master,' Finn protested. 'He's even worse than Flavius Aetius, because Uther enjoys killing his victims. The Roman dog was too orderly and too cold for such hot passions. I won't leave you, Myrddion.'

'You must,' Myrddion insisted. 'You're a father now, so your responsibilities extend further than your own desires. You must tell your children what you've seen and heard. You are the Truth-teller, so you must survive and be free of any further stains on your honour. If Uther seeks me out, he'll demand duties of me that I'd prefer not to contemplate. I don't want to worry about you, your wife and your babe as well as my other companions. Serve me well, my friend, by leaving me to my destiny.'

A thin, almost inaudible whimper caught his attention. 'Hush, Finn. Listen! Something is alive in that pile of corpses to the left of the gate.'

Two of Uther's warriors picked up the flaccid body of a woman whose head lolled unnaturally and whose throat had obviously been cut, to judge from the veil of blood that had soaked her robe from neck to hem. Beneath her body, and partially protected by the curled chest of a youth, a small child began to cry thinly from its nest of ruined flesh.

As quick as the flash of a merlin's wings as it glides in for the kill, Myrddion swooped under the arms of the nearest warrior and plucked the infant from the blood-soaked earth. The child was wholly saturated with its mother's blood, so the healer couldn't tell easily if it had suffered any injuries. As he tried to remove its sticky swaddling bands, Brangaine appeared at his side as if by magic, and whisked the child from Myrddion's hands.

'I'll see to the little one back at the inn, master,' she said, and Myrddion knew better than to refuse her. She had already wrapped maternal arms around the whimpering child.

Another mouth to feed, a cynical voice whispered in Myrddion's brain, but he closed a mental door on that insidious thought with a sharp, dismissive slam.

'Why are you here, Brangaine? It's far too dangerous, and you've left Willa unattended.'

'The prince has been seeking you, master, and Gron looks likely to give you up. He's a snake, that man, with no decent feelings except to whine and complain about everything in his smug existence. I came to warn you.'

Brangaine scowled at her master with a look that would have curdled milk, so Myrddion attempted to soothe her injured feelings by sending her back to the inn to cleanse the infant and discover if the child had suffered any hurt. Then, his duty done, he turned to continue the search for those who remained alive among the drifts of bodies.

By coercing any able-bodied person who passed into helping

him, Myrddion managed to free the pitifully few survivors who still breathed. In their pursuit of plunder, Uther's warriors had moved on to pick over the corpses of Saxon invaders in the lower town, having no pecuniary interest in the half-dressed men and women who had been caught up in the merciless battle. The killing field at the wall revealed a total of one hundred and fifty-one dead. Only two slightly wounded children remained alive, and Myrddion was heartsick to contemplate the thoroughness displayed by the Saxon attackers. Unprotected flesh was helpless against swinging axes and iron swords.

In the lower town, Myrddion and his assistants must perforce cope with cruel burns, grossly swollen flesh and bodies that were blistered, splitting and glistening with internal fire. As Annwynn had done so many years before after the destruction of the Blue Hag inn in Segontium, Myrddion plied his henbane and poppy liberally, for few patients survived the kiss of the flames.

And so, some hours later, Myrddion was dispirited and on edge when a warrior from Uther's personal guard found him treating the last of the survivors. The prince's orders to the young man had been curt and to the point.

'Instruct the healer whose name I cannot recall to attend on me at the house of Gotti, the trader, before nightfall. Warn him that he'll feel my wrath if I am forced to search for him.'

The attitude of the messenger was derisive in both tone and stance, for the slight young healer who stood before him seemed incapable of any threat to either himself or the prince. As the son of a minor Atrabate lord, the warrior was very full of his own importance, although he had not yet learned to be suspicious of superficial appearances. Myrddion recognised his immaturity immediately, although the young man affected a close-cropped, ruddy beard in the Roman style.

'Before I ask you to present your message to me once again, young man, what is your name? I don't like to receive instructions from persons I haven't met.'

As he spoke, Myrddion's eyes remained fixed on the burned leg of a young matron, barely fifteen years of age, whose face was blackened with soot, except where tears had cut long runnels down her cheeks before dripping onto her scorched robe.

'It's Ulfin. Now hear the words of Prince Pendragon, Master of the West and scourge of the Saxons,' the young man snapped crossly, as he tried to regain the initiative.

'I am aware of your master. What is your message?' The healer spoke with such calm presence of mind that Ulfin became both flustered and angry. He was of a similar age to Myrddion, and trying desperately to disguise his nervousness and frustration, but something that flashed in the slanted black eyes as they glanced up at him made the warrior feel queasy for a moment. However, the smiling mouth soon restored his initial impression of guileless, harmless youth, and he repeated the message more slowly.

'I will come when I have finished dressing this young woman's burns. A few moments mean nothing to Prince Uther, but they are crucial to her chances of surviving her injuries.' Without waiting for an answer, Myrddion returned to wrapping an unguent-smeared bandage around the painful blistering on the girl's foot and leg.

'My lord instructed me to bring you to him immediately!' Ulfin exclaimed sullenly, his right foot stamping childishly on the roadway where Myrddion was working. 'The prince will make us both suffer if you keep him waiting.'

'I said I would come when I finish this dressing – and I'm almost done. I would point out to you that Uther Pendragon is your lord, not mine. He is also indebted to me, so I counsel you to be courteous.'

The warrior would have protested, but Myrddion turned an unresponsive back towards him and continued to wrap the girl's calf with careful deliberation. Ulfin began to pace as his fertile imagination sought an excuse for his tardiness. Uther would not be amused and Myrddion had won a new enemy.

'There, it's all done now,' Myrddion whispered to his patient. 'You've been a brave girl, and soon you will feel much, much better. Have no fears, for I will see you before I depart for the north.'

With his usual attention to detail, Myrddion washed his hands thoroughly in a bowl of warm water, cleaned his blood-rimmed nails and plaited his hair, which had begun to escape its thong. Then he gave instructions to Finn and Crodoc to care for their patients, straightened his robes and turned back to face the young warrior.

'Very well, Ulfin, I'm ready. I'm a stranger here, so show me to the house of Gotti.'

Obviously, Ulfin thought, as he led the way back into the city. No man who knows him keeps the Son of the Dragon waiting.

The Gotti house was a two-storeyed, clay-brick structure that owed more to the Roman subura than to fine villas. From the entrance, Myrddion could see a long corridor that opened into a familiar internal atrium, complete with statuary. As he was being searched for weapons, he noted that this open garden was long and thin, and that the Gotti household apparently adhered to the practice of growing edible foodstuffs in a city, if the glimpse of neat rows of herbs, potted lemon trees and some young cabbage heads were any indication. Once Uther's guards had completed an efficient body search, Myrddion was conducted into the triclinium, where the shutters were wide open to catch any stray rays of sunshine.

'You've taken your time, healer. Was my messenger not sufficiently persuasive? As for you, Ulfin, we'll discuss time management at a later date.'

Uther lounged on a couch, totally at ease for all he had lived free from Roman customs for many years. Myrddion examined the prince's clean-shaven cheeks and the wildly spiralling curls that were still as vigorous as they were in his memory. But Uther was now into middle age, and his face showed every vice that had been imprinted over the elegant bones and sculpted features of his face. An invisible aura of power hung around his head and shoulders, and Myrddion could almost hear the crackle of lightning.

The healer upbraided himself. Look into his eyes, fool! There's more than power in there – there's rage and a cold hatred as well. Apart from his brother, Uther hates almost everything.

Warned, Myrddion bowed his head with exquisite courtesy, judging the depth of his obeisance to a nicety. Uther was no king, but nor was he merely noble. A wise man would always treat that unpredictable nature with care.

'Your servant was admirably clear and brief, lord. It wasn't his fault that I have kept you waiting. I was partway through bandaging a young woman's burns, so the delay was my fault entirely. Has the scar from your old wound faded?'

This final question deflected a gathering storm on Uther's handsome features. He bared his forearm and Myrddion bent to examine a long, white furrow in the golden skin where a boar's tusk had ripped apart the flesh and muscle.

'As you can see, healer, your skills served me well. Now, reacquaint me with your name, for I like to know the details of my servants' lives so that I might judge their characters. Ah, I see you have yet to learn how to guard those black brows of yours. Yes, you'll serve me, healer, or I'll be forced to apply pressure. No true leader permits a useful tool to pass unused through his fingers.'

'Alas, lord, I am waited for in Segontium, so I may not remain here.' Myrddion's voice was implacable, but still courteous. His eyes roved over Uther's face, and a chillier part of the young man's complex nature admired the prince's icy calm.

'You'll serve me, healer, because I'll find something that will persuade you. What is your name? I have no wish to call you by your trade, so answer me fairly.'

'I am Myrddion Merlinus, previously called Emrys, Prince Uther. I have been healer to many kings, most recently to Flavius Aetius, the former *magister militum* of Rome.'

'Impressive, but what do I care for failed generals who have met their fate? I'm more interested in your Roman name. Now I hear it again, I remember wondering at it before.' As Uther's mouth twisted with something that Myrddion decided to ignore, the healer determined to think carefully before he explained anything personal to this formidable man.

'I'm the bastard son of a father who refuses to acknowledge me, so since his name is no longer material I have taken the name of his hunting hawk, a bird that declined to be tamed. And although you are scathing of my old master, I would remind you, my lord, that Aetius was always successful as a battle commander. He forced Attila, the Hungvari, to his knees at the Battle of the Catalaunian Plain, and was only assassinated at the hands of a fear-crazed emperor. Hubris is a dangerous sin, my lord, whether we are generals, princes or mere healers.'

'Is that a warning, Myrddion?' Uther chuckled, and the healer had no idea whether humour or sarcasm was the source of the prince's amusement. 'Like Aetius, Valentinian is dead, so why should I waste a moment's thought on the strategies of other, failed minds? Still, you manage to pique my curiosity. You're a man of many skills, Myrddion Merlinus, so I'll not set you free to roam at will. You'll accompany me to Venta Belgarum. My brother's birth celebrations are due, so you'll make an excellent gift for Ambrosius Imperator.'

'You are gracious to say so, 'Prince Uther, but I must decline your invitation. I am promised to accompany my servant, Finn Trutheller, to his new mistress, Annwynn of Segontium. Once there, I intend to spend a little time with my family and my king, Melvyn ap Melvig of the Deceangli.'

Uther frowned, lowering his huge, leonine head so that his blue eyes examined the healer from under his golden brows. His eyes were flat and expressionless, as featureless as shallow puddles of pale water.

'I should be insulted by your refusal of my offer of preferment, but I accept that you are a prideful young man, Myrddion. But you must be made to listen to my demands so that pride doesn't lead you into error.'

In the small, ominous silence that followed, Myrddion read much into Uther's words. For a short moment, he thought that the prince would permit him to leave Verulamium unscathed, but then the blue eyes slowly rose and Myrddion was forced to repress a shudder.

'No, my fine hunting bird, you will learn to come to my glove, or you'll be caged. I thought you would understand me, Myrddion Merlinus. Truthteller can go to the devil for all I care, but you will journey to Venta Belgarum with me, either on the back of your horse – or in chains.'

'Of what use is an unwilling servant?'

Uther considered Myrddion's question seriously. 'Depending on the servant, his usefulness will be gauged by me. I'm losing patience with you, Myrddion Merlinus, and I've nearly decided to drag you to Venta Belgarum in chains. Any patriotic tribesman would consider my proposal to be an honour. The reverse of patriotism is treason, a crime punishable by death, and at least you'd not be in a position to give succour to the Saxon cause.'

Myrddion recalled Willa's warning and realised that he had no recourse but to accept Uther's decision, but his honour demanded that some concessions should be wrung from his opponent. His shoulders squared as he prepared to do battle against the wit of the prince.

'I am prepared to swear allegiance to Ambrosius Imperator and to the crown, Prince Uther, subject to several conditions. I am no traitor, but my journeys have convinced me that we must find some equilibrium and commonality with the Saxons who have invaded our lands. I agree that they must not be permitted to overrun our homeland, or everything we cherish will be eroded away. But I'll not willingly swear allegiance to a man who would coerce me or threaten me, my lord. I am not a peasant and I find it insulting to be forced into labour by a stronger, more ruthless hand than my own.'

Just when Myrddion expected Uther to become enraged, the prince grinned. 'Bargaining, are we? I don't give a tinker's curse if you swear allegiance to me or not, as long as I am obeyed. I'm of a mind that you will be important in the coming wars, whether you choose it or not. Decide, Myrddion Merlinus! Do you come to Venta Belgarum? Or do you die?'

Myrddion looked around the triclinium at the hard faces of Uther's guard, especially at a tall young man who stood directly behind Uther's couch. In the faces around him, all he could read was disinterest, harshness and unquestioning obedience to their master. The healer knew he was weakened by his affection for the friends and servants who had followed him to the far ends of the known world.

'I will journey to Venta Belgarum with you, Prince Uther. My fellow healer Cadoc and the Greek Praxiteles will accompany me, but Finn Truthteller and my other servants will need a cart and a horse to journey to the north. And they'll need provisions. I'll not leave a young family to perish on the wild, distant roads leading to Segontium.'

Uther laughed. His ruddy lips glistened with amusement and something darker that lurked close to the surface of his nature, but the prince was honestly amused by Myrddion's attempt to bargain with him.

'Find a horse and cart, Botha. I care not where they come from, just root them out and present them to Master Truthteller with my compliments. Ulfin, you can be of some use and terrify the Gotti into parting with sufficient food to feed the travellers. If you do well, perhaps I'll forget how slow you've been to obey my instructions – perhaps!'

The tall young guard nodded and would have left the triclinium with Ulfin hot on his heels, but Uther had not quite completed his instructions. 'Make it fast, Botha! I am bored with Verulamium, now that it has yielded up its Saxon attackers. I'll be on the road to Venta Belgarum by the morrow and I want my healer with me.'

'I understand, my lord – and I live to serve,' Botha replied in a voice that was firm and deep. As the two warriors turned to leave, Ulfin tried not to run from Uther's presence.

As if Myrddion had ceased to exist, Uther returned to his beaker of wine and the healer realised that the audience was over.

Finn Truthteller was inconsolable when Myrddion insisted on sharing everything he owned with his former assistant. Botha had arrived within a brief hour, driving a lumbering farm cart drawn by two huge horses that tossed their pale manes and stamped their gigantic, hair-fringed hooves. Cadoc eyed the beasts with approval and Finn would have exchanged them for the oxen had Myrddion not refused his offer outright.

Cadoc was disappointed.

Bridie wept, which set her infant to crying lustily, until the Flower Maiden echoed to the noise of wails and tears. When

Myrddion produced a purse holding four golden coins, Bridie's cries of grief became even louder as Truthteller attempted to refuse such largesse.

'I'll not take it, master. That purse is yours, and it was earned at enormous personal cost. I would have remained a madman wandering the mountains of Cymru were it not for you, so how can I take your hard-earned coin?'

'Please, Finn. You've earned my gratitude over many weary miles of patient service. And so has Bridie. Her limp should remind you every day of how much she has relinquished by obeying my wishes. Regardless of your protestations, my friend, you leave with my blessing. And, if they are willing, I want you to take Rhedyn and Brangaine and the children with you for their continued safety.'

Brangaine was torn between the choices suddenly open to her, for Willa's huge green eyes haunted her, waking and sleeping, and the child's safety consumed her thoughts. But almost as compelling was her fear of being an unattached female without any means of earning a living when she lacked a master to give her status. Now, faced with two unsatisfactory options, she was struck dumb with the weight of her responsibilities. Eventually, she opened her mouth to agree to head north to Segontium, but Willa pushed her way forward to face her master. The child's face was very serious and earnest as she made her foster mother's decision for her.

'Lord Myrddion, my mother would agree to leave with Finn for my sake.' The child's rusty voice was oddly persuasive and Myrddion recognised the same tone of command that he used at times when hard decisions must be made. 'She does not wish to leave you, but she loves me enough to throw away her security. But she need not, for I'll not go to Segontium whatever you say. Venta Belgarum is where she who must not be named wishes me to be . . . even though

I am frightened. We are all her tools and I have come to realise that she saved my life for some purpose.' She turned to Brangaine. 'I must go with the master to Venta Belgarum, because the Mother wills it.'

Brangaine's shoulders slumped in the light of her daughter's vivid, insistent eyes. Then she turned to face Myrddion while her arms wound tightly around the child.

'What should I do, master? What should I do?'

'I don't know, Brangaine, but perhaps Willa is right. Perhaps our destiny has always led to Venta Belgarum, and although we try to avoid our separate fates the Mother will have her way, no matter how we struggle to gainsay her.'

'Aye, master, I know.'

Then Brangaine wept, as if Willa had already been torn from her arms.

Rhedyn elected to stay with Brangaine to help with the children, so in the end just Finn Truthteller and his young family took road for Segantium. The only person who was overjoyed to see them climb into their wagon and set the horses in motion was Gron, the innkeeper. All day, he had been predicting dire consequences to the inn for sheltering the healers, until his wife longed to brain him with her best iron cooking pot.

'After they've gone, the eyes of Uther Pendragon will turn away from us. At least some of them are leaving, but I'll not rest easy until I see the back of all of those cursed healers.'

'You'd not have to worry about coming to the prince's attention if you didn't water the wine,' Fionnuala hissed, her plump breasts quivering with the dislike she often felt for her spouse. 'These healers have brought custom to the Flower Maiden . . . and if they go, you'll have nothing to complain about, will you? Be careful what you wish for, husband.'

Gron eyed his angry wife out of the corners of his eyes and tried to look affronted, which failed dismally because of the shifty look that was etched into his cadaverous face.

But later, when Myrddion paid their account at the inn and made arrangements for their departure, Gron felt a strange reluctance to pad the bill in his usual custom. The landlord would breathe more easily once the healers had gone, but perhaps there were worse dangers ahead than strange, outland travellers.

Venta Belgarum was far away, and Uther soon chafed at the slow speed of the journey. The prince usually drove his troops mercilessly so that they seemed to appear, fully armed and thirsting for blood, under the walls of any Saxon fortress they encountered. Like smoke, the tribesmen came and went at will. Unfortunately, Myrddion's oxen were unmoved by Uther's desire for haste and plodded along in the rear at their usual slow pace. Eventually, Uther decided to desert the healer's party, leaving them with a guard of half a dozen mounted cavalrymen while he sped onward like an arrow loosened from a bow. On his order, the foot soldiers broke into a brisk trot and Myrddion marvelled anew at the discipline and fortitude of men who marched to war with their weapons in a pack upon their backs. As they ran, the warriors sang lustily and Myrddion's heart trembled in his chest as tuneful voices sang tales of long gone days when his people ruled his wild and beautiful land unopposed.

> Gold-hilted in his hand I see his sword;
>   Two spears he holds, with spearheads grim and green;
> Around his shield the yellow gold is poured,
>   And in its midst a silver boss is seen.

Other, lighter voices answered as they disappeared into the grey dust of the roadway.

Fair Fergus ruin on us all hath brought!
We crossed the ocean, and to him gave heed;
His honour with a cup of ale was bought;
From him hath passed the fame of each high deed.

'Their song gives me the shivers, Myrddion. It doesn't seem right, somehow, to run towards the enemy belting out a song of death,' Cadoc muttered.

Myrddion listened from the back of his horse until the eerie music passed away into the low hills. 'They sing a song from Hibernia that tells of the exile of the sons of Usnach. Perhaps we should take their message as a warning. If Uther doesn't stop the enemy, then we will be exiles in a far land, forever torn from everything we love.'

'There's a cheerful thought,' Cadoc whispered under his breath.

After passing the next small township, the wagons travelled slowly along a narrow, ill-kept road leading out of Durocobrivae, and this part of the journey soon became uncomfortable and slow. The ribbon of compacted earth and fieldstone plunged south through uneven country, making little concession for travellers who sought an easy route into the south-west. Spring rains rendered the road both muddy and treacherous, especially when going downhill, and the women were forced to alight from the carts and trudge beside them with their long skirts dragging in the mud.

Now that the journey had actually begun, Willa had cheered immediately and her face was wreathed in smiles when Botha, who had been charged with ensuring that the healers reached Ambrosius's capital, swung the girl up onto his horse to ride in front of him. With her immature back pressed against the burly guardsman's torso, she sat and laughed aloud at the efforts of the sliding oxen, the sudden flight of a flock of ducks and the trailing branches of thick oaken copses that caught in her hair. Myrddion felt his spirit lighten as he watched her happily devouring these wild places as if she had never experienced the terrors of bad dreams.

Cold, filthy and weary, the small party imagined themselves to be the only travellers in this savage place until the landscape cleared and they found themselves fording a swift river.

'Where are we, Botha?' Myrddion asked, wringing out his black cloak, which had become saturated when he was unhorsed in the river. 'I swear we've seen no one since we left Durocobrivae.'

Botha pointed to the north with one hand. 'There's a hamlet across that way, but I don't think it even has a name. This road eventually meets another goat track that takes us south to Calleva Atrebatum, where we'll join a major thoroughfare that leads into Venta Belgarum. The journey becomes easier after that.'

'Promise?' Cadoc snapped irritably as he stripped off his wet boots and tried to warm his chilled feet.

'Not if we don't get these beasts moving,' Botha replied tersely. 'Gods, but I hate oxen!'

'At least that's something we can agree on,' Cadoc retorted, and the slow journey resumed.

Day blurred into day, for oxen travel at their own pace and no application of whips or quirts will speed their steady plodding. Just when Myrddion believed he would scream with boredom and frustration, Calleva Atrebatum hove into view.

The large Romanised town rested in a small nest of low hills and presented an orderly, well-kept visage to strangers. The cheerful faces of the local peasants, the neat conical cottages on well-tended farms and the fat-tailed sheep that grazed on the low slopes brought sudden tears to Myrddion's eyes. His memories of these lands had comforted him during their travels because of their fruitfulness and plenty. The tuneful whistling of a cowherd driving his beasts to fresh pastures filled some of the emptiness that existed in the young healer's heart. Perhaps service in Ambrosius's court mightn't be so very bad if the sights, sounds and smells of home surrounded the healers with a promise of better days ahead.

Botha had been charged with shepherding his charges to Venta Belgarum at the best possible speed, so he only permitted a single night of rest in a comfortable inn on the outskirts of Calleva Atrebatum. Hot food was a boon and straw-filled pallets luxurious treats after weeks on the road. By now, Finn must be far away and Myrddion ached for the companionship and calm common sense of the laconic herbmaster. He also missed the gurgling smile of Bridie's infant, although Brangaine's newest orphan was a lusty child who cried ceaselessly when he was wet, hungry or tired. Fortunately for his chances of survival, the little boy could eat well-chewed food, for milk was only rarely available. In Calleva Atrebatum, Myrddion immediately took comfort from a long, relaxing soak in the still-functioning Roman baths, the custom that he missed most from his adventures in the Middle Sea.

Over a bowl of warm soup, Myrddion tried to discover the private secrets of Uther Pendragon by questioning Botha, but at first the prince's most trusted guardsman refused to be drawn.

'I know what you're about, healer, so don't try to trick or bribe me. I would take any insult to my master in bad part.'

'I'll ask my questions to your face, Botha, for I've nothing to conceal. I'm fearful of Prince Uther, and I'd be pleased to find some evidence that he's not the machine of war that men describe in whispers behind his back.'

Botha laughed harshly, but then he relented. 'My master is much as he has been described. What would you have me say, Myrddion Merlinus? Uther Pendragon is a man who has been shaped by cruel times. He is a warrior who has been hammered out by suffering to save his country, but only by spending his own blood profligately. He is in the saddle for many months of each year. Against the wishes of his brother, he has not wed, nor has he acknowledged any children that might warm his old age. His thoughts are ever fixed upon striking the Saxons at their heart and I've never known a man so determined and inflexible in his chosen purpose. If you would feel his wrath, then mention the name of Vortigern, the murderer and traitor, for my master lays all the ills that afflict our land at the feet of that bloodstained bastard.'

CHAPTER IV

THE MASTER OF THE SUN

Phoebus, who first environed the round world with
the rays of his wisdom so that he might rightly win the
sole honour of the name of Sol, was infatuated with
the love of Leucothoe, to his own disgrace and her
destruction, and, through the repeated change of the
eclipse, he frequently came to lack his own light, of
which the whole world felt the loss.

Twelfth century English prose

Like a young Roman matron, Venta Belgarum rested inland from
the large harbour of Portus Adurni, with a low hill on one flank and
a wide river on the other. The air of this rich provincial town was
sweet and the climate was temperate for the isles of Britain, so the
river valley produced an abundance of fruit, vegetables and
livestock. Few peasants ever slept with their bellies cleaving to their
spines, and both floods and drought were rare. To add further
blessings to her citizens, the port had become the chief conduit of
trade with the continent now that Dubris had become a Saxon
enclave. Myrddion understood why those thanes with an eye to the

future turned their ambitions towards Venta Belgarum with both lust and envy.

The town itself had been blessed by Roman occupation. The roads were wide and well designed, the public buildings were constructed from quarried stone and it was obvious that a clear sense of order in town planning had been developed for centuries, leaving only pre-Roman and post-Roman commercial and domestic architecture to sprawl in the mild sunshine. The Roman buildings were perfectly aligned and self-contained. Here, in a position of prominence, stood Ambrosius's hall and the seat of his government.

The forecourt of the hall was not large, but it possessed the distinction of being completely paved in the Roman style. The wagons groaned to a halt and Botha ordered two cavalrymen to drive the vehicles to a house near the city walls where Uther had ordered that the healers should be domiciled. With sound common sense, Botha had ordered this detour to the centre of the busy town so that Myrddion should see with his own eyes the glories of the High King's rule.

The Great Hall of Ambrosius was constructed of timber and its design was inclined to hark back to the distant past, so the imperator had ordered that the vast doors be suitably painted. As carved dragons of amazing intricacy had been adzed out of the timber, the red colours of the legions figured prominently in conjunction with thin strips of beaten bronze, copper and brass. Every wooden surface was covered with complex, intertwined patterns that had no ending and no beginning: much like the nature of the High King himself, with a firm foundation in the tribal past but strengthened by Roman invention.

'As soon as you have bathed and dressed, you must return with your two guardsmen to this hall, where Prince Uther will introduce you and your party to the High King. Do I have your oath that you will not try to escape?'

'Aye. Your prince kept his word and allowed my assistant to go back to Segontium. I will not repay his trust by breaking faith with him.'

Botha nodded his handsome, broad-boned head. 'Fairly said. You have until sunset. At that time, my master will expect you, in company with your remaining assistant and your servant, to be ready and waiting outside the hall. Prince Uther has no interest in your women, so they may stay with the children.'

'We will be there, Botha.'

The route to the living quarters allotted to the healers was not long, but it was complex, for it wound through a network of streets that lacked Roman order and method. Myrddion recalled the grid patterns of Rome and the simplicity of finding a path from one landmark to another in the City of the Seven Hills, so the way through the outer, serpentine roads of Venta Belgarum was difficult to remember. Myrddion asked Praxiteles to memorise it, as he was more used than his master to finding his way through the circuitous marketplaces of the east.

The house that would become Myrddion's home for many years was a low, sprawling structure of stone and timber that had been constructed in the Roman style, and had probably once been the abode of a minor official attached to the legions. Myrddion was surprised by the lack of windows, for the building was quite old and harked back to a Roman domestic architecture that presented blank walls to frustrate possible enemies. Any light that filtered into the small rooms emanated from an open atrium that was small, overgrown and badly in need of weeding. Long before the carts were unloaded, Rhedyn's thoughtful eyes were already fixed on a large patch of thistles that served as the lungs of the villa.

Generally speaking, its rooms were cramped but comfortable, although Myrddion discovered a dusty, spider-webbed scriptorium, complete with scroll niches and shelves that were perfect for the storage of the young man's precious glass jars. As this room was larger than most, Myrddion reasoned that the original owner of the villa was a man who made his living in some clerical capacity.

Like children with a new toy, the healers explored the whole building. There were simple baths and a functioning hypocaust in the back of the structure, although the plunge pools were empty and the fires to heat the water were long dead. The women found the separate kitchen and Brangaine's eyes grew starry with delight when she spied the overgrown remnants of a herb garden.

'We will need servants,' Praxiteles stated laconically as he ran his fingers over a dusty divan. 'We'll have to do a great deal of work to set this house to rights.'

'Aye, but first we must wash and dress for our meeting with the High King. Is there a well?'

'Yes, master, and there are pipes that go somewhere into the foundations,' Cadoc answered swiftly, having raced through all the rooms and the dusty patches of unhealthy grass that were hemmed in around the villa by a low rock wall. 'But I think they're made of lead.'

'They'll need changing then,' Myrddion muttered. 'Find your best tunics, you two, and join me. Our guards will know where the nearest baths are.'

Unfortunately, the Roman baths had been demolished years earlier, so the three men were forced to sluice themselves clean with cold water from the well. No one enjoyed this experience overmuch, although the sun was still shining. Makeshift towelling dried their hair and bodies, while Brangaine and Rhedyn entered into the spirit of the occasion by dusting and cleaning their best robes. Even Myrddion's worn boots were cleansed of the dried mud that had fouled them on the long journey.

Within the prescribed two hours, just as the sun began to set in the west, the three companions were escorted into the hall of Ambrosius. Myrddion wore his best black tunic, leggings and cloak, held together with a huge damascene brooch given to him by a grateful Syrian trader whose nephew's life he had saved. The funereal colour of Myrddion's dress was mitigated by the fineness of his gems. Two gold and ruby rings adorned his hands, an ancient arm ring gifted by his great-grandfather encircled his wrist, and an electrum spike added a barbaric touch in one ear. His face was smooth in the Roman style, for Myrddion loathed the sensation of hairiness and had plucked away much of his beard when he was maturing. His extreme male beauty was feminised by his waist-length black hair, enlivened only by a streak of white that sprang from the right side of his forehead.

Cadoc had cleaned his leathers, taking particular care with the brass plates that had protected his torso when he was a soldier. His good tunic was snow white with age and vigorous washing, and his boots were clean. His leather satchel, worn proudly over his shoulder, added an air of distinction to his appearance. Out of a streak of vanity, the scarred man had plaited his red hair into the fore and side plaits of a warrior and bound the ends with strips of copper.

Praxiteles had few possessions of any material worth, having sold his ancestral gems when he lost his trading business in Constantinople years earlier. But poverty and the need to earn his bread as a servant had no power to diminish the impact of his thick moustaches, which were as white as the clouds over Venta Belgarum. His hair was bound around his head and was the same distinctive colour, but long streaks of jet amongst the braids gave his face an exotic cast, accentuated by his golden-brown skin. On the journey to the west, he had taken what coin he had earned in Myrddion's service and purchased undyed tunics that had been embroidered at neck and hem in the Greek style. The impression of hale old age and intelligence expressed in his deep brown eyes, the sun-leached wrinkles on his face and his upright, vigorous stance spoke more eloquently of far places and hotter suns than any use of mere decoration.

In their separate ways, the three men were oddities, so the courtiers who clustered in the anteroom of Ambrosius's court of justice eyed them carefully from the corners of their eyes.

The inner doors opened with a flourish at the appointed hour and the powerful lords of the south ambled into the large audience room. Like a stream of water impeded by stones, the aristocratic guests washed around the three outlanders in a curious but silent flood, leaving them to stand awkwardly in the midst of Uther's personal guard as they awaited their instructions.

Myrddion quickly grew impatient at the delay and the contempt that it implied, but he succeeded in maintaining his calm demeanour. Tantrums and temper would not advance his cause. He understood the Roman perspective, and trusted he would be able to reason with whatever the High King and his brother had in store for him.

Uther appeared at the open doors to the inner room, as cat-footed as usual and with Botha at his shoulder. With a single, beckoning gesture, he called the three men forward. Half dazzled by the number of oil lamps within the large audience room, they entered Ambrosius's seat of power.

As Myrddion advanced he kept his head down, so his first impression was that the uneven flags beneath his feet were unusually clean. No traces of mud, scatterings of leaves or drifts of dust were permitted to gather on Ambrosius's floor. As he raised his eyes, he saw that the room was long, rectangular and naturally inclined to be dark, for no apertures permitted cold air to bring discomfort to the imperator. Ambrosius had ordered that oil lamps, sconces, a circular fire-pit and numerous torches be lit so that mellow, golden light bounced off the reflective surfaces of the guardsmen's armour and the goblet of rare glass held in the hands of a slim lad who stood beside two large hunting dogs. A sweet, almost floral scent perfumed the air from the oil lamps and softened the undecorated severity of the room.

'Are these the men who are your latest find, brother?' A tenor voice spoke in very pure Latin. 'Bring them into the light, for you've piqued my curiosity.'

Myrddion moved forward with Cadoc and Praxiteles a little behind. Without examining his new master, the healer knelt gracefully before abasing himself in the Celtic fashion.

'Rise!' the voice ordered imperiously in Celt. 'I can't judge your worth if I can't see your faces.'

Myrddion obeyed, surveying the figure that sat on an opulent, fur-covered Roman stool before him. Ambrosius needed no throne or dais to demonstrate his power and his authority. Mere appearance was sufficient to impress.

Myrddion could now gauge the similarities, and the differences, between these two extraordinary brothers. Uther was the taller of the two and was almost a giant, even by northern standards, but his brother was more compact and animated. Ambrosius's body seemed to crackle with invisible fires and the force of a powerful intellect that could not be hidden by flesh, muscle or bone. His long-fingered, expressive hands were moving, tapping and stroking the arm of his chair, while his feet, in their simple Roman sandals, seemed to be invested with lives of their own.

'Brother, the young man who stands before you is a healer of significant skill. He saved my arm six years ago, as you know, for all that he hails from the barbaric wilds of Gwynedd. His name is Myrddion Emrys or Merlinus, and he has latterly returned from the Middle Sea. He is my birthday gift to you.'

A flicker of distaste chased itself across the broad cheekbones and forehead of the man who sat on the Roman stool.

'Really, Uther! You can't treat men like birth gifts, as he's hardly yours to give.'

'Yes, he is! I bargained with him, and I believe he'll fulfil his side of the agreement. He's now yours to keep.'

'You must forgive my brother, Myrddion Merlinus. He has laboured for many years to keep our borders safe from the invaders, so his manners have been neglected in many ways. To what lands did you travel in your journey to the Middle Sea?'

The imperator's face showed a flush of excitement and Myrddion was reminded that Ambrosius had been forced to wander through many lands during his own youth as he fled from the wrath of Vortigern. Ambrosius's hair was the same reddish blond as his brother's, but he kept his curls under control by cutting them ruthlessly short in the Roman military style. Below a pair of thick, well-shaped eyebrows, two eyes of a vivid shade of blue surveyed Myrddion eagerly from head to toe.

So blue! Barbarian eyes! Then Myrddion amended his snap decision when he saw a flash of controlled intelligence in their seemingly hollow depths. No. They were Roman eyes.

'From Gesoriacum, we travelled extensively through the lands of the Franks and the Visigoths,' Myrddion replied in equally pure Latin, causing Ambrosius to raise one inquisitive eyebrow in surprise. 'From Massilia, we journeyed to Rome, the north of Italia, Ravenna and thence to Constantinople.'

'Then you have travelled far,' Ambrosius replied, his face carefully neutral, although his hands and feet were in constant motion as if they mirrored his furious mental activity. 'You will have seen the world as it is.'

'Aye, lord king. I've seen too much of it for comfort, I fear.'

'As have I,' Ambrosius murmured as his busy fingers toyed with the fringe on a cushion. 'We will speak in private at a later time, for I would welcome news of the world. Couriers come rarely to Venta Belgarum.'

'As you wish, highness, so shall it be,' Myrddion answered in his easy, mellifluous voice.

'The healer has seen battle, and has proved his skills in the north as well as in the Middle Sea,' Uther added, his mouth twisted as if he tasted something foul. 'He served Vortigern during the wars with Vortimer, and he knew Hengist and Horsa.'

Why is he trying to set Ambrosius against me? Myrddion thought, as he saw the slight frown on Ambrosius's face and noted the sudden tension in the High King's body that was released in the swift jerking of one expressive foot. He tried to speak calmly.

'All too true, I'm afraid. When I was but ten years old Vortigern tried to kill me, believing I was the son of a demon. The king's sorcerers claimed that I had the gift of prophesy and should be offered for sacrifice, but Vortigern relented and slew his magicians in my stead. In the process, he killed my grandmother, who was the High Priestess of the Mother and a daughter of the king of the Deceangli tribe. Earlier, I had treated Horsa, whose leg had been broken in a fall from his horse. Hengist was grateful for my services to his brother and helped me escape from Vortigern's wrath.'

When Myrddion paused for breath, Ambrosius asked several rapid-fire questions.

'Why did the regicide think you had a demon for a sire? And how could you know anything of healing at such a young age?'

He doubts me and tries to trap me. Be careful, Myrddion, and keep your wits about you.

The healer's smile was as open and guileless as a child's. For the first time, he began to use his expressive hands for emphasis.

'My mother claimed a demon had forced itself upon her when she was a young girl. As it turned out, she lied, but she was very young and was terrified into making this excuse when a Roman dignitary raped her after being washed ashore during a storm near her home. Only her wits and her courage saved her life. Melvig ap Melwy, the king of our tribe, was her grandfather. Fortunately, he took a liking to me and chose to believe the fiction. Because of the lie, I couldn't learn the ways of the warrior as my birth dictated, so my grandmother apprenticed me to the herbmaster Annwynn of Segontium when I was only eight.

'So how did you come to serve Vortigern? I would have thought that you would hate him as much as I do, if he killed your grandmother.'

Myrddion recognised the same distrust growing in Ambrosius's eyes as had always lived in the heart of his brother. Vortigern had wounded their family deeply, but Myrddion saw a way to turn this enmity to his advantage.

'I loathed the man, highness, and one of my happiest days was when I saw him burn to death inside his fortress. But that is another story, my lord. To answer your question, Mistress Annwynn taught me the trade of healing and later gifted me with a box of scrolls that had belonged to her own master. She was illiterate and knew that I could use them to instruct her in their wisdom. From the scrolls, we learned the principles of Hippocrates, which enjoin all healers to do no harm in their craft, and that all men deserve a chance to live after the carnage of the battlefield. When Vortigern's army was defeated in a battle near Tomen-y-mur with great loss of life, my mistress insisted that we offer our services to save as many as we could. I was reluctant, but my mistress is a true healer and will allow no one to suffer if she can assist them in any way.'

Ambrosius grunted, but his keen eyes were a little less hard.

'Once Vortigern's army was rested and his men dispersed, he refused to permit me to depart with my mistress. He could see into the hearts of men, even mine, and he had no softness or mercy in him. He threatened to kill Annwynn if I didn't obey. But, if I'm honest, I must admit that he also offered an added inducement. He offered to tell me the identity of my father if I served him loyally. Ultimately, I served him out of fear – but I also served him for my own purposes.'

'Ah,' Ambrosius said, and Myrddion realised he had passed a test of some kind. 'Yes, Vortigern understood the virtues and vices that we hold in our secret hearts. He was the very devil.'

'He was worse than the Christian devil, for he brought our people into a conflict with the barbarians that will last as long as we live. I believe they would have come anyway, but to invite men as noble and skilled as Hengist and Horsa into our midst was crazy. Like a fox among the chickens, they sank their roots into Dyfed and the gods alone know when we will ever drive them out. Vortigern's motives were selfish, and weren't governed by the needs of his people – long may the bastard burn.'

'Aye, if the gods truly exist,' Ambrosius replied. 'But I'm sure we've near to killed the gaiety of this evening with our talk of old times and brutal men. You may now present your assistants to me. I can tell by their dress that they also have stories that might beguile our evening.'

Myrddion gestured to Cadoc, who advanced two steps, abased himself and then stood under the sharp regard of the High King.

'This is Cadoc ap Cadwy, a Briton from the Forest of Dean in Cymru, who served Vortigern in the battle of Tomen-y-mur. I met him on the first day we arrived at Vortigern's camp. He had been burned, and was our first patient. As his injuries meant he couldn't wield a sword, spear or bow with his old proficiency, he became my apprentice and has followed me in my wanderings ever since. He is a man who holds my absolute trust, and he is also my friend.'

Myrddion's simple declaration of affection caused Cadoc's eyes to moisten, which Ambrosius recognised at once. 'You may show me your scars, Cadoc,' the High King demanded.

Cadoc winced, for his old wounds were a source of shame to the Celt. They opened the hidden box of unhappy memories that he kept firmly closed in the depths of his brain. Efficiently, he stripped off his leather breastplate and the laced tunic beneath it to expose the puckered cicatrices that marked one side of his face, neck, shoulder and part of his upper arm. With arms spread widely, he turned slowly so that the king's guests in the audience hall could see the full extent of the wicked damage that had been inflicted by hot oil during the battle. More than a few warriors winced, and their faces blanched as they imagined the pain of such a gross wound.

'I apologise, Cadoc ap Cadwy. I was arrogant and discourteous to ask you to expose your old scars for the amusement of a foolish, thoughtless man. I beg your pardon,' Ambrosius said, and no one present doubted that the High King regretted his impulsive demand, for few men could have obeyed and still retained a shred of dignity.

Cadoc dressed slowly and deliberately with a calm, expressionless face. Once the worst of his deformities were covered, he looked up into the High King's face and spoke man to man.

'I accept the spirit of your apology, lord king. I know that few people understand the scarring that can be caused by exposure to fire, so I know that you intended no slight towards me. In truth, I remember very little of pain at that time, for my master kept me very busy and I had little time to dwell on my hurts. In the years that have passed since then, I have reconciled myself to the loss of full movement and am grateful that I lived through it. I have seen the world as my master's apprentice and learned a new trade, and I now save life rather than take it. I am content with my lot.'

'You speak like a lordling, Cadoc. How can this be so? Were your kin high born?'

Cadoc laughed aloud and his cheerful face was transformed. No one who beheld that cheeky expression thought of the scar that twisted his eyebrow and left shiny areas of bright pink across his cheekbone.

'My da became an innkeeper in Caerleon, my lord, but he was born in the wilds where he sent me to be raised. He was no peasant, it's true, but he was a common man without letters. Master Myrddion gave me a smattering of Greek so I could read the scrolls, and he showed me how speech, especially when it is shaped courteously, can smooth a man's path through life. I was a common foot soldier, sire, although I was born with a ready and impertinent tongue. Now I'm a healer – and I am very good at my trade!'

'Well said, Cadoc. A man can be measured by his actions more than by what he says he can do. What did you think of Rome – as a plain man of the people?'

'It's very large and the people live moderately well, my lord, but something is rotten within it. The city is too old and too accustomed to power to realise that times have changed.'

Ambrosius chewed his bottom lip and his fingers danced over the woollen fringe on the hide cushion of his chair.

'But is it still a beautiful place? I remember its cleanliness and its loveliness.'

'Ah, but did you live in the subura, my lord? In the back alleys, Rome chokes on its own filth. Venta Belgarum is sweet and clean even in the peasants' huts, but Rome has too many people to be kept well. She's old, my lord, and nigh to her death.'

'Never!' Uther snapped from his brother's side. 'Rome will endure, even when we are all dust. I don't believe her might can ever be extinguished.'

Diplomatically, and without answering except to nod ambiguously, Cadoc stepped back behind his master and Myrddion smoothly filled the awkward little silence.

'And this man is my servant, Praxiteles, who elected to follow me back to the west when I left Constantinople. Lest it be thought that he is below the society of cultured men, I should explain that Praxiteles was a wealthy trader and shipowner until chance stripped him of his fortune. He speaks many languages and is literate. I depend on him to care for my possessions and my people, and I would happily trust him with my life.'

'High praise, Praxiteles of Constantinople,' Ambrosius said softly. 'I notice that you use no gens to indicate your family line. Do your ancestors matter so little that you deny them?'

Praxiteles could have been insulted by the High King's tone and question. If so, he masked his feelings.

'I am of the house of Scipio, your highness. When my great-grandfather came to Constantinople, he married the daughter of a Greek shipping family from Ephesus, so Greek and Roman blood runs together through my veins. But when I lost my fortune and my wife died, I put aside the past, believing that my God had a purpose for my suffering. When I met my new master, I knew that God intended me to serve this man and a dutiful servant has no use for ancestry or pride. My daughters were grown, settled and safe. My grandsons stand high in their own lands, so I am free to see a wider world and learn the lessons that God has planned for me.'

Uther sniffed with contempt, for servants had no place in his world except to clean his boots, see to his every bodily comfort and keep their mouths shut. By contrast, the king had a keen empathy that resulted in an understanding of the humblest of those who served him. As Ambrosius spoke to Praxiteles without a trace of pretension or arrogance, Myrddion compared the two brothers. Uther was lacking in some essential element, which made him more beast than man, but Ambrosius seemed, on first acquaintance, to be a ruler whom Myrdion could respect, and perhaps even come to love.

I must remember that these two powerful men are brothers, Myrddion thought. Part of Uther must dwell in Ambrosius and vice versa, he decided, as Praxiteles backed away from the High King to stand behind Myrddion's left shoulder.

'Much as I disapprove of owning anyone, Uther, I find that I am taken with my birthday gift from you. I thank you, brother, for I've a feeling that we will both profit from the services of this man and his friends.' The king turned back to Myrddion. 'You have housing? Good. Then you may hire servants at my expense, Myrddion Merlinus, and set up your practice. My only demand at this stage is that you will call on me every day at sunset. In the event of a war, you will provide the core of my healers, and I expect you to train a group of young men who will serve my interests thus, again at my expense. Is such a bargain acceptable to you, Myrddion of Segontium?'

With his mind exploring how easy life would become with new apprentices and servants provided by the king, and the coin earned in serving the sick of Venta Belgarum, Myrddion realised that Ambrosius's proposal was more than fair. It was lavish!

'How could I refuse such generosity, my lord? I am your man for life, and I am prepared to swear my allegiance to you, if you should so wish?'

'No, Myrddion. A handshake between us is sufficient for men such as you and I.'

Ambrosius rose to his feet and offered his naked right hand to the Celtic healer. Uther seemed alarmed at his brother's carelessness and Botha's hand dived to his sword hilt, but Ambrosius brushed their concerns aside and gripped Myrddion's arm at the wrist.

And so they stood, hands clasped, and Myrddion realised that he had aligned himself to this man for the rest of his life.

The audience was over.

* * *

Several hours had passed and the three companions had returned to their house. The women had worked hard, but the old villa was still hardly habitable, so the party set up beds in the scriptorium for warmth and fell asleep almost immediately. Myrddion had informed Rhedyn and Brangaine that more servants would be arriving at the High King's expense on the morrow, and everyone would be set to work, including himself. With excited whispers, the women settled down with the children.

Even when he heard Praxiteles's soft snoring and a faint buzz coming from Cadoc's open mouth, Myrddion discovered that sleep stubbornly eluded him. Like a rat in a cage, his mind chased itself as he dissected every word of his audience with Ambrosius. The High King was so different from his brother. His hands and feet were never quite still, indicating a highly strung nature and an active mind, but early lessons had taught him to disguise his feelings. That broad Roman face his almost every thought, except for telltale muscles along the jaw and the ridges of his eyebrows. Only a skilled observer would be able to discern Ambrosius's secret thoughts, but Myrddion had learned to interpret many of the signs of inner conflict present in the minds of unpredictable rulers.

After the audience, Myrddion had sent Praxiteles and Cadoc back to the house while he awaited the promised private meeting with Ambrosius. During this enforced observation of the court, he realised quickly that many in the assembly of notables and tribal leaders were currying favour and jostling for preferment. As he studied Ambrosius's methods of dealing with requests for land, the disposition of inheritances and border disputes, Myrddion was reminded of the formalities and efficiencies of the Roman courts. Only one scribe laboured to take notes of the various decisions that were made here, so Myrddion hoped that Ambrosius had a retentive memory. The emperor of the east had been an elderly and dithering ruler, but the empress and the clerics who supported him were

highly organised. As Ambrosius frowned over one petition demanding a solution to a particularly difficult question of succession, the
young healer was appalled at the raised voices, the shouted insults
and the lack of order that seemed normal in this particular hall of
justice. Ambrosius's decisions were crisp and intelligent, and on
several occasions he demanded more proof before he arrived at his
decision, but the High King was struggling with archaic, traditional
systems that were based on the principle that all well-born Celts
were free to express their views. Myrddion's quick glance at Uther
confirmed the younger brother's reservations about the established
rituals of the legal process.

Uther would do away with all argument and act independently
if he ever became High King, Myrddion decided. And I understand
his impatience, although I deplore the very idea of autocratic
decision-making. Because he is intrinsically fair, Ambrosius is hard
pressed to retain control of his temper. His weakness is his decency
and his balance. He avoids arriving at a decision until all the evidence
is to hand. It will be the death of him if he doesn't take care.

After calling the youth with the wine cup to his side on several
occasions, Ambrosius came to a decision that pleased few of the
petitioners. He rose to his feet, pleaded weariness and sent
the whole jostling pack away with a curt instruction to return the
following day.

Men who would be kings do not understand the tedious, banal
duties of governance, Myrddion thought, as he bowed low and
hovered on the fringes of the departing crowd. He was unsure
whether he, too, was meant to leave the hall.

'Not you, Myrddion! We have further matters to discuss.'

Once the room was empty but for Uther, the guard and the
sleepy youth with the wine cup, the High King stretched luxuriously
and ran his hands through his cropped hair in a habit that was
obviously a sign of his impatience.

'Thanks be to all the gods that those yapping fools have gone,' he murmured. 'Myrddion, come to my private apartments. And as for you, Beric, it's off to bed for you.' The High King clapped the boy on his slim back with obvious affection as the youth bowed and relinquished the wine goblet to his master.

'Uther, can you scare up some food and drink for us? I'm sorry to give you a servant's task, but I'm too tired to explain what I like to some sleepy house servant – and I don't want to be disturbed. Ulfin will protect me and taste my food, won't you?'

Ulfin appeared out of the ranks of the guard, bowed obediently and waited for his master's instructions.

'Also, brother, can you discover what those infernal idiots were talking about when they were going on about Reece pen Ryall's death? I smell secrets in their lying words. Can you ferret them out for me?'

'If they're hiding anything, I'll discover it, Ambrosius. I agree, those two young men are up to something.'

'Good. Myrddion, Ulfin – come with me.' Ambrosius turned on his heel and strode off into the shadows at the back of the hall. Almost running, Ulfin and Myrddion had to hurry to keep up.

As they followed the king's broad-shouldered figure down a number of narrow corridors and onwards to a set of wooden stairs, Myrddion had an opportunity to examine his new master from behind. As the High King lacked his brother's long legs, Myrddion had considered him less powerful. Now, he saw the breadth of shoulder, the long torso and the powerful arms, so that Ambrosius's well-muscled legs seemed truncated, given that he had a body meant for a much taller man. The High King's sandalled feet came down on his heels, so that the leather soles made audible thuds with each step. So did the great ones walk as they demonstrated their superiority with the force of every stride.

His tunic was simple and unadorned, but the wool was so fine and beautifully woven that his dress bore the unmistakable stamp of quality. A simple coronet of golden laurel leaves was on his head and the ribbons that bound it at the back swayed and bounced with the speed of his movements. At each stride, a small chime rang melodiously, and Myrddion, searching for its source, noticed a bangle of gold about the imperator's wrist. The jewellery was adorned with small, perfectly formed bells that hung from it at regular intervals. This bangle was almost feminine in appearance and function. It puzzled Myrddion and he made a mental note to ask Ulfin or Botha about it when he had the opportunity. Other than this, Ambrosius wore no other ornaments except for a large gold and chalcedony ring on his thumb.

Eventually, Ambrosius thrust open a wooden door.

'Come in, Myrddion, and find somewhere comfortable to sit. Ulfin, make yourself useful and find a decent wine for my guest.'

Myrddion stood in the doorway and surveyed the room before him with undisguised curiosity.

The floor was wooden and much stained and discoloured by years of hard usage. A series of rag and wool rugs softened the greasy surface and provided splashes of colour to brighten the rather dour atmosphere. A number of chairs and divans provided comfortable seating and brilliantly dyed cushions were added for the easing of chilled flesh and aching muscles. A low table was lit by a large, intricate oil lamp in the Roman style, and Ulfin used a taper of compressed straw to light several wall sconces that caused the room to leap into sharp focus. A brazier filled with hot coals rested on a thin plate of iron and provided a blanket of warmth that invited Myrddion to enter the room.

A doorless opening on one side revealed a small sleeping chamber furnished with a simple wooden bed with a base of woven leather straps to support the High King's body in comfort. On a small table beside the bed, a water jug of beaten silver had been placed, accompanied by several fine pottery bowls filled with nuts and fruit and a large platter ready for food. Altogether, the room promised warmth, luxury and a comfortable beauty that depended on the quality of its furnishings rather than the quantity.

Myrddion was invited to sit on a gleaming hand-rubbed stool that had sturdy back supports. Immediately, the young healer felt at home, as Ambrosius threw himself onto a long divan and crossed his ankles on the low table.

'Well, Myrddion, what do you think of my hall of justice?'

Fortunately for Myrddion, a servant entered at that moment with a woven rush tray on which stood a number of covered pottery bowls. 'Ulfin!' Ambrosius ordered, and the warrior took the pottery covers from each bowl so that Myrddion could see a number of stews, slivers of meat, joints of fowl and vegetables. Then, using a delicate eating knife, Ulfin proceeded to taste a small portion from every dish.

'If you're thinking that I don't trust the food that comes from my own kitchens, Myrddion, you're quite correct. The Saxons desire my death, but I have enemies in any number of places, including the Pict nations, in Cymru and even among the ambitious kinglets in the south.'

'I understand, my lord. Poison has been the weapon of choice of usurpers for as long as men have coveted the possessions of others. Vortimer died of poison and his assassin, Queen Rowena, was in turn a victim of this silent killer. Some men whisper that you ordered her death, highness, if you will forgive my bluntness.'

Myrddion waited, his heart almost stilled in his chest with apprehension, as Ambrosius digested his critical words. Then the High King chose to laugh, and handed his guest a horn mug of pale wine.

'You're right to speak your mind on this matter. It has long been rumoured that I ordered the Saxon queen to be murdered by stealth. I'm innocent of the charge, but I have no regrets that the deed was done. Someone close to me paid the Glywising aristocrat to oversee the killing. I could take a guess – but I won't! I make no apologies for my eagerness to see Vortigern and his woman removed from Cymru but, strangely, no one ever came forward and claimed credit for the deed. I'd have happily paid a reward to her murderer.'

'I was there when Rowena died, my lord. The serving woman who poisoned the queen's cosmetics paid fearsomely for her part in the plot. Rowena forgave the girl at the end and I had a feeling that the queen was happy enough to die, if it ensured the safety of her sons. She was ravished and beaten by Vortimer, you know, when he held her as a hostage at Glevum. I saw the bruises, and any fool could gauge that her treatment at her stepson's hands took a terrible toll on her will to live. She understood blood price, you see, for the northerners believe that each death must be paid for. If so, she paid the price in full.'

Ambrosius gestured towards the food tray and handed Myrddion an eating knife. His brows were knitted together. 'You look like a beardless boy, but you have seen an abundance of the cruel deeds that have been enacted in our lands.'

He smiled softly as he recalled past wrongs. 'My half-brother, Vortimer, was driven to madness by the ambition of avaricious men, and so much blood has been spilled in pursuit of this throne.'

Ambrosius toyed with the bangle on his wrist and the bells tinkled softly.

'My mother's second husband, Vortigern, killed my brother Constans and caused us to be sent into exile. Her bangle reminds me now of the love she held for us and how she became a sacrifice to her husband's ambitions. I have known terrible times, Myrddion Merlinus, but you have experienced things that even I will never know. I wish to harness that experience and use it to my advantage.

Don't frown so – I'll always tell you my intentions to your face.'

Myrddion nodded his head. In his frankness, Ambrosius was difficult to gainsay, for such candour was unusual in such a powerful man.

'So, I return to my first question before we were interrupted. What did you think of my hall of justice?'

Instinctively, Myrddion decided to answer the king's question with the frankness that Ambrosius seemed to prefer. 'You need more scribes to keep a record of the words uttered by the petitioners and your responses, all of them, so that you're not forced to depend on your memory alone. This would ensure that you have a record of the conflicts that occur in your realm, and allow such knowledge to serve you well at some future time.'

'Agreed, Myrddion. I understand your meaning. There's always a dearth of good scribes, but I will set my warriors the task of finding as many as possible. Do you have any thoughts on the matter?'

'The Christian church has learned men in abundance who can meet your needs, if you can make the appropriate arrangements with them. I'm not of that faith, but I advocate using every tool at your disposal. Such a liaison could provide a further advantage to you in that they could become future allies to your cause.'

'Your words are clever, so I'll take your advice. Uther was wise to divert you from your journey to Segontium, as you are proving valuable to me already. Have you any other suggestions or criticisms?'

Myrddion stared at his thumbs, concentrating on the ruby ring he had been gifted at birth.

'There are two other ways you can enforce your judgements during disputes between the nobles. First, you need a seneschal with the authority to intervene during unseemly and confusing displays of temper such as we saw tonight. In my view, such an individual should have the power to censure and punish, for your task is merely to judge and arrive at decisions, rather than to control the behaviour of petitioners.'

'That's also good advice. I shall think on it. What is your other suggestion?' The High King's eyes glowed in the light of the lamp and Myrddion wondered how he had ever thought those mild blue eyes were shallow.

'You need a spy network, not only in the Saxon camps, but also in the halls of your allies. You should know in advance which lords have ambitions, and those who do not. In this fashion, you can protect your own position and secure the safety of the realm.'

'Ah!' Ambrosius sighed deeply, and lines of worry etched his handsome face. 'I'm aware that this throne hangs by a thread, for if I should die I have no son to follow me. Only my brother stands between the people and a civil war for the throne. Between these four walls, I confess I've thought long and hard about a spy network, but Uther lacks the subtlety to organise such a structure, so I would be forced to employ an outlander to assume that role. Yet Uther is the only man in these wide lands whom I fully trust. I'm sure you'll forgive me if I state the obvious, but I speak truthfully. My brother Constans trusted Vortigern, our stepfather, and perished because of his faith in that friendship. I'll not make the same error.'

'I understand, lord.'

'But your suggestions do have merit, Myrddion Merlinus, so I will consider your advice carefully.' Then the king grinned and poured another cup of wine. 'Now, tell me of Constantinople, the Jewel of the East. How I loved that city when I was a boy.'

As wary friends, the two men spoke of far-off cities and strange customs until their meal was finished. Even then, Ambrosius would have continued the conversation, but he saw that Myrddion's eyes were heavy and the healer was stifling yawns of weariness.

'But I keep you from your bed, healer, in my eagerness to speak of the past. I've been discourteous and I beg your pardon for it. Go to your rest, and I will look forward to sunset tomorrow when you can tell me of the death of Flavius Aetius. It seems crazed to me. What sensible ruler robs himself of his most able defender?'

After murmuring all the courtesies of a guest, Myrddion excused himself and Ulfin guided him out of the High King's hall, instructing a dour warrior to ensure that the healer was escorted safely to his house. Now, as he chased sleep, Myrddion permitted himself to wonder at the nature of Ambrosius Imperator, a man who seemed so open and reasonable, and yet had survived even the unscrupulous manipulations of a man such as Vortigern.

'There must be more to him than the face he exposes to the world,' Myrddion whispered into his pillow as sleep finally dragged him down into the peaceful darkness.

THE HOUSE OF THE HEALERS
IN VENTA BELGARUM

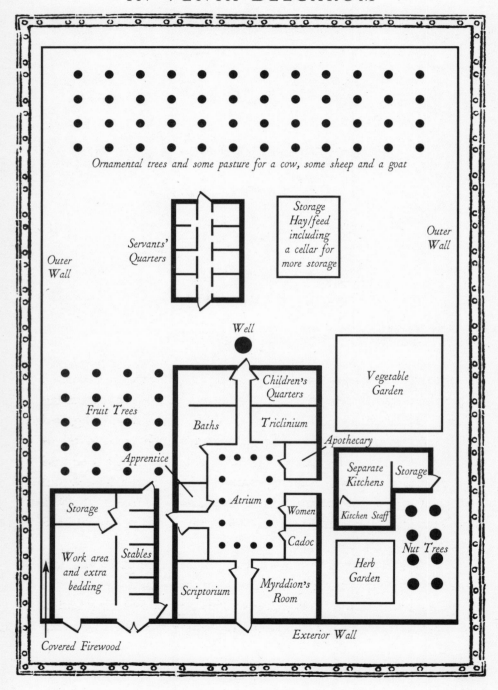

Ornamental trees and some pasture for a cow, some sheep and a goat

Servants' Quarters

Storage Hay/feed including a cellar for more storage

Outer Wall

Outer Wall

Well

Children's Quarters

Vegetable Garden

Fruit Trees

Baths

Triclinium

Apothecary

Apprentice

Separate Kitchens

Storage

Atrium

Women

Kitchen Staff

Storage

Cadoc

Stables

Herb Garden

Nut Trees

Work area and extra bedding

Scriptorium

Myrddion's Room

Covered Firewood

Exterior Wall

CHAPTER V

A CELTIC WOMAN

'Twas I plucked the apple down
From the bough above and ate;
Folly, while they stay alive,
Woman never will forsake.

Anonymous Celtic poem

The morrow dawned with all the promise and rich aroma of spring. The air was crisp with a hint of chill, but the clouds scudding through the bright blue sky were more fluffy than threatening, and the sturdy farmers of Venta Belgarum were fully employed in weeding around the new shoots thrusting through the furrows and tending to the birthing of the new season's lambs and calves. When Praxiteles sallied forth before dawn in search of servants, he was forced to accept men and women whom he would normally have rejected as ludicrously unsuitable.

A ragtag group of raddled whores, old men, cripples and lay-abouts eventually assembled in the large, unkempt kitchen for Myrddion's inspection. The group was an unprepossessing bunch and many carried old injuries that had doomed them to grinding poverty in the past. Myrddion noted one man with a twisted leg that had obviously been broken and set incorrectly long ago. Another had been born with a twisted spine. Although Myrddion realised that the man must be very strong to have survived for so long, he deplored the circumstances that doomed the sufferer to a life of hardship because of an accident of birth.

Depressed by the group before him, the young healer sighed audibly, and then addressed his new staff. 'I am a healer, a man who has dedicated his life to the alleviation of illness and pain, so I understand how difficult survival must have been for all of you. Therefore, I have decided that you will have a safe haven in this house of healers where the generosity of the High King will pay your wages. You can be assured that I'll turn no one away because of age or infirmity. I am searching for effort, devotion and an earnest desire to better your lot in life.'

The prospective servants should have been grateful. Instead, they stared, gape-mouthed, at Myrddion as if he were a lunatic. What sensible person hires the old and the twisted? Most of them had only come with Praxiteles in the hope of a free meal. Several of the men, especially those few not yet grown to middle age, began to sneer behind their hands at such transparent foolishness.

For his part, Myrddion continued to smile casually, but his tall frame seemed to grow until it dominated the rough mud walls of the kitchen and his shadow, in the dawn firelight, hung over the room like a creature out of night terrors.

'You will hear it whispered that I am the son of a demon. Do not believe such foolish stories, for I am far worse than the mere scion of a chaos monster as insubstantial as dreams. I can see into your secret hearts, for I am the grandchild of the High Priestess of Ceridwen in Cymru. She died to protect me, and told her people that the goddess had gifted me with an added eye to hunt out wickedness, sloth and dishonesty.'

Cadoc stared at his master with nearly as much surprise as the men and women who watched him with varying degrees of horror. This Myrddion who was claiming to be ruthless and manipulative was new to him. Cadoc was confused, for his master had always been kind and generous towards his servants, treating them with the same courtesy as he extended to kings.

'If you labour hard in my service to the best of your abilities, you will have a roof over your heads, food in your bellies and coin in your purses. But if you betray me, I will cast you adrift on the mercies of Venta Belgarum where all men will know that your hearts are as twisted as your bodies. Do you understand me?'

Raggedly, the new servants nodded their agreement with varying degrees of awe, concern or scorn.

'I will now speak to each of you privately and allocate tasks according to your skills and aptitude. But first, Praxiteles is my steward and he must be obeyed at all times. He is responsible for my household, and when he instructs you to carry out your duties he is speaking with my authority. Cadoc is a healer and, again, he speaks with my authority. Rhedyn and Brangaine are skilled workers with the sick and the injured, and will always be addressed respectfully. If they require a service from you, their requests must be accommodated to the best of your ability. Perhaps some of you will show an aptitude for your duties that will earn preferment for you. If so, the choice will ultimately be yours. As for now, a hot stew will chase away the last of the night for those of you who are hungry, while I will begin my interviews with you individually.'

The odd assortment of men and women, young and old, was silent with apprehension. Myrddion pointed to the youngest of the men, who was cursed with a shrivelled arm and had been so unwise as to sneer openly when the healer first began to speak. The man flinched visibly, but he followed his new master into the house, along the corridor and into the scriptorium where Myrddion seated himself among the boxes and crates that held his possessions.

'What is your name?' Myrddion's voice was curt.

The man ducked his head and fixed his gaze on his dirty, bare feet. 'I'm called Fingal, or the fair stranger. My mother made a joke when she named me, master. I was born with this arm, so she considered me to be worse than useless. As I am!'

'Show me the limb, Fingal,' Myrddion demanded, and Fingal exposed his left arm from the sleeve in which it was usually hidden. The forearm was grossly shortened and under-developed, and the muscles were wasted from lack of use over many years. The hand itself was small and the vestigial fingers were so short as to be almost entirely useless. But Myrddion noted that the man's thumb was normal in both size and appearance. Although the whole arm was some three or four inches shorter than his hale arm, the crippled limb still retained considerable strength above the elbow, so Fingal obviously used the upper muscles to wedge objects against his body in order to manipulate them with his good right hand.

'Despite a certain degree of incapacity, you are still fortunate, Fingal,' Myrddion said. 'You may have been told that you are useless, but you have good muscle in your upper arm and a thumb that will allow you to hold objects against the stumps of your fingers. If you can stop thinking of yourself as useless and start seeing yourself as a man, we might be able to teach you to have some respectable mobility in that arm. It will never be pretty, but I think it can become serviceable. I can design a wrist strap that will assist you to manipulate a spade or a fork and then you'll be able to work like an able-bodied man.'

Fingal said nothing, but his face spoke volumes of the doubt, the resentment and the frail hope that fuelled his inner rage.

'Answer me fairly. Do you wish to be treated like a man rather than a cripple?'

'Yes,' Fingal snarled resentfully. 'I want to be treated like a sodding man. Wouldn't you?'

'Ah, so now we have signs of anger. I'm glad to see you aren't lacking in spirit. Well, Fingal, you shall fill the role of chief gardener. There's a little land around this house – not a lot, mind you, but enough. I want the wall built higher and there is a need for trees to be planted. Fruit trees will add to our self-sufficiency, as will vegetable gardens. A herb plot is important to healers for growing our medications, and I would like to have a beautiful atrium where we can pipe our own water. I will provide the coin for everything you need. But first, the servants' quarters at the rear of the property are in a dreadful condition. Your first task is to make them habitable.'

Fingal was confused and overwhelmed by the range of his new responsibilities. Unused to being seen as a man with abilities, he stammered out a rather doubtful affirmative.

'Good. Now choose four men or women who you think will have the muscle, the patience and the temperament to work with you and obey your orders. You will be in charge of the gardening so the choice must be yours, as you will also bear the responsibility for any errors made by your staff. Most of the new servants have been damaged in one way or another, so I expect you to treat them fairly and generously. Once you've made your choice of assistants, send them to me.'

Fingal watched as Myrddion wrote his name on a clean scroll and added the letters that described his new position. Myrddion carefully explained what he had written and then warned Fingal that he had meant everything he said in the kitchen.

'I am giving you a chance, Fingal. It's up to you how you use it.'

Convinced that his new master must surely be mad, Fingal returned to the kitchen, where his fellows were devouring a hot stew prepared by Brangaine. As she placed a bowl before him, Fingal thanked her absently, for he was already assessing the potential usefulness of the ten persons seated on the floor. He selected an older man who was whipcord thin but still retained most of his teeth and was tanned to the colour of old oak. After that, he chose a boy who was obviously wanting in his wits, a girl disfigured by a strawberry mark that covered half her face, and another greybeard. All were sent to Myrddion.

So Ciabhan, Horn, Berwyn and Aeddan went down on Myrddion's list as outside servants, and Fingal led them away to assess the renovations needed to refresh the old servants' quarters.

Myrddion discovered that one sullen woman of some thirty years was deaf, having suffered a bout of the spotting illness when she was a young girl. She could speak much more clearly than other poor souls who had been born without hearing, and had become adept at watching lips to discover what the speaker wished to communicate, but the tragedy of her life was that she had been sold into prostitution by her family in the mistaken belief that she was unsuitable for any other function. Four children had been born to her, and each had been sold as soon as it was weaned. Finally, when her looks had begun to fade and her anger had affected her value to her customers, they had thrown her onto the street.

'What is your name, woman?' Myrddion asked in a gentler tone than he had used with Fingal, taking pains to move his lips slowly and precisely.

'I am Aude,' she replied with the slight thickness of the tongue that was common to the deaf. Aude had marvellous hair that was both thick and curly. The colour was somewhere between honey and flame, and Myrddion was reminded of Tegwen, his first woman, who had served him with love and utter trustworthiness. This woman's face was lined with privation, but although dirt was deeply ingrained into her skin the young healer was touched by the pride that had prompted her to wash her hands and face as clean as she could make them.

'You will be in charge of the children in the house, Aude,' Myrddion decided. 'Can you weave and spin yarn?'

'Yes, master,' she replied hesitantly. The speed with which she had divined his meaning convinced Myrddion that she was far more intelligent than her mulish expression and short responses suggested. 'But I've not used wool or flax for many years.'

'All that happened in the ugly past is finished now, and this house is your new life. As well as the children, you will be in charge of our bandages and look after the cleanliness of the house. You will have three women to help you, so select them carefully and send them to me.'

So the names of Aude, an old ex-slave called Kady, and two widows, Dubh and Hasair, were added to Myrddion's list.

Dyfri, the man who had been crippled because of a badly set leg, was put in charge of Myrddion's scriptorium where he was given the responsibility of caring for all the herbs and potions that Myrddion used in his trade. Cadoc would teach him the many menial but important labours that were the backbone of the healer's art.

'Your leg is no impediment to carrying out the duties of a herbmaster, Dyfri. In case you make the mistake of believing that you can take the king's coin and do very little, understand that you must work from dawn to dusk, and you must obey Cadoc in all things, while applying yourself to your tasks. However, a good herbmaster can earn a substantial living anywhere in these isles.'

For the first time, Myrddion saw genuine gratitude in the man's plain, rather cherubic face. 'I know I can do what you ask, Master Myrddion. I'll learn as fast as can be.'

'Good. Cadoc will set you to work at once. And tell him that I want him to design a better crutch than that stick you are using. It doesn't work well at all.'

The final woman was a slatternly, loud-mouthed, middle-aged

drab. There was nothing bewitching or intoxicating about the scarred, florid face that Maeve presented sullenly to the world. Because she had always been plain, she had hawked her body on the streets for as long as she could remember. Pimps and customers had left her face and body liberally scarred from their fists and their knives, so she was even more unprepossessing than in her youth. Few men now responded to her advances, so desperation had brought her to Myrddion's door.

'I want you to work in my kitchens, Maeve. And if you know of another woman who would help you with cooking and cleaning duties, then I could use her also. I don't care where she comes from or what she's done in the past, but you will soon know my requirements. Are you prepared to work from dawn to dusk for your coin, Maeve?'

'Aye, master. And I do know of another woman who will help me. Her name is Mavourna, and she is my friend. We who've spread our legs in alleyways know where we stand in the world. We're just conveniences for any man with an itch.'

'Never refer to yourself in such a way again, Maeve. You may make a valuable servant yet.'

'I'm sorry, master, if I spoke crudely. Perhaps I'm not even fit for your kitchens.'

'We'll see, Maeve.'

All that remained was to find a duty for the man with the twisted spine. Caerwyn was an embittered man, with his hunched shoulders and the hump on his bent back, but his arms were corded with hard muscle, as were his powerful thighs, for he had found every possible way to counteract his deformity.

'You are the strongest of my new servants, Caerwyn, so to you must fall the most menial and difficult work. Don't take my decision amiss, for you could prove to be my most valuable worker. No villa will function without an able-bodied man, and I don't jest when I describe you thus. Firewood must be chopped for the kitchen ovens, great cauldrons must be moved, scoured and filled, and I would be lying if I said you wouldn't be called upon to move heavy objects that the women can't manage. Can you accept such tasks without offence? It is honest and important work, although only I will understand the true value of what you do.'

Caerwyn stared at Myrddion to ascertain whether he was being patronised. When he saw nothing but respect in the healer's open face, he nodded awkwardly with a hint of moisture in eyes that were soft, long-lashed and as brown as the hide of a roe deer. Myrddion was heartened by the twisted man's display of emotion.

'Aye. I can do that and more, master. To work like a man without the insult of charity or pity is enough for me.'

'Don't make your final decision before you know how much I'll expect of you,' Myrddion joked, and then the audience was over.

And so the house of Myrddion Merlinus began to buzz with activity as thirteen unlikely new servants began to work for a new and very peculiar master. Perhaps the number could have been unlucky, but Myrddion would send no one away, even to propitiate the gods or the superstitions of foolish men.

In the early evening, just before the glowing sun disappeared into the west through the ruddy clouds, Myrddion returned to Ambrosius's house, mindful of his promise to his new master. Within moments of joining the noisy throng pushing from the antechamber into the hall of justice, Myrddion became aware that Uther wasn't the only brother capable of blinding speed, once Ambrosius had made up his mind. Three scribes sat at small folding tables, armed with scrolls and writing materials, ready for the fray. With amusement, Myrddion noticed that the youngest scribe wore the robes and tonsure of a Christian priest.

Ambrosius learns fast, he thought. And he must be persuasive if the chief prelate of Venta Belgarum gives him the services of such a valuable young cleric.

As a pushy aristocrat from the Reece pen Ryall inheritance dispute of the previous evening began to thrust himself forward to the front of the audience, an old man advanced to the centre of the hall armed with a long staff tipped with gold. Briskly, he pounded the flagging three times and ordered the warring family members to present themselves.

'Who is the old gentleman with the staff?' Myrddion hissed at a warrior who stood beside him. The man eyed the healer doubtfully.

'The old man is Madoc pen Madag, the king of the Cantii who were. My master gave shelter to the people of the tribe when they left the southeast, and King Madoc has been appointed as Ambrosius's seneschal this very day. We have been told that all petitioners will have to get past old Madoc before they trouble the king.'

In almost the same instant, the petitioner glared at the seneschal. 'Who are you to give orders to noblemen?' he snapped rudely.

Madoc pen Madag fixed his portly, crude inquisitor with a hard, agate stare. 'From this day onward, I have been appointed as the seneschal to the High King of the Britons. You know very well who I am, sir. I will forgive your rudeness for the moment, but Lord Ambrosius's guard will remove you from this session if it continues. Am I understood?'

A low hum of whispers filled the long room, while the stout petitioner reddened unattractively. Fortunately, one of his companions nudged him with an elbow in his ample belly when he opened his mouth to protest.

'The court of Ambrosius, High King of the Britons, is now in session,' the seneschal's commanding voice roared out, easily the most powerful part of his ageing body. 'The heirs to the house of Reece pen Ryall will step forth and be recognised. As seneschal, I tell you that all men will speak through me if they wish to be heard in this court. Unseemly shouting or argument will result in your summary removal and your claims will not be heard.' The family of Reece pen Ryall settled instantly when Ulfin and Botha stepped forward to flank the old man and, rather to everyone's surprise, the audience began smoothly.

Ambrosius was rarely called upon to speak, and he swiftly made his decision and gave his judgement. Skilled in the handling of petitioners, old Madoc knew exactly what queries he needed to put to the warring parties, so the truth came to light far more swiftly than any of those present would have believed possible during the previous night's entertainment. Rather to everyone's surprise, the business of the evening was quickly concluded.

When Myrddion joined Ambrosius in his apartments, the king immediately demanded the healer's opinion of his changes. Myrddion noted the High King's glowing face and excited pacing and gave an honest, enthusiastic response.

'You've done wonders in one day, master. And the choice of Madoc was inspired. With one blow, you give the Cantii tribe due honour, and win yourself an experienced negotiator who will simplify your own life. I offer you my congratulations, master.'

Ambrosius blushed to the roots of his fair hair at the generous words, and Myrddion wondered how much direct praise the High King had received throughout his life. Very little, I suppose, he thought sadly. Beggared kinsmen seeking shelter are rarely regarded with approval. Ambrosius and Uther must be strong to have survived such an unpromising start in life.

Then Ambrosius insisted on a full accounting of Myrddion's day, including his selection of servants, the roles ascribed to them and the reasons for his choices. Somewhat puzzled by the king's interest. Myrddion answered as best he could, while Ambrosius insisted on full descriptions of all his new charges.

'It seems to me that you've taken on the old, the halt and the lame, Myrddion. Now that I think on it, Cadoc, Praxiteles and your women aren't completely whole either. Do you seek to aid those whom you can't heal?'

'I have never considered my actions from that perspective, lord. Situations arise and I respond, but I've rarely been let down by those who work with me. The most damaged person will still have his usefulness. For example, Fingal has been handicapped since birth, but he has learned many ways to use that malformed hand, and I was surprised how competent he was at his work once I'd designed a leather arm support for him. He was the man most likely to rebel against my rules, so I put him in a position of responsibility straight away. It's been less than a day, but I believe he's whipping his crew into shape already and seems to be working harder than I'd have believed possible. And anyway, master, you've done the same thing when you took an ancient king and made him your seneschal.'

'I suppose so.' Ambrosius looked thoughtfully at his wine. 'Let us drink a toast to my new spymaster. I've thought all day on this thorny problem, and only one person springs to mind whom I can trust to serve my interests. You, Myrddion Merlinus, are that man.'

'Why me?' Myrddion gasped. 'I don't know anybody, and I've only just returned after a long period in foreign lands.'

'So? No one of note will believe that someone as young and as dedicated to the task of healing as you are would be employed in such a secret world. And you *did* serve Vortigern's cause. I'm certain that you will find willing eyes and ears among those you have assisted back to health in the past. You are the perfect man for the task.'

The king paused and looked directly into Myrddion's eyes. The young man felt the full force of his charm and wavered under its spell. 'Hear me, Myrddion, and believe what I say. I'm honest enough to admit that I can't trust you entirely, but the fault isn't yours. I have learned much about you, for a Demon Seed is remembered with both affection and fear. I have enquired into the details of your life and I will soon be in possession of everything I need to know.'

'I don't fear any exploration of my past, master, but who can know a man's inner heart? Even if I agreed to serve you in this matter, I may misjudge the men I choose. I could do more harm than good.'

Ambrosius grinned widely as if Myrddion had passed some kind of test. When he spoke again, it was as though Myrddion's fears were of no moment. 'I will require you to keep me fully informed of all the networks you create, but I won't interfere or broadcast your role in my court. It's in my best interests to keep you secret, and therefore safe. But you must forgive me if I sometimes doubt you. I have little reason to trust anyone, but I have discovered that we share a quality of otherness and loneliness, and so I believe I know you. Besides, if you make errors, how can I hold you to blame? I make mistakes myself.'

'But building a spy network takes time and much expenditure of gold. I know you have the wealth, but how will I find the time to cross the land seeking men who'll risk their lives to live in the shadow of the Saxons? How will I find men who'll spy on our own tribal kings, which is probably the most important role of all? Methinks you ask too much, Lord Ambrosius.'

'Do I? Well, my need is pressing, my young friend, so I have little time to pick and choose. A spymaster must be clever – as you are. A spymaster must be an accurate judge of men – as you are. Will you serve me, Myrddion?'

'But you have only known me for two days. You say that you don't trust easily, but by the Mother whose name must not be spoken, I'm amazed that you put such dependence on an itinerant healer. I feel the weight of your expectations, my lord.'

'The choice will be yours, Myrddion, so answer me fairly,' Ambrosius said easily, hiding any concern or eagerness he might feel.

The young man sighed. He really didn't want to commit himself to so many projects at once. He had never envisioned having to train healers to replace his own commitment to his trade, running a large household or setting up a practice in a major city. The quiet beaches of Segontium would have been sufficient to fill the void in his hollow heart.

But a worm of ambition began to stir at the back of his brain as his fertile imagination set to work on the problem. 'I could possibly set up a network in Cymru *if* I utilise my knowledge of my homeland,' he responded cautiously. 'But if I attempt to run before I can see the ground I walk upon, then rabbit holes will surely trip me up and your network will fail.'

Ambrosius grinned, and Myrddion realised that he had never expected the healer to agree to his proposal. Now, well pleased with half a loaf when he had expected none, the High King was prepared to lavish gold upon the project. Outmanoeuvred by an expert conspirator, Myrddion glumly agreed.

'Ah, my merlin! Like the bird after which you are named, you will fly very, very high in my service, and I pray I am here to see the wonders that you will build above us on the heights. I also know that men should beware, for you have the raptor's eye and very sharp claws to catch at your prey. That makes you start, doesn't it? I expect a spy network to operate in Cymru by next summer.'

'You may expect, master, but there's no guarantee that you'll get,' Myrddion replied caustically, disturbed by Ambrosius's use of the metaphor that Myrddion had chosen for himself.

'See? Who else would politely suggest that I should go to Hades for my presumption? Aye, Myrddion, you'll build me a spy network that will endure long after I am dust.'

* * *

Disturbed and more than a little angry with the High King and with himself, Myrddion strode briskly through the corridors in order to leave by a side door and escape from the quiet hall. As he pushed the heavy iron latch open, a hand snaked out from the shadows and gripped his wrist painfully. Uther Pendragon loomed out of the darkness, eyes reddened with weariness and cold fire.

'Take care, healer, lest you slip off your perch and fall. It would be a tragedy if my brother lost such a promising servant through a thoughtless accident.'

'Lord Uther! How may I help you?'

Uther smiled without mirth, and Myrddion noticed that the prince's canines were unnaturally long. 'You're becoming altogether too cosy with my brother for an itinerant healer who has only been in Venta Belgarum for two days. Perhaps I'll believe that you've ensorcelled him, if your influence continues to grow.'

'I obey my master – exactly as you instructed, Prince Uther. I do no more than that.'

Uther punched Myrddion hard on the chest and, for a moment, the young healer's sight darkened. Finally, he was able to draw a deep breath. 'I have no influence over the High King, my prince. He manipulates me as much as he does everyone else who serves him. Personally, I would be grateful to return to Segontium and resume my travels. You have the power to send me away, and I'll not argue with you if you should do so.' He straightened painfully and tried to calm his ragged breathing. More than anything, he wanted to strike at the prince's sneering face.

'Just remember that I'll be watching everything you do, Myrddion Merlinus. If I decide that you're a danger to my brother, you'll be a dead man.'

Uther pushed Myrddion hard and the healer barely escaped striking his face against the stone outer wall. Slowly, Myrddion turned and bowed low to the prince before forcing himself to walk through the door at a steady, unhurried pace when every instinct told him to run.

The man is green with jealousy, his inner voice told him, and he resents every moment I spend with his brother. Perhaps I'm best served if I go to the north on my master's business for a time.

A month was a long time in Venta Belgarum, but it was forever when the walls had ears and every shadow held a sly observer who was eager to inform Uther Pendragon of every action Myrddion took. Somehow, the healer ran his household, sorted out the many petty squabbles that arose, and terrified Fingal when the servant was caught pawing drunkenly at Berwyn while the girl screamed hysterically at his unwanted attentions. Fingal had worked hard in his position as chief gardener and had proved that he had the capacity to control a crew of workers, for the servants' quarters were already repaired and watertight. Unfortunately, the young man had never held a position of responsibility before, and his lapse, when it came, was an unforgivable breach of trust.

The next morning, after being locked in the empty baths to sober up, a shivering and very repentant Fingal found himself summoned to the scriptorium, which now glowed with beeswax, fresh whitewash and clean glass containers filled with mysterious objects. When Fingal lifted his aching head to face his master, his heart sank. Myrddion's black eyes were as hard as rain-washed pebbles and his mouth was set in an uncompromising line.

'What do you have to say for yourself, Fingal? You frightened a girl who was under your instruction, who believed you valued her hard work. Do you think that your role in my household gives you any right to force yourself upon her?'

'I'm sorry, master. I was drunk.'

'So you believe you are permitted to rape girls when you drink. Is that what you're telling me?'

Vainly, Fingal searched for an excuse, but he was finally forced to resort to the truth. 'No, master, I took advantage because I thought I could get away with it. Berwyn's ugly, so I thought she'd welcome the attentions of a man.' His voice sank to a whisper. 'Even half a man like me.'

Myrddion looked exasperated, and Fingal felt a small glimmer of hope. Anything was better than that frozen, icy glare.

'You're not half a man, so stop feeling sorry for yourself. And who are you to pass judgement on an affliction that has dogged Berwyn's life since birth? Of all men, you should understand her position. Ah, now you look contrite because your wits aren't addled with cheap cider. So, what punishment should I give you? What would you do in my shoes?'

Fingal was certain that his crime warranted expulsion from the house of the healers and his heart ached already for the loneliness that would follow such a punishment. Haltingly, he conveyed his thoughts to his master.

'Yes, Fingal, I should cast you out as a lesson to the other servants that I'll not be disobeyed. But you've been honest with me, so I'll give you a choice. First, you must beg Berwyn's pardon – and mean it! Then, if you can bear ten cuts of Cadoc's leather belt across your back, you may remain in my employ.'

Cadoc twitched from his position beside the door. He was unsure whether he was capable of whipping a man, especially as ten blows would break Fingal's skin and cause blood to flow.

On the other hand, Fingal was elated. 'I'll take your punishment, master, and more. I'm sorry for what I've done, and I'll never drink again.'

'That's not what this punishment is for, Fingal. You may drink, by all means. I do myself. But attempted rape is another matter altogether.'

With a firm step, Fingal led the way into the bare atrium where the rest of the servants were gathered, having divined Myrddion's intentions in the mysterious rumour mill enjoyed by all good workers. They listened attentively as Myrddion explained Fingal's choice of punishment and showed their approval of their master's wisdom with serious nods and the odd smile. When Fingal begged Berwyn's pardon on his knees and with his head bowed low, they rumbled their satisfaction. Poor Berwyn burst into tears.

Then, like a man preparing for execution, Fingal stripped the coarse, stained tunic from his upper body. The two leather straps that were designed to help his grip when using hoes or picks remained attached to his wrist and forearm, for Fingal never removed Myrddion's gift that freed him from his infirmity.

Inwardly, Myrddion steeled himself for the ordeal ahead. 'Your belt, Cadoc, if you please,' he demanded calmly, his eyes fixed on Fingal's upper body.

The servants were amazed, for they divined that their master proposed to conduct the punishment himself.

One by one, the blows fell. At first they didn't feel so very bad to the sufferer, but the abused flesh bruised and swelled quickly, and even though Myrddion tried to avoid areas he had already struck the skin was splitting by the time the sixth blow was inflicted. Both Myrddion and Fingal suffered throughout the last four blows, but the servant managed to stay on his feet until the bitter end, although blood flowed from his bitten lip and he moaned deep in his throat.

When the last blow was finally struck, Fingal fell to his knees and panted noisily through his open mouth. Crisply, Myrddion ordered that he should be carried to the servants' quarters and laid, face down, on his simple pallet. Then Myrddion spread a healing unguent over bandages with his own hand, and carefully wrapped Fingal's injuries. He mixed poppy juice with hot water and encouraged Fingal to drink. Finally, when the servant was drowsy, he rose to leave.

Fingal gripped Myrddion's robe with his good hand. 'Swear, master, that you'll not cast me out while I sleep.'

'You have borne your punishment like a man, Fingal, so I'll not cast you out.' Myrddion's voice was stern and gruff, as if he were on the verge of tears. 'But you must never force me to do such injury to you again.'

Content, Fingal slid into a painless sleep, secure in the belief that his master did not lie. Only Cadoc knew that Myrddion drank three glasses of wine that night in order to face the bad dreams that would descend on him while he slept. Even then, Cadoc sensed that his master wept during the night.

Four days later, with a saddlebag containing a purse of gold, and without a single warrior for protection and company, Myrddion rode away into the north on the High King's business. Venta Belgarum wouldn't see the healer again until winter had come and gone.

Venta Belgarum lounged in the heat of an unusually warm summer. The cobbled and flagged streets lay in a haze that shimmered like standing water. The citizens could barely move in the sweltering noontime, and children risked drowning as they frolicked in the silver shallows of the river with shrill cries of excitement and joy.

A cloud of dust spoke of unexpected visitors long before the cavalcade came into view. The hard roadway had become a dust bowl in the unrelenting heat as the mud of spring was caught between the flagging and the gravel, baked hard by the sun, and then crushed to powder by the wheels of many wagons. Horsed warriors indicated that this was no trading caravan, fresh from the west. Cadoc was at the open market outside the city's walls among the common peasantry, and he hastened to the gates with them to goggle at their betters.

The healer recognised the small, compact horses and the distinctive plaits of the Brigante tribe as the warriors rode past, guarding four wagons that were piled high with spoils, boxes, iron trunks and supplies. The last wagon contained women, all in chains and most of them dark-haired, black-eyed and barbaric with body painting formed from blue tattoos.

'Picts!' Cadoc muttered under his breath with disgust, for no true Briton could countenance the fierce blue people who had been driven beyond the walls, yet still attacked the northern tribes during the spring in their eagerness for plunder and revenge. Men spoke quietly about the endless enmity of the Pictish people. A thousand years might fly by, but their hatred would endure forever.

Conspicuous in the wagon was a woman whose brown hair was liberally streaked with reddish tinges and curled wildly in the way of the Celtic women of the north. She was slim and comely, but her arms were marred by ugly tattoos at the wrists and the upper arms so that she appeared to wear heavy manacles. As she passed, Cadoc saw that her eyes were a brilliant sea green and she possessed a smattering of freckles across her nose and on the swelling of her upper breasts. None among the observers doubted that this woman had Celtic origins.

'Who is she?' he asked a foot soldier who was slogging along the roadway in the rear of the captives' wagon. The man grimaced as he tried to draw air into his straining lungs.

'Who? The tribal bitch? She's a hostage from beyond the Vallum Antonini, taken by the Picts when she was a child. We captured them all when a Pict army marched south into Brigante country.'

'Shut your yap, idiot, and keep moving,' a handsome man on a horse shouted, riding straight at Cadoc as if to crush him under the hooves of his horse. 'You're not here to amuse these clods. The High King awaits us.'

Cadoc bowed his head just sufficiently to suggest courtesy, and the Brigante warrior spurred his horse back to the front of the column.

'Who was that oaf?' Cadoc asked no one in particular.

'Be grateful you've still got your head, man,' a grizzled trader muttered as he nudged Cadoc in the ribs and gave him a conspiratorial wink. 'That's Luka, the eldest son of the Brigante king. He fights, he whores and he drinks. He does all of them well – but he's a killer in battle. And he's a notorious hothead.'

'I'll surely remember Prince Luka,' Cadoc muttered with a snarl. Like any proud warrior, he was affronted by Luka's rudeness and his ready disposition to misjudge people.

'Do that, friend! But I'd still pray that he never sets eyes on you again.'

As Cadoc made his way through the jostling throng towards the quieter streets that led to the house of the healers, he mulled over what he had seen. Experience told him that a great battle had been fought in the north and the Brigante had succeeded in defeating the Picts. No less than the king's son was escorting the plunder of war south to Venta Belgarum, where a tribute of women as well as red gold would be presented to Ambrosius Imperator. More important, the High King was finally making an impression on the arrogant tribes of the north.

Then Cadoc remembered the face of the Celtic woman and the sharp glitter of her snake-green eyes. Was she still as she had been born? Or was she now a Pict and committed to continuing the hatred against her father's people forever?

I wish my master were here. He could warn Ambrosius to take precautions with this woman. I don't trust the slut at all, Cadoc thought grimly. Then the house enfolded him with the myriad small decisions that fell to him while his master was away. Yet he couldn't quite forget the woman's shining eyes and the single glance that followed him through the day and into the fabric of his dreams.

Myrddion's chart of
pre-Arthurian Wales

SETEIA AEST

MONA

Canovium   • Deva

Segontium   Dinas Emrys

GWYNEDD

Tomen-y-mur

• Caer Gai   Forden

Pennal

Bravonium

POWYS

Llanio

Magnis •

GLYWISING

Llandovery

DYFED   Fortress   • Y Gaer   Glevum

Caer Fyrddin   GWENT

Burrium

Venta Silurum

• Nidum   Isca

Abone

SABRINA AEST   Aquae
Sulis

THE BATTLE BETWEEN THE PICTS AND THE BRIGANTE IN NORTHERN BRITAIN

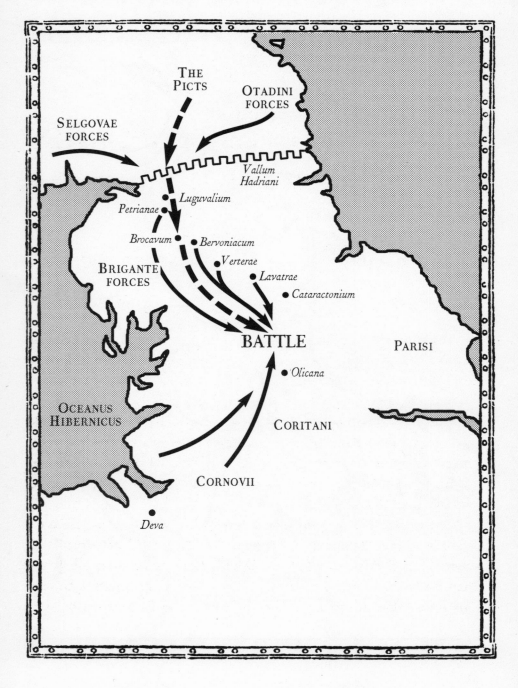

CHAPTER VI

PLOTS, COUNTERPLOTS AND BLOODY THOUGHTS

It is well known, that among the blind the one-eyed man is king.

Erasmus, *Adagia*

As the sun set bloodily in the west, Ambrosius accepted his tribute from his most northerly allies. The High King had dressed with unusual care, and wore the ancient torc that had graced the throats of his ancestors in its time, as well as the unclean flesh of Vortigern. The barbaric rope of gold, finished with uncut sapphires, struck a discordant note in the elegant attire of a Roman nobleman of a previous century. Unconscious of any irony in his dress, Ambrosius waited on his simple chair for Prince Luka of the Brigante to arrive at his hall of judgement.

The prince had a mixed reputation, so Ambrosius was curious to see if the man matched the stories that filtered down from the north. Luka refused to use his father's nomen, or even his given name, Llywelyn, being consumed by a fierce determination to win his own fame. Aspiring to the throne of the Brigante tribe was

insufficient for him, for he rightly dismissed his eventual inheritance as an accident of birth. Ambrosius approved of such pride, but
he was concerned and intrigued by Luka's reputation for hot
temper, excess and wild, elemental charm, for such character flaws
were dangerous in an ally.

I'll know soon enough, Ambrosius thought, as he exchanged
glances with his brother. At least Uther has been less grumpy of
late, although I have missed the company of the healer. The young
man has the power to soothe, and his brain is sharper than Uther's
blade – and that's saying something. It's a pity that Uther is jealous
of anyone who stands with me as an intellectual equal.

Just as Uther was becoming restive and angry at the delay in
their visitor's arrival, the ornate doors to the hall were opened with
a flourish and Prince Luka entered, flanked by his personal guard,
who had surrendered their weapons in the antechamber. Although
the newcomers were unarmed, they still looked hard, dangerous
and savage – especially the prince.

'I welcome you, Luka of the Brigante tribe. I have heard whispers
of trouble in the north and I hope you will inform me of any danger
to my lands. I am pleased that, at last, the Brigante, the Atrebates
and the other great tribes of the south can meet and exchange
loyalties after many years of silence and distrust.'

As Ambrosius welcomed his visitor with his usual grace and
warmth, his eyes narrowed on the hawk-sharp face that was lowered
in a deep obeisance. Luka managed to appear compliant and
independent at once, not only in the ready and deep bow he made
so gracefully, but also in the quick measuring glance that examined
the High King from head to toe as he rose to his feet. Ambrosius
began to look for what lay beneath the superficial, blatantly osten-
tatious savagery of the young prince's appearance.

'Please be seated, Prince Luka, for there is no need to stand on
ceremony on this day. Uther – a chair for our guest.'

This simple request established the notion in the minds of witnesses in the audience chamber that Uther and Luka were equal in standing at Ambrosius's court. What Uther thought of this situation was impossible to guess. His face unreadable, he nodded curtly at one of the young men in his train.

Prince Luka accepted the simple stool brought forward by the nervous servant, and then visibly relaxed. Ambrosius registered the amber-brown eyes that gazed at him with candour and an unsettling assessment. Of little more than average height, Luka made up for his lack of inches with a muscular, slender form and quick-moving hands that were as animated as Ambrosius's own. The prince's fingers were long, scarred by sword practice and many years on horseback, and Ambrosius could see them caressing a woman with equal skill. Under the High King's regard, Luka fiddled with his intricately worked electrum torc, so Ambrosius became conscious of the prince's love of display. A brace of arm-rings of massy gold, as well as several large, barbaric and vivid finger-rings decked Luka's body with easy panache.

'Lord, the Picts attacked from beyond Hadrian's Wall in strength. Summer was well advanced, so they caught us by surprise. Far beyond the Vallum Antonini, they had obviously planned their invasion secretly and carefully, depending on speed and surprise to counteract the lateness of the season. After carving through the Otadini and the Selgovae tribes, they drove deeply into our lands before we could muster the levies, so many warriors died to blunt their advance.'

'An unusual and subtle strategy for Picts to use,' Ambrosius murmured. 'Someone in the north has been thinking hard, knowing our eyes have turned towards the east and the Saxons with the approach of summer.'

'Aye, lord,' Luka agreed. 'We had fortified the fortresses of Lavatrae, Bravoniacum and Cataractonium, so we were outfoxed entirely when Talorc, the Pict king, attacked Luguvalium, then Brocavum, before driving his army through the mountains towards Olicana and access to the green lands of the south. But their speed was their undoing, as well as the reason for their initial success. We have long used the old Roman fortresses of Verterae and Petrianae, and Talorc bypassed these two citadels without leaving a force behind that could keep our troops pinned down.'

'A mistake.' Uther snickered from behind Ambrosius. 'It's stupid to leave your rear unguarded. I wish I'd been there to enjoy the fun.'

'I doubt it was fun, brother. I can imagine that the loss of life must have been frightful,' Ambrosius chided gently, and he saw the sudden furrow of distaste between the Brigante's eyes. So Luka was more than just a fighting animal, the High King thought.

'The men of all the fortresses marched to intercept the Picts, while leaving only token forces to guard the eastern marches. My father gambled on a single, decisive battle that would finish the Picts for generations – or destroy us.'

'Tell us, Luka,' Uther murmured eagerly, for he was engrossed in the Brigante's story.

'We drove north through Olicana and made a forced march towards a river valley that could impede the Pict advance. Mountains ringed the valley, and the wild sea cliffs lay to the west, so we trusted our brothers from the fortresses to guard our backs. We met the Picts on the banks of the river, and the clash of men on horseback shuddered through the two armies. Our levies ground together like stone on stone so that no side had an advantage and the battle continued long and fierce. The Blue Men gave no quarter and fought until they perished.

'Then, just as I was beginning to despair of breaking the Pictish ranks, the troops of Verterae and Lavatrae poured out of the hills, both afoot and on horseback. Their impetus, as they charged down the long hill to engage the enemy, cut a huge hole in the rear of the Pict army and gave us heart to continue the struggle. Step by bloody step, we gained ground and managed to pin the Picts into a deadly circle.'

'Did Talorc surrender and parlay for terms, or retreat like a sensible man?' Ambrosius asked, easily able to visualise the blood-churned mud and the heaped corpses of a desperate struggle to survive the conflict.

'We offered them terms, my lord. I know the Brigante tribe has a reputation for ferocity, but we are honourable men. Once we knew the battle was won, my father called a truce and sent me to offer them a chance of surrender without humiliation, but Talorc spat in my face. I had to use all my weapons' skill to escape unscathed, for the Picts were prepared to break the truce. Once I rejoined our force, my father ordered the net closed and we slew their men until our arms were almost too heavy to lift our swords.'

'Terrible,' Ambrosius murmured, for he regretted the loss of so many warriors.

'Aye, it *was* terrible. But our losses were light compared with those inflicted on the enemy. Many widows beyond the two walls will wail in sorrow when their men come home no more. And they will sing songs of the death of Talorc for generations, for he refused to surrender and died where he stood. We despise the Picts out of long habit, but I would be blind if I didn't admire Talorc's fierce courage in the face of certain death. Only when the king had perished did the will of the Picts break, and they started to run. We allowed them to pass back into the north, but only a few hundred men will return out of the thousands who marched into Brigante lands only weeks before.'

'I take it that you captured the baggage train,' Uther interrupted, eager to determine the value of the Pictish war chests.

'Aye. As the emissary for my father, Lord King Ambrosius, I beg you to accept one fifth of all that was taken from the dead and the dying. What remains will succour our widows and orphans, as well as fortify our borders, for we believe the Saxons will consider the aftermath of this conflict with the Picts to be an opportune time to attack us.'

Luka gestured towards one of his guard, who struck the closed doors with his fist. A group of warriors entered, bowed under the weight of the wooden chests, bound with iron bands, that they laid at Ambrosius's feet. One of the warriors opened the lids and exposed piles of looted valuables that filled the chests to the brims. Under the ruddy light of the torches, the gold, silver and bronze that had been stripped from the dead seemed to have been washed with the sheen of blood.

'I have heard that you took hostages as well,' Uther cut in over Ambrosius's courteous thanks, causing the High King to dart an admonishing glance in his direction.

'Behold the household of Talorc, king of the Picts,' Luka cried in a ringing voice as a group of women was herded into the audience chamber. They entered on naked feet, for they were chained and humbled, so the links of their shackles rang dully as they swayed into the circle of lamplight.

The Pict women were quite short, but they were proud and very shapely. They wore their tattoos with pride and stared at their new masters with palpable scorn. Even as Luka introduced the Pict queen, an older woman whose hair was liberally streaked with grey, Ambrosius found his eyes drawn to a red-haired woman who was unmistakably Celt in appearance. Her green eyes were insolent and angry, and she scorned to hide her partial nakedness with her long tattooed hands.

The woman's lissome body and the endearing freckles across her nose, forearms and breasts impressed Ambrosius. Even the sharp enmity in her eyes caused his loins to tighten painfully.

Ambrosius had always trodden carefully around the fairer sex, for he had a healthy respect for the reputed female penchant for slyness and manipulation. Even the need for an heir was not overly pressing, as Uther could step into his shoes should accident, assassination or death in battle send the High King prematurely to the River Styx. Not that Ambrosius planned to pay the Ferryman early: far from it. The king nurtured grandiose plans for the future of the people of the west, ambitions that would take time to bring to fruition. Unlike his brother, he recognised that there were many Saxon thanes of character and pragmatism who might well enter into alliances under some form of truce. Further, he believed that little actually separated Saxon and Celt but blind prejudice, for even their gods and customs were similar. With patience, Ambrosius believed he could blunt the violence of the past and build a lasting accord with Saxons of goodwill.

Even as his mind ranged over the many possibilities open to him, he continued to stare at the Celtic woman intently. Finally Luka interrupted his liege's abstracted concentration.

'What do you require us to do with the captives, my king?'

'They may stay or go as their hearts dictate. I'll not turn noble-women into slaves. They are free to find new husbands or masters if they wish to remain in Venta Belgarum. Let each woman who chooses to leave be given a horse and enough supplies to last for a week. She may then return to her home as best she may.'

The noblewomen whispered together with a sound like wind soughing through dried grasses. Their faces were closed and blank and their bodies were rigid with revulsion.

'Then we will depart this heathen place,' the Pict queen decided in a voice that was deep, resonant and charged with sexual promise, although she must have been past the age of childbearing. 'The mountains of the north wind call to us and my husband's shade demands to be set free of the chains of this world.'

The other women swayed and nodded, so that Ambrosius imagined that he gazed at flower women, heather women, blue with their tattoos and the midnight blackness of their manes.

'My lord,' Luka protested. 'These women are from noble families who will be prepared to pay a ransom for their safe return. You cast away gold that would enrich your war coffers.'

'I don't make war against females,' Ambrosius snapped. 'And who is that Celtic woman? She's obviously not a Pict, so she has no business being chained.'

'She damned well acted like a Pict when she bit me,' Luka responded roughly, still smarting from the king's rebuff. 'She was married to one of the lordlings. But don't ask me which one, as I can't pronounce their heathen names.'

'Stand forth, woman. I know you understand me. Who are you, and what are your antecedents?'

Ambrosius's tone left no room for disobedience, so the Celt stepped to the front of the cluster of women with her chin lifted in pride. Her steps were graceful and turned her slightest movement into a promise.

'My husband's name was Garnaid, lord of the area north of what the Romans called Camelon, beyond the Vallum Antonini. The Romans ceded us those lands, believing us to be too barbaric to dwell on softer, more civilised soil. And you could not dislodge us, no matter how hard your ancestors tried. But some of us still dwell in the lands of the Selgovae and Damnonii, in an uneasy truce with the tribal kings and suffering much poverty. Some Otadini tribesmen hunt us like vermin, yet you consider *them* to be noble.'

Her voice was light and lilting, although she spoke Celt with a limping accent, as if she had been stolen from her people a long time ago.

'I repeat, woman, what is your name and where do you come from?'

'I am Bridei, once called Andrewina Ruadh when I lived in my father's house near Rerigonius Sinus. I grew up within a stone's throw of the wild sea, a daughter of the Novantae tribe. When I was ten years old, I was stolen, or rescued, by a raiding party from beyond the northern wall, and became a replacement for a murdered daughter. In the north, I learned what it is to be free and no chattel of ambitious men. There, I married as I chose and bore sons, so I thank you for permitting me to return to my bairns.'

'But you're not a Pict!' Ambrosius exclaimed, affronted that a well-born female would prefer the travails of the icy north.

'And you're a Roman, Ambrosius Imperator, and not a true Celt in blood. As such, you belong in Rome, don't you? No? Like you, I choose to be where my heart dictates. I am now a Pict.'

'By birth and bloodline, you are Celt until it is established whether your kin will take you back. If none is found alive, or your family should reject you, then you may go where you choose. In the meantime, you may serve in my kitchens.'

Bridei flashed Ambrosius a malicious glance that could blight the immature ears of wheat. The High King smiled a little at her defiance, although Uther clenched his fists at her arrogance and decided that this woman should meet with an unfortunate accident.

'I'll not be a servant to my people's enemies. You'll have to chain me.'

'Of course, my lady,' Ambrosius agreed equably. 'If such is your desire.'

Then, as the women were ushered out of his hall, the High King turned his back on her to talk to Luka and Uther. Bridei was led away in chains. Her heart ached for her sons, but her pride did not permit her to weep.

Myrddion lay curled in his cloak in a thick nest of dried leaves outside Tomen-y-mur as he waited to ride into that benighted town. He had ridden far, visiting the towns of Glevum, Venta Silurum, Isca, Nidum and Caer Fyrddin. At first, he had been unsure of ever finding eyes and ears for Ambrosius, but he had been mistaken. Years of war had taken their toll on the British people, and kings and commoners alike gave thanks for the night that Vortigern had perished at Dinas Emrys. They were vocal in their praise of peace, at least in his hearing, and at Isca Myrddion even heard the tale of Vortigern's burning, told with much elaboration, by an old soldier who claimed to have been at the fortress when the old monster died. Initially, Myrddion had wanted to hide in embarrassment, but he covered his hair with the cowl of his cloak, sat quietly at the back of the inn and listened in amazement as the unlikely tale unfolded.

'It was a lucky day when the gods took pity on us,' the warrior explained to a rapt audience. 'We'd suffered sorely from the tyrant's cruelty and it seemed we'd be killing each other for years. Civil war was like to turn Cymru into a wasteland full of weeping widows and starving children. Let's face it, what harm does Ambrosius do to us? We send our share of tribute and the levies, and we're left to live our lives as we want. But under Vortigern's iron fist? I remember it well, mind, so I'm glad the bastard's safely dead.'

'But how did it happen, Ewen? I'm told he died in a storm,' a plump-faced farmer asked, pouring ale from a brimming pottery jug into a mug clutched in Ewen's gnarled fist. Gratified with the response, Ewen took a deep quaff of the ale and brushed his grey moustaches clean. He preened visibly.

'I tell you that the good god Bran sent the lightning that struck Vortigern. It burned him up in seconds. Ugh! What he looked like afterwards! We were sick when we tried to move the king's corpse. He fell apart like over-cooked meat.'

Ewen continued to elaborate on his grisly tale to the groans, cheers or grimaces of the crowd, but Myrddion had heard enough.

Yet the flashy lie was of use, for it ensured that Myrddion's mentor, Eddius, remained safe, despite lighting the fire that caused the death of King Vortigern. Nor did Myrddion have the heart to blame Eddius for his sin of regicide. Eddius's wife, Olwyn, Myrddion's grandmother, had been killed by the king's own hand and her blood had cried out for vengeance from beyond the grave.

'A pretty fallacy,' he whispered.

The man next to him glanced up at Myrddion sharply and then, surprised, narrowed his eyes in recognition.

'I know you, master.' The man spoke softly and deferentially, for he remembered the sunburst ruby on Myrddion's index finger. 'You were the healer at Tomen-y-mur. You're the Demon Seed.'

'Were you there, my friend?' Myrddion sighed. He had already found some men and women who were eager to serve him because he had saved their lives after one of the many battles fought during Vortigern's time. Their admiration made them eager to repay him, and Myrddion sometimes believed he was taking advantage of their gratitude.

'Yes, I helped to erect your first tent at Tomen-y-mur. My brother died at the hands of that bastard, Balbas, who was supposed to be caring for him. God rot the cur! I hope he starves for the greed and ineptitude that killed my brother. You took Aelwen into your tent and tried to help him, but his blood was already poisoned.'

'I'm sorry, friend. Every healer regrets the lives he cannot save.'

The warrior shook his plaits and clasped both hands together so tightly that the knuckles shone whitely.

'He didn't suffer, because you gave him something to ease his way into the shades – or so you said. You let me stay with him and hold his hand until he drew his last breath. I never thanked you, for I couldn't think for sorrow. At the time, I wanted the whole world to burn to cinders so everyone would suffer as I did, so I couldn't say a word. Forgive me for being so ungrateful.'

'There's nothing to forgive. I've seen every form of grief, so I understand how paralysing it is. What is your name?'

'Aled. We were Aelwen and Aled of Isca, or Caerleon as we call it. A pair of boys who were set for trouble – that was us. We were never apart in life, so I miss him more than I can say. I'm married now, with two boys of my own, and I serve the Silure king, but nothing fills the hole left by the loss of Aelwen.'

'I understand. I felt the same when my grandmother died, but the grief grows dim with the passage of the years, and leaves behind only the memories of the good days. You'll see, Aled. The Mother hasn't forsaken you.'

Embarrassed, Aled turned the conversation to Myrddion's presence in Cymru. Stories had grown around the Demon Seed and his name was often mentioned in conjunction with Vortigern. But he had been absent for so long that rumour suggested that his infernal father had either spirited him away to the Otherworld or driven him mad.

'As you can see, Aled, I am neither crazed nor demon-cursed. I am still a simple healer.'

'Aye,' Aled snorted with scorn. 'And I'm the High King of the Britons.'

Myrddion laughed gently. 'No. You are surely not Ambrosius, Aled. In fact, the High King is my master now, and I'm here at his behest on a matter of great secrecy.'

Aled raised one sceptical eyebrow. Venta Belgarum was far away, but only foolish braggarts claimed familiarity with Ambrosius Imperator.

'I swear I never took you for a man who would happily serve a foreign king.'

'I wasn't, Aled. But I've seen the Middle Sea since I was last in Cymru and my opinions have changed. You can't imagine the wars and bloodshed that take place as migrating tribes pour into the void the Romans leave when they abandon the lands they ruled. Bridges, roads, buildings, aqueducts and the law itself are cast away. The Saxons are as nothing when compared with some of the tribes across the Litus Saxonicum. No, I serve Ambrosius because he represents law, order and strength for our people.'

'I will agree with you that we need no more Vortimers or Catigerns to tear the tribes and clans apart, but it goes against the grain, master, to welcome a stranger.'

Myrddion chose his next words carefully, because Aled was exactly the type of man he needed: a cool-thinking, rational patriot.

'Ambrosius's mother was both Roman and tribal, which many men forget, but I have talked with him and I can swear that he has always thought of these isles as his homeland. Late at night, he speaks of his years of exile in Brittany, Rome and Constantinople. He still thinks of those places, which he could have considered his home, as foreign and beautiful. But like me during my journey to Constantinople, he longed for the dim blue skies of Britain.'

'Perhaps,' Aled growled. 'Perhaps I'm being a fool to set such store by nine generations of family behind me on the same soil. But our family lands belonged to other peoples, including the Picts, before we Celts settled in Britain. I suppose the world is changing and we must change with it.'

The warrior's expression was thoughtful, so Myrddion rose to buy another pitcher of ale. When he retuned, Aled was sunk in gloom.

'By your description of Gaul, we could be at war for years. May the Mother save us.'

'No, Aled, we must act to save ourselves. I'm in the service of Ambrosius, and I'm searching for like-minded men, including some who speak Saxon, who are prepared to serve as listeners within and without the kingdom.'

Myrddion carefully refrained from using the ugly word *spy*, but Aled's back straightened and a cloud settled on his brows.

'A spy in the Saxon towns I understand, but you must call it by what it is, Master Myrddion.' Aled's voice was crisp with his displeasure. 'But why should any loyal tribesman provide you with information about his own people that will be used for the benefit of Ambrosius Imperator? Such information smacks of treason, and brings dishonour to the informant's own tribe.'

'You said it yourself, Aled. We don't want another Vortimer, hungry to assume his father's throne. Good kings need fear nothing from Ambrosius Imperator. Believe me, he knows the Saxons are unpredictable and cruel enemies. He needs no others.'

Aled nodded tersely, but his shoulders remained stiff and unbending.

'The men who have already committed themselves to this task have sworn an oath to me, not to Ambrosius,' Myrddion continued as persuasively as he knew how. 'I will decide how the information I receive should be used. If you insist on describing my mission accurately, it is my task to be the spymaster, so you must decide whether I have the integrity to carry out my role. I hope I have already proved to you that I can be trusted.'

Aled remained silent for almost ten minutes as he considered Myrddion's proposition. He drank slowly, stared at his strong right hand, flexed it and looked into the middle distance with eyes that saw nothing but his secret thoughts. Myrddion sat quietly and permitted the warrior to consider his options. Finally, Aled made a decision, wiped his hand on his jerkin and offered it to the healer.

'I'll serve you, Myrddion of Segontium – but only you. I'll trust you to act honourably with any information I give you, so long as you swear to be guided by what is good for our lands.'

'I can make such an oath easily.' Myrddion grinned. 'I owe nothing to Ambrosius and his brother, and I yearn to see a king who is totally committed to the tribes and their survival ruling the west as one peaceful nation. I can swear to you that I will always remain true to this good earth and the people who till the soil and shepherd its beasts, and I refuse to bend the knee to *any* man who is drunk with power. The Saxons are the enemy and their advance must be stopped.'

So, in diverse ways, Myrddion travelled through the south, finding a man here and another there, men who swore an oath to serve him personally rather than pledge loyalty to the High King. At first, Myrddion was awed by the responsibility that these strong men placed in his hands, but his reasonable, inner self whispered that sensible warriors prefer leaders who are close at hand, access- ible and human, for few ordinary people understand the political jostling for power of kings.

In Caer Fyrddin, Cletus One Ear and his eldest son swore to serve Myrddion because of the shared skein of kinship. Aunt Fillagh wept copious tears to see her great-nephew again, now so strong and powerful, and in private she shared her memories of his birth with her husband. Even though time had weakened her eyesight and her memory, she recalled a powerful sense of destiny that had been woven around the comely young man's form and face.

'You'll see, Cletus. Our Myrddion will be the most powerful man in the land, more important than even the High King. Olwyn would have been so proud to see him rise so high.'

'Aye! One day, we'll boast that the boy is kin to us. I thank Fortuna that I found his bulla for him.'

'You found the locket, husband, but his accursed mother found the sunburst ring. Did you see it upon his finger?'

Cletus puffed up with natural pride. Many years had passed but, with an ageing man's memory, he recalled long ago days more clearly than the happenings of yesterday.

At Isca, Aled had informed Myrddion of a rumour concerning a man from Venta Silurum who had been orphaned by Saxon raiders from the Demetae hills. After killing his parents, the raiding party had enslaved the young man. Eventually, the captive escaped from the Saxons when he was some twenty years old and had run wild like a savage ever since. Unable to live in normal human society, and fuelled by a hatred so scarfing and hot that he could barely contain it, this Gruffydd kept to the wild places and hunted Saxons with a ruthlessness that was becoming legendary.

'He was somewhere north of Tomen-y-mur when I last heard of him. He was nearly recaptured after he murdered a Saxon trader on the road out of Caer Fyrddin, so he took to his heels and disappeared into the north. I can't imagine how he lives, but if you can find him and mend his maddened brain, you'll have a Saxon-speaker with an axe to grind.'

So Myrddion headed into the north.

He avoided the dangerous areas around the old fortress that the Romans had called Moridunum, and rode hard towards Segontium and his old family home. When he reached the mountains, he found the hill people who provided one of the skeins in the rope of his blood. These people were very short and squat and seemed to be stunted by the harsh winds, the bone-numbing cold and a life of grinding privation as they eked out what food could be grown in such inhospitable places. They gazed at their tall young visitor with glazed eyes that filled with superstitious terror as they noted the growing streak of white on his right brow and the sense of otherness that enveloped him like an invisible cloak. When forced to face him, they accepted his coin and shared what they had with him for the sake of his great-grandmother and her sister Rhyll, whose names were still remembered with affection and awe. But they never explained their fear of him, or invited him into their homes, which were little more than flintstone circles topped with thatch to keep out the snow. Perhaps they feared that he would curse them, all unknowing, but whatever their reasons, Myrddion wore his loneliness like a Christian hair shirt.

At Caer Gai, Myrddion found a ruined house of some size, perhaps built by the Romans to guard the way into the north. An oak tree, many hundreds of years old, had been riven by lightning, and the softer wooden core had been devoured by time, so Myrddion sheltered for a night in the cavern at its base. A thick bed of rotted wood and long dead leaves formed a comfortable pallet and a nearby tarn provided icy water, allowing Myrddion to dine on a stew of dried meat fleshed out with tender greens and some wild parsnips. The peace of the mountains settled into his heart, the winds sang in the flutes of the stone ruins like a choir of children and the young healer could have wept for the beauty of the wild places.

Tomen-y-mur was a walled town, built high over the coast and the wild winds of the sea. As Myrddion trotted through an eerie silence towards his mother's house, he took solace from the sight of hunting birds as they soared far above him, although they were too distant for his eyes to discern whether they were hawks, merlins or falcons. He saw one great eagle as it rode the thermals rising from a valley, its wings effortlessly accommodating the swirling air, and his heart lightened as if these wild things spoke to him of a future worth his labours. Yet he was aware of dread as well, and feared meeting his mother, now in her forties, who had hated him all his life.

He passed through the sheltered valley where Vortigern's army had licked its wounds and a younger Myrddion had learned his craft in a bloody leather apron, gore-smeared to the elbows as he saved what lives he could. There was the copse of trees where his tent had stood. The earth was very green where the dead had been buried and wild flowers still flourished in great shrivelling drifts, although autumn was now giving way to winter.

'The dead seem to give new life from within their graves. Truly, the Christian priests speak honestly when they say all flesh is grass.' Myrddion spoke aloud to break a silence so profound that he ached from the emptiness of the sky, the mountains and the distant view of the sea.

The route to Tomen-y-mur took comparatively little time. Myrddion traversed the slopes where he had loved his first woman, although he couldn't remember her face or anything about her, other than her name. He berated himself for this failure, cursing the casual affections of men and his own callousness. He had been besotted with her hair, he remembered at last, so wild and red, tied up with a strip of coloured rag. There, where dead flowers still raised desiccated heads towards the cold sun, he had marvelled at that thick, curling hair and luxuriated in her body and the sweet nothingness that it promised.

But no matter how memory distracted him, Tomen-y-mur eventually called to him from the end of a narrow road that was little more than a goat track, an eyrie of small huts with dark beetling walls and a view of the grey sea. The first snow came in a flurry of wind as he approached the gates on a dark afternoon, so he spurred his horse through the narrow gap opened by a spluttering keeper whose curses followed him along the muddy street.

Tomen-y-mur boasted a single inn, a hovel where the smoke-filled interior and general coating of oily grime over every surface revolted the young healer. The town was a byway, and few sensible folk braved its isolation. Myrddion shuddered to think of his mother trapped on a farm outside such a place, where she would have been starved for companionship and beauty.

The small room was filled to bursting by a press of men from various trades. Myrddion could smell the shepherds before he saw them, for their untanned cloaks of sheeps' wool reeked nearly as badly as the odour of unwashed flesh, ordure and piss combined. With a barely disguised shudder, Myrddion approached a hulking man behind a plank bar who was pouring jugs of something resembling ale from large barrels. His fat, hairy fingers filled Myrddion with disgust, especially when he saw the man wipe his streaming nose on his sleeve, hawk, and then spit onto the dirt floor.

'You're a stranger,' the innkeeper said unnecessarily. His face was marred by a fierce squint and his belly was gross. Myrddion remembered Gron at Verulamium and compared the two men mentally. At least this man seemed slightly cheerier, but no less venal.

'Aye. I'm from Segontium, although I've been travelling for six years. I've come to see my mother, Lady Branwyn, who lives in these parts, and to hunt up a man called Gruffydd.'

The innkeeper eyed Myrddion closely, pursed his lips and decided to grin, exposing a mouthful of rotting teeth. 'Well, boyo, you're out of luck on both counts. Gruffydd comes here sometimes, but he's not in tonight. As for the lady Branwyn – your mother, is she? – she's mad!'

Several men stared at Myrddion and one nudged his neighbour with a dirty elbow. 'Are you the Demon Seed, then?' he asked roughly.

'Are you speaking to me?' Myrddion asked politely, but his raised eyebrow and chilly demeanour flustered the shepherd into incoherent half-sentences.

'Er . . . yes . . . er . . . begging your pardon, sir,' the man stammered, and the innkeeper shot a withering look of contempt at him.

'Don't be minding him. He talks to himself, if there's no one else available to listen to him, and he never knows when to keep his sodding tongue behind his teeth. He spends too much time with sheep, if you take my meaning.' The innkeeper leered unattractively.

'I am Myrddion Merlinus of Segontium, and I am the healer at the court of Ambrosius Imperator, High King of the west. Do my credentials meet with your approval?'

'It's not for me to argue with my betters, sir,' the innkeeper intoned, ducking his head apologetically. 'Will you be needing a room? A meal? The girl will see to it, or I'll tan her hide. And I'll see if I can find Gruffydd for you, sir. You'd do honour to my inn if you were to stay here.'

Having discovered that arrogance – or the Aspar manner, as Myrddion had tagged it in memory of his birth father – was an effective and speedy route to achieving his desires, the tired healer relinquished his horse to the ostler and trudged up rickety stairs to an attic room. When the maidservant opened the door for him he sighed dispiritedly, for the space was filthy with bird droppings, the regurgitations of at least one owl and the dust of years. The girl heard his reaction and shyly offered to help.

'If my master is willing, I can clean your room, especially if you're staying for a while. You're the first guest of the house for . . . well . . . years.'

'I thank you for your offer, and I'd appreciate anything you can do. At the moment I need hot water, as soon as possible.'

'And food, sir, would that please you?'

Without thinking, Myrddion answered more bluntly than was his usual fashion. 'Will I survive the experience?'

The maid visibly straightened. 'My mother is the cook, sir. Perhaps it's not what you're used to, but she doesn't use rotten vegetables or meat that has turned. She uses clean salt and cooks the meat through to the bone. She doesn't scrimp with the portions either. We're poor, sir, but we don't cheat, not even fat-arse Brychan, who's none too clean in his habits. Me and my ma do what we can with what we've got to keep the inn tidy, but there's only so many hours, sir.'

Myrddion was ashamed. How many more times would he fail to see the world from the point of view of the weak and the helpless? 'I'm sorry, lass. Bring me whatever will heat the heart of a cold and bad-tempered man. My only defence is that I've been thwarted all day and I took my anger out on you.' He fumbled in his purse and retrieved a copper coin. 'I'll pay to have Brychan's attic cleaned and will be grateful for whatever you can do to make me comfortable.'

The girl took the coin and held it carefully, as if it would vanish of its own volition. 'I've never had a real coin before, sir.'

'Don't you receive wages for your work in the inn?' Myrddion asked curiously.

'Oh, no, sir. I'm Brychan's bastard, as are my two little sisters. Mam works to keep us in his favour though he's got another woman now, a real sow who never moves her lazy rump.'

Myrddion's brows knitted with dislike of the greasy innkeeper. He understood the plight of a woman with three young daughters, and he supposed a roof over their heads and food in their bellies was worth any compromise, given the grim alternatives.

'I'll pay your sisters to work for me as well. What's your name, lass?'

'Brychan says my name's heathen, but Mam came from across the water with her da when she was a babe. She called me Cait, sir, which is short for Caitlin, but I answer to anything.'

Myrddion picked up her hand and unclenched her fingers to examine her palm. The fine-boned hand was seamed with scars and calluses, and was heavily muscled as well, but her nails were clean and well shaped, like small pink shells. The skin was hard, but the fingers were long and he could feel that the bones beneath the flesh were beautiful. Without thinking, he raised her hand to his lips and kissed the work-worn palm.

Cait flushed and was suspicious, but Myrddion waved her

concerns away. 'I don't need someone to warm my bed, nor do I require anything of you but some hard work and honesty. Can you do that for me, Cait?'

'Aye, sir,' she replied and lowered her head as she backed away, already half in love with the kindness and grace he had shown towards her. 'I'll arrange to get you some hot water and food for your dinner then, shall I?'

'Bridei Ruadh,' Ambrosius whispered with little more sound than the exhalation of a sigh. 'Why won't you kiss me? You give me your body willingly enough, but not your mouth. Am I so vile?'

Bridei lay under Ambrosius's spent body, her reddish-brown hair spread across the fine sleeping pallet like a bloodstain that was almost dry. Her jaw and the white column of her throat spasmed briefly as she thought of her lost children, and then she smiled sleepily in the way she knew moved the High King.

'I'm still a servant, my lord, no matter what you might say. I share your bed but I am your possession, regardless of your words. The only thing I have that is mine is my soul, which is still Pict – and I cannot give my soul to my enemy. You have my heart, but I keep my spirit jealously, so I cannot kiss you. Ask for anything else, but not that.'

Ambrosius rolled away from her so that his long, powerful spine was all she could see of him, except for his curly, closely cropped hair. She was torn between a desire to stroke the long bow of his back and an impulse to take up the eating knife that was so casually laid on a low table and plunge the weapon deep into his muscular flesh.

But she knew the knife was not long enough to cause the High King permanent harm, nor did her wilful heart truly desire to kill him. She would never see her children again if she committed such a deed, and she hoped, against all reason, that he would tire of her one day and send her away. But, like the Picts who had shaped both her youth and her womanhood, she was patient.

Bridei had heard an owl call outside the High King's shutters on three successive nights. Its wings had beaten at the wood as if it sought entry, and she wondered if Ceridwen had turned her smile upon her suffering daughter at last. She kissed Ambrosius's stiff spine and felt his resolution weaken. After a few seconds, he rolled over and enfolded her in his powerful arms.

Two days had passed in Tomen-y-mur and Myrddion chafed under his enforced inactivity. Deep snow had fallen, and the dirty town was transformed under a blanket of powdery whiteness that softened the hard flint surfaces and disguised the mean streets. The healer passed his time by transcribing the names of the complex network of agents that was starting to form under his clever hands onto a scroll.

On the second afternoon in his newly scoured room, he huddled over the brazier that rested in an iron tray beside his feet and tried not to remember the warm, balmy winds of Constantinople. Cait had brought some heated mead, and although the cloying sweetness was not to Myrddion's taste at least the hot beaker warmed his hands. Just when he thought he might be able to continue with his writing, Brychan stuck his untidy head round the door and announced that Gruffydd had drifted into the inn.

'Invite the gentleman to join me, Brychan, and bring a jug of beer and two cups. If Gruffydd tries to refuse, explain to him that he will be paid for his trouble whether he decides to oblige me or not.'

'That one will come for the free beer,' Brychan snorted and disappeared.

Rallying his drooping spirits, Myrddion combed his hair and tied it back, more to appear older than out of any vanity. He called for Cait and asked her to beg her mother for something filling to eat, explaining that he would be entertaining an indigent guest who would probably have a voracious appetite. Cait nodded her understanding of his requirements, and on her way down the shadowy stairs passed a disreputable man coming up in company with Brychan, who was carrying a pottery jug of ale and two earthenware mugs.

Myrddion rose to his feet as his guest entered, although he was obliged to bend almost double because of the low-set rafters. 'Please be seated, Gruffydd,' he said politely, pointing to the only seat in the room. 'As you're my guest, I'll sit on my pallet.' He did so as he spoke, and watched his quarry fold his compact body onto the poorly constructed stool.

Sitting down, Gruffydd looked boneless and unthreatening, apparently completely at ease. When any other man would have been wary and suspicious, he managed to present himself as a disinterested dullard. His eyes seemed empty of any thoughts of consequence, his hair was a wild tangle with a complement of twigs caught in the untamed curls, and his clothing, if such rags merited the word, were slovenly and food-spotted.

Pouring a mug of beer for his visitor, the healer noticed the scars around the thickly muscled neck. Gruffydd took a deep gulp of the sour brew, grimaced, and then grinned dourly.

'You're looking at my slave scars, whoever-you-are. So why don't you stare your fill? Perhaps you should see this one if you're so damned curious.' With one grimy hand, he dragged down his tunic and exposed a healed scar shaped like the iron spearhead that had been heated and pressed to his breast. The hair had never grown over the ugly cicatrice and Myrddion winced as he imagined the agony that such a wound would have caused.

But even worse were the marks left on Gruffydd's neck by a metal shackle. He must have worn one for years to have been left with such hideous scars. Aghast, Myrddion realised that, unlike the Romans, the Saxons clearly did not line their iron neck rings with strips of hide to protect the flesh.

'Want to see more?' Gruffydd drawled, and yanked off his shirt to expose his body to the waist. Then he stood up and turned his back on Myrddion, stretching his arms wide. Layer upon painful layer, scar tissue had built up, criss-crossing the whole broad back until there was no unblemished skin between his neck and his crude leather trews.

'Enough, Gruffydd! Get dressed, please. Whatever you wanted to prove to me, you've done it. The Saxons were cruel masters, but you managed to survive.'

Gruffydd replaced the rags that covered his abused flesh and settled back on his stool like a disreputable heap of rubbish, his face sinking into its previous vacuous expression.

Myrddion went straight to the point. 'I need someone who hates the Saxons but has the capacity to pretend to be one, or at least to be sympathetic to their cause. Are you such a man?'

'Who wants to know? Why should I bother to listen to you, except for your superlative beer?'

At that moment, Cait entered with a wicker tray steaming with rich aromas. Myrddion's mouth began to water as she laid down a large pottery bowl filled with some kind of stew before unloading several slabs of flat bread, two small wooden bowls, two wooden spoons and, with a flourish, a whole roasted chicken still bubbling from the fire, with crispy, slightly blackened skin.

'Your mother's a wonder, Cait. Please give her my congratulations and my thanks.'

Cait smiled with a flash of attractive dimples. 'I'll tell her, Master Myrddion. It's little enough praise she gets from Brychan, so she'll be grateful.' Then, with a little bow, the girl was gone.

'I'll say this for you. You look like a girl, but you've got the women jumping after you. What's your secret?' Gruffydd punctuated his approval by ripping a leg from the chicken and starting to eat.

'There's no secret. My name is Myrddion Merlinus Emrys and I hail from Segontium. I'm a healer in the service of Ambrosius Imperator in Venta Belgarum, and I've been charged with a special mission for my master. Don't hold my youth against me. I've travelled widely, and I promise I'm not the soft, sentimental fool you take me for.'

'Possibly. I'll hold my decision on you in abeyance while I enjoy this food,' Gruffydd replied laconically through a mouthful of chicken.

'You still haven't answered my question, Gruffydd. Must I repeat myself?'

Gruffydd lowered the chicken bone into his bowl and wiped his greasy fingers on his thighs. He sighed.

'It seems a pity to spoil good food,' he said reflectively to his bowl, then raised his eyes slowly to engage those of Myrddion. 'Hate the Saxons? What I feel goes beyond hate. My mother was repeatedly raped in front of me. I was only nine, and I'd lived a comfortable life until then, as my da was a successful trader and landowner. I'd never even imagined such brutality. She bled, she fought, she cried for my father – and afterwards, they cut her throat and made me watch. But worst of all, they called her a stupid whore. No, I don't hate them. The word's too weak for what I feel.'

Gruffydd's eyes danced with little fires of madness, but the healer was impressed with the rigid control that held the man's fury in check. Harnessed correctly, Gruffydd could become a very useful tool.

'I want to hear the whole story, Gruffydd. Then we can eat in peace, and I will decide what should be asked of you. What happened to you and your father after your mother died?'

Gruffydd laughed softly, without mirth. 'I cried, but they just thought me a coward and a fool. And so I was allowed to live, may the gods help me to forget. I wish I'd died with my father.'

Myrddion said nothing. Although his face remained blank, his heart ached for the little boy who had been so grossly traumatised. Gruffydd was fortunate that the Saxons had considered him harmless.

'They dragged my father away and I never saw him again. His hands were soft because he'd never been a warrior or worked in the fields. Later, I heard that they called him a woman because his muscles were so soft. It was then I was told that they had used him like one, although he tried to fight them. Even when he resisted, the animals thought his struggles were amusing, and enjoyed him even more. Then, when they became tired of his struggles, he was handed over to their women as a plaything. Gods, but I wish they'd killed him cleanly. Women can seem as soft as new butter and as sweet as honey, but they have demons inside them that mere men cannot see. He lived for two weeks under their torture and I was told, with much mirth, that he was made to suffer for every man those hellcats had lost during the years after Vortigern's death.'

Myrddion shuddered, but said nothing. The flow of Gruffydd's narrative was in full spate and the healer would do nothing to halt that ugly rush of memories. To know a man fully, Myrddion knew that he must understand the worst parts of his soul.

'They shackled me, branded me and made me their animal. In those days, I still had some beauty, so I came to discover that Saxons aren't above pederasty. With a collar round my neck and a leash to make me obey, I was forced to perform for the brutes as their fancy took them. But I managed to stay alive.'

Gruffydd's chest was straining and his big hands clenched and unclenched as if they searched for a Saxon neck to break.

'I outlived my beauty, but I refused to stop fighting them. I was beaten again and again until I prayed for death, but if the gods do exist they didn't care what happened to me. Eventually, the Saxons forced me to work as a field slave because I wasn't pretty enough for anything else. I moved rocks and performed the manual, numbing tasks that any ox or horse would do – but I survived. I learned to speak like a Saxon, because I had to think about something other than killing them all. I learned to hide what I was thinking, but I swore every night that I would make every Saxon man, woman and child who crossed my path pay for what had been done to my family and to me. I found that revenge is a powerful incentive to keep a man alive.'

'Aye. When no other hope exists, hatred can fill the void,' Myrddion whispered, remembering a cold evening when he waited to be executed at Vortigern's whim. The memory led inexorably to his beloved grandmother, Olwyn, as she lay under a shroud after she had been murdered by the Celtic king. Myrddion understood Gruffydd's hatred, and how it scoured the soul clean of anything resembling softness.

'I managed to escape after six years,' Gruffydd continued. 'My master decided that one of his blows had addled my wits, so I said nothing to disabuse him. He turned his back on me one day when we were away from his hall and his warriors. He considered me to be an ox and not worth noticing, so I smashed his head in with a large rock I was pulling out of his newly ploughed field. Then I turned his head to a bloody paste.

'They loosed their dogs after me, so I killed them. They sent men after me and I killed them as well, because I wasn't prepared to run. I *wanted* to be hunted. I took their weapons, one by one, and I killed Saxons until even their blood sickened me. I suppose I was mad, but I didn't care. I'd be dead now if an itinerant priest hadn't found me, tied me down and hidden me until I began to come back to my senses. He spirited me out of Dyfed as an acolyte, although I can't remember much about it. I suppose he was a good priest and he was a gifted man of the woods, which is why he avoided being captured by the Saxons. He taught me woodcraft and forced me to come back to myself by reminding me that my mother would want me to remain alive. When he was killed by robbers in Towy, I was free to act as I chose.'

Myrddion listened in silence.

'I can do nothing for you, Myrddion-three-names. I kill Saxons because it's the only way I can sleep soundly, and to forget the eyes of my mother when her throat was cut. I was never told how my father died. Nor did I ever learn the details of his torture, so my mind creates one horror after another. I can pretend to be a man, but I'm still the ox, lashed to the plough, or living on food slops that are more rotten than the scraps that have been fed to the pigs. I pretend to be human, but I'm not.'

The silence was so profound that Myrddion could hear the crackle of coals in the brazier. The smoke might have made his eyes water, but he knew that the tears that threatened were caused by empathy and sadness.

Gruffydd drank deeply, his fingers quite steady. His face was vacuous once more, as iron self-control forced the unsleeping horrors in his tortured memory to retreat behind invisible shutters. Yet despite all the dictates of common sense, Myrddion knew, beyond room for any doubt, that this slovenly and murderous man was crucial to the future of the land and to his own fate.

Outside the crude attic shutters, a flurry of snow struck the inn and a cold breeze stirred the air in the small room. The Mother seemed to whisper to Myrddion that he had been born for a great purpose, and she was placing his tools in his hands one by one. Here sat the first weapon, a man made dangerous by impossible cruelty and aching loneliness.

'You know what you must do, my child,' her voice murmured in the stray draughts of gelid air. 'If you disobey me, your world will be swept away forever. The choice is yours!'

CHAPTER VII

UNDER THE OAK TREE

I am called a dog because I fawn on those who give me anything.
I yelp at those who refuse, and I set my teeth in rascals.

Diogenes, *Kosmopolites*

A rough hand on one shoulder woke the healer with a nervous jerk. Myrddion surged upright, his eyes blinking away his dream.

'You fell asleep, Myrddion-three-names. You're lucky I'm an honest man, or I would have taken everything you have. Who were you speaking to in your dreams?'

'The gods,' Myrddion said, and rubbed his tired eyes. 'I've been plagued by night terrors since childhood, but thankfully I rarely recall them. And yes, I'm glad of your honesty, my friend. Only a fool sleeps in front of a stranger, and I'm not usually so careless.'

Gruffydd growled from deep in his throat. 'Here was I thinking you had something murderous for me to do and you were feeling guilty. I'll tell you now that I'm no assassin. I kill for no man, nor do I take coin for my dead. I may be ruined, but I'm not a mongrel dog.'

'It seems to me that you're intensely human,' Myrddion

interjected, trying to deflect Gruffydd's obvious anger. 'Only a human can really hate effectively, for beasts forget the hand that whips them or slays their mothers. Only people remember wrongs done to them. It is our strength, and our curse.'

Confused, Gruffydd stared at the healer.

'You may shake your head all you wish, Gruffydd, but I was raised to believe I wasn't human. Even children taunted me with the insulting name of Demon Seed. But I suspected that no child of a demon could feel the hurt, the humiliation and the rage I felt when I was treated as being of no account. I have felt the desire for revenge so keenly that I believed I would vomit with the rankness of it, but I have learned that a cold brain concocts a more fitting punishment for life's ills than the crude heat of bloodletting.'

Gruffydd snorted with derision. He had been told, by what kinfolk he still possessed, that his bitterness was blighting his life. This young man had no words to change the patterns of behaviour that brought Gruffydd some kind of release.

'I know, I know. But one day a Saxon will be faster than you are and he will kill you. Other than a measure of personal satisfaction, what will you have achieved when the shades claim you?'

'I don't care,' Gruffydd snarled viciously. 'Now, if you've finished trying to suborn me, I'll be on my way, for I've eaten as much as my gut can hold.'

'I can show you a way to hunt in the daylight, and how to kill whole armies rather than single men. I can provide more bloody satisfaction than you can dine on for the rest of your life. You can gorge on your revenge until you sicken of it, although I'd prefer that you remain on the borders of our lands for half of the year and keep your sanity. But I'll understand if you don't have the stomach for subterfuge.'

For the first time, Gruffydd looked vaguely interested, even though his brows were knit with irritation that such a young man should call his courage into doubt. When he eventually spoke, his voice was drenched with sarcasm.

'Who are you, boy, to lecture me on the niceties of revenge? You're hardly out of your teens and you don't know the Saxons like I do.'

At least he's talking to me, Myrddion thought wryly, trying to retain a surface calm. He was heartily sick of arguing with this obdurate and embittered man, but he remembered the voice of the Mother in his dream and was left with a painful sense of urgency. Some of his feelings must have shown in his expression because Gruffydd began to chuckle.

'Don't like your own medicine, do you, healer?'

'Not over much, Gruffydd. And I'm no boy. I wear my face smooth in the Roman style but beware that I don't lose patience and leave you to die. The Mother told me that you were already fated to die under an oak tree, pinned to its trunk as a sacrifice to the northern god Baldur. The crows would have eaten your eyes while you were still alive, you fool, but the Mother has sent me to save you from this fate. She has plans to use you for another purpose. In my dream, she told me that your destiny is to have a great influence on the future of this land – whether you will it so or not. Beware, Gruffydd, for I'd not care to gainsay the Mother when she walks the cold roads of winter in her guise as the Hag. Listen to me, fool, and consider how much more satisfying your life would be if she shines her holy eyes upon you.'

'This is superstitious nonsense!' Gruffydd growled. 'Where was the Mother when my parents screamed for her help? When I tried to pray to her, she turned her face away from me. I saved *myself*, so be damned to her and all the other gods who let my mother die in pain.'

Myrddion felt the fingers of the Mother caressing his shoulders like smooth, water-washed bones of ivory. He felt her invisible serpents as they wound around his arms once again, as if a memory of babyhood still lived in his brain. Unbidden, unwanted and unstoppable, the words came vomiting from somewhere in the pit of *her* stomach. Gruffydd flinched, but Myrddion was no longer able to see the shambling man's fear.

'You will carry a sword, Man of Blood. It is very long and rich in gems, with a dragon on the hilt that devours the blade. You stand behind a giant whom I shall bring into birth, and you will rise high in the eyes of the tribes in the shadows of the giant's hand. Do not deny me, Man of Blood. You will father children but your heart will be lost to the dragonlet, and in the child's eyes you will learn what it is to be a man. Do not mock with a doubting heart, for I tested you in pain and loss so you could carry that sword as your reward. If you disobey me, I will come for you before the winter storms are done.'

Myrddion fell heavily as Gruffydd's clenched fist struck him squarely in the chest. Dragged back to his senses by pain, he lay supine on the wooden floor and stared up at the red-eyed man standing over him, who rashly began to draw his knife.

'Stop, Gruffydd,' Myrddion panted. 'Stay your hand. Whatever I said, I have no knowledge of it. It was not I who spoke. Another's voice used my mouth, and the message I uttered was for you alone.' He curled into a ball while he coughed uncontrollably and tried to draw a full breath into lungs jarred by Gruffydd's blow. With resignation, he accepted that his life could be forfeit.

Gruffydd was bone pale, and he sat down on the stool with a thud as if his legs could no longer bear his weight. The man's grimy hands were trembling, and the wickedly sharp knife fell unnoticed to the floor.

Whatever I said has terrified him, Myrddion thought. He didn't dare to speak aloud, so he made no sound except to gasp hoarsely as his breathing gradually came under control.

And so silence reigned in the attic room, except for a cold stream of air that froze the warm breath of both men, so that vapour escaped from their lips as if they were out in the snow and the driving wind. Even the brazier spluttered under the vicious draught until, gradually and impossibly, the wind died in the small space and the room was warm once again.

'What happened? What sword? What dragonlet? I don't understand what you want of me.'

'I don't know, Gruffydd,' Myrddion said wearily. 'I told you that I didn't say a word. Another presence has spoken through my voice, but you must obey if it wants you.'

'I must sleep,' Gruffydd muttered, shaking his shaggy head in confusion. 'I'll come tomorrow, before noon, when the light is stronger and I can't see the shadows on your wall.'

Then, like a wight, the man rose and slipped out of the attic on silent feet. One moment, Gruffydd was sitting on a stool, the next he had disappeared. 'The man's a ghost,' Myrddion whispered, and then struggled to his feet, wincing as he moved.

He removed his tunic and peered down at his chest. A huge bruise was already beginning to form around a lump that was swelling on his breastbone.

'The bastard's broken something,' Myrddion cursed, and hunted up one of his own salves. Then he rolled himself carefully into a blanket and stretched out on his pallet. Even though his stomach growled with hunger, he was asleep almost immediately.

'Your guest ate well, Master Myrddion,' Cait said cheerfully as she scraped out the dead coals from the brazier into an old leather bucket. Myrddion rolled over on his pallet and groaned as he felt the pull of a cracked sternum.

'Are you unwell, master? Can I help you?'

'I'll live, Cait. Although the next time my visitor swings a punch at me, I hope to duck in time. That Gruffydd's deceptively strong.'

'Gruffydd?' Cait blushed a becoming shade of pink. Then, just as quickly, her cheeks paled. 'If he hit you, he'll be having me to answer to. It's bad enough that he never washes and smells like some old animal, but I can forgive that, since he's a man and knows no better. But to strike you, master, who does no harm to anyone, is an unforgivable sin.'

The lass is smitten – and with Gruffydd of all people, Myrddion thought in amazement, while keeping his face prudently neutral. I wonder if he knows?

'I fear I may have annoyed him, but he'll return by noon and he'll be much more amenable. Didn't you recognise him when you served us last night?'

'I didn't look, sir. I'm no harlot and Mam says to keep my eyes down around strange men. Not that you'd permit anything to happen to me, but a girl must be careful.' Then Cait was gone, and the room was colder without her sunny presence.

Myrddion dressed slowly and washed in the warm water that Cait had brought in a glazed bowl that was the wonder of the inn. Only special guests were given the honour of using this large receptacle, a sign of the innkeeper's supposed wealth. When Myrddion examined the bruise on his chest, he saw that the swelling had receded but the flesh was now a nasty shade of black and purple. Once he was dressed, he felt more optimistic.

He found his woollen cloak and hurried down the stairs to the kitchen, where he was warmly welcomed. After breaking his fast, he made his way into Brychan's dirty kingdom where the first tipplers were already propped on benches against the wall, supping bad ale.

'Your friend Gruffydd is here and he's asking for you,' the host whispered conspiratorially. 'And he's not in a very good mood, so who do you want him to kill?'

'You, if you persist with stupid questions,' Myrddion snapped. 'I've a feeling he'd happily do it for me. Where is he?'

'In the corner. The darkest one, where such dogs belong, far away from decent folk.'

'My thanks, Brychan,' Myrddion grunted, knowing that the small courtesy would appease the innkeeper after his flash of temper. Brychan expected men of means to be difficult.

A few long strides took Myrddion to the corner seat where Gruffydd slouched, more shadow than man. The gleam of upraised eyes was the only sign of movement in the black puddle of his form.

'You're here,' Gruffydd said unnecessarily. 'Sit you down then, and explain what happened last night.'

Myrddion stroked his breastbone through his thick woollen shirt. The bruise still ached. 'I'd appreciate it if you didn't shut me up with your fist if I should start to speak again. Besides, the walls in this inn have ears. Let's walk together. No matter how cold it is in the open air, it's much cleaner than this flea-trap.'

'It is that,' Gruffydd replied, and surged onto his feet with more animation than usual.

'I feel like a walk in the open, but perhaps a ride would be even better,' Myrddion whispered softly. 'I take it you have a horse?' Gruffydd was sober, prickly and distracted on this grey morning, and the healer had no plans to annoy him further.

'Aye, I keep a horse. She's not young and she's failing in her wind, but she'll survive a short gallop, I expect. I had enough of being afoot when I was owned by the Saxons.'

A short time later the two men ventured out through the town gates into a landscape that was more mud than snow. Rather than risk the horses on the treacherous road, Myrddion led the way into the dark of the forest where tall trees blotted out the grey skies and skeletal branches rattled in the light wind. The thinner saplings had been cut down for firewood but superstition had spared the larger oaks in deference to memories of ancient rituals dating back to the druids. Such ceremonies were older than time. There, in the echoing stillness, only the hooves of the horses made any noise on the flinty scree, while the bare limbs of elm and aspen trees raised naked hands to a chill sky.

At the centre of the wood, Myrddion drew his horse to a halt beside a forest giant so ancient that half its branches were dead and its trunk groaned dangerously in the bitter cold. Yet it seemed to be clinging tenaciously to life, just like the land around Tomen-y-mur.

'Why this tree?' Gruffydd asked, his teeth chattering from within his ragged cloak.

'I don't know. I just seemed to recognise it when I saw it.'

Myrddion forced his horse closer to the oak so he could pat its seamed and shaggy bark. A streak of sap stained his wool-wrapped hands with a wet stickiness not unlike drying blood.

Gruffydd shuddered.

'I'll serve you, Myrddion Merlinus. Not because I want to, nor even to take revenge on the Saxons, but because I'm afraid to gainsay the Mother. I swear I saw her shadow on the wall behind you when you spoke last night. May the gods help me, but this is the tree where I will be hanged if I refuse you. I thought I had no faith left in me, but I was awake all night trying to decide what to do. As the Mother said, perhaps your proposition will give some purpose to my suffering. Now tell me what you want of me.' He laughed with a sound that was so hoarse and metallic that it could have come from Hades itself. 'Or what she wants of me.'

Myrddion decided, on the spur of the moment, to reject the use of a subtle approach to persuade Gruffydd. The man was frightened and confused, so Myrddion must convince him that what he asked made sense. Only the unvarnished truth would serve him now.

'You speak Saxon, so you can pass on valuable information about troop movements to me. You can listen in inns and discover what the Saxons are thinking and where they'll strike at us next. I'll not lie. The work will be dangerous and could easily be the death of you. But you will be doing a great deal to help resist the Saxon advance into our lands. One way or another you will cause the death of many of them; they will curse the bad luck that seems to follow them whenever they attack us. We will ambush them before they can destroy our cities and murder other families like yours.'

'I can journey into the Saxon lands, but whether I can live among them without vomiting is another matter altogether.'

'I have complete faith in your ability to dissemble, Gruffydd, for you have fooled the Saxons for the best part of your life. What are a few more years, if your work undoes Saxon plotting to overrun our lands? Ultimately, Ambrosius will be paying in gold for your services, although your allegiance will be given to me, rather than directly to the High King. I will relay your discoveries to the appropriate authorities.'

'Does the High King know he has a sorcerer for a healer?' Gruffydd laughed coarsely.

Myrddion whitened, and Gruffydd realised he had gone too far.

'I'm not a sorcerer. Some twist in my blood through my mother's kin has cursed me with these waking fits. Far sight, the hill people call it, and they count those who suffer it blessed. But I'd not have it, if I were given any choice. Absolve me from the sin of sorcery at least, although I have suborned you to join my service at the Mother's bidding. Hate me if you wish, but acquit me of that particular abomination.'

Gruffydd cursed the curiosity that had led him to speak so unwisely. He remembered the tale being whispered in the taproom, of the two magicians who had been sacrificed at Dinas Emrys in Myrddion's stead when the healer was a child, so he understood the depths of the young man's revulsion. Myrddion had been very young when two grown men had died because of his sight. Gruffydd said nothing further, leaving Myrddion to his own turbulent thoughts.

For a whole week, Myrddion and Gruffydd spent the short, dim days together as Myrddion explained where the major Saxon enclaves could be found and showed Gruffydd his maps of the rich lands south of Londinium. Gruffydd had never imagined such wondrous things, and quickly memorised the network of roads that linked the settlements of the south. Despite his scepticism, the fledgling agent realised that the young healer had a gift for subterfuge and the skills to bring Ambrosius's plan to fruition. He also had the wealth to ease Gruffydd's path into the east.

'You are the only Saxon-speaking spy I've found thus far, so you are a vital strand in my web of information. Your gift for being able to remain undetected and unnoticed in odd corners will be priceless, but first we must do something about those scars, or devise some way of explaining them away.'

'They could cause difficulties, couldn't they? A ragged scarf and a sturdy woollen undershirt, well stained to discourage the squeamish among the Saxons, and several layers of disreputable clothes should see me safe enough.' Gruffydd grinned engagingly and revealed surprisingly good teeth.

'Here's enough coin to smooth your way, but it's not gold, I'm afraid, because that would attract too much attention. But there should be enough silver and copper here to purchase everything you need, starting with a decent horse. I will arrange for you to be paid a regular stipend in gold that will be hidden at a secret place or left in the care of some person you can trust. You will be well paid for your endeavours. When you need more coin for expenses, you need only visit me at the house of healers under the guise of being in poor health. Similarly, approach me there if you must speak to me urgently.'

Gruffydd chortled. 'I like my horse. But I'll grant she's like to drop dead on me, so she'll need replacing eventually. You think of everything, Myrddion; it's a pleasure doing business with you.'

'You will usually find me in Venta Belgarum, because Ambrosius has give me a list of tasks that I'm unlikely to finish for years. In the meantime, I plan to design a means of communication whereby our circle alone can divine the meaning of our words. But such a system will take time to devise, so you must have patience with me in the meantime.

Gruffydd found himself grinning rather foolishly. Suddenly, his life was being stretched purposefully out in front of him. He now had a future, which was an inconceivable thought a month earlier. He even felt the first stirrings of excitement; an emotion that he thought had disappeared with the deaths of his parents.

'Just take care, Gruffydd. You're precious to me, and not only because you're my only Saxon-speaking spy. The Mother has told me of her plans for you, so I'll pray to her to keep you safe. Besides, Cait will claw out my eyes if anyone should hurt you on my account.'

Gruffydd flushed blotchily above his straggling beard. 'It's like to be the other way round. I've been thinking that she's smitten with you, rather than me.' As his face turned scarlet he looked absurdly young, causing Myrddion to remind himself that they were roughly the same age.

The healer laughed deprecatingly. 'No, Gruffydd, I can assure you that I'm only someone who has been kind to her. It's you, for some reason that I can't fathom, who's captured her heart. And if ever a girl needed a good man to give her a decent life, it's Cait. Fortunately, now that you are in the employ of the High King, you'll earn sufficient coin to take a wife, but I'm certain that you'll need to accept her mother and her sisters into your life as well.'

* * *

Myrddion's thoughts turned increasingly towards the last thing he must do before he could return to Venta Belgarum and kinder weather. He had not seen his mother for over six years, and although they had no love for each other the ties of birth remained important to the young man. What he could tell her about Flavius Ardabur Aspar, and his home across the Middle Sea, might also relieve her irrational terrors and, perhaps, ameliorate her madness.

One dark morning, with a heavy heart, Myrddion finally mounted his horse and set off for Maelgwr's farm, where Branwyn and her brood dwelled with her second husband. Brychan had provided sketchy directions based on landmarks such as fallen trees and cairns of flint, so the young healer worried that he would miss one of the many signs and lose his way. On the other hand, guiltily, he knew he would welcome such an excuse to avoid the inevitable confrontation.

'Why am I going to see her?' Myrddion asked his horse as it trudged into a vicious, icy wind that blew straight from the sea. 'The gods know she'll not make me welcome. You'll be lucky to receive even a nosebag of grain, whereas I'm more likely to wear her eating knife between my shoulder blades.'

The rutted track spoke mutely of isolation. Few wagons made the journey into this wild place, which had plentiful supplies of clean water but soil that was more shale and flint than good, brown loam. Presently, in a deep fold in the hills where the water was caught in a rough-cut limestone basin, Myrddion saw a ramshackle shepherd's hut with smoke pouring out of a hole in the roof, and turned his horse towards it.

As he dismounted, a man who was completely swathed in sheep-skins pushed open the rotting door to greet his visitor. A heavy, twisted crook of wood hung by its hook over one shoulder and a shaggy dog growled at Myrddion from between the shepherd's wide-spread feet.

'Who are you, and what are you doing up here? I'll tell you outright that I've nothing worth stealing.'

'I'm seeking the villa of Maelgwr and his noble wife Branwyn. I am her son, Myrddion Merlinus Emrys.'

The shepherd ducked his head respectfully, but he made the sign to ward off evil when he thought Myrddion wouldn't notice.

'Come in then, young sir. I've got hard cheese, mead and some flat bread that's not too old. I've also got a haunch of cold mutton. A wild dog killed the old ewe two nights ago and nothing goes to waste in these hills. You're welcome to share what I have.'

Myrddion hobbled his horse where some dry grass thrust its way through a thin powdering of snow. Stamping his feet and stripping off his knitted gloves, he thanked the shepherd for his generosity and ducked through the low entry.

Inside, the unprepossessing hut was spartan but clean. A pallet of straw was laid out close to the central fire, and a tripod above the low blaze carried a heavy iron pot filled with hot water. Pointing to his pallet as a seat, the shepherd used a long hook to tilt the pot while he filled two coarse bowls with water to which he added viscous mead, releasing the smell of old honey that was both sweet and aromatic. A flat rock served as a platter for a heel of cheese, some rather mouldy bread and a slab of meat that had been carved from the unfortunate ewe's leg.

Myrddion refused the food, explaining that he had eaten at the inn in Tomen-y-mur, but he accepted the hot mead with his usual grace. Warming his blue-tinged fingers before the fire, he lifted the mug, which was steaming pleasantly in the dim light. The liquid was very sweet, and too cloying for Myrddion's tastes, but he soon felt the warmth loosen the cold knot in his belly.

'I thank you, my friend. Your hospitality to strangers is laudable, and it makes a nonsense of Tomen-y-mur's reputation for being churlish and backward.'

The shepherd scratched his greasy hair and looked puzzled. 'Begging your pardon, master, but I only understand the half of what you said. I'm an ignorant man, but I'm a Christian and I share what I have with others. The priest tells us that we should give if we hope to receive. My name is Goll. I'm told that it means one-eyed, so my mother must have been confused. I've worked for Maelgwr for long years, and his brother Maelgwn before him, God rest his soul, and it suits me well enough. I like sheep and there's more to looking after them than you'd think. Sheep aren't very knowing, not like my Tomos here, so I have to help them with the lambing, keep them out of the cold, find new grass for them and cut winter feed for them in the autumn. My days are full.'

The shepherd talked on, but eventually he ran out of words and Myrddion was able to ask some questions. 'Is Maelgwr a good master? Does he treat you well?'

'Aye, he's a good enough master, I suppose, although he's not like his brother. Now, there was a fine man. He was fair with his workers – too fair at times, if you take my meaning. But when he died . . .' Goll crossed himself in the Christian fashion. 'Well, we take the rough with the smooth at Tomen-y-mur.' He paused. 'You know how it is, sir. Masters come and masters go, but the sheep still need crutching and shearing.'

'I understand, Goll. No master would care to live out here, but it's quiet and peaceful. Do you ever see the mistress?'

Goll snorted, but then he remembered that Myrddion was her son. 'She's very unhappy, sir, I don't doubt. Never a body to speak to, and women set store by friends, don't they? I never married because no woman would be willing to share this life. It's said that your mother wasn't willing to come to Tomen-y-mur in the first place, so her fits and starts are only natural, I suppose.'

Even Goll looked doubtful at his excuses, so Myrddion hurried on with his questions. 'I've heard that Maelgwr isn't happy in his marriage and looks to ... more pleasant pastures for his amusements,' he hinted delicately. By suggesting he knew more than he did, he hoped to break down the shepherd's natural reserve.

Goll shuffled his feet and gulped down his warm mead. The healer realised his host was acutely uncomfortable and was unwilling to gossip over the foibles of his betters. 'I'll confess my reasons for asking these questions, Goll. I've heard that Maelgwr would like to be rid of my mother, but until her grandfather died he didn't dare to defy the king of the Deceangli. Now I'm afraid he may send her to the shades before her time.'

Goll looked honestly shocked, and Myrddion could tell that he had never considered that his master might resort to murder to resolve his marital problems. But mixed with the shock was fear, as though the shepherd wanted his sharp-eyed visitor gone before he found himself in a situation where he could lose his head.

'Never mind, Goll. It was wrong of me to ask you to inform on your master. I won't breathe a word of what you've said today – I'd be in near as much trouble as you if they suspected me of meddling in my mother's marriage.'

The shepherd bit on nail until it bled and worry etched sharp creases between his gentle eyes. After a pause he began, 'A redhaired slut works as a house servant, and there are many who say that my master visits her room late at night. The girl sleeps alone, which is rare enough to be a matter of gossip, but I've never seen anything myself. I can't say what goes on in that house because I stay out here, away from it, where no man can blame me for what might happen.'

Myrddion rose to his feet and offered Goll his hand. 'I thank you for your mead and for your honesty. Now, how do I find Maelgwr's house?'

With Goll's directions echoing in his head, Myrddion forced his horse into an unwilling trot, and after an hour he reached a long, low building at the brow of a hill a few miles from the sea. On the flat land below the house, neat fields edged with stone walls indicated some decent earth, and under a light sprinkling of snow Myrddion could see neatly ploughed furrows ready for the new growth of spring.

The house on the hill was dun-coloured, sprawling and far less well kept than the fields below. As a weak sun tried to burst through black clouds that were pregnant with snow, a woman bustled out of the main doors carrying two buckets, which she began to fill from a well set into the muddy forecourt of the flint-and-mud-sheathed house. Smoke drifted into the air from kitchens at the rear of the building, and snug barns appeared to house horses and milking cows. In the weak noontime sun, chickens picked desultorily at grain scattered on the bare earth or scrounged for long-dead seedpods around the farm buildings. Myrddion noticed that all the care and efficiency in the place seemed to be lavished on the outbuildings rather than the main villa, and he sighed at this evidence of his mother's condition.

The servant moved back towards the house carrying the two full buckets, which slopped water with every step. She appeared to be completely oblivious of the presence of a stranger, so Myrddion swung down from his horse and stood directly in front of her.

'I am Myrddion Merlinus Emrys and I wish to speak to my mother, the lady Branwyn.'

'I don't know about that,' the woman drawled, looking at him with vacuous eyes. 'The master doesn't welcome visitors, so you'd best be on your way.' She attempted to brush past him, splashing water on his boots and trews.

'Be careful, woman!' Myrddion added a toe-curling oath, not his normal habit in front of servants, but this particular female was both truculent and dismissive.

'If you want to beg for food, go to the kitchens at the back of the villa,' she snarled, and Myrddion felt his hackles begin to rise. Perhaps he was nervous of the meeting with Branwyn, but whatever the cause, the woman's arrant discourtesy rankled.

Without any further thought, he snatched the buckets from her and upended them, splashing several curious chickens that set up indignant squawking and much flapping of wings. Then, gripping her by the shoulders, he shook her roughly and forced her to look at him.

'I don't know what passes for manners from servants in this place, but I believe I made myself perfectly clear. I intend to speak to Maelgwr and I don't mean when he gets around to noticing my presence. You will take word to him immediately that I desire to see him. I will wait for him in the triclinium and I require a glass of decent wine from you – if you are capable of finding any.'

Ardabur Aspar would have smiled to see how much his bastard son resembled him at that moment. The servant saw the raised eyebrow and the palpable scorn in those black eyes, and for the first time she spotted the two ruby rings on his fingers. She paled visibly and tried to curtsey, which was difficult considering Myrddion was still restraining her.

'Do you understand, woman? I mean now!'

'Aye, sir. The master's in the orchards and I'll send for him immediately. Come in, come in. Begging your pardon for making you wait, but I didn't realise who you were.'

Myrddion followed her into the house and onwards to the best room, where she dusted down a dirty plank bench with her skirts before scurrying away, apologising as she went.

Myrddion gazed around the well-proportioned room, where signs of past luxury could still be discovered in the faded whitewash and furniture that was well crafted and beautiful, although it was scuffed now and scratched for lack of maintenance. Several obvious cobwebs adorned the corners of the triclinium and the number of dead insects in the silken traps indicated that they were well established. Branwyn was no chatelaine, but she had never been so slatternly as to allow this level of dirt to occur in her house. His heart sank.

With an insolent swish of fine fabric, a red-haired girl flounced into the triclinium. She was dressed in an inappropriate shade of clear, strong yellow, and Myrddion recognised the garment as one of Branwyn's bride gifts from Melvig ap Melwy, her grandfather. The girl carried an earthenware bottle and a common pottery mug that she slammed down on the table. Lifting her chin, she surveyed Myrddion from head to toe, taking in his muddy boots and customary black attire. She sniffed dismissively.

'If you've come after money from your mother, you're out of luck. Maelgwr is of no mind to waste his coin on the bastard son of a moon-mad old crone.'

'I bid you good day as well, mistress,' Myrddion replied sardonically, and swept her a bow that even Aspar would have admired. 'Where is your master?'

The slattern blushed unbecomingly. Her flushed cheeks and the abominable colour of the dress did her red hair no favours. She was also far too full-breasted for the style and Myrddion suppressed a sneer at the sight of her flesh as it welled out of the straining fabric. The colour had looked well against Branwyn's dark hair and brown eyes, but this young trull turned the garment into a strumpet's garb. It was also sweat-strained at the armpits and grubby at the hem.

'I serve the mistress and I decide what orders are given in this house,' she snapped. Her confidence and arrogance made Myrddion's heart plummet even further, for his mother must be in even worse health than he had feared if this young madam was caring for her.

'Where are the children? Before you decide to answer impolitely, young lady, I would inform you that I serve as well – only my master is Ambrosius, High King of the Britons. I am his personal healer, Myrddion Merlinus Emrys. You may have heard of me, but I fear you have the advantage over me. Exactly who *are* you, mistress?'

Finally aware that she had met her match, the hoyden tossed her head with what rags of pride Myrddion had left her. 'I am Seirian, and I am the mistress of this house while the lady Branwyn is . . . indisposed.'

'I repeat my question, Seirian. Where are the children? I've a mind to meet my brothers and sisters.'

'The boys are fostered to local landlords and traders. The girls work at spinning and weaving and carry out other tasks where they are needed.'

'Aren't the small ones being taught their letters?' he asked, although he already guessed at the answer.

'And why would they be learning to read? They'll only be married off to bring wealth to this house. That's their only purpose.'

Myrddion felt heartily sorry for any children in Seirian's care. 'For the gods' sake, woman, they are the great-grandchildren of a king. Their children could rule at Canovium, if chance or the plague were to kill Melvyn and his sons. Are you so stupid that you don't understand that Lady Branwyn is the daughter of the High Priestess of the north? Where are your wits that you see no point in educating her children?'

'My master decides these things, not I,' she whispered sullenly, biting her lip.

'I see.' Myrddion lifted the wine jar and poured a little of the viscous liquid into the mug. The coarse pottery rim was gritty, as if the glaze was poorly applied, but this small inconvenience fled into insignificance as he washed the wine around his mouth before discourteously spitting the liquid out onto the flagging.

'Cat's piss would taste better than that brew. Is this the best that the master drinks?'

The slattern's venomous glance was more instructive than any lies she might tell, so any guilt at fouling the flagstones was quickly forgotten.

'You could at least have fetched me the master's wine, for I'm persuaded that he'd not wish the High King's healer to drink such swill. I'll not even use this mug, for I can't believe my mother would purchase such inferior rubbish.'

Seirian's flush had deepened to somewhere between puce and crimson. Having lost the duel of insults, she flounced out of the triclinium, leaving Myrddion to consider how far Branwyn had fallen when she had married her second husband.

Left to his own devices, Myrddion had some time to consider his own lapse in good manners, as well as the appalling behaviour of a girl not yet in her twenties and obviously unmarried, who felt secure enough to be rude to the eldest son of her mistress. Was Branwyn held in such little esteem?

All those years before, both he and King Melvig had told Maelgwr that they would be very concerned if Branwyn's health should deteriorate. Since then, Myrddion had been absent for six years, and Melvig had been dead for nearly seven, so Maelgwr probably felt free to act as he chose. But had he done anything to harm Branwyn?

At that crucial point in Myrddion's argument with himself, the master of the farm entered the triclinium, in all his dirt, without bothering to wash his hands. Fortunately, Maelgwr didn't bother to offer his grimy paw to his stepson. Neither man liked what he saw.

The years had padded Maelgwr's slender body with a soft blurring of flesh, while a double chin, plump beringed fingers, a heavy paunch and a rosy nose spoke eloquently of years of good living. The dirt on his hands indicated that he was not above trimming his orchard trees or weeding around the blackberry canes, but his soft leather boots and a cloak of finely woven blue wool attested to a streak of vanity in his personality. At the moment, as he slung his cloak onto a divan, he expressed his displeasure by his pout and the faint, greasy sneer under the greeting he offered without the slightest hint of sincerity.

He's up to something that's not to his credit, Myrddion thought, as he rose gracefully to his feet.

'I must apologise for Seirian and the other house servants if they offended you,' Maelgwr said, as Seirian entered the room with a new wine flask and two horn cups. 'Please join me.'

Myrddion nodded, realising that his silence was unnerving Maelgwr more than any intemperate words could. The healer watched carefully as his host poured the wine into the cups, to ensure that nothing was added. He was determined that he would not eat in this house unless the food was prepared by his own hands.

'Now.' Maelgwr handed a full cup of wine to Myrddion and gulped at his own. 'How may I assist you, stepson?'

Myrddion sipped slowly on his wine. The vintage was soft and smooth, definitely superior to the vinegar piss he had been offered earlier.

'I'm here to visit my mother. Is that so strange? I've been away in Gaul, Rome and Constantinople for some time, and on my return I became the High King's personal healer. I have come into the north on the orders of Ambrosius, so I have taken this opportunity to visit unannounced. I hope I've not inconvenienced you?'

Both men showed their canines as they smiled with a wholly false bonhomie.

'My house is your house,' Maelgwr replied grandiloquently, although his smile wavered a little. 'But I'm sure you realise that my darling Branwyn often wanders in her wits. Do you think it is wise to see her, given that she feels so much animosity towards you?'

Myrddion smiled with the same feigned friendliness and trust.

'Yes, I do. As I've already explained, I am a healer, and I am now in possession of some information that may improve her health.'

Maelgwr proceeded to flatter, explain and complain as he detailed the difficulties of arranging such a visit as Myrddion requested. For his part, the healer sipped his excellent wine and permitted his host to babble. Obviously, Maelgwr was unwilling for the son to see his mother, while Myrddion was equally determined to batter down the door of her sleeping room if necessary. At the back of his mind, he wondered why so many impediments were being raised to deny him access to his mother.

Finally, as Maelgwr embarked on yet another complicated description of his wife's many mental ailments, Myrddion decided that enough was enough.

'Show me to her room at once. Maelgwr. I may be able to lift some of the weight from your shoulders, and I cannot think of a single reason to refuse me – unless you have something to hide.'

Maelgwr blanched and tried to remonstrate, but the younger man cut through the babble with ruthless efficiency by placing his cup on the greasy table and walking off towards the atrium.

'I take it my mother's quarters are this way?' he asked over his shoulder, and began to stride down the colonnade. Maelgwr hurried to catch up on his plump legs, and led Myrddion to a small, mean room at the very back of the large rambling house. Impatiently, Myrddion unlatched the door. It was locked on the outside.

'Is my mother kept penned in day and night?' he demanded.

'Only when she is unwell,' Maelgwr answered, trying to suggest that this state of affairs was rarely necessary. 'Or if she tries to hurt herself.'

'Surely that is the precise time when she should be closely watched,' the healer responded. 'You may go now, stepfather, for I believe I can handle my mother by myself. Should she be out of her wits, I'll give her a draught of poppy juice to settle her. And I would appreciate your leaving the door open, if you please. I believe that a feeling of constraint increases the distress of the mentally disturbed.'

Maelgwr was hardly a stupid man. He must have realised that Myrddion wished to be certain that no one could lurk outside the door to listen to his conversation with his mother. However, the healer had manoeuvred him into a position where he had no choice other than to obey. As Maelgwr retreated back into the house, Myrddion took the precaution of placing a heavy footstool against the door to prevent it from being treacherously closed. Then, on quiet feet, he entered his mother's room. Long before he reached her pallet, the sharp reek of urine assaulted his sensitive nose.

Branwyn was a tiny mound on a filthy pallet, curled into the fetal position and barely visible except for a hank of long, greasy, matted hair. As he approached she lifted her head, took in his appearance and then cowered back into her soiled blanket.

'It's you! It's you! I knew you'd come for me. You said you'd kill me. But I don't want to die.'

Myrddion spread his hands wide with the palms upward to show that he carried no weapons.

'It's Myrddion, Mother. I've met him, the beast who raped you. Did you hear me, Mother? I know his name.'

'You're the demon — and you're lying to me.'

'No, Mother! See? I am still a young man, far too young to be your demon. Perhaps I am the Demon Seed, but I certainly have no desire to kill you. You must know me. After all, you tried to kill *me*. But all is forgiven, Mother, so let me help you to sit up. No, don't flinch away. I'm a healer now, and I can make you feel much better.'

'Nothing can make me well,' Branwyn wailed as he lifted her gently and supported her shoulders while he positioned two odiforous pillows under her torso and neck to support her upper body. Some trace of sanity enlivened her eyes, and as Myrddion assessed her condition he felt his anger begin to rise.

He had feared to meet her. He remembered the proud, vicious woman he had last seen at King Melvig's funeral. That creature bore no resemblance to the pathetic shell who now looked up at him with forlorn eyes.

Her face had fallen inwards, so only the beak of her nose, her high cheekbones and the fine line of her jaw remained. Sunken cheeks and a toothless mouth suggested great old age, although she could be no more than thirty-seven summers.

The hands that tugged at his tunic were skeletally thin and black with bruises. Still more contusions marred her upper arms, where the loose skin barely covered her bones. As Myrddion lowered the blanket and eased the dirty, sodden shift away from her body, marks of abuse were clear on her yellowish flesh. Nor were these marks the signs of self-abuse. Hands of different sizes had punched, slapped and pinched this pathetic creature, then left her in her soiled clothing behind a locked door. Many of the bruises were black, purple and fresh, but others were green and yellow. The injuries had been inflicted over a long period of time.

'Don't fret, Mother. I'll organise some warm water to clean you, a shift to cover you and some salve for these injuries. You will soon feel much more like yourself.'

A crafty look slid through the sick woman's eyes.

'You won't try to poison me, will you? I know your game. You'll bring me poisoned milk so you can lie with my husband in peace. I won't drink it, I tell you. I won't eat anything that comes from your hands. My son said you'd try to kill me – and he's right.'

'Yes, he is.' Myrddion wanted to weep for this ruined old woman who had starved herself almost to death rather than perish at Seirian's hands. 'I'll set everything to rights now, Mother, never fear.

Myrddion is here, and even the goddess won't save anyone who tries to harm you.'

Despite his self-control, Myrddion's eyes filled with tears. His mother continued to babble about a red-haired woman who would, according to her son's prophecy, try to kill her. Once again, Myrddion cursed his ignorance of anything he said when the fits came upon him, especially in this particular instance. Could he have saved his mother her suffering if he'd known what had been predicted?

'I promise, Mother. At last you'll be safe.'

Then, fuelled with murderous rage at the callous treatment Branwyn had endured, Myrddion stalked out of the stinking room and along the corridor, roaring for Maelgwr and Seirian as he went. The small girls in the atrium, their heads bent over piles of washed wool, shivered as he passed and turned their faces away from a countenance that was white with fury. They huddled together for comfort as the Demon Seed headed for the triclinium.

Behind him, Branwyn screamed once, thinly, like a small bird caught in the talons of a hawk.

'My mother is close to death from starvation and lack of water, but I see few symptoms of madness. And there is ample evidence that she has been slapped, kicked, pinched and punched. You are fortunate that I didn't bring my weapons, because if I had my sword in my possession right now, I'd separate your head from your shoulders.'

Maelgwr cowered back against the triclinium wall. He was unsurprised: after all, he had known what the healer would find when he entered Branwyn's room. However, for nigh on twenty years he had heard tales of this Demon Seed who was known for his equable temper, his intellect and his reasoning. His mother had tried to brain him, and yet he had spoken in her defence when she had been brought before the king of the Deceangli tribe for punishment. What fool would do that? Maelgwr had expected anger from the young man, he had even expected a demand for reparation, but he had never anticipated such white-hot rage. This Myrddion Merlinus was shaking with fury, his hands were clenched into fists and his eyes were black holes burned into his white face.

'Who has done this thing to my mother? Who has tortured her? Was it you, Maelgwr? Are you so lost to honour that you are entertained by pain? No, not you! You wanted to be rid of her, regardless of the fact that you were very fortunate to receive such a dowry, or to have such marriageable children that you could sell for profit as you now possess – because of *her*. You just wanted to see her gone like a used-up wineskin that's not even worth refilling.'

'Kill him to shut him up, Maelgwr,' Seirian whispered. 'He's alone, so why are you so squeamish? Who's going to know what happens to him?' The servant girl leaned against a pillar of the colonnade in her stained finery. If she had expected Myrddion to show some trace of fear, then she misjudged him, for the healer rounded on her like a striking serpent.

'Now I see it. You're the one who inflicts the pain – you, and the women who fear you! You made a mistake when you wore my mother's dress, because I remember everything she owned. I could tell what you were before you even opened your mouth.' Seirian started to protest, but Myrddion raised one hand and pointed at her with a finger that was suddenly steady. 'Be silent, woman, or you'll never exercise that vicious tongue again.'

'Yes, be silent, Seirian. Truly, you're not helping,' Maelgwr pleaded, and Myrddion saw beyond the bluster and the veneer of strength to the vain and ageing man who cowered under the skin.

'I have lived a very long time in places that are far more terrible than Tomen-y-mur ... and I have survived.' Myrddion spoke in a soft and deliberate voice more chilling than his earlier ranting. 'The High King knows where I am, for I am on his business. And many citizens in Tomen-y-mur know where I am for they directed me to your master's house. Would you have him kill them all? The High King is Roman and we have an understanding, for I also have Roman blood. He will tear the pair of you into bloody pieces until you admit sins that you've never committed just to stop the agony. You sought to rise to my mother's place with no more thought for the consequences than a moth that singes its wings in the fireplace. Now, send me a trustworthy woman, hot water, clean cloth and the satchel from my horse. And pray that the mistress doesn't die from your abuse, or I'll be forced to kill you myself.'

What is happening to me? Myrddion thought. I've never felt such anger before. I swear I would happily kill the bitch, and enjoy it, at the least provocation.

Fortunately for the house of Maelgwr, Branwyn accepted food from Myrddion's hands, which surprised him more than anything else. Her flaming, scarfing madness seemed to have burned itself away, as if her mind had decided that all her small wounds had finally atoned for her surrender to Aspar on Segontium's beach so many years ago. Now, she was as compliant as a child, and as wide-eyed, as if the voices in her head had loosened their hold and returned her to infancy. If she recognised Myrddion, it was without the ugly memories, as if he were one of her mother's kin come to save her from an ignoble fate.

'Where's Mother?' she asked him several times. 'Where's Olwyn?'

Patiently, Myrddion explained that Olwyn was dead but still looked down on Branwyn and cared for her. After she had been washed and her stinking bedding had been dragged away to be replaced by fresh wool and clean blankets, he picked her up in his arms and laid her down beneath the new coverlets. Her body was so wasted and light that she really could have been a child, and only her long limbs suggested that she had ever been a young woman at all.

Myrddion was like a whirlwind when he was fired by strong emotion. On horseback, he scoured the small hamlets along the coast until he found a widow who his instincts told him was both good and of strong character. Without kin to care for her, the woman was near to starving herself, so Myrddion hired her to care for his mother and his sisters. On the journey back to Maelgwr's farm, he warned Grannie Mairwen what she could expect to deal with as a part of her duties, and the stern Ordovice woman tightened her lips in understanding.

'The lady Branwyn is your first concern, but I would like you to watch over my sisters as well. I trust nobody in that house and intend to repay them in kind for their ill treatment of my mother. This gold coin will give you standing, and you will receive another for each year of your service. Should my mother perish of other than natural causes, send a message to Goll the shepherd. He is a friend and will bring me down on their filthy heads. Should you feel fearful of my stepfather or his woman, go directly to Goll, who will know what to do to ensure your safety.'

'Aye, master. I'll take every care, both of them and of myself. Your mother will want for nothing.'

Myrddion took another two gold coins from his leather pouch. 'Speak to Goll and hire a man of your choice to act as your personal body servant. I will sleep more soundly, Grannie Mairwen, if I know you have a strong young man on hand to work for you and to give you protection. Please agree, so my mind can be at rest. Don't be concerned about Maelgwr's feelings because he will obey my instructions out of fear if for no other reason.'

Myrddion smiled as he watched Grannie Mairwen with Branwyn. In her presence, his mother was calm and sweet-tempered, only becoming fractious when she was left alone for too long. Mairwen loved to talk and tell stories, of which she had a seemingly endless supply, and even Myrddion's sisters would creep into their mother's room and listen, although they took care to stay beyond Branwyn's reach. Myrddion sighed as he imagined his mother's murderous attacks on her children in the past, and wondered what harm her mania had done to these innocent girls.

'What damage Aspar did!' he told the empty air of the atrium. 'But he'll never pay for his manifold sins.'

Such is life, his inner voice told him. But for now, it's time to depart and be about my duties.

Maelgwr and Seirian were left in no doubt what would happen to them if his mother suffered or perished at their hands. Unwillingly, Myrddion gave Maelgwr another gold coin to ensure that his mother was kept supplied with the necessities of life. Perhaps greed would work in tandem with the dread of Ambrosius's axe to keep Branwyn safe.

Then Myrddion rode away, knowing in his heart that Branwyn would forget him within the hour.

After a brief stop at Goll's hut to offer him payment if he would ensure that Myrddion was informed about his mother's health, Myrddion returned to Tomen-y-mur. Then, with little regret, but carrying a heavy weight on his heart, the healer started his return journey to the south. Winter was finally releasing its icy hold on the earth and was promising a season of plenty in the coming spring.

'I can soon be a healer again,' Myrddion whispered to his horse. The white and black sheep on the green hillsides, the burgeoning fields and the sweet smell of mud and turned earth filled him with relief. The sadness of Tomen-y-mur had weighed heavily on his heart and he desired nothing more than to sleep in his own room surrounded by people he knew and loved.

Venta Belgarum lay in wait behind walls that glowed golden in the late afternoon sun. A trick of the light edged the dressed Roman stone and its wooden palisades with a line of scarlet, like the flashes of a soldier's red cloak or a memory of the legion's pennons and eagles. Myrddion could almost hear the echoes of brazen horns rallying the centuries to march against their enemies. In the freshening wind that spoke of warmer weather to come, Myrddion heard fragments of screams, shouted orders and the cries of beasts in extremity, and he knew what lay ahead.

THE BATTLE OF VERULAMIUM

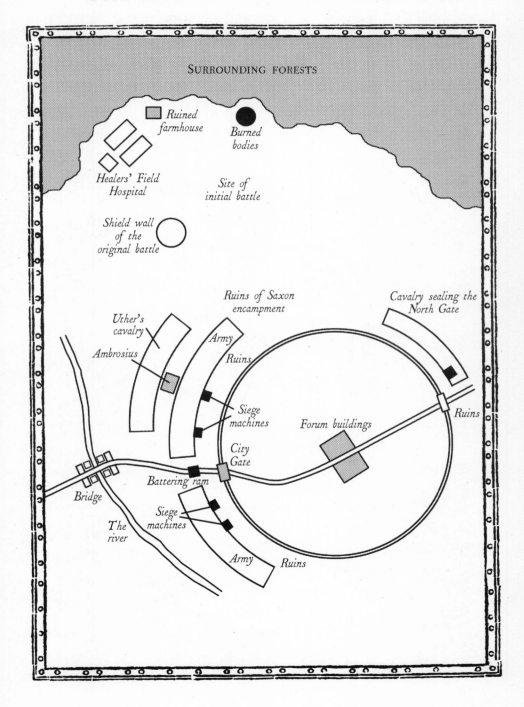

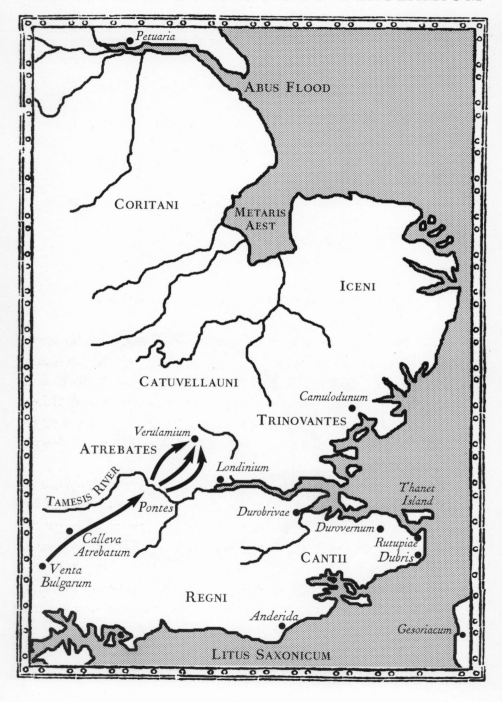

CHAPTER VIII

BACK ON THE ROAD

Qui desiderat pacem, praeparet bellum.
[Let him who desires peace, prepare for war].

Vegetius Renatus, *Epitome institutionum Rei Militaris*

As he approached the walls of Calleva Atrebatum, the healer saw a huge contingent of foot soldiers marching out of the city gates and heading in his direction. Cavalry rode on the edges of the force and Myrddion could see the twin banners of Ambrosius and Uther snapping in the light breeze at the head of the column. Moving to the very edge of the roadway, he halted his horse as the army began to flow past him.

After half an hour, the baggage train hove into view and Myrddion saw Cadoc handling the reins on the first of the two wagons used by the healers. As Cadoc recognised the stationary horseman he gave a wild battle yell, and a wide grin enlivened Myrddion's face. Everything would *now* be well. His searing anger, the incomprehensible pressure of the Mother and the impossible task of building a spy network in Cymru would be as nothing if he and Cadoc were about to travel together once again in the train of an army.

As Cadoc drew the horses to a halt, Myrddion noted the presence of Dyfri and Aude, while Praxiteles drove the second wagon with Rhedyn and Brangaine alongside him. He threw himself from his horse while Cadoc leapt from his wagon, and the two men gripped each other hard by the forearms before embracing. Then they stepped apart, grinning like fools, and slapped each other on the back with exaggerated and embarrassed force.

'What's Ambrosius about?' Myrddion asked, once he had satisfied himself that his household in Venta Belgarum was safe and well. 'The whole army seems to be on the move. And siege machines! What city is about to feel the wrath of Uther?'

'Verulamium has been occupied by a detachment of Saxons who attacked as soon as the winter snows were finished. Apparently, their thane is a man called Thorketil whose ceols recently arrived from the north and sailed up the Tamesis river. He must have been certain that the Celts were thoroughly cowed, for he immediately took control of all the roads leading to and from Londinium and has been sending his scouts further afield with each new day. Verulamium never stood a chance. Thorketil's strategy was very similar to Uther's, for he attacked the civilians in the countryside and the hamlets until the citizens of Verulamium opened their gates and begged for mercy. May they take pleasure in their captivity! All news from the city has dried up, so only prayers to the Tuatha de Danaan can help the poor fools until we get there.'

'What's known of this Thorketil?' Myrddion asked, for the name was not remotely Saxon in nature.

'It's said that he comes from the north of Frisia, close to Jutland, so perhaps he is more Jute than Saxon.' Cadoc shrugged expressively. 'He calls himself the Vessel of Thor and claims that the God of War fills his body and soul in battle and this inner strength brings success to his people. His fearsome reputation runs ahead of him, and so the High King must stop him, if only to prove that the gods haven't turned against us.'

'So – we are bound for Verulamium?'

'Aye,' Cadoc replied as he hoisted himself back up onto the wagon. 'For good or ill, we go to Verulamium.'

The healers hadn't served at a battle since the Catalaunian Plain at Châlons, and Myrddion had hoped never to experience such carnage again. Still, his heart lifted as he rode beside the wagons, for they were setting off on the familiar journey that led to the old, recognisable patterns of violent death. He understood this small world of blood and violence where he fought with all his physical and intellectual strength to drive the twins of chaos away from his tents. Better this life of action than death, destruction and the strange dreams of foreboding he had experienced during the past few months.

Before the armies reached Pontes, where a tributary of the Tamesis river headed off to the north east, the cavalry broke away from the main force and began to ride direct to Verulamium at speed with Uther at their head. Myrddion was relieved to see the tall figure disappear into the wood, for although neither brother had approached him since he had joined the baggage train, Uther had eyes in the back of his head and would have been advised of the healer's return almost immediately. At Pontes the rest of the army divided, the main body following the tributary towards Verulamium while a century, or a contingent of eighty men, remained with the baggage train, which could not stray off the roads with safety and needed to stick to the broad paths leading to Londinium. Left unprotected, it would soon have been stripped bare by the local Saxons.

Myrddion sought out the captain of the century when they paused to rest during the first evening. The healer took heart from the fact that the soldier in charge was a hard-bitten, laconic Romano-Celt who had been raised in the Roman way and treated warfare as a matter of good logistics and ruthless maintenance of discipline. Then, with a jolt, he realised that Ambrosius must need the siege machines very badly to deprive himself of his most able troops to ensure their safe delivery.

'And who might you be?' the captain snapped as he strode from where he was checking the supplies and kit of the ten squads of soldiers who made up his command. He was short and very dark, squat in the body, and endowed with a heavily muscled set of powerful shoulders that were abnormally broad. A beak-like nose dominated his face above lips so thin as to be almost invisible.

'I am Myrddion Merlinus, healer to Ambrosius,' Myrddion replied crisply, wondering with a wry, internal grin if he should salute this professional warrior.

'The Demon Seed! I've heard of you. So what do you want? I'm busy.'

'May I ask your name, captain? We'll be together for some time on this journey and, as I'm a civilian, I wouldn't want to offend you by using the wrong military term of address.'

'Septimus will do. Captain Septimus. Now, I repeat, what do you want?'

'Will we go all the way to Londinium before we begin to head north? If so, we will be entering enemy territory and may be forced to fight every inch of the way to protect the baggage train. I know the siege machines have been broken down so they are more manoeuvrable, but we'd be crazy to march blithely into the dragon's lair.'

'Really? The High King didn't leave any instructions that I was to consult you, or anyone else, so leave these considerations to your betters.'

Fuming inwardly, Myrddion produced his map case containing

the charts he had drawn when they passed through the outskirts of Londinium a year earlier. He unrolled the precious hides on the soft grass near a covered fire and hunkered down on his haunches to point out a broken line west of the city.

'This is little more than a goat track, but it bypasses Londinium and brings us out just south of our destination. There are no rivers to cross and it would be possible to widen the path to allow us to pass. The Saxons would not expect us to take this route, and I'm reasonably certain they don't even know of its existence. If we were to travel by night as well as by day, we would reach Verulamium shortly after the main force, a feat that would surely impress Ambrosius with your efficiency.'

Septimus looked at Myrddion's crude map with scepticism. He moved it with one work-calloused finger so he could examine it from a different angle. From his expression, it was obvious that he had little reading skill.

'What if the path becomes impassable?' he grunted.

'Call yourself a Roman?' Myrddion joked, hoping the dour little man would take no offence. 'Caesar built a road through the deepest forests of Gaul, plus bridges, as he chased the barbarians back across the Rhenus. Your engineers are more than equal to the task. The High King needs siege machines and his best troops if he is to survive this campaign, and I promise you that if we don't follow this road, our small force will be annihilated.'

Septimus bridled, but his eyes narrowed in thought. 'You know the way?'

'I know where the path starts, and where it finishes,' Myrddion replied. 'I'll happily take the chance if it ensures the safety of the women who are travelling with me.'

'I'll make up my mind when we get to the place where the path starts,' Septimus retorted, before rising and stalking away from the fire.

'Lord of Light, give me strength!' Myrddion muttered sardonically at the Roman's equivocation as he picked up the scroll of maps.

The soldiers round the fire-pit had been rolled up in their thin blankets attempting to sleep like all sensible men of war when the conversation had started. Now they opened their eyes and watched narrowly as Myrddion's tall figure strode off.

'I smell lots of tree felling and digging,' one of the older soldiers snapped. 'Sod that black crow, boys, for he's too clever by half. Still, I suppose digging's better than dying defending these sodding siege machines.'

'You're such a ray of sodding sunshine, Targo. Why didn't you stay in Hispania with the legion instead of signing on to fight with Ambrosius? God knows you're old enough to seek a quieter life.' The younger man, who came from Eburacum and had escaped with his parents when the Saxons first arrived in the north, had a more sanguine view of army life.

'If you'd been to Hispania, you wouldn't ask such a stupid question. The place is overrun with Goths, Visigoths, Vandals and Mithras alone knows what else. Old Gaul is divided up like your old patched tunic, Tullo, and they're all trying to kill each other. As for Italia – shite, it's done for, and all sensible men are trying to find a nice quiet part of the world where they can retire in peace.'

'So why are you here, Targo? It seems to me that we've got our own problems.'

'I didn't fancy going to the east. It's all too strange and mad out there in the wilds – the people are all god-crazy.' The scarred veteran made the age-old circular action with one finger near his temple. 'I figured if I came as far into the west as I could I might have an easier life, but here we are off to war again. At least I understand this time which side I'm fighting on, which is nice for a change.'

'And the High King is away from that Pict whore. Ambrosius has gone moon-mad over that woman,' one of the other warriors muttered. His dress was like the armour of his fellows, largely Roman in style, but the plaits in his hair marked him as a tribesman born and bred.

'Aye, Blaise,' Targo grunted dourly. 'The brothers are odd. Too much mixed blood, I reckon.' The old soldier seemed oblivious of the implied insult to all the Celts in his vicinity. Accustomed to the Roman's pungent and pointed observations, his fellows swallowed their bile, because the ageing warrior usually spoke sense. 'Neither of them appears normal in the way they approach their dealings with women. Their types seem to go clean mad when they fall in love, and their balls turn their brains into mush.'

'Go to sleep, you sons of whores.' Septimus appeared and poured a helmetful of water onto the fire, which hissed like a dying snake. 'You'll get to exercise something other than your tongues when the dawn comes tomorrow.'

'When this little exercise is over, I'm going north,' Targo sniped to the empty air where Septimus had stood only a moment before. 'It might be cold, but I'm right sick of marching.'

'How long have you been a soldier, Targo?' Blaise murmured sleepily from his cocoon of blankets.

'Shite, boy, I've no idea. My old father sent me off to the legions when I was eleven. Must be thirty years or more since then. Too long by far!'

The night became still and quiet as the mounds of soldiers slept by turns and the sentries stood in the shadows of the trees, invisible in the darkness. The camp was full of small sounds of violence as the night hunters went about their bloody business of survival, but the larger predators knew to avoid the place, for the things that rested there reeked of blood-letting, old death and the promise of new killing.

* * *

Myrddion halted at a point where a faint trail led off on the left of the Roman road. Septimus approached at a trot and the healer pointed into the waist-high grass and saplings through which a goat track led into the north.

'The wagons can pass through this mess, as long as we're careful,' he explained. 'But it would be best if some scouts and engineers moved ahead of our convoy to warn us if the track becomes difficult to traverse.'

Septimus looked at the main Roman road, flattened by the passage of many feet and beasts, and then stared with profound doubt down the overgrown path. Only a fool would cheerfully exchange one for the other.

So that makes me a fool, he thought sourly. 'Very well, healer, we'll give it a try. I've been thinking about being ambushed along the way and my back is beginning to prickle already. We'll trust to your pathway.'

With the practical efficiency that was the stamp of his leadership, Septimus sent a contubernium of ten men ahead as forward scouts along the route his force would be taking. He then divided sixty of his troops on both sides of the convoy to warn of any Saxon ambush. Another contubernium of ten men was assigned to protect the rear, prudently placed to prevent unfortunate surprises. Once his men were dispersed, Septimus ordered Cadoc to turn his wagon onto the track.

'Thank all the gods in the Otherworld that we ditched those sodding oxen,' Cadoc called to Myrddion, who had urged his horse alongside the team. 'Those useless slabs of brainless meat would be hopeless in this terrain.'

After the spring thaw and the warming of the earth, the path was overgrown with new growth. There had been plentiful rain, so the close air under the trees was alive with gnats, disturbed wasps and other winged insects that Myrddion couldn't name. Their stings and bites made a misery of the journey for soldiers, beasts and drivers alike, so Myrddion cautioned the men to smear any exposed flesh with mud to ward off the worst of the swarms.

No marshes impeded their progress, but on several occasions the party was forced to push the wagons through deep, clinging mud beside ponds of standing water. To unfamiliar eyes, the scene was pretty, with wild flowers, sedge and water weed in those places where the sunlight broke through the forest cover. Dragonflies caught the sun's rays in little prisms of blue, gold or green, while the noontime air was hushed, except for the sound of insects and the low hum of wings. Myrddion wondered at the peace and tranquillity of this quiet world, which was only rarely disturbed by the odd cowman or shepherd as he drove his beasts to market. The purveyors of war's ugly trade did not belong in this beautiful glen where the shadows were deep and the dark blue and green hues of the trees and leaves burgeoned soft and new after winter's long and frozen silences.

After the second day's hard slog, the soldiers were almost too exhausted to eat their cold rations before they rolled themselves into their thin blankets and curled up under the wagons. Myrddion was covered in mud from head to toe because on several occasions the wagons had become bogged down, and only saplings under the heavy wooden wheels could provide the traction that allowed the heaving, sweating men and horses to move the dead weight. Too tired to wash, Myrddion walked up the narrow track that had almost succeeded in doing what few armies ever could – break the resolve of Roman military might.

Frustrated, he kicked at a rock on the roadway and swore crudely when the obstacle didn't move. Not only did his foot hurt, but the rock was one more problem that might have to be dug up before they could continue their journey. As he massaged his foot, Myrddion considered the problems of battle and the difficulties of protecting baggage trains.

'They are always the object of the enemy,' he muttered to himself. 'Money, machines, food, weapons, healers – the rear is where the most valuable components of a war are kept. And it moves so damned slowly. Ambrosius and Uther go charging off to Verulamium without spare rations or any other supplies needed to fight a protracted battle. They take only the basic materials of war – the men who fight and die, and the arms they need to protect themselves. There has to be a better way of managing logistics.'

Unfortunately, the night had no answer.

Suddenly a gravelly voice whispered in his ear. 'Careful how you go, healer, or you're a dead man.'

'Shite!' Myrddion spun and reached for the small scalpel he always kept in his boot. 'Who in Hades are you?'

'I don't matter, healer. I was watching out, enjoying the night, like, and I wondered if I could sneak up on a Demon Seed. It seems I can!' The short, heavily muscled man smiled darkly, while Myrddion peered through the moonlight gloom and recognised the unmistakable outlines of a Roman foot soldier.

'I'm embarrassed,' Myrddion murmured. 'No man likes to be caught talking to himself.'

'It's only a problem if you're expecting an answer,' the old soldier replied laconically. 'But you're right in what you said. What sort of general goes galloping off and leaves the rear to make its own way to the war? These brothers seem to have more hair than wit.'

He smiled again in the darkness with a flash of eyes and bared teeth. 'I know you're a friend of the High King, so don't bother to answer that. According to old Septimus – and he's been in Britain for years – Ambrosius usually thinks his actions out before he makes a move.'

'What would *you* do, friend, if *you* were in charge?' Myrddion asked the shadowy figure somewhat testily. Like all men, he felt free to criticise his friends, but he resented anyone else who voiced the same opinions aloud.

'Marius, the soldier's general, sorted this nonsense out years ago. He decided that his men would carry almost everything they required, in pieces if necessary, and still move at the speed of a forced march – even over god-awful terrain. I'm not saying it would work here, mind, not in Britain where the ground's like quicksand and the rain keeps pissing down.'

The two men had been strolling up a slight rise as they talked, and now paused at the summit. 'Well, what do you know?' the warrior said. 'There's the sodding North Road. Well done, healer! We'll arrive in Verulamium long before anyone expects us to get there.'

The soldier pointed one gnarled finger and Myrddion peered in the direction he indicated. 'I don't see anything except a few white stones,' he said.

'Look! Can't you see, healer? Only the legions ever made anything as straight as that. Those white stones are distance markers.'

The soldier's arm and hand tracked the line of a break in the treetops through the faint moonlight. Yes! The steadiness of that moving finger pointed out the inescapable, sword-straight deline-ation of a purpose-built road.

'That's the end of my sleep for tonight,' the solder growled. 'If Septimus has half a brain, and he does, we'll be back to footslogging as soon as I tell him. Now is the perfect time to get onto the sodding road. We don't want to break out there exhausted, and in the full light of day. I can almost smell the Saxons to the north and they're big buggers. A little man like me has to aim at their balls.'

Laughing quietly, the soldier turned to return to the wagons, but Myrddion gripped his left arm in passing. 'Your name, friend? You never told me your name.'

'Only the men I fight and bleed with have a need to know that.

But you're well met by moonlight, healer.' Then the soldier disappeared into the long grass without a sound.

Septimus roused the soldiers immediately, and ordered the baggage train to resume its slow movement. Clearing a path through the underbrush by the light of makeshift torches was a tiring and a slow process, and each foot of ground covered was achieved with scraped knees and sundry small injuries. By the time the moon had set and faint light rimmed the eastern sky, the baggage train was achingly close to the Roman road. Then, when only a matter of a hundred feet separated them from the wide thoroughfare, Septimus ordered the soldiers to hew down the obstructing tree branches and saplings, disguise the wagons, and rest during the hours of daylight.

Myrddion argued. Four days had passed since Ambrosius had left with the main column and the healer worried at the number of wounded men who would inevitably perish while they slept.

'And how many will die if we're ambushed on this fine wide road over yonder? Perhaps yourself? How will you save anyone if you're dead or wounded?' Septimus growled, and Myrddion was forced to admit that he had allowed his emotions to overrun his normal rational self.

I seem to be out of balance lately, he thought ruefully, as he joined Cadoc under the wagon.

As soon as dusk fell, the soldiers stripped away the concealing branches and the wagons juddered and swayed into movement. The horses strained, the soldiers pushed from behind, and as if regretfully relinquishing its hold on the baggage train, the path vomited the convoy onto the road that would take them to Verulamium.

All through the night, freed of mud, thick grass and the brutally uneven ground, the wagons made a good pace towards their destination while the soldiers trotted beside them. The miles were steadily devoured by that bone-numbing action that Caesar had used so brilliantly to defeat the savages of Gaul. Without complaint, at a speed between a walk and a trot, the soldiers held formation while maintaining an intent watch on the nearby copses for any sign of Saxons.

With the approach of dawn, Myrddion knew that one last push would bring them to their destination. As they climbed the final hill, he was aware that only a stretch of flattish ground, a few miles in width, separated them from Verulamium.

'You! Yes, healer, I'm talking to you. Let's check the terrain. The sun will be up shortly, and then we'll see what we'll see. Blaise, come along too, and keep your eyes peeled.'

Septimus was in his usual foul mood, but Myrddion was eager to be at Verulamium, so he hoped to persuade the dour Roman to continue if the road ahead should prove to be clear. The two men stood on the brow of the hill, with Blaise a little in the rear, as the light slanted upward on their right, gilding the crowns of a deep forest to the east. Gradually, that feeble glow brightened, revealing the details of the long valley and the river that ran through it, serene and still with the increasing light of the dawn.

'Well, the bridge is still in position down there,' Septimus grunted with a soldier's grasp of essential details. The beauty of the valley was of no consequence to the jaded eyes of a professional warrior because it offered neither threat nor advantage.

'There's smoke in the hills,' Myrddion said with equal curtness, and pointed to long, dissipating rags of grey that stained the lightening sky over Verulamium. 'There's been some fighting outside the city, but the walls are still standing.'

Septimus gnawed at a hangnail on his thumb as he thought. Then, with the speed that was customary to him, he shouted for Blaise.

'Back to the wagons, boy! We'll rest for a short time until the road is fully lit to give the horses the heart for the downhill run. Then, we march – at the double! The wagons must make best speed, hear? The machines are needed at Verulamium.'

Blaise spun on his heel without question and trotted back to the waiting convoy.

'There's burned earth down there,' Myrddion whispered. 'The defenders have been using hot oil over the walls, and the Mother knows how I hate burns injuries. Most soldiers die of shock, but those who linger suffer dreadfully.'

'There's been a battle, healer, so there will be plenty of work for you to do. Look downstream.' The Roman pointed to his left, where the gory evidence of a desperate conflict was slowly being revealed in the strengthening light.

A brown stain marked a large area of green field, churned by the feet of horses and desperate men. The distance was too great for detail, but Myrddion had experienced enough battles to recognise the physical signs of their aftermath.

'It's obvious that the Saxons came out of Verulamium and fought Ambrosius there,' Septimus muttered. 'The churned earth leads back to the city and, as there's a siege going on, I'll wager Verulamium is still in Saxon hands.'

'How so?' Myrddion could barely make out the details of the force surrounding the city, but he could imagine the swift annihilation that would ensue if they drove blithely into the middle of a Saxon camp.

'I can tell that you've not followed Uther,' Septimus's voice held neither fear nor admiration, but was simply a recitation of fact. 'His forces wouldn't run into a captured enemy city. Ambrosius's foot soldiers would have forced the Saxons back into their holes once Uther broke their backs with his cavalry.'

'What if you're wrong?' Myrddion's voice was thick with

reservations, although he was eager to reach the High King's troops.

'I'm not wrong! Ambrosius has been forced to mount a siege on Verulamium, a strategy which will be slow, costly and difficult.' Septimus's voice spoke of his hatred for sieges more loudly than words. 'We must get down there as soon as we can.'

For once, the Roman and the healer were in perfect agreement as they retraced their steps to the wagons and the column.

The teams of horses were weary, but the drivers were ruthless in their application of whips and reins as they forced the beasts into a surge that would take full advantage of the downward grade. Myrddion spurred his horse and soon outstripped the column and the wagons. He needed to know if the bridge had any enemy defenders, and whether they would make their presence known as he approached. His horse's hooves hit the rough-sawn slabs of the bridge with a loud clatter as the shadows of the night were finally vanquished by a bloody sunrise. With his heart in his mouth, Myrddion urged his horse at a gallop up a low bank on the other side of the river.

Suddenly, cavalrymen appeared through the smoke on the small, agile horses that spoke of the flinty mountains of Myrddion's home.

'Who goes there?' a rasping voice bellowed.

'Myrddion of Segontium, healer to Ambrosius,' he panted, the breath almost jolted from his body by his headlong rush. Behind him the column was approaching the bridge in a disciplined run and, behind them, Myrddion caught a glimpse of Cadoc's red hair atop one of the wagons as the rays of the rising sun limned him with fire.

'We have brought the baggage train to you,' Myrddion shouted unnecessarily.

'You're badly needed,' the leading cavalryman snapped, and turned to where the smoke haze was building over Verulamium.

* * *

Battlefields are a special, unique kind of hell. The Christians believe that hell is fire and heat filled with unimaginable horrors of physical pain, while the Romans believe that it is cold, shadowy and without substance. Neither comes close to the truth.

The hell that is battlefields is hard, grinding and muscle-cracking work. The soldier, if he is to have any chance of survival, must be strong at the shoulders and forearms so he can hold his shield and swing his sword past that point of exhaustion when every rational thought tells him to drop his guard. He must have legs made for running, but also knees that can lock hard to assume the position, in concert with his fellow warriors, to absorb the shock of a charging enemy, whether on foot or on horseback. He must possess deft feet that can grip the earth, no matter how thick the bloody mud might be, and yet still be able to spin and pirouette in the dance of sanctioned murder.

Battlefields are noisy, distracting and filthy places. The sound deafens the ears, in grunts of effort, screams of rage, prayers to callous gods, whimpers of pain, the clash of metal kissing, cutting and killing and the endless rumbling and drumming of horses' hooves, wheels of wagons and siege machines and the feet of running men. To survive, a soldier must be able to ignore the sounds and smells that assault him, and focus only on the man who stands toe to toe against him. He must narrow his focus so that his enemy is the only person who is real, for every muscle twitch or movement can be a warning of danger. So the battlefield belongs to the strong, the dexterous and the focused, those men whose temperaments and physiques have been honed for survival.

Myrddion rode through the battlefield outside Verulamium and thought darkly of the temperaments of those men who killed for their bread. Across the river, and on level ground to the left of the approaches to Verulamium, Ambrosius's cavalry had met the Saxon defenders of the city who had ventured outside the perimeter to win glory by claiming Celtic heads. The healer saw clearly defined circles, dug with heels and shields into a field that had been designed to grow vegetables. And now the tender shoots of lime green and emerald, as fresh as jewels against the brown loam of the field, were flattened, smashed and uprooted by careless boots. Here, the shield wall had been formed in ever narrowing circles round the thane standing proudly at the centre of his warriors. There, where hooves had cut wide furrows into the turned earth, as straight as a plough-share, the Celtic cavalry had attacked from two sides at once. A day before, on the morning of the battle, men had been scythed like corn, and their blood had blurred the shoots of surviving growth with sanguine stains that would only disappear after the next heavy rain.

Myrddion kicked his horse towards the smoke rising from piles of burning bodies beyond a ruined farmhouse in the distance. Experience told him that the wounded would be found somewhere near the shelter of that building, where the dark rain clouds would be held at bay by a partial sod roof. With Cadoc and Praxiteles driving the wagons on easier ground through the muddy field, Myrddion knew he could set up a tent hospital quickly and efficiently. He hated to think of what injuries awaited him.

While Praxiteles set up the tent in the lee of the farmhouse, Cadoc set off with the emptied wagon towards Verulamium, with Rhedyn aboard to assist in transporting the wounded men from the siege of the city to this position of relative safety. Although the city walls were less than half a mile from the healers' tent, the short distance would be difficult to cover by warriors suffering serious wounds. Initially, Cadoc's task was to bring them back to Myrddion's care as quickly and as carefully as possible.

On makeshift stretchers made from cloaks slung between spear shafts, the wounded from the earlier battle were borne from the farmhouse to the healer's tent. Brangaine had already found what

197

women were available to assist with the nursing, and the myriad tasks of building cleansing fires, heating water and assembling the salves and painkillers of the healer's art were in train. Myrddion missed Finn's calming, experienced presence but Dyfri, even with his crippled leg, was quick to provide Myrddion's every need. As the wounded arrived, the bloody work began.

Few seriously wounded men on either side remained alive, for the battle had been fierce and those warriors with gross sword or axe wounds had bled to death long before the baggage train had reached the outskirts of Verulamium. Some chance remained for those suffering bow injuries, concussions, or wounds received during the cavalry attack. Broken bones would heal, arrows could be cut from strong young flesh and head wounds would either heal – or not. Myrddion laboured with scalpels, pincers, forceps and needles over his folding surgical table, his hair plaited down his back and his body stripped to the waist under his leather apron. During this critical time nearly as many would die as would live, for Myrddion could not prevent the foul humours in the air from poisoning any breach in the bodies of the sick. The inflammation of infection, the early signs of gangrene and the reek of cauterisation were all around him.

By the time Cadoc returned with the first casualties from the walls of Verulamium, Myrddion had finished with the first wave of seriously injured patients, and was stitching and bandaging minor wounds on warriors who had managed to transport themselves to his tents. Praxiteles took the reins of the wagon after the casualties had been unloaded and set off for the wall to collect the next batch of wounded men, while Cadoc set to work alongside his master in the primitive surgery.

And so the day passed as the healers fought their own battle against pain and death.

In the cool of the evening, Myrddion received a summary order to treat the High King for a minor injury. The impatient messenger gave Myrddion no choice, and because the young healer had experienced the sad truth that kings do not wait on the needs of ordinary men, he packed his satchel and followed the courier outside to where a young officer awaited him. Smoothly, Cadoc took up a new needle and finished stitching the long slice on a soldier's arm that Myrddion had been treating before the interruption.

'Where is Lord Ambrosius?' Myrddion asked as he mounted his horse in the darkness.

'In his tent. The main walls are still resisting the catapults, but the engineers predict the gates will fall to the rams before morning. The High King intends to lead the charge into Verulamium.'

Something in the officer's voice caught Myrddion's attention. 'Is that you, Ulfin?'

The man turned in his saddle to look at him. Myrddion could barely make out his eyes in the shadow of his helmet.

'Yes, healer, it's Ulfin. So you survived in the north? A few of us hoped you'd meet with a nasty accident.'

Knowing that Ulfin was Uther's creature, Myrddion ignored the insult. 'What is amiss with the king? Is his wound serious?'

Ulfin shrugged and dug his heels savagely into his horse's belly. The startled beast leapt away and Myrddion was forced to follow at a brisk gallop.

Even though darkness had fallen, the main Celtic encampment was well lit. What did Ambrosius have to hide? Thorketil knew the size of the force that opposed him and trusted to the vicious, individual contests within Verulamium's narrow streets to win the day for him once the Celts gained entrance to the city. Meanwhile, Ambrosius needed light to bombard the town with the hastily reconstructed siege machines, while a long battering ram, protected by a stout roof of timber, pounded steadily on the thick iron-braced gates. Periodically, the Saxons poured burning oil down on the battering ram, leaving a steady stream of blistered and suffering men in its wake. Dourly, the Celts replaced the injured men and continued to assault the gates.

Myrddion wished that he had the leisure to consult his precious scrolls. The Greeks had mastered the use of fire as a tool of terror, and their healers had devised a wide pharmacopoeia to combat the results on human flesh. 'There is too little time,' he whispered, as Ulfin drew his horse to a halt before the large command tent that the brothers used while conducting their campaigns.

'Don't take this amiss, healer, but the health of my masters is my chief concern,' Ulfin muttered as he roughly searched the healer from head to toe. He raised his eyebrows when he found the scalpel in its narrow leather sheath within Myrddion's boot.

Myrddion laughed. 'Would you begrudge me my protection, Ulfin? I wield little blades like this every day in the course of my work. If I had wished to harm you, there'd have been an extra grin below your face before you even tried to search me. Enough. Take me to your masters.'

Ulfin grunted, unconvinced that Myrddion was really capable of violence. The scalpel was replaced, and Ulfin held the leather tent flap open so that the healer could enter.

Ambrosius was holding a pad of cloth to the right side of his face as he examined a chart of the inner city. Uther hovered behind him like a huge, black shadow, and Myrddion felt dark wings begin to beat in the back of his mind, as if the curse of prophecy stirred in the coils of his brain.

'I am here as you asked, my lord.' He bowed over Ambrosius's hand and kissed the large ring on his master's thumb. The huge pearl in its centre looked like a blinded eye.

'Myrddion!' Ambrosius exclaimed with obvious pleasure. 'I'd heard you had joined the column and I was glad. Somehow, our twisted fates are clearer whenever you're around. Take heed, brother, should you ever stand in my shoes. This healer brings good luck to us and must be held close to your heart. With him beside us, we shall never fail.'

'I wish it were so, my lord,' Myrddion answered carefully, noting the flash of Uther's eyes in the shadows. 'Now, show me what's amiss with your face.'

'It's a trifle, Myrddion! A little love tap from an amorous Saxon! But it's hot, and I'm being cautious for I have no intention of missing the final defeat of Thorketil. He'll bow to me or I'll have his head.' Ambrosius lowered the pad.

The wound was neither deep nor dangerous, but it was spectacular. From the right eyebrow to the jaw, narrowly missing the corner of the eye, a long slice showed where an axe had almost cloven Ambrosius's head in two.

'Damn me, but he almost got me,' he said with an admiring smile. 'At the last moment, I saw his eye twitch to the right, so I threw myself to the left. I almost made it. Uther spitted the poor sod, didn't you, brother?'

'He'll not use his head again,' Uther said laconically.

Myrddion recognised the telltale redness at the points where the muscles of Ambrosius's face were most active.

'Your wound is becoming infected, highness. The Saxon used a fouled blade, probably on purpose. So the enemy grows ruthless.'

'Any enemy is ruthless. Set to work then, Myrddion, and do what you must. I'll not complain, and Uther won't separate your head from your shoulders if you hurt me.' Ambrosius carefully turned his head to engage his brother's eyes. 'Will you, Uther?'

Like a chained bear, Uther growled softly in the back of his throat.

Hot water and an open flame were brought swiftly, and Myrddion sterilised his blade. Although Ambrosius bit his lips until they bled, he did not blench as the healer quickly reopened the wound. Then, while the cauterising iron sizzled in the coals of the fire, Myrddion staunched the flow of fresh blood.

'You'll have an impressive scar, master, for I have to burn your flesh to scour out the infection,' he whispered as he removed a small flask from his satchel and measured out several drops into Ambrosius's wine cup. 'But first you will have to drink this poppy juice in a little wine.'

'I'll not be drugged,' Ambrosius groaned, moving his lips carefully. 'I'll need my full wits tomorrow.'

'And you'll have them, master. But the Saxon blade came close to your eye, and even a stone golem would flinch from a white-hot blade there. I can't afford to have you move. So drink, my lord, and I'll fix this *love tap* in a trice.'

'Aye, you don't lie,' the High King said, meeting Myrddion's eyes with an intense blue stare. 'Do your worst, Myrddion. I'll thank you in the morning.'

Then, with a flourish, the king drank his wine and grinned at his healer. A world of trust lived in that action, and Myrddion realised that he loved Ambrosius.

'You will start to drowse shortly, my lord, and then I'll begin. But I fear you'll not be pretty when I finish.'

Outside the tent, the engineers continued to loose the catapults, sending a deadly rain of stones, old iron and fiery, fat-soaked bundles of wool into Verulamium. If he listened carefully, Myrddion could almost hear the screams of pain.

THE CELTIC TRIBES OF BRITAIN

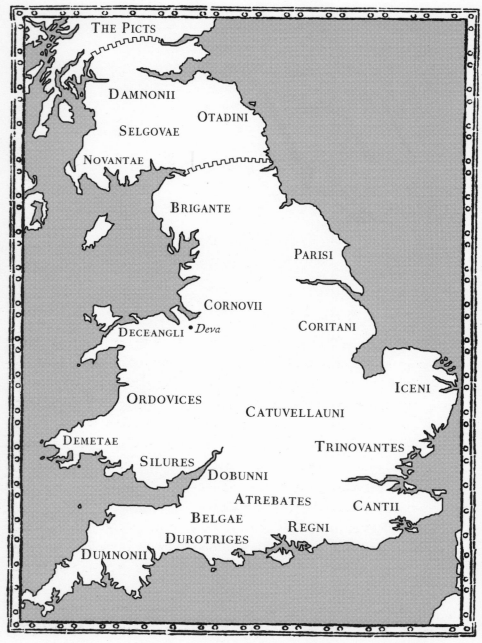

NB: The lands controlled by the various tribes in the map above are approximations only, for the details have been lost in the mists of time and the relative geographic positions of territory controlled by the Saxon invaders.

CHAPTER IX

THORNY BURDENS

Ave, Imperator, morituri te salutant.
[Hail, Emperor, we who are about to die salute you.]

Suetonius, 'The Life of Claudius'

Myrddion was still awake when the final assault on Verulamium began. From the dim tent hospital, quiet now in the last moments of darkness before the dawn, the sound of the ram carried clearly from the city gates. The dull thuds were regular and Myrddion could tell from the hollow echo that reverberated through the aftermath of each blow that the wood and iron resisting Ambrosius's efforts for so long were finally starting to weaken. Like a faltering heartbeat, the main gates of the city were about to fail.

Myrddion could imagine the scene.

Boom! The ram had a cap of thick iron, bound at the end of a long wooden trunk that swung forward and back in a cradle, powered by the cracking muscles of the engineers and common soldiers who controlled the swing of its pendulum.

Boom! The iron cap was shaped and decorated with a ram's head, horns lowered to strike the gate in the traditional Roman style.

In that final darkness, trembling on the edge of success, the sweating, exhausted soldiers must have prayed each time that the next swing of that brooding, threatening head would shatter the crossbar that held the poised army at bay.

Boom! As flags of light rose over the darkness of the city, Myrddion left his quiet domain and climbed a low rise. From this vantage point, he would know when the gates submitted to iron and muscle, and then Praxiteles and Aude would take the empty wagons to the city walls. Then, as the inevitable casualties mounted, Myrddion would lose any visual perspective of the course of the battle as he fought his own fierce struggle against death. Now, as golden light spread in thin sheets over the forests, the Roman road and the humped shapes of the city, Myrddion experienced the tranquillity of a man who knows his purpose and is content. But such peace is fleeting in the affairs of men.

A grey and foggy dawn was followed by a clear and cloudless morning, as if the gods wished to observe the sport of mortals unimpeded by clouds or rain. The battering ram destroyed the gate at last, and the engineers drew the iron-shod machine back while the cavalry forced their way through the smashed obstruction with scant regard for life or limb. Uther led the charge, and even Thorketil hesitated to confront a warrior, taller than a Saxon, who wielded weapons with the ferocity of his namesake – the dragon.

With Ambrosius at their head, the foot soldiers attacked immediately after his archers turned the sky black with a protracted rain of arrows. While the Saxons on the parapets were forced to keep their heads down and their shields up, the centuries began to pour through the ruined gates and fan out into pre-planned formations that Ambrosius had devised during the night after his face had been stitched and dressed by Myrddion. One group of warriors, experienced climbers, scaled ladders with their shields held above their heads, while a small contingent of archers continued to pepper the defending Saxons on the walls with arrows. Then, once the walls were swept clean of the enemy, the archers recovered what arrows they could and mounted the parapets to rain death down on Saxon heads in the long, straight streets below.

Ambrosius had pored over the old plans of this ancient Roman civil centre. From his patient studies, he knew every thoroughfare in Verulamium, and Thorketil's defensive positions soon became apparent. While Uther used his cavalrymen like a cudgel, and rode down citizens and enemies alike, the foot soldiers used the old strategies of the legions to clean out every nest of Saxons with calculated efficiency. The Tortoise, the Wedge and the Fighting Square were all employed by Ambrosius as a net of iron tightened around the Vessel of Thor.

Once Uther secured the eastern gate, the battle was effectively over. Thorketil had no intention of surrendering, and nor had his warriors, who set fire to every building they relinquished to the advancing foot soldiers. Perhaps the thane intended the blaze to trap the Celts between stone and fiery death, for the wind initially favoured the Saxons and blew filthy smoke to blind Ambrosius's eyes, but then it changed and sent disaster leaping to the east, from building to building and then from thatch to rafters, as the fire drove the Saxons back towards Uther's waiting cavalry.

From his vantage point on the small knoll Myrddion watched the carnage, distanced from the screams, the roaring of flame and the howls of defiant Saxons. The city was burning fiercely, and the Saxons fled from this enemy that was far more potent than Ambrosius's troops. When Uther eventually trapped them in the old forum, Thorketil screamed defiance from lungs that were hoarse with smoke.

'To me! To me! No surrender!' the thane howled recklessly, and swung his axe and sword like a berserker, careless of the safety of friend or foe.

'No mercy,' Ambrosius roared in response. 'Kill them all.' And so, with ruthless efficiency, his soldiers killed every Saxon they could find.

Myrddion laboured for two days with Cadoc and Dyfri by his side, sleeping in snatches as they struggled to save whatever lives they could. Of that time of sorrow Myrddion remembered very little, not even the faces of the men who were carried in extremities of pain to his surgical table. If he thought at all while his deft hands worked in the old familiar patterns, he was focused on the treatments available to him and the alleviation of pain, for a field surgeon knows that shock kills more quickly than the grossest of wounds. And so the long day passed, in the rumble of wagons, the smell of cauterised flesh and the sharp, metallic reek of blood.

After the warriors were treated, he turned his skills towards the civilians who had been used as human shields during Thorketil's final stand. The children with their hair burned away and their throats so blistered they were unable to cry tore at Myrddion's heart more than any adult could. As one by one they suffocated and died, he stood in blood and ministered to the dying until the poppy juice and the henbane were spent and Cadoc was sent to scour nearby villages for any replacement drugs that might still be available.

And even then, Myrddion wasn't permitted the luxury of sleep.

On the first night, he received an unexpected visitor. The veteran who had shared Myrddion's night of musing on the goat track opened the tent flap and limped into the surgery. The ageing soldier had not come alone, for he carried the senseless body of a woman who had been crushed by falling masonry during the siege.

'I'll wait till you've treated the lass's injuries, healer. See to her first, because she has little ones who need her.' The Roman mercenary's face was a sickly yellow in the dying light.

'How do you know, soldier-no-name?' Myrddion asked briskly as he assisted the smaller man to heft the woman onto his surgical table.

'Because they followed me the whole way. There's a boy, who's no more than five, and a girl who's about eight, I would guess.'

Myrddion cursed under his breath, but his hands were very gentle as he cut the woman's robe away from her back. A huge bruise covered her spine from the back of her neck down to the tailbone.

'I think her spine is broken, and if I'm correct she'll die no matter what I try to do for her,' Myrddion whispered, as he checked the feeling in her legs. The limbs were unresponsive. 'I think her skull is broken as well. But at least she's not in any pain.' Turning to Brangaine, he nodded at his assistant. 'Prepare a pallet for this woman, and let her children remain with her. There's nothing we can do.'

The soldier peered into Myrddion's face. 'Tears, healer? Is death so sad when it comes in sweet oblivion?'

'No, damn your eyes! I'm not saddened, I'm furious! I wish I knew enough to treat her, but the broken spine is beyond the skills of any healer. Only the gods could save her now, and they never choose to help the innocent.'

As if to avert the tears that threatened to unman him, Myrddion roughly ordered the soldier to remove his sandals and greaves so that his burned leg could be treated.

'I'll need to open the flesh or the blisters will split. It's better to do the job with a clean scalpel than risk infection. The skin will be breached, even if I do nothing.'

'Cut away then, healer,' the soldier said. 'What will happen to the lass's children?'

'If no relatives can be found to take the little ones into their home, my women will take them back with us to Venta Belgarum.

I'm beginning to collect a whole menagerie of children as we travel from one battle to another. I don't seem able to leave innocents behind when we collect them on the road.'

'I would have felt obliged to take care of the children myself if you hadn't out-volunteered me. I must be growing old and soft. In past times, I always understood that the Fates have mapped out our lives before we are born, which explains why children often die before they're fully grown. I never worried myself over civilians in those days. The legions keep a man occupied, and the newest recruit soon learns that it doesn't pay to dwell on situations that simple soldiers can't change. Arggh, but I'm sick of marching, killing and then marching away again. I want a fireside of my own before it's too late, and a woman to warm my feet in the winter. I think I'll head off north when I've served out the year. I've had a gutful of Venta Belgarum and places like Verulamium, because I've learned the hard way that a soldier whose heart isn't in the fighting any more is a dead man walking.'

This is an unusual man, Myrddion decided. Most patients watch their treatment studiously, as if close scrutiny will dispel the possibility of further injury or death. The soldier stared straight ahead, and his voice never wavered as Myrddion cut the blisters and cleansed the charred edges of skin.

'Verulamium is finished, healer, and it will become a place for wild dogs, madmen and dead Saxons,' the veteran went on. 'I doubt the town will be rebuilt, for the heart of the people has been ripped out.'

'There, and your treatment is also finished! The wound is clean, and you'll heal well, my friend.' Myrddion tied down the end of a bandage that now covered the veteran's leg from ankle to knee. 'Cadoc will give you more salve, and I'd like to check the burns in two days' time. You must keep the injuries clean.'

The soldier looked down at his bronzed leg with its incongruous white dressing and grinned crookedly. 'You're very good at what you do, Myrddion Merlinus, I'll say that for you. I hope you find an answer to your puzzle over baggage trains.'

Myrddion raised his eyes to the older man's face and saw wisdom and humour reflected in the brown eyes that studied him so closely. 'I hope you find the fireside you seek, my friend. In many ways, I wish that I were in your shoes.'

'Those long feet of yours wouldn't fit.' The veteran clambered to his feet without wincing, and offered Myrddion his hand. 'I'm Targo,' he said. 'We may not have fought together, and I seem to have done the bleeding for both of us – but we *have* served together, haven't we? I'll listen for word of you in the years to come. Perhaps we might meet again some day.'

'And I will listen for your name, friend Targo.'

The days passed slowly as Verulamium was cleansed and the civilian population began the long trudge into the west with everything that the fires had failed to destroy. Myrddion received no word of the innkeeper Gron and his cheerful wife, Fionnuala, while the Flower Maiden inn was a blackened shell when the healer sought out his erstwhile hosts. The young man recalled that the sojourn with them had been the last time the company of healers had been together before Finn and Bridie departed for Segontium. He felt a longing for those relatively carefree days before he had become embroiled in the games of kings once again but, like the inn, the past was a slate that had been wiped clean, and he knew that no man or woman can totally recapture their past.

If Myrddion was harried and sad, Ambrosius was ebullient. When the healer arrived to check the deep furrow that now bisected his face, the High King insisted that he take a cup of wine with him while he gave a full report on the condition of Ambrosius's wound. Myrddion did his best to employ layman's terms, but the king was no ordinary patient. The healer was soon explaining the efficacy of radish paste, seaweed, poultices of berries and mashed leaves, and the relative merits of henbane, mandrake, and other sundry poisons.

'In future, I'll take care to remain on good terms with you, my friend,' the High King murmured. 'You could poison us all, even if Ulfin tasted every dish, if what you say is true.'

'Of course. The very simplest poisons are pretty mushrooms, harmless-looking berries and innocuous roots that resemble parsnips. They all kill over a period of time, and there's no real cure to save those unfortunates who ingest them. But poison isn't my way, lord. It's a filthy death and my hands were not fashioned to kill.'

Ambrosius laughed merrily, but Myrddion felt the shadows of doom hover over his head once again. Not Ambrosius, he thought desperately. Not poison! Heaven help us!

'Bring Pascent to my tent, Uther. I'd like Myrddion to meet him and form an opinion about his malady. A promising young man needs all the friends he can find.'

As Uther stalked out of the High King's tent, leaving a strong waft of disapproval in his wake, Ambrosius continued to speak animatedly as his clever mind clutched at a new diversion.

'We found Pascent chained to a statue of Mars in the old forum. He'd obviously been caught in the city when the Saxons overran it, and Thorketil was keeping him for later amusement. He'd been cuffed around a little and was parched with thirst, but has suffered no lasting hurt. However, he claims to remember nothing of his captivity in Verulamium. Perhaps you can find a way to open the doors that are chained shut within his memory.'

'Perhaps, lord. I have noticed that sudden shocks, terrible brutality or even guilt can wipe the brain clean of every detail, even the previous life of the sufferer. And although he retained his memory, an apprentice of mine was afflicted by dreadful dreams for years after he was forced to watch and report on Saxon justice. The mind is an amazing instrument, my king.'

Ambrosius's eyes sharpened, and he insisted on a full recounting of the story. Myrddion entered into Ambrosius's spirit of curiosity and embellished the saga of Finn Truthteller with such vividness that Ambrosius sat like a child, transfixed by the fascination of the tale.

'Of course I've heard of the Night of the Long Knives. Who hasn't? And Catigern was acting for me when the brothers drove the Saxons out of the Cantii lands. I never liked Catigern overmuch because he allowed his hungers and ambitions to show in his eyes – I'm certain he'd have turned on me after he had assassinated his brother. Gods, but he was a true son of his twisted father! Still, no matter what vices Catigern possessed, it must have been a gruesome death to suffocate under the body of his victim.'

Just as the High King sobered at the thought of dying in the grave of a rotting corpse, Uther shouldered his way into the tent, followed by a handsome young man dressed simply and with distinction in fine wool. The man wore no jewellery, and Myrddion deduced that the Saxons must have stripped him of his wealth. His thumb and the third finger of his left hand bore white marks where rings had been, and a narrow band of untanned skin around his bronzed throat suggested that he had worn a torc for many years.

'Myrddion Merlinus, this is Pascent, a survivor of Saxon captivity. He has taken this name because it sounds familiar, but he has no idea of his true identity. Uther is sure, from his accent, that he is one of your fellow tribesmen, for his voice has the cadence of your northern accents. He speaks very pure Latin with an odd inflection, so I'm sure he has been well educated.'

Pascent was a tall young man of about twenty years. His skin was tanned to an attractive golden colour that indicated health and vigour, except where purpling bruises marked his brow and jaw. His eyes were as blue as those of Ambrosius, and Myrddion wondered if some Roman ancestry created this extraordinary colouring. By contrast, Pascent's hair was sun-kissed brown and he wore it in a thick shock that fell disarmingly over one eye. With a rueful grin, he pushed his hand through his thick, blunt-cut fall of hair in an action that seemed to be habitual.

'Good morning, Pascent. May I ask you some questions and examine your head?' Myrddion asked courteously.

Pascent looked uncomfortable, but Ambrosius explained Myrddion's calling and expressed the hope that his renowned healer could restore Pascent's memory. The young man blushed and then agreed, although he kept his eyes lowered.

Carefully and thoroughly, Myrddion checked Pascent's skull with his sensitive fingertips for any kind of knot or breach that could account for his memory loss. The young man was visibly nervous and upset, but he suffered Myrddion to peer into his eyes for signs of bleeding or cloudiness. As soon as the examination was over, Pascent lowered his head again.

Myrddion came to the conclusion that Pascent was as healthy a young man as he had ever examined. 'You have been trained in the ways of the warrior, I see,' he added, casually picking up each of Pascent's hands and pointing out the calluses of constant weapons practice on the forefinger, second finger, thumb and palm. Suddenly interested, Uther peered over Myrddion's shoulder and grunted in agreement.

'Aye, the boy has been trained to fight with either hand,' he murmured, and his feral eyes narrowed with suspicion. For once, Myrddion's sympathies were with the prince.

Pascent answered Myrddion's questions willingly enough, with frankness and an open expression that was almost endearing, but the healer suspected such easy charm, especially when the boy seemed so nervous. Some trick of the light reminded Myrddion of someone else, but for once he could not draw a name out of the past.

By the time Myrddion left the presence of the High King, tiny worms of suspicion were beginning to feed at the back of his mind. He could identify no tangible reasons for his unease, but his instincts screamed that something about Pascent rang false. The young man seemed genuine, but Myrddion had observed the manner and presence of his own father, Aspar, and he had trusted and loved his Flavia to the point of madness. These two powerful persons used charm as an offensive weapon that lulled suspicions and manipulated emotions. To his cost, Myrddion had learned to distrust the easy seduction of a smiling, sympathetic face.

Pascent's hands were hard and muscular, and were far too strong to be the hands of the pampered prince the absent jewellery suggested. This young man was a seasoned warrior who had been trained from childhood to kill, for his calluses told the tale of his life and such signs couldn't lie. Pascent was a great deal more than a Celt who had been fortunate enough to be captured rather than killed. But who was it he reminded Myrddion of?

'Those vertical scars on his right thumb are familiar. For my life, I wish I could remember,' Myrddion said aloud, causing a sentry to snap to attention behind him. But the healer was too occupied with his thoughts to notice. The morning was crisp and cleanly washed with spring showers, and Myrddion must begin the task of preparing his patients for the long trek to Venta Belgarum. Putting his suspicions behind him, he decided that Uther could be relied upon to watch the new claimant for his brother's affections through those resentful, untrusting and jealous eyes.

Two months passed in the tedium of the void left after the brief and inconclusive battle. After a slow journey to Venta Belgarum, using the longer but smoother route via Durocobrivae to spare the wounded, Myrddion at last returned to the house of the healers.

Late one night, Gruffydd appeared at his door. He looked as disreputable as ever; but Myrddion was heartened by the clarity and reason in his brown eyes.

With his dirty boots on Myrddion's table in the scriptorium and a wine cup cradled carelessly on his chest, Gruffydd examined Myrddion closely.

'Damn me, but you still look sixteen, Myrddion. I don't know how you can sit so quietly, surrounded by gods know how many poisons and magical things. What's in the glass jar?'

'It's a two-headed fish – a freak of nature,' Myrddion said as he turned to follow Gruffydd's pointing finger. 'Such oddities interest me.'

'Ugh!' Gruffydd looked slightly queasy as he picked up the jar. 'But if this sort of thing amuses you, who am I to criticise?'

'I imagine you have a purpose that brings you to my house under cover of darkness,' Myrddion said softly, 'other than my choice of distractions to beguile my time.'

'Aye, I do. I've just ridden from Londinium, travelling off the main roads to avoid attention.' Gruffydd chuckled dourly. 'Verulamium was retaken by the Saxons as soon as Ambrosius was out of sight, but I don't suppose the High King will be surprised. The skirmish he fought for Verulamium was only to remind the Saxons that the he won't easily be driven out.'

'Did the tactic succeed?' Myrddion sighed inwardly at the waste of life for such a transitory gesture. 'Better to strike at the Saxon heartland and be done with it.'

'Yes ... and no. Ambrosius used a simple strategy. The Saxons are very superstitious, so they won't sleep within the ruins of Verulamium for fear of Thorketil's wight, which some fools say still haunts the place. Wild beasts roam the ruins and will continue to rule there until the thanes forget Ambrosius's lesson. But the Saxons have secured the roads, so Ambrosius will find no easy route into the north, not even along the goat track I heard you found. We mustn't underestimate our enemies, Myrddion. The thanes aren't fools, but they were surprised by the speed with which Ambrosius engaged their forces after travelling overland, so they intend to secure as many of the major roads as they can.'

'What's your advice then, Gruffydd?'

Gruffydd drained his cup and lifted his muddy boots from the table. He leaned forward, his face suddenly animated.

'Ambrosius must fortify the towns that are the keys to the northern and western roads. He must use the existing fortresses, and strengthen those towns that control the passage of men and goods. It's the only way to stop the Saxons from cutting us up piecemeal. Venonae, Ratae, Lactodorum and Lindum are vital. I've not travelled into the north yet, although when I leave here I'm off to Petuaria to check on the sons of Hengist and Horsa. Melandra, Lavatrae and Cataractonium are strong, but other former Roman fortresses are currently home to only wild dogs and wandering shepherds. Ambrosius must start to think of the lands beyond Calleva Atrebatum. At present, he is too distant from the tribal kings of the north and west, leaders who must be forced to play their part in the protection of the Celtic lands.'

Myrddion could imagine the fortresses, strung like stone pearls along the mountain spine that split their island into eastern and western halves. Those abandoned towers of yesteryear were the key to domination of the wide roads leading northward to Hadrian's Wall. Gruffydd was right, and the spy had placed his blunt finger directly on the flaw that existed in Ambrosius's strategic thinking. If the Celts didn't take control of the fortresses, then the Saxons would.

'Leave it with me, Gruffydd. I agree with you, and I wish I had another thirty of you to prowl around the Saxon fringes for me. But for now you're going to be stretched very thin, so I'll apologise in advance.'

He pressed a purse into Gruffydd's unwilling hands. The erstwhile Saxon captive hated to accept coin for what he perceived to be his duty to his people, but Myrddion insisted. 'You must live, you must eat, you must ride a decent horse and you must drink ale in all sorts of disreputable places. All of these activities require you to possess a supply of coin. Besides, you may be able to find me more Saxon speakers if you have gold to pay them – and then I will have ears in the east to help you. But please, Gruffydd, I must ask that you be careful of your life. The Mother will guard you – but she'll need a little assistance in those flea-pits that you frequent.'

After Gruffydd slipped away, nothing remained of his presence except for a faint odour of horse and sweat, some tracks of mud on Myrddion's table and the position of the double-headed fish, whose eyes were now turned towards the wall. It seemed as if the spy had never existed.

In that momentous year, Venta Belgarum was enjoying a warm summer that buoyed the spirits of citizens and warriors alike. The victory at Verulamium had heartened the west and galvanised a feeling of optimism. Whenever Ambrosius rode out to the hunt or to meet the southern tribal kings at Corinium, the people cheered him, threw their caps in the air and tossed field flowers at the feet of his horse. The applause of the citizens was more tepid for his saturnine brother, but such enthusiasm lightened even Uther's bleak spirits. Only Myrddion seemed to worry that the young man, Pascent, spent too much time in the High King's company.

Myrddion also met the Celtic woman, or the Pict bitch as Uther most frequently described her.

At the earliest opportunity, Myrddion had requested an urgent and private audience with the High King. The intimacy of their previous nightly meetings had dissipated, for Ambrosius had become interested in new experiences and diversions, but Myrddion still held the king's ear and his service at Verulamium was not forgotten. Radiating disapproval, Ulfin led Myrddion to the royal apartments after the evening judgements in the Great Hall.

Ambrosius sat at ease, and Myrddion was surprised to see that he was already eating delicacies from a massy silver platter. Ulfin had not been required to taste the food.

'You're welcome, my young friend. I see that you've brought your maps, so we shall have a cup of wine together before you tell me how I should run my kingdom.'

Ambrosius smiled to rob his words of any sting, but Myrddion flushed anyway, and wondered at the change in the king's personality that had occurred while he was away.

A woman swayed forward out of the shadows and poured two cups of wine from the jug on the table. Myrddion registered the mane of curling red hair, the disarming freckles and the graceful form of a woman who seemed completely at home in the king's private rooms.

Ah, so Cadoc was right! This must be Uther's Pict bitch, he thought. He accepted the proffered wine cup and, as surreptitiously as possible, used his sharp sense of smell to gauge the quality and safety of the wine as he lifted the goblet to his lips.

'Ignore my lady, Myrddion. You may speak freely in front of Andrewina Ruadh, for she's unlikely to leave Venta Belgarum in the near future. I intend to keep her close to me.'

Madness! Where is Ambrosius's reason hiding? She's the enemy!

Myrddion bowed low to the Pict bitch and shook his head with a smile.

'No, my lord, we shall have our discussion at a later time. I would speak freely if I was risking my own skin alone, but my news affects the continued health of others, so I must request that we speak in private.'

Ambrosius's brows drew together with unusual pique, but before he could order Myrddion to obey him Andrewina Ruadh bowed and begged permission to depart. 'I am a mere woman, lord king, and have no understanding of politics,' she said, and smiled so deprecatingly and prettily that Myrddion should have been charmed. But all the healer's hackles rose as he stared into her vivid green eyes. There was no lack of understanding there.

'Very well, Andrewina, you may leave. But you will return when my healer concludes his business.' Ambrosius's eyes followed the woman's sweet shape all the way to the door and Myrddion's heart sank as he observed the glaze in his master's eyes.

The king is besotted with her, and she's more Pict than any of us.

But Myrddion too understood the games of kings, so he cordially bid the lady good night. He offered her a deep, respectful bow and watched with relief as Ambrosius's brow slowly cleared.

'I should be cross, healer, but I understand your sensitive nature. Tell me all, then, and don't spare me in the telling. I've already had Uther nagging me like a fishwife over Andrewina, so I may as well hear all the bad news at the same time.'

Ignoring the trace of petulance that remained in Ambrosius's voice, Myrddion gave a full report of Gruffydd's findings. The High King grinned when he heard that the Saxon thanes believed the ruins of Verulamium were haunted, but his fair brows contracted with the news that the roads were impassable and the woods were thick with invaders.

'By Mithras, must I scour these barbarians out of my lands, year after year?'

'Yes, my lord, you must. They will not retreat, just as you will not permit them to take our lands. Where can any of us go? So this war is in a state of impasse and, if we are lucky, it will last as long as we live. What is the alternative? Do we move further and further west until the Oceanus Hibernicus is at our backs? Or should we run to the north as the Picts were forced to do? Those dour people would relish a chance to take vengeance on us for the hundreds of years of what they believe to be tyranny and invasion. You must act, lord, now that our fledgling spy system shows us a way to confine the Saxons within a narrow strip of the lands in the east.'

Ambrosius bit at his thumb and Myrddion noticed that the nails on his master's fingers were chewed to the quick. Sympathy softened his eyes for a moment, for no man could be envious of a High King whose decisions had such wide ramifications for the security of the realm. Then his expression hardened. In recent times, Ambrosius had been acting out of character with increasing frequency, as his passion for the Pict bitch indicated. He had welcomed Pascent into his household and now, in the teeth of his brother's disapproval, he was becoming careless of his long-held, justifiable fears of treason. He must be forced to see sense.

'My man suggests you fortify all the towns that dominate the roads leading into the north and the west. The result will add to our security and keep our lines of communication open. Now, at considerable risk to himself, he journeys to Petuaria where Hengist has taken a foothold. He urges you to resurrect the old Roman forts on the mountain spine, using the tribal kings to man them. The concept of fortifying Venta Belgarum in isolation is a strategy I can't support, master, for you must see the land of the Britons as a whole and set the wheels in motion to secure it all, not just the part that you know and love. To succeed in your ambitions, you must convince the tribal kings of the north to support your cause.'

'What would you have me do, Myrddion? My troops will be stretched to breaking point if I spread my armies to fortify those places you suggest. I can see the logic in your strategy, but I have only so many warriors at my disposal. The tribal kings show no desire to come to my assistance.'

Myrddion had spent many hours devising a path through this particular conundrum. Ambrosius must be forced to think with vision, and the goal must be to unify the tribes into one cohesive nation.

'Tribal kings such as my great-grandfather have provided men and gold to supreme rulers when the common need became obvious, master, and most agree with the concept of united tribes when a serious outside threat stiffens their spines. The difference here is that they must agree to unite in peace in order to avoid future wars. You must call the kings to a meeting, explain the Saxon strategy and offer your vassals a chance for glory and autonomy by making them responsible for certain fortifications. The cost for you will be minimal, you will bind the tribes to a common cause, and together you can pin the Saxons to those parts of the eastern coast where they currently prevail. Those tribes who have been displaced by the Saxons will welcome the opportunity to make our enemies pay for their stolen acres. How can such a plan hurt you, even if the tribes are recalcitrant? You will soon learn who your friends are.'

'And I'll also know who my enemies are. Yes, you may be correct. I might learn much about my alliances from such a meeting.' Ambrosius's face creased into a wide white smile and the healer detected traces of Uther's lupine expression in the High King's obvious pleasure. Even Ambrosius was capable of gloating amusement as he considered the machinations involved in dragging the tribal kings to heel. 'I'll call the kings to Venta Belgarum, although not all will come.'

'But they must be *forced* to attend this meeting, my lord. I suggest you hold the meeting at a central city, one that will be acceptable to any tribal confederation. The kings must be brought to perceive themselves as allies, rather than as separate rulers responsible only for their own boundaries. So the site of the meeting must be chosen carefully so that none of them will feel offended.'

'Where would you hold it, Myrddion? I'm ashamed to admit that I'm not familiar with the towns of the north after spending so many years abroad.'

Myrddion had spent hours considering this very question, so he had an answer at his fingertips. 'Deva, master. Call the kings to Deva. The city has a Roman history and is a trading port. Most important, it is neutral and no king can lay claim to its allegiance. It lies halfway between Venta Belgarum and the wall, and its choice would indicate your willingness to stir out of your safe haven in the south. You already have useful ties with the Brigante, but look further, towards the Otadini and the Selgovae who protect the mountains between the Vallum Antonini and the Vallum Hadriani. No High King has sought favour with them before, but who better to guard your back while limiting Saxon and Jute advances into the north?'

Ambrosius poured another cup of wine and waved Myrddion towards the delicacies set out on the large silver platter. Gingerly, Myrddion chose the roasted leg of a small bird and nibbled at the crisp, sweet flesh while his master considered his suggestions. Once he saw his way clear, Ambrosius made his decision swiftly.

'Deva it is, then. I'll send out couriers tomorrow to all the tribes, no matter how small, to call their kings to Deva. Have you been there, Myrddion? No? Well, you shall lead the way. Uther will accompany you on the journey and he will organise the security measures, but you'll be responsible for selecting a meeting place and determining the agenda for the meeting itself. Don't fail me, Myrddion, because our success or otherwise at Deva will determine the future of our people for decades to come.'

Myrddion was aghast.

'How can I fulfil such a major undertaking, master? I'm a humble healer. Your seneschal would be a far more suitable choice.'

'Perhaps so, but he's as old as the mountains and twice as stubborn. Nor will his old bones permit him to ride for days on end. On the other hand, you always fulfil any task I set for you. Like your namesake, you fly very high. No, if you truly desire the kings to be assembled in order to negotiate a new treaty between the tribes, then you must obey me and do the necessary work.'

There was a pause, and then Myrddion made up his mind.

'Very well, master, I will journey to Deva. No doubt I will have disagreements with your brother about deadlines and procedures, though, for Prince Uther distrusts me.'

'I'm prepared to speak to my brother and stress that you are acting in my name, if that will make your task easier. But you're still frowning, healer.'

'I should remain silent, master, for you may not be pleased if I voice my opinions with candour.'

Ambrosius grimaced. 'I absolve you from any blame, healer, but someone has to be honest with me. Do your reservations rest with me personally, or with the state of the west?'

'With you, master, but you'll not thank me if I'm blunt.'

Ambrosius frowned thunderously and Myrddion decided that he would be equally damned whether he spoke out or not. Finally, the king sat upright, poured out another cup of wine, took a deep breath and nodded to his healer. 'Speak the truth. I'll not resent honesty.'

Myrddion took a deep shuddering breath and silently asked the Mother to guide his words, for he realised the dangers of meddling in the affairs of the complex man who sat so easily in his company.

'Of late, my lord, I have been concerned that you have cast caution to the four winds and risked harm both to your person and to the realm. Tonight, for instance, you ate and drank from the hands of a Pict hostage who is, I'll admit, a beautiful and an engaging woman. As well, Pascent comes and goes from your presence at will, and we have yet to verify his identity. Your people depend upon your judgement entirely, master, so we are forced to wonder if the kingdom would survive unscathed if you were to die at treasonous hands. I don't know Andrewina Ruadh, or Bridei, or whatever her name really is, and she might be a perfectly innocent victim of Pict enslavement. But she might not be an innocent, my lord. As for Pascent, we don't even know his true name – and he is eerily familiar to me. Truly, Lord Ambrosius, you are taking unnecessary risks with your life.'

Two spots of high colour appeared on Ambrosius's cheeks and Ulfin, in the corner of the room, made a snorting sound as he snickered under his breath at Myrddion's effrontery. Ambrosius leapt to his feet and, for a moment, Myrddion thought that the High King might reach out his slightly trembling fingers and throttle his healer, but the fit of fury passed quickly, although Ambrosius stood over the younger man in a pose that was both threatening and threatened.

'You dare too much, Myrddion, with your misplaced loyalty to my throne. Whom I take into my bed is my business, and whom I harbour as a friend is my decision.'

Then Ambrosius spun away and stalked over to Ulfin with an oath. Curtly, and with scorn, he ordered the smirking warrior out of the room. 'You will gossip at your peril, Ulfin. No doubt you'll report my healer's lapse to my brother, but you leap above your station when you laugh at me in my presence. Now get out of my sight!'

The door closed on Ulfin's fleeing form, and Ambrosius rounded on Myrddion. 'Would you begrudge me the love of a woman or the companionship of a friend? I have lived for nearly forty years, alone and friendless, and I am weary of measuring every word and constantly doubting any person who offers their hand to me. Are *all* men and women false? Must I relinquish *everything* for the good of my people?'

The final question was asked in a voice that actually trembled with an excess of emotion. Myrddion understood. He, too, knew the texture and taste of loneliness, and he too hungered for the sweet anodyne of a woman's arms. But Myrddion Merlinus was not a king.

'I don't know, master. Truly I don't. If Andrewina is the love of your heart, how can I deny her to you? But you cannot marry her or father children on her, for the tribal kings would see such a love as signs of weakness. I merely ask you to take more care. Please, lord, for I fear some deeper malignancy rises against you. The Saxons will not rejoice if you wring agreement from the kings, so it is entirely possible that they have already placed an assassin among the members of your court.'

'I am a man, Myrddion. I'm not a god, and I cannot live an emasculated life forever.' Tears were actually forming in the king's eyes, and Myrddion was beginning to regret having initiated this conversation. 'I'm becoming tired, for I have been beset with responsibilities for my entire life.'

'You were born to bear these burdens, my lord. When men desire a throne, they forget the crushing weight that a crown can place on the head that bears it. I can't answer you, because I don't walk in your shoes. I simply beg you to beware the motives of everyone around you, even me. Trust your brother only, for you can be certain that he alone would die for you. Oaths and pro-testations of love or loyalty are easily uttered and are gone in the whisper of a breath, but blood will remain true.'

Ambrosius's shoulders slumped in defeat; he knew that Myrddion spoke the truth. 'I will think on your words, Myrddion Merlinus, but you must leave me now, for Deva awaits your pleasure.'

'I'm sorry for the pain I have caused you, Lord Ambrosius.' Myrddion bowed and began to back out of the king's presence. 'Perhaps I shouldn't have spoken.'

But Ambrosius had no answer for his loyal servant. He sat down and rested his arms against his knees, clenching his fingers together as if fearing his grip on something nameless would weaken unless he tightened his hands until his bones shone whitely in the lamp-light. The mellow glow haloed his fair hair with a coronet of gold, and Myrddion's last glimpse of the king's face caught an expression of desperation and recklessness that made his heart sink.

Ambrosius wearies of the kingship and its heavy burdens, the healer thought as his footsteps echoed down the long corridors of the king's hall. There will be no saving the kingdom if Uther is allowed to rule.

Myrddion wiped his sweating brow and examined the engineers' work with a nervous, calculating eye. Although the sawn columns and wooden rafters were ugly when compared with the elegance of the original Roman amphitheatre on the site, the newly built outer walls of stone gave the building an impression of permanence and imposing height. The roof was supported by heavy uprights of oak, and tiered stone seats mounted the raked floors inside the amphi-theatre, providing ample room for the dozens of kings who would arrive in the next few weeks.

Myrddion had achieved wonders out of nothing.

His idea was simple. Only Ambrosius and his seneschal would stand, or sit, in the area where plays and amusements had once been enacted. No questions of precedence or prestige would arise concerning other seating within the building, for the tribal kings would be accommodated in a circle whereby no one would be closer to the High King than any of his peers. Any tribal lordling who anticipated a fierce squabble over which tribes were being favoured in the presence of the king would discover that every group would be equal, no matter how small.

'When will this . . . this very large room be finally finished?'

Uther asked from behind the healer. His voice was curt, but Myrddion recognised a trace of respect in the question that Uther directed at him.

He turned and saw that Uther was staring up at the rafters with an incredulous expression on his face. Secretly grinning, Myrddion pointed towards a group of local carpenters who were busily reinforcing the roofing beams.

'See, lord prince? Once the roofing supports are in place, thatch will be laid to make the circular hall watertight. The servants will need to work by day and night to make this space comfortable, but I'm certain Ambrosius's hall will be ready in time for the meeting of the tribal kings.'

'Humph! It'll be damned uncomfortable, even in summer, which is almost gone. I'd rather not sit on those stone benches for too long. It's a recipe for bone ache or constipation.'

'Women are already sewing cushions stuffed with lambs' wool, my lord, and I've scoured the town for cloth in many different colours. The kings will be comfortable. Their banners can be hung on the upper walls once they decide where they will sit. As soon as the roof has been completed, a team of women will scour the area clean.'

'Humph!' Uther repeated dourly.

'The kings, of course, will be billeted in suitable lodgings,' Myrddion added. 'I've almost completed the organisation of comfortable beds, good cooks and plentiful wine. The housing of their retinues is more difficult for I've no idea who is coming, or how many guards will accompany them. Still, the city fathers and the magistrates are co-operating, for their position as a neutral city was reinforced when the decision was made to site Ambrosius's hall here. Because of its trading advantages, Deva is a wealthy city and the magistrates know she is a tempting target for ambitious kings.'

'Humph!' Uther responded once more.

'Do the security measures go well?' Myrddion asked carefully. 'Deva has very good walls, and the harbour is an effective bar to all but the most determined of enemies.'

'Between you and me, healer, Deva is a nightmare to secure.'

Uther's voice was almost friendly as he explained the difficulties involved in keeping his brother safe. According to Uther, walls were only effective if the gates could be closed against potential attack, but Deva was such an open city that the gates were never locked. He growled about the citizenry's inability to appreciate the most basic concepts of defence. Accustomed as they were to protection from the legions, and then cushioned by their position as the trading hub of the central lands, Deva's citizens were unwilling to contemplate any action that would kill off business.

'Idiots!' Uther muttered. 'I've tried to explain that the presence of so many kings will be a huge temptation to assassins, but the city leaders look at me as if I've grown an extra head.'

'Any external attack would have to come by sea, and the Saxons would be forced to sail their ceols around the southern coast of Britain to assail this town. Such an offensive is unlikely.'

Uther stared hard at Myrddion to satisfy himself that the healer was serious, and neither critical nor laughing at him. Satisfied that Myrddion regarded the problem of Ambrosius's safety with the caution and respect it deserved, the prince checked the large structure, noting that two doors permitted entry and exit. He nodded with satisfaction.

'My lord, I am worried that any attack on our king will not come from an external source but will be planned by persons closer to home. I am particularly concerned about the status of Pascent and Andrewina Ruadh. I'm sure I remember Pascent's face from somewhere in my past, but I've been away from Britain for so long that I can't remember who he is or where my memories come from. And I know Andrewina Ruadh appears to be biddable and seems content with her lot, but women long for their children in ways that men will never understand. I can't believe she stays with my lord willingly when her sons are far away and her husband is dishonoured and lacks a mourner.'

'I just don't like the bitch!' Uther snapped. 'And I don't like Pascent. Something about that young man smells bad. I wonder if they could be in collusion.'

Myrddion considered Uther's suggestion, but decided that a pact between a quasi-Pict and a Celt seemed unlikely. 'I doubt it, Prince Uther, but you've watched them and you'd know more of their activities than I do.'

'No, possibly not . . . but it's a neat answer, for I neither like them nor trust them. But then, I don't like many people, you included. Still, *you* do have your uses. Your plan for the fortresses is good, and I'm aware that we must control the Roman roads.'

And so Myrddion and Prince Uther came to an uneasy truce. Both were profoundly suspicious of two people who were enjoying the favour of the High King. And both were passionate in their opposition to Saxon incursions into the tribal lands, although each had quite different reasons for his position. Uther had gradually come to acknowledge the healer's considerable abilities, while Myrddion grudgingly accepted that the prince was very good at what he knew best – those skills pertaining to war and killing Saxons. The truce was fragile, but both men realised that they now had the basis of a working relationship.

Deva was a beautiful town, nestled at the very end of Seteia Aest where the waves lapped the stone wharves built by the Twentieth Legion centuries before. The city was gracious, with paved streets and a fair aspect, while the wind was sweet with salt, seaweed and the perfumes of flowers and trees. Wherever Myrddion gazed, every vista pleased the eye.

But Deva possessed a greater treasure than a fair setting and healthy air. Myrddion had discovered the original legion hospital, a facility that was mostly deserted except for one aged healer who had worked in its echoing rooms since he was a young boy. Scoured by the sea breezes of the smells of old pain and death, it was a living memorial to what could be done to alleviate the effects of illness. Myrddion explored its rooms whenever he had a free moment, and he was particularly taken with the use of piped water within the structure. He was happy to see that the original builders had not used lead in their building materials but had settled for clay. While Roman surgeons weren't always clean and hygienic, the presence of water pipes and channelling suggested that the healers of Deva had been advanced in their thinking.

Sunny, perfect days followed each beautiful morning as Ambrosius's hall rose and the preparations for an historic and momentous meeting continued. Within the echoing, circular interior, the kings would decide whether Ambrosius would become a true High King, ruling the united tribes from the Vallum Antonini to Vectis island on the Litus Saxonicum. Then, as a true *dux bellorum*, Ambrosius would possess the authority to rule, and to drive the Saxons into the cold waters of the northern seas.

At long last, the Celts could become a nation, the Britons, who would grow to be a confederation of tribes fired by an ambition to preserve their world, even if they must die to achieve it.

'Ave, Ambrosius,' Myrddion whispered. 'May you live long and rule well.'

CHAPTER X

THE ROUND HALL
OF THE CELTS

History is, indeed, little more than the register of the crimes, follies, and misfortunes of mankind.

Gibbon, *The Decline and Fall of the Roman Empire*

The first king to enter Deva in state was Melvyn ap Melvig of the Deceangli tribe, Myrddion's own kinsman and the brother of his grandmother, Olwyn. Heavily armoured and lavishly bejewelled, he arrived at the head of a modest contingent of warriors. King Melvyn was grey with age and his back was bowed from the twin blows of fate that had taken his two eldest sons in a plague two years earlier. Far from home when disaster had struck, Myrddion never knew how bitterly Melvyn had regretted his kinsman's absence when his own boys had withered and died.

Where was the family healer when he was really needed?

Now, wearing a simple diadem adorned with cabochon sapphires and river pearls, Melvyn was a rather sad figure. His face was set in the deep lines of old age and even his beard and moustaches were white and thinning with the years. But the remembered hazel eyes were still kind as he swung from the saddle and advanced to embrace his great-nephew.

'Well met, Myrddion. I didn't expect to see you here, nor did I imagine you would greet us in the name of Ambrosius Imperator. I heard from the healer who returned to Segontium that you had arrived in Britain, so I expected you to reappear out of nowhere one day. But, as always, you've surprised me.'

At Myrddion's side, Prince Uther waited impatiently for a formal introduction. Feeling the prince's palpable irritation, Myrddion introduced his great-uncle to Uther, who swept Melvyn away to his quarters, assuring him that the High King was arriving that very day and would be pleased to dine with him that evening.

Myrddion grinned appreciatively. Uther was on his very best behaviour, and while no one could accuse him of being charming, he was struggling to be friendly and unthreatening. Of course, no one was deceived by that shark-like smile, but the prince's determination to please the local kings in the name of his brother underscored the importance of the meeting.

Over the next two days, tribal kings and princelings rode into Deva, where Prince Uther and Myrddion met them. Uther had blanched at the suggestion that Ambrosius should stand in the open where an arrow could strike him down, while Myrddion perceived political and psychological advantages in keeping the High King away from the gaze of the crowd until the great meeting began. Thus, a mystique would be created, and a theatrical anticipation would add glitter to the ultimate moment of formal welcome.

The largest contingent of warriors rode with King Lot of the Otadini tribe, who arrived with his wife, Queen Morgause, and one hundred seasoned warriors. Initially, Myrddion swore at the size of the contingent and wondered aloud where he could billet such a group.

'Just do it, healer,' Uther ordered under his breath. 'Did you expect such a powerful king to travel across half of Britain without protection?'

King Lot was a large, fleshy man who dressed with an epicurean flamboyance that rivalled any of the gilded young men of Rome. Favouring expensive, bold colours and dripping with gold, silver and furs, Lot cut an impressive figure. Even his bulk added to the suggestion of raw power that surrounded him. From his huge, hair-spotted hands to his hulking shoulders and thick, bowed legs, Lot's appearance suggested the strength and endurance of an oak tree. Although he wasn't tall, and his reddish hair was fast receding from a low, broad forehead, the impression of physical mass usually silenced any opposition when he bothered to speak his mind.

Under Lot's watchful eyes, his troops seemed highly disciplined, and their small hill horses were proudly decorated with elaborately woven saddle blankets and ornamented harnesses while their manes and tails were plaited with silver wire. These tribesmen wore their polished body armour with the easy grace of men well used to riding many miles burdened with boiled oxhide shields and bronzed weapons. Even Uther clicked his tongue admiringly as he noted the wary eyes, rigid backs and stern demeanours of highly trained cavalrymen.

Myrddion was interested in Lot's wife, for he had been told that Queen Morgause was a great beauty and the younger daughter of the famed king Gorlois, the Boar of Cornwall. Rumour suggested that she ruled in all domestic matters within the Otadini lands and was as formidable as her husband. As he stepped forward to assist her to dismount, the healer stared up at her cowled figure and wondered how a woman could demand, and receive, so much earthly power.

Then Queen Morgause swung out of the saddle, ignoring his steadying hand as she thrust the hood back from her heavy fur cloak, and Myrddion understood her glamour.

Morgause was very tall for a woman and was extremely slender, although she had already born a clutch of sons. Her eyes were deeply set within finely sculpted cheekbones, but their changeable colour, somewhere between blue, green and hazel, threw them into prominence under her highly arched brows. Her hair was dark and vigorous, almost crackling with life in the slight breeze and braided with great intricacy around her small head, although wisps had escaped to curl around her delicate face. Her lips were rich, pink and pouting in a mouth that was made for seduction, and Myrddion felt a visceral, wholly sexual desire as her eyes settled on his face. She smiled slowly and luxuriantly, revealing small white teeth that seemed unnaturally sharp.

'Your highness,' he murmured and bowed very low to break the spell of those beautiful eyes. Later, Myrddion was surprised to discover that Prince Uther had been untouched by Morgause's beauty, calling her a 'harpy in the making'. Uther was never impressed by females, and took his sex where he found it with the careless greed of an unthinking animal.

'She's dangerous, that one,' he hissed at Myrddion as they escorted the Otadini rulers to their billet. 'Ostensibly, she's come to see her father and her sister who are arriving from Cornwall later today. But, according to my sources, she loves to meddle. Lot only stirred himself to attend the meeting because of her insistence.'

'Then she will be useful to us,' Myrddion replied quietly. 'Whatever her reasons for making such an arduous journey, we benefit from her presence. It's certain that the other kings would not have promised to come if Lot hadn't stirred from his fortress in Bremenium.'

'Yes, but useful for how long? The bitch aims high, and she'd have the throne of the High King for her bucolic husband in an instant, if she could inveigle it out from under Ambrosius.'

'There's no chance of that,' Myrddion said softly, for several

Otadini cavalrymen had come within earshot. Uther would never learn tact.

King Gorlois arrived from the south on the same pleasant afternoon, so Myrddion was kept busy organising more sleeping quarters. Fortunately, the Dumnonii contingent was smaller than Lot's – but no less deadly. From their first formal greeting, Myrddion was drawn to Gorlois, whose open face and warm brown eyes encouraged friendliness. Myrddion wasn't deceived by Gorlois's natural grace, for he could see the marks of ruthlessness and power in the king's heavy brows and in the deep creases that dragged down the mobile mouth. But Gorlois had qualities of courtesy and warmth that were as engaging as they were potentially dangerous.

Gorlois is gregarious and open, Myrddion concluded. For all his muscles, he is a thinker, and it's a potent mix in tandem with his obvious fighting skills. His warriors love him and they believe him to be invincible.

The woman who rode into Deva with her father was a totally different matter. On a late afternoon, as the sun sent its last shimmer of scarlet to catch at her raven-black hair and lighten her lambent dark eyes, she was as seductive as her sister, but her extraordinary beauty was brittle, hard and capricious. Morgan, the lily of Cornwall, was a creature of the shadows that, even in the waning sun, already seemed to gather in her loosened hair.

Myrddion assisted Morgan to dismount, and with a start of surprise Uther saw that the healer and the daughter of Gorlois were very similar in appearance. Both wore their black hair long, both were slender and both possessed a vivid strand of white hair that sprang from their right temples. Myrddion and Morgan, whom some people already called the *fei* for her peculiar ideas on the old religion, were like two sides of the same coin.

'Welcome to Deva, my lady. May your visit be productive and pleasant,' Myrddion murmured with his usual quiet grace as Uther greeted Gorlois. 'The city is the richer for your beauty.'

One slim white hand pushed playfully at Myrddion's chest. A narrow blue serpent had been tattooed around the slender wrist, and he wondered why she should deliberately mar her fair skin. In the lengthening shadows, its red tongue seemed to flicker with life.

'Ah! The famed Myrddion Merlinus, the Demon Spawn! I am honoured, my lord, that you deign to welcome a mere woman.'

Recognising the sardonic humour in her dark eyes, Myrddion permitted his admiration to show in this duel of courtesy. He bowed. 'How could I fail to pay homage to one who is already famed for her beauty and her talents? You're hardly a mere woman, my lady.'

'Your complimentary words hide your caution, Myrddion Merlinus,' she riposted neatly. Her sudden laughter was like the sound of tinkling silver bells or the singing of live water over rocks. 'Perhaps we shall be friends – or even worthy adversaries?'

'Perhaps, my lady.' Myrddion turned away, his thoughts in turmoil. Morgause, who had seemed so seductive only a few hours earlier, was swiftly paling into insignificance in the glow of Morgan's smiling countenance and clever dark eyes.

'Gorlois and his daughters are extraordinary people,' Myrddion whispered to Uther. 'Imagine what a son he could sire.'

Uther snorted with scorn and surprise. 'I cannot understand why you admire that Morgan creature,' he snapped irritably. 'The woman is like a death watch beetle, all hard carapace and glitter.'

Myrddion showed his bemusement. 'I never expected such poetry from you, my lord. Your skills on the battlefield are legendary, but now you prove that perception must be added to your talents. I'd prefer to call Morgan a slender serpent, like the vipers I saw in Italia. They are tiny, black and quite lovely in their deadliness.'

'I can read character in a face like any other man,' Uther snarled. 'You're jesting with me – and I'm not amused by it.'

'I apologise, Prince Uther, for I meant no disrespect. Indeed, I agree with you, so it's fortunate that you don't feel the tug of her glamour. I *do* feel it, and it makes me afraid. Perhaps this council poses more potential difficulties than I originally thought.'

'It's too late to feel nervous about what you started, healer. We have made the necessary preparations and Ambrosius is committed, so we must do our best to ensure that the meeting is a success.'

Over the next twenty-four hours, the tribal kings continued to arrive. Prince Luka represented the Brigante, and Myrddion wondered why his father kept himself distant from the great courts of the land. He filed the question away in his memory for later consideration and welcomed the tempestuous young man with a courtesy and respect that Uther did not bother to express. Luka grinned at Myrddion and the healer perceived a fleeting trace of gratitude in the Brigante's mobile face.

From the lands of the Ordovice, King Bryn ap Synnel came with his son Llanwith pen Bryn. As Myrddion had known these two powerful men during the years of his youth, when Bryn had been one of King Melvig's most valued friends, he was able to greet them with sincere warmth.

And so they came, the kings of the Durotriges of the south, the Atrebates, the Dobunni, the angry and sullen Demetae and the fresh-faced Silures. The dispossessed came as well, flint-eyed and rigidly polite, concealing a persistent simmer of anger over their lost lands – the Cantii, the Trinovantes, the Iceni and the Parisi. Almost as sullen in their demeanour were the leaders of those tribes who faced the menace of the invaders directly, namely the kings of the Catuvellauni, the Coritani and the Regni, men who held on to their broad acres with ever-weakening fingers. Finally came the tribes who rarely ventured out of their own lands. The Cornovii king left his mysterious forests and their deep valleys to make the short trip to Deva in company with the romanised

Belgae of the verdant southwest. From the icy north on the edges of Caledonia, the Damnonii, the Selgovae and the Novantae tribes rode their shaggy-coated hill ponies into Deva with a peculiar, alien dignity.

And so they came, for this gathering was to be the first meeting of the tribes who made up the fragmented nation of the Britons, and Deva marvelled at the wonders that journeyed to her door.

The day of the Great Council arrived as the first leaves of autumn fell from the city's trees in little drifts of gold, scarlet and orange. The vivid green of the hazels, lindens and oaks was sprinkled with a dusting of yellow and lime, while nut and fruiting trees were groaning with the weight of apples, pears and apricots that had sprung to sweetness in a warm summer. The golden days seemed endless, but Myrddion remembered that the fairest gifts of nature could also hide the direst punishments.

At first, the kings were puzzled by the shape and nature of the newly furnished hall. Myrddion's teams of women had worked industriously, so comfortable cushions softened the hard stone seats, while hangings of coloured wool warmed the grey flint and granite walls. The chequered cloaks of the tribesmen added to the splashes of colour that enlivened the cold stone. Myrddion heard Morgan's laughter rise over the mumbled conversations of kings like a white gull taking flight. Searching through the blaze of colour and the flash of gems, he saw her slim form clad in funereal black so that the smooth column of her throat seemed very white below the blur of her face.

She is amused by this circular space, he thought. She understands its implications.

Some little time elapsed as the kings decided where to sit with their guards and servants behind and above them, while men-at-arms raised their tribal banners on the back walls. Fanciful birds and beasts, flowers and symbols of power rampaged there, adding their barbaric splendour to the regimented Roman structure. In the hum of excited voices and the air of expectancy and solemnity that slowly mounted in this vast glittering throng, Myrddion saw tangible proof that his own hard work had come to a splendid conclusion.

Then the babble of voices slowly died as Ambrosius entered the space at the centre of the amphitheatre with Botha in his wake. Fully armed, the bodyguard bore a simple Roman curule chair, free of ornamentation or cushions, which he placed in the centre of the floor. Then he, Uther and Ulfin placed themselves in a loose semi-circle facing the kings, with their weapons obvious in a meeting place where all other arms were forbidden.

Ambrosius had accepted Myrddion's advice and was dressed with stark simplicity in the Roman manner, clad in a tunic of snowy whiteness, a toga with a narrow edge of purple and his jewelled bangle as his only ornamentation. Although the High King had protested, Myrddion had urged Ambrosius to forgo wearing the imperial crown of Maximus.

'You will alienate the tribal kings if you rub your status and your breeding into their faces. This is not the court of Ravenna, Rome or Constantinople. These kings believe themselves to be higher born than you are. You will lose dignitas by trying to out-glitter them, and the crown of Maximus will only remind them of their defeat at the hands of Rome's military might.'

'But I *am* better born than any tribal king,' Ambrosius had protested. 'To be other than myself is to shame my ancestors.'

'That is vainglory, my lord, and not worthy of your status. I know your ancestors were noble and great-hearted, but each of these men can trace his ancestry back for nine generations of pure tribal blood, which is their measure of legitimacy. You will always be an outsider in their eyes, so to compete with them would be a fundamental error. They know you were raised as a Roman, so dress as they expect. Such an admission will do you no harm with the Roman towns, for several magistrates and city fathers have come to our meeting from Aquae Sulis and Eburacum as well as Deva, and all three have retained forces trained in Roman military tactics. While they will sit in the second tier of the hall, they are important to us, for we need them as allies. By association, the Belgae are almost as Roman in manner as you are. You must be what you are, for that is your strength, but don't rub the kings' noses in your superiority.'

'You want me to place myself on their level and create a bond between us?' Ambrosius's face had begun to show a dawning of understanding.

'Exactly, my lord,' Myrddion replied, his face wreathed in a smile of relief.

And so the kings watched intently as Ambrosius took his seat before them with an open, welcoming face. The crown of Maximus, which had come to symbolise many bitter memories of defeat, was safely locked in an iron box in the king's private quarters.

When Ambrosius finally rose to his feet, the room became silent with expectation, apprehension and an undercurrent of resistance. Ambrosius looked like a king, perhaps even an emperor, in his simplicity and steadfast air of permanence. His firm jaw, his direct gaze and his scar, still livid and angry, marked him as a man of action. His appearance did him no harm in the eyes of the tribal kings, who wore their own puckered marks of sword, arrow or axe with pride.

'Brothers and fellow kings, I welcome each of you to my hall on this momentous day, one that will change our destinies and our history forever. We have come from the four corners of the tribal lands of the Britons, over many weary miles, to address a common cause, namely a defence against a deadly enemy. If any of you see no reason for our assembly, if any of you do not fear for the safety of your borders, then speak out now before we address the issue of the Saxon menace to our collective peoples.'

An uncomfortable silence fell. Myrddion had warned Ambrosius that the kings might be unwilling to speak freely.

'I know that some of you might hesitate to express your opinions openly. But look around you, fellow rulers. While this hall was originally a gift from our erstwhile Roman conquerors, it is now a circular space where no man stands higher than another, not even a High King. It has been changed to suit our specific needs. All men are equal within this space, whether your lands are large or small, rich or poor, and no man who speaks his mind will be ignored, ridiculed or punished for his honesty. Do not fear to offend me, for we are all equal in strength, brotherhood and dignity within this hall.'

Several kings looked doubtful, while Lot was loudly scornful. But a few lords of the smaller tribes nodded slowly as they began to absorb the implications of Ambrosius's promise.

'Now is the time, Ambrosius,' Myrddion whispered. 'Force out any opposition.'

'I ask any man who sees little point in this assembly to come forward.'

Immediately, the king of the Demetae tribe, a saturnine warrior with waist-long plaits, rose to his feet and advanced into the circle to address his peers.

'I, Cadwallon ap Cael, believe that meetings of strangers cannot effect a great deal of change. I have heard that the Cantii and the Parisi are enraged because they have been driven out of their soft arable lands, and must accept charity, shelter and bread from brother kings.' He glanced at the Cantii and Parisi contingents, sitting stiffly on their soft cushions, and sneered bitterly. 'We of the Demetae were unfortunate to have been the recipients of Vortigern's most lasting legacy. We are forced to live, cheek by jowl, with *invited* Saxon settlers who spawn on our best land and take what they cannot purchase. Where were the united kings when Vortigern invited Hengist and Horsa into our lands? Was there any protest from the united kings when Demetae fortresses such as Moridunum were stolen by the Saxons? You were grateful you hadn't been placed in our position, so you abandoned us to our fate and tried to forget that we exist.'

The silence in the room was absolute, broken only by the hollow echo of Cadwallon's booted heels as he resumed his seat. His face was thunderous, but his neighbours were angrier still, and would have launched into justifications and recriminations had Ambrosius not raised his hands and demanded silence.

'Cadwallon ap Cael speaks truthfully. The Cantii would not have been defeated by Hengist had he not been invited into Cymru by the regicide. The Parisi would not have been driven out of the north had my forces not defeated Hengist near Durovernum. We could chase reasons for what has come to pass all day, and never find an end to the blame. What has happened in the past is now our history, and we don't have the luxury to change anything that has gone before. What is important are the decisions that are made at *this* meeting, and what those choices can mean for our future.'

Clutching at Ambrosius's words to soothe their collective guilts, the greater number of the kings nodded wisely while Cadwallon elected to lounge on his cushions and jeer at their discomfort.

Ambrosius continued. 'We must clear the air before this meeting can begin. Personally, I applaud Cadwallon ap Cael for his brutal honesty – which is a challenge to us all. But we need more straight speech if we are to reach an accord.'

King Lot rose to his feet, stepped into the circle and embraced the seated kings with widespread arms. From his vantage point, Myrddion recognised the oratorical skill in the Otadini's gesture and the bluff, direct way he engaged his audience's eyes before he began to speak.

'I thank Ambrosius for bringing us to this gathering, but for those of us from the lands to the north of the Vallum Hadriani, any threat will most likely come from the northern Picts rather than the Jutes or the Saxons. I embarked on the journey to the south to attend this meeting only because I would meet my kinfolk here, rather than out of any conviction that the Otadini tribe needs the assistance of any other allies. Unfortunately for most of you, we are too distant for the Saxons to bother with us.'

'Are you a proud Briton, or are you not?' one of the Iceni lords shouted angrily as he struggled to his feet, for he bore an old axe wound that made movement difficult. 'When we routed the Romans, your Otadini tribe was noticeably absent. Even when Boudicca was executed, ages ago, the kings of Britain said nothing. Too distant? Wait till the Jutes come battering at *your* gates. I'm told that their homeland makes your weather seem warm. And they will eventually arrive to defeat you and yours.'

'Silence!' Ambrosius demanded. 'If we shout at each other and scream imprecations, all we'll achieve is a schism that will never be healed, and in time the Saxons will destroy us piecemeal, just as they are doing at present.' He waited until Lot swaggered back to his seat and the Iceni warrior sullenly resumed his place. 'Our thanks must go to King Lot for stating the truth as the northern tribes see it – for without honesty this moot will fail. Our gratitude should also go to our Iceni friend for publicly expressing his anger. I know his feelings are commonly held in the east, but they have thus far been unspoken. This hall is where we speak what we truly believe, without fear of recrimination or reprisals.'

Gorlois rose to his feet with a big man's power, but chose to stand among the kings rather than speak from the centre of the room. Perhaps because he was reported to be a man of vision, straight speaking and loyalty, he lost neither dignity nor impact by this decision.

'I chose to attend this meeting because I fear for a future without loyal friends at my back. Now I look for guidance and leadership that, in the past, has been sorely lacking amongst the Britons. I also took heart from the High King's decision to select Deva as the location for this meeting. The city is central within the tribal lands, for just as the Iceni and the Otadini tribes are as far to the north and east as our tribal lands extend, so my lands are equally distant in the southwest. I have fought alongside my neighbours and watched our brothers defeated piecemeal because we had no overriding strategy to protect the tribes as a whole. Also, I recall the years of Vortigern and his sons, and no man now living would choose to return to those days of blood, vengeance and tribute. So I have come to this meeting to listen and to contribute towards its success in forging a lasting and united Britain where we are all equal. I pray to all the gods that we leave Deva with a workable answer to the Saxon menace. If we don't arrive at a treaty that commits us to communal defence, then our tenure of this land is finished.'

Most of the kings and their retinues responded with cheers, drumming their shod feet on the stone floors and clapping their hands. So fierce and heartfelt was the response to Gorlois's thoughtful speech that Myrddion began to think that the Boar of Cornwall could hold the key to the future.

'I acknowledge the truth in the words of King Gorlois,' Ambrosius said, saluting the Dumnonii in the Roman way with one clenched fist upon his chest. 'No man stands higher in my esteem than the Boar of Cornwall, who is a true son of our gods.'

He paused, so that the silence gave emphasis to the words that followed. 'I have come to this meeting to speak my thoughts on the matters before us, but for those kings who have not heard the details, I call upon my brother, Prince Uther, to describe the battle and the subsequent siege of Verulamium, a conflict which has proved that the Saxon incursions can be stopped. Not easily, but our enemy is not invincible.'

Prince Uther lacked subtlety, but he had such leashed violence in his nature that he could demand the attention of his listeners. That, coupled with a soldier's understanding of what the warrior kings would know of campaigning, held him in good stead as he outlined the attack on the Saxon forces outside the city of Verulamium. The lords listened intently as Uther described how the use of his cavalry had achieved a brutal victory over the enemy. Then, to spontaneous acclaim from his audience, Uther launched into a workmanlike description of the siege and the fall of the city. Unused to such approval from his peers, he resumed his place with an expression of surprised and embarrassed pleasure.

Ambrosius stood up. 'And so we defeated the Saxons at Verulamium. Now Myrddion Merlinus of Segontium, whom some of you know, will explain the aftermath of our great victory.'

Myrddion shot his master a startled glance. It had never occurred to him that Ambrosius might ask him to speak at the assembly, for he had no standing in this company. Any suggestions for united defences would come more appropriately from Ambrosius himself.

But if I must do this thing, then I shall do it properly, Myrddion thought, as he descended the steps from his position behind the High King. The eyes of the crowd fixed on his tall, black-clad figure, and his sensitive ears caught a rumble of disapproval. Because after all is said and done, I am still a bastard.

The great room was dark, windows being superfluous given the haste and necessary security of Myrddion's plans. Ambrosius had ordered that perfumed torches and huge bowls of oil be lit to illuminate the vast space, including a circle of lamps round the centre of the hall. Myrddion stepped carefully into the circle and the flames caught the blue in his hair, the glitter of his eyes and the gold of his gems. As he raised his hand to quieten the crowd, the mellow light caught at his sun ring and turned the heart of the gem into a pinpoint of fire that captured the eyes of his audience. Silence fell – and a stillness that was both exciting and terrifying at the same time.

'Yes. I am the Demon Seed, or the Devil's Spawn, or whatever name you care to call me. I am a bastard, and you are affronted that I should be permitted to stand before you and address this regal company. Yet here I am, Myrddion Merlinus, named for both my fathers, and I speak the truth, even if you will revile me for it. I was named after the Lord of Light, who accepted me at my birth when no man stepped forward to claim me as his son. My second name I chose for myself after a hunting bird that my father could not tame. I am myself, and my sires have no bearing on whom or what I am. Accept me or reject me for whatever reasons comfort you, but your stance will not change what I know to be the truth.'

The circular room stood still and wanting.

'Verulamium was retaken by the Saxons once we had left, although its new masters are plagued by superstitions that prevent them from inhabiting its ruined streets. You should remember that the Saxons are afraid of wights and demons, and our increasing knowledge of their weaknesses is one of our great advantages over the invaders. To date, only Hengist has taken the trouble to attempt an understanding of our strategy and tactics.'

The crowd growled, and Myrddion knew his words had struck home. He capitalised on his brief advantage.

'But our enemies aren't fools. Yes, they refuse to surrender in battle and they needlessly waste the lives of their men. They prefer to fight as individuals to win glory, and they tear down stone buildings to raise inferior structures. They believe their added height and reach make them superior in all things. But these beliefs are merely customs. They are deeply rooted in the northern way of life, but they will change with time as the Saxons learn who we are and the advantages of our way of life. They will copy our siege machines and learn our methods of combat, because they are as clever as we are. We, too, originally came from the cold north and even our gods are much the same as theirs. Whether we like it or not, we were invaders once and, historically, we are closer to the Saxons than we ever were to the Romans. At root, the Saxons are our cousins, and are only separated from us by the passage of time and by geography that does not allow us to recognise the best attributes of each other's way of life.'

The crowd howled its contempt, and King Lot leapt to his feet.

'This is nonsense!' he shouted. 'This is treason! The Saxons are barbarians and are nothing like us.'

'Treason, King Lot? To speak the truth is hardly an attack on the crown. When I look at you impartially, my lord, I see a man whose height, girth and colouring is much like that of our enemies. I have been to Gaul, where I met and served the Frankish kings in peace and war. I served with the Visigoth king at the Battle of the Catalaunian Plain and I deeply mourned his death. I know these tribal men take the same pride in their ancestry within their own lands as we do. In many ways the similarities between us make us brothers of a sort, and across the Litus Saxonicum their friends and families are fighting to hold their own lands from new invaders even as we speak. They are motivated by the same forces that brought us to these isles and made us the masters here.'

Lot shouted his objections to a chorus of agreement from his neighbours. 'Why do you thrust such unpalatable facts down our throats, Myrddion Merlinus? Do you want to dishearten us? Do you want us to crawl into bed with our enemies? Are you in their pay?'

Myrddion stiffened at the insult, and quelled his natural revulsion with difficulty. 'Not at all, my lord. I serve the sick and the dying, and my oath of loyalty is to Ambrosius Imperator for the length of our lives. I have served many masters, but my heart belongs in these isles and I'll never betray my people. But we must understand our foes so we can take advantage of their weaknesses and learn how to defeat them – finally and irrevocably. When you go into battle, do you do so with a blindfold on your eyes and one arm bound to your side? Of course not! Admitting that the Saxons are acting as we did when our people crossed the sea from Armorica, which our brothers call Brittany, is not treason – it's just stating the inescapable truth. It means we can out-think them, because we've already been successful in driving out the Picts in the past.'

The crowd lapsed into sullen attention. 'What you say is true,' Gorlois called from his seat. 'Our ancestors took this fair land from the Picts hundreds of years ago. We succeeded because we worked as one people and we isolated the Pictish tribes from each other.'

Myrddion shot him a grateful glance. 'The Saxons seek to achieve the same results by taking and holding the Roman routes so they can isolate our peoples from each other. They have an advantage that our ancestors didn't have: straight, well-made roads that link our towns and allow our troops to move quickly and safely with a certain degree of impunity. But roads can belong to anyone with the muscle and the intelligence to take them and hold them. The Saxons intend to overrun the defences of the nearest of the tribes through their use of these routes, consolidate their victories and then move on to their next victims. It will take time for them to achieve their aims, but they have all the years they need to defeat us.'

'No! Never! It will not happen!'

The kings shouted and roared, and Ambrosius winced. Perhaps ordering Myrddion to speak had been a tactical error after all. The High King almost stepped in to intervene, but Myrddion was quick to regain the initiative, raising his voice to be heard over the opposition.

'How can we stop them? Earlier, King Lot, you decided that you were too far from the invaders to be open to the threat of attack. Ask yourself, is this true? I am led to believe that there is a fine, broad road that runs from Londinium to the steps of your hall. It is a Roman road, and it is now controlled by the Saxons who guard Verulamium.'

'Then the road must be taken back,' Lot roared.

'Aye, but who should do the taking? And who should be responsible for holding it to ensure your continued safety? The Catuvellauni? The Coritani? The Brigante? The High King? No, King Lot, everyone here must become involved in retaking these essential thoroughfares from the invaders, and every tribe must be involved in holding the roads for our own use. Further, we must reinforce the Roman fortresses that the legions built, for our present needs are exactly the same as those of our Roman conquerors.'

Uproar broke out again, but by this time more than a few kings were beginning to understand Myrddion's confrontational style of explanation. In particular, Gorlois had grasped the importance of the roads and the fortresses that commanded the defensive positions along them, for there was a thoroughfare from Corinium to Durnovaria that made his own lands susceptible to attack.

As smoothly as silk as it runs through the fingers, Myrddion ceded the floor to Ambrosius as, like Gorlois, the tribal kings thought of the roads that could easily bring an enemy to their own walls. The High King raised his hands for silence.

'My healer has a unique means of gaining your attention, but I believe he proved his point. As one united nation, we must control the roads for the good of all the tribes, just as we must repair and inhabit the Roman fortresses that were built to protect those roads. Everyone must play their part, for every tribe represented here is under threat, no matter how distant that threat might seem. If we fail to find a common purpose, the Saxons will use our disunity to drive us into the sea, using our own roads and resources to defeat us.'

Although the kings would continue to argue about who was responsible for what, the day was already won. Ambrosius was endorsed as the High King of all the Britons, the concept of united tribes came into being and it was accepted that Deva should become the location where all great moots would take place in the future. The only business that remained to be finalised was the smaller details of the new accord.

At last, Myrddion could rest, and perhaps the insistent voice in his head would be silent.

'Well, Gruffydd, you did it,' Myrddion whispered to the empty hall once the last of the kings had departed for a celebratory banquet. 'Your simple idea is now the defensive plan of the Britons, so I thank the Mother for the day you crossed my path. You have already proved the virtue of her choice.'

A peal of laughter interrupted Myrddion's words and he turned to see Morgan's mocking, amused expression. Dressed in unrelieved black with an amulet of great intricacy hanging between her breasts, she cut a barbaric figure as she moved out of the shadows near the door. Myrddion focused on the amulet and noticed that it was a huge obsidian eye. Her lips were very red and she flicked her tongue across them like a large black cat considering a tasty mouse pinned in a corner before her. Even her nails, which were stained with exotic henna, seemed to flex, ready to toy with Myrddion, and to draw blood while she caressed him.

'Beware of hubris, Myrddion Merlinus. You may have won a great victory today, but you'll pay for every demand your High King has wrung from us. Don't blame the Mother, or this Gruffydd person, for what you have done. You have given our power to your Roman master.'

'There is no other defence for our people, Morgan. Can't you see how vital it is for the tribal kings to be united?'

'Of course. I don't deny your assessment of our situation, but being right is ultimately no defence in tribal politics. My father considers that you are a very clever adviser to the High King and our people, while King Lot has determined that you are an impediment to his ambitions. You gather enemies and friends in equal measure. Beware, for I dreamed that you carried a sword that dripped with blood, and that the gore swept over the whole land like a tidal wave that eventually drowned us all. You wield too much influence for any one man and, rightly or wrongly, you are fated to be the cause of our demise.'

'You're out of luck, lady,' Myrddion hissed. 'I'll not permit myself to be frightened by night terrors. Nor will I accept that hubris drives me, for I've seen the effects of that sin too often to fall prey to it. I prefer to believe that I am a patriot, and my fate matters very little in the greater plans of the Mother.'

'You are a *dabbler*! You enjoy puzzles, don't you? *You* decided that the disunity of the tribal kings was a problem that needed a workable solution, so you devised one. You enjoy being the hidden puppet-master, don't you? One day, Myrddion, you will solve one problem too many for your own advantage, and then you will learn that you must pay a price for that pride. Yes, one day your curiosity will drive you a step too far.'

Myrddion shook his head in denial but he knew, in his secret heart, that Morgan had found a weakness in his character. He tried not to hurt other people, but he knew he loved to succeed, to fill a void in his soul caused by the years of scorn that had poisoned his childhood. Was he truly as uncaring as Isaac, a Jewish healer he had met when he was in Rome, who was driven to solve the mystery of disease by intellectual curiosity alone? Was he prepared to allow men and women to die so he could ultimately be proved to have been right? Perhaps Morgan spoke the truth.

'Aye, you understand my warning. I can see the guilt in your eyes.'

She laughed again and toyed with her victim like the feline she was. 'At the moment, your own desires and the needs of the realm coincide. But in search of the greater good, you will eventually be driven to compromise your principles. You can't have it all, Myrddion. After a fashion, I admire your ethics, but in many ways you are deluded. One day you will make too many sacrifices of other souls in order to achieve what *you* perceive is best for us. Like mine, Myrddion, your heart is cold.'

It's not! It's not, Myrddion's conscience screamed inwardly. I'd never allow an innocent to die in order to be proved right.

'You remain silent, Myrddion Merlinus, because you can't gainsay me. Aren't we a pair, you and I? We should be lovers rather than enemies, but I believe we'd tear each other to pieces as eagerly as we caressed.'

Myrddion couldn't speak. He felt as if his tongue had cleaved to the roof of his mouth and even his breath was dependent on this hated, seductive voice that laid bare his greatest weaknesses.

'Still, I wonder if I'm being hasty. Perhaps there would be profit for us both if I welcomed you into my bed. No king – no High King – could resist us if we worked in concert.'

A vista of power suddenly stretched itself within Myrddion's mind and some part of him considered Morgan's half-serious proposal with a terrible sincerity. Gasping, and almost in tears, he pulled himself back from the imaginary pit that had opened at his feet.

'No, woman, you'll not corrupt me. I'll not betray my master for a promise of delight and power. Uther was right – he can recognise a dangerous whore when he sees one. I'm just a healer, and so I will remain in spite of your temptations and threats.'

Morgan turned pale with anger. 'My dreams are true, and I have no doubt that you'll drown us all in blood.'

'I obey the Mother, Morgan, the goddess who caused me to be born. I'll pay any price that she exacts from me to save our people from enslavement, and I'll not be tempted by your dreams or your fair, soft flesh, for you'd rot my soul away from within.'

Myrddion turned his back on Morgan, so he couldn't be ensnared by those glittering eyes that promised pleasures that equally sickened and excited him. He heard her soft footsteps on the stone floor as she turned, now laughing softly, and swayed off into the shadows of the great circular hall. When he turned back, she was a dark shape disappearing up towards the doors leading out of the council chamber into the growing night.

As Myrddion left the amphitheatre by the opposite set of doors, he tasted salt in his mouth and vomited uncontrollably over the granite steps. Even when his stomach was empty, he continued to retch painfully until he felt light-headed with the voiding of more than just his last good meal.

The trees outside the amphitheatre tilted crazily as he leaned against a pillar. Although full darkness had not yet blanketed Deva and the lamps had not been lit in all the darkening official buildings, an owl leapt into the air out of a copse of hazels in front of him with a clatter of wings and an impression of great eyes and sharp talons.

'A curse is coming, Grandmother Olwyn. But what can I do? Help me, Mother of us all. Help me to be strong.'

But the blanket of night and something darker that hovered over Deva could not be averted. Wind caused the hazels to shudder and a sudden chill stripped a few more leaves from their branches.

'All things must end,' Myrddion whispered, but he had no idea why he spoke such a doom aloud, now that his master was poised on the very edge of success. The skies bled out the last of the day and Myrddion turned wearily towards the banquet hall and the resumption of his duties.

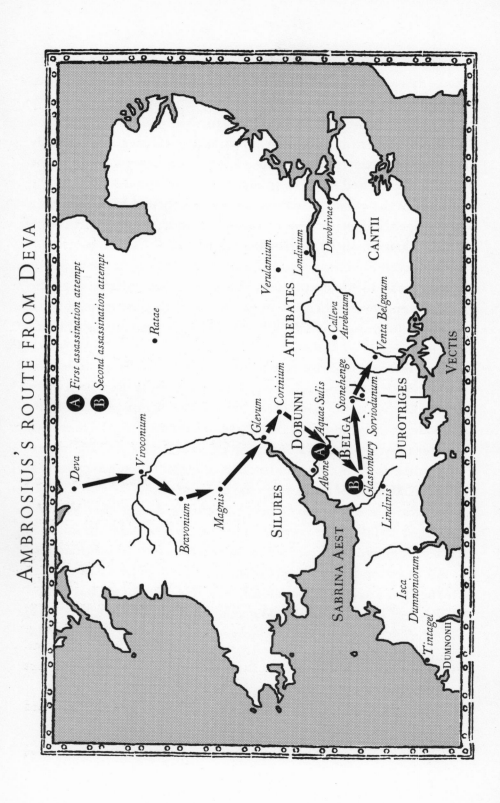

Ambrosius's route from Deva

Ⓐ *First assassination attempt*
Ⓑ *Second assassination attempt*

CHAPTER XI

ALL THINGS MUST END

Overall, through the regions of earth,
Walls stand rime-covered and swept by the winds.
The battlements crumble, the wine-halls decay:
Joyless and silent the heroes are sleeping
Where the proud host fell by the walls they defended.

Anonymous old English poem, *The Wanderer*

The banqueting hall was located in the old forum, and as Myrddion approached the merry gathering his eyes were dazzled by the hundreds of lamps, many torches and several fire-pits that warmed the cold stone and lit the dark spaces. A statue of Jupiter, somewhat the worse for wear, presided over the feast from a heavy marble base, while a sculpture of Constantine guarded the exit from the hall. The faces of both sculptures were heavily weathered and Jupiter had lost his nose in some conflict during the latter years of the Roman occupation. Now the crowd of feasting men around their plinths ignored them as if they had never swayed the fortunes of the known world.

Uther greeted Myrddion with an expression resembling good

humour. 'You did a good job in the council meeting, healer. When you started to speak, I considered removing your head from your shoulders just to shut you up, but then you set us all on end. Praise to Mithras, you put that fat fool Lot in his place and scared him silly with the suggestion that he could be under attack. Then, as the final coup, you left every person in the room looking to my brother for guidance. Well done!'

Uther slapped Myrddion on the back with bone-aching force. Surprised, the healer wondered if the prince was already drunk, but decided that Uther's over-bright eyes and uncharacteristic bonhomie were signs of excitement at being unleashed to kill Saxons along the whole length of the tribal lands.

'Have a cup of wine, healer. My brother has seen sense and is employing Ulfin as his taster once again, the Pict bitch has been sent back to Venta Belgarum and I only have Pascent to worry about. In short, I'm inclined to be pleased with you.'

Myrddion accepted the finely chased wine cup in the spirit in which it was offered. 'But is Lord Ambrosius pleased with *me*? As Ulfin no doubt told you, the High King resented my meddling in his affairs, but I'm pleased he is taking some precautions at last.'

'Ambrosius enjoyed today's proceedings,' Uther explained. 'We're both in your debt, but don't worry. You'll do something to upset me, so consider tonight to be a brief holiday for us both.'

Despite his misgivings and the pall that hung over him after his conversation with Morgan, Myrddion laughed and drank deeply. The heavy red wine warmed his stomach and eased some of the darkness in his thoughts. Servants bustled around the two men, bearing heaped trays of food or heavy wine jugs. The tables groaned under the best fare that Deva could offer, and Myrddion examined the banquet through the eyes of a man who had planned every detail carefully.

In unusual accord, the kings sat together in geographic groups, for these men would be required to work with each other in defence of the roads and fortresses within their tribal areas. Nor could any king complain about the richness or variety of the food offered for their delectation. Whole geese stuffed with chestnuts, onions, tasty mushrooms and whole boiled eggs vied with every type of fowl, sides of venison, tasty rabbits and haunches of beef. Richly gravied stews swam with mutton, lamb and bacon fat. Bowls of fruit, both fresh and cooked with honey, tempted the heartiest of appetites with sweetness, while the fruits of the sea cooked in pastry or glazed and stuffed with sweetbreads were spread on steaming platters.

But, try as he might, Myrddion could stomach nothing. Perhaps the long day had sucked the hunger out of him. Perhaps he was too weary to eat, having planned this feast for many anxious days. Whatever the reason, the healer drank one cup of wine too many and found his bed early, hoping that a night's sleep would repair what months of effort had taken away.

Several days passed in argument, eventual accord and feasting. Venonae, Ratae, Lindum, Melandra, Templebrough, Olicana, Verterae, Lavatrae and Cataractonium were apportioned among the tribes, to be manned and strengthened into functioning, efficient fortresses. In the south, Venta Silurum, Durnovaria, Calleva Atrebatum, Portus Adurni and Glevum were selected as towns of major importance which must be garrisoned by warriors who could take offensive action should the need arise. All told, each tribe was made responsible for at least one fortress, including the smaller towers along the two northern walls that would give protection against incursions by the Picts and limit those places where ceols and long ships could find safe harbour.

Much of the argument centred on the fortresses that had already fallen into Saxon, Angle or Jute hands. The consensus was that the

Saxons should be precluded from the use of any lands stolen from the Cantii, but logic ultimately prevailed over sentiment. The expenditure of lives and coin required to retake Verulamium was agreed to be unprofitable, just as the location of Londinium was determined to be too distant to warrant consideration.

'In any event the land is dead flat in Londinium,' Uther explained. 'The Roman fortress on the Tamesis is too small to be of any use to us now, and any attempt to retain control over the city would be a nightmare. While the streets are broad, too many people dwell cheek by jowl in such density that our warriors would be killed in swathes in any attempt to drive the Saxons out. Besides, many tribal traders still dwell there, so the city is not wholly Saxon. In time, perhaps, Londinium might become a neutral city, protected for its trading links with the continent. If you order me, your highnesses, I'll capture Londinium, but I'd lose it again as soon as I departed to fight another battle elsewhere. Like Verulamium, we'd lose more men than the campaign would be worth.'

'Then it's your belief that Londinium and Verulamium are lost?' Ambrosius said. 'Is that correct?'

His brother nodded regretfully. Ambrosius pressed home his advantage over the kings as they digested the unpalatable truth.

'Understand me. We must not trade with the Saxons nor admit foreign merchants into our lands, for so it was that Londinium was originally taken by stealth. Portus Adurni and Magnus Portus will become our trading centres, for Dubris is lost to us. With apologies to our Cantii neighbours, I cannot see any tribal force being able to dislodge the Saxons from those wide, temperate lands of the south. Once again, the landscape is our enemy because of its open, flat terrain. But Anderida must be held, for that fortress exposes Anderida Silva and our southern cities to attack from the barbarians. If the Cantii and Regni tribes are agreeable, the southern coast can still be held.'

Although many of the kings had never heard of these strange, exotic-sounding places, they caught Ambrosius's urgency, and so certain key sites became priorities for defensive action by the Britons.

It was soon determined that Anderida, Eburacum, Lindum and Durobrivae were essential to the survival of the united tribes. Piece by piece, an agreement was hammered out, and recorded by the scribes provided by the Christian bishops of the south. Even though many of the tribal kings could not write, they could press their intaglio rings into hot wax or make their marks beside the inscriptions of their names.

From his usual vantage point, Myrddion regretted that the common tongue had no written form, requiring all the records to be translated into Latin. He was unsurprised that so few kings could write, because he understood that many noblemen shared his great-grandfather's view of literacy. That venerable old king, Melvig ap Melwy, had considered that education weakened a strong man's mind, his personal resolve and his ability to make decisions. Myrddion's own education signified that King Melvig considered him disbarred by his illegitimacy from a career as a warrior or a ruler.

Myrddion sighed with regret. Until the kings saw the benefits of learning, they would remain as backward in their thinking as their enemies.

After a week of good food, better wine, carousing and wenching, the kings returned to their own halls secure in the knowledge that someone had taken the helm of the ship of state. They may only be oarsmen on that vessel, but the ship now had a purpose and a direction in which to steer. Myrddion bade them farewell with a feeling of anticlimax. Had it really been so easy?

'So all our fears were unfounded,' he commented to Uther as Gorlois, the last king to depart, rode away from Deva towards the southwest. The city was left feeling curiously empty after two weeks of hustle and bustle as the political centre of the British nation.

'Thanks to the gods! We're not out of the woods yet, and we're still far from home,' Uther replied. 'I won't sleep soundly until we're back in Venta Belgarum.'

'So when do we leave?' Myrddion asked, his voice pitched casually to hide his eagerness to be home.

'In four days. Ambrosius has taken it into his head to ride to Glastonbury, where he intends to give thanks to all the gods, including the Christian lord. Personally, Glastonbury gives me the horrors. Something old lives in that place. Don't ask me what it is, because I leave all matters of fancy to you.'

Uther was only half joking. Indeed, he often relegated matters pertaining to religion, superstition or the arcane to the healer for solving. This admission was, of itself, a sign that Uther had relented towards Myrddion. Their truce, fragile as it was, had warmed Ambrosius's heart, for the High King considered that their co-operation was of significant importance to the safety of the realm.

In the days before they left, Myrddion was kept busy liaising with the city fathers over the future care of the hall while negotiating, in Ambrosius's name, the payment for outstanding expenses incurred by the tribal kings during their attendance at the moot. While Ambrosius went riding with Pascent and his nobles under the watchful eye of Uther, Myrddion organised the baggage train for their homeward journey, purchased supplies and made arrangements for the scribes to return to Venta Belgarum and their monasteries. There they would produce the master copy of the accord for Ambrosius, along with additional copies for the other kings who had attended the moot.

'They won't be able to read it, you know,' Ambrosius told him one evening over a late-night supper.

'What they do with the accord doesn't matter, my lord,' Myrddion replied. 'They will be tied even closer to you by the magic of writing. It's a simple ploy, I know, but it sets their words in iron, an oath that is not easily broken.'

'You're to be congratulated, healer,' Pascent murmured from his cosy spot near the fire-pit. The nights were becoming chilly, and Pascent's blue fingers indicated that he felt the cold more than his masters.

'Why?' Myrddion asked. Pascent rarely spoke to him, so he was intrigued by the young man's professed admiration.

'At the meeting, you tore into the tribal kings for the sole purpose of driving them into Lord Ambrosius's arms. Truly, a good defence is a powerful attack.'

'You give me too much credit, Pascent. I merely spoke the truth as I saw it. Honesty can sometimes be a painful thing.'

'Aye, unvarnished truth can be a knife in the side,' Pascent murmured in agreement. 'Kings can rarely afford such a luxury, for subterfuge is their protection and their greatest skill.'

So young – and so embittered! 'Have you remembered anything about your past as yet?'

'No.' The youth coloured and idly rubbed his long scarred fingers together. 'And I'm beginning to despair that I'll ever discover who I am.'

'Perhaps the journey to Glastonbury will spark a memory,' Ambrosius contributed, his strong face softened by sympathy. 'Most tribal lords make a pilgrimage to that holy centre of learning at some time during their lives.'

'I hope so, master.'

Yet Pascent was a gay, enthusiastic companion once the party rode away from Deva over a scattered carpet of tossed flowers, amid the cheers of its citizens. Riding behind the main group, Myrddion could understand Ambrosius's attachment to the younger man. Even a freshening wind that required the king to don his fur-lined gloves couldn't dampen the mood of festivity that transformed the long journey into a pleasant interlude.

From Deva, they followed a secondary Roman road that skirted the deep green and midnight-blue forests of Arden to arrive at the Ordovice centre of Viroconium. There, at the behest of King Bryn, Llanwith pen Bryn joined their party to strengthen tribal ties with the High King and to receive instruction in the ways of a great court. Nervous and uneasy with the Roman brothers, Prince Llanwith gravitated to the only person he knew, Myrddion Merlinus.

As Viroconium fell behind, the landscape became wilder and more rugged. To the west, Myrddion could see the high grey mountains that called to him with a siren-song of home. As they crossed a number of swiftly flowing rivers via stone Roman bridges and forded any number of streamlets in every fold in the terrain, he became accustomed to the constant music of rushing water. His eyes were charmed by flowering gorse, the gold of autumnal trees and the delicate skeletal bones of aspens that had already dropped their leaves in long swathes of rust. The fat-tailed sheep that clung to every slope spoke of a peaceful countryside, and every village was inhabited by rosy-cheeked peasants who gazed on the panoply of the High King with eyes that were round with wonder.

'It's good to be so close to home,' Myrddion murmured to no one in particular.

Llanwith, who was some few years older than the healer, lounged in the saddle with the ease of a born horseman. A deft kick in the ribs guided his horse beside Myrddion's.

'If you miss Segontium so much, why don't you return there?'

Myrddion stared into the middle distance where a circular slate hut with a thatched roof was bleeding a trail of white smoke. The croft was well kept, and neat beds of vegetables were proof of careful husbandry. This journey was filling him with peace and a deep longing that he knew would be with him until he returned to the grey mountains and the sea that he loved.

'Ambrosius would not release me, nor would I break my oath of fealty. Initially, I was forced to serve, but I have come to accept that the High King is our greatest hope of salvation. He is an extraordinary man, Llanwith. Yes, he may be more Roman than Celt, but he loves this land and he has committed his life to serving it. A crown lies heavy on a head, and I've seen how little he relishes the constraints of rule, but his love for the Celtic peoples ennobles him. I will happily serve him for the rest of my life.'

For a moment, Llanwith rode beside the healer without speaking. Myrddion permitted the silence to lengthen, for few men can bear to endure a void and must rush to fill it. Over the years, he had discovered much to his advantage by this simple ploy.

'But he seems to be very distant, Myrddion. We are used to rulers who are passionate, sometimes wilful and always excitable. Vortigern was such a man. For all his fits and starts, and despite his violence and acts of barbarism, we could still understand him. The Roman says all the right things and his manner is correct and pleasant, but Bryn and Melvyn complain that they cannot fathom the passions that stir his heart. Damn me, but I wish he'd lose his temper or act on a whim, just so I could read his true character.'

Ahead, a shepherd whistled piercingly from the hill with his crook hung over one shoulder. Shaggy with the thickening coats that marked the onset of the colder weather, two black and white dogs ran towards a small flock of sheep from opposite directions as they obeyed orders quite invisible to the High King and his retinue.

'I am Ambrosius's dog, and my task is to herd the sheep back to the fold. Although I betray my master when I discuss his private nature, I can promise you that he is a true son of the Atrebates, as passionate as you, friend Llanwith, but he has learned to hide his emotions for his personal protection. He longs to love as his heart dictates, but he cannot do so. He hungers to trust the men and women who serve him, but he cannot do so. Would you have him assassinated because he was careless among those people in whom he places his trust?'

Myrddion's reputation for wisdom and learning was such that the Ordovice prince paid serious consideration to his argument. Llanwith furrowed his thick brows and toyed with his luxurious beard in an action that was habitual when he was deeply consumed by thought.

'So you're saying that he must take care to appear almost inhuman in his calm and reasonable demeanour if he has any hope of survival as ruler of the Britons.'

'That's exactly what I'm saying. And would you choose to live in that way?' Myrddion's eyes were still fixed on the distant figure of the shepherd, who was following his flock towards a natural pen formed by a fold in the land and secured by a rather flimsy fence.

'So the united kings are the sheep, while you and Prince Uther are Ambrosius's dogs. I can think in metaphors too, my friend. Unlike my father, I can read.'

'Yes, Llanwith. Noble sheep, but they are still beasts to be herded and protected from wolves and human predators. I thank the Mother that my birth freed me of the burden of rule. Caring for servants is quite onerous enough.'

'You're a cold fish at times, friend, but I like you none the less.' Then Llanwith laughed, and an already bright day suddenly developed an added gloss.

Myrddion had never had a friend who was his equal, yet owed him nothing. Although Llanwith had shaken him for a brief moment with his reference to the coldness of his nature, so like Morgan's barbed attack, he was beginning to depend on the bluff camaraderie of the Ordovice prince. In the evenings, Llanwith always appeared at the healer's fireside with a flask of red wine and muddy boots which he rested on any available surface. His uncritical, open face masked a keen intellect that was honed by wide reading on topics that he enjoyed discussing with Myrddion. They would often argue about military matters, for Llanwith was convinced that an eventual defeat of the Saxons would require new strategies utilising a combination of the disciplined approach of the Romans and the wild flair of the Celts. Myrddion admitted that Llanwith was his master in strategy and took pleasure in describing the Battle of the Catalaunian Plain in detail for the prince's enjoyment. In the weeks that followed, Myrddion came to look forward to these conversations, for they eased the hollow of loneliness that lay behind his breastbone.

'What about women, Myrddion?' Llanwith asked one evening, as rain pattered softly on their leather roof and intruded into the tent in long, damp runnels. 'Have you ever been in love?'

'Yes, once, but I prefer to forget the experience,' Myrddion said shortly. 'I've learned to survive without sex.'

Llanwith gave an explosive snort of laughter.

'Why? Do you confuse sex and love, my friend? One can exist quite pleasantly without the other. Why do you live like a Christian priest when the land is full of willing women who'd be happy to share your bed? I've seen how the women look at you.' A sudden suspicion made Llanwith pause. 'You don't prefer men, do you? I'm not criticising, for we all have kinfolk who follow the Greek fashion in matters of love.'

'No, not at all,' Myrddion responded with a little scowl of affront. 'I know you'll laugh at me, but women frighten me more than a little. Except for one girl who loved me for myself, I've always been the means to an end for those females who have crossed my path. In Deva, Morgan tried to seduce me with promises of power, but no simple physical release is worth what I would have suffered afterwards.'

'For Gwyddion's sake, and I use the name of the trickster god deliberately, what do you think the war that exists between men and women is all about? Men rule the roost, so women must be devious to protect their own interests. Men have brought this fate on their own heads because they don't realise that women can be friends as well as lovers – indeed, many men would argue that they're about as important as a good horse. I learned early that women have brains and hearts as well as breasts, so they'll do anything for you if you respect and honour them. But if you hurt them or deride them, they'll look to have their revenge on you in any of a number of unpleasant ways. Women can be devils.'

'You can say what you like, Llanwith, and you can reason with me until the seas boil, but I have experienced how dangerous the slaking of one's sexual desires can be. My own mother was driven mad by a man who forced himself on her, and I'd rather not do that to any woman.'

'Nor would I, and nor would any true man. But rape is domination, not sex, and I'd never confuse the two. I swear, Myrddion, that you'll become a twisted, unfeeling soul without the solace of women in your life. Don't you enjoy lying with a willing woman? I've heard that some men are as sexual as an old tree branch, so you needn't fear to be honest. We *are* friends, you know.'

Myrddion sighed. Friendship appeared to be making demands on his privacy.

'Very well, Llanwith. I desire women like any other man and, yes, I hunger for willing bed partners. Does that satisfy you?'

'For the moment. I can see that I will be forced to stir myself.'

Llanwith changed the subject before the two men could find themselves at odds with each other. Myrddion was grateful for the respite, but a niggling feeling at the back of his mind warned him that Llanwith hadn't finished with his belated sexual education.

The retinue reached Glevum via one of the minor roads, and Myrddion shuddered to see the damage from fire and siege that was still etched upon the town's venerable walls. Most of the damage inside the new gates had been repaired, and Ambrosius was eager to see all the places where the battle between Vortigern and Vortimer had taken place. Although the sun shone warmly and a gentle light played gracefully over the long grasses of the flat earth by the river, the trailing willows reminded the healer of that grim night when Vortigern's forces outflanked the army of his son. At Ambrosius's insistence, Myrddion recounted the stages of the battle, and pointed out the spot from where Vortimer's siege machines had attacked the moving shields devised by Myrddion to protect Vortigern's warriors from the bombardment of boulders, old iron and fire. When he described the advance of those clumsy covered platforms, and how they were disassembled to make a simple bridge over the river, Ambrosius insisted on pacing out the attack.

'It was brilliant tactics! Vortigern was a genius in his way. Who designed and constructed these machines?'

The High King's eyes were intense, and Myrddion was certain that Ambrosius was filing the information away within his retentive memory until the time came when he would use it to meet his own strategic requirements.

'I did, my lord, but I wasn't really sure what I was doing at the time. I was simply developing a vague idea into a practical concept.'

'Aye, I expected as much. I'll instruct Uther to provide you with a scroll so you can draw those machines for me to study. The time may come when we'll need ideas like these.'

After Glevum, the road widened and was soon busy with local traffic. Warriors, peasant farmers, traders, priests and cattle being herded to market shared the straight thoroughfare with Ambrosius's retinue. Word spread quickly, and when the travellers reached Aquae Sulis the population met the High King outside the widely opened gates with heaped flowers, excellent wine and ales, music and crowds of excited citizenry. Myrddion was amazed to see the fusion of Roman and tribal architecture that existed amicably within the city walls.

'Aquae Sulis, home of the Roman west and a place where anything is on sale,' Llanwith chortled and gave Myrddion a wink. 'Ambrosius will be occupied by the city fathers tonight, leaving us free to play.'

'Don't be ridiculous, Llanwith. I've new supplies to purchase and organise. I'll be too busy to spend my time tomcatting with you.'

'Just come to the baths then, Myrddion,' Llanwith wheedled, with his eyes rolling comically in emphasis. 'You haven't lived if you've never experienced a real Roman bath.'

'I practised my craft in Rome for a year, you clod. Do you think I stayed dirty for all that time? The Romans are masters at cleanliness and comfort. Still, I must admit that a bath would be relaxing.'

'See how easily you're corrupted when it's something you really want?' Llanwith retorted and bore Myrddion away.

The baths were a welcome relief after a long journey on horseback. The waters of Aquae Sulis were believed to have healing properties, and lounging in the tepidarium and drinking a cup of wine Myrddion acknowledged how tense he had been as his muscles slowly began to relax. Llanwith gambolled in the steaming waters like a large, hairy seal, completely indifferent to his nakedness, while Myrddion was content to rest his head against a mosaic of fanciful sea creatures and dream away the evening under the vaulted roof.

But Llanwith had different plans for their continued pleasure, and all too soon Myrddion was dragged away, rosy with cleanliness, along the broad streets of Aquae Sulis.

'I know a house nearby, very exclusive, where the women are clean and very talented.' Llanwith winked broadly. Although Myrddion protested that he had no desire for a woman, gainsaying Llanwith pen Bryn was like trying to stop the tide, an impossible task. Unwillingly, the healer was dragged into a stylish atrium, sweet with the perfume of late flowering trees and exotic oils that burned like small stars in wall sconces.

A number of men and women lounged around a fanciful fountain of Triton blowing a conch shell which expelled a glittering shower of water. The women came in every size and colouring, and were dressed in peplums and robes of delicately woven, imported materials that revealed glimpses of their bodies. Musicians played in a discreet corner and Myrddion caugh snatches of conversations that ranged from the recent meeting of the tribal kings to living conditions in Rome, which were deteriorating after the murder of Flavius Petronius Maximus, to the latest fashions among the wealthier citizens of Aquae Sulis itself. Surprised, Myrddion eavesdropped on one young woman's recitation of a poem by Sappho, a Greek woman from the isle of Lesbos, whose writings were considered both licentious and blasphemous throughout the lands of the Middle Sea. Myrddion had never expected such signs of sophistication and learning in a brothel.

'Surprised, friend? You needn't be. The Romans have always understood casual sex and have raised it to an art form, at least for the great ones of the land. These ladies are hardly the drabs that follow armies or ply their trade in filthy back alleys.'

Llanwith grinned irrepressibly. He had found a young red-haired girl with a shapely, lush body that she kept almost hidden under a yellow robe, and before Myrddion had time to protest he had scanned the crowd and beckoned to a tall, black-haired woman with deep brown eyes.

'What's your name, darling? My friend here is Myrddion Merlinus, healer and factotum of Ambrosius Imperator, our master. He's shy, is our Myrddion, but he loves to talk.'

'My name is Carwen, masters, named for my white skin.' The girl dimpled prettily.

'White love,' Myrddion said awkwardly, knowing he was babbling to fill the silence. 'It's a pretty name for a lovely girl.'

Carwen laughed and Myrddion was reminded of Morgan, but this girl's eyes were kind as well as brilliant, and her merriment held no trace of sarcasm.

'You do me honour, my lord, which is undeserved. I doubt my sire was concerned with the meaning of my name when he sold me at six years of age for the price of a flask of wine. But, praise to Lady Venus, my new mistress saw a trace of beauty in the urchin I was, and it was she who saw to my education.'

Myrddion's mouth turned down with distaste, but Carwen punched him lightly on the chest and laughed, although Myrddion caught an edge of disappointment in her eyes.

'Not that kind of education, Myrddion Merlinus. My mistress, Longus Longinia, is more Roman than anyone living in the Seven Hills and has modelled her house on the villas of the great courtesans of Rome. We were taught to speak and read Latin, and were instructed in music, literature and dance. Poetry is my forte, especially licentious verse, but my heart belongs to Horace, I'm afraid. We were even encouraged to develop religious beliefs to cater to the whims of our customers. I am Christian, and I am well versed in the story of Mary Magdalene, a whore who was saved by the Christus.'

Myrddion couldn't help but look doubtful, for he felt that Carwen was in some way laughing at him, even as she pressed another cup of light white wine into his hands.

'But you were right, matters of the bed were also part of my education, for my task in life is to please my customers, to converse with them while soothing their guilts and catering to their greatest needs. I serve unhappy men, like you, who fear to expose themselves to women of their own class. And sometimes they are old and ugly, but who am I to judge them? At heart they are lonely and lost, and

I help them to bear their unhappy lives. Is this wrong, Myrddion Merlinus?'

Myrddion was forced to face his prejudices, and as he looked at Carwen's intelligent, beautiful face and mulled over her arguments he found little to revile. What compromises had he made to serve the greater good? Too many to name. And who, at times, had caused the greater harm? He had no doubt at all that he had. No, Carwen was a fair woman who earned her bread as best she could.

Her knee, pressed against his thigh as they sat on a marble bench, seemed hot against his skin. Her eyes were very bright and the pupils were enlarged so that his reflection swam in them when he looked at her. Despite himself, he raised one hand to stroke her heart-shaped face and felt the soft, peach-like down on her skin with a kind of heightened sympathy mingled with sharp sexual awareness. When Carwen captured his hand and kissed the sensitive palm and each individual finger, he felt his loins tighten with desire.

'Come with me, Myrddion Merlinus. Don't think . . . just be, my lord.'

Carwen rose, holding the captured hand that still tingled from the touch of her lips. With his mind torn between desire and revulsion, he followed her to a gracious staircase leading to the small bedchambers above the public rooms, where she pulled him over the threshold into her special domain.

The room was soft with pretty hangings that had been decorated with her own hands, and an elusive perfume rose from the wide bed. Carwen's eyes were very wide and deep, and Myrddion had the strange notion that the Mother looked at him out of their warm broad depths. He had no power to stop her as she stripped the black leathers off his body and sighed at the milk-white beauty of his skin before she pressed him down into a nest of cushions.

Later, Myrddion would remember little of the hours he spent in that room. Carwen's body was perfect and as white as his, except for the brown aureoles of her nipples which hungered for his mouth. For the first time, he learned the pleasures to be found in giving as well as receiving, and he marvelled that the act was so much more than a mad, passionate coupling of hot bodies and even hotter love. At last, the healer who knew so much about the human body came to understand Llanwith's assertions that there is a glory in muscles, brain, nerves and pleasure-centres that has no bearing whatsoever on love. He imagined, as he lay spent and happy in Carwen's arms, how pleasant love must be when it was allied with sexual attraction. At the end, he could only feel pity for Flavia, who had used her seductive appeal as a tool to earn a comfortable life.

Who then is the courtesan? Carwen, who is honest, intelligent and giving, or Flavia, who prides herself on her bloodlines but will welcome anyone between her legs who will give her the comforts and status she craves?

Myrddion wouldn't have willingly moved from the warmth of Carwen's flanks firmly pressed against his, but a great knocking downstairs disturbed the sweet lethargy of successful lovemaking. Booted feet and demanding voices found their way to her door.

'Up, healer!' A rough voice heightened with a thread of panic called him from the bed. 'You're needed!'

Before he could cover his nakedness, Uther burst into the small sanctuary, ran his eyes over the scene, and threw Myrddion's trews at him.

'Get dressed, damn you! Ambrosius is ill and calling for you.'

Uther's eyes were reddened with impotent fury, so Myrddion didn't pause to ask questions. He threw on his clothing, snatched up the satchel that always accompanied him, and bent hastily to kiss Carwen.

'I've not paid yet, lady, but I must leave with the prince before he explodes,' he murmured in her ear. 'I will return soon with your money.'

'It's all been done, my lord, at the orders of Prince Llanwith. Come again, Myrddion, should Aquae Sulis cross your path. I will be waiting for you.'

Myrddion ran in Uther's wake as Llanwith emerged from another room, tousled and looking even more like a bear than usual. He held a knife in one hand, while his other laced his trews into place.

Through clenched teeth, Uther spoke over his shoulder as the men clattered down the stairs. 'I fear poison, healer. My brother is racked with convulsions and I fear he will die. Make haste, or I'll hurry you with the flat of my sword.'

'There's no need, Uther. I'd happily give my own life for the safety of your brother. Lead on while Llanwith fetches a green glass jar from my saddle bags. Please, Llanwith?'

'At once, Myrddion.'

Llanwith reached the door of the villa even faster than Uther, an amazing feat for such a big man, and disappeared into the early morning half-light.

As Myrddion and Uther emerged, a guard closed around them and the party set off at a soldier's run, until Myrddion was panting with the strain. Nor did the pace slacken until they passed through the city gates and reached Ambrosius's leather tent, which was surrounded by soldiers who were stirring like an ant's nest disturbed by a playful boy.

Under a waning moon, the light was ruddy with torches. At the tent flap, Myrddion drew a deep breath as he felt the doom he had dreaded settle over his heart.

'Not Ambrosius!' he thought with a sickening sensation that began in his stomach and seemed to freeze his blood. Then, before his courage could fail him, the healer thrust the tent flap aside and steeled himself to do battle with the forces of treason.

CHAPTER XII

BEYOND TEARS

In sorrow of soul they laid on the pyre
Their mighty leader, their well-loved lord.
The warriors kindled the bale on the barrow,
Wakened the greatest of funeral fires.
Dark o'er the blaze the wood-smoke mounted,
The winds were still, and the sound of weeping
Rose with the roar of the surging flame
Till the heat of the fire had broken the body.

Anonymous Anglo-Saxon poem, *Beowulf*

The interior of the tent was too still, too theatrical, to be quite real,
Myrddion decided as he thrust his way into the large space.
Although he was pale and feverish, Ambrosius's eyes still blazed
with so much life that he gave the illusion of being the only person
in the tent. Awkward and nervous, Pascent stood at the head of the
High King's folding cot, wringing his hands in distress, while Ulfin
lay curled in one corner of the tent. The bodyguard was pallid, and
sweating in his own vomit.

'Remove the food taster. He's obviously as sick as his master,'

Myrddion ordered Botha who, in turn, nodded at two of Uther's guard. Ulfin was carried away. 'Feed him saline water ... salt in water ... as much as he can stomach. Then, if he doesn't purge himself, stick your fingers down his throat,' Myrddion instructed Botha, who nodded impassively. 'And keep him warm. Shock kills.'

Myrddion scanned the tent and saw evidence of a meal of stew and bread. A flagon of wine sat on the folding table, close to an upturned chair. He summoned another of Uther's bodyguards.

'Remove the food and drink and keep it in a safe place until I can examine it. You, Pascent, as you're unaffected, I need to know what the others ate that you didn't touch.'

Uther's lips drew back from his teeth and he growled deep in his throat like a dog. 'Answer quickly, or you'll wish you'd died at the hands of the Saxons.'

'Don't you think I'd have taken pains to eat some of the poison if I was the assassin?' the young man retorted, his eyes as shallow as marbled glass. 'I was fortunate because I arrived late for dinner. I wasn't here to serve the king as was my custom. You know that I always wait on Ambrosius, my prince, but I was delayed. When I arrived, I spooned out some stew for myself, but hadn't begun to eat it when Ulfin was struck down.'

'Go to your tent, boy, if you know what's good for you,' Uther snarled. 'And stay out of my way. If you stir before I'm ready for you, I will kill you slowly, deeming you to be trying to escape. Do you understand?'

'How could I not, sir?' the young man replied stiffly, and left the High King's tent with a rigid back and an expression of affront. He bowed punctiliously to each person as he passed out through the flap, in company with a tall, sardonic warrior.

'Could we arrange for one of the servants to clear up this mess?' Myrddion asked Uther. 'Where in Hades is Llanwith? I need that emetic.'

'Explain!' Uther demanded abruptly, even as he cast a length of cloth over Ulfin's vomit and made sure a bowl was close to his brother's hand.

'I use senna as an emetic to purge the stomach and bowels of poison. It will scour the body clean, providing the poison hasn't been absorbed into the blood.'

As the healer spoke, Llanwith shoved his way into the tent, with a sweating brow that spoke of frantic exertion. 'Is this the jar you wanted, Myrddion? It took an age for me to find it.'

Ambrosius began to shake, great tremors stiffening his muscles and causing his body to convulse while his eyes pleaded for more life. His hands twisted in the cushions until the knuckles shone white with spasms of pain.

'Hold him down, Uther, and place his belt between his teeth so he can't hurt himself. Llanwith, search out a clean pannikin from one of the warriors. No one could poison all the guard.'

Llanwith ran out of the tent and returned clutching a primitive drinking cup.

'Now, hold it still for me.' Carefully and calmly, Myrddion filled the cup with water from his flask. Then, with painful care, he measured a number of drops from the green glass jar into the fluid. He used the point of his own eating knife to stir the oily mixture.

The convulsion had passed and Ambrosius was attempting to catch his breath, his face twisted into a rictus of pain. Yet the blue eyes were calm when Myrddion approached, and the healer felt the weight of the High King's trust.

'Uther will help you to drink, master. You will be vilely ill, but don't fuss or feel unmanly. Fortunately, you have already been sick and some of the poison has been expelled. Now we'll try to remove the rest.'

'I've ... soiled myself,' Ambrosius panted in embarrassment.

'Not to worry, my lord. You're in my charge now, and I desire you to drink the water that Uther will raise to your lips. Every drop. It will taste terrible, but you shouldn't care about that.'

As gentle as any mother, Uther bent over his brother and lifted him into a sitting position before raising the beaker of emetic to his lips. The king grimaced at the oily, vile taste but gamely forced the liquid down before reclining, exhausted, against the pillows. When the purgative was all ingested, the High King began to vomit uncontrollably until his stomach was completely empty. Throughout this painful interlude, Uther supported his brother's head, his face creased with love and a nagging anxiety that he failed to hide from the sharp eyes of the healer.

When Ambrosius's spasms had finished, Myrddion and Uther stripped him, cleansed his body with warm water, changed the bedding and then wrapped him in heavy woollen blankets. Exhausted from the convulsions, the High King drifted into a light doze.

'What now?' Uther demanded, as Myrddion began to repack his satchel.

'We wait, Prince Uther. I suspect the assassin is a novice, and he used too much poison out of ignorance. Both Ulfin and Ambrosius vomited the worst of the toxin out of their systems almost immediately, and I'm confident my purgative will have removed the rest. It's difficult to tell what damage has been caused, but whatever poison was used, it was quite potent.'

'So where are you going?' Uther snapped through lips that were a thin wound in his drawn face. 'Ambrosius needs you.'

'I am going to feed Ambrosius's meal, piece by piece, to the city hounds. When one begins to show symptoms of poisoning. I'll know how it was done and possibly be able to isolate the poison, which I hope will lead me to the culprit.' Myrddion's eyes rested on the salt box on the table. 'I'll take that box as well. I can't imagine that the salt is poisoned, but I'm not taking any chances. I'll return as soon as I have some information for you. The assassin must be caught or he will try again, so Ambrosius Imperator must be protected at all times. Who can care for him more zealously than you?' Myrddion looked into Uther's deceptively shallow eyes. 'One more thing, Prince Uther. It is possible that the assassin might also make an attempt on *your* life, so you should look to your own safety.'

Uther smoothed his brother's wet hair back from his pasty forehead. Deep lavender shadows were scored under Ambrosius's closed eyes and Myrddion prayed that the king had the deep wells of strength necessary to fight off this tangible proof of hidden malice.

'I thank you, Myrddion Merlinus. Let me know the moment you isolate the poison. You may use Botha to enforce your will, as he is oath-bound to me and my house for life.' Uther was unaccustomed to depending on anyone, and the words were dredged up with acute embarrassment.

Followed by Llanwith, Myrddion slid through the tent flap and made his way to the tent where the remains of Ambrosius's meal had been taken. They found Botha there, and the healer asked him how Ulfin was faring.

'He's better, lord Myrddion. I had no trust in anything belonging to other men, so I used my own supply of salt and water. Once his stomach was completely voided, he regained his colour and seems much improved. Of course, he only tasted each item of food in the meal, while Lord Ambrosius ate a grown man's share.'

'Yes, so we must pray that my purgative worked in time. I hope we can quickly discover what poison was used, and how it was delivered to the king.'

Botha nodded, and his understanding was clearly written in his intelligent eyes. 'Poisoning is unmanly. It's a woman's weapon for those who lack the courage to attack their enemies face to face.'

'Aye. This is a spiteful crime, and almost impossible to solve because the assassin acts with stealth. You are forced to wait for them to make a mistake and thus reveal their identity.'

Before the hour was out, one of the hounds showed signs of poisoning after eating some of the stew from Ambrosius's plate. Myrddion used his scalpel to give the poor animal a quick death, and the source of the poison was determined when another dog died after eating fresh meat that had been sprinkled with Ambrosius's salt.

'It's the salt!' Myrddion exclaimed to Botha, who was standing alongside him. 'So we know that the poison is red in colour, and I can make a reasoned guess at what it is. But I can't be certain, for I don't traffic in potions of death.'

'This assassin was cowardly – and clever,' Llanwith muttered, while Botha spat on the earth with a strong, honest man's revulsion. 'Who would notice someone tampering with the salt box? It's a horrible thought to know that Ambrosius was poisoned by his own hand.'

Later, in Uther's tent, the prince was ominously quiet when Myrddion reported his findings.

'I believe our king was poisoned with realgar, but I can't be sure. I've heard of it being used by assassins in Rome, Greece and, notably, in the north. The perpetrator was unfamiliar with its use because he made the crucial mistake of using an amount that was too large and too pure, so that Ambrosius vomited almost immediately and most of the poison was expelled before it could kill him, praise be to all the gods.' Myrddion could read fear and dread in equal measure in Uther's lupine eyes. 'Poisoners usually take care to destroy any evidence of their potions. Search the camp by all means, but there's little chance that we'll find our assassin. Still, it's worth a try, because any attempt as blatant as this one suggests to me that he won't be deterred by failure, and will surely try again at the first opportunity.'

Given something constructive to do, Uther stroked his brother's face before stalking out of the sickroom, bent on a ferocious search of the whole camp. Heaven help any man or woman caught with a suspicious potion, Myrddion thought.

'Assist me to rise, Myrddion,' Ambrosius called from his sickbed. The healer almost smiled: his master had only been pretending to sleep. 'I'm sure you have some restorative that will permit me to travel. I have no intention of dying in Aquae Sulis, so we must break camp and be gone by noon tomorrow.' The king's face was still very pale and his pulse was febrile, but his eyes were as sharp and as determined as ever. 'Try to restrain Uther from harming Pascent, for the boy wasn't even present when I ate.'

'Of course, my king. I have sent Pascent to his tent, where he must remain while Uther searches for any hidden substances. As for your fitness to travel, I have tisanes that will help with the nausea, stomach cramps and diarrhoea, and we must thank the Mother that your ill-wisher is a tyro in the cowardly art of assassination. He used far too much poison and you expelled it before it could irreparably harm your organs. Otherwise we would be building your funeral pyre.'

'So much for food tasters and the protection they offer. How is Ulfin, incidentally? I'd forgotten him during my own travails, and he has always been a selfless servant of this family.'

Myrddion grinned at his king. Ambrosius was so natural when he was free of protocol and public scrutiny and could speak his mind without guile or dissembling.

'Ulfin hated swallowing the great quantities of salty water needed to cleanse his body of the toxins.' Myrddion smiled. 'He vomited until his throat was raw, but he will be well in a day or two.'

'You don't like Ulfin over much, do you, Myrddion?' Ambrosius whispered, as he watched his healer fill a cup with hot water to steep some chopped leaves that he had produced from a jar.

'No, my king, I don't like him at all. Botha, Uther's man, is the very best of servants and warriors, and shows excellent judgement – but Ulfin is a sneak.' Myrddion gasped as he burned his finger in the hot steam from the kettle. 'I apologise, my lord. The Mother punishes me for arrogance and ill-will. I suppose I've had too little sleep.'

Ambrosius struggled into a sitting position, although he paled a little with a spasm of pain. 'I want your promise, Myrddion Merlinus, that you will obey me if any further harm should befall me in the near future.'

'Nothing will harm you, Ambrosius, for we are on our guard now.'

The eyes of the High King captured Myrddion's and held them fast in their bright blue intensity. Myrddion marvelled that he had ever thought those blue eyes were cold, for the fierce, clear depths burned with an urgent passion.

'I want your promise, Myrddion Merlinus. And then I will tell you what I demand of you.'

'You ask much, lord. Perhaps too much.'

The High King's gaze would not set Myrddion free. He felt Ambrosius's compulsion and need burn into his brain. 'Do you care for me at all, healer? I have more trust in you than any other man on this earth, with the exception of my brother.'

'Yes, I care for you, Ambrosius. And yes, if I must prove my fealty, I will swear to obey you, although my mind warns me that I will suffer for it.'

Ambrosius lay back on the pillows and closed his eyes, exhausted by this simple exercise in force of will. The brief tide of energy drained out of him and the High King was a sick and ageing man again, one whose beauty was fading under the twin flails of illness and duty.

'Uther will rule once I pass into the shades. He has the calculation, the coldness and the ruthlessness in his nature that will permit him to be a High King. But Uther sees the world in black and white, and people are either friends or enemies. Nor does he try to understand the motives of those men and women who are closest to him. I fear for him once he is free to be wholly himself.' Ambrosius opened his compelling eyes. 'Try to understand him, Myrddion. Uther never knew the softness of our mother, for our father died when he was very young and then she wed Vortigern.'

Ambrosius's face contorted with distaste and anger, and Myrddion recalled that the High King's mother, Severa, had been Vortigern's wife before he married Rowena. Shite! Myrddion thought sickly. Vortimer and Ambrosius were half-brothers.

'Constans, our older brother, was murdered by Vortigern so that he could usurp the throne. Uther and I both adored Constans as all younger siblings do. So before he was nine years old, Uther was forced to accept that the world is a place where trust withers on the vine and love kills.'

Even if he had known what to say or how to respond, Myrddion dared not interrupt these confidences. Whether the king's mood was impulsive or coldly reasoned, Myrddion couldn't tell.

'We travelled together for a long, long time after we fled from Vortigern, forced to live off the charity of our kinfolk. Uther hated every slight and longed to return home, although he rarely complained. But something hardened in him during those years of rootlessness and shame. When we returned to Venta Belgarum, we came with mercenaries and even Vortigern hesitated to attack me from the front. His reputation was in tatters by then, and all sensible men shied away from the Regicide – but Uther had already learned how to hate. We had so little in our childhood, apart from each other, that he takes what he wants with greedy hands, and even I have difficulty keeping him under control.'

'Lord Ambrosius, Prince Uther is my . . .'

'No, Myrddion, you have to understand. Uther can be a great

man. He has the capacity to lead the tribal kings to victory, even more ably than I ever could. But he could also become a monster without a calm and reasonable voice that would warn him of pitfalls placed in his path.'

'Let's hope that you live for a very long time,' Myrddion replied, attempting to display a jollity he didn't feel.

'Don't treat me like a child, healer, for a good king plans for every contingency. Uther is my beloved brother and heir, but there is a dark space within him that the throne will set free. You must stay with him, whatever the cost. You must guide him into safe channels of action in order to hold the accord together. But most important of all, you must ensure he begets an heir.'

Myrddion's jaw dropped. What did Ambrosius think he could do to sway an elemental force like Uther Pendragon?'

'He would never listen to me,' he protested. 'Inevitably, he'd separate my head from my shoulders, for there's no love lost between us. Even as I try to fulfil my oath to you, I'll be digging my own grave.'

Ambrosius managed to chuckle with a rusty, painful humour dredged up from an abused throat and lungs. 'Not he, Myrddion,' he croaked. 'Uther has one great weakness. He loves his brother, so fetch me a scroll and ink. Make sure the pen is sharp and new, as my hand is unsteady. I must set my wishes in Latin so that Uther will be bound by his affection for me, and I will tell him that he is to keep you close to him, for my sake.'

'Lord . . .' Myrddion began, but he saw the iron in the High King's eyes and knew that all arguments were fruitless. 'I'll send for the scroll and some writing materials.'

'Good. I know the fate I am laying upon you, and I'd not damn you to such a future if I had any choice in the matter.' Then Ambrosius laughed with a trace of his old gaiety. 'Perhaps I'm thinking with the superstitions of an old granddam, while I'm fated to live for decades.'

'Aye, lord,' Myrddion replied cheerfully, and found a servant to obey the High King's wishes. Something in the nagging, doleful voice in his skull warned him that the horrors of the last twenty-four hours weren't yet over. Myrddion remembered the owl at sunset in Deva, and shivered as a sudden premonition began to press on his heart.

Spare me from service to Uther Pendragon, Mother. I fear that he will steal my soul.

The road to Glastonbury was clearly marked, for untold numbers of pilgrims had made the journey along this path as they sought communion in this special place with its long hierarchy of gods. Once, according to distant memory, Glastonbury had been an island in an inland sea, and several warriors who had been to the ancient sanctuary were eager to show Myrddion petrified shells that they had found and strung on thongs round their necks. Myrddion marvelled at the perfect, stone-like beauty of these small, coiled shells that were near as old as the hills that rose in green mounds around them. Surely the gods had decreed that this strange valley was a sacred place, raised from living waters to praise the various gods who had been worshipped there for years beyond counting.

Still waxen in colour, Ambrosius had taken to his horse on the second day of the journey, scorning to approach holy Glastonbury like a mendicant on a stretcher.

'I am the High King of the Britons and I'll come to the bishop as one – on my two good legs.'

Neither Uther nor Myrddion dared to gainsay him.

For fear of poison, Ambrosius ate boiled eggs and drank only water and new milk purchased from local peasants and delivered to Ambrosius in Uther's own hands. On several occasions, Uther milked the cows himself. Myrddion approved of these simple precautions for medical reasons, because Ambrosius was far from well and this simple fare could only be beneficial for him. Myrddion personally boiled all the drinking water and guarded it zealously so that there was no opportunity for malice that could harm his master. But the journey to Glastonbury was slow, and every day on the road increased Myrddion's forebodings.

On the eve of their intended arrival at the monastery, disaster stole into the camp and turned their precautions to nothing. In the distance, the tor rose from the valley floor and the stone tower on its crown was an accusatory finger pointing to the gods.

As had become customary, Myrddion and Uther served all meals to the king. As the cup bearer, Pascent was only permitted to bring the king's goblet and plate to Myrddion or the prince, while his every movement was watched closely as Ambrosius ate. Pascent dined in the High King's company, but the steely suspicions of Prince Uther, who harboured serious doubts about the boy, killed the Saxon captive's appetite. Out of loyalty, Ambrosius still demanded Pascent's presence whenever they made camp and refused to listen to Uther's carping. The High King swore that laughter would heal him more quickly than medicine, but Myrddion nursed his own doubts about the young man and watched every move of his deft fingers when he was in Ambrosius's tent.

That night, just as Myrddion was sinking into sleep, Botha appeared in his tent and shook him to wakefulness with a rough hand. 'The High King has taken a turn for the worse. Come quickly, as our lord is like to die.'

Myrddion snatched up his satchel without pausing to ask questions. In a camp that was suddenly stirring anxiously, he ran between the dying fires on bare feet until he reached Ambrosius's tent. The scene inside caused his heart to sink.

Ambrosius had vomited and soiled himself in his extremity. His hands and feet were ice-cold and his circulation was low, and

Myrddion could clearly see a frightening blueness in the king's nails and lips as if his patient was suffering from a disease of the heart.

'Open your mouth, lord,' he ordered. 'I must check your throat and your breathing.'

Like a tired, fretful child, Ambrosius obeyed between spasms of vomiting. His mouth was reddened and, with a sick lurch of his stomach, Myrddion saw patches of redness at his wrists, elbows, knees and ankles. Several blood vessels in his eyes had burst, giving his eyeballs an ugly red cast.

'I'm so thirsty that I could drink the river dry, Myrddion,' he whispered. 'I remind you of your oath to me.'

'It hasn't come to that yet, my lord. I intend to fight to keep you healthy with every ounce of my strength.'

Ambrosius laughed weakly then turned his head away as his stomach spasmed. 'God, my gut is afire.' Without pausing to think, Myrddion began to mix a few drops of poppy into his boiled water and assisted the king to drink.

'This potion will make you drowsy, lord, but it will take away your pain. I must consult my scrolls to find the answer to this particular illness. Don't be afraid, Ambrosius, my true friend, for I will find it.'

'If I am to sleep, I need Uther now. He's rampaging through the camp, seeking invisible enemies.' Turning to Botha, the king pointed across to a small table. 'There's a scroll in my chest. Please bring it to me, and then find my brother and escort him here.'

By the time Botha returned, the pupils of Ambrosius's eyes had widened and his pain was gradually receding. He was drifting in and out of sleep as Myrddion wrapped him in heated woollen blankets. With a great effort of will, the king roused himself when Uther entered the tent.

'Brother,' he said softly. 'Hold my hand until I sleep. Botha has a scroll that must be read if this illness closes my eyes for ever. I ask for your promise that you will ensure the accord of the united kings holds firm, and that you will send Andrewina Ruadh home to her children. All else is for you to decide.'

Uther held his brother's hand and swore that he would promise anything, if only Ambrosius could be returned to health. His eyes were stark and fearful, and Myrddion remembered that Uther had no kin in the isles other than his brother, who was fading even as they watched.

As soon as Ambrosius was deeply asleep, Uther left Botha to guard the High King and bodily dragged Myrddion out of the tent. His hands were very strong as he gripped Myrddion's loose tunic, but the healer could feel that the iron fingers were trembling.

'You told me that he'd survived the poison! That he was feeling better! What has caused this illness? What have you *done*?'

'I've done nothing, Prince Uther! You know that! I drank the water before Ambrosius, and you milked a cow but yesterday. The eggs he ate had not been breached. Now I must consult my scrolls, for these symptoms are puzzling, and new to me.'

Unconsciously, Uther had continued to shake Myrddion as a terrier shakes a rat. Suddenly, he seemed to come to his senses and loosened his hold on the healer's tunic to run his sweating, shaking hands down his own overshirt.

'Poison? Again? How?'

'I don't know, lord, but you must give me time to consult my scrolls and perhaps I will discover something. You must gather your wits, Uther. You're no use to your brother if you run amok through the camp. Let me go to my tent.' Myrddion paused, then said, 'You would also be advised to find Pascent and put him under guard. No one but him has been with us while Ambrosius was eating.'

'It's already done, healer. Find out what's wrong with my brother. Go!'

Myrddion had been unable to take his sandalwood box of scrolls with him on the journey to Deva, but he rarely travelled without a number of herbal references he had been assembling since he had first become Annwynn's apprentice. That redoubtable old woman knew everything there was to know about plants, nuts, flowers, roots and fruit, both their curative and their toxic properties, but to his regret Myrddion could not remember even a quarter of it.

Now, in the chaos of his tent, with Llanwith trying to help but simply getting in his way, Myrddion hunted through his precious herbal scrolls until a sudden thought crossed his mind.

'Llanwith, do something useful and bring me every piece of baggage that Pascent possesses. I don't care if he complains, and I know that Uther has already searched him. Don't argue! Just bring me everything. Oh, and be careful, Llanwith. You don't know what you'll be touching.'

Llanwith looked thoroughly alarmed and grabbed a pair of Myrddion's leather riding gloves, which proved to be a very tight fit. Then, with a puzzled expression and panic in his quick movements, he was gone.

Uther returned to Myrddion's tent just as the Ordovice prince arrived with two saddlebags held gingerly in his gloved hands. Myrddion looked up from the scroll he was trying to read by the fitful light of an oil lamp.

'What have you discovered?' Uther demanded. 'Do you suspect Pascent?'

'I told you why. As for the reason I'm searching his possessions, it's because I'm desperate. Perhaps there's something in his bags that seems harmless, but isn't.' He lifted the first bag gingerly. 'May I have my gloves back, Llanwith? I hope they're not too stretched by those hams that pass for your hands.'

Wordlessly, Llanwith stripped off the leather gloves and Myrddion immediately donned them, carefully pressing each finger firmly into place. Then he upended the saddlebags on to the sod floor.

Three pairs of blank eyes examined the resultant mess on the ground. Spare tunics, leggings, a small drawstring pouch of soft leather, a knitted cap with wilted flowers tucked into it, a scrap of fine rag and a spare, worn leather belt lay innocently on the churned grass. With one booted foot, Myrddion moved a rolled tunic and revealed a battered cup, a flask and a worn eating knife.

'Perhaps the flask has something in it,' Uther decided, and picked up the leather container. After removing the brass stopper, he upended the flask and discovered it was empty.

'Shite! Shite! Shite! There's nothing here that could have harmed Ambrosius,' Uther swore, and then repeated a particularly coarse description of Pascent's parentage. Myrddion's mind twitched momentarily, but then the half-memory slid away.

'Let me think!' Myrddion begged. 'Please stop talking and give me a moment to think.' He stared at each item, lifted it, smelled it and then discarded it with a grunt of disgust. When he came to the knitted cap, he examined it inside and out, and then turned his attention to the wilted flowers. They were very pretty, somewhat daisy-like, with six or seven petals on each flower and a cluster of yellow stamens in the centre. The petals were still a clear yellow although the plants were bruised.

Myrddion's eyes darted from the petals to the cup, and then to the scrap of cloth. 'Where did you find the cow yesterday, Uther?'

'You know where. It came from that cottage in the small clearing, miles from anywhere in particular. We had to collect the cow from the fields before I milked it.' Uther looked thoroughly irritated under his surprise. Llanwith tensed, expecting an explosion of temper.

'You collected the cow yourself?' Myrddion's eyes were very bright.

'No, I sent Pascent. He couldn't poison the milk while it was still in the cow, and if he'd milked it himself, always supposing he could, Ambrosius would never have touched it.'

'So that's where he found the meadow saffron,' Myrddion whispered. 'Was anyone sick in the cottage?'

'A young girl was poorly, but I don't see what that's got to do with anything. The brat probably caught a chill.'

'She probably drank milk from a cow that had been eating meadow saffron. It's a pretty flower, isn't it? But the milk of cows or goats that have been eating it can kill a young child.'

Llanwith pen Bryn and Uther stared at the wilted, bruised flowers as if they had suddenly turned into serpents.

'But Ambrosius isn't an infant. He's a grown man and unlikely to be poisoned so easily,' Llanwith protested. 'The peasant's daughter wasn't dying.'

'But she wasn't already suffering from a previous poisoning, was she? Ambrosius's body has been weakened, so the toxic elements of the plant were far more effective on him. Pascent must have known of its effects, since he collected some of the flowers and thrust them into his cap. He couldn't be sure that the milk was contaminated, but he didn't warn you of any possible danger, did he, Uther?'

Uther's expression was thunderous. 'No, he fucking did not!' The crudity hung on the air with the promise of sudden death.

'How did you recognise those flowers, Myrddion?' Llanwith asked. '*I* didn't know what they were. Would Pascent, or whoever he is? Could the poisoning be an accident?'

'Annwynn pointed meadow saffron out to me many years ago. I'd forgotten all about it until now, but Pascent picked those flowers for a reason,' Myrddion replied carefully. 'I recall that she told me that every part of the meadow saffron plant is poisonous – the leaves, the stalk and the sap are all toxic. He might have used some decoction as well. But how?'

He lifted the cap and sniffed it delicately. His nostrils twitched. Uther and Llanwith watched him, gape-mouthed, as he used a pair of medical forceps to lift a scrap of rose wool which seemed a little stiff and stained.

'Of course,' Myrddion whispered. 'It must have been a crime of convenience, committed on the spur of the moment, but done so brilliantly and naturally that none of us even suspected what was happening.'

Uther took one angry, threatening step forward with his hands clenched into fists. 'Stop talking in riddles and make some sense. Can Ambrosius be saved from this . . . this . . . meadow saffron?'

'Perhaps – but more likely not. You want the truth, don't you? If Pascent has done what I suspect, the king will suffer progressive paralysis until his heart stops and he dies. We must pray that I am wrong.'

'But there has to be an antidote. Can't you purge my brother again?' Uther was desperate and angry in his appeal, and Llanwith tensed unconsciously. Myrddion seemed unmoved.

'There is no antidote – only time and the body's strength. If enough poison has been given, death always results.'

Uther closed his eyes and tried to regain his self-control. Myrddion's words were a death knell, but he still clutched at the one constant in this tragedy. 'How did Pascent do it? I understand the bit about the cow, but he never touched Ambrosius's cup or plate once food or drink was placed in them.'

'I'm not sure yet. As far as I can see, he was acting as circumstances permitted. So many things could have gone wrong for him. A cow cropping meadow saffron doesn't mean that the milk is unsafe immediately. The beast has to digest the poison before it is effective. From what I remember, the toxins won't hurt the animal, but they can kill its calf if it is very young. Pascent would seem to have gambled in every way, so hatred has to motivate him far more than

I can read from his facial expressions. He's never shown an obvious flicker of dislike towards your brother.'

'I don't understand anything you're trying to explain,' Uther replied, his frustration obvious in both voice and body. 'You're saying that a cow's milk can be poisoned because it eats a flower? Who could ever believe that?'

'For the moment, Uther, you must keep Pascent under close watch – and you mustn't execute him out of hand. We need his confession, or the union of kings will believe any number of rumours if Ambrosius should happen to die. What we must ensure is that we avoid talk that you have murdered your own brother to steal his throne. It would be disastrous for you, especially if Pascent is killed out of hand without direct evidence of his guilt. But one detail is quite clear.'

Pale with anger, his jaw muscles rippling as he held his temper in check, the prince rounded on Myrddion. 'And what might that be, healer?'

'Pascent seems to understand the land and its pitfalls. Of one thing I'm certain – peasants understand the dangers of meadow saffron, but noblemen have little or no knowledge of flora and fauna.'

Then Myrddion left the tent to return to his patient. As the sun rose on a chilly autumn morning complete with the first gentle mists of the seasons, the healer was concerned to discover that Ambrosius had weakened further. He complained that his legs refused to move and that his hands couldn't clench when he tried to make them. Although pain still periodically racked his belly, the king's mind remained very clear.

'I'll not live, Myrddion, will I?' Ambrosius whispered. 'Don't bother with kind lies, because the body knows its own fate and I can feel the paralysis rising towards my heart. I'm not frightened to die, but I have so much left that I want to do. I should have been more assiduous in my father's faith. Then, perhaps, I'd not fear the end of things so keenly. But my mother worshipped the old Roman gods and so I've hovered between Christianity and the old worship all my life.'

The High King was in a mood to talk, so Myrddion waited with his tincture of poppy until he tired.

'You need only ask and Botha will ride to fetch a priest from the monastery at Glastonbury. We are so close to the community that he can be back by noon.'

A look of yearning sweetened Ambrosius's face. 'Aye, I'd like that. Whether it's the Christian God, or Bran, or Zeus, or the gods of the Saxons who intend to rule our world, it would please me to be shriven as I was when I was a boy and my father still lived.'

Myrddion nodded at Botha, who left the tent without a word.

'I should like to know why I'm dying. It's a very odd feeling to experience the onset of death while my mind is still so clear. I cannot understand who hated me enough to kill me, my Myrddion. I can tell by your expression that you know, or suspect, but you don't wish to wound me. Would you have me draw my last breath while still wondering?'

Myrddion stared at his long, sensitive fingers and wished he could find a comforting lie, but Ambrosius had already ordered him to be honest with him, now that his time was limited.

'You know who did this deed, Myrddion. I can tell.'

'Aye, lord. I know who poisoned you, but I cannot fathom the reason or the method. Only Pascent can answer your questions.'

At first, Ambrosius's face was thunderstruck, but his expression gradually changed to a deep and bitter disappointment. He tried to pull himself up on to a pile of cushions and Ulfin hurried to assist him.

'I trusted him and held him close when Uther urged me to exercise caution . . . or order his execution. You tried to warn me, as well. But why would Pascent want me dead? Consider it one of the last wishes of a dying man, but I want to face my murderer so that I can cross the River Styx, or go to the Otherworld, or to Paradise, understanding the reason for my death.'

Ambrosius paused, panting after such a long, impassioned speech, and Myrddion feared for his heart. 'Bring him to me, Myrddion,' he gasped. Then the king grinned with his old, reckless charm that meant he was acting without reflection. 'I can see by your face that you wish me to die peacefully and without further burdens on my spirit. Perhaps you are right and a wiser man would listen, but I have tried to be reasonable for all of my adult life . . . and yet I have come to a violent end. You will do as I order, for I will be quite safe with Ulfin to guard me.'

Unwilling and saddened, Myrddion walked to the tent where Pascent had been quartered with one of Uther's trusted officers. Warriors guarded the tent flap, and within, another hardbitten, laconic soldier watched the young man with a sharp eye.

'He can't be left alone,' the soldier said conversationally, when Myrddion entered. 'Prince Uther has ordered me to guard him from *all* harm, including you, healer.'

'Do you believe I plan to set him free? Or slit his throat? The High King lives and demands the presence of his poisoner. Will you disobey Ambrosius Imperator?'

'As long as he's guarded and safe, I'll take him wherever the High King desires – straight to Hades for preference.'

'Then bring him with sufficient guard to ensure he cannot run. I want his hands bound, for I'm offended that a common felon should stand freely like a man before the master of us all.'

'So the woman-killer isn't dead yet,' Pascent whispered softly, but with venom. 'Never place your trust in poisons. I'd have used a blade, except the Roman was too cowardly and far too careful to come within my reach.'

'No, you feared to die, Pascent, so you'd rather kill in secret and protect your own skin. Gag him,' Myrddion ordered contemptuously. 'His voice turns my stomach.'

'With pleasure,' the soldier responded, and was none too gentle as he rammed a wad of cloth in the young man's mouth and bound his wrists behind his back.

'Bring him with you, and send one of your warriors to tell the prince where Pascent is being taken. Tell Uther he is being moved on the High King's orders.'

Roughly, Pascent was escorted to Ambrosius's tent. Uther and Llanwith appeared within moments, and the prince insisted that three men remain to guard the captive, who was now sporting a swelling over one eye from a heavy kick after he had slipped and fallen.

'Ah, Pascent,' Ambrosius began sadly, and then he saw the venom in the young man's blue eyes. Abruptly, he turned to Uther. 'Remove his gag so he can tell me why I am so loathed.'

With his own hands, Uther dragged the plug of cloth from Pascent's mouth, narrowly avoiding being bitten in the process. The prince merely laughed at Pascent's obvious hatred. 'Like all dogs, this creature has sharp teeth, brother, and the same understanding of honour as a mongrel hound.'

'How dare either of you censure *me* or lecture *me* about honour? You have none! You are cowardly Romans . . . the last branches from a rotten tree, and the sooner you are both dead, the cleaner the air of Britain will be.'

Ambrosius was genuinely puzzled. 'I don't understand, Pascent. You've tried to kill me on two occasions, and I have no notion why you should do so. Yet I can only suppose you allowed yourself to be captured by Saxons purely to place yourself close to me.'

'The Vessel of Thor was happy to oblige me at Verulamium, although he never believed you could defeat him. Gods, but I tried to explain to the fool that you have Loki's own luck, and would see him worm-food before the day was out. The Saxons still don't understand their enemy. I knew that I had only to wait, protected by my bruises, and I would win back the honour that I once had. And you believed everything I told you because I knew how to act like a lordling.'

'I was never convinced, you nameless dog,' Uther snapped, and slapped Pascent with a stinging blow across the mouth. 'I'll not use the alias that you took as your own, for I always knew you to be a cuckoo in the nest.'

The blow was not overly heavy, but the young man's lip split, and he spat a gobbet of blood on to the cloth-covered floor. Then he smiled insolently at Uther with his bleeding mouth, but didn't deign to answer him. Instead, he turned to face Myrddion with an air of reckless arrogance that entirely changed his countenance.

'I suffered a moment of doubt when you turned up, healer. I was sure that you'd remember me, but my appearance must have changed in the eight years since we last met.' Pascent grinned unpleasantly, displaying such triumph that Myrddion longed to emulate Uther and slap the young man's handsome face. 'I suppose I was little more than a boy at the time, so I bear you no ill-will for your memory loss. Even though you were a danger to me, I was determined to leave you in peace. After all, it was you who made sure we survived the horrors of Dinas Emrys.'

'Shite!' Myrddion swore. 'I never saw it, fool that I am! You were fourteen, near fifteen, on that terrible night. Have I saved you so you can murder all our hopes? Are you so Saxon that you would destroy half your birthright?'

Uther strode forward and shook Myrddion bodily. The healer's eyes were filled with tears, as once again he saw the long road that led from one generous action to a terrible outcome. Although

Uther shook him until his teeth rattled, Myrddion was lost in the terrible machinations of fate.

A sharp slap bought the healer back to himself. Uther's hand had left a red imprint across Myrddion's pale face. 'Who *is* he?' Uther demanded.

'I have never given a damn about the wars between the Saxons and the Celts,' the captive snarled, his face twisted into an ugly rictus of hate. 'I am a little portion of both, so how can I go to war against myself? The only person I ever truly cared about was my mother.'

Myrddion laughed hysterically, and Pascent bowed awkwardly in the healer's direction, given that his hands were bound. 'And now you can kill me, for I've done what I swore to do in the years before I became a man.'

'Of course you have,' Myrddion replied shrilly. 'How could your honour not insist that you carry out a crime such as this?' He turned back to Ambrosius, and his eyes were terrible with a dark knowledge.

'My lord Ambrosius, High King of the west, this young man is Vengis, the eldest son of Vortigern and Rowena, a Saxon woman, who both perished at Dinas Emrys. He has come seeking blood price for the poisoning of his mother.'

CHAPTER XIII

THE KING OF WINTER

We owe respect to the living; to the dead we owe nothing but truth.

Voltaire, *Lettres sur Oedipe*

The oil lamps flickered in the darkening tent. Storm clouds were gathering, and a mist of rain obscured the sun. As he lay on his soft woollen pillows, Ambrosius's face was so pale that he already looked like a corpse with his blued lips and haggard face, while the lamplight bleached the gold of his hair to the colour of pale ash. The light cast upwards from the lamp closest to him was reflected in his bloodshot eyes, so that Myrddion could fancy that his master was a reincarnation of Charon, calling for the lost souls he would carry to the Underworld on his time-warped, split and weathered ferry boat.

Uther's face was obscured by shadow. As if seeking the solace of darkness, he had stepped backward when Myrddion had introduced Vengis, so that his body alone expressed the powerful emotions that caused his huge hands to clench and unclench as he sought for something he could rend and pound into the dust.

At the centre of the lamplight, his chin streaked with blood, Vengis talked and talked. Having hidden behind an affable mask of innocence for long, wearisome months, the young man relished the opportunity to justify his crime, to glory in his vengeance and to boast, like a common felon, about how clever he had been. Guilty and shocked, Myrddion had no choice but to listen.

'You'll kill me, or your brother will, once you have taken your last vile breath,' Vengis stated proudly at Ambrosius's recumbent form. 'I have no illusions that my death will be either quick or painless. I could have eaten the pretty flowers in my cap if I had wished to escape the so-called justice of your court, but only a coward tries to escape the outcome that has been hungered for during year after lonely year of exile, as I wandered in the cold north with neither kinfolk nor friends to offer shelter. There is nothing you can do to me that could be as terrible as the years that have passed since the death of my mother at Dinas Emrys.'

'How did you poison me? I know about the salt, but I doubt that you've had any experience as a secret murderer, which probably explains why you botched your first attempt. My brother and my healer took every precaution possible during the journey to Glastonbury.'

Vengis glanced at Myrddion, who returned his gaze and nodded in understanding.

'You've figured it out, Demon Seed, haven't you? My father used to call you the Black Raven of Cymru, and often said that you were the worthy son of a devil sire. But I never believed him because you tried hard to save my mother's life. Still, I've cursed you often enough on this journey as you blocked my plans at every turn. Loki was laughing in Udgaad and did not see fit to smile upon me until two days ago, at a time when I was almost mad with despair. When I saw the cow in the meadow, the beast was cropping meadow saffron. I couldn't believe my luck. Of course, I didn't know whether the beast had been feeding on the plant for hours or days, so I took a few of the flower stems and placed them in my cap, just in case the cow's milk wasn't toxic. Uther had no idea what it was, even when he joked that I wore flowers in my cap like a girl. I almost laughed aloud at the dolt, and had to pretend that he had hurt my feelings. It's easy to see that Prince Uther has never had to work at menial tasks like a beggar, just to prove his loyalty. My brother Katigern and I had to slave for the thane who took us in, for no amount of royal blood compensated for being born the sons of an animal like Vortigern. But the thane did me a favour, as it turned out, for I learned to keep his fine milking cows away from clumps of meadow saffron.'

Vengis paused for a moment as his tongue explored a loosened tooth.

'Even so, only infants die of the small amounts of poison that are ingested in the milk of a cow.' Uther's voice grated like the sound of a whetstone dragged down a pitted blade. 'At least, that's what the healer says.'

'Myrddion is correct ... as always. But you were all so busy protecting the food the woman-killer ate that no one ever thought to check the cup. You poured the water yourself, Demon Seed. You gave me the means to kill your master and helped me to break the accord of the united kings.' Vengis giggled childishly, and Myrddion's blood ran cold.

'You took some of the stems and the leaves and pulverised them in water,' Myrddion interrupted. 'Then you steeped the meadow saffron for as long as you could. Am I correct?'

Vengis nodded.

'You used an old cup as a container and you'd have tossed it away later, when you eventually found the opportunity. You soaked the liquid up in a scrap of wool or very fine cloth and then put it in your jerkin. You took a great personal risk, Vengis.'

'There was no risk to me. I only had to wait and act as I always did. I brought you the king's cup and plate, as was my duty. How easy to wipe them clean and then squeeze the fluid, just a little, into the bottom of the goblet. Neither of you looked. For all your caution, Myrddion Merlinus, you never checked the cup, although you took it from me and filled it with water. The Gates of Hades were already opening for the High King, and you were still waiting for someone – me – to tamper with the food.'

'Idiot!' Uther hissed in Myrddion's direction.

'But I gave you the plate, Uther pen nobody. As always, you were ignorant of anything that didn't involve brute force. A dragon? You? Where was your fabled ability to smell a Saxon, or half of one, anyway? I'd carefully wiped the plate over with my cloth, so it would have seemed very clean. You didn't even notice what I was doing, and just ordered me away from Ambrosius while he ate off the poisoned plate. Too late! Too late!'

Vengis laughed again and the sound wasn't quite sane. Myrddion wondered how long the poison of vengeance took to madden even the strongest of men ... and Vengis was strong with his father's venom.

'So do what you wish with me, for I don't care. If Ambrosius dies, any pain will be worth it. If he lives, my brother will hunt him down once he has risen to the position of thane.'

'But I didn't order the death of Rowena,' Ambrosius whispered, his face genuinely pained. 'Why did you believe I'd do such a thing?'

Vengis's eyes opened very wide, as if such a possibility had never occurred to him. Since boyhood, he had nurtured a rumour in his heart, and now to be told it wasn't true was more than he could accept.

'You're lying. My father swore that you had ordered her murder,' he snarled, his face twisting like that of a child hovering on the point of tears. 'The servant woman exposed the plot, and she named the traitorous Silure nobleman who was in your pay.'

Myrddion felt sick. He remembered poor Willow, hanging in the executioner's hands, her neck broken and her body streaked with blood. She would have said anything to satisfy her terrible master, Vortigern, and feed his prejudices to the end. She may even have believed it, for Vortigern had never doubted that Ambrosius was his enemy.

'So you have decided that the violence will never end, Vengis, as more and more blood price will be demanded until men forget that we ever existed? Must we kill and bleed by turn until the end of time?'

'Take him away and make very, very sure the bastard is kept safe and well,' Uther ordered, and the young man was dragged away.

In the silence that followed, Ambrosius searched his brother's face with a sad, defeated understanding. 'Did you order the death of Queen Rowena, Uther?' he asked quietly, one hand outstretched towards his brother, who fell to his knees at the sufferer's bedside. Uther took the proffered palm and kissed it, while Myrddion felt a wave of shame that he should witness such a private moment.

'Yes, brother, I did. And in doing so, I've caused your death. The Saxon bitch killed Vortimer, who was your ally and our half-brother. While he was a weak man, he was our creature and our blood, so the woman could not be permitted to go unpunished for her crime. I knew you would forbid me to order her assassination, so I didn't tell you. Her death exposed and maddened Vortigern, as I hoped it would, but I never thought that her sons would live to avenge her. To be honest, I never considered them at all.'

'What did you think her sons would do?' Ambrosius whispered with exasperation. 'Welcome their freedom from their parents? Stay at Dinas Emrys to be murdered by Vortigern's enemies?'

From the shadows, Myrddion realised that Uther could hardly speak for weeping. His shoulders heaved over his bowed head, which was buried in the pillows beside the High King's. Ambrosius raised his hand with difficulty and stroked his brother's wildly curling hair.

'Don't weep for what is done, Uther. Please, no guilt or shame should attach to you, for the goddess Fortuna has decided that the skein of my life must be shortened. Simply promise, in reparation, that you will obey my instructions in the scroll I have given to Botha. I will hold you to it from beyond the grave.'

Touched by Ambrosius's greatness of heart and sickened by the cosmic joke that the gods had played on them all, Myrddion left the tent to await the return of Botha with a priest. He prayed that they would be quick.

A dark noon had given way to a stormy afternoon when two tired horses splashed their way into the camp in the teeth of driving rain. Scorning the violence of the elements, Botha wore his usual serviceable cloak, while his plaits streamed behind him in the wild, wind-torn air as he dragged his exhausted horse to a halt. By comparison, the cowled figure who sat astride a smaller horse was a compact figure muffled against the storm. As Myrddion raised a hand to assist the man to dismount, he was surprised to feel hard muscle through the coarse homespun of cloak and robe. A square, muscular hand with beautiful fingers gripped Myrddion's forearm.

'Thank you, my son. May the Lord protect us poor sinners during this sad time. Does the High King still live?'

'Aye, lord. But he is failing, and I have neither the knowledge nor the potions to save him. I can only ease his pain.'

'I am no lord, young man, only a humble priest of the high God.' The priest's hand, unadorned but for a worn thumb ring of orange gold, raised the cowl to reveal a face so Roman and so pure in its features that Myrddion could almost smell the scent of oranges and taste the light patina of dust raised by thousands of hurrying feet in the subura. Once again, he remembered the sun that had warmed him to the bone when he had served the sick and dying among the Seven Hills of Rome.

A pair of warm brown eyes looked through Myrddion, and the healer fancied that the priest saw every weakness and sin that marked his soul. The man had shaved his head in the Aryan tonsure but his remaining hair, cut militarily short, was raven black and frosted with grey. Feeling unsettled and superstitious, a condition he found disconcerting, the healer led the way into the tent of the High King, where Uther still crouched on the floor beside his brother. Myrddion turned away so he would not shame the prince by seeing his soundless tears.

'I have come, my lord, to give you the consolation of our Master who promises you rest after all your struggles.'

Uther looked up, having dragged one forearm over his streaming face so he could examine the priest with dry eyes. Carefully, the Roman removed his sopping cloak to reveal a satchel, much like Myrddion's own, slung over one shoulder. From it the priest took out a narrow length of fine cloth decorated with gilt, which he kissed reverently before placing it around his damp shoulders. Then he retrieved a small vial of oil and a golden cross rich with coloured cabochon gems that danced in the lamplight.

For the first time, Myrddion saw and heard the ritual of Extreme Unction, as Ambrosius bared his soul in confession in a faltering, thready voice. He would have left the tent, but Ambrosius became so distressed that Uther ordered him to remain. Like a long, slow wave of music, the Latin ritual lifted the gloom that hovered over the bed and the dying man who lay so still upon it, transfiguring the leather tent into a place of light and hope. Myrddion was almost swept away by the beauty of the prayers for Ambrosius's soul, spoken in a Latin so pure that the healer wondered what gens had fathered such an extraordinary man.

'You may sleep now, lord king, in the knowledge that my Master, Jesus of Nazareth, will take your hand and lead you into the presence of God. All your trials are over and you can, at last, rest in joy and peace.'

'What is your name, priest?' Uther asked with uncharacteristic humility.

'I am Lucius, father of the flock of Glastonbury and a poor penitent.'

'You are Roman,' Ambrosius whispered, each word dragged out of him by the fierce will that forced his heart to beat.

'I *was* Roman, but now I am nothing but the instrument of my God,' Lucius replied, and stepped back from the king's bed.

'You must swear to obey my . . . wishes in the scrolls, Uther.'

'I swear . . . but you don't have to leave me. Fight to live! Don't give up! We have always been together, brother, so what use is a crown to me if you are dead?'

'Hush, Uther. All my hopes are in your hands now and you must do what has to be done.' Ambrosius slowly turned his gaze towards his healer, narrowing his eyes in the failing light. 'Myrddion Merlinus? I hold you to your oath . . . and beg that you care for Andrewina Ruadh. I ask also that you remember me when the kings meet at Deva . . . I swear, that day was . . .'

Then the king's breath stopped. His chest laboured to expand and contract as his eyes rolled backward in his head and his body stiffened. Then, as Lucius moved forward and stroked the waxen forehead, the body of the High King slowly relaxed, took another breath . . . then another . . . and, suddenly, the tent was utterly silent.

Myrddion turned away so he would not dishonour his king by weeping. Lucius placed one comforting hand upon his slumped shoulder and ushered him out of the quiet tent, now empty of the personality that had saved a kingdom.

In the icy, driving rain, the healer turned his face up to the black sky and wept unashamedly. No moon could pierce the heavy cloud cover, and Myrddion wondered if the sun would ever shine again. The sun king had ruled in the summer of their hopes, and as the cold winds had come after his great triumph at Deva his spirit had been stolen away.

'What will we do without him?' Myrddion spoke softly to the priest. 'We are lost, and the isles of Britain will surely fall to the Saxons in time. Ambrosius was the best Roman I ever knew and he loved this land with his whole heart.'

Beside him, Lucius of Glastonbury stood like a bulwark against the gusting wind. His robe was plastered against his body, revealing a physique that had been shaped by hard, unrelenting work. When he spoke, his voice rose over the persistent howling of the storm.

'But Ambrosius was also a Briton. He was born here, and he dreamed throughout his long exile of his desire to return. What else matters? Your friend is at rest now, Myrddion Merlinus. If you choose to weep, then do so for yourself, for I fear the days ahead will be harsh for men of goodwill.' He dropped his voice so that only the healer could hear him. 'The king of winter has come.'

Uther was inconsolable. With a strong man's pride, he refused to weep in public, but Myrddion had heard the muffled sound of heart-wrenching misery coming from the High King's tent. The young healer had no difficulty imagining Uther pressing his tear-stained face into his brother chest's as the corpse, draped in a pure linen shroud by Botha's blunt, clever fingers, was laid out on the king's camp bed.

What could Myrddion do? In the back of his mind, Ambrosius's voice seemed to whisper, 'Help him. He is desolate, and who can know what he will do to ease the agony of guilt that devours his heart?'

Had the prince read the scroll penned by Ambrosius's own hand? Dare he intrude on the mourning of such an unpredictable man?

'Who lives for ever, anyway?' Myrddion whispered aloud, and thrust his way into the tent where the corpse of Ambrosius lay, waiting for the fire that would devour his mortal remains.

'Please accept my condolences for your loss, my lord. Ambrosius Imperator was the best of men, my heart's master and a ruler who was both just and kind. My craft betrayed me, for I couldn't find any way to save his life. I beg your forgiveness, my lord.'

Uther was sitting on a low stool with his back to the tent flap. His body offered no clue to his responsiveness to Myrddion's words. Then, just as the healer turned to go, the new king rose to his full, impressive height, and rounded on the younger man.

Uther's face was hollow with grief and as expressionless as a marble effigy. Except for his narrowed lips and puffy eyes, few men would realise that this prince of the realm was ravaged by his only selfless emotion, his devotion to his brother.

'Ambrosius has forced me to accept you as my chief adviser, so give me the benefit of your wisdom, healer.' Every word dripped with sarcasm and Myrddion knew that he stood on a tightrope above a bottomless chasm. One wrong step and Uther's reddened eyes promised a bloody explosion of ungovernable rage, oath or no oath.

'Ambrosius, my dear master, must go to the fire in a place fitting for a ruler who was both wise and devoted to his people. The kings must be called to an appointed place where his funeral pyre will be remembered throughout the ages.'

Safe ground!

Uther turned his bloody thoughts away from retribution and

impotent pain to the task of giving honour to his beloved brother. 'Where do you suggest? I'm loath to desecrate my brother's peace by transporting his mortal remains to Venta Belgarum, although I will have to be crowned in its church, as custom dictates. Where else can my brother be honoured?'

Myrddion thought furiously. Glastonbury was too Christian to be chosen. According to Llanwith, the church was tiny and very dilapidated, not a fitting monument to Ambrosius's glory, at least in Uther's eyes. Besides, the kings who followed the old religion and those chieftains from the Roman settlements would be offended by any preference given to the Christian God.

'The Giant's Carol, my king. That ancient, mighty circle of stones is an appropriate place to send the spirit of Ambrosius soaring into the sun. The purpose of the Dance has been lost in the mists of time, but the land is flat, so the pyre will be visible for many, many leagues. I have been there and have felt the power of its great age. My master will be honoured in a fitting manner, and the tribal kings will never forget Ambrosius Imperator.'

'The Dance? You would build his funeral pyre at the Dance?' Myrddion began to fear that Uther was offended, for the new king began to pace distractedly back and forth across the floor of the tent. 'There's very little wood on the plain and my brother must have a pyre of unsurpassed size and magnificence.'

'You are the heir, Lord Uther. I propose that the warriors, the peasants and the tribal kings who share the boundaries of their kingdoms with the Giant's Carol should gather the wood needed to honour their martyred king. You have the power to ask this boon of them but, lord, I would suggest that you don't demand it of them. Leave the kings with no choice other than to show their sorrow in a practical fashion. If you are subtle, your request can be used as a test of loyalty to the throne.'

'I'm a plain-spoken man, Merlinus, and I lack the patience to pander to the egos of those squabbling fools. If the tribal kings argue, I will teach them to be more respectful in future. My brother will be sent to the Otherworld with all the dignity and ceremony that can be arranged at short notice. That is *your* skill, Merlinus. You will do for Ambrosius's cremation what you achieved for him at Deva, and I'll not complain at the cost.'

Myrddion was in an invidious situation. If he refused to play his part in the plan Uther had proposed, the new king would be enraged. His love for and loyalty to the memory of Ambrosius was also a factor, for he was as determined as Uther to ensure that men who spoke of the funeral of Ambrosius in years to come would do so in voices hushed with awe.

'Very well, I will honour my master with a ceremony that shall be remembered as long as Britons live in these isles. Should I write to the tribal kings and explain the murder of the High King, and order their presence at his cremation and the execution of his assassin? They should be invited to your coronation as well, my king, and there would be no harm in reminding them that nothing has changed as far as they are concerned. They will still be expected to honour the accord on pain of oath-breaking.'

Uther looked irritated for a moment, for he realised that the healer was manoeuvring him towards a tactful approach to the tribal kings when he longed to relieve his pent-up fury on any chieftain who dared to defy him. As he watched him, Myrddion could see awareness and chagrin written clearly on the saturnine face, but then Uther chuckled quietly to himself as he decided on the orders he would give his new counsellor.

'I keep forgetting that you're skilled in Latin, healer. You will word the message very clearly so that each of those nobodies realises that I'm holding him to account. Oh, you can dress it up as politely as you like – by all means. But make sure that there is an iron fist behind your fair and courteous words.'

Myrddion breathed a sigh of relief, but the respite was short-lived. Uther straightened his brother's chair and sat rigidly, his emotions under check and replaced by the coldness that Ambrosius had recognised.

'It's time for plain speaking between us, Myrddion Merlinus. Have you read the scroll, my brother's last gift to me?'

'No, my king, I have not. Such messages are private, but Lord Ambrosius made me vow to serve you and offered me the protection of his word if I should do so. I know nothing other than what he told me.'

Uther's expression remained unchanged. 'He asked me to keep you close at hand as my chief counsellor, because he thought that you were a man who could be trusted to keep your head in difficult situations. He insisted that your loyalties were completely with the Britons and that you'd never betray me. Was he correct?'

For a moment, Myrddion almost retorted that he'd hardly deny Ambrosius's faith in him, even if that trust was misplaced. Fortunately, prudence intervened.

'I am oath-bound to you, King Uther, for good or ill. Just like Botha, I take my vows seriously. Besides, I am committed to the saving of life, not the taking of it.'

'Naturally you'd agree, whatever your private thoughts might be. Don't colour up, healer. I know you're loyal, even though I have no liking for you. You're a storm crow if ever there was one, and if it were not for my promise to Ambrosius, I'd remove you. In truth, you're too damned clever and too resourceful to be a safe servant, but I also am oath-bound, just like you.'

Myrddion thought quickly and moved to Uther's seated figure, bowed deeply and then fell to his knees. 'Your candour does you credit, King Uther. Though my vow is already given, I offer it again in the full knowledge of what I do. I swear by my hope of redemption and on everything that I hold dear to devote myself to your interests and the interests of the Britons until death takes us.'

Then Myrddion abased himself for the first time in his life and placed Uther's foot upon the back of his neck, like a slave of no worth. A voice seemed to whisper approval in the back of his skull and he was reassured that this act of self-sacrifice was what the Mother required of him.

'Get up, healer. You've proved your point, and I'm convinced you are sincere. But should I suspect that you've broken faith with me, I'll have you killed. Do we understand each other?'

Myrddion rose smoothly to his feet and two spots of colour marked his pale cheeks. 'I too am the direct descendant of kings, my lord, and my oath is as strong as iron and as long as life.'

'Good. Then we'll manage to co-exist for Ambrosius's sake. But I am the High King, and though you may advise me I will make the decisions, not you. For now, I expect you to fulfil the duties you were carrying out at my brother's command. The spy network has already proved its usefulness, and the training of healers is also critical. After my brother ascends to the gods, and I have been formally crowned in Venta Belgarum, you and I are going to war. The Saxons will learn that Uther Pendragon will brook no incursions into his lands, nor allow settlers to devour his soil, acre by acre. I plan to create a corridor of scoured and burned earth from Portus Lemanis to the outskirts of Londinium. The Saxons will be persuaded to stay in the lands they presently occupy and will be suffered to encroach no further. This I swear over the body of my brother. Now, leave me to mourn him. We will begin the journey to the Giant's Carol on the morrow, so a fine wagon must be made sufficiently beautiful to bear his body. The common people will be encouraged to observe the passing of the High King.'

'May I suggest that Lord Ambrosius's body should lie in state to accentuate the great loss to the realm?'

'Do whatever honours the memory of Ambrosius, but be ready to depart from this cursed place tomorrow. And before I forget, Vengis will be chained to the wagon and he will walk behind the man he killed. He will go to his death with my brother. In the flames!'

Half a dozen cavalrymen were sent into the countryside to collect holly and mistletoe. Myrddion warned them to ensure that the latter was not permitted to touch the earth, for all herbalists knew that mistletoe lost its efficacy if it became earth-bound.

'Why use mistletoe?' Botha asked, as Myrddion relayed his orders.

'It was sacred to the Druids as the symbol of rebirth. It will not have its berries yet, the little white globes that men say bear the semen of the reborn king. But the people will understand the message and its meaning.'

Botha's heavy, clever face was illuminated with admiration. 'Aye, I had forgotten the old stories from my childhood. I will find carpenters to erect a plinth on which to lay my lord's body in a nest of mistletoe. The simple people will believe that Ambrosius Imperator will come again.'

'Alas, he'll not return, but your plans are good, Botha. A canopy must also be created to protect the corpse from this infernal rain. And then we'll deck the whole wagon with holly, ivy, lacy foliage and whatever flowers may be found. The king's body must be washed, his hair dressed and his flesh protected by his ceremonial armour. His sword must be placed in his hands, so that all men who see his corpse will remember the day the High King's cortège passed them by.'

Botha nodded, and Myrddion was confident that every detail would be carried out to his exacting standards. 'I will wash the king myself, healer. I have nothing else to give him but my labour.'

'I will also need sufficient riders to travel to the courts of the tribal kings with Uther's command to attend Ambrosius's funeral pyre at the Giant's Carol. They must ride day and night, pausing only to change horses, for the messages must reach the kings within four days. They will ride in pairs, and each rider will lead a spare horse to guard against accident to either rider or horse. We will pause at Glastonbury, where the High King will lie in state before travelling to the Giant's Carol. Then, in eight days, his body will be consigned to the flames. Be sure that the couriers have good memories, for every word must be exact.'

Once again, Botha nodded, and Myrddion was comforted by the warrior's calm strength.

'Do you require anything else, my lord?'

'Aye, Botha, but don't give me titles that are undeserved. I will need Ulfin and two other men to ride to the Carol and begin the building of a huge pyre in the centre of the stones. They will demand wood from the Dumnonii, the Belgae and the Durotriges, and they may cut down whole forests for all I care.'

Myrddion's voice was harsher than usual, for he had so many tasks to complete that his head was spinning. He had scarcely slept for three days and the strain was beginning to fray his nerves.

'I'll go with Ulfin to keep his concentration where it belongs – on the building of the pyre,' Llanwith rumbled from behind the healer.

'Shite, Llanwith, you're too quiet on your feet for such a big man. You startled me.'

Llanwith chuckled. 'Ulfin responds well to orders, but the villagers who live around the Carol will take more notice of a prince of the Ordovice than of a mere warrior. Besides, it's obvious to me that you need some assistance. Our new king is placing too much on your shoulders.'

Botha strode away, obviously determined to hear nothing about his master that would force him to take offence. Myrddion watched his broad, retreating back with genuine respect. 'Botha's an extraordinary man,' he said. 'He conjures up whatever I need.'

'He is a different prospect from his master, may the gods be praised,' Llanwith added irreverently. 'Uther overloads you in the hope that you'll fail.'

Myrddion sighed. Llanwith was almost certainly correct, and the healer could imagine years of labour stretching out before him as he juggled the twin tasks of obeying his king and fulfilling his oath of fealty.

'May the gods help me, but Lucius was right. The years ahead will be difficult.'

Eight days later, when those kings whose lands were close enough to enable them to attend the cremation had ridden the doleful miles to the Giant's Carol, Ambrosius Imperator was given to the cleansing flames. The weather had worsened in the intervening week and autumn was gripping the land with unseasonal chills, driving rain and grey skies. The farmers could not harvest their crops easily, for the mud was choking the furrows and the fruit seemed likely to rot on the trees. The peasants crossed themselves or gripped their amulets, and prayed that the spirit of the dead king would be sent on his way with honour so that the land would not be blighted by his restless spirit.

On the road to the Carol, men and women, cherry-cheeked in the chill wind, brought offerings of grain, fruit and vegetables to Uther in order to quieten the soul of his murdered brother. Kneeling on the muddy road and oblivious of the staining of their homespun, the villagers offered up prayers and songs in sorrowing wails, so that the journey from Glastonbury became a long tapestry of weeping faces and frightened eyes. Myrddion huddled in his black cloak and absorbed the sorrow and the superstition of the people of the south.

Lucius had led the prayers at Glastonbury, and although Uther was initially contemptuous of the old timber church that seemed to lean inward with the passage of untold years, Lucius explained that it was believed to have been built by Joseph of Arimathea, or the Trader, who had known the blessed son of God. Mollified, Uther permitted his brother's body to be laid on the altar, while tenor and baritone voices intoned hymns of praise and consolation that spiralled upward towards the menacing tor and the old tower that pointed like God's finger towards the faded sun.

Myrddion had climbed the tor and viewed the seven encircling lines of earthworks that traced its flanks. 'The Virgin's Teat,' he whispered, and felt the fingers of the Mother stir the hairs at the base of his skull. 'It's old . . . so old that the tower is relatively new. Men and women have worshipped here as long as they have walked the earth.'

Feeling the poetry and power of stone and tree, water and earth, Myrddion was filled with a strange, inexplicable peace. From the tor, he could see another, lower hill that had been crowned by a single tree that had been twisted by the wind so that it resembled a gnarled hand. Turning to his right, he was confronted by a low, green valley in which the church, the farms of the abbey, the blacksmith's forge and the farmers' pastures nestled within a network of waterways. To the north of the tor, he could see the entry to the valley through which pilgrims made their way to this sacred place, while to the east the Roman road carved a clean, straight line through the landscape. Off in the distance, and many miles away, he could just make out a glimpse of a tumulus or another tor.

Something caught in his throat like an echo of passion or a memory of pain. Swiftly, he dragged his eyes away from the blue-grey distance, intoned a prayer to the Mother, and departed.

And now, stern of face and stiff in the saddle, or marching with the pride of fighting men, Ambrosius's cortège and his warriors came at last to the great plain that dwarfed the massive stones in its windswept vastness.

Some vestigial, tribal memory caused Uther to order that camp should be made outside the huge circular mound that surrounded the circles of standing stones and trilithons. Careless of the labour that his warriors must undertake at the end of a long, cold day, he strode through the gap in the mound, calling for Myrddion to accompany him.

'I perceive your purpose in choosing this place,' he said approvingly as they strode past a single stone buried in the earth at a slant, pointing towards the circles and the growing tower of wood at their very heart. 'The flames will be seen to the seas in one direction and to the mountains in the other. If Ambrosius and Lucius are right, then my brother himself will see his funeral pyre from Paradise. Your choice pleases me.'

'Thank you, my lord. I wished to honour my master with as much ceremony as I could.'

Uther turned back and grinned wolfishly at his healer. 'Let's hope that Ulfin and the Ordovice prince are building a pyre that is worthy of the monument.'

Myrddion's brows contracted for a moment at Uther's casual insult to Llanwith by naming Ulfin, a simple warrior, before the prince. Unfortunately, Uther would never recognise his insults for what they were. The new king would always be careless of the feelings of others and now, as his thirty-eighth year approached, he would never change.

They strode past the chalk circles cut into the emerald green sod, shocking in their pristine white contrast. They moved through the small bluestone circle where the stones were the size of a small man and entered the last great circle. The grey sky spun dizzily as Myrddion turned to take in the whole magnificence of the Giant's Carol.

The stone uprights were roughly chopped out of living rock, and were three times the height of a man. Atop these vast irregular monoliths rested precariously laid, flatter stones that, if they could be seen from above, formed a huge circle. Myrddion's brain struggled to fathom how these gigantic blocks of rock could have been levered into position by human hands.

'How did they build this structure?' Uther asked, his voice hushed with awe. 'How could these stones have been caused to fly into position?'

'Legend tells us that Myrddion, the Lord of Light for whom I am named, set these stones in place at the beginning of recorded time. I cannot say how the circle was built, Lord Uther, for only a god could lift their vast weight. The legends also tell us that they were moved here from a spot many leagues away in the mountains of Cymru.'

Within the circle, even larger groups of uprights capped with other cyclopean stones formed a rough horseshoe. Here lay a large, almost flat monolith that looked like an altar that had been cast down by a giant. Around the altar, the circle danced and spun.

Off centre, a tower of wood rose high above the massive trilithons and dwarfed even their huge, grey mass. Using horses, ropes, levers and the cracking muscles of warriors and peasants, whole logs were being raised towards the heavens. Llanwith balanced himself precariously and shouted instructions as another log cut roughly to size was hauled up, spinning crazily, by the use of a framework of timber and ropes. Other sturdy men stood with Llanwith as they waited to manoeuvre each log into position.

King and healer watched the process, which seemed simple from below yet was fraught with danger above. Once Llanwith was satisfied that the log was in place, he shouted at Ulfin to take his place and climbed gingerly down the tall pyre to bow deeply to the new king.

'Is the pyre almost finished, Llanwith?' Uther demanded, squinting as the sun burned into his eyes from just above the horizon.

'There's one more log to place in a locking position. That will secure the whole construction and the platform can be winched up to the very top of the pyre,' Llanwith replied, wiping his streaming forehead with his arm. 'The work's gone well for such a massive pyre, although five men have been killed and a score have been injured. We could have used your expertise if you had been here when the accidents happened, Myrddion, for we had no idea how to treat crush injuries.'

Myrddion would have hurried off to treat the poor souls who had been injured had Llanwith not detained him. 'The wounded and the dead have been sent back to their families. No stain of blood or pain should be permitted to mar the pyre of King Ambrosius.'

For the next two days, while the tribal kings gathered, Myrddion concentrated on preparing for the rite of cremation, including shrouding the corpse in the finest cloth that Uther possessed. This task was unpleasant, for Ambrosius had been dead for many days, and although the weather was not warm the body was waxen, livid and very unlike the living, breathing Ambrosius. Myrddion used precious oils which Uther had received as a funeral gift from Gorlois to sweeten the cadaver and drive away the worst of the distinctive reek of corrupted flesh.

The days had shortened with the approach of winter, and Uther decreed that the ceremony should be conducted just before nightfall. Those kings in attendance would be invited to attend Uther's coronation as his guests, as he could offer no hospitality at the Giant's Carol. Myrddion admired the decision, reinforcing as it did the perception that the new king was smoothly assuming his brother's throne.

Most of the kings came, except for those beyond the wall who had sent couriers to express their shock and sympathy at the murder of Ambrosius Imperator and make excuses for their non-attendance.

'Words are cheap,' Uther said curtly. 'Provide me with a list of those kings who are not present. I will be particularly diligent in ensuring that their tributes are paid on time.'

A fitful sun broke through the thick cloud cover as the kings, their retinues and an unusually large number of common citizens and peasants gathered at the great monument. The stiff wind that had howled across the great plain all day had finally dropped, which the kings took as a sign of the gods' approval. Ambrosius's body had been placed atop the great tower of wood, which had been drenched with oil on the lower tiers to ensure that the wood would burn fiercely. The kings had tokens of their fealty such as precious oils, sheaves of grain, garlands of flowers and boughs of fruit trees with the mature fruit still on them, and these were placed between the logs along with the villagers' gifts.

The crowd was hushed, and Myrddion mounted the altar stone so all those present could see and hear him.

'Hail, lords of the west. My master, Prince Uther, who will be crowned before you at Venta Belgarum, wishes you to attest to his judgment of the murderer of Ambrosius Imperator. Hail, Uther, lord of the west.'

Recognising their cue, Uther's guard roared out, 'Hail, Uther, lord of the west!' a salutation which the kings were forced to follow.

Uther had dressed with care. Over his usual snowy tunic and purple-edged cloak, he had flung a wolf pelt that added a violent edge to his conservative dress. Unlike his brother, who had shunned decoration, Uther wore arm-rings of gold, several rings on his fingers, a golden band across his forehead indicating his status and a huge round pin to hold the wolf pelt in place. The heavy gems, the fur, his exuberant hair and his great height suggested barbaric magnificence with a warning of menace.

'King of the Britons,' Uther Pendragon roared. 'Behold the man who slew our high king – not face to face like a warrior, but like a thief in the night – with poison. His name is Vengis and he is the eldest son of the Regicide, Vortigern, and his Saxon woman. This creature has betrayed his birth and served the interests of our enemies. He confessed his vile crimes against us to Ambrosius himself, in our presence, before the High King died. The men who will now stand before you heard that confession. Stand forth!'

Myrddion, Llanwith and the three warriors who had been guarding the assassin stepped forward and swore to the truth of Uther's assertions. Then Myrddion told the assembly that he had recognised Vengis at the very last, and described the night of Vortigern's death and his sons' flight into the Saxon camps. The crowd growled sullenly.

'I demand death for this traitor who preyed upon the generosity of Ambrosius, and then struck at the heart of the man who loved him,' Uther howled. His repressed rage poured forth like hot ash and the kings trembled at his passion. 'I demand your permission to burn him with his victim.'

Vengis was dragged forward.

His face was bleeding, as were his feet from the cruel stones of the road, and his mouth leaked a trail of blood. Uther had ordered that the murderer's tongue be cut out so that the reasons for his crime could not be spoken. The killer was making a valiant attempt to be brave, but no man can face the pain of burning with equanimity.

'Aye,' Gorlois of Cornwall shouted, remembering the wisdom and generosity displayed by Ambrosius.

'Aye,' shouted the kings, one by one, and the young man's bladder voided in terror.

At a nod from Uther, Vengis was dragged halfway up the pyre and bound to the logs with his arms and legs spread wide. Myrddion followed and pretended to test the bonds while he held grimly to the log structure with one arm, trying not to think about the long fall to the hard earth if his grip should fail.

The young man's eyes were wild with terror and pain as Myrddion thrust Vengis's own scrap of rag into his mouth. From below, Uther watched with a grin of approval, as if this final humiliation was a just punishment.

'Swallow the fluid that is soaked into the cloth, Vengis,' Myrddion hissed into his ear. 'It has the juice of the poppy in it, and you'll not feel the flames if you do as I say. I am betraying my new master by offering you mercy, but the choice is ultimately yours. You may spit out the cloth if you wish, but I have assuaged my conscience by offering you an anodyne.'

Then Myrddion climbed down to stand behind the kings, who gradually became silent as the light faded.

In the stillness, Myrddion could hear his heartbeats, like hammer blows, as he watched Vengis. The lad had not spat out the drug-soaked rag. Myrddion prayed that he would not lose consciousness before Uther lit the fire, for then his traitorous mercy might be suspected.

Fortunately, Uther was impatient to taste his revenge. With due ceremony, he used a long torch to light the four corners of the pyre, and as the light finally fled the sky the wood on the lowest levels began to catch, fuelled by the gifts from commoners and kings. With a great rush of heat, the tower began to burn fiercely as flame and smoke reached upward and obscured Vengis's bound form. At the top, the white-shrouded figure of the High King seemed to twist in the shimmer of heat.

Ah, Ambrosius! You would have killed Vengis cleanly if you were here, for you would have understood his pain. I hope you are not offended by my intervention. Myrddion's thoughts rose with the howling flames, and for a moment he saw Vengis's face, head thrown back and bloody mouth gaping open. But the poppy had done its work and the blue eyes, so like those of his victim, were closed and blinded.

The pyre could be seen for many miles and men would later remember the pillar of flame that climbed into the night sky like a promise of the doom to come. Years later, they would remember Ambrosius's death as the beginning of the west's troubles, and curse Vengis and his line for ever.

But such anger was in the future. That night, as ash and cinders swirled through the Giant's Carol, the kings imagined that the stones came to life and danced once again. They went to their tents in superstitious awe, while the smell of burning flesh pursued them into sleep.

Only Myrddion and Uther, flanked by Botha and Ulfin, remained awake as the pyre collapsed inward with a great whoosh of ash and charred wood. As Uther exulted in the carnage, Myrddion wept and remembered the kindness of Ambrosius's blue eyes.

Shortly afterwards, the cold rain came, stinging their exposed flesh and driving them back to their tents. The night was washed clean so that, in the cold morning, only ash and a burned section of sod remained to remind Myrddion that Ambrosius had ever lived at all.

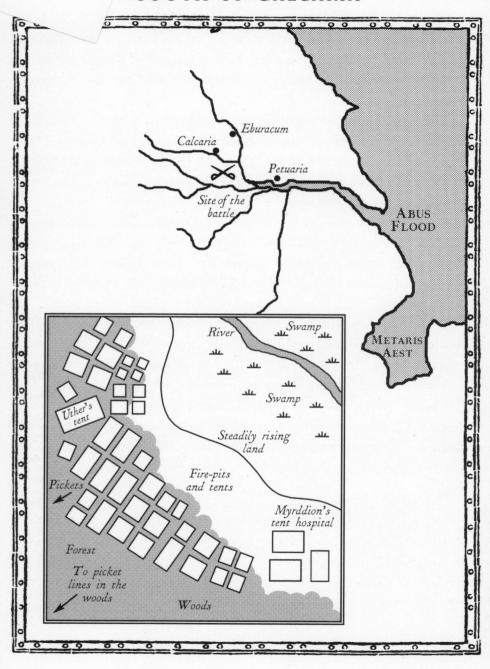

CHAPTER XIV

THE DOGS OF WAR

For all men kill the thing they love.

Oscar Wilde, *The Ballad of Reading Gaol*

More than two years later, Myrddion stared out at a silver web of marshes edging a long, slow river that led to Calcaria in the north, and as he stared at the detritus of battle he felt the deaths of a multitude of men press down upon his heart. The shallow slick of the marsh was red with the last dregs of the sun in a dusk that seemed interminable. Hours had passed since the Saxons had been driven into the river with a profligate waste of life. Cadoc and two younger healers were still wading through the foot-deep mud and rushes as they searched for any warriors who might have survived the battle, although Myrddion had little hope that the fierce fighting had left many men alive. The long half-light of summer seemed so peaceful in this landscape of nodding bulrushes and strange flowering plants that lived between earth and deep water, while insects still hummed and darted in the last of the light. The healer felt the mud grate under the soles of his boots and stared into the flags of daylight with eyes that were tired and dispirited.

The years in Uther's service had been so very, very hard.

'Hold him!' Cadoc shouted abruptly. 'In the name of all things good, pack the wound with mud, anything, until our master can treat him on the table. You!' he roared, as he pointed to two warriors calmly splashing towards the higher ground. 'Move your lazy arses and help us with this man. He's still alive.'

When will this ordeal be over, Mother? Myrddion asked quietly while he dragged his feet out of the sucking mud with a weary surge of energy. While he wasted his time daydreaming about horrors, a man was lying, sorely wounded, who needed his assistance.

The two warriors grumbled all the way to the healers' tents. The filthy scarecrow they carried between them was unrecognisable as either Saxon or Briton, for the slurry of blood and mud that caked his hair and blurred his features was so thick that he looked more like an earth golem than a man. Only his smallish stature pointed to the likelihood that he was a friend who had remained alive in a marsh full of dead men, one of the few who had struggled to reach the higher ground and the deep woods that hid Uther's encampment and masked his numbers.

'Be quick!' Myrddion summoned his flagging will and forced the two warriors onward while Cadoc and his companions continued to search for the last of the survivors. 'I'll be damned if I'll let him die after surviving this long in that stinking shit.'

Andrewina Ruadh had come running with Rhedyn on her heels. Slower because of his crutch, crippled Dyfri followed, and all three stared at Myrddion in surprise. They were unused to his cursing, and were equally perplexed by his distracted, irritated expression. Over this last summer their master had become increasingly silent, so that even the irrepressible Cadoc had been unable to lift his spirits or make him smile.

'Summon bearers to take him to the surgery. These dolts will kill him if they continue to carry him like a sack of old turnips.'

Two men materialised out of the nearest tent and ran to obey their master's orders. Indifferent to the blood and caked filth that stained their clean robes, they carefully carried the wounded warrior to the hospital tent.

'I need hot and warm water, clean cloths, and something to cut these rags off his body,' Myrddion ordered, struggling to regain his usual crisp decisiveness. He stripped off his own mud-fouled tunic and sluiced his body with river water, wincing at the sudden chill against his goose-pimpled skin. Andrewina Ruadh, who was now simply known as Ruadh, handed him a length of old linen which he used to dry his torso. Then he donned his leather apron, which the women had cleaned since the bloodbath of surgery had finished in the middle hours of the afternoon.

'My thanks, Ruadh,' he whispered before turning to the other woman. 'Rhedyn – lay out my tools without touching the blades.' He felt the older woman stiffen, so he tried to smile in apology, although the muscles of his face felt stiff and unnatural. 'I'm sorry, Rhedyn. I know you'd never do such a thing. I'm just tired.'

'It's been a long day, master,' Rhedyn replied softly, accepting his apology. Her plain face and grey hair showed the marks of her hard labour as his assistant, but her eyes were clear and content. She had put aside the ugly and dangerous status of camp follower when she had first decided to follow the boy healer who treated her like a person of value. Now, eleven years later, she had travelled the world and gained an extended family of the heart, so she worshipped the man who had given her respect and purpose. But now she was worried about him, so she gave him little pats and caresses as she helped him to tie back his long hair.

Before lifting the wounded man on to the surgical table, the bearers lowered him gently on a length of oilskin outside the tent and carefully removed his leathers and armour. What could not be unlaced was cut away with old scalpels, until some tanned flesh was exposed to permit Myrddion's careful examination.

The warrior was powerfully built with long, whipcord muscles that indicated stamina, and Myrddion deduced that he was probably a cavalryman judging by the calluses on his hands. The battle had been fought on foot, for horses were useless in this landscape of mud and forest.

But who or what the survivor was would be immaterial if he died.

Ruadh handed him a large bowl of warm water and a precious piece of sea sponge which he used to sluice the body as clean as possible. Working in tandem with her master, Ruadh used cloth to dry the cleansed areas of skin as quickly as possible, paying particular attention to the man's face and his flaccid penis. When Myrddion raised one eyebrow at her, Ruadh coloured and explained that men cared about their manhood only fractionally less than their honour.

Myrddion laughed naturally for the first time that day, and Ruadh congratulated herself silently for giving a man she loved so much a moment's respite from his black moods.

Now that his patient's face was clean, Myrddion recognised one of Uther's strongest and most vocal allies.

'It's Prince Luka of the Brigante, Ruadh. We must save him if we can. Fetch Dyfri and ask him to prepare stimulants – the man's lost too much blood.'

Luka's initial wound appeared to have been a deep puncture in the shoulder which had obviously not totally incapacitated the hard-bitten warrior. But it must have slowed him down, as a number of cuts and slashes across his forearms, hands and knuckles showed he had narrowly avoided killing blows. The real damage had been done by a blunt instrument that had struck him on the forehead. Myrddion gently pressed his fingers round the ugly, odd-shaped bruise and was concerned when he sensed a faint irregularity in the skull. Brain fever killed slowly but inexorably, so Myrddion checked the back of the head, the ears and the mouth with great care.

'Why do you always check the side of the skull opposite to the wound, master?' Ruadh asked as she helped a bearer to lift Luka's unconscious body on to the battlefield table.

'I have observed that there is often damage to the brain on the opposite side of the skull to where the initial blow fell. I've seen it many times when the bone has been breached and the patient has unexpectedly died. In the past, I have occasionally carried out a post-mortem examination on the skulls of such patients.'

'You've opened the skull?' Ruadh gasped, wide-eyed, as her hands worked unconsciously to staunch the slow leak of blood from the shoulder wound.

'Aye. Perhaps I have sinned, but the warriors I examined were mostly Saxon and all were very, very dead. What I learned has helped me to save other lives, but I would be obliged if you remained silent on this matter. The Christian Church forbids us to cut open any corpses and who knows how Uther would react to such information about me.'

'I could more easily die than betray you, master,' Ruadh replied earnestly. 'But what did you find?'

Any person not initiated into the alien world of battlefield medicine would have found this conversation very disconcerting, but Myrddion's fingers didn't hesitate as he explored Luka's shoulder wound and cleaned it thoroughly of the mud that had fouled it. His scalpel opened the wound still further and, with a grunt of satisfaction, he used his forceps to retrieve a fragment of leather that had been driven into the injury. In truth, healers often spoke of other things as they struggled with death over the supine bodies of damaged men. Perhaps it was the only way they could remain sane.

'The brain, which is the source of our thoughts – indeed, all of our senses – is greyish pink, and very soft. It is a network of blood vessels and I don't understand a fraction of how it works. The skull protects it as a glass or pottery container protects our unguents and liquids from harm. What happens when you shake a jar of cream? Or you thump the jar on one side? The contents always hit the other side of the jar with some force. If the cream was our brain, there would be damage where the jar was struck and further injuries where the cream bounced against the other side of the glass.'

'Your knowledge is amazing, my lord.' Ruadh's eyes were so starry with adoration that Myrddion flinched. 'In some ways, it opens my eyes to the mysteries of the gods.'

'I can stitch this shoulder wound now, Ruadh, so I need needles and gut.'

As she prepared his tools, Myrddion looked across at her and smiled, for he was eager to divert the topic of conversation into safer areas. 'Do you ever regret the loss of your children, far away to the north of the Vallum Antonini? When Uther freed you to return to your home, I never understood why you stayed in the south. I'm grateful, of course, because you're a budding herbmaster who could one day rival the great Annwynn herself, and she is the best I've ever known. But you have cut yourself off from your childhood kin as well as your own children. Why would you be so . . . rash?'

As he spoke, Myrddion's fingers deftly packed seaweed paste and radish into the wound and stitched it temporarily with a single knot. Ruadh assisted with eyes and fingers that were calm and still.

'I loved King Ambrosius in my way, so the Pict life was barred to me for ever once I realised how I felt about him. If I was a true wife and mother, I should have killed him while he slept – indeed, I planned to do so when he took me to his bed for the first time. I even had a small fruit knife that could have been used to stab him through his sleeping eyes. But I couldn't do it. I'm not squeamish, as you know, but I looked at Ambrosius's care-worn face and remembered his gentleness, and I couldn't make my hands obey me. He was sweet and loving, my lord, for all he was a king. I regret that I never kissed him, for to do so would be the last betrayal of my dead husband and my lost children. But I wish I had, Master Myrddion, so that he would know that I had come to love him before he died.'

By now, Myrddion had stitched most of the nastier superficial wounds on Luka's arms and Ruadh had begun to bandage them with neat expertise.

'I still don't understand why Ambrosius's death didn't set you free.'

'I felt in my heart that I had betrayed the Picts, while I had rejected my tribal kin years ago. I was lost – until the day you took me in because of the love you had for my dead lord.'

'So your place here is based on personal honour?' Myrddion laughed. 'Many men say that women can't really understand the concept.'

Ruadh's fingers stilled, trembled, and then resumed their careful, efficient movements.

'Those clods would be wrong, master. Women have their own code, which is as rigid and unbending as anything a man can devise. But few men try to understand us as my lord Ambrosius did. He was a rare king . . . and an even rarer man.'

'Aye, he was that.'

Together, they examined the huge lump on Luka's forehead and decided that the elaborate boss of a shield had probably caused it, hence the strangely mottled purpling.

'What can we do, master?'

Myrddion shook his head regretfully. 'Nothing, Ruadh,' he whispered. 'We must keep him very still and force liquids down his throat – milk for preference – and hope that he wakens of his own volition. I'll not despair until I have no other option.'

'Then I'll pray to the Blessed Virgin for him – and for you. Perhaps God might still have plans for this young man. After all, he is still alive when thousands of others have perished.'

Several more men were found alive, but all succumbed to their wounds without regaining consciousness. As his bearers carried away the last of the bodies for communal burial, Myrddion regretted that battlefields could not be organised to save as many lives as possible. The healer had hired a score of body servants and trained them in the rudiments of first aid so that they could stop bleeding and carry wounded men off the battlefield after the fiercest of the fighting had left behind its trail of dead and wounded warriors. Lives were saved by this simple expedient, and Cadoc's tasks were made significantly easier as he need no longer expend his energies in bringing back the injured himself. A significant proportion of Myrddion's apprentice healers were youths, and the training herbmasters were either women or men like Dyfri who were crippled in some way. The healers no longer depended on warriors to provide the brute strength needed at the field hospitals. The extra hands saved lives.

As full darkness fell, Luka's condition remained unchanged. Myrddion was tired, not from recent physical exertion, but from years in the saddle and at battlefields that blurred together in his memory. But worst by far was the need to mitigate the endless caprices of Uther Pendragon.

After his initial grief, and his crowning amid the magnificence of the newly built Christian church in Venta Belgarum, Uther began a campaign of attrition against both the recalcitrant tribal kings and the Saxon thanes. Gone were the days of the judgment halls where justice was dispensed with mercy as well as punishment. Despite Myrddion's best efforts, Uther made snap decisions about petitioners, whether they were the humblest peasants or the most offensive noblemen. More than once, Myrddion had risked his head by intervening when Uther had flagrantly ignored reason to either settle old scores or exercise a rather skewed ruling.

During the two winters that he had spent in Uther's service, Myrddion had ridden countless miles as he tightened and extended his spy network, while checking that the tribal kings were fortifying the outposts in accordance with their oaths to the High King. He was now viewed as Uther's creature, so the prejudice and dislike he had suffered in his youth were laid on him anew – and two-fold. The tribes feared Uther, but they obeyed him sullenly, for the gods alone could guess what he would do if he was gainsaid – or betrayed.

So Myrddion suffered a crushing isolation that was only assuaged when he dwelled in the house of the healers, where laughter and a spirit of enquiry still reigned. In his scriptorium, Myrddion could study, assemble his opus on herbal curatives, train eager young men to serve on the battlefield and enjoy the company and laughter of children. Had he not possessed this peaceful haven, Myrddion suspected that he would have broken his oath to Ambrosius, and run.

In the darkness, as Myrddion checked several scores of patients who seemed likely to survive, Botha sought him out. The tall captain of Uther's personal guard carried a nasty slash across the thigh which had almost castrated him, but Myrddion imagined that the unfortunate Saxon never had a chance to repeat the blow. Botha was a superlative warrior and a man whose life was ruled by a finely honed sense of honour which governed all aspects of his life.

'The High King wants you, Myrddion, and you know how quickly he expects you to obey,' he said with a wry grin. Both men were slaves to Uther's whims.

With a flash of irritation, Myrddion permitted himself to scowl.

'Then he'll have to wait until I dress that cut on your thigh. It's very high and likely to become infected because the muscles bunch with your every movement. Strip to your loincloth, Botha. If you argue, we'll only be delayed further.'

When, tightly bandaged and on tenterhooks, Botha finally ushered Myrddion into the High King's tent, Uther was pacing irritably. Something in the king's eyes gave Myrddion a frisson of apprehension.

'You took your time, Botha. You've permitted the healer to flout my orders, as usual.'

Myrddion winced. His relationship with the High King was strained, not only because their characters were diametrically opposite, but also because Myrddion had been the only person to see Uther weep over his brother's corpse. The king couldn't tolerate the constant reminder of what he perceived as a gross weakness.

'Botha has been wounded, highness,' Myrddion answered for both of them. 'I doubt you were even aware of it, but your servant's blood could have been poisoned without treatment because of the mud in the wound. The decision to delay was mine, and I apologise for that error.'

Uther grunted, then threw himself grumpily into a folding chair among a scattering of scrolls and maps. His handsome face settled into lines of discontent, made ugly by something sly and disappointed behind his blue eyes.

'We routed the bastards, but we still can't break through to Petuaria. That son of a whore, Hengist, knew what he was about when he led his people to this godforsaken stretch of coastline. They breed like ticks in the marshes and all their battle plans are shaped by the landscape. I'll learn to fly before we dislodge Hengist's sons out of the old Parisi lands.'

Prudently, Botha and Myrddion remained silent.

'We've lost too many men by playing the Saxons at their own game. The Roman-trained centuries don't work effectively in marshland and the cavalry was wasted in the deep forests, except for night reconnaissance. As for siege machines? Bah! All we need now is bad weather.'

Once again, he expected no reply. Myrddion recognised the king's continual switching from one source of annoyance to another: Uther was fuelling his frustrations. The healer knew from painful experience that any sort of imprudence might yet follow.

'Leonates of the Dobunni has seen fit to ignore me. And Gorlois has refused to send troops to assist us. He could have cost us the battle. I'll not be mocked, Myrddion.'

The healer watched the mounting warning signs that he had come to dread. Under his thick yellow brows, Uther's eyes were mere slits, obscuring the colour of the irises and giving his face a bestial appearance. His nostrils were flared as if he smelled something vile and his mouth had fallen in so that every word spat out of those almost invisible lips showed his teeth in a feral snarl. The High King was working himself up into a tantrum and only the gods knew what would be the result.

'Gorlois has never failed to send troops to our campaigns in the south. Perhaps he deemed that this attack was better dealt with by the Brigante tribe. I cannot read the Boar's mind, but he has always been loyal, my king. As for Leonates, he was ill throughout the winter with lung disease, so perhaps he has been unable to send levies to assist you. His son, Leodegran, is still in his teens and is probably overwhelmed by his father's illness.'

'No excuse. The boy is a sybaritic pup and if he wishes to rule one day, he should take care to maintain his alliance with me.'

Myrddion dropped his eyes and bowed respectfully. 'Of course, my lord. I shall look into the matter of Leonates's health.'

'As for Gorlois, how dare he decide which campaigns he will fight and which he will not? He's not the High King, although I've heard whispers that many of the tribal kings would be happy to see him take the crown of Maximus. Even his name irritates me. If he continues to decide when and where he'll send his levies, then he'll discover that a dragon can burn a wild boar to a crisp.'

Myrddion almost laughed, although Uther's expression was far from humorous. At times the High King's intemperate words were ludicrous, but in other circumstances they were monstrous. The healer set to work to soothe his bad temper, while Botha tidied the disordered tent and hunted up some of the red Hispanic wines that Uther loved. Cosseted, coddled and placated, Uther's mood improved so much that he demanded that his current woman be sent to his tent, and as the doe-eyed girl slipped through the flap to the sweet susurration of her robe, Botha and Myrddion sighed and departed.

But Myrddion could not rest peacefully. All his persuasion had failed to still the worm of suppressed rage that ate into the king's brain because the Saxons had thwarted him, so instead of seeking his bed he went to the healers' tents to check on the condition of Luka of the Brigante, who still lay like a dead man on his cot. He paused by the rolled-up side of the largest tent and stared down towards the swamp where little corpse lights seemed to flicker. During his journeys in the Middle Sea, Myrddion had been told that the phenomenon was caused by pockets of gas that escaped from deep underground, but even his rational understanding was jarred by the eerie flicker of coloured light where so many corpses still lay pressed into the mud.

Just as Myrddion began to turn away, a long ululating cry raised the hair on his arms as it rose over the sleeping camp like a night creature taking to the wing. The agonised sound didn't belong to a golem or a wight that sought to terrify the living. A human throat had produced that high keening in an excess of pain.

Several fruitless moments were spent in trying to find his satchel, so panicked was Myrddion by the terrifying noise. Cadoc emerged from under a wagon half dressed and cursing. But the sound had been cut off abruptly as it rose to an inhuman pitch, as if the lungs and vocal cords that produced it had been severed.

Cadoc and Myrddion hurried towards the camp, although neither man could place the origin of the scream. Where a tangle of warriors jostled in the circle of tents along the forest edge, the two healers skidded to a halt. Rudely wakened men grabbed their weapons and asked each other unanswerable questions, while the horses made their fear known with whinnies and stamping of feet from the picket lines hidden deep in the woods.

'What in Hades was that?' Cadoc muttered as his eyes scanned the partly dressed warriors who had boiled out of tents or from their sleeping blankets around the fire-pits.

'I've no notion, but they . . . he . . . she . . . was in extremity. Some-one needs us badly.'

'We'll be unlikely to find them in this crowd,' Cadoc snapped, for his good humour had fled with the end of his comforting dreams.

Gradually, order was restored. Officers calmed their men and explained that a camp follower had experienced a bad dream and was now settled back to sleep. Disgruntled men cursed all women on campaign and returned to their slumbers around the dying fires. Finally, peace settled over the High King's camp.

Myrddion and Cadoc had barely returned to the healers' tents pitched on the rise above the swamps when Botha and two guardsmen appeared out of the darkness on silent feet.

'You're wanted, Myrddion,' Botha ordered in a crisp whisper. 'Come now, and bring your satchel with you.' His face was particularly impassive, and the healer felt the shorter hairs on the back of his neck stir with apprehension. 'No noise, hear?'

'What's amiss, Botha?'

The captain ignored Myrddion's hissed question and skirted the camp on silent feet. Defiantly, Cadoc ignored a frown from one of the guards and hurried after his master.

Pushing their way through thick underbrush, the small party approached the High King's tent by the most indirect route, taking care to move as soundlessly as possible.

'Is the High King taken ill?' Myrddion tried again.

Botha stopped in his tracks, turned and hissed at him to keep his mouth shut. Myrddion's eyebrows rose, for Botha rarely lost control or showed any emotion. Something must be very wrong if even his composure was fraying. The party moved forward once more, but both healers watched the dark and threatening shadows out of the corners of their eyes.

Uther's tent was set on the highest point of a small hill in the forest and some clearing of trees had been necessary to assemble his tent within the allotted space. Smaller tents were placed in a semicircle that clustered around the High King's skirts, and the main body of his force was bivouacked below him. This arrangement was unusual in that kings usually set up their bivouacs in the centre of their forces to ensure their security, but Uther always valued the high ground and Myrddion was never surprised at the risks he took.

What did surprise him was the route taken by Botha and the guards to reach the king's tent. What were they trying to hide?

The tent loomed out of the shadows, and Botha stopped. 'Go in, healer, and I'll wait outside for your call,' he said, a little shamefaced. Myrddion wondered why the captain was reluctant to accompany him.

The smell alerted the healer immediately, even before his eyes adjusted to the gloom within the tent. A single oil lamp burned on the sod floor near the camp bed, and the shadows seemed to be thick with something menacing and alien. Both healers advanced into the tent, and the coppery smell of fresh blood led them into the small halo of light.

Myrddion put his left hand on a chair which had been upended in a violent struggle and recoiled at the feel of fresh blood across his palm. As his eyes adjusted to the darkness, he recognised the shape of Uther in the far corner of the tent, cleaning his hands on a scrap of cloth. Without pausing to think, Myrddion approached him.

'Are you well, lord? Let me see your hands in case you've suffered some hurt.'

'Stay away, damn you! If I'd wanted you, I'd have called for you.'

Uther's voice was hoarse and ragged with the last traces of an explosion of temper. The king plunged his hands into a basin of water and Myrddion watched the liquid darken in the dim light. Without being told, the healer knew that the stain would glow red in the lamplight.

Shite, what has Uther done? Which poor soul has he harmed this time? Myrddion's thoughts chased themselves in circles. Cadoc's comforting presence at his back awoke the healer to another danger. His colleague would not survive knowledge of any misdeeds committed by the king.

I must get him out of here without alerting him any further than he already is. Gruffly, Myrddion ordered his assistant out of the tent, and when his friend opened his mouth to protest his temper began to fray and his voice became unusually curt.

'Wait outside for me, I said,' he hissed. 'Don't argue, for I'm trying to protect you! And ask Botha to come in.'

Without another word, but with a glance that spoke volumes, Cadoc left the tent.

As Botha entered the tent with downcast eyes, Myrddion turned back to the king. 'You have blood on your arm, my lord. Show me the wound so I can assess the harm that has been done to you. Tell Botha to summon the guard. If an assassin is on the loose, we can't afford another murder. The realm wouldn't survive the instability that would arise were you to die.'

'Stay where you are, fool. I'm not bleeding. The bitch bit me, but it's of no account.'

Shite! The curse skidded through Myrddion's brain and his unwilling eyes scanned the tent for Uther's woman. A small heap lay under a blanket in the darkest corner of the tent, and Myrddion felt his gorge rise.

'Botha?' Myrddion whispered as he turned his back on the king and picked his way through scattered and broken furniture towards the still form under the coarse wool. The tiny figure seemed smaller than a child, while a spreading black stain, darker than the shadows, seeped into the blanket.

Botha didn't need any prompting. With a careful hand, he flicked the covering aside and stepped backward with a slow sigh. Practical to the end, he turned, approached Uther and helped him to remove a fine linen shirt that was spattered with blood, bundled it into a ball and disappeared out of the tent without a backward glance.

While Uther dressed himself with something approaching good humour, Myrddion knelt beside the small woman. Her long black hair was thick with blood, which still seeped sluggishly out of deep wounds on her forehead. There were indentations in her skull and shattered bones in her forearms and hands. As Myrddion pulled the blanket down lower, he saw that her small pert face was mis-shapen and swollen, as if she had been badly beaten. Her eyes were wide and gazed out at something very far away that no mortal would ever see until the shades came for him with flowers or whips of fire.

'There, there, little one,' Myrddion whispered as he stroked her bloody, broken palm where fine bones had pierced the skin, careless of her caking blood as it transferred to his hand. Although his fingers were sticky, he still felt for the large vein in her neck. He knew he would find no pulse, for he was certain that no life remained in the boneless, slack-mouthed little creature. The stink of urine and faeces almost overpowered the reek of blood.

Beside the body, a heavy pottery flagon lay in pieces as if it had been dropped by careless fingers. The coarse shards were stained with blood and lees of red wine had soaked into the sod.

'Is she dead?' Uther asked conversationally, pouring himself a cup of wine. His voice was quite calm, almost jovial, as he picked up his chair, uttering a mild oath when he felt the blood on it. Casually, he wiped his soiled hand on his tunic. 'She's more of a problem dead than alive. Gods, that girl would try the patience of one of the Christian saints, and she could nag a man to his death.'

'*Her* death, certainly, my king.' Although Myrddion had tried hard to strip his voice of any censure, he knew he had failed. Uther looked up at him with narrowed eyes from under his golden eyebrows.

'It's not your place to comment on what I do with my property, healer. Moderate your tone or get out! Since you've meddled in my business, I'd prefer that you were of some assistance, but I can easily dispense with your services.'

The smile on Uther's lips was particularly lupine, almost well fed, as if the frustrations of the previous day's battle had been exorcised.

'Where is Botha when I need him? This tent is a pigsty, and something has to be done with *that* before it starts to stink up my space. Shite . . . and now her father will be annoyed, I suppose. I knew that his plan to foist his daughter upon me was a mistake all round, so I don't see how he can legitimately complain. She was a pretty little thing, but she had no more sense than a child.'

'Who *is* her father, lord?' Myrddion asked with a sinking feeling in his gut. He was sickeningly aware that the High King was beyond his control, and all he could do was try to protect him from the consequences of his actions. But, under his urgency, Myrddion wanted to scream and sob with a revulsion that was soul deep.

What am I doing? Mother . . . Ambrosius . . . how could you ask this of me?'

'Her name was Carys,' Uther replied sourly. 'But she wasn't as easy to love as her name promised.' He glared at Myrddion. 'Where the hell is Botha? I'm hungry, but first I want this mess cleaned up.'

'Who is Carys's father, lord?' Myrddion repeated gently, and despite the depth of his despair his voice adopted the practised, soothing tones that he used to quieten badly injured patients.

'He's Calgacus minor, the son of Calgacus major, the king of the Novantae tribe. He's a pompous idiot who sets great store by an ancestor who resisted the Roman advance into the north at the Battle of Mons Graupius, centuries ago. He says his ridiculous name means *sword wielder* or something equally grandiose,' Uther was explaining as Botha re-entered the tent.

'At last, Botha! Where have you been all this time? I'm hungry.'

'Burning your shirt, master.' Botha managed to look stern, self-effacing, disapproving and obedient at the same time. 'I presumed you didn't want the world and his wife to know what happened to your woman?'

'No, damn your eyes! I don't want the Novantae to pull out of the accord, but I really don't see what Calgacus expected to happen when he foisted his idiot daughter and her servants on my house.' Uther looked irritably at his hands and picked at some dried blood under his nails. Myrddion took some heart from the king's attempt at justification, although his excuses were half-hearted. Then, as he watched, the healer saw Uther's face change as a sudden thought struck him. 'I'd forgotten about that gaggle of women she takes with her everywhere she goes. They're aware that Carys was with me.'

'Calgacus minor must be convinced that his daughter was slain by Saxons,' Myrddion mumbled in a voice that seemed to come from some hollow place in his soul. 'The tribes between the walls are vital to your plans, my king, unless you wish to spend every spring and summer fighting in the north. Why in the name of everything holy did you kill her?'

Botha took the bowl of bloody water and the stained cloth and disappeared, to be replaced by Ulfin, who took in the situation at a single glance. Myrddion's stomach threatened to empty at the bland look in the warrior's eyes.

'The silly bitch complained that the ring I gave her was paltry,' Uther muttered. 'She said she was with child, so I should marry her and produce a legitimate heir. I don't have the time for such nonsense, and I don't want a snotty brat trailing around my palace at Venta Belgarum. Look at what Vortimer tried to do to his father. Brats grow up and threaten their sire's safety, so I'll have no doubtful heirs waiting to sever *my* windpipe when I'm not looking. Shite, any peasant bitch knows how to rid herself of an unwanted embarrassment, but Carys went on and on about the hero she carried in her womb. I will *not* tolerate a pregnant bitch making claims on me. Her father would get thoughts above his station – and nobody tells me what to do. I didn't hit her hard at first, but then I lost my temper when she threatened to complain to him.'

Two dead if the child is included, Myrddion thought morosely. No wonder the poor little thing was curled up – it was to protect the babe in her belly.

'What did she expect when she tried to coerce me? Her death is her own fault,' Uther continued petulantly, as if Carys's ugly murder were an inexcusable inconvenience embarked upon solely to upset her master and king. To his everlasting shame, Myrddion said nothing.

'Ulfin, take Carys's maidservants to a place near the Saxon dead and ensure that they have a nasty accident. Kill some horses if you need to and use a couple of Saxon bodies to give credence to the tale.' Uther paced as his mind worked swiftly. 'And put a few bodies from our own dead with them, cleaned up and armoured. With luck, it will look as if the women were captured and good Celts died trying to rescue them. Do you have any problems with obeying my orders, Ulfin?'

Ulfin shook his head without any visible signs of concern, while Myrddion wondered if he would have time to warn the unfortunate young women before the warrior organised their execution. Many mothers north of the wall would weep if Uther had his way.

'Don't even think about it, Myrddion,' Uther snapped as he recognised the desperate plan written on the healer's face. 'If your honour pains you, do what Botha does and refuse to dwell on any orders that compromise you. I value Botha a damned sight more than I care about you, so I accept his squeamishness. But not yours! Your task is to clean her up, stitch her into a shroud and organise a wagon to return her body to her father with a long letter of explanation. I'll leave it to you to word the message in such a way as to cement Calgacus's loyalty to me while inflaming the anger of his warriors. I can already tell that her sacrifice is going to be very useful to me, now that she's safely dead and I've had a chance to think about it.'

With shaking knees and nauseated by his complicity, Myrddion wrapped the childlike figure into the blanket once more. Uther was so cold and so calculating in his brutality that his murderous plan would probably succeed. After all, what could Calgacus do, so far from the place of his daughter's death? And who would dare to call the High King of the Britons a liar?

'Her body should remain here until your troops find the bodies of her maidservants. People will talk if I carry her corpse to the healers' tent now.'

'That's the spirit, Myrddion. Now you can get on with your tasks. I'll send her body before cockcrow, by which time my warriors will have discovered the atrocity. Be sure to show the necessary shock and outrage! Oh, and one other matter comes to mind. I want my ring returned before her body stiffens.'

Gulping as he tried not to vomit, Myrddion eased a large freshwater pearl off the dead girl's middle finger. When he handed it to Uther, the king put the jewel on his little finger, admired it for a brief moment, and then dropped it into a casket which he secreted in his scroll case.

'Now get out, and do something to clean up that cowardly face of yours. You'll set my guard to talking if you can't control yourself. Anyone would think you'd never seen a little blood before.'

Back at the healers' tent, Myrddion drank two goblets of powerful Hispanic wine and ordered Cadoc to wake him before dawn. Aghast at his master's ashen appearance, Cadoc would have asked awkward questions, but Myrddion pleaded exhaustion and fell on to his pallet fully clothed and gritty with mud. When he finally fell asleep, Ruadh carefully removed his boots.

Waking was agony, Myrddion decided as Cadoc roused him by shaking his shoulder. The face of his assistant was perplexed, unsettled and suspicious. 'What's amiss, Cadoc? I can tell you're bursting with information.'

'Apparently the High King's woman and her servants were stolen by a band of Saxons at dead of night, although how they pierced the defences beggars the imagination. Uther sent out troops to find them and a skirmish followed, during which the women were murdered by the Saxons. All the Saxons were killed.'

Myrddion turned his face into his pillow and tried not to cry with shame and chagrin.

'I hope this news is only a rumour, Cadoc. I'd not wish such a fate on gently raised young women.'

'It's not a rumour, master. Their corpses have been retrieved and the body of Uther's lover has been sent to our women to be cleansed, stitched into a shroud and sent back to her father by wagon.'

Unwillingly, Myrddion struggled to his feet and searched for his boots. 'I'd best help Ruadh, Brangaine and Rhedyn complete the rituals. We will pray to the Mother for them.' Somehow, Myrddion couldn't force himself to meet Cadoc's honest eyes.

'Well, master, here's the strange thing. I saw the dead warriors when they were brought into camp slung over the backs of their horses. Shite, Myrddion, I'd swear that I treated one of these men yesterday and he died before my eyes. Something's going on, master, and I'm not a fool.'

Myrddion hung his head with shame. 'Say nothing, Cadoc, if your value your life. I beg you, stay clear of this whole mess and keep as far away from Uther Pendragon as you can. I'll do everything that is necessary.'

The healer would have brushed past his friend but Cadoc moved to bar his way. 'You can't protect me for ever, lord. I know that Uther killed that woman, and then set up this charade to hide his guilt.' Cadoc lowered his hands on to Myrddion's shoulders and forced him to meet his eyes. 'And you knew, didn't you, master? How could you protect such a man?'

Myrddion wished he had time for the luxury of tears, but he had a scroll to write to preserve Ambrosius's dream. 'Unfortunately, I am oath-bound to both Ambrosius and Uther. I don't expect you to understand, because I can't make sense of it myself. At this moment, I would prefer to be blind so that I couldn't see what I am forced to do. But I'm not, and my oaths compel me to comply with Uther's demands. I wish I was anywhere but here, even back in Rome where my hands and my soul were still clean.'

With a pang, Myrddion longed for the calm, pragmatic presence of Praxiteles, whose age and intelligence would have provided some comfort. Cadoc had been too faithful and too true to be soiled by this dishonour.

Cadoc dropped his hands and lowered his eyes. 'That oath will be the end of you, master. I will keep my mouth shut, but not to save my own neck – only to spare you pain. Please, master, you must avoid that man whenever you can.'

'I wish I could, but he won't let me.' Myrddion's anguished cry begged Cadoc to understand the trap that was closed around the healer's neck. These was no going back.

As the sun rose redly over the marshes and carrion birds flapped from corpse to corpse, Myrdion sat at a camp table and wrote a hasty scroll which would be sealed with Uther's intaglio ring. The lie came easily to his pen, probably because no one in the north would ever read it other than a scribe or a priest, and they would be obligated to repeat the falsehood word for word, regardless of what they might believe. In this case, Myrddion was confident the Novantae king would accept his explanation. Further, to reinforce the words on the scroll and to ensure the message reached the Novantae intact, a courier would be required to recite its contents as well.

So, in Britain, an inability to read or write was no drawback for a king.

'Calgacus minor was a fool,' the healer whispered softly. 'A daughter should not be risked so that a parent can secure preferment. I wonder if Calgacus will weep for Carys, or is she just a lost opportunity to further his ambition?' Myrddion realised that he was talking to himself, and unwisely at that. Perhaps I'm a little mad, he thought, and stared out over the land as he tried to reach the calm centre that lived within his spirit.

At first, all he could see in the new morning was a vista of carrion birds, several wild dogs and the mud-coloured bodies that barely disturbed the nodding heads of the reeds. But then he raised his eyes above the swamps and beyond the river and saw fields laid out like a flat green carpet, broken by glints of distant water that spoke eloquently of rich pastures and smallholdings in Saxon hands.

'I can't bring myself to hate Hengist's kin,' he whispered again. 'I wish them gone, perhaps, but the kind of loathing that Uther feels for them is so . . . so pointless and destructive.'

Those distant lands were a wide green sea, and Myrddion fancied that if he had the strong wings of his namesake, the merlin, he would be able to view the flat grey sea beyond. Neither ocean nor land cared if he suffered, or if Uther was a dark and twisted monster under his tall, handsome form. The peasants who tilled that soil wanted peace, a surcease from the floods that tried to reclaim their fields in bad weather, and children and grandchildren to speak their names aloud after they were dead. Only fools and healers chose to live in a half-world of pain and suffering.

For a brief moment, Myrddion savoured an idyll of rural life, and then he laughed at his own foolishness. Until he was released from his oath, he must play at dice with a smiling, unpredictable demon and try to save as many lives as he could while doing his best to preserve the ways of the Britons. Myrddion was fully aware that he would eventually come to loathe himself.

'There's no help for it,' he sighed, and at last peace released the tensions in his shoulders and the pain in his heart. But even as he dreamed in the warming sunshine, nothing could heal the fresh wounds in his spirit.

CHAPTER XV

THE BOAR OF CORNWALL

In a short while the generation of the living are changed
and like runners pass on the torch of life.

Lucretius, *De Rerum Natura*

Gorlois and his wife sat before a warming fire and broke bread
sweetened with new honey as they talked in the desultory fashion
of husbands and wives who have been happy together for many
peaceful years. The low golden flame from the fireplace lit Ygerne's
face, and as Gorlois examined those beloved features he marvelled
anew at the radiance that shone out of her eyes and sweetened her
expressive mouth. How wondrous that a man far from his first
youth, and one who had never been a handsome figure, should be
loved by such a woman.

In the quiet that is too serene to be disturbed by mere words,
Ygerne inwardly thanked the Christian God for her blessed life.
The only shadow to mar the contentment of her days was that her
dear husband had no sons to rule after him, but Gorlois himself
seemed untroubled, insisting that his brother's son, Bors, would be
a successful king, while their daughter Morgause had mothered

sons who would surely become kings in the future. Even his beloved Morgan, while set to remain childless if she had her way, was more powerful than many lords by dint of her gifts of prophecy and charm.

'I am so fortunate, Gorlois, and so happy,' Ygerne whispered.

Gorlois wiped a smear of honey from the corner of her mouth and then licked his finger clean.

'I never told you how frightened I was when I came to Tintagel for the first time. I was terrified by waking dreams of something horrible that I couldn't see . . . but then you came, and I felt safe again.'

'I'd never permit anyone or anything to harm you, my lady. Every year with you has been a joy for me.'

Ygerne lowered the fragment of bread and honey that she was about to eat and examined the face of her beloved, drawing pleasure from every feature. Gorlois's hair was greying fast, but his body was still hard and slab-muscled, although little wrinkles had begun to appear around his eyes, neck and hands and the skin had begun to sag slightly around his flat belly and buttocks. Never a vain man, Gorlois was unconcerned except for his fear that Ygerne would tire of an old man. As if she could read his mind, Ygerne reached across the table and pressed his nut-brown hand.

'You think yourself unworthy of me, husband, as if I was something rare and precious. I am a pretty face, a superficial, accidental arrangement of features that some people find pleasing. But my face isn't my heart, my lord, which belongs to you alone. I have never seen a man I could love except you, and I swear that I never will. I'm simply Pridenow's daughter, not particularly clever or accomplished, but a woman who has been smiled upon at birth by the Christian God and the Tuatha de Danann.'

Unused to displaying such overt affection, Ygerne blushed, and her beauty almost stopped Gorlois's heart from beating.

She was a superb wife and a loving mother, and over the years even the stiff-necked Dobunni had come to worship Gorlois's gentle queen.

'We have been summoned to Venta Belgarum by the High King, my beloved. He has demanded the presence of Morgan and yourself as well, although I cannot understand why he should wish to see you. The High King shows little interest in women and even less inclination to wed – indeed, the united kings worry that he has no heir to take his place if he should fall in battle. He is angry with me, I know, because I did not send troops to the northern campaign. Frankly, beloved, I don't have so many men that I can afford to waste them in the north.'

'Is Uther so reckless that he spends good warriors like copper coins?' Ygerne asked, unconsciously placing her finger on the salient argument behind her husband's refusal to obey his king's demands. Gorlois had come to recognise that a shrewd strategic intelligence lay behind her guileless blue eyes.

'Uther will send whole phalanxes of seasoned warriors to certain death in order to bludgeon his enemies into submission. He's not reckless, but something rather worse. His troops are of less account than his horses, his tents or his weapons, and he uses them ruthlessly to achieve his ends. I'll place my men under his control when we are threatened in the south, but I won't strip my villages bare of boys and old men for the benefit of other tribes.'

Ygerne gazed into Gorlois's congested face. Her husband was angry now, with the slow, inexorable rage that his enemies feared. Once he was committed, he couldn't be deflected.

'You trifle with the unity of the kings, my lord, although I understand your reasons. But surely our men must fight the length of the mountain spine if we are to defeat the Saxons.'

Ygerne looked so serious that Gorlois stroked her cheek affectionately and his dark mood lifted.

'That's true, my lady. I flirt with disaster, but what am I to do? Uther is not Ambrosius. I swore my oaths to Ambrosius's plans for our people, and while Uther hates the Saxons like poison, he detests most other people as well, even good Britons. He's dangerous, my dear, and I'd not take you anywhere near him if I had any choice in the matter.'

Ygerne laughed a little, but her eyes were sombre. 'I'm an old woman, husband, and as you say, the High King is not swayed by the words of women. I am prepared to accede to his wishes and travel to Venta Belgarum under your protection. I'd not have you suffer because you try to safeguard me. After all, what can he do to me?'

'I dislike the idea of the vulgar crowds gawking at you, sweetheart. Morgan will enjoy such an excursion, but I'm loath to drag you away from the quiet of Tintagel. I know you are safe here, for all our people would be prepared to die for you.'

'You're a dear man, Gorlois, but why would anyone stare at me? I'm past the age of maidenly beauty and relinquished any pride in my appearance many years ago. But the crowds will certainly find much in Morgan to marvel at. That girl worries me, husband. She'll not marry, and she dabbles in spells that I fear to even imagine. She should have been a boy, and then the study of sword and spear would have assuaged her need to excel.'

'Aye, sweetheart, our Morgan is a wondrous woman, and I'd have no fears if Uther took a fancy to her. I'd back our girl against the dragon, and that's the truth.' Gorlois shook his loosened hair as if to banish a wicked thought. 'She'd cut his throat if he laid a finger upon her.'

Ygerne smiled with that bewitching curve of her full mouth that always stirred her husband to passion. 'She's more likely to turn him into a toad, if I know my girl,' she said. 'Or she'd try, at the very least.'

Then she crowed with merriment as her husband picked her up bodily and carried her off to their warm bed and his even warmer embrace.

Later, as her husband dozed under the furs, Ygerne stared up at the oak rafters and listened to the winds of autumn as they swirled around Tintagel. Venta Belgarum! The name rolled off her tongue with a sweet softness, like a loving word or a caress. Once she had feared to venture away from this wild coast and its broad rich lands, but now a frisson of excitement raised the hair on her arms. Perhaps the queen of the Dumnonii could assist her husband in his duel of words with Uther Pendragon. And if, later, she wept during her dreams, she did not remember the images of blood and fate which were weaving a rope around her, stronger by far than her own beautiful hair.

The same winds cleansed the streets of Venta Belgarum, lifting any accumulated litter and sweeping it into dark corners. They stirred the fruit trees in the healers' small orchard and threatened to strip the boughs of their ripe fruit. In his narrow sleeping room, Myrddion dreamed, pillowed by Ruadh's breasts.

With great reluctance, the healer had sunk his scruples and taken the Celtic woman to his bed. She was warm and loving, and Myrddion was starved of the adoration that can live in a woman's eyes. If he wished that Ruadh were Flavia, he was too gentlemanly and too kind to allow such a wish to take root. Ruadh had lost everything women value, so he could not deny her this simple release, even though his common sense warned him that any emotional entanglement could be very dangerous.

In the room that Brangaine shared with Willa, the eleven-year-old child tossed, moaned and wept in the grip of a painful dream. Brangaine woke and rose from her pallet to collect a mug of water from the well, and when she returned Willa's face was wet with tears. Lovingly, Brangaine watched over her darling's sleep.

Willa was tall for a girl and as slender and graceful as a young aspen in the forest. Her hair was now a glossy chestnut mane that fell thickly past her tiny waist without a hint of curl. Her small breasts had budded, and her hands were beautiful and animated, even in the throes of her dream. So entrancing were her fingers with their almond-shaped, delicate nails that few men saw her scars. Even her feet were slender and beautiful, and accentuated an air of fragility and delicacy that inspired most males with a desire to protect her from the evils of the world.

The closed, fluttering eyelids covered irises that were as bright and as green as fine Roman glass, with silky, hidden depths that seemed to beckon the watcher into her soul. Her sweet mouth and even teeth mitigated a nose that was a fraction too long and too narrow for perfection, yet this flaw accentuated her beauty so that her immature face and form was both innocent and angelic. Her loveliness terrified her foster-mother and she took enormous pains to keep young Willa as far from the haunts of men as possible.

Besides Brangaine, only Cadoc was fully awake in the whole of the sleeping household. Unable to sleep, and too anxious to rest, he had checked their only patient, Prince Luka, by lamplight.

The Brigante lord had remained in a deep sleep for two weeks while they had transported the wounded home from the north. When Luka had finally woken from his long dream, he was disoriented and his muscles were too weak to permit him to stand. Now, recuperating in Myrddion's house, he was slowly returning to health while the healers examined the effects of a blow to the head on the normal functions of the human body.

Cadoc grinned affectionately as he left the sleeping prince to his rest. The Brigante was lucky that his head was so hard. A lesser man would have died before the apple harvest was completed. Even now, although he still suffered from headaches, Luka was making jokes and pining for a horse or a woman – in whatever order.

Rarely had Cadoc been so irritable and so sleepless. The house was very still and the city had hunkered down to rest, like some great beast finally grown weary of light, drink and danger. Cadoc cleaned every surgical tool he could find by lamplight and then began to reorder the scriptorium, trying to burn away the sleeplessness that stemmed from a deep-seated anxiety. His master, the healer of all healers, was spiralling down into a dangerous, bleak depression. Cadoc had watched his friend's distracted, inverted mood gradually darken as he grappled with Uther's increasingly high-handed behaviour. Cadoc was afraid that Myrddion was walking along the edge of a deep chasm where the friable earth was crumbling under his booted feet, and would tumble into the depths of a killing despair at the slightest error of judgement.

'Vortigern was a monstrous man, but he could be understood. That dirty son of a whore liked being the High King and intended to stay on the throne of Maximus, whatever the cost. He could be as crooked as a rock adder, but he was sane.'

Cadoc spoke aloud in the bleak silence of his thoughts. After midnight, the old villa seemed full of unquiet spirits, and Cadoc, superstitious despite his practical upbringing, drew comfort from the sound of his own voice.

'Ah, Cadoc!' A dimly lit form stepped out from the darkness of the colonnade. 'You're becoming poetic in your old age.'

Cadoc almost dropped a precious jar of powdered aconite, a poison that Myrddion was using for experiments. He spun awkwardly, clutching his jars to his naked chest as Brangaine appeared before him, swathed in a long sleeping robe and carrying a totally inadequate oil lamp. The mellow light was kind to her ageing face, softening the grey in her hair and erasing the lines that seamed her eyes and the edges of her once-full lips.

'Blood of the gods, woman, you scared me shiteless,' Cadoc

swore as his heart threatened to burst out of his chest. Gradually, his breathing slowed, and he lowered his tense body down on to the nearest stool.

'Two of us – and we're both wakeful in the night. Misery loves company, Cadoc, so I sought out the other watcher in our household. We may as well worry together as apart, so I'll fetch some warm milk to soothe us.'

When Brangaine returned with two shallow bowls of heated and sweetened milk, Cadoc had cleared some of the clutter he had created in his orgy of cleaning, so the two colleagues could sit on their stools and warm their hands around their bowls. Brangaine noted the deep furrows between Cadoc's usually merry eyes and sighed sadly.

'I heard you talking about the Burning Man, Cadoc, and I thought of my husband, who was killed in Vortigern's ranks beyond Tomen-y-mur. The High King was a violent, dangerous and superstitious creature, but he was a true king for all that he stole the crown for his own purposes. Lord Ambrosius might have expected too much of our master but he was always kind to him in his own way. Ruadh has also told us how gentle he was when he was alone with her.'

'Aye, Ambrosius was a fair man,' Cadoc murmured as he sipped his sweetened milk.

'But the son of the dragon is another matter altogether! I can barely say his name without feeling sick. The man kills because he can – without even Vortigern's excuses of superstition and ambition. Perhaps I could understand him if he was crazed or perverted, but he's cold and inhuman, Cadoc. He's only looked at me once, and my blood fair froze in my veins.'

'Our master weakens,' Cadoc whispered. 'Something happened at Calcaria that made him heartsick.'

'We all know that Uther killed the little Carys, Cadoc, so say it aloud. Myrddion knew the truth and covered up the murder. It's killing him slowly, so you must face the worst, Cadoc, like us women who were forced to cleanse the poor little body that Uther dumped on us like so much spoiled meat. Saxons don't leave a woman unraped, or let their victims cool until the bodies are rigid and cold before they abandon them for their enemies to find. We know, Rhedyn, Ruadh and I, and no one had to tell us how the poor little thing perished, or that she was pregnant with the king's child.'

'Beware,' Cadoc hissed, 'for you'll be killed if you're heard. To say what you have said is treason.'

'It is the truth. The Mother *and* the Virgin Mary saw Carys die and they will ensure that Uther is repaid for his sins,' Brangaine hissed in turn, and her eyes were suddenly hard and bright like river pebbles under shining water. 'And her women perished after her, I'm told, the victims of Saxon murderers. Nonsense! Not even a five-year-old child would believe such drivel.'

Cadoc's powerful hands turned his bowl of milk again and again. Brangaine watched his restless fingers and understood his concerns.

'Yes, our master knew that Uther gave the orders that led to the death of the girls, and that Ulfin creature carried out the deed for him. This loss of innocent lives is devouring our master from the inside out. I've seen his eyes – aieee! But I worry, for I can feel the days shortening and the hands of the goddess are drawing us all towards her. She's the Blue Hag now, and her face is ageing into winter. She'll have what she wants, and we mortals must suffer for it.'

Cadoc stared at Brangaine with eyes as round and smooth as brown glass beads. Brangaine was not particularly religious. In fact, she teetered between Christianity and the old religions as the mood took her, and sometimes combined both. During their years together, Brangaine had been a rock of common sense and was rarely disturbed by the emotional storms of the other women in the house. Her love was saved for Willa, her master Myrddion

Merlinus, and the toddler Cathan who had been found at Verulamium. But Venta Belgarum was a filthy cesspit beneath its fair and superficial beauty, so brutalized children were often dumped at the doors of the House of the Healers. As always, Myrddion had no heart to turn innocents away, so the rooms of the old villa reverberated with the shy laughter of little ones as they learned to play. Though she showed affection to all, Brangaine's devotion was hard won, and her heart was given to only three.

'We must protect him, Brangaine, if he can be saved. Damn me, but now he must send word to those tribal kings who are able to leave their winter halls that they are required to attend a feast to celebrate the solstice. What a farce! The High King has no wife, so the rites of rebirth are as cold as a witch's tit in a snowstorm. And the master also worries that the Boar of Cornwall has drawn the High King's ire. I've told him that he cannot save everyone, but you know how the boy is. He gives his word and it's iron-clad.'

'He's not a boy, Cadoc. He's a man. Ruadh has gone to his bed, and with luck she'll quicken, and that might divert his mind. Perhaps we'll escape this cursed place if she carries his seed. He'd not allow any child of his blood to be born under the dragon's claws.'

Brangaine spoke so prosaically that Cadoc almost missed the message under the words.

'So you women have decided that the master should become a father? You take liberties, Brangaine! Myrddion wouldn't wish to bring new life into this place, or to be responsible for an infant while he is following Uther's battles through the countryside. You have no right to meddle.'

Brangaine tried to stare Cadoc down, but eventually her eyes dropped with a kind of shame. The women had forgotten their master's trade in their neat plan to remove themselves from Venta Belgarum and the dangers of Uther Pendragon.

'For shame, Brangaine! What were you thinking of?'

'Willa!' she hissed. 'My girl is racked by night terrors. Can't you feel something horrid drawing closer to us all?'

Cadoc finished his milk and slammed the bowl down on a shelf so that the jars on the table shuddered. 'I think about the master, about our comfortable life and our useful work; I think about my friend having to swallow the insults and violence of the High King in order to keep us all safe; I worry about how we can save Uther's soldiers from his total disregard for life, as does the master, and I care about our servants who'd not survive long if Myrddion deserted them.'

Brangaine's cheeks flooded with shame and she backed out of the small room like a chastised child. But in her secret heart she had no regrets about the argument with Cadoc, for she hungered for the wild hills of Powys and the safety they promised for her and the children.

At this time of early winter, the house of the healers was neither a carefree nor a truly happy place, although Myrddion took great pleasure from watching the children's games and from the sounds of laughter that echoed through the old Roman colonnades. The kitchen women were cheerful and seemed content to relinquish their old trade on the streets, while the house servants were happy to spend their time whitewashing the outer walls of the villa in the fashion of the houses in Gaul that had so captivated Myrddion during his travels. A veneer of contentment covered the cracks that were appearing in Myrddion's carefully constructed life.

He was kept busy organising the minutiae of Uther's impending feast. The potential for social disaster was huge, and Myrddion would not have been human had he not resented being treated like a servant in charge of the kitchens. He had sent the carefully worded invitations out to all the kings from Deva to the Litus Saxonicum, knowing in his heart that Uther's use of ceremony was designed to bring Gorlois and young prince Leodegran to heel. The order to bring wives and older children was a careful threat that Myrddion did his best to nullify with graceful language, and other than to decide where the guests would sit in order of precedence he left the working of the feast to those able stewards who had served Ambrosius. His small act of defiance went unnoticed by Uther, who used Myrddion with the casual disregard he would apportion to a tethered and collared hound.

So easily can nations be turned to rubble!

One by one, the kings and their retinues came to Venta Belgarum in the first month of a mild winter. The city enjoyed the crisp cold of early morning frosts and days that were short and dim. The sun had no bite, but only a gentle kiss on bare faces. No snow had fallen, but soft rain cleansed the roof tiles of the Roman buildings and scoured the cobbled streets of summer's refuse.

The day the Boar of Cornwall came to the city, the people on the streets gawped at his magnificence. He had been a familiar figure in Venta Belgarum during Ambrosius's rule, but for this particular visit he had decided to arrive in unaccustomed pomp and splendour. He wore a coat of metal links polished to the buttery shine of silver that should have been far too heavy for any ordinary man to wear because of its great weight. A cloak of many otter skins, glossy and waterproof, had been stitched together by Ygerne's busy fingers, although she had been obliged to protect her hands during the heavy work with stout leather gloves. She had fashioned the lining from a fine fabric gifted to the Boar as part of her dowry and it shone with the refulgence of shell whenever he moved. The collar was wholly of winter fox, snowy and thick, and she had arranged the legs to clasp at her husband's throat with bands of orange gold. From behind, the head glittered with two raw green stones of crystalline amber, taken from the sea's bounty on Gorlois's rough coasts. Green amber and heavy gold massed in his dark hair so that the king of the Dumnonii seemed almost god-like in his power and strength.

Ragged cheers followed him through the gates, but the Dumnonii king maintained a stern, sober countenance. He attended this meeting unwillingly, and Myrddion admired the integrity which was written on every line of his face.

In his retinue, cradled within a circle of armed men, rode two of his dearest possessions, his wife and his daughter.

Every citizen of Venta Belgarum had heard of Queen Ygerne's beauty, rendered legendary because none had ever seen her face. As for her daughter, Morgan, the population spoke in whispers about her attempts to master magic. Men sniggered in the inns about rumours of multiple lovers, despite her noble blood, but not one of those leering dullards would dream of making any ribald comments within her hearing. She might have turned them into snakes, foretold their deaths, or, worse still, informed her father that commoners had sullied her name. The rawest recruit in Gorlois's army knew that the king would gut anyone who insulted his daughters.

Hooded and shrouded in heavy wool, the two women rode through the streets of Venta Belgarum, conscious of the many pairs of eyes that searched for a hint of flesh or the flash of an eye. Neither woman lifted her gloved hands from the reins of her horse or lowered her hood to satisfy the curious gazes of the vulgar crowd. The guard closed around them tightly, their eyes hard and bright with dislike.

In the great forecourt before the king's hall the retinue drew to a disciplined halt, and Gorlois dismounted and looked round. The large, paved space was surrounded on three sides by roads and buildings that seemed to lean in homage towards the hall and the palace. Uther had ordered the archaic carvings around his tall doors painted a vivid brick red with an edging of liquid gold, because the ancient, complex, interlaced design was based upon his totem of entwined dragons. The magnificence of this rambling wooden building, two storeys in places, was in stark contrast to a squat and square grey-stone church that sat incongruously next to the barbaric splendour of Uther's residence. Under his breath, Gorlois swore pungently, for he understood the symbolism in Uther's latest gesture.

'Obey me without question, for I am the Dragon,' he whispered.

The brass-sheathed doors opened and a tall, slender figure in deepest black walked towards the king with his head bowed low in homage. Gorlois immediately recognised the jet-black unplaited hair marked with its streak of white. Insulted to the core, the Boar of Cornwall realised that Uther Pendragon had not deigned to greet his guests in person.

Myrddion saw the muscles in the face of the Dumnonii king tighten with suppressed anger as he scowled. The healer had argued in vain with the High King, explaining that such a calculated slap on the face would not be forgiven, but, Uther had merely flared his nostrils and turned away.

'Say whatever is necessary, Myrddion. After all, that's your purpose and the reason you've been foisted upon me. You may let the Boar know I am displeased with him.'

In frustration, Myrddion had protested. 'I recall that the Romans counselled us to hold our friends close, my lord, but to keep our enemies even closer.'

'Don't address me in such a familiar fashion, healer. What my brother has created, I can also destroy. Remember your place.'

Despairingly, Myrddion had obeyed. Now, as he kneeled on the ice-slick stones, he prayed to the Mother that such humiliations would not become the pattern of his life.

'Forgive the High King for his absence, my lord, but affairs of state have delayed him. Welcome to Venta Belgarum for the winter solstice, King Gorlois, and I hope your sojourn in this city will be pleasant and happy.'

Gorlois read the chagrin in the healer's face. He remembered the Demon Seed very well from the accord at Deva and admired the young man's intelligence and tact. Although under his calm façade he was toweringly angry at Uther's slight, he was too wise to cast blame on the man who carried the unwelcome message.

'Get on your feet, Myrddion Merlinus, for it is unseemly for a man of your learning and intelligence to grovel in the dirt.' Gorlois stepped closer and whispered, 'You are not responsible for your master's manners.'

'Or lack of them,' Myrddion responded softly, knowing that Uther had spies watching and listening behind him. 'Take care, my lord, for every stone in Venta Belgarum has ears.'

Normally, he would never have spoken so openly, for many lives rested upon his compliance with Uther's wishes. But the healer's pride had been trampled in the mud and his extra sense was twitching in his brain. He felt the coming storm that was gathering behind Gorlois's snapping dark eyes.

'My lord.' A gentle voice interrupted them. 'Please help me to dismount and introduce me to this young gentleman, of whom you have told me so much. The whole world has heard of Myrddion Merlinus, so I hope I don't offend.'

That voice! Mother, have you come to earth to give me hope?

The cowled figure was tall and slender for a woman, and Myrddion could see the faintest trace of a creamy white cheek. But the voice seduced. Husky, deep for a woman and lilting in cadence, it sank into any true man's bones with a promise of unimaginable intimacy. Against his volition, his expressive right eyebrow rose.

Gorlois's hard expression softened immediately. 'My dear, allow me the pleasure of presenting Myrddion Merlinus, who has the unenviable task of advising the High King of the Britons. Myrddion, this is the queen of the Dumnonii and the Flower of Tintagel – Ygerne the Fair.'

Laughter sweet and unaffected issued from under the cowl. 'My lord, you do me too much honour, indeed you do. Lord Myrddion will expect a paragon, when all he will find is a middle-aged mother of two grown girls.'

Then, as the sun sent down a fortuitous slant of weak golden light, Ygerne lifted the hood back from her face.

Myrddion couldn't help his reaction and was grateful that the massed citizenry could only see the queen's cloaked back. His breath hissed in, and he bowed from the waist to hide his traitorous eyes.

No wonder Gorlois hides her away, he thought. So must Helen have appeared to Paris when he betrayed Troy to possess that unsurpassed beauty. By the gods, she is all women at their purest!

Fortunately, Gorlois couldn't see Myrddion's eyes until the young man had calmed somewhat. He had taken his wife's gloved hand and raised it to his lips, and Myrddion realised that Gorlois adored his wife with a passion rarely, if ever, seen in marriage. Ygerne coloured prettily, and Myrddion took the opportunity to examine her face as dispassionately as her beauty would allow.

Taken feature by feature, the queen should not have been so beautiful. Her nose was delicately modelled but not short, her cheekbones were very high and her eyes were of an indeterminate colour somewhere between blue and green, but neither. Her eyebrows were delicately arched but not remarkable, and her chin and jaw were firm but not exceptional. Her slightly loosened braids defied any description of their colour, being composed of every light shade right through to chestnut.

She is a chameleon, Myrddion thought. Every trick of the light catches her anew so that she is never the same. She is one of the fairest women who ever lived.

'My wife will be lovely until death takes her,' Gorlois stated proudly, and the faces of his warriors reflected his adoration.

Myrddion murmured a graceful compliment, his mind spinning madly out of control as he led Gorlois, Ygerne, Morgan and a small group of personal guards and servants into the palace and along the passageways to a suite of rooms that were comfortable, but not opulent. The Dumnonii guard was billeted on the outskirts of the city.

Bemused, Myrddion left the royal lovers and sought out Uther as he had been ordered. Fractious as always, the High King was pacing his quarters like a wild beast, while Ulfin and Botha attempted to seem busy in the luxurious apartment.

'Well? What did Gorlois have to say? What does the fair Ygerne look like? And is that Morgan witch behaving herself? You've kept me waiting, healer.'

'Lord Gorlois said nothing except to introduce me to his wife, who is a great beauty. Morgan stayed modestly cowled, and said nothing at all. Gorlois made no complaint about his men's being quartered so far away. In fact, I wasn't required to insist on his billets because he had already selected only a few body servants to accompany him into your palace. As always, the Boar of Cornwall was contained, courteous and graceful in everything he said and did.'

Uther growled like a big cat that Myrddion had seen at the circus in Rome. His blue eyes had exactly the same inhuman calculation as the lion had shown as it stalked a terrified felon in the arena. Even his curling, luxuriant hair was more like a mane than human locks.

'What will he do? What will he do?' Uther asked no one in particular. 'He'll not brook insult, but he's far too clever to expose himself to my justice. That . . . man! Gorlois would be king, I know it. He'd put his arse on my throne and his head into the crown of Maximus. Never! I'll embrace Hades before *that* day comes.'

'Truly, my king, I don't believe that Gorlois harbours any desire for your crown,' Myrddion protested as mildly as he could. 'He shows no signs of duplicity and my spies in Tintagel would know. He is simply more devoted to the people in the Dumnonii lands than to the rest of Britain.'

'We'll see!' Uther snapped. 'The banquet will be our first meeting. I've organised various hunts and amusements for the kings over the next ten days, but I'll be too busy to meet any of them until that night. Make sure they all understand that.'

Gods! When will Uther learn that the mailed fist smashes the nut and makes it difficult to swallow for the shell grit?

But Myrddion's face said nothing, although Uther knew precisely what he thought. In his quiet corner, Botha watched the two formidable men circle each other with words and his heart grew cold for the sanctity of his oath to his king. In the warrior's imagination, Myrddion was a long, slim blade, sharp and light, but wicked in its flashing speed. His king was a heavy Celt sword, used to crush and hack through cringing flesh, and had no fear of the lighter blade or the narrow hand that wielded it, trusting to his animal instincts to outguess the healer's intelligence. But Uther Pendragon was wrong. Botha could feel the power growing inside Myrddion Merlinus like a sea creature rising towards the light.

'As you ask, so I shall obey, my lord,' Myrddion replied enigmatically and Botha recognised the double meaning in the passive reply. The warrior was oath-bound to the High King, and knew he should speak his fears aloud to his master. On the other hand, he understood the frustration and the passions that drove Myrddion Merlinus because he had felt those same emotions often enough during the years he had served Uther Pendragon. He considered the question carefully, and decided that his personal code of honour did not demand that he should explain Myrddion's growing resistance to a king who also had eyes to see and ears to hear.

So Myrddion left the king's presence to explain to Gorlois and those kings already in residence that Uther was too busy to join them. He did so with delicate, wry humour, in a way that left no one in any doubt that Uther's healer did not approve of the situation. Gorlois quaffed his wine thoughtfully and joked with Leodegran and Llanwith pen Bryn with an absent, abstracted good humour and tried to interpret the fear that flitted through the black eyes of Myrddion Merlinus.

That night, in Ruadh's arms, the horses of terror galloped through Myrddion's dreams. Ygerne screamed shrilly through eyes that were wild with horror; Gorlois wept tears of blood above a severed neck wound; Morgan grew suddenly old and smiled widely to reveal that her tongue was now a hissing serpent . . . and an infant slimed with the blood of birth opened inhuman grey eyes and smiled at him with such trust that his heart almost broke in two.

Just when the images were more than he could bear to watch, they were blown away by an unnatural, freezing black wind and a cowled shape appeared. Whether it was man or woman, Myrddion could not tell. Human or god, he could not say. But his brain froze with terror.

'You must do what must be done, my poor suffering son. When this child is born, then you will be free – for a time.'

'Master . . . mistress . . . do not ask such dishonour of me, for I can go no further . . . I'll die of shame. Why did you give me life to do such things as I know are coming? I'll not obey! I'll not do this thing!'

The voice in his ears was neither male nor female but was greater than either. It replied gently, but Myrddion knew that all the storms of this world, and the screams of every living thing upon it, could not drown out a single word.

'You will do what must be done because you were made for this time. The road has been hard, my son, and will be harder still before

I permit you to die, but everything I ask is necessary, and nothing will compromise your honour. Others will break their oaths, although you will suffer for it, but you will finally be free.'

Then the figure lifted the cowl and Myrddion saw a succession of faces beneath the hood. There was his grandmother, Olwyn, gently smiling at him; Aetius sneered; Petronius Maximus nodded ruefully; Flavia's lips trembled; face after face came and went in the blackness under the cowl.

Then other faces he did not know replaced the friends and enemies of his youth. Old and young, they flashed past his wondering gaze. A tawny-haired woman was replaced by a breathtaking beauty with golden hair and cerulean eyes. A gnarled old mercenary gave way to a huge, brooding barbarian. A woman with ice-white hair and eyes too blue to be anything but a dream smiled at him with heart-stopping love. And then the faces were gone, and Myrddion knew that his dream was almost over.

A final face began to loom out of the pitch blackness, a face that seemed to belong to Uther Pendragon. There was the hair: wild, tawny and spiralled with curls. There was the same firm jaw and noble brow, but Uther never possessed such delicacy of cheekbone or nose. And then the eyes opened, and Myrddion saw that they were winter-grey and as chill as the northern ice packs.

'May the heavens protect me,' Myrddion screamed. 'Who are you?'

'I am what you desire most, the creature of your brain,' the face answered, but Myrddion screamed anew. For this face spoke with the seductive voice of Queen Ygerne of the Dumnonii, wife of the Boar of Cornwall.

CHAPTER XVI

A CURSE OF *LOVE*

The easiest thing of all is to deceive oneself; for what a man wishes he generally believes to be true.

Demosthenes, *Olynthiaca*

Still shaking within the shadow of his dream, Myrddion attempted to fasten the strings of his tunic with fingers that trembled uncontrollably. Ruadh's eyes were clouded with concern as she assisted him by smoothing the sable fabric over his broad shoulders and straightening the glossy leather hem around his trim hips. She knelt and laced his boots while Myrddion tried unsuccessfully to compose himself.

'Master, you must take a few drops of poppy in hot water tonight. These dreams must not continue, beloved, else you will go mad.'

Absently, Myrddion stroked her red hair with fingers that had lost their natural dexterity. He felt her wince when his nails caught in a tangle of her curls, so he pulled away from her.

'There will be no poppy, tonight or ever, for no soporifics can protect me from my dreams. In fact, they will only come with more intensity should I try to drug them away. You must avoid me for a time, Ruadh, for my affections can be poisonous. Although I don't intend it, those whom I care for always seem to die or be spirited away. I have too much esteem for you to risk your life, so leave me to my duties and my misery.'

Self-pity closed his throat and almost made him weep. He felt useless, unmanly and weak.

Ruadh rose gracefully to her feet. Those closest to Myrddion had grown fond of her but to the court of Uther Pendragon she would always be the Pict bitch who was the last love of Ambrosius Imperator. Now, sword-straight and proud, she met her lover's eyes directly, until Myrddion was forced to turn away.

'I'm no coward, Myrddion. Nor do I fear the animosity of the gods, for they have already taken everything from me but my life. Yet in answer to my prayers they have been sufficiently kind to have given you to me, so their curses can actually be blessings. I'll not leave you, master, although staying at your side may bring about my death. Don't try to persuade me or reject me, for it will not work, no matter what you say out of kindness. Such actions would be unnecessarily cruel and we'll both suffer because of your scruples. For a change, I will choose my own fate, for I will run no more!'

Then she grinned impishly to dispel the mood of gravity that her words had created.

'Besides, who would help you to dress in the mornings? You'd wear your tunic awry or inside out without my help, or put your left boot onto your right foot.'

'As always, my lady, you speak truly,' Myrddion answered seriously and bowed respectfully. 'You make my days bearable.'

'Get away with you and your sweet tongue, Myrddion Merlinus, for you'd charm the birds out of the trees.' She slapped him playfully across the buttocks as she slipped out of the sleeping chamber. 'You must hurry, beloved, for Uther awaits you.'

'Sod him. He can wait.'

'I heard that,' she called back to him across the colonnade.

Wanting to respond childishly, Myrddion suddenly discovered that he was smiling, and that he was actually hungry. Bless Ruadh! She always finds a way to cure my worst horrors. I wish I loved her as much as she loves me.

A wise man understands his own heart and Myrddion had long realised how his women had manipulated him into this relationship with Ruadh. He had understood their motives and been quietly amused, but a wholly physical need had demanded the warmth of Ruadh in his bed and he had accepted their meddling without complaint. With clinical detachment, he had carefully examined his feelings for Ruadh and had discovered that he admired many qualities in her character, from her courage to her irrepressible sense of humour; but he also recognised that although his affection for her was deep and genuine, her loss would not cause him lasting loneliness.

'Perhaps I lack the capacity for anything deeper,' he whispered aloud. He enjoyed their sexual compatibility and was comforted by the release of all the pent-up furies of each day that was spent with Uther Pendragon. Besides, he could talk to her as an equal and vent his frustrations into a sympathetic ear. With mingled ruefulness and arrogance, he supposed he was using her in his way, as men are wont to do, but the current situation suited them both.

You think too much, and you're a fool, he berated himself as he collected his map of the southern Saxon towns. He had received troubling news from Gruffydd overnight, and Uther must be informed immediately. First things first, Myrddion!

The tribal kings had ridden out at dawn on a wild boar hunt, a symbolism that was lost on no one, least of all Gorlois, the man it was supposed to threaten. Myrddion, therefore, was free to talk common sense to Uther. The noble ladies and their children were gathered in a warm room at the rear of the palace, sewing, playing at dice and amusing each other with gossip. Against all the odds, Venta Belgarum was at peace, at least for the moment.

Just as he raised his fist to rap on the timber frame at the entrance to Uther's apartments, Botha tugged the heavy wooden door open. A deep furrow of worry creased the warrior's eyes, usually the only sign that the captain betrayed of cracks in his composure.

'Our master's in a tear this morning, Myrddion. He had a bad dream last night and he's considering consulting a wise woman. Take care what you say, for he's wound up as tight as a wire garrotte.'

'Who's there, Botha? If it's the healer, he'd better have good news.' Uther's shouted voice sent a small tremor up the fingers of Botha's hand as it rested on Myrddion's forearm. The fingers tightened on his flesh in warning, then fell away.

With a sangfroid he didn't feel, and a cheerful nonchalance that was completely feigned, Myrddion strode briskly into Uther's apartments. The dream-ravaged, depressed healer had vanished and a firm, fair statesman had taken his place.

'Good morning, highness. Botha tells me that your sleep has been disturbed. I also had the night terrors last evening. But they pass, because they are only the messages of an unquiet brain.'

'So you are an expert in dreams as well, are you?' Uther sneered, sipped on his wine, grimaced and then threw the wine cup at Ulfin's face. 'This shit is sour. Find me something decent – or are you trying to poison me?'

Ulfin blanched and hurried away. 'And find that wise woman while you're about it,' Uther shouted after him.

'I can mix a sleeping draught that will banish all your night horrors, my king,' Myrddion murmured in an attempt to placate his master.

'*You* drink it, for I'll not touch it. I remember how my brother died.'

'You insult me, my lord!' Myrddion protested rigidly. 'I am oath-bound to protect you.'

'Take it any way that pleases you, healer. Now, what brings you to me so early? Come on, out with it! I can see that you're bursting with news.'

As Uther resumed pacing back and forth across his sumptuous bedchamber, Myrddion wished he had stayed in bed a little longer. Anything he told the High King would be rejected out of hand while Uther was in this difficult mood.

Uther stopped pacing abruptly as Myrddion remained silent. 'Do you mean to disobey me, Merlinus?' The High King's voice was suddenly quiet and silky. Uther was always more dangerous when his voice became gentle and soothing.

Myrddion took a deep, settling breath. 'No, my lord. Of course not. I received an urgent message from my spy in the Saxon east who is currently in Londinium. An unknown man came to my door before cockcrow late last night and was gone just as quickly, so I was unable to question him. But the hand that penned the Latin belonged to Gruffydd, whose intelligence has been so valuable to us in the past. I am forced to take his warnings seriously.'

Uther started to pace again, but without the frenetic energy of a few minutes earlier. His face was focused inward, and his eyes had become chill. The High King was always at his best in a crisis.

'Well? You'd best tell me, unless you expect me to cool my heels all day while you decide what you think I want you to say. So – out with it.'

Myrddion untangled Uther's sentence and shook his head swiftly. 'I never prevaricate, master, nor do I attempt to weaken Gruffydd's warnings. His messages are always too important to our cause to trifle with. Nor would I insult you by misrepresenting information that could be dangerous to you.'

Myrddion spread his map of the southeastern cities across

Uther's table and the High King stopped to examine it. The soldier in the king gave a little nod of approval at the placement of rivers, forests and villages on the rudimentary chart.

'According to Gruffydd, ceols are preparing to sail out of Portus Lemanis to carry men to Anderida. They plan to dig in near its gates and lay siege during the winter months so they can make a concerted attack on the fortress during the spring when our warriors will have depleted their winter stores of grain. We'll be unable to dislodge the Saxons if they become too entrenched, so we shall have to intercept them. Our enemies are like beetles boring into wood, or the lice that infest clean wool.'

Uther rubbed his freshly shaved jaw with a sword-calloused forefinger. 'They breed too damned fast,' he said as he moved his finger from his city to the fortress, attempting to judge the distance between them. 'Anderida is close to my defensive lines, so I can only assume that the Saxons are trying to provoke me. They'll not have my fortress – not now and not ever! But why are they sailing now? They've always been reluctant to venture out to sea in the winter.'

'It's true that they'd not sail from Gesoriacum at this time of year, my lord, for that journey would be madness in the storms of winter. But they can hug the east coast if they sail from Portus Lemanis, and then trust in the gods to make a decent landfall. They are learning to act unpredictably, damn them.'

Uther snickered softly but Myrddion read no humour in the grating sound.

'So they think that they can outfox the dragon. Well, we'll see. Perhaps I'll keep them waiting in the cold until spring, and then we'll discover how well they manage against my cohorts. Perhaps I'll march earlier.'

'Is it wise to wait so long, my lord?' Myrddion asked as mildly as he could. Uther's scorn for proffered advice, coupled with his refusal to accept opinions that ran counter to his own strategic assessments, made him a very difficult master to counsel.

'Not really, but I am considering an answer for them that will kill two birds with one stone. I'll let you know my decision when my plans are ready for implementation.'

Myrddion was instantly alarmed. Uther's countenance was almost coy and his eyes seemed to contemplate a secret that he was savouring, a tasty titbit to enjoy. From harsh experience, the healer knew that such obvious machinations by the High King usually spelt pain and danger for someone close to hand.

Gorlois? Of course! He'll send Gorlois to stop the rot at Anderida.

At that moment, Ulfin returned with a wineskin and handed his master a fresh cup, which Uther drank abstractedly. Other than Ulfin's laboured breathing, for the guard had run to obey his master, Myrddion's crisp voice was the only sound in the tense room. One finger pointed at the map as Uther stared down, his attention focused on the healer's information.

But try as he might, Myrddion couldn't draw Uther out, so the High King's plans remained concealed, a conundrum for Myrddion to puzzle over while the king was plotting. Just as the healer was preparing to put his suspicions into words, a knock interrupted them and Ulfin ushered in a woman who bore all the outward characteristics of a country housewife. The wise woman had come.

Myrddion's knowledge of women was too subtle to expect that all soothsayers famed for their prescience should look like crones, but even so, this woman's appearance surprised him. She was small and round with very red cheeks that gave her face the appearance of a ripe apple. A white scrap of rag covered all her hair and her plump face was almost youthful in its lack of wrinkles. Merry brown eyes surveyed the king sympathetically, before she lifted her skirts to honour her master with a low curtsey.

'What is your name, woman, and where do you dwell?' Uther demanded, after Botha had ruthlessly searched her from head to toe.

'My name is Muirne, the Sea Bright, and I was born in Hibernia. When I was a wee girl I married a man from Powys, but he died in Lord Ambrosius's service. I was forced to settle in Venta Belgarum, far from my kin, for the sake of my little ones. I've kept hunger from the door with my ma's cures for fever and the ague, and with a little fortune-telling, my king. My old ma always said that the seeing was a family curse, but it's kept me and my little ones fed for many a cold winter's night. They be grown now, so it's sad I am to be so far from the green lands of my birth. But a woman cannot be complaining.'

'No one here will care or listen,' Uther said bluntly.

'As you say, my lord, no one will listen. So . . . why do you come to me when the whole city knows that Mistress Morgan, who would choose to be a Druid like the wise ones who perished on Mona island so long ago, would gladly assist the High King with whatever ails him?'

'I don't trust the bitch,' Uther replied curtly, but the fluid cadences of Muirne's voice seemed to have soothed the worst of his anger. Myrddion could see no evil in her face, so he hoped she would not say anything to draw down Uther's rage upon her hapless head.

'Then tell me what you want, macushla, and I'll try to help you.'

In a manner that was completely out of character, Uther sat and proceeded to recount his dream with neither shame nor argument. He ignored her use of the familiar diminutive, *macushla*, a word that Myrddion imagined had never before been addressed to Uther, and in contrast with his dealings with the tribal kings, his guard and Myrddion, he spoke with surprising candour.

'In my dream, I stood in a wheat field where the healthy young plants came to my knees. While I stood there, spears rose out of the stalks and grew upwards towards the sun. I was forced to retreat from the field or be impaled on the long, leaf-shaped blades of iron.'

The wise woman, Muirne, nodded her head and her eyes became duller and darker. Myrddion imagined that he felt her mind probing outwards towards the king, seeking a breach in the shield that he used to disguise his worst and deepest feelings.

'At the edge of the field, two women barred my way and foiled my chance of escaping to safety. I reached for my sword, but it had vanished in the way of dreams. One of the women laughed and I knew from her voice that she was that Morgan bitch. She offered me a plate of apples and said: "Now you'll live forever, Uther, if that is what you desire, Child-killer."

'I took an apple and bit into it. Oh, but it was the sweetest, juiciest apple I've ever tasted. But the woman simply laughed with triumph and spun in a circle until she was only a puff of rancid-smelling air. I looked down at the apple and the flesh went black and shrivelled in my hand.

'The other woman smiled sadly under her cowl and lifted her arms to embrace me. I knew I'd be safe if I loved her and protected her, but I noticed her swollen belly and she told me that the child was mine. I was furious because she had no face and sought to trap me because I am the High King, so I wrenched a spear out of the wheat and stabbed her in the swelling of her pregnancy.' Myrddion's gorge rose at the murderous image. 'The spear went right through her body, and I felt sure that she and her hell-spawn would die, but she lowered her hands and said: "So it shall be. The child will prevail."'

Uther's gaze settled on the face of the wise woman. 'Then the sun seemed to split and I woke up.'

Muirne rocked on her heels and her face grew as pale as an old sun-bleached shell.

'Lord, I beg you not to blame me for my reading of your dream. Surely, the gods touched you in your sleep to warn you of troubles that lie ahead. In your heart, you know the messages that came to you in these dreams as well as I do, but I fear that you will order my death for speaking of the fate that might befall you.'

Uther looked thunderous and impatient by turns, and Myrddion held his breath. 'I don't know the meaning of my dreams, woman: you've been brought here to explain them to me. I'm a soldier, not a soothsayer. I don't intend to have you killed, whatever you might say, but I warn you that I'll know if you lie to me. I'll surely punish you for *that* presumption.'

Uther's voice was so controlled that Myrddion was immediately on his guard. The healer understood his master, and he knew that he couldn't trust this stranger king one single inch. Poor Muirne! Uther will keep his oath, but he has only promised that she won't die. There are worse things than death.

'The wheat field is our land, which has suddenly become your enemy and begins to turn against you. That you could pluck a spear from it should be a good sign, master, but the presence of the women changes the meaning to a threat. You mustn't use the war between our people and the barbarians in any way to further your ambitions. The spear, and your actions against the pregnant woman, will turn on you and you will fail in your purpose.'

'Who is this woman who claims that an infant will defeat me?' Uther's voice remained calm, but his soft voice only deepened Myrddion's nervousness.

'Does it matter, my lord? Your dream merely acknowledges that you will try to kill the fruit of your loins. Morgan said as much when she called you a child-killer. Do not fall into this error, my lord, if you wish to secure your throne. Kill no children! The Morgan in your dream offers you immortality because of it, but you discover that the gift is poisoned and you will be remembered forever as a monster *if* you fall into this trap. The gods are warning you clearly, my lord, for I take the cowled figure to be the Mother, and the other gods fear her fury as much as we mortals do.'

'Your answers are plausible, woman, but what if I've already killed a child? Is my fate already decided and set in stone?'

Myrddion could see the cogs of Uther's mind grinding out the unspoken name, *Carys*, and the healer hoped that the High King felt a twinge of regret, if not of shame, for the pregnant girl's murder.

Muirne shook her head so vehemently that Myrddion feared it would fly clean off her shoulders. The ghastly image caused his heart to race and his hands to tremble. 'No, lord. No. The subject of your dream has not happened. I can swear to you that the growing grain signifies things that are yet to come, so the gods wish you to take heed of their messages.'

'Enough!' Uther whispered. Then the room grew very still as he rested his hand on his chin and thought out her warnings. 'Give this woman a piece of gold and take her to an apartment in the palace.' He half turned and spoke softly to Botha. 'She stays with me until her usefulness is over.' He turned back to Muirne. 'Do not weep, Sea Bright. If your words are true, then you will be able to warn me of the danger when the time comes. You are a wise woman, aren't you? I'm loath to allow you to speak unwisely to those who might be curious about my affairs, so you must dwell with me until I decide otherwise.'

As Muirne turned to go, Myrddion smiled slightly in relief. He gripped her forearm in farewell, and was horrified to feel her death in her bones. He almost recoiled from the knowledge, but an inner voice told him to offer her his own words of comfort. She would have need of his wisdom.

'Do not try to take advantage of your position, Muirne, for your words put you in conflict with the Mother. You should drink only milk and water, and you must pray to the Mother's snakes to guide your eyes – and your tongue.' Then Ulfin hustled the little woman away, and Uther rounded on his healer.

'Why did you try to warn her, Myrddion Merlinus?' His voice had returned to its usual harsh tones and his face had resumed the familiar expression that Myrddion knew and dreaded. 'Was it professional jealousy because I ignored your advice and consulted a soothsayer? Perhaps I wanted an unbiased opinion from her.'

'She is doomed to die in your service, master, so I had to warn her that she is playing with fire – the fire of the goddess, at that.'

'We'll see. And don't speak about what you've heard, will you? Of course you won't, for you've too many servants you care about to wish *me* any ill-will. So what does this Muirne creature matter? At the very least, she'll be useful for a time.'

But will you listen to her advice, Uther? Never, Myrddion thought desperately as he escaped out into the clean fresh air. You'll go your own way as you always do.

'I'm getting up now, damn you, Cadoc. I don't care what Myrddion says, because I've lain abed so long that I want to scream with boredom.'

Luka swung his legs over the side of the divan on which he lay, a simple wooden structure that was strung with leather straps to keep his wool-stuffed pallet off the stone floor. His toes gripped the uneven surface, and Cadoc winced as the warrior exerted all his reduced strength to surge to his feet. Once upright, he teetered dangerously as he struggled to gain his balance, while Cadoc and Brangaine fussed around him like mother hens. They would have supported his elbows if he had permitted them to do so, but he waved them off with a crude oath.

With one painful step after another, Luka made his awkward, staggering way to the door frame, his sleeping robe flapping ludicrously around his brown legs. Finally, he stood trembling at the entrance to the colonnade, his face transformed with pride and joy.

'See? I made it!' he crowed to Cadoc and Brangaine with a boy's delight.

'That won't mean much if you sicken again because you're over-tired,' Cadoc responded tetchily. However, he found it difficult to dredge up any real disapproval for Luka's efforts. Any healer worth his salt is heartened by patients who passionately desire to be returned to health.

Footsteps on the scuffed marble of the colonnade warned the trio that the master was in the house. While Luka was keen to demonstrate his new strength, both Cadoc and Brangaine prepared for objections from Myrddion. To the healer, Luka was already something of a medical miracle after surviving his head injury, for few men lived long after such a blow as he had received.

'You're out of bed, Prince Luka,' Myrddion said mildly. 'How do you feel?'

'Tired – but upright! And you can forget the title. Any man who cleans my shit and piss for months knows me as well as my mother and should address me in the same fashion.'

'Very well, Luka.' Myrddion smiled. 'Now, tell me, how is your balance and your vision?'

Luka grinned in response and Myrddion realised that few men, and even fewer women, would be able to resist Luka's charm when he was in the mood to exert it.

After receiving satisfactory answers to a series of pertinent questions, Myrddion decided that Luka was well enough to spend most of his days out of bed, provided he didn't undertake any strenuous exercise. With luck, he might also be able to attend the solstice banquet, as long as he promised to forgo heavy food or drink. And, if his condition continued to improve, he should be sufficiently recovered to attend the meeting of kings that was to be held three days after the solstice, a promise that Luka accepted with rueful good humour.

'Won't that be lovely? The council will be all boring talk from tedious men who are determined to miss the blindingly obvious. The answers are very clear, too transparent for half those old dodderers. We need to squash the Saxons like bugs. All of us – in a concerted effort.'

'Are you so eager to return to my tender care with a new set of wounds, Luka? I hope we'll commit ourselves to an extended war in the south, but I don't fancy your chances of being ready to ride very quickly. You've only just learned to walk again.'

Myrddion's admonitions were half in jest, but for all Luka's confident aspect his face was paling even as they joked. The Brigante was exhausted and was swaying dangerously.

'It's off to bed with you now, Luka, and no arguments, please. Cadoc will support you, because you're likely to faint at any moment. If you plan to disagree with me, we'll argue it out from your bed.'

Then, before Luka could protest, Cadoc had swept him up, carried him to his pallet and tucked him firmly between warmed blankets into which Brangaine had slipped a heated brick. Myrddion drew up a rather rickety stool and sat down beside the bed, and the two men engaged in conversation.

'You're troubled,' Luka offered after half an hour of casual talk. Myrddion had learned that Luka was courageous, honest, blunt, and at times foolhardy when his personal honour was at stake. He raised one eyebrow at the Brigante prince, but he felt comfortable with the young man in a way that he rarely did with other men of his own age.

Perhaps, the healer acknowledged, Luka is more truly my equal in status than Cadoc, or Ambrosius, or even Cleoxenes. I was far beneath the latter two in experience and power, while Cadoc, for all his courage and willingness to learn, does not share my understanding of the noble classes. What a vain creature I'm becoming!

So Myrddion unbent a little, and if he spoke more freely than was wise, Luka never betrayed him.

'Uther is even more unpredictable than usual, the Saxons are sailing for the fortress of Anderida and Gorlois has managed to offend the High King's sensitive feelings. Is that enough trouble to manage at once?'

'It's more than enough,' Luka responded. 'How did you get caught up in such a knot of intrigue, Myrddion? You don't seem to be the kind of man who pursues power.'

For reasons unclear to himself, Myrddion found it easy to confide in Luka, and would have explained about his oath to Ambrosius had Llanwith pen Bryn not strolled into the small room with the easy grace of a large man who is perfectly in tune with his body.

Luka and Llanwith were acquaintances, for they were destined from birth to be part of the next generation of kings, but they had never socialised outside the parameters of formal feasts and tribal meetings. The men looked at each other warmly, but warily. Luka held the high ground, as he was a patient and therefore needed tender handling, but Llanwith had been unusually well educated and was curious to learn more about the heir to the throne of one of the largest and most powerful tribes in all the isles. Through jokes and good-natured rivalry, he could learn much of Luka's character.

'Luka, prince of the Brigante. I thought you were dead!'

'I like you too!' Luka retorted. 'As you can see, not only am I alive, but I'm in full possession of my wits and I'm on the mend. I'm lucky enough to have a very thick skull.'

Llanwith grinned and checked under the covers with scant regard for Luka's possible embarrassment. Myrddion envied the Ordovice prince his casual social skills.

'There's no woman lurking under the blankets with you? Here's a wonder. I was told you were the greatest . . . er . . . swordsman . . . in the west, and here you are in an empty bed. For shame, Luka! Your reputation will suffer for this.'

Despite Llanwith's teasing tone, Myrddion was worried that Luka would take offence, but instead he gave a cheeky grin, lifted the covers and patted his pallet.

'If you promise to take a bath, you can join me – if you're so worried about my reputation.' The saucy, very feminine wink that accompanied this invitation caused all three men to burst into spontaneous laughter. Luka was a natural mimic.

'I wasn't aware you nurture an inclination towards men,' Myrddion retorted before he realised what he had said. 'You must have a penchant for hair, Luka, because Llanwith has enough for three men – and I'm only referring to his back.'

Llanwith's brown eyes glowed with amusement. 'I'll donate some of my excess hair to you if you like, healer. You're uncommonly smooth-skinned for a Briton.'

'I've always followed the Roman fashion,' Myrddion replied with perfect seriousness. 'I started plucking my body hair as a youth, and I've continued the practice ever since.'

'You don't pull it out by the roots, do you?' Luka exclaimed, his eyes wide as he considered the work entailed in carrying out this operation. 'Even around your balls?'

'It must take for ever,' Llanwith said curiously, examining Myrddion's face with the keen interest of a man of intelligence. 'Doesn't it hurt?'

'It was painful when I first started doing it,' Myrddion told them, 'but my hair seems to have got the message over the years, and it hardly ever grows now, except for the toughest parts of my face.'

'But why do it?' Luka asked. 'Don't you want to look like a man?'

'Why? I can't be a warrior because I'm a bastard. I worship the

Mother, which is largely a female practice, and I'm a healer, so my personal grooming affects my patients. So why not?'

Despite the common sense in his answers, Myrddion's challenge had a bitter edge, causing both Llanwith and Luka to feel vaguely ashamed of their social gaffe. Their expressions sobered instantly.

'Besides, I wish to appear as different as possible from my master,' Myrddion continued. 'It's bad enough to be called Uther's storm crow behind my back.'

'True. He is the High King, so there's no help for you in that regard, but I can understand that you would wish to distance yourself from him. That man's . . .'

Luka interrupted before Llanwith allowed unwise words to pass his lips. 'The word for the High King is unpredictable,' he said firmly.

At that awkward point the three men parted, but Luka begged the others to return during the evening, for the nights drag on when an active man is forced to lie abed.

'While your healers and servants are very worthy people, there's not a beddable girl or a decent conversationalist among the whole bunch,' he said, leering comically. 'I'm starved for amusement.'

So their good mood was restored and promises were made, both spoken and silent, and it was clear to them all that a friendship was beginning to form between the three men.

'Is this what you expect of me, Mother? A trine? I enjoy their company and they lighten my heart, but I'm fearful of speaking unwisely in their presence. I'm afraid of betraying myself.'

Myrddion spoke aloud, but only Rhedyn, who was collecting feverwort from the scriptorium cupboard, was close enough to hear his words. The woman smiled softly, for her master was in sore need of good companions.

When Myrddion returned to the king's hall, the hunt had finished and servants were dressing a huge boar for the table. Inevitably,

Gorlois had killed the monster in a fearsome contest of brute strength and courage, and the carcass would take pride of place at the coming Samhain feast.

Myrddion paused in the shadows to listen to the servants while they singed the hair off the coarse hide.

'What a beast! Look at the size of those tusks,' the oldest man murmured as he measured the wicked, curved teeth along the length of his palm.

'Aye, it's huge. Yet King Gorlois attacked it with only a spear and a knife for weapons. On foot and alone, he planted his spear in the earth before him and braced it against his leg. Then, in its eagerness to destroy him, the boar leapt straight on to the weapon and impaled itself. Can you see the wound?'

The speaker had acted as one of the beaters, and his task had been to drive the boar towards the nobles who made up the hunting party. Two of his friends had bled to death when they were slashed by those wicked, sharp tusks. The speaker himself had been forced to climb a tree to escape the animal's initial charge, so he had witnessed the conflict between it and Gorlois from the safety of a thick tree branch.

'Only a man of enormous strength could have held that spear in place as the boar tried to climb down the blade to reach him. It drove the barb into its own heart. Gods, but Gorlois is a true man.'

'Aye, his kind is rare,' the older servant replied. 'Would that the High King were as noble.'

'Shut your mouth or we'll both be served up for the High King's pleasure like this dead meat. Gods, but you're a talkative fool.'

Myrddion slipped away, considering how far Uther's reputation had decayed and yet increased. Common men now feared him more than any other warrior in the west, but that fear had no admiration in it, only dread.

Aye, Uther is surely a dragon. And he will come to regret his treatment of the lowest among us, Myrddion thought. After all, they are the ones who bleed for us in battle. If the king continues in this high-handed fashion, they will desert him.

Myrddion's evening was not destined to be uneventful. He had scarcely entered the great hall before Gorlois left his conversation with the other kings and approached him with a personal request. Myrddion noticed that a smear of boar's blood still stained the king's leather jerkin at the neckline. The beast had almost reached his throat.

'My wife is unwell and has a mild fever, so I'd like you to examine her. It's probably nothing, but I'd be comforted by your opinion, master healer.'

'I shall visit her highness at once. For propriety's sake, I trust she keeps her daughter and maidservants with her?'

'I'd not trust even you with her otherwise.' Gorlois grinned easily, but Myrddion wasn't deceived by the king's warm brown eyes. A glint of steel behind those bland irises warned Myrddion that Gorlois meant every word he said.

Myrddion made his way to the Dumnonii rooms. The spartan apartment had been softened by hangings of an attractive rose shade, and something aromatic burned in a brazier beside a couch on which the queen sat, surrounded by her younger attendants. The atmosphere in the room touched the sensitivity in Myrddion's soul and reminded him poignantly of his grandmother. Ygerne and Olwyn were much the same age, although his grandmother had been dead for many years. Olwyn had been lovely as well, although she had lacked the strange glamour of this slender woman. Even Morgan's robes of unrelieved black and her downturned, angry brows could not dispel the aura of gentleness and beauty that embraced Queen Ygerne.

When she admitted him into this feminine sanctum, Morgan

made her reservations very clear. 'Father acts unwisely to send Uther's creature to help us. I'm perfectly capable of caring for my mother. As you may know, I understand more of herb lore than most healers – including you.'

'You may speak truly, Lady Morgan. However, I have been ordered by your father to satisfy myself and him that Queen Ygerne suffers no serious illness. I must obey him.'

Morgan scowled even more darkly at Myrddion's natural courtesy, but she stepped away so he could make a low bow of respect to the queen.

'If you would allow me, highness?' Myrddion lifted one slender wrist and felt for the pulse points in the Greek fashion. He could feel the steady beat of her blood under his sensitive fingers, and the perfume that rose from her skin, her hair and her clothing was intoxicating.

Releasing her hand, he laid his palm against her broad, high forehead in the age-old test for fever. Her skin was cool to the touch and a little dry, and her eyes were clear and showed no signs of discoloration or the hot glitter of illness.

'Leave us,' Ygerne ordered her maids. 'You may stay, Morgan, but do me the courtesy of remaining silent. I wish to speak to Myrddion Merlinus free from bad-natured ears and the possibility of gossip.'

'Really, Mother! Your servants would never inform on *you*,' Morgan retorted.

'I can find no sign of illness, your highness. In fact, I would say you are in superbly good health.'

Ygerne looked down into her lap, while her nervous fingers busily folded and refolded a strip of delicate fabric that she kept tucked into her sleeve. 'My illness is not of the body, Myrddion. I need to consult you on another matter. Forgive my frankness, but I have heard that you have the gift of prophecy, which is a matter of interest to me. Is this rumour true?'

Myrddion was puzzled, but not offended. He had no idea what Ygerne wanted of him, but he answered as honestly as he could, for to deny the rumours would be foolish. He was fully aware that most Celts were familiar with the story of Dinas Emrys and the Demon Seed.

'I have had dreams that profess to be prophecy, my lady, and I have fallen into a waking fit on several occasions. I hate the very thought of these fits, and would prefer they did not happen.'

'I understand more truly than you might think, Myrddion. My father, Pridenow, has been dead for many years, but he swore that the sight passed through his bloodline and I shouldn't be frightened if unbidden images came to me, sleeping or awake. I am fortunate, for I have rarely felt this inner ... touch ... so I have largely been left in peace. My daughter, Morgause, feels it not at all, but Morgan claims that unbidden warnings have come to her on many occasions from the time of her earliest childhood. I cannot understand it, so I have prayed to the Virgin most earnestly to explain this gift. She chooses to ignore me.'

'I am a man of science, your highness, like the old Greeks. I study the natural world to try to understand its secrets, so I endeavour to probe the world of my five senses as carefully and as dispassionately as I can. But I have never understood the secret of the sight, although I cannot doubt that some people are so afflicted, and often against their will. Perhaps it is just another sense that some people are able to use, like hearing or touch. Some people have a very poor sense of smell, and others cannot see very clearly. We are all different, my lady. Why do you ask?'

'When I was a girl and I first journeyed to Tintagel, I was terrified by unbidden visions that came to me during the night. When I first saw my beloved Gorlois, I dreamed that he carried a terrible wound across his throat. I remember the terror I felt at the time, but the visions gradually disappeared and I have been left in peace for many years – until I journeyed to Venta Belgarum. The dreams and images have now returned tenfold.'

'Your highness, I . . .' Myrddion began, but the queen cut him off with an impatient gesture of her hand.

'You must say nothing of this conversation to Gorlois. He'd worry, and I'll not have my lord disturbed by a woman's foolishness. But I have seen his head with blood pouring from a severed neck, and I smell decay spreading like a sickening perfume in the folds of his cloak. I have dreams of a bloody child, Myrddion, and the night horrors will not release me. I am sure that my happiness is over for ever and the long road of my life leads me towards a dreadful threshold. What can I do?'

Her eyes were huge and a tear shivered on her long, dark lashes. Ygerne had no need for cosmetics and her pink lips trembled like rose petals torn by the wind. Myrddion wanted to ease her mind at any cost, so great was her power over him. Every beat of his heart strove to protect her, but he recognised the vision of the child with its echoes of Uther's dream and his own, and his flesh cooled with presentiment.

'If there is one thing in which I have total belief, your highness, it is our ability to choose our separate fates. *Nothing* is certain: no visions or dreams can confine our actions. We choose to listen to them, or to reject them, and so the future cannot be set. Even random chance cannot be purely accidental, for if we examine each incident carefully, we can tell that what *seems* to be the caprice of Fortuna is actually the outcome of many small, seemingly unrelated choices that have come together under the guise of chance. You must pray to your god, my lady, and remember that the sight can only be *insight*, and nothing more.'

Ygerne sighed deeply and closed her eyes, and her whole body relaxed. Then, as her extraordinarily changeable eyes opened,

Myrddion glimpsed something in their depths that disturbed him. He was conscious of Morgan's presence hovering behind him like a grim carrion bird, and felt the hair rise at the back of his neck.

'Your explanation has eased my spirit, master healer. Yes, intent is important. As you say, it is insight and not sight. I will pray and consider what you have said, Myrddion Merlinus, for you are wise beyond your years. Forgive me for causing you so much trouble over a woman's formless fears.'

'No, my lady. It is you who should forgive me. I have no definitive answers, so my words are simply my attempt to explain the gifts of Ceridwen. I could easily be wrong.'

'I could forgive you anything, Myrddion. Your heart is pure, having no stain upon it.'

As Myrddion backed way, bowing low with true reverence, he considered his reaction to Queen Ygerne. Few women had touched him beyond the immediate desires of sexual fulfilment, and he had never met a female whose appeal was so intellectual, and yet so profoundly physical. Her goodness was so vulnerable that he feared for her safety as she moved like an unprotected innocent in the violent vortex of Venta Belgarum with its deceits, caprices and savagery.

That night, as he spent himself in Ruadh's willing body, it was Ygerne's face that he saw. Somehow, the Dumnonii queen had wormed her way into his soul.

CHAPTER XVII

UTHER'S BANE

No sooner had the king cast his eyes upon her [Ygerne] among the rest of the ladies, than he fell passionately in love with her, and little regarding the rest, made her the subject of all his thoughts.

> Geoffrey of Monmouth, *The History of the Kings of Britain*

Time passed and the three friends grew to enjoy each other's company in the uneasy inactivity of Venta Belgarum. The snows had come, but the falls were light and served only to conceal the harsh rectangular lines of the city. Even the grey walls of the stone buildings seemed softened by the shimmering white dusting on each protruding rock, while in the streets rubbish was soon buried under a pristine snowy blanket. The winds had dropped, but the sun was invisible behind dove-grey cloud cover that was pregnant with snow flurries yet to fall.

On the day of the solstice feast, Myrddion awoke early and was fed and abroad before the light had driven back the black shadows of a still night. As he walked to the citadel, he noticed that almost every doorway was decorated by a trail of mistletoe, heavy with white berries, to signify the birth of the King of the New Year. As the old year died, the enfeebled king of the earth would be transformed into a rosy boy, and so the solstice marked the great cycle of birth and death that was enacted in the depths of winter. So the High King and his queen should dance and rejoice at the Samhain fires, for they represented the fertility of the land.

'But Uther has no wife and no desire for a son who, like Vortigern's offspring, might lust after the crown of Maximus. What a travesty! Uther will oversee a sterile ceremony without a holy bride. Gods, help us in this time of need.'

When several workers who were clearing snow from a stable door with wooden shovels began to stare at him with rolling eyes, Myrddion realised that he was speaking aloud. He shook himself mentally. What was wrong with him?

When he arrived at the king's hall, it was to find that the days of preparation and thankless labour were finally bearing fruit. Harassed servants were distractedly carrying baskets of fish to the kitchens, safe in swathes of fresh green grass. Rock oysters were being kept fresh in wooden bowls of salted water, while a huddle of servants were basting, carving, cutting and dicing vegetables, fruit, every kind of fowl and huge slabs of venison that were turning on spits. Pride of place was taken by Gorlois's boar as it turned slowly on a great iron stake over a slow fire. It was far too large for the kitchens, so an exterior cover had been employed and two servants were turning the carcass with hands protected by stout leather gloves. Periodically, the boar's skin was basted with a viscous liquid that Myrddion recognised as honey.

The smells of slow-cooking meat made Myrddion salivate while, driven half mad by the aroma, a collection of hopeful hounds sat just beyond range of stones thrown by a kitchen boy whose sole task was to keep them at bay. Myrddion's heart lifted as he watched the scurry of busy men and women with faces wreathed in smiles as they prepared for the holy feast.

'You're sunk in thought, Myrddion?'

The healer turned slowly.

Botha was leaning negligently against the wall of a half-timbered hut used to store dry wood. His cloak was very muddy around the hem and the healer wondered what his master had desired of the bodyguard so early in the day.

'You're out and about before cockcrow, Botha. Is anything amiss?'

'No, healer, all is well. I've been seeing to the welfare of Bishop Lucius of Glastonbury, who appeared in response to a call from his master, Bishop Paulus of Venta Belgarum, whom you might know as Caomh the Gentle. His presence has put our master out of temper, for the Christian Church has decided that the solstice coincides with the birth of their Jesus, the undead god. Uther is not best pleased and now must celebrate the occasion in the stone church two days hence. He is an occasional Christian, but like most warriors he prefers to give his allegiance to Mithras rather than a god who preaches peace.'

'A difficulty for you, I know, Botha. But Lucius gave Ambrosius peace as he was dying, so Uther must be grateful to him. Besides, the prelate appears to be an unusual man, one who understands what it is to fight and to kill. I trust him, although I'm no adherent of the Christian faith. He has a presence ... a serenity, one that inspires confidence.'

'Aye, healer. Still, our master causes upsets throughout the city when he is annoyed, so I've billeted Lucius with Paulus, and I'm hoping that both men will avoid attending the feast tonight. Tact should keep them within their own stout walls and away from a pagan celebration.'

'Pagan?' Myrddion's eyebrow rose. 'I consider the Old Faith is still the true faith, but I concede that I'm in the minority. What if Uther should insist on the presence of his bishop? That might cause embarrassment for Bishop Paulus. I'd like to speak to Lucius, if the bishop will permit him to converse with a pagan. I confess that his erudition and strength of character intrigue me. Would my approach be welcome?'

'I can't see why not, healer. You are a power in this city, and you stand at the left hand of the High King. Lucius and Paulus are probably as curious about you as you are about them. They deal with non-believers all the time, although they insist that theirs is the one true faith.'

'I think I'll pay a visit to Lucius, then, while I have the leisure,' Myrddion decided. Botha nodded impassively, and pointed the way to the Roman-style building that housed the senior prelates of the west.

Myrddion traversed the icy streets, trying to avoid the mud and slush that had so befouled Botha's cloak. The stone-built house was a sombre, windowless building that looked as though it faced inward to a central atrium. The heavy double doors sported a huge brass knocker shaped to represent the head of a fanciful beast with an iron ring through its nose, polished to a glittering brightness.

Myrddion used the iron warning bell to pound on the door and listened as the echoes reverberated through the inner halls.

After a short interval, the heavy door was dragged open by an elderly priest who was tonsured in the Roman fashion and whose hands and lips were blue with cold. With a pang of sympathy, Myrddion realised that the ancient's feet were bare on the cold paving.

'I have come to speak to Bishop Lucius of Glastonbury. My name is Myrddion Merlinus of Segontium, sometimes called Caer Narfon.'

The old man examined Myrddion closely with red, rheumy eyes, but he chose not to speak. A single knotted finger was raised, and the priest pattered away on his cold feet into the colonnade, leaving Myrddion standing on the threshold.

Once again, the healer had to wait for some little time before he heard approaching footsteps and saw Lucius striding towards the entry with the stooped, elderly priest hurrying in his wake. Although his robes were unbleached homespun tied at the waist with a frayed, plaited rope of coarse wool, Lucius carried himself like a warrior dressed in stylish armour and fine linen. His simple leather sandals left much of his feet bare and his head was uncovered, yet he gave no impression of being cold or uncomfortable.

'Myrddion Merlinus, I remember you well.' Lucius's voice was a smooth and pleasant baritone and, once again, Myrddion was struck by the purity of the bishop's Latin. 'How may I assist you, my son?'

'My apologies for disturbing you, but I wished to thank you for the compassion that you extended to my beloved master Ambrosius. I never had the opportunity to speak privately to you, for Uther moves like the wind when he decides to act. Perforce, I had to oversee my dead lord's funeral pyre at the Giant's Carol.'

'I understand, good Myrddion,' Lucius replied, his eyes fixed on the healer's face. 'But that's not why you have come to me, is it?'

'I'm not sure why I came, except that I felt impelled to speak to you again when Botha told me that you had arrived in Venta Belgarum.'

'Then enter, my friend, and come into the atrium. Perhaps good Father Ednyfed here would be so kind as to find some hot milk for us to drink.'

Father Ednyfed looked up at Myrddion like an eager, twisted and elderly black bird. His weak eyes were bright with interest.

'I would not wish to presume on Father Ednyfed's kindness. The floor must be very cold on his bare feet.'

Father Ednyfed shook his head vigorously, causing Lucius to smile and nod to his priest. 'Perhaps you would be so kind, Brother Ednyfed.'

The old priest pattered away with more sprightliness than his bent back and gnarled limbs suggested. Myrddion's sympathetic eyes followed the figure in its rusty brown robe. 'Why does your priest forgo sandals and mittens? He is too old to bear the full force of a cold winter.'

Lucius smiled reflectively and a world of sympathy and understanding filled his eyes.

'Your concern does you credit, but Ednyfed chooses to feel the cold and to remain mute. He expiates a sin that cannot be washed away with prayer alone – at least, in his understanding.'

'Why would any god demand such suffering?' Myrddion whispered.

'My Lord demands nothing. Ednyfed offers his old bones and his silence willingly. I'll not come between him and his belief in his salvation.'

Ednyfed reappeared at Lucius's elbow, bearing a tray unsteadily in his old hands.

'Thank you, my brother. The milk is very welcome.'

Ednyfed offered milk to Myrddion, then bent painfully and kissed Lucius's ring. Myrddion looked away, embarrassed by this humble display of devotion.

As the ancient priest departed, Lucius cupped his hands around his bowl and his piercing eyes examined Myrddion carefully as the young man tried to find a comfortable position on a hard stone bench.

'You're troubled, healer. I can see that your shoulders are bowed under some weight that you weren't carrying when last we met. How may I help you?'

Myrddion shook his head irritably. 'I don't know, Lucius. I suppose, if I were of your Christian flock, I would probably wish to make my confession to your God and free my soul from burdens of knowledge that have soured me and stained my honour. I have seen such things . . . and said nothing, for the sake of an oath that binds me to my dead master and his wishes.'

Lucius nodded in understanding. 'There is a terrible contradiction between the call of personal honour and the demands of the realm,' he said carefully, balancing the needs of the young man who sat so quietly before him and the strictures of his faith. 'You tread a dangerous road between twin evils, and with only a small slip your soul can be stained forever.'

He smiled at Myrddion, whose eyes had begun to tear up as he recognised the understanding in the prelate's face.

'I cannot hear your confession, nor can I give you the absolution that your heart desires. But I can listen, Myrddion, for I was pagan once and I know that God worked through me, even then, to lead my stumbling feet along the paths that he had destined for me. You may speak freely, for I'll never betray a word said in this house. You have my oath as a bishop, a Roman and the son of a family who always took pride in the glory of their name.'

There was no good reason for Myrddion to unburden himself, other than his trust in the word of this compelling and interesting man. So, after all the years of silence and discipline that had held his emotions in check, Myrddion began to speak of what he had seen and done in the last two years of service to Uther Pendragon. At first, the words came slowly and painfully, but quickly turned into a flood as the healer felt the weight of his shame and guilt lift off his shoulders.

So this is why confession is so attractive to Christians, Myrddion thought.

'Yet more troubles are to come, Lucius. I don't know if you believe in prophecy and the sight. I imagine your beliefs preclude such superstitions, but I know that such things exist, whether we will them to or not. I am being pushed and pulled towards a dreadful event where I will have to balance the weight of my soul against the needs of our people in the west. Uther is a necessary evil, for only he can save the land from Saxon invasion at this time in our history.

No other claimant exists who can hold Ambrosius's fragile accord together, so what am I to do?'

Lucius rose to his feet, his stern, beautiful face furrowed with care. His eyes, so black and lustrous, were far away in time and space as if he measured the lessons of the past before he spoke.

'Uther is a dangerous man because he hates so thoroughly and so viciously. Nothing is beyond him – not murder, nor blasphemy nor the destruction of the whole land if it will serve his purpose. But his hatred is held in check by self-interest, which is your only hope. For too many years, he was a nameless warrior who had been cast out of his own lands. He'll not risk such exile again, which gives you a weapon that can be used to hold his worst excesses in check.'

'Aye, that is true,' Myrddion replied slowly, his mind working swiftly and his eyes glowing with growing hope. 'Perhaps I can play on that fear and keep him focused on the Saxons, rather than the madness that lies at his heart.'

'Don't mistake wickedness for madness, Myrddion. Like the creature he is named for, Uther is coldly savage and his hatreds are the same. He isn't demented, but merely evil. That flaw, too, can be useful to you if you can forget the nonsense about his monstrousness, for evil is largely impotent.'

Myrddion nodded slowly and thought of Uther's demand that Carys's jewel be returned to him. That small theft was evil, not mad.

'So what can I do in the trials that lie ahead?'

'For good or ill, you hold a certain power over Uther Pendragon because of the oath he gave to his brother. You will need to base your decisions on what is good for the realm. Perhaps you will need to trample your personal honour into the dust at times, simply to save and serve the people. In that eventuality, I wouldn't care to stand in your shoes. You are still young, and you have many bitter roads to travel before you die.'

Myrddion rose to his feet, for the fog had cleared from his brain. Lucius had placed his strong, slender forefinger upon the crux of Myrddion's problem. Now that he understood that his personal honour was less important than the welfare of the Britons as a whole, his path, thorny and painful as it was, seemed clearer.

'Thank you, Bishop Lucius. No other man could have seen my dilemma for what it was, or defined it so clearly. May I speak to you again should I have the need, for there is a great loneliness in the power that Ambrosius thrust upon me?'

'Of course, my son. If it is any consolation, Ambrosius Imperator must have trusted you more than any man alive to lay such burdens upon you. Perhaps he was unfair, but he had so little time and he loved this land. As do you.'

'As do I,' Myrddion replied sadly, and took his leave.

The busy afternoon passed in a blur of organisation. Onto Myrddion's broad and unwilling shoulders fell the task of deciding the order of precedence and trying to prevent the very real threat of any tribal king's feeling himself overlooked and insulted. For prudence's sake, Myrddion placed Gorlois, his queen and his daughter halfway down a table where they were flanked by Llanwith pen Bryn on one side and Luka of the Brigante on the other. Thus Myrddion hoped to relieve Uther's suspicions of a fancied plot between Gorlois and Leodegran by placing them far apart, and thereby avoid any direct conflict with the High King.

Once he had covered every eventuality that could be foreseen, Myrddion checked the solstice pyre in the forecourt before scurrying to the house of the healers to bathe and dress in his most sumptuous clothes. With his head still spinning with nasty possibilities, he dressed with the help of Ruadh and Cadoc, who had polished his jewellery to a brilliant gleam. Praxiteles would attend as his table servant and the old trader had found snowy linens in which to dress, although Myrddion imagined he would be chilled to the bone.

'You're too old to wear linen in the dead of winter,' he chided his friend with real concern. 'You'll catch your death in that frigid hall.'

Praxiteles grinned and parted his snowy robe to reveal crude but effective fur breeches and boots, roughly laced up his legs. 'Under my finery, I assure you that I'm very warm, master. And don't fear for ructions during the ceremony, for I'll do what I need to do to keep the meal moving smoothly.'

Myrddion had chosen to wear his customary black, but the women had found a length of finely spun wool that provided a grand, if funereal, long robe over his leather breeches and boots. A belt of silver links lay around his narrow hips and Brangaine brought in the fish necklace of electrum that had belonged to his grandmother, and fastened it round his neck when he wasn't looking.

'I can't wear this,' Myrddion exclaimed, flicking the glittering links with his forefinger. 'This necklace is sacred to the Mother, and I am a man. Attending this feast will be difficult enough without offending *her*.'

'The Mother will attend the ceremony whatever you do or say,' Ruadh answered for them all. 'Wear her mark so that all men know you for what you are. Give Uther something to ponder over.'

Myrddion snorted with scorn. 'He'll not recognise this piece of jewellery, nor understand its significance. Uther is a clod where religion and portents are concerned.'

'But others will recognise her sign and tell him what it is. Head up, master, for you go to war for all of us this night. Start the new year under her favour.'

Against his misgivings, Myrddion submitted to their argument, thrust his rings upon his fingers and permitted the women to bind his hair with silver wire. With his sable-trimmed cloak tossed negligently over his shoulders, he felt equipped for some invisible battle and ventured out into the night, followed by Praxiteles who bore a bright, flaming torch.

As he passed the homes of the common folk of Venta Belgarum, the citizens were shocked by his appearance. The torch elongated his shadow until he seemed to be a veritable giant, while his black garb melded with the shadows so that he was almost invisible except for the pallor of his face and hands. But the reflection of the torchlight on the electrum scales of the fish necklace burned with a cold white fire and marked him as a creature of the darkness.

Myrddion entered the hall from the side, choosing to forgo the impact of a showy arrival through the great gilded doors. After checking the area devoted to the feast for one last time, he joined the noble guests as they milled in the anteroom, awaiting the High King's pleasure.

Nervously, Myrddion examined the throng of brilliantly dressed guests. Servants wove their way through clusters of gossiping kings and their spouses to offer wine, chilled juices and tempting titbits designed to whet hearty appetites.

So far, so good. No one has grown restive . . . yet. Why is Uther keeping everyone waiting?

'Ho, Myrddion,' Llanwith called from a dim corner where Luka was seated on a purloined stool, looking a little pale. 'When does the feast begin? I swear that half the guests will be drunk if we don't eat soon.'

Myrddion shrugged noncommittally as he joined his two friends. 'I have no idea, Llanwith. I imagine the High King is making a point about something.'

He explained the reasons for their seating arrangements and wrung a promise from them to act as a buffer between Gorlois and the High King.

'How do you expect us to deflect Uther if he is in a temper?'

405

Luka asked plaintively. He was feeling weary, hot and very hungry.

'Just do your best. You're a long way from the head table, so the problem shouldn't arise.'

'Promises, promises,' Luka muttered.

At that moment, the inner doors to the hall swung open and Botha summoned the kings to take their places for the solstice feast. As the guests were ravenous, they showed little concern for status and order of entry. Indeed, Botha had to press himself against the door jamb as the kings, their wives and their retinues made a concerted dash for their places at the tables.

'Like hogs come to their master's trough,' Llanwith muttered darkly, but Myrddion refrained from making any comment. Ensuring that Llanwith had spotted the dark head of Gorlois in the crowd, Myrddion slipped away to a minor table at the back of the feasting hall where he sat with several city notables, on the fringes of this grand occasion.

His choice of position had not been motivated by false modesty. From his seat, he could watch all the actions of his master at the opposite end of the room as well as observe the tribal kings as they ate. When Praxiteles offered him heavy red wine from a gilded jug, Myrddion placed his hand across his goblet and asked for water, which Praxiteles hurried away to procure.

'We are honoured by your presence, master healer,' the town magistrate murmured politely. His heavy chain of office hung round his scrawny neck and Myrddion recognised the Roman workmanship in the decoration. Once he had been introduced to the civic leaders at the table and their overawed wives, he settled down to a programme of careful observation.

A group of musicians played drums, pipes and lutes for the pleasure of the crowd, while servants in blood-red livery moved around the room bearing huge jugs of wine.

But still Uther Pendragon was absent from the ceremony.

Then, just when the High King's absence was becoming an insult to the tribal kings, Uther entered in a robe of red slashed with gold. He wore the heavy crown of Maximus, which was studded with huge, blood-red garnets so that, under the glow of many oil lamps, Uther's hair appeared to bleed. Flanked by Bishop Paulus, who looked distinctly uncomfortable, and Ambrosius's seneschal, the old king of the Cantii tribe, the High King seated himself, with Botha and Ulfin standing directly behind his chair.

A murmur that began like a long, slow wave of noise washed across the room. Then, as if every voice had been cut off by a sharp knife, the room grew silent. The musicians laid their instruments to one side in response to a subtle movement of Botha's hand.

'Behold, kings of the tribes of Britain, the High King comes amongst us on this, the solstice, in the dying days of the year. Hail to Uther Pendragon, High King of the Britons.'

Botha's voice had been impressive in its strength and solemnity and, as one, the kings and their retinues rose to their feet and lifted their wine cups high.

'Hail to Uther Pendragon, High King of the Britons.'

Half a hundred voices shouted out the salutation, as if the noise would drown out any doubts that Uther might harbour about them. The rafters shook in response and the flames in the lamps dipped and swayed as if a strong wind had passed over them.

The tribal kings seated themselves, the musicians began to play a rousing tune better suited to a battle than a feast, and the food was carried into the dining hall on great steaming platters by staggering servants. Under a façade of merriment and good fellowship, almost frenetic in its nature, a mood of unease was building because of the stern, unbending visage of the High King. His face could have been carved out of a great slab of amber, it seemed so stiff . . . and so still.

Uther's eyes roved around the hall, capturing the unwilling attention of one king after another. When his cold gaze passed on, that unfortunate king would gulp his wine and address himself to his food with a feigned gusto that was wholly false. Myrddion was willing to wager that the fine venison and pickled vegetables tasted like dust and ashes inside their dry mouths.

Of the whole throng, only Gorlois met Uther's gaze directly, although Llanwith and Luka avoided the king's examination by maintaining animated conversations with the ladies next to them. Gorlois actually had the temerity to raise his wine cup in a silent toast to Uther, whose brows met in annoyance before acknowledging the toast.

Ave, Gorlois. It's past time that Uther received a taste of his own treatment, Myrddion thought grimly.

The air seemed to crackle between the two formidable men, so that Llanwith felt the hairs rise on his arms. Uther's eyes swivelled towards Gorlois's ladies in a gesture meant to threaten and subdue. The blue eyes glittered like ice in his rugged, impassive face.

Morgan felt the power of his gaze and lifted her chin in defiance. She had dressed with care for this particular feast, understanding that her beloved father was under threat. Her hair hung down her back in a thick black wave of gleaming ebony, except for the silver lock that sprang from her right forehead. She had emphasised that forelock by plaiting it with silver wire, and her earrings were heavy baubles of the same metal, so flattering to her colouring, and strung with pearls of great price. Her dress was black, trimmed with sable for warmth, but the décolletage was laced low so that the swell of her perfect breasts was visible. With palms and nails stained with expensive imported henna and the skilful addition of lip rouge so that her mouth was a red wound in her milk-white face, she was a splendid, erotic figure.

But Morgan's eyes, so like those of her father, were almost black in the flickering light and she seemed mocking, challenging and wise beyond her years. Myrddion could see her raised profile, so pregnant with messages for the High King that he imagined he heard her response to Uther penetrate his brain.

Do not touch me or mine, or I will make you suffer for eternity.

Uther's anger was palpable as he raised his wine cup, drank deeply, then rammed the goblet down on the table with sufficient force to bend the soft gold. Bishop Paulus jumped with fright, and watched his earthly master out of nervous, uncertain eyes.

The High King's medusa stare moved to Gorlois's most treasured possession, Queen Ygerne, who was speaking animatedly to Prince Luka about the need for noblewomen to better the lot of their servants and farmers. Luka had been dazzled by Ygerne at first and had been content to watch her smiling face, paying little attention to what she said. But her warmth, eagerness and intelligence had soon captured his attention, and he realised she was a woman of tenderness, as well as a creature of inexplicable glamour.

Uther laid eyes on Ygerne for the first time and saw the Dumnonii queen at her absolute best. Knowing that her husband was beset on all sides by the High King's enmity and the passive acceptance of the situation by his peers, she had dressed with exceptional care. She understood that a soft, pale rose shade suited her admirably and had sacrificed a bolt of imported cloth from her dowry for the occasion, with underskirts of cream and pale dove-grey. Her dress was modest but the fragile, valuable cloth was light, revealing the slender beauty of her form and accentuating the whiteness of her throat as it rose out of the antique gems that formed a heavy collar of rubies and garnets at her neck.

Above this flower-coloured confection, her pale face captured every flicker of the lamplight, accentuating the changeable nature of her expression. Her high cheekbones were polished by the light, as were her broad forehead and delicate, narrow nose. She was too distant for Uther to see the true colour of her eyes, but he was sure that they were pale. Her mouth drew the High King's eyes with its uncoloured, cosmetic-free voluptuousness and seemed to drag his gaze towards the concealed swelling of her breasts.

Across that room of colour, laughter and raucous noise, Myrddion saw Uther bite his lip until the healer feared that blood could come gushing out. He followed the track of Uther's stare and saw Ygerne, unconscious of the scrutiny of the High King's pale eyes as she laughed at one of Luka's jokes. She tossed her head in unconscious coquetry, and even beneath the gauzy rose veil her luxurious hair was trying to escape from her plaits. Corkscrews of curl softened the fine bones of her face, and even Myrddion wondered what it would feel like to loosen those bindings and set that long, wonderful hair free so he could bury his face in it.

Myrddion swivelled his gaze back to Uther.

'Oh, Mother! No!'

The councillors and the magistrate stared at Myrddion, aghast at the words that had unconsciously burst from his mouth.

For under Uther's fixed stare was the lust of a man who has kept his bodily desires under rigid control for decades. Unbidden, Ygerne had wakened something that had slept within the basic nature of the High King, something filled with longing and desire that had never been satisfied by any living woman. Perhaps it was a buried memory of a long dead mother. Perhaps it was the idealisation of womanhood treasured by a callow youth. But there, whatever its source, was a compulsion so foreign to the coldness of Uther's nature that Myrddion could feel the heat in his master's eyes from across the whole length of the hall. The king was entrapped in the woman's face, a forbidden woman who would never smile upon him.

Myrddion swore with crude pungency and the ladies at his table drew away from him with distaste and shock. Apologising absently, the healer watched Ygerne's eyes turn from Luka's face and rise in response to the urgency of Uther's stare.

She saw, she understood and, as all women do, she *knew*.

For a moment, the queen's eyes widened with recognition, and Myrddion saw a tremor run through her whole body and reach her hands, which clutched the table edge with white-knuckled panic.

She sees the lust of the king, Myrddion thought, his mouth parched with panic. What will she do?

The blush started at her throat and rose upwards in a delicate wave. Many women of pale complexion look blotchy when they flush, but Ygerne could colour and simply appear lovelier as the veins so close to the skin suffused her face with rose-petal pink. The queen's eyes dropped to break the contact, unwittingly exposing the length and delicacy of her lashes so that, if possible, she was more beautiful than before. Pinned by the king's stare, she sat like an effigy under the crazed intensity of his blue gaze, until Morgan whispered in her father's ear, her eyes masked and hard.

Gorlois summed up the situation at a glance and would have risen to his feet had Llanwith not stamped forcibly on his foot, causing him to wince in pain. Ygerne turned to her husband, hung on his arm and whispered urgently into his ear. As the Dumnonii king bent to listen, his brows knitted together and his head shook in rejection, but Ygerne pressed herself against him and Myrddion could tell that she strained every muscle of her body to keep her husband seated.

With a quick word to her daughter, Ygerne rose and Morgan swathed her in a heavy cloak. With a deep bow to the High King's table, both women moved swiftly from the feasting hall, while one of Gorlois's guards followed in their wake.

The small scene had taken little more than a moment and most of the guests had been oblivious of the lightning-charged danger in the hall. Gorlois's tanned face was pale and his eyes burned like coals in the linen-whiteness of his face, so that Myrddion rose and hurried towards their table. He was too late. Uther was standing up, and the room gradually became silent.

'King Gorlois, your lovely queen leaves our feast early. Why?'
The demand was harsh and Gorlois flinched. He swallowed audibly.

'My Ygerne sometimes experiences sudden headaches which
come upon her when she is over-excited. Your excellent food, your
wine and your entertainment have been far too rich for a lady used
to the quiet halls of Tintagel. She begs your pardon for any
discourtesy, but my daughter, Morgan, will prepare a sleeping
draught for her. Tomorrow, I am sure, she will be well again.'

Uther's expression was impossible to read but the message in his
words was crystal clear.

'I shall depend upon it, Gorlois, have no fear.'

The High King's mood for the remainder of the feast was sullen
and introverted, although his guests enjoyed his bounty with gusto.
The small incident that had caused Queen Ygerne and Morgan to
flee from the hall had been noticed by very few except for those at
the centre of the storm. The tables groaned with food and cups
overflowed with wine, while laughter, music and shouts rose to the
great oaken rafters like flocks of coloured birds. Among that gilded
throng, Myrddion was sunk in gloom as he watched Uther's face
with a sick fascination. Against all reason, the High King refused to
enjoy the luxury and opulence of his own feast, while his eyes
watched the doorway that had swallowed Ygerne. Perhaps she
would return!

Gorlois glowered, and all the combined jokes and sensible
suggestions of Luka and Llanwith could not defuse his brooding,
growing anger. The High King had stared at his queen as if he
wished to devour her, and the Boar was insulted to his very soul.

Oblivious of the currents of anger, resentment and distrust that
ran beneath the glittering feast, the crowd poured out into the
forecourt at Uther's command, leaving behind scattered bones and
food scraps all over the tables and the marble floors. Uther's dogs

scented meat and began to scavenge among the scraps once the crowd had deserted the hall for the Samhain fires.

With a murmur of wonder at the size of the structure, the crowd clustered around the base of the pyre in air so cold and crisp that their breath steamed. Then, while servants brought baskets of farewell gifts for the god of the old year, the lords and ladies stepped forward with sheaves of wheat, fruit, dried flowers and other symbols of renewal and hope.

'How ironic,' Llanwith whispered in Myrddion's ear. 'We celebrate rebirth but Uther is childless and like to remain so. When he eventually dies, whether in battle, by accident or even of old age, all this will be swept away in a tide of Saxon migration.' His widespread arm encompassed the whole of the west, and Myrddion could feel the mourning in the Ordovice prince's bear-like stance.

The healer raised one hand to rest it lightly on Llanwith's forearm. 'I will do everything I can to save our land, Llanwith. We will negotiate these dangerous roads safely if you can keep faith with me. Uther is not immortal, nor is he infallible. Anything but!'

'Silence, Myrddion!' Luka hissed from behind Myrddion's back. 'You speak treason, and the High King has taken the torch to light the fire.'

The healer felt oddly comforted by the closeness of good friends.

As Luka whispered his warning, Uther turned to face the assembled dignitaries. 'Kings of the west, the old year dies and a new one struggles to be born. Although our enemies assail us, the gods are with us, for they carved these isles from the wild oceans in a time before time, and they will not leave our land to the mercy of harsh foreign deities. As you are aware, I have no wife to share my bed, bear my sons or light the solstice fire with me. As a soldier and the guardian of our borders, I have lacked the time or the leisure to court a woman. Yet the gods may relent and send me a wife. As I light this fire, I pray that they will stand beside us in the battles to come, and that they will take pity on us poor, suffering and lonely mortals. Let the old year burn, and may the new year rise in glory from the ashes.'

Although he is rough and uncouth in most encounters, Uther has a gilded tongue when he wants to use it, Myrddion thought. But what does he mean by those words? Let the gods provide? Uther's never looked to the gods for anything, and trusts only cold iron to speak for him.

Uther thrust his torch into each corner of the pyre as, all over Venta Belgarum, smaller fires were lit to welcome the maven, the god of the new year. The night sprang awake with a ruddy face, and the streets became alive with running citizens, wild dancing and the mad joy of celebration. Many children would be conceived on this night and no husband would argue the parentage, for the darkness was the prelude to a new dawn and a change that even the simplest citizen acknowledged as the Samhain fires roared, collapsed and sank into embers of russet, blood and gold.

Although he tried to bury himself in sensation; although he struggled to find some release in the soft breasts and warm thighs of Ruadh; although he tortured his mind with memories of Flavia and her hot, sweet mouth, Myrddion found his body was cold and unresponsive. With muttered apologies, he rolled away from Ruadh's body as cold as a smooth block of stone. Yet fire burned in his belly as he felt the Mother run her fingers through his ribcage, along the twisted veins and arteries through which his blood pumped, until she lodged herself within the convoluted caverns of his brain.

'She has come!' he screamed aloud on the edge of sleep. Ruadh curled herself into a fetal ball and prayed for the first light of dawning.

CHAPTER XVIII

LOSS

Who can find a virtuous woman? For her price is far above rubies.

Proverbs, 31:10

'I must have her – the witch has ensorcelled me and I can think of nothing else. I see her eyes whenever I sleep. Every woman I touch palls in my arms because she is not Ygerne. I must have Gorlois's woman, whatever the cost – or I'll go mad!'

Uther paced his bedchamber like a wild stag in rut, shaking his heavy head of hair as if carrying a crown of antlers that hungered to bury themselves in Gorlois's broad chest. His hands clenched and unclenched, his eyes were frenzied and his appetite was gone, so that even the calm and reasonable Botha shivered at his master's growing desperation.

'He's like to act in some crazed fashion to gain the woman, alienating all his allies in the process,' Botha had whispered to Myrddion as they talked outside the king's apartment. 'He'll not be deflected, Myrddion, for you know how our master thinks. He'll not be satisfied until he possesses what he lusts after.'

'And Gorlois will not sacrifice his wife for safety's sake,' Myrddion told the worried captain. 'Ygerne would kill herself before she'd allow Uther to touch her. Does Uther want her because she belongs to a man he envies or is it that she is an exceptionally beautiful woman? What a coil. I've tried to puzzle a way out of this mess, but there's none that I can see.'

'All you can do is your best, Healer. Uther has tried to approach Ygerne in the ladies' bower, but she eludes him like a ghost. Her daughter inflames the situation further by sniping at him in her patronising fashion at every opportunity, but today the kings will meet and our master is on the brink of an explosion of rage. You know the symptoms as well as I do.'

'Intimately!' Myrddion snapped. He squared his shoulders and pushed the door open.

'You've finally seen fit to join your king,' Uther sneered, and paused in his rabid pacing as Myrddion entered his apartment. 'How kind of you to find time to see me.'

Ignoring his sarcasm, Myrddion bowed deeply. 'Are you unwell, my lord? Can I be of assistance?'

With a burst of dangerous energy, Uther rounded on the healer and prodded Myrddion on the chest with one forefinger to punctuate each sentence. It was only with the greatest difficulty that Myrddion refrained from backing away or, worse still, striking Uther's hand away.

'The meeting of the tribal kings is to be held within the hour. But at the moment I have no intelligence concerning their expected response to my instructions. Nor do I know what the Saxons are about. And Gorlois defies me by hiding his wife away from me. What do you propose to do about *that*? You're supposed to be my adviser, so advise me.'

'The latest news arrived during the early hours of this morning, at some risk to the messenger, master. The Saxons have landed at Anderida and they have surrounded the fortress. Unexpectedly, their warriors have begun to dig beneath the walls while your loyal subjects rain burning oil and arrows down upon them. Still, the Saxons have not been deterred from their siege and the fortress is dangerously low on fresh food. The advice I have received is that our warriors are reduced to eating their horses even as we speak.'

'So? Let them wait! I will execute the whole garrison if they surrender – those few that the Saxons leave alive. More important, what have you discovered concerning Gorlois's plans? He plots treason, doesn't he?'

Myrddion shook his head. 'No, my lord, that's untrue. I have been through the reports of every spy embedded in the Dumnonii retinue and I have no doubt that Gorlois remains true to the west and to the High King. He desires only to return to Tintagel with his wife and daughter.'

Uther grinned like a wolf and something starving gleamed in his blue eyes. 'He'll not go to Tintagel – on my oath. Not alive and breathing!'

'Master . . .' Myrddion felt the air drain out of the room. 'Gorlois is your strongest ally and your powerful left hand. Do not remove one arm, like the Roman emperor Valentinian who killed Flavius Aetius, his last great general. Rome suffers now because of that foolish execution and the emperor eventually perished in a welter of his own blood. You are needed in this land, my lord, and the west will fail without you. To sweep Gorlois away to the shades, for the sake of a pretty face, is sheer madness.'

Uther struck Myrddion across the face with his clenched fist. If the king had expected Myrddion to fall, however, he was mistaken, for although the healer was driven backwards for several stumbling steps he somehow managed to keep his balance. Myrddion's eyes were black wounds in his white face, except for where a red mark was imprinted on his brow and a thin snake of blood escaped from a split in his dark eyebrow.

'You shouldn't strike at friends, lord, for you have too few to antagonise those who support you. I am oath-bound and cannot retaliate.'

'You?' Uther snarled and shook his stinging knuckles, where the skin had been split by the hard bones of Myrddion's brow. 'The day I fear a healer is the day I consign myself to death.'

Botha would have spoken and moved forward to intervene, but Myrddion raised his left hand and motioned him to hold his position. 'Do not interfere, Botha. Your trial of faith is years in the coming, so leave me to mine.'

Uther howled and struck Myrddion once again, this time dropping the healer to his knees. Shaking his head slowly, and with his face leaking blood from the mouth, Myrddion rose to his feet, but his hands were still not curled into fists. A part of his brain knew that Uther was baiting him out of a frustrated hunger to shed blood, but the king also hoped to be given the justification to sweep his adviser into oblivion and free himself from his oath to his brother.

Myrddion's split lips opened as he raised his head. He spat a gobbet of blood to the floor and stared the High King down with eyes that were changing . . . changing . . . and growing colder than the ice packs of the north, more pitiless than anything Uther had ever seen. Myrddion felt the goddess coming and the old fitting began to rise in his mind like the slow uncoiling of her serpents. Yet this time, the shivering creature that was Myrddion was permitted to hear and remember every word that he was forced to utter.

'Woe to you, Uther Pendragon. You have been given a crown, but it will never be enough for you.' Myrddion's voice continued as Uther cocked his fist to strike him once again. 'Strike me if you wish, but you have set the wheels in motion and Fortuna will now oversee the attainment of all your desires. The wheel turns, and you cannot – will not – stop it.'

'What are you raving about?' Uther's voice seemed to come from far away, while Myrddion's voice grew louder and stronger, to fill the whole apartment with a reverberating sound that was hardly human.

'You will have your woman and may you take much pleasure in her, for she will bring a dowry with her that sows the seeds of your impotence. Although you will fight the Saxons to a stand-still, you will waste your strength in years of war for no honour and little glory. But you *will* take pleasure in the terror you bring into being, out of spite and in raddled old age, and you will kill the only creature on this earth who loves you . . . all to create a failed myth of power.'

'I am the High King. I *am* Pendragon, so I am no myth, you drivelling fool,' Uther hissed, but his fists loosened and he took a half-step backward away from Myrddion's accusatory eyes.

'You will keep the throne warmed for a man who is far better than you . . . one who will eclipse you without effort or fear. Every-thing you are will be written on your face by the time of your death and men will rejoice when you take your last breath. You will die alone and unmourned, and a witch will seal your spirit away into eternal darkness.'

The room was so still that Myrddion's ragged breathing was shockingly loud.

'So what of you? I'll see you worm food before that fate comes to me.'

Myrddion laughed and the sound was rusty, like the complaint of hinges on a ruined door to a tomb, or the lid of a sarcophagus being dragged open by impious hands. 'I will outlive you by decades to see all that you hate most come into being. Fear not, Uther Pendragon, for you'll not be forgotten, but men will whisper your name in tandem with the hated Vortigern's as those kings who paved the way for something better. Your crown and your sword will belong to another man whom you'll bring into being out of the blood and tempests in your soul.'

Incensed, Uther struck Myrddion again, and this time the healer's head snapped backward, so that Botha feared that his neck had been broken by the violence of the blow. Slowly, like a young tree struck by lightning, Myrddion fell until he was only a black puddle of cloth on Uther's floor. 'Shovel this mess away,' Uther ordered with hunted, shamefaced eyes. 'I have a meeting to attend.'

'I'm sorry, Master Myrddion,' a voice whispered from far away. Across a vast divide of blackness, the healer heard the voice and wondered vaguely why the phlegmatic captain of the king's guard would need to beg his pardon in such an ashamed voice. But the effort of thinking was too difficult. Myrddion slipped back into womb-like darkness.

When he awoke the second time, Myrddion tried to open eyes that felt as if they had been stitched shut. Painfully, he struggled to pull apart his gummed lashes while a soft, soothing voice hushed him and placed a cool damp cloth over his face. When the hand lifted away the moist compress, Myrddion discovered that his eyes opened easily and Ruadh's concerned, frowning features swam into focus.

'Why are you here, Ruadh? Where am I? I don't understand what's happening.'

'You're in a small room in King Uther's hall and I was called to tend to you by Captain Botha over half a day ago. It's the evening of the third day of the New Year – the tribal kings are meeting and it seems we are going to war. And you, my beloved, must lie still because you have been very ill. I feared that you'd never wake again.'

Disoriented and alarmed, Myrddion's expert fingers explored the left side of his face, which ached with painful insistence. He found a knot at his temple on the hard skull bone that protected the softer, weaker temple below it. 'I was very lucky,' he whispered.

'An inch lower and I could have been killed. I feel like I've been kicked by a horse.'

Then, because his eyes hurt so much, he closed them for the welcome dark, while his exploratory fingers continued to rove over the swollen contours of his face. He needed no eyes to see what the king had done to him when enraged beyond cool reason. His trained fingers found the split in his eyebrow, the contusion on his cheekbone that bruised his eye and the deep cut across his jawline. Because he understood the value of strong teeth, he checked each one and sighed with relief when he was sure that none was damaged, broken or loosened in its socket.

'He was trying to provoke me,' he whispered as he hungered for the luxury of healing sleep. His common sense told him that matters between the High King and himself were finally at breaking point.

'I understand, master, for Botha told us that he was certain Uther wanted you to strike him in turn, so that he would be at liberty to order your execution. Do you remember what you said to him? Brangaine has told me of your fits, but she also explained that you never remember what you have said.'

Myrddion stirred on the pallet, which was filled with straw that scratched him through the coarse homespun fabric. 'I remember every word I spoke on this occasion.'

The healer felt, rather than saw, Ruadh's raised eyebrows and he wearily opened his eyes again to explain. 'I don't know if what I said was prophetic or not – or if I was just repeating whatever entered my head during a fit of temper. I do know that I said terrible things to the High King, so I'm surprised that I'm still alive and breathing.'

Ruadh laughed shakily, and Myrddion sensed the tears that lay below her amusement. 'He must place a high value on you, for you are ordered to take the healers to Anderida to care for his troops. We have waited for you to come back to us.'

'I'll not go. Let Uther and his damned war go to the shades

unmourned. I don't care any more for oaths, honour or threats, so I'm going home, regardless of what the High King tries to extort from me. I've had enough of him.'

'Oh, master!' Ruadh's face changed, and now Myrddion could see the tears that spilled unchecked over her eyelids and ran down her face. 'You can't refuse, my lord, for Uther will not permit you to challenge his sovereignty.'

'Help me to my feet, woman, and you'll see Myrddion the healer walk away from Venta Belgarum and everyone in it.' Without waiting for assistance, he dragged himself to his feet and stood swaying, his blackened and swollen face contorted with purpose. 'I've had enough,' he said unnecessarily.

Leaning on Ruadh's shoulder, he staggered to the doorway of the mean, dusty room, which was clearly used to store broken furniture, bales of rotten fabric and other rubbish. No evidence could have been clearer of Myrddion's fall from grace and favour. He had been dumped unceremoniously on a filthy pallet in a disused storeroom. No guards barred his path as he made his painful, weaving way through the echoing corridors until they reached the dark silence of the cobbled forecourt. Under a sallow moon, the citadel seemed empty, and Venta Belgarum stilled with a frightened hush that waited on its master's next order. Painfully, but with determination, Myrddion forced his trembling legs to carry him down the winding streets that led to the House of the Healers.

The few people who were abroad in the night to see Myrddion's damaged face chose to avoid his eyes, as if even a shared glance could contaminate them. The fear generated by an autocratic ruler extended down into the meanest streets, forced its law-abiding citizens indoors and caused them to huddle around their fires holding their children close to their breasts. Myrddion could sense a dangerous rift in the maintenance of order within Venta Belgarum, and the miasma of fear and tension only firmed his determination to flee with all his staff at the earliest opportunity.

The house of the healers was dark, although wagons had been loaded and the familiar, welcoming buildings still offered an aura of safety and comfort. The door gaped inward and Myrddion leaned on the frame for a moment, his senses swimming from his efforts to propel himself forward.

'Come, master, you must sleep if we are to embark on *any* journey,' Ruadh murmured. 'Regardless of our destination.'

Her face reflected her despair and she looked much older than usual, so Myrddion wondered if she had told him everything she knew or suspected. Then Praxiteles came and took his right arm and Cadoc moved to his left, and both men carefully and tenderly helped him to his room where he could surrender to the sweet anodyne of unconsciousness.

Before the dawn stole into his bedchamber, Myrddion was roused from a deep sleep by eerie, heart-rending screams that tore apart the silence of early morning. With a jerk, he surged out of his warm covers and staggered to his feet. Shouts, curses and the terrified crying of children followed the initial disturbance, so that the cacophony chased the last dregs of sleep out of his brain.

With some of his old vigour, Myrddion slipped the wooden latch on his door and hurried into the colonnade that led to the women's quarters. In the atrium, now sweet with herbs and dried flowers, armed men crushed the tender mint, thyme and lavender beneath the soles of their booted feet.

'At whose command do you disturb the order of this house?' Myrddion shouted at the melee. Around him, the women crowded close, as if they could draw comfort from his proximity.

Close-cowled, helmeted faces swung in his direction and Myrddion recognised Ulfin in the vanguard of Uther's personal guard. He looked for Botha's calming presence, but the tall warrior was absent. Myrddion felt his stomach lurch, for Ulfin would obey his master to the letter and would be pitiless in the execution of his orders.

'I believe you're seeking me, Ulfin. There's no need to terrify the women and children. I'll willingly accompany you to wherever you want me to go.'

'No, healer. My orders don't only affect you,' Ulfin replied with a superior, sneering twist of his lips. 'You're ordered to Anderida with the other healers.'

'Then why do you invade my house before full light? Why do you terrify innocents with bared swords, unbidden and uninvited?'

'My orders are specific, Myrddion Merlinus. My master wishes to ensure that you accompany the army to Anderida, and to ensure your obedience I have been instructed to relay a personal message to you from the High King.'

'Then give me your message without delay, so you can get out of my house.' Myrddion's voice was ragged, for his quick intelligence could imagine several extremely unpleasant reasons why Ulfin would invade his home with armed men.

'My master bade me tell you his decision. You have seen fit to defy his legitimate orders as the High King of the Britons and, as he no longer trusts you to obey his instructions, you will relinquish two hostages to ensure your future compliance with his wishes.'

Into the dumbstruck silence, Brangaine's cry cut like a razor. 'Master! This cur has tied Willa and Rhedyn and plans to take them to King Uther.'

Over my dead and bleeding body, Myrddion thought savagely.

'How dare you break into my house, Ulfin? Had you knocked, you would have been admitted like any other civilised citizen. I am loyal to the throne and always have been. I do not deserve to be treated like a common felon.'

Ulfin shrugged carelessly. 'My master gave me my orders and they take precedence over all other considerations.'

'But Rhedyn is one of my trusted assistants, so she cannot be spared if we are going to war. Would you tie my hands behind my back by robbing me of a trained healer? Your master didn't ask for her by name, did he?'

Ulfin shrugged again and Myrddion knew that he had guessed correctly. Ulfin had been ordered to take women hostages because Myrddion would not permit the helpless to suffer. In a swift, ruthless show of force, Uther had ensured Myrddion's co-operation.

'Then you choose the hostages, healer. I don't care who comes, as long as they're female and relatively young. I'll not be palmed off with old crones already close to death.'

'Take me,' Brangaine cried. 'Take me for Willa! Please, master.'

'No,' Ulfin said with a nasty grin. 'The girl's no healer, so she's coming. My master will take to her, so choose another. I don't care who.'

'I'll go,' the girl with the strawberry scar on her face volunteered. Berwyn was a fine worker, but, as a gardener and house servant, her skills were not essential. Mute and ill, Myrddion could only nod his thanks for her sacrifice.

Swiftly, Willa and Berwyn were lashed together by a rope attached to each girl's neck, and their wrists were tightly bound. Willa's eyes were very calm and she smiled at her foster-mother with a tremulous curve of her sweet young lips. With a pang, Myrddion recalled the fear she had expressed when they had first arrived in Dubris, and he felt deathly afraid for her.

'No!' Brangaine screamed. 'I'll not let you take her!'

With a careless wave of one hand, Ulfin signalled to an officer of the guard, who held Brangaine by both shoulders while another warrior trussed her up like a chicken and dumped her bodily on the ground. She dissolved into a flood of weeping.

'Remember, healer, your girls remain safe as long as you obey the orders of the High King. I expect I'll see you at Anderida.'

Then, without any apology for the booted feet that left the atrium in a shambles, Ulfin led the guardsmen and their captives out of the house of the healers, leaving shocked silence in their wake.

'Well, that's torn it,' Cadoc muttered, hurrying to cut Brangaine free with a knife he had secreted in his boot. 'Do we go after the guard and try to rescue our people, master?'

The servants looked horrified at the suggestion, but hope bloomed in Brangaine's wet eyes. Regretfully, Myrddion shook his head. 'There's no chance of succeeding against trained warriors. We'd only perish in the attempt and then Willa and Berwyn would be put to death. Their only hope of safety depends on my obedience. At first light, I'll try to reason with Uther, but I suggest we pack for war.'

Then, because Myrddion understood his king so well, he ordered Praxiteles to remain behind when the other servants dispersed to carry out his instructions. The sound of Brangaine's weeping and Cathan's frightened questions were muffled as Ruadh closed the door behind them.

Myrddion turned to Praxiteles and smiled softly at his faithful servant. 'Friend, do you plan to defy me if I order you to carry out a distasteful retreat that has little honour in it?'

Praxiteles was his usual pragmatic self, although he was a little pale under the warm olive of his skin. 'I will obey as long as your instructions are reasonable, Myrddion. You have always been a thoughtful master and you can't help the excesses of a wicked king.'

'That's as may be, Praxiteles,' Myrddion murmured regretfully. 'I have aided and abetted a tyrant for far too long, but I'm damned if I can see any other option that can help us with our predicament now. I'll continue to serve him until Willa and Berwyn return, but I'll not allow him an opportunity to enforce my obedience again.'

Praxiteles waited patiently while the healer stared at the crushed herbs and considered his options.

'I am vulnerable to Uther's threats because of my loyalty to the children and the older servants who have nowhere else to go if I should be forced to flee,' Myrddion glumly.

'Aye, Master,' Praxiteles answered with his usual calm.

'While I have innocents around me who can be harmed, Uther has a means of forcing me to obey him, no matter how brutal and outrageous his demands. He has me trapped.' Myrddion closed his fist over some broken fronds of mint and the air was suddenly cleansed with the scent of the crushed herb. 'I must extricate myself. I'll have to order you to wait until the army marches out of Venta Belgarum for Anderida. We healers will be forced to travel in the baggage train, and I expect us to be absent for months. Nothing good will come from this campaign, I know it.'

'What task do you plan for me, Myrddion?' Praxiteles moved so he could engage Myrddion's eyes. 'Do you have any special instructions for me?'

'Yes, my friend, I do. I intend to send you to Segontium with the remainder of the household women and Cathan. You will also take any of the men who are willing to travel north with you, and pay off those servants who wish to remain here in Venta Belgarum. They can stay in the house, but I caution you to take everything of any value with you, save only for my jars and herbs. I want the women gone to a place where they will be safe from the clutches of Uther Pendragon. Uther will not ride so far into alien country for the sake of some runaway servants. He only travels into the north to fight and to kill.'

Praxiteles nodded his understanding. 'And what should I do in Segontium, Myrddion? Wherever that might be.'

Despite the dangers inherent in his proposal, Myrddion laughed. 'You're going to hate the cold up north, Praxiteles, but you'll love to be near the sea again. You'll take my money chest and purchase a house in the town, where you'll find Finn Truthteller and Bridie. As soon as practicable, I'll send Cadoc, Brangaine, Rhedyn and

Ruadh to join you, for I cannot bear the thought that Uther might harm those I love. As soon as we are out of sight, my friend, make good your escape and run far and fast.'

Praxiteles extended one brown hand and raised Myrddion's chin so he could survey the damage caused by Uther's fists.

'He lost his temper, Myrddion, and he'll be enraged when you defy him. Remember his lack of self-control the next time you enter into a battle of wits with the High King. I'll do what you ask because it's the only sensible solution to your dilemma, but you must understand that you'll be alone in a hostile court for some time, perhaps for years. Make friends if you must, but only with those men whom Uther cannot harm.' Then he smiled kindly at his master. 'It's back to sleep with you now, and I will take care of Brangaine. The worst night must give way to a new morning, so with luck the light of day will bring better news.'

'I hope so, but somehow I doubt that Uther will soften his views.'

In the morning, the poplace was astir like the frantic scrambling of insects exposed to the harsh light of day when a rotting tree trunk is turned over on the forest floor. Like the beatles and nameless crawling things that are suddenly prey to the sharp beaks of birds or the attacks of other predators, Venta Belgarum's citizenry filled the streets as they nervously tried to grasp the implications of the new threat. Uther had ordered that all able-bodied men should follow him to Anderida, so the city boiled with preparations. To fortify himself for the confrontation to come, Myrddion paused to purchase a leg of roasted chicken and a mug of ale from an inn facing the forecourt of the hall. As he sat beside a roaring fire and the feeling began to return to his frozen hands and feet, he asked the innkeeper for any news of Gorlois and the tribal kings.

'Why, master healer, there be great doings in the meeting of the kings. The Boar of the Dumnonii has been given permission to send his womenfolk back to Tintagel, as long as he strips his land of men to swell the king's army. Gorlois has sworn to obey this order, for Uther insists that the Dumnonii king should command the cavalry. I know that I'll sleep better knowing that Cornwall marches to Anderida, I'll swear to that. If anyone can rout the Saxons, it would be King Gorlois.'

'Aye, but what of the other kings?' Myrddion tried to appear casual in his questioning, but the sharp-eyed innkeeper wasn't deceived.

'Bless you, healer, of course they will obey our lord. The Dragon is like to hold a grudge against any that refused to comply with his wishes. Oh, yes, they fawned all over him, I'm told, and couriers have been sent to all the kingdoms to summon men to swell our ranks.'

'It's far too cold at the moment to lift a siege. Many men will die of exposure,' Myrddion mumbled. Even now, cold winds tried to force their way through the shutters and a flurry of icy rain battered at the closed door with the pattering sound of sleet.

'Soldiers die all the time. Our greatest fear at the moment is that the Saxons will surround us.'

Myrddion nodded in agreement. 'We don't want them here, but the weather is turning nasty and the road to Anderida Silva is long and harsh. It's possible that we could lose so many men on the journey that our purpose will be blunted before we even start the campaign.'

He addressed himself to eating his chicken leg, despite the pain in his jaw from the effort of chewing. When he had finished – regretfully, for a roaring fire was blazing fiercely – he presented a copper coin with the head of Maximus stamped upon it in payment for his meal. The innkeeper grinned widely at this excess and offered fulsome thanks as Myrddion slipped through the door and out into a flurry of snow.

Botha intercepted him before he could reach the king's apartment and dragged him forcibly into a small bedchamber across the corridor. 'Are you mad, healer? Didn't you learn anything yesterday when the king took to you with his fists?'

'He's ordered Ulfin to take two of my women hostage to ensure my good behaviour. I must try to make him see sense.' Myrddion tried to push past the captain, but Botha stood firm.

'Do you want to die, or do you want your girls to be raped – or worse? For pity's sake, man! If Uther sees your bruised face before you've healed, he's likely to remember the fate you predicted for him before he knocked you senseless. If you keep your head down, everything will eventually return to normal.'

Botha's voice and manner were unusually jumpy, a fact that simply heightened Myrddion's anxiety and firmed his conviction to discuss the matter with Uther. But he had scarcely begun to protest before Botha dealt him a stinging slap.

'That's just pride talking, Myrddion Merlinus, and not common sense. You know our master, none better. And you must realise that you'll waste your breath reasoning with him until he's killed the Saxons at Anderida. After that, he'll be in a better mood.'

Glumly, Myrddion slumped back against the rough wall of the small room. In his heart, he knew that Botha spoke good sense and that Uther was unpredictable because of rage at him, lust for an unattainable woman and anger at the Saxons. Frustrated on all levels, the High King would strike out until his blinding fury was assuaged.

'Very well, I'll listen to your advice, Botha, but you must promise to keep the captives as safe as possible. Those poor girls shouldn't suffer because the king resents my existence. Promise me, and I'll return to the house of the healers and pack for Anderida.'

Botha rubbed his jaw with his forefinger and Myrddion heard the harsh rasp of whiskers against the sword calluses on his hand. 'Aye, I'll do all I can to keep the lasses safe, although the girl called Willa sits mute and refuses to eat. If you send me any messages from her mother, I'll make certain they reach her.'

So Myrddion returned home to begin preparations for the journey to the east. He was familiar with the landscape from his travels in the service of both Ambrosius and Uther, so he understood the strategic importance of Anderida. The Roman fort, stone-walled and gated to the east and west, was protected by the sea to the south and was positioned to defend a long sweep of coastline where the Romans had expected invasion from the continent.

As he examined his map of the area, Myrddion marvelled at the wily engineers who had built their fort with a swamp at its back, a perfect defence for Roman legionaries who would have felt ill at ease so far from home on the chilly coast of southern Britain. Behind the swamp, the forests of Anderida Silva rose in densely covered hills that formed an effective barrier to all but cavalry.

No major roads led to the fortress, so a novice commander might decide that it lacked strategic importance. But such a con-clusion would be an error, because Anderida, and the hills to its west, guarded the verdant fields of Vectis, Magnus Portus, Noviomagus and Portus Adurni that were the funnel through which the tribes traded with the Franks and the Visigoths across the Litus Saxonicum. More important, if the ports should be occupied by the Saxons Venta Belgarum would inevitably fall and a spearhead would be driven, hard and true, into the loins of the west. The tribal kings would never recover from such a disaster.

'The fortress of Anderida must remain in Celtic hands for as long as possible,' Myrddion explained to Cadoc, prodding the map penned on the hide scroll with an emphatic forefinger. 'Look at what it protects. Beyond Anderida Silva is Calleva Atrebatum, and only the gods could help us if that city should fall, for it straddles the Roman roads in all four directions. We'd be trapped between Scylla and Charybdis.'

'Scylla and what?' Cadoc said blankly.

'A rock and a whirlpool. We'd be easy meat for our enemies – they could isolate us and slice us up like a side of beef. And where would we be then, if we didn't have a savage like Uther who is the only king with the stomach for what must be done? I wish, however, that he didn't enjoy slaughter quite so much.'

'Death and destruction seem to ease his rages, master. So we go, I take it, to save Willa and Berwyn from what might be a nasty end.'

'Yes. The first contingent of troops marches out tomorrow and the reinforcements will be called to their bivouac outside Noviomagus. By the time we arrive in the baggage train, the Dumnonii, Belgae and Dobunni troops will have joined the warriors from Uther's Atrebates tribe. The High King is playing for keeps, and I believe he intends to slaughter the entire Saxon force.'

'Then there will be much red work for us to do,' Cadoc answered stolidly. 'It's time to pack for a prolonged campaign.'

Four weeks later, on a cold and moonless night when snow lay lightly over the forest floor of Anderida Silva and frozen branches creaked and groaned under the icy weight of winter, Myrddion huddled inside his heavy furs. From a low hill, he looked down at the silent host that had spread out into two great horns as they prepared to attack the two Saxon camps besieging the Celtic fortress. Even now, the Saxons were busily burrowing below the frozen stone walls of the fort or pounding on the wooden gates on the eastern and western flanks. The silent fortress seemed far too small from this distance to warrant the loss of life that would follow the engagement of the warring forces.

Uther's encampment was in darkness, for even in these icy conditions the High King had ordered that no fires should be lit unless there was no other option. Men were huddled in mounds of snow and the horses were picketed out of sight in the forest. Every scout sent out from the Saxon lines and every courier had been summarily executed, although few of the latter revealed the contents of the messages they carried for their commanders in Londinium. Even Uther admitted to a thrill of admiration for the courage of these Saxon warriors, but he killed them anyway.

'The Saxons must know we're here,' Myrdion whispered aloud, more for comfort than with any expectation of a reply. Cadoc was snoring under the lead wagon and the night was deceptively still.

Snow crunched under a booted foot and Myrddion turned awkwardly in his cocoon of furs. A black figure, powerful and heavily muffled, approached his position through the charcoal tree trunks.

'Who goes there?' the healer hissed, feeling rather foolish at the melodramatic choice of words.

'A friend, Merlinus. I'm Gorlois of the Dumnonii.'

'King Gorlois? Lord, why do you come to me? I'd expect you to steer well clear of Uther's storm crow.'

'Walk with me, Merlinus. Have no fear, for I don't plan to end your life by stealth, nor do I blame you for the sins of your master. Uther Pendragon is a law unto himself.'

The dark figure beckoned Myrddion into the treeline where they were unlikely to be overheard. As he moved to join him, Myrddion reflected on the ironies of life. Of all those who might have sought him out, here was Gorlois, the man he least wished to meet. He was almost sure that the Boar of Cornwall would harbour a grudge against him because of his position at Uther Pendragon's court.

Fortunately, he was wrong. With an impatient gesture of one hand, Gorlois pulled back his cowl and lowered himself gingerly onto his haunches.

'Get down, Myrddion, for I'd prefer not to be seen in your company. I'm watched all the time, even when I go for a piss. It took ten minutes to throw off my watchers when I went to the latrine this time, so even those clods will eventually realise where I am. Come closer.'

'How may I assist you, my lord? I must tell you that I have fallen out of favour with the High King, although he's forced to keep me safe through his oath to his brother.'

Gorlois laughed softly. 'I expect you wonder about stray arrows though, don't you?'

Myrddion nodded, for there was no need for further explanation.

'It's so still and peaceful here, but the Saxons have created a little Christian hell outside Anderida itself. I am expected to ride in the vanguard to smash the enemy against the fortress gates tomorrow, so I also fear the stray arrow or the knife blade from behind. As I said, I am constantly watched, and Uther smiles at me as if he is contemplating a pleasant, easily digestible meal. I fear he intends to dine over my corpse before the week is out, but he'll discover that I'm a source of stomach ache if he tries and doesn't succeed.'

'I'm sorry, my lord, but I have no authority with Uther Pendragon after the last alteration between us. If I spoke in your favour, he would assume that you were guilty of treason and act accordingly.'

'No, you misunderstand me, healer.' Gorlois examined his nails intently as if some secret rested within them. 'I don't expect to die in the coming battle because Uther needs me at the head of his cavalry, but if he wants my death after that, then he'll contrive it. I have no hope that he'll see reason.'

Gorlois picked up a handful of snow and pressed it between his fingers. With the grin of a light-hearted boy, he tasted the snow on his tongue and sighed deeply.

'Life's so good, isn't it, healer? Every breath, every smell on the breeze, the taste of clean snow on my tongue . . . if I'm fated to die, I'll miss the joy of living. Still, I'm over fifty summers by my reckoning and still hale and strong, and that happy state cannot last forever. I would be content to die in battle if I were spared the slow decline into infirmity, because no man wants to recognise pity in the eyes of his wife and children.'

Myrddion remembered his great-grandfather, Melvig, who had lived to a remarkable old age; he had suffered as his strength declined. Myrddion nodded his head in understanding.

'But if I should perish, my Ygerne will be exposed to the lust of Uther Pendragon. Because he has no shame, he makes his intentions quite blatant. I was surprised that he permitted her to return to Tintagel. I suppose he hopes to lay siege to her when I'm removed as an impediment.'

'I'm afraid so, lord. Uther is crazed on the topic of Ygerne, although all his advisers have tried to dissuade him. It's a sudden infatuation that rose out of nowhere, and I've tried to fathom it, but I don't understand his reasoning. Uther has never shown any inclination to take a wife, so perhaps he desires your queen because she is unattainable?'

Gorlois snickered, but his laughter was scant on humour. 'Many men have desired my wife, but she remains faithful. I believe she would kill herself before she permitted *any* other man to lie with her. She doesn't understand her own beauty and believes herself to be old, but her loveliness is still bewitching and will bring Uther to ruin if he continues to pursue her.'

'Aye, I believe you. Uther can't rape your wife without destroying all personal credibility. Once you're dead, his path to Ygerne is clear, but even a High King cannot take a tribal queen by force.'

'You read my fears correctly, Myrddion. So ... if I should die in battle, I beg that you try to protect her. She lacks any comprehension of the wickedness in the world and will not understand Uther's ruthlessness. I'm terrified for her.'

Myrddion rose to his feet with a little grunt of effort. As he straightened his spine, he stared up at the dark sky where the stars were obliterated by heavy cloud cover and he could smell more snowfalls in the air. His mind ranged to distant Tintagel, a place he had never been, and tried to imagine the Lily of Cornwall and her marvellous, changeable eyes in her home beside the turbulent ocean. His own black eyes were pained.

'I should tell you, Gorlois, that I prophesied for Uther in Venta Belgarum and I threatened him that he would achieve his heart's desire, but lose his soul in the getting. I fear I predicted your death. The goddess speaks in riddles when she speaks through my mouth, so I might be talking nonsense. But I promise you, Gorlois, that whatever happens I will serve your wife with all my strength. I will risk my life for her, and ensure she sees out her days in peace and plenty. Something whispers to me that she will survive Uther Pendragon and all his viciousness. After all, she is the daughter of Pridenow, warrior of renown.'

Gorlois sighed. 'Aye, Pridenow was her sire, and Morgan will protect her in her own way.' His eyes were ineffably sad. 'You've comforted me, healer, because I believe you'll try to keep your word. If a doomed man can give you a boon, then ask, for I am in your debt.'

As true warriors, king and healer stood together for a brief moment while the moon broke through the pregnant, threatening clouds to touch their faces with a rime of argent. As if on cue, snow began to fall once again, forcing Gorlois to raise his cowl. With surprising gentleness, he smiled at Myrddion out of the thick wool.

'Ave, healer. Perhaps I'll see you beyond the shadows.'

Myrddion discovered that he couldn't trust his voice, so Gorlois disappeared into the dark of the trees without a farewell. Then the moon disappeared again and darkness blanketed the land as if a shroud had been spread over the earth.

'Ave, Gorlois,' Myrddion whispered. 'Men will remember you as long as courage and loyalty count for anything.'

Then the healer returned to the wagons to watch over his small flock until the dawn came creeping out of the eastern sky.

CHAPTER XIX

THE JUDAS KISS

If you gaze for long into an abyss, the abyss gazes also into you.

Nietzsche, *Beyond Good and Evil*, iv

Snow fell and turned the cavalry into grey ghosts of horsemen. It filled holes in the landscape so that every stride was a test of faith for men and beasts, while it muffled the thunder of the charge as well, so that the phantom wave of armed men was almost upon the Saxons before they were detected.

A battlefield in the dead of winter, in flurries of snow, is a silent, unearthly dance where blood disappears into the pristine whiteness and the dead become little mounds on the flat plain. Even the clash of swords and spears is muted and eerie, and the cries of wounded men are distant and inhuman, like the far-off screams of hunting gulls.

Only in the press of bodies, as boots and hooves struggle for purchase on black ice, is warfare fresh and real. As always, blood spray, spilled brains and hacked flesh are the offerings to the gods of war, although the snow soon covers the excesses of human savagery. A horse thrashes in a welter of snow, spilled entrails and blood until its throat is cut in a bright arc of scarlet. All too soon, its remains are covered by a thin white shroud. Even the blood freezes, and continues to leave a delicate tracery on tree trunks and stone walls. Winter death has a grim beauty, as delicate as a dying breath.

From the distant treeline, Myrddion surveyed the silent battle-field and prayed to all the gods that Gorlois would live. Behind him, under cover, Cadoc set the fires to heat water and provide some warmth for the dying, but heavy flurries of snow from the passing storm obscured the two fronts of the battle so that neither healer could guess at the outcome.

Gorlois had led the cavalry charge against the eastern gate and his orders had been concise and clear-cut. The gate to the fortress must not be breached by the besieging Saxons, and everyone who stood between Gorlois's force and the wall must die. Meanwhile, Uther would lead a combined cavalry and infantry charge against the western gate. As expected, Uther's horsemen carved through the Saxon force like a hot knife blade through snow.

'Who's winning?' Cadoc asked as he coaxed another fragile flame to life in his hoard of kindling. He swore vilely as an un-expected skirl of wind caused the flame to lick his fingers with a sting of heat.

'I can't see clearly,' Myrddion replied. 'But the foot soldiers in Uther's command are maintaining disciplined ranks so I suppose the Saxons at the western gate have been decimated. As for Gorlois, the fortress walls hide what is happening on that side of the citadel.'

Cadoc grunted sceptically. 'I'll warrant that Gorlois's force was smaller than the squadrons of the High King,' he muttered, as he sucked on his burnt fingers.

'Shove your fingers in the snow, Cadoc. The cold will ease the pain of your burn,' Myrddion said absently. 'Damn me, but I can't see a thing, so all we can do is wait until we discover whether the wounded are Saxon or Celt. As the victors will probably kill the enemy wounded, we'll soon know the outcome of the battle. We may even have to fight for our lives.'

'Let's just count the casualties,' Cadoc agreed glumly.

Myrddion was almost relieved when the wounded began to arrive on foot, on horseback or carried by their companions. Exposure to the elements was a major cause of mortality, even in the balmiest of summers. In a winter snowstorm, among warriors who were already chilled from a night without fire, it was potentially disastrous. While Myrddion admired Uther's ability to make quick, confident decisions, he deplored the High King's disregard for the welfare of the men who fought under his standard.

'Here comes the first of them,' Cadoc shouted. He marshalled the apprentice healers to their working positions while the women collected bandages, water and the precious medicines that would save the lives of wounded patients. Myrddion turned regretfully from his vantage point and positioned himself at the forefront of the waiting healers as a line of trudging, staggering men floundered towards them through the deepening snow.

At a signal from Cadoc, the bearers moved towards the warriors and assisted the exhausted men to reach the relative warmth of the tents. In such brutal conditions, only the walking wounded had any chance of reaching the healers without assistance, but the frigid conditions had served one positive purpose, as Myrddion discovered when the first patients were prepared for treatment.

Cold slowed the rapid blood flow that was normally the most devastating of killers. Once Anderida was relieved and the gates were opened, Myrddion could send in a cadre of apprentice healers to care for the wounded and dying in relative warmth. But until that hour arrived, his tents could only accept those who managed to stagger through the winter snows. An increasing number succeeded in reaching the field hospital without bleeding to death.

Blue with exposure and trembling from shock, some wounded men stumbled into the tent bearing hideous wounds that should have caused almost instant death from blood loss. Myrddion quickly assessed the potentially fatal slash wounds, and then set to work at speed, directing the younger apprentices to clean and stitch the wounds speedily so that patients could be given some small chance of survival.

As always, Myrddion chose to labour over those patients where his unerring skill was vital, usually the most dangerous puncture wounds where arrows were still embedded in the flesh. Of all the healers, only Myrddion was sufficiently deft and confident with a scalpel to offer a reasonable hope of success. With a few considered strokes of the blade, he could carve a barbed arrowhead out through the entry point, where alternative treatments might prove to be life-threatening.

In some cases, where it was the only option, the healer was forced to remove the arrowhead on the reverse side of the body. In this treatment, Myrddion could prepare a path for the arrow by opening healthy skin and carefully avoiding the tangled skeins of blood vessels and muscle until he could grip the iron tip of the arrowhead with fingers or forceps. He would then draw the arrow through the body. These through wounds were easier procedures for both healer and patient than any other option, because the barbs couldn't lacerate the flesh.

Considering the size of the opposing forces and the ferocity of the battle, all too few men arrived at the tents of the healers. When a courier brought the news that Anderida was secured, Myrddion sent healers and wagons to the two battlefields and the really grim treatments began. As usual, few Saxons were found alive, and none of those who were, no matter how hideously wounded, was permitted to set foot inside the citadel.

'Pain is the killer,' Myrddion repeated many times to his assistants.

Battlefield experiences over many years had taught him well, and he used every hard-won lesson to thwart the snow, the cold and the chill wind that turned his feet to ice. But even the worst days eventually end.

The High King sent no orders and, to Myrddion, this lack was a blessing. Despite Uther's crimes, he was necessary to the survival of the western kingdoms. But, worryingly, few patients had come from the eastern gate where the fighting had been fiercest, so no news had been received of Gorlois's fate. Myrddion was forced to take the pragmatic view that this lack of news was positive.

The hour must have been very late when the cortège made its way to the healer's tents. Cadoc saw the torches first, a snake of horsemen bearing improvised bundles of sticks bound with oil-soaked cloth that had been set alight to guide the way. Myrddion knew what had happened long before the horsemen reached the higher ground.

Eerily, the flickering lights did little to pierce the darkness, even though the snow had ceased to fall. Heavy cloud cover blackened the heavens so that even the glistening whiteness of snow banks barely managed to lift the gloom. The horsemen were black shapes against the grey, and the red glow of the torches touched helmets or mailed shoulders with a bloody glow. Within the twin ranks of horsemen a single beast plodded stoically, its hide shining with blood. A darker shape lay across its back, and Myrddion swiftly washed his bloody hands, cleansed his face with a handful of snow to sharpen his wits and waited outside the main tent for the cortège to arrive.

As he had already guessed, the horsemen were part of Gorlois's personal guard. They led the king's horse, which was faltering from weariness and a slew of shallow wounds, as it bore its dead master to a point where his body could be prepared for the funeral pyre. Myrddion swallowed and prepared himself to do his duty.

'Myrddion Merlinus?' a dark-visaged, bearded warrior shouted as the horsemen halted under the sanguine light of their torches.

'I've come to meet you, for I can guess your purpose,' Myrddion responded sadly. 'You carry the body of Gorlois who was the King of the Dumnonii tribe. This night is one for mourning, for the noble Gorlois was a man of unimpeachable honour.'

'You speak the truth, Storm Crow.' Myrddion ignored the insult, for he saw the stark sorrow in the eyes of the middle-aged warrior. 'I am Bors, who will rule in Gorlois's stead, but I'm only half the man my uncle was, and I cannot conceive how any man could fill his boots or lift his sword.'

Myrddion sighed and bowed his head as several warriors dismounted and lifted the king's shrouded corpse from the back of his shivering horse.

'Care for the master's steed also, Myrddion, if healing a wounded animal doesn't insult you. Fleet-foot is his name. He bore my cousin proudly, and suffered painful wounds without complaint during many campaigns. I'll return him to the green fields of Cornwall where he will sire stallions to carry my own sons.'

The warrior's voice was heavy with loss, yet he remained proud and fierce, so that Myrddion saw the seeds of another great Dumnonii king in the dark, bearded face.

'Cadoc will care for Fleet-foot without shame, for this horse is also a warrior as brave as any man who lives or dies on the fields of war. I shall personally see to the preparation of King Gorlois's body. Have no fear, for Gorlois was my friend and I will treat him like my own kin.'

'I don't doubt you, Myrddion, but I do distrust the High King. I will leave a contingent of officers to guard my lord until such time as his ashes are offered to the sun.' Myrddion nodded in agreement, for he understood the bitter distrust and the slow-burning anger in the eyes of Prince Bors. Gorlois had survived a hundred skirmishes, but now, conveniently, he was dead.

With due honour, the body of Gorlois was carried into the surgical tent and laid out on Myrddion's table. Ruadh began to remove the heavy armour from the corpse while Myrddion eased the crested helmet up from the king's snarling face. As his fingers smoothed the stiffening muscles of the mouth into a half-smile, Myrddion felt an ache of regret. These last offices for an honourable and noble man should be performed by Gorlois's wife and daughters, but they were far away, so the healer vowed that the corpse of the Dumnonii king would be treated with all the respect and love that his own family would have brought to the task.

Once the body was bared for washing by Ruadh and Brangaine, Myrddion examined it with the care of a healer dedicated to his trade. The many contusions and small cuts that the warrior had suffered during the battle, despite his armour, would have meant an uncomfortable night for Gorlois if he had survived, but such were his fighting skills that the king had taken only two serious wounds. And one of them had been performed on the body after Gorlois had died.

His brain racing, Myrddion straightened up. 'Gorlois's body tells us clearly what happened to him,' Myrddion explained to Ruadh and Brangaine as he lifted the king's powerful hand, which was stained with dried blood to a point well above the elbow. Obviously, Gorlois had killed many Saxons during the assault, for he had worn gauntlets and the blood had soaked through those protective leathers. What facial flesh had been visible between helmet and visor was similarly blood-spattered, and the fine spray of opposing warriors' arterial blood had soaked armour, tunic and the wool beneath to reach the skin.

'He was bathed in the blood of his enemies,' Ruadh murmured, and her green eyes shone with admiration, for her Pictish upbringing still had the power to stir her sensibilities, especially with its emphasis on raw, indomitable courage on the battlefield. Sympathetically, Myrddion wondered if she thought of her lost children who still lived beyond the wall.

'Gorlois was a superlative warrior – a master with sword and knife.' Myrddion stared at both women across the king's body. 'But if you look at his wounds, you can see that he was killed from behind.'

The healer pointed to a deep, blue-tinged and puckered puncture wound that entered Gorlois's body below the left armpit where the armour was weakest. A long, narrow knife thrust had breached Gorlois's ribs and lacerated his heart.

'He was killed by a friend,' Myrddion concluded, even as his mind rebelled at the evidence written on Gorlois's body.

'How so?' Brangaine asked. Her hooded eyes were wide in surprise.

'He was held from behind and stabbed with the left hand. Let me show you.'

Myrddion stood behind Brangaine, gripped her round the neck with his right arm and then stabbed upward with an empty left hand. The two women could see, from the angle of penetration, that a knife thrust would have pierced the heart.

'Perhaps an enemy warrior outflanked him,' Ruadh suggested, her voice still analytical. None of them believed that Gorlois would retreat.

'But why, then, would his killer turn him over after he fell and slice his throat open to ensure that he was dead? All warriors know when they have delivered a killing blow. See? Gorlois scarcely bled from the throat wound, and if his heart had still been beating the arterial spray would have drenched his corpse even more heavily than it's already stained. That stroke was made after Gorlois had stopped breathing.'

Myrddion pointed to the gaping wound that ran from left to

right across Gorlois's throat. Clearly, the killer had either continued to hold Gorlois upright and changed knife hands – a highly unlikely action – or he had bent over the king's dead body and sliced his throat open like a butcher slaughtering a deer.

'His killer was left-handed,' Ruadh said unnecessarily.

'Perhaps. But he used both hands for this sword stroke.'

Myrddion assessed the long, even slice on the king's throat as he indicated the entry point under the left ear. 'See? A wider blade was used for this blow – a sword, judging by the shape of the wound. Like Uther's guardsmen, this killer fights without the use of a shield, so he can carry a weapon in each hand.'

Ruadh gently kissed the grey-blue mouth. 'Ave, Brave Heart. Your enemy feared that you'd survive even this treachery.' Her left hand touched the wound in the king's side. 'He was making sure.'

'I'll leave him to your ministrations, ladies, for his men will wish to send him to his ancestors with due reverence, preferably in Cornwall. He must be washed completely, perfumed and sewn into a shroud. I'll send a bearer to clean the king's armour, Brangaine, if you would wash his linens.'

'If the sun ever shines again,' the older woman whispered, and sighed. Except for a single message received through Botha, she had heard nothing of Willa and Berwyn, and her heart was aching.

Only the nobility eschew the use of a shield in battle, Myrddion thought furiously. Saxons occasionally use axes and swords in tandem, but Uther's guard are trained to fight with knife and sword. How could one of Uther's guardsmen approach so close to the king in the midst of his own cavalry?

A small, cold voice answered Myrddion's unspoken question from within.

The king's guardsmen, and especially Uther's couriers, can go anywhere they choose, both on the battlefield and off it, for their movements are governed wholly by the will of the High King. It would be interesting to discover where Ulfin was during the attack on the eastern gate.

Myrddion acquitted Botha of the assassination. The captain of the guard would have obeyed his master, albeit unwillingly, but he would have killed Gorlois from the front.

'I'll see how Cadoc is managing with Gorlois's horse,' he said to the women, and left the tent.

Watching as Cadoc stitched shallow slashes across the rump of the shivering beast, Myrddion had scarcely established that Fleetfoot would live when Ulfin appeared out of the darkness like a bird of ill-omen.

'You're wanted, healer. Don't even consider taking your time, because Uther has decided your patients can survive without you for an hour or two.'

'Tell the women where I am,' Myrddion hissed at Cadoc before turning towards the wagon. 'I'll collect my warm cloak and healer's bag if I'm to be gone so long, and I'll check on how our young apprentices are dealing with the wounded inside the citadel as well. I refuse to freeze my arse off for Uther Pendragon, or for you, Ulfin. And you have my permission to repeat my words to him as, no doubt, you always do.'

Ulfin fumed impotently, and watched the healer closely as he gathered his belongings. But Myrddion had spent too many months among the thieves and hired thugs of Rome to have learned nothing, and his scalpel went into the small sheath inside his boot in an impressive act of sleight of hand. Then, armed and feeling unnaturally dangerous, he mounted the horse that the guardsman had brought for him.

The battlefield was unusually quiet, considering the carnage. A mound of Saxon dead had been flung unceremoniously to one side after the bodies had been expertly stripped of anything of value. A wagon was already filling with booty: weapons, and chests of torcs, arm-rings and other precious objects. The casualties among the Atrebates warriors were minimal, and Myrddion would have expected a mood of elation to buoy up the High King's camp. They had won the battle but few men were celebrating, and Uther's warriors simply plodded through the snow as they collected the dead in silence. The grey-faced men were almost somnambulistic in their movements, and an unnatural hush blanketed the activity around the open gates of the garrison.

'How were conditions in the fortress?' Myrddion asked Ulfin. 'The survivors seem quite strong and hale.'

'They were eating horse meat when the siege was lifted, so no one was actually starving. But Anderida has suffered her share of dead from stray arrows used by the Saxon peasantry, or from disease. We've been lucky that the siege was raised so promptly.'

'Disease?' Myrddion asked sharply, for any fevers and plagues were dangers to the whole army of the west.

'Mostly the colds and breathing illnesses of winter,' Ulfin sneered. 'There's nothing for you, Storm Crow.'

'My name is Myrddion Merlinus, Ulfin, and I insist you use it.' Myrddion's voice was haughty and cold. 'I am no farmer or peasant for you to bully, and I doubt that I'll be out of favour with your master forever.'

Ulfin grunted with amusement.

'Very well then, Master Myrddion. Any illness that exists inside the fortress is no concern of yours, for they have their own healers.'

Ulfin pulled his horse to a stop outside a stone-walled building in the centre of the circular fort. Warriors entered and left the building in a constant stream, so Myrddion deduced that Uther had made his headquarters at the hub of this Celtic hive. Strong winds were blowing from the sea with a tang of salt and seaweed, and the healer recalled the dunes that rose above the straits separating Segontium from Mona island. He longed to see those cold, grey waters again and feel the ancient peace of his home seep into his bones.

The healer dismounted and followed Ulfin into the building, past Botha and several guardsmen, into a windowless inner room where Uther paced with his customary impatience. 'Well, Storm Crow? I've done what you wanted and we have driven the Saxons away from Anderida. Now, for matters of urgency.'

Myrddion drew in a shuddering breath. Here it comes, he thought fatalistically. Will I survive this trial of strength?

'I have been told that Gorlois's corpse rests in the tents of the healers. I trust that all due deference is being given to the mortal remains of the Boar of Cornwall? He died well, I hear.'

Now it comes. Uther has completed the first step towards achieving his ends.

'No, my lord, Gorlois died from a cowardly knife thrust that pierced his heart from behind,' Myrddion stated in a flat, unemotional voice. 'Before his death, he had killed so many Saxons while securing the eastern gates of Anderida for you that he was slick with blood.'

'His widow will mourn him, no doubt,' Uther responded dismissively, although his eyes searched Myrddion's face for some reaction. 'But not for long, as I intend to take her to wife in honour of Gorlois's great sacrifice for the west.'

'May I speak freely, sire?'

'You may, but remember whom you address, and the future of those little girls who wait in hope in Venta Belgarum.' Uther's cold voice was a threat to the bravest heart, but Myrddion felt oddly immune, as if he were following a predestined path.

'She'll not take you willingly, Uther. Despite their high birth and their arranged marriage, Gorlois and Ygerne loved each other to the exclusion of all others. She will die before she takes you into her bed.'

Uther's handsome, impassive face twisted with a powerful emotion that Myrddion didn't recognise. 'So you'd counsel me not to return Gorlois's body to Tintagel in person?'

'Frankly, my lord, she'd presume you were invading her husband's fortress, lock the gates and let you cool your heels outside forever.'

'Damn you, healer. You never seem to give me pleasant advice,' Uther snapped, but without his usual repressed fury. 'Just once I'd like one useful solution from you.'

'Do you want the truth? Or a palatable lie?' Myrddion retorted. He was tired of fencing with Uther and only the fate of Berwyn and Willa kept his voice neutral.

'I'm afraid that you're accurate on this occasion. Well, to Hades with convention or the opinions of the tribal kings. I want Ygerne and I'll have her, so find a way to get me into Tintagel without having to lay siege to one of my allies. Do you understand me, Storm Crow?'

'I understand you, but I won't do it. I'll not be a party to the rape of a newly widowed queen.' Myrddion held his breath. He had never refused Uther outright before and his flesh crawled in expectation of a knife in the ribs or another blow to the head.

Uther snickered quietly and Myrddion's blood chilled. 'You'll obey my orders, Storm Crow, or I'll use little Willa in Ygerne's stead until you do what I ask. After I've finished with her, I'll give her to my guard. How long do you think she'll last? She's a pretty little thing – but not very strong.'

Although Myrddion had expected a similar threat, the actuality of pack rape, threatened by a High King, was so dishonourable that he took a backward step in spite of his best efforts to stand firm. Uther saw his involuntary action and grinned with triumph.

'And when Willa is dead, I'll start on the ugly little servant. I'll warrant she'll fight back, which I'll enjoy. She'll last longer too, because she's a sturdy little beast, and that should please my men.

Best of all, these women have no standing with the tribal kings and no one will protest at what happens to either of them. You're the only man who cares whether they live or die.' Uther paused and swallowed his wine with one gulp. 'Don't doubt my intentions, Storm Crow. I never threaten without delivering.' He turned to his servant. 'More wine, Ulfin.'

As the king's guardsman sprang to obey his master's order, Myrddion tried to think.

'There's no way out for you, Myrddion Merlinus,' Uther continued smoothly. 'The girls, your healers and yourself will perish nastily unless you devise a way to smuggle me into Tintagel and learn to live with the consequences.'

'Better men than you have tried to kill me since my infancy, but the goddess has decreed that I shall live until I am a very old man. Truly, you would earn my thanks if you decided to carry out your threat.'

Gods, Uther has thought this out. He knows I'll be forced to obey because I can't bear the thought of Willa and Berwyn being raped and tortured. But how can I live if I betray Ygerne and the dead Gorlois, for my honour will be trampled in the dust. If I'm honest, I don't want to die before my time.

Myrddion's thoughts were written on his agonised face and Uther fed on the healer's indecision. The king gloated openly, and his blue eyes were almost colourless with enjoyment as he sensed the moment of victory over his adviser.

'I don't even know the geography of Tintagel,' Myrddion protested and knew, as he spoke, that he was capitulating. The bitterness of failure rose in his gorge until he could taste the sour bile of vomit.

'That's easily remedied,' Uther said with his chin raised in triumph. 'Botha!' he bellowed in the direction of the outer door.

'Master?' The captain of the guard entered the room hastily and read Myrddion's shame at a single glance. Dropping his eyes, he bowed to his master and awaited his instructions.

'Show the healer our plans of Tintagel and explain its particular problems.'

Still impassive, Botha collected a scroll from Uther's campaign table and rolled it out with a deft flick of his wrist. 'As you can see, healer, Tintagel is a leaf-shaped peninsula surrounded by sheer cliffs that plunge down to the sea on all sides. A narrow neck of land links the castle with the mainland and a very narrow bridge of wood crosses this expanse of rocks and the wildness of the sea. The garrison has been constructed on the landward side to protect this entrance, so any attack becomes bogged down before the bridge is even reached.'

'You're suggesting that it would be impossible to take Tintagel by force,' Myrddion said, interested in the puzzle despite his abhorrence of the task.

'It's an impossible siege in the short term,' Botha agreed. 'The defenders have their own wells and can fish the seas with impunity, so an attacking army might have to wait outside Tintagel for a year or more.'

'So force of arms is pointless and that's why you need me,' Myrddion muttered bitterly, swivelling his eyes to stare at Uther with growing understanding. 'I must discover a strategy to attack a fortress held by two defenceless women.'

'Yes, that's precisely what I require of you. You gave no less assistance to my brother – or to Vortigern before him.' Uther's voice was stony and inflexible, warning Myrddion that no pleas would be accepted. 'You will obey me – with alacrity.'

'Neither Vortigern nor Ambrosius required me to act like a barbarian who makes war on women. Even Vortigern's idea of warfare was clean, by comparison.'

Myrddion's words were unwise and he was speaking without

reflection, but Uther wasn't provoked. The High King knew that his healer might protest all he chose, but he would ultimately be forced to comply with his master's wishes.

'I will need your map, and I will need time to think,' Myrddion whispered, so that Uther had to strain to hear him. 'I can't pull Tintagel Castle onto the mainland by magic, because I don't have any charms that I can use, even if such things existed. Only stealth will open the citadel to you and, as it has never fallen, I must have time to find its weaknesses.'

Myrddion knew that his voice lacked conviction and he accepted that he had surrendered to Uther's threats. But he still intended to play for time.

'You have the hours of darkness in which to complete your task, so pray that there's no sun tomorrow, if you require more time. King Bors will be ordered to secure the fortress and bury the dead to keep him out of the way. Nor will any Dumnonii courier be permitted to reach Tintagel with the sad news of Gorlois's death. You'll think hard, Myrddion Merlinus, for many lives depend on your intelligence and your capacity for deceit.'

The healer staggered out of Uther's rooms and ran into the open air. To the amusement of the guardsmen who lounged around Uther's headquarters, he vomited violently into the pristine snow. Try as he might to quell his stomach, his body was racked by spasms until his throat was raw and his stomach was empty. He felt as if he had been poisoned.

'Come, master healer, your time is short,' Botha's voice said softly from behind him. The captain laid a sympathetic hand on the younger man's shoulder. 'I'll accompany you to your tent.'

Carefully, and almost tenderly, Botha assisted Myrddion to mount his horse and then led him back through the garrison. The moon broke out of the cloud cover and Myrddion realised that time was painfully short. What could he do? How could he hope to protect the queen, without damning Willa and Berwyn to Uther's retribution?

'How can you serve this king, Botha? How can you listen to such monstrosities with a still and patient face?'

Botha turned in the saddle and halted his mount by pulling on the reins. 'He is my master and I am oath-bound to him, right or wrong. Usually, my king is mindful of my honour and doesn't ask anything that would compromise me, and so I'm able to serve, albeit with a heavy heart. My lord Uther is the High King. He will save our people from the Saxon menace, and while I shudder at the measures he uses to fight this war, I will die to preserve him. Please try to understand that while I try to retain my honour, my oath comes first.'

'I don't know how I can live with what Uther expects of me. We both know I'll obey him. Because my mother was raped, I can attest that no good comes from such violence. But I'm trapped, so whom do I sacrifice? Those whom I know and love? Or those persons who deserve my respect? Whatever happens, I am damned if I do and damned if I don't.'

Something in Myrddion's voice caused Botha to pause, to think and then to respond with a fierce urgency. Perhaps the captain of the guard feared the healer would attempt to kill himself to escape the Gordian knot that Uther had bound around him.

'But your birth was the result of a rape, Master Myrddion, so some good came out of an evil action, given all the lives you have saved as a healer. Our destinies are in the hands of the gods, if such things exist, but I believe there must be a balance in the vast distances of time and space, which demands that good must eventually prevail over wickedness and thwart the evil ones in the end. I am bound to believe this truth, or else my life would have no purpose. You must trust in your own goddess, and save as many innocents as you can.'

Myrddion hiccuped with distress, and Botha couldn't tell if the healer laughed or wept – or both. 'So, also, said Bishop Lucius of Glastonbury when he advised me. A man of war and a man of God have both seen my conundrum far more clearly than I have. I've tried to choose reason over emotion my whole life, because I've always found that it's dangerous to love or to trust too much.'

'You touch upon the riddles of the gods, Myrddion. Ultimately, we survive on faith or we fall into the abyss. In my judgement, you're a man who possesses strong feelings, but then I'm not the one who is required to stand in your shoes. Whatever choice is made, you must stand by it.' Botha laughed deprecatingly. 'We argue philosophy in the teeth of a tempest.'

Myrddion didn't dare to close his eyes after Botha left him in the healers' tents, despite having been awake for nearly two days. He feared that he lacked the strength to bear the assault of the night terrors that would come.

So, weary and bowed with care, he sat with the corpse of Gorlois and explained to the shade of the great warrior how he would betray a selfless love. Myrddion begged the dead king's pardon, because he could see the answer to Uther Pendragon's demands so clearly that he wondered that the High King had not found the solution for himself. Near dawn, as the eastern sky began to stain with the faintest touch of rose, a feeling of peace stole into his heart. Either the goddess, Gorlois or his own inner voice finally accepted what had to be done and lifted some of the weight of responsibility from his conscience.

'You are not to blame,' the voice whispered. 'Ultimately, some good can come from Uther's wickedness and you will be given a second chance to redeem yourself. Place no trust in kings and believe only in the human desire for truth and beauty that cannot be gainsaid, even by the masters of the earth. Be at peace.'

Myrddion suspected that his inner voice was only wishful

thinking, but he still accepted its comfort. Then, exhausted by worry and work, he closed his eyes and fell into a deep healing sleep, his tired head resting on Gorlois's cold breast.

The snow clouds had thinned and weak sunshine broke through the cover to gild the shrouded land. Strangely, there were no birds calling and the winds had ceased to rattle the bare branches of the forest trees. Only a hunting vixen, over-late in her search for food, padded through the snow like a white ghost. She smelled the taint of death on the air, the scent that men brought with them to disturb the quiet of the forests, so she hastened to the den and her two cubs, which were almost old enough to fend for themselves. She carried a plump pheasant in her jaws to keep their hunger at bay and shivered at the delicious taste of blood in her mouth.

Behind her, the light brightened as another day dawned.

TINTAGEL CASTLE

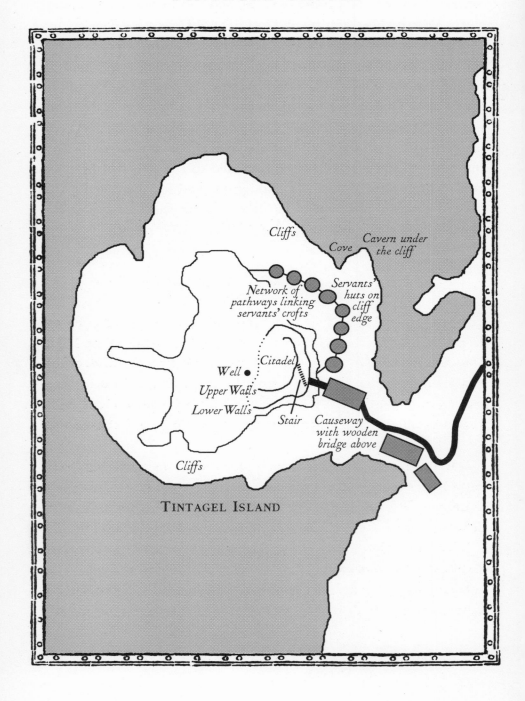

Cliffs

Cove

Cavern under the cliff

Network of pathways linking servants' crofts

Servants' huts on cliff edge

Citadel

Well

Upper Walls

Lower Walls

Stair

Causeway with wooden bridge above

Cliffs

TINTAGEL ISLAND

CHAPTER XX

TINTAGEL

In nature there are neither rewards nor punishments,
there are only consequences.

Ingersol, R.G., *Lectures and Essays*

Dragged into Uther's presence with scant regard for his dignity or
his position, Myrddion swayed with weariness in front of the High
King. Uther's bloodshot eyes were sunk deeply into his head, proof
of a restless night. The corners of the High King's mouth were
drawn down while the bones of his skull were prominent with
weariness, exposing a death's head that predicted a withered old
age.

'Well, healer? While you were resting, I was awaiting your
solution. It's a pity your servant had to be cuffed around a little, but
he denied Ulfin entry into the tent where you were sleeping beside
Gorlois's corpse. Perhaps the Boar has tempted you to join him?'

'It's a cowardly act to punish an unarmed servant for a perceived
slight,' Myrddion protested hotly. 'I hope that Cadoc has not come
to lasting harm for my sake, but I'm also certain that there will be
an accounting one day for atrocities done by others in your name.'

'Brave words, Storm Crow! It's fortunate that your friend will live, although he may have suffered lasting injury to his hand. However, as you are about to give me the information I want, I'll permit you to treat him so he can be returned to health. I still need competent healers.'

Uther's eyes were both cold and excited, for he knew he had finally taken Myrddion's measure. Cadoc's injury was a timely reminder to the healer of Uther's ascendency.

How does he know that I've devised a solution to his problem? Myrddion thought with a sick realisation that he had no way out of his predicament. His mind returned again to Cadoc's plight, for his faithful friend would be robbed of a means of earning his bread if Myrddion couldn't repair his injured hand.

'Whatever I have to say is for your ears alone, King Uther. The treachery I've planned is sickening to me, so to discuss it publicly is both shameful and foolish.'

Negligently, Uther dismissed his guard with a wave of his hand, except for Ulfin who had been the architect of Cadoc's punishment. With a baleful stare in the warrior's direction, Myrddion addressed the man as the contemptible vermin he was.

'I won't forget the injuries you inflicted on my friend's hand, Ulfin, for you appreciate how much a healer depends upon agile fingers. Pray that I can set his bones so his tendons can do his bidding, else I might be inclined to foretell your future.'

'I'm not afraid of you, healer, even if men say you're a prophet of doom,' Ulfin scoffed with a sneer. 'A bag of wind cannot harm a true warrior.'

'You're not worth my attention, warrior or no,' Myrddion snapped as he turned his back on the guardsman with the same imperious arrogance displayed by Melvig ap Melwy, his great-grandfather. The slight was so pointed that Ulfin flushed along his flat cheekbones.

'As for your problem, your highness, you must enter Tintagel disguised as Gorlois, King of Cornwall. There is no other way to breach the citadel. The battle for the eastern gate of Anderida was a bloodbath, I'm told, so there will be armour and tunics aplenty belonging to Gorlois's guard. They must be cleansed and used in your deception.'

From his cushioned chair, Uther peered up at Myrddion from under his golden eyebrows. 'True! But even if I deck out my men in the Boar's colours, I look nothing like Gorlois. For starters, I'm six inches taller than he was.'

'A man's height is immaterial when he's on a horse, and you'll be riding Gorlois's destrier. Bors begged me to heal his uncle's horse, and it's in the care of my wounded servant. Every man in Tintagel's garrison must know their king's stallion, so you will ride Fleet-foot into the citadel. But I beg that the horse be permitted to survive, for I gave my word to King Bors that I would protect it.'

'Very well,' Uther replied coldly. 'I don't want the animal anyway.'

'The Boar's helmet and visor will disguise most of your face and your distinctive hair will be hidden. I will dye your brows black temporarily, but you must keep your eyes hidden as much as possible. Their colour is too distinctive.'

Uther nodded smugly. So far, Myrddion was making sense and the High King could see how the ruse would work.

'If you arrive at Tintagel's garrison in full darkness, preferably during the fogs that plague the coast, you will be further disguised. I expect you'll have no difficulty filling Gorlois's leathers and armour, for you are as broad-shouldered as he. Your legs will be a problem, but you should pass muster if you can hold them against your horse when you're in sight of his men.'

A shadow passed across Uther's tired face. 'But our voices are quite different. I could not sound like Gorlois, no matter how hard I tried.'

Myrddion grimaced without mirth. 'I've thought of an answer to that, sire. I'll bandage your throat so the dressings are obvious and they will tell Tintagel's guards without words that you have been wounded. A little dried blood will support the fiction, as long as you remember to croak any orders you give when you're within earshot of the garrison. You're wounded, so no one will wonder that you're eager to be comforted by your queen.'

Uther nodded. 'It's imperative that no word reaches Tintagel that Gorlois has perished. I've taken steps in that direction.'

'I'm sure you have,' Myrddion replied dryly, imagining the stiffening corpses of murdered couriers abandoned on the western road for the carrion birds. 'Cloak your servants heavily. The weather is so vile at Tintagel that no one will question their identity. I don't know the exact means by which Gorlois announced his approach to the garrison.'

'I'll discover it, never fear,' Uther answered decisively and gestured to Ulfin, who left the headquarters at a trot. 'I have a Dumnonii courier in Anderida who is still alive, so Ulfin will discover what I need to know.'

Myrddion felt ill. 'Is another good man about to go to the shadows unmourned?'

'He won't be unmourned, Myrddion. Since you seem to care so much for the Boar's warriors, you have my permission to say whatever prayers for the dead are necessary as you accompany me to Tintagel.'

Shock caused the colour to leach out of Myrddion's cheeks. 'Me? Why do you need me to go to Tintagel? I must tend to Cadoc and continue to care for those wounded in the battle. Don't ask me to participate in Queen Ygerne's betrayal . . . please. Leave me in peace now that I've told you how to achieve your desires.'

'To inform on me as soon as I turn my back? Do you take me for a fool, Storm Crow? Besides, I'm told that the Lady Ygerne has a soft spot for you. It's perfectly plain to me that Gorlois would need a healer on such a long trek home after being wounded.'

Uther's face was elated, excited and predatory, and Myrddion knew that any pleas would simply feed his enjoyment of the healer's discomfort.

'Very well. If you insist, I will ride to Tintagel with you, but please give me leave to attend to Cadoc's wounds before we depart.'

'Agreed, Storm Crow.' Uther smiled and sipped at a goblet of wine. With a graceful flick of the fingers, he casually picked up the scroll with its plan of Tintagel fortress. 'I've memorised what is known of the king's apartments, but we have many miles to travel, so the fiction needn't begin until we reach the Dumnonii lands. We will then become warriors of their tribe.' His gaze abruptly hardened. 'There is one other matter I require of you, Myrddion. I want the severed head of Gorlois.'

Myrddion felt his knees tremble. 'Why, lord? Why would you want to desecrate the corpse of a brave and noble man? I don't understand.'

'You aren't privy to *all* my thoughts, healer. Just provide me with the head of the Dumnonii king in a leather bag. I don't want it stinking before we arrive in Tintagel, so pack snow around it. I'm sure you know how to decapitate a dead body, for I'm told you did as much for your kinsman, the Deceangli king.'

'That ceremony was carried out as part of an ancient ritual, my lord, and it was done with reverence. Not like . . . *this*.'

'Do it any way you please – just do it. I require you and the head to be ready to depart for Tintagel by dawn tomorrow.'

Dismissed at last from Uther's presence, Myrddion stumbled out of the High King's headquarters. Botha's sympathetic eyes followed him as he trudged out of Anderida through the soiled grey snow. Myrddion chose to walk to the tents of the healers in order to regain his composure before he reached his companions.

Regardless of the cost to himself, they must not learn of Uther's perfidy, for such knowledge was dangerous and their lives could be forfeit. Praying that he could play his part like a man, the healer drew on his last reserves of strength, and was comforted only by the remembered words of Bishop Lucius: 'You will need to base your decisions on what is good for the realm.'

Myrddion recalled the grave expression on Lucius's face as he offered advice to Myrddion before the fateful solstice feast. Lucius had been brutally frank. Myrddion must trample his personal honour into the mud of Anderida, deliberately, in full knowledge of the consequences of his actions. Uther had been destined to rule, and the healer's choices had been taken from him, one by one.

When Myrddion entered the healers' tent, Cadoc was huddled over a bowl of snow with his broken hand buried in the cold, melting mess. Surprised, Ruadh looked up from the slivers of wood she was shaping into splints to immobilise her friend's fingers.

'Thank all the gods that you've come! I'm not equal to setting bones, while Cadoc is contemplating suicide because he believes his hand will never work properly again.'

'Show me,' Myrddion demanded with some of his old authority, and Cadoc lifted his hand out of the basin and laid it on a clean cloth on the surgical table. Myrddion noticed that the body of the Dumnonii king had been moved to an improvised bier and was covered with a fine fur cloak. Two Dumnonii guards stood at each end of the shrouded corpse.

'Ah,' Myrddion murmured, and grinned at Cadoc as he probed his assistant's knuckles and finger joints with his own sensitive fingertips. 'See? The bones haven't pierced the skin, so your chances of healing properly are excellent.'

Without warning, Myrddion pulled on Cadoc's forefinger and felt the knuckle bones slide back into position. Taken by surprise, Cadoc barely had time to scream.

'That knuckle was only dislocated. That's one finger that Ulfin didn't break, and with a thumb and a forefinger you can still hold a scalpel, praise be to the gods of healing.'

'That hurt!' Cadoc protested, but Ruadh noticed that the spectres had retreated from his warm brown eyes.

'Now for the others. Brace yourself, Cadoc, or you'll frighten our patients.'

Obediently, Cadoc bit down on a plug of leather while Myrddion rapidly set the other three fingers. Of them all, only the last joint caused some difficulty. Shaken, waxen with pain but still bright-eyed under a thin wash of unshed tears, Cadoc looked up at his master hopefully as Myrddion bound and splinted the last of the damaged digits.

'You're lucky that Ulfin is a thug and a bully who'd rather prolong agony than do his job properly. You have several disloca-tions because he was bent on making you suffer rather than destroying your hands. The break in the little finger is the only one that troubles me and you might experience some difficulty in moving it. I won't know for sure until the splints come off, but I believe you'll still be a healer once the bones knit together.'

'Then I must give my thanks to Bran, Don and all the great ones. I'd sooner be dead than crippled, even though I sound like a coward. But what of you, Myrddion? Something has shaken you, so don't try to deny it.'

'Come outside, both of you. I'd rather not speak in front of these good men.'

The day was barely born, but after a promising beginning of weak sunshine the cloud cover had returned as if to hide Anderida and the plots and counterplots that were being spun within it. Myrddion looked up at the flinty sky and spied a few flakes of snow beginning to fall.

'I will be leaving Anderida in company with King Uther and his men early tomorrow. Once we've gone, you are ordered to put the wounded into wagons and take them to the fortress. They'll be warm within its walls, and the apprentices can care for them well enough.'

'Why?' Cadoc asked flatly, his clever eyes fixed on Myrddion's face.

'Because I'm ordering you to take one wagon with all the tools of our trade to Segontium, out of harm's way. Don't shake your heads. I'm being forced to carry out despicable tasks for the High King because he regards you as hostages. He is aware of my affection for you all, and knows he can force me into compliance by making threats against your lives. You must take Brangaine, Rhedyn, Dyfri and Ruadh and flee before he realises you've escaped his clutches.'

'Brangaine won't leave Venta Belgarum as long as Willa is held in captivity,' Cadoc warned his master. 'And I'm reluctant to go, although I'd be prepared to take the others to a place of safety if you allow me to return to your service.'

'No!' Myrddion's voice was strengthening. 'I'll be forced to serve Uther for as long as my friends are close at hand, for he's a dragon in thought and deed. You are in ever-present danger in my service, and I insist that you flee. You may recall that your hand was broken to ensure that I complied with every detail of Uther's plan. In the hard years that lie ahead, I cannot spend every moment looking over my shoulder for fear of what he might do to you.'

'I'll not leave you,' Ruadh said. Her mouth pursed stubbornly and Myrddion read a willingness to die in her green eyes. 'The others must go, but Uther is a strange creature and I don't believe he'd kill his brother's woman. I don't care, anyway. You may say what you choose, master, but I intend to stay.'

'You may have to tie her down, Cadoc, for I can't risk more blood on my soul,' Myrddion said so softly that his voice was little more than a whisper. 'Praxiteles has already left Venta Belgarum with the rest of the household, and he'll meet you in Segontium on your arrival.'

The snowflakes began to fall faster and whitened Myrddion's black hair. For a moment, Cadoc saw Myrddion as he would become in future years, tall and aristocratic like a king out of ancient days. The scarred healer shivered as the breeze suddenly increased in strength.

'How will we manage without you, Myrddion?' Cadoc whispered, tears streaking his fire-scarred face.

'Why, Cadoc, you'll survive very well. Llanwith pen Bryn will gladly employ a healer of your quality, and I will see you whenever I am sent out of Venta Belgarum. I'm not planning to die, and nor shall I vanish like a puff of smoke. For everyone's safety, I wish to ensure that many leagues lie between Uther Pendragon and the ones I love. Grant me the peace to sleep easily at night, Cadoc.'

'But he can still find us in Segontium, master,' Cadoc whispered, scrambling for some means to stay by the side of the only person he had ever selflessly loved. 'Distance would mean nothing to Uther Pendragon.'

'But he won't. Uther prefers the south and only ventures into the north on campaigns. He never even looks at subordinates, unless he has some duty for them, so he wouldn't recognise you even if you were treating him. Fortunately for me, the Dragon has a simple, arrow-straight mind and no real talent for subterfuge.'

Both Ruadh and Cadoc looked doubtful, so Myrddion hurried to explain. 'Yes, he's a beast, but I've never known him to disguise his feelings very well. His tactics are brutal and direct, and while they're extremely effective, he's not clever. No, he'll not pursue you to Segontium, or trouble himself to think of you once you've gone.'

Ruadh gripped Myrddion's hand tightly. 'The price that is asked of you is too high. Damn the goddess! And damn all the gods if they force you to live unloved and empty. Such servitude should not be any man's fate.' She wailed the final words, so one of Gorlois's guards moved at the flap of the tent to check for danger in the snowy morning gloom.

Myrddion tried to smile nonchalantly and waved the guard away. The warrior eyed the healers with narrowed, suspicious eyes, but he eventually returned to his post.

'I'm the Demon Seed, remember, and I've been alone for half my life. Now, will you please do this service for me? If you love me, you'll agree when I beg this sacrifice of you.'

Unable to speak the hated words of acquiescence aloud, Cadoc could only nod. Ruadh refused, and Myrddion felt a deep pang as if the goddess had already determined his lover's fate.

'I have one other unpleasant duty to perform, and for that task I must ask you to leave me with Gorlois and the guards. But first, Cadoc, would you fetch my sword for me?'

'Your sword? You've never used it before. You rarely bother to even wear it,' Cadoc protested. Myrddion had been gifted with King Melvig ap Melwy's sword when he had cut the head from his kinsman's body, but Cadoc knew that the healer had never used the sword during the many years it had been in his possession.

'Just obey me, Cadoc. Truly, it is best if you have no knowledge of what I do.'

Unwillingly, Cadoc trudged off through the thickening snowfall towards the wagons while Ruadh cast a defiant glance in Myrddion's direction and headed for the second tent where the bearers were caring for the wounded. Myrddion sighed again and tried to remember the last time he had been truly happy. As he looked out at the dimming landscape, the trees were like the corpses of summer, and the grey sea, just visible beyond Anderida, was a charcoal slab that looked solid from this distance. The healer shivered inside his black cloak and wondered if he would be at peace this side of the grave.

Then, with squared shoulders, he elbowed his way into the surgical tent. He demanded time alone with the corpse of Gorlois, and such was his reputation that the guards reluctantly agreed. When Cadoc returned with his great-grandfather's sword, Myrddion winced at the burning cold of the gold-plated scabbard and the sanguine glitter of its bloody jewels.

'Leave me now, Cadoc, and keep the guards occupied for at least an hour. I'll inform you when they can return.'

With a reluctant, confused expression, Cadoc obeyed.

Myrddion stood over Gorlois's corpse for a moment as he recreated in his mind the ritual he had seen carried out by the Druids at Canovium. Then, before he could lose his nerve, he swiftly exposed the neck. Raising Melvig's sword above his head, he prayed that Gorlois's soul would speed like an eagle high above the winter clouds and onwards into the heart of the sun. Then he allowed the blade to fall.

The corpse was rewrapped with a pile of clean dressings and bandages fashioned to form the shape of Gorlois's head. Only a few minutes sufficed to stitch the shroud together and re-cover the remains with the fur blanket. The ruse was too hurried to fool Bors for long but, with luck, Uther's troop would be gone, as would Cadoc and the women, before the desecration was discovered.

Myrddion placed Gorlois's head in a leather bag and packed it with snow before heading off to collect the dead king's armour and linens. Secrecy still mattered, and although the hand that had struck off the Dumnonii king's head seemed cursed forever, perhaps Willa and Berwyn would be freed because Myrddion had obeyed the High King. He would do his utmost to ensure that Bors remained ignorant of Uther's plans for as long as possible.

With those items he prized most stored in his satchel, carrying the leather bag and wearing his sword, Myrddion saddled Fleet-foot and loaded the destrier with Gorlois's armour. Then, before he lost his courage, he led the horse away from the tents. He was grateful for the heavily falling snow which filled his tracks and rendered horse and man almost invisible. Inside the fortress, he took refuge in the stables and gave Botha the severed head for delivery to Uther Pendragon. Ulfin collected the armour with the contemptuous sneer that was his habitual greeting to the healer.

'I have done all that was asked of me, but I require horses for myself and furs to keep me warm. I have not dared to bring my own belongings, lest King Bors should become suspicious. Uther must provide for me.'

While Ulfin shrugged with disinterest, Botha nodded slowly.

'I'll find everything you need, healer. I'll also bring you stew and wine, if you choose to stay in the stables for the night. It's wild outside today and the king wishes to leave before dawn, so you need to rest.'

'Aye, so I must, for there are many miles to ride in the days to come.'

The straw was malodorous and the scratching in the corners of the stables warned Myrddion that he shared his bed with rats. But he was beyond caring, for a man can only tolerate so much horror and loss before his mind becomes sated and his senses numbed. Exhausted, he determined to ignore the rodents on the oaken beams of the tack room, trusting that the Mother would protect her errant son. He fell into a deep sleep amid the straw.

Outside, the snow had stopped at nightfall, to be replaced by a northern wind so bitter that every surface turned to ice. But in the straw, Myrddion slept on and on. He did not dream.

The road to the west had proved to be harsher than anything that Myrddion had ever encountered during his arduous journey to the Middle Sea. Uther travelled fast and left foundering horses at every outpost as he continued his headlong rush to reach Tintagel before rumour travelled on the winds and warned Queen Ygerne that her happiness was over. Men and horses were rarely rested, and then only because Fleet-foot was integral to Myrddion's ruse and the destrier's strength must be preserved until the troop entered the precincts of the fortress. Confused and fractious, the stallion had not been ridden during the journey to ensure he could carry out his role in the entrapment of Ygerne.

At the borders of the Dumnonii lands, the troop halted to rest, although Uther fumed at the necessary delay. Beside a shallow, ice-choked stream, the men were instructed to wash their bodies thoroughly, replait their wet hair in the fashion of Gorlois's guard, and finally dress their shivering bodies in the cleaned and refurbished armour of the dead Dumnonii warriors. Wrapped in heavy, chequered Dumnonii cloaks that muffled their shapes and faces, Uther's guardsmen turned into Gorlois's warriors under Myrddion's watchful eyes, but the healer felt no sense of triumph at the success of his plan.

Uther paced around the clearing in a fever of impatience. It was only with the greatest difficulty that Myrddion was able to force the High King to harness his mad energy and submit to having his brows darkened.

'What's that muck?' Uther growled, eyeing a small pot filled with a dark, greasy substance.

'It's called stiblum, master, a woman's cosmetic that is used to darken the area around the eyes and eyebrows. Ruadh permitted me to take her prized pot with the promise that I'd return it. Stand still and let me darken your brows. Then I'll add some to the pouches under your eyes to suggest illness, and that will draw attention away from their colour.'

Once he had finished his ministrations, Myrddion stepped away from the High King and watched as he donned a dead man's clothes and armour. Gorlois's trews were hopelessly short, so Uther changed back into his own serviceable leathers. He retained his own boots and lacings because his feet were so much larger than the Dumnonii king's, but the armour fitted perfectly, and once heavily cloaked Uther was thoroughly disguised.

'Now for the final touches,' Myrddion told him. 'Ulfin must plait all that hair into a cap and wind it round your head. Even one stray curl will spoil the fiction we've created.'

Ulfin scowled and began the arduous ask of plaiting Uther's mane of hair with a thunderous face. Although his intellect wasn't swift, he was acutely aware that Myrddion was enjoying both the spectacle and his own discomfiture whenever Uther cuffed him for pulling too painfully on strands of the High King's curls.

Once Ulfin had finished, Myrddion drew a long bandage from his satchel and bound the king's throat and part of his head to create the effect of a neck wound. Slushy mud was used to soil the clean cloth and support the appearance of an old wound. Uther provided a small amount of blood by cutting his thumb and pressing the wounded digit onto the cloth until Myrddion was satisfied that the bandage looked authentic.

'What of me, lord? Do you suggest that I should disguise myself?' Myrddion asked, his feet crunching nervously in the dry snow.

'Why? Everybody knows Uther's Storm Crow. We can only hope the garrison will assume that you've been sent by me to care for their master.' Uther grinned whitely and Myrddion was reminded that the king had perfect teeth.

'Try not to smile, my lord. Gorlois had a tooth missing in the front of his mouth.'

Once they were dressed and muffled, the troop took to the road again, still riding hard but pausing regularly to rest the horses. Despite the freezing winds, the peasants gave ragged cheers at their lord's passing whenever the warriors galloped through villages along the route. On each occasion, Uther raised his left hand in salute, obeying Myrddion's orders that he must courteously acknowledge any peasants who recognised him.

As the grey day dragged towards darkness, the trees began to grow sparser, except in hollows where the wind could not reach them. Those trees that raised their heads into the sea winds were contorted into bent, crippled shapes that suggested rows of trolls or strange earth demons that waved their naked branches in warning at the passing warriors.

Carefully avoiding low branches in the deepening night, the troop followed the narrow tracks that wound towards the sea. The route had been carved out by horsemen and carts over countless years, for no Roman roads had been built along these fierce shores where naval landings were impossible and the sea was a wild, untamed thing. Occasionally, strong moonlight revealed the odd cove of pebbles lying between frowning cliffs and Myrddion could make out occasional glimmers of light that spoke of small fishing villages existing on the perilous edge of the great ocean. Land and sea had a wild beauty, and Myrddion discovered that he understood the contradictions in Gorlois's character far better for having seen his country. Strong, vigorous and fierce, Gorlois had been more than a match for this wild coast, yet its alien beauty was echoed in the sentimentality and protectiveness that had softened the harsher edges of the Dumnonii king's nature.

'A savage and lovely place,' Myrddion whispered aloud, but the sound of the horses' hooves covered his momentary slip of the tongue. Prudently, Uther had ordered complete silence in the Dumnonii lands unless they were challenged. Dreading their arrival, yet wishing that this devil's ride would soon be over, Myrddion clung to his mount like a limpet and tried to keep his mind blank.

The troop paused at a great cliff that plunged hundreds of feet down to the boiling sea below. To both left and right, promontories thrust fingers out into the crashing cauldron of waves, but Tintagel on the left was shrouded in darkness as spume, fog and sea mist turned its peninsula into an indistinct outline.

On the mainland below them, and reached only by a steep, treacherous path, the unmortared stone walls of the garrison shivered under gusts of the fierce wind. 'May the gods be with us, for that path is deadly,' Myrddion panted to Uther. 'It's solid ice, so we won't be able to gallop on it.'

'Sound the horn,' the High King ordered, and lowered his visor. Somehow, chameleon-like, he hunched his broad shoulders within his fur-edged, chequered cloak. Myrddion was forced to blink his wind-dried eyes, because Gorlois had returned to life in front of him.

The ram's horn sounded, eerie and plaintive, as the troop rode down the path with its dizzying descent. Only Fleet-foot moved ahead briskly, confident on home ground and familiar with every treacherous twist in the approach to the garrison. Recklessly, Myrddion urged his own horse to follow in Uther's wake, careless of the black ice that caused a beast behind him to slide dangerously on its haunches. The horn sounded again, and torches sprang into life in the garrison as several armed men reached the small court before it, huddled in heavy furs to withstand the wind that howled from the black sea.

'Make way!' Myrddion shouted, his voice blown into rags by the gale. 'Gorlois comes home to Tintagel, so make way!'

Uther scarcely paused at the garrison and raised his left fist in Gorlois's customary salute. A part of Myrddion was amazed at how acutely Uther must have observed his Dumnonii rival, for the action was a perfect mimicry of the Boar's salutations.

'I am home,' Uther croaked in a voice that was scarcely audible. 'A Saxon nearly got me, but I'm hard to kill.'

The guards laughed at their master's gallows humour and Uther rode on as his troop clattered behind him, sawing at their horses' bits to keep their heads up in the treacherous conditions. They rode into the sea mist, and were suddenly confronted by dizzying drops on either side of a narrow wooden bridge.

Uther didn't hesitate. Fleet-foot knew his stable was near and that he would be fed sweet hay and clean water to reward him after the long ride. Given his head, and as eager as his rider, the stallion leapt away as Myrddion and Uther's personal guard clattered behind. Hooves on the wooden planks of the bridge sounded hollowly, and one horse screamed shrilly as the whole structure shivered slightly in the gale. Then they were across and a steep, winding path led them upward, up and up – towards raw flint walls that towered above them until Myrddion felt dizzy and sick, and could only grip his horse's mane for dear life with whitened knuckles.

A hastily opened gate welcomed them into a dark, narrow forecourt, and Tintagel was taken.

While the guard disposed of the few men protecting the lower gate with disciplined efficiency, Uther dismounted and tossed the reins of Gorlois's horse to a boy who had come from the small stables, his eyes blurred with sleep. Myrddion watched the boy's expression change to one of terror as he saw the two gatekeepers die in fountains of their own arterial blood.

'Bar the gates and then follow me,' Uther hissed at Ulfin. 'Your men may have any women they find in the fortress, save only for the queen and her hell-born daughter. But tell them to be quiet about it, for any undue noise will rouse the garrison and we can do without an assault.'

'Aye, lord,' Ulfin grunted, and beckoned Botha to his side to relay his master's orders. Out of unexpected and uncharacteristic sensitivity, Uther had capitalised on Ulfin's unquestioning obedience, and left his captain in a subordinate role that spared Botha from compromising his personal code. Myrddion grudgingly admitted that his treatment of Botha was one of the rare decencies in the High King's behaviour.

Perhaps there's hope for him after all, Myrddion thought. The healer trusted that the captain's cool head would save as many lives in Tintagel as possible, so he took his satchel from his saddle and gripped the free hand of the stable boy who was still frozen with fright, although he clutched Fleet-foot's reins with the other.

'Listen to me, boy. Do you want to live? You do? Then obey me to the letter. Take the horses into the stables, and treat them as you would for your master. Stay with them, groom them, and feed them grain from your store, for they have travelled many long miles. But whatever you hear, do not leave the stables and you might survive the night. Do you understand?'

The youth stared up into Myrddion's eyes and nodded dumbly. The healer handed over his own horse and gathered the reins of several others, until the stable lad began to function in his customary, comforting routine, although his face was ashen under the wind-torn moon. The mist that had disguised their approach had been blown away on this bare outcrop of stone, and they were surrounded by the thunder of crashing waves and howling winds below the inner wall and the citadel.

High king and healer surveyed legendary Tintagel. The fortress was small and primitive, and built of unmortared stone that was lined with a thick stucco of mud, dung and straw. Roughly circular in shape, with protruding additions that had grown randomly around a central tower, the fortress had an archaic set of thatched roofs over a framework of undressed oaken branches. Tintagel's great age was clearly written in the primitive building methods that were stitched together with younger, more sophisticated rooms, built by the ancestors of King Gorlois.

Below the parapet of stone that covered the flat top of the castle grounds, narrow paths snaked between knee-high grass blown flat and desiccated by the wind. The paths wound perilously around the sloping walls of the cliffs to small conical huts of stone that clung to the dizzying edges of the sheer drop to the waves below. Here the servants of the citadel lived, bred and died, generation upon generation, flowing back to the forgotten past when the tribe first crossed the Litus Saxonicum and defeated the blue-tattooed Picts. Tintagel had been ancient even then, and no man had set foot on her solid stones without the permission of her lord and master.

Until now.

Uther had disappeared, so Myrddion began the journey to the core of the labyrinthine fortress, remembering ancient legends of the Mother's dwelling, another maze below the earth with a monster at its heart. Putting aside his superstitions, he climbed any stone stairs he came to, reasoning that Ygerne's nest would be in the centre of the fortress at its highest point. Then, out of the claustrophobic silence of the winding corridors, he heard a woman wail in a shrill, unearthly crescendo of horror. Cursing, he followed the keening sound until, suddenly, it was cut off.

'Where do you think you're going, Merlinus?' Ulfin whispered from behind the healer's back. Myrddion felt the sharp point of a knife blade against his kidneys.

'Do you plan to murder me from behind now that my usefulness is over? I promise you that if you send me to the Mother before my time, your days will be haunted by my unquiet spirit.'

'I repeat, healer. Where are you going?'

'I'm searching for Morgan before some idiot kills or rapes her. Uther Pendragon doesn't need the whole Otadini tribe and their allies pouring over the wall with a thirst for his blood. Those mad northerners have very precise concepts of the duties owed to ravaged kinswomen.'

The knife was withdrawn a fraction, and Myrddion began to check each of the four rooms running off a central set of worn stone steps that led to the highest point of the tower. The rooms were oddly shaped and very small and should have been cold and forbidding, for the walls were sealed with ancient mud to deflect stray breezes. Raw wooden shutters kept out the gusting, spiralling winds. However, the dun-coloured walls were mellowed to some extent by hanging fabrics of soft colours: rose, yellow-gold and verdant green reminded Myrddion of fields of rampant wild flowers. Perhaps Ygerne had woven these hangings with her own hands during the long years while she waited for her husband to return from his many battles. The threads were vegetable-dyed, so that the hangings shimmered and moved with a semblance of life that infused something plain and unadorned with subtle, changeable beauty, much like the colouring of the queen herself.

Respectfully, Myrddion closed each door carefully. Only two remained for his attention and the healer feared to push on the old, hand-polished wood of the first. He pressed his ear to the door instead, knowing that Uther would not welcome any interruption if he was in the room with Ygerne, yet terrified that the queen might be seriously injured, even dying. His bargain with the High King had not included violence to the person of King Gorlois's wife.

There was no sound, only the loud beating of Myrddion's frightened heart. Cautiously, he pushed open the door, which complained with a squeal of ancient metal straps. Conscious of Ulfin's threatening presence at his back, Myrddion inched his way carefully into the darkened room.

Something brushed his arm with a sting of fire and Myrdion instinctively threw himself sideways. A dark shape flew at Ulfin, all claws and wild hair, wielding a small knife with such deadly intent that it almost caught the seasoned warrior in the eye. The blade skidded along his forehead and the smaller figure stumbled. Too fast for Myrddion to intervene, Ulfin gripped the figure, twisted it in his arms and was about to break its neck when Myrddion's wits returned.

'Not for your life, Ulfin! It's Morgan! Morgan, the queen's daughter! Remember Uther's orders.'

'You bitch!' Ulfin growled from the back of his throat as blood from a ragged slash across his forehead dripped into his eyes. 'I'll make you pay for that cut.'

Before Myrddion could stop him, the guardsman broke the hand that held the knife with a deliberate twist of the fragile bones.

'Gods, you're an idiot!' Myrddion cursed as Ulfin pushed the shocked woman back into the room and threw her onto a narrow bed more suited to a servant than a princess. Myrddion had time to notice the cell-like, spartan nature of the room, which possessed little furniture except for a pair of clothes chests and a single stool. A small pottery jar filled with dried flowers rested on the thick stone sill of the shuttered window. It was the only sign of femininity that Myrddion had ever observed in the Dumnonii witch.

'Let me see to Morgan's hand, Ulfin. By all that's holy, don't make her suffer. Don't bring the wrath of the Mother down on us.'

'Get out, healer, unless you like to watch.' Ulfin raised one hand to his forehead and wiped away the blood while his left hand pinned the struggling, silent woman on the bed. 'The bitch has scarred me for life, so I'll treat her like the whore she is. Get out, unless you want to share her.'

As Ulfin's free hand was already busy stripping away his tunic and unlacing his leather breeches, Myrddion sobbed and backed away from the ugly scene. Once outside the room, he slid down to the icy floor and prayed to the Mother for those women in Tintagel who were being forced to suffer as the spoils of war. As he prayed, the screams in the last room began again, higher and higher, and the noise was infused with such loss that Myrddion covered his ears and beat his head against the floor until his blood soaked into the old boards.

When the two rooms were finally silent, Myrddion was still unable to move. Images ran through his mind like thread on a spindle: bloody babies, bleeding feet, an old man in a huge bed covered with a white fur, a girl crucified over an open window, a woman with savage eyes and pointed teeth and, at the end of a long parade of horrors, a sword with a dragon on the hilt. It leaked blood from one end of the metal to the other in a thick, viscous stream.

Just when he thought that he could bear no more, Myrddion felt a touch inside his mind that was as gentle as a Judas kiss. 'You've done what had to be done, good son of my heart. As your reward, you will suffer my dreams no longer. Rise up now, for my daughters will need your ministrations.'

The voice was neither male nor female, and Myrddion wondered why the whole fortress was not awakened by the androgynous thunder of it.

'So this is the voice of the Mother – or God – or *something*. Or, perhaps, I've gone mad.'

Both rooms were still, not with healing sleep or peace, but as if the gale outside had left this spike of stone at the very centre of a greater, cataclysmic whirlwind. Myrddion sat against the wall and waited. His time had come at last.

CHAPTER XXI

THE WOMAN OF GLASS

Oderint dum metuant.
[Let them hate, so long as they fear.]

Accius Lucius, *Atreus*

When Ulfin finally stalked out of Morgan's room, Myrddion's head had sunk upon his bent knees in exhaustion and he almost slept. Ulfin kicked him viciously on the thigh.

'She's all yours, if you want her. The bitch is as cold as the winds that blow from the Western Isles.'

Myrddion clambered painfully to his feet as Ulfin swaggered away, fastening his heavy leather body armour as he went. 'Watch your back, Ulfin, for I swear that you'll die in the most grotesque way you can imagine. Nor will you recognise the blade when it comes after you.'

Ulfin turned slowly and grinned nastily at the healer. Morgan's knife wound had ceased to bleed but the edges of the skin were ragged and would scar badly. Let him wear her mark with pride, Myrddion thought savagely.

'Do you prophesy again, healer? Or is it just more hot air?'

'It's a promise, Ulfin.'

As the warrior began to strut away, Myrddion made a vow to himself. He determined that while he couldn't take Ulfin's life with his own hands, he'd not lift a finger to treat the guardsman or alleviate his suffering if his wound should begin to rot.

'You're like an old toothless dotard who mumbles nothing but empty words,' the warrior sniped back over his shoulder. 'See to the hell-bitch, if you don't want to use her yourself.' Then Ulfin disappeared down the stone stairs that led to the lower rooms. His footsteps clattered on the hollowed stone treads with the sound of dry bones clicking together.

Myrddion crossed the threshold of Morgan's room cautiously, but no threat lurked in the deep shadows to harm him. Inside the claustrophobic space, Gorlois's daughter was a dark shadow on her bed, rolled into a coarse blanket so that only a hank of long black hair was visible.

'Come, Lady Morgan, I'll not harm you, but your wrist needs treatment if you wish to use your hand properly in the future. Don't be afraid of me. You know I'm only a tool of the Mother – for good or for ill – so we serve the same mistress.'

Morgan surged up and the rough cover slid away from her white, naked body. Ivory flesh, black hair and a soft fur triangle between her legs were carelessly exposed, as were the bruises caused by the hands and knees that had been used to force her into physical submission. Purple and blue, the marks of Ulfin's large paws and sharp fingernails covered her breasts, her thighs and the narrow column of her throat. A single bite mark that had drawn blood revealed the brand of Ulfin's ugly mouth on Morgan's pale breast.

But Myrddion had no time to be either embarrassed or ashamed by Morgan's nakedness, for her burning black eyes bored into his from a face that was swollen, bruised, tear-stained, but undefeated. Her fury was a live, cold thing, more intense than Uther's rages, so that Myrddion took a step back from such all-consuming loathing.

'I beg your pardon, Lady Morgan. Ulfin is . . .' His voice trailed away for a moment, then strengthened as he focused on the task before him. 'I must treat your wrist, my lady, so no historionics.'

Still her intense, unwavering stare never left his face. Uncertain whether shock or pain had stolen her voice, Myrddion crossed to the small window, opened the shutters and grasped several handfuls of salty snow from irregularities in the lichen-encrusted stones. Outside, the black night was full of howling voices in the icy gale.

Myrddion lifted Morgan's wrist and packed a handful of snow around the swelling that distorted its delicacy. After initial resistance, she permitted his touch and even held the snow in place. Then they sat together in silence while Myrddion tucked the woollen blanket around her with gentle, sexless care.

Eventually, shocked and hurt, her loss of dignity defeated even Morgan's rage. 'You must promise me, prophet, if such you be, that he will die screaming for what he has done tonight,' she whispered so quietly that Myrddion bent his dark head close to hers to hear her thready voice. 'I can't live cleanly while that animal breathes my air.'

'Ulfin dines on the leavings of his master. He is an extension of Uther Pendragon's inner darkness, so I promise that he rushes towards an inevitable, bloody fate. I don't need to prophesy to know he'll be punished. Can't you see the doom and stupidity that dull his small eyes? If such an extreme is possible, I hate Ulfin even more than you do.'

Before Morgan could retreat into the cold space of her anger and abasement, the healer gently probed the narrow bones of her wrist and found the break where the hand bones met the complex network of tendons and veins in the wrist. He hunted through his satchel for his poppy tincture, then found a jug of water and poured a little into a plain pottery beaker. Using his body to hide his actions, he added several drops of the tincture and swirled the beaker until it disappeared.

'Drink, Morgan. You know my Greek oath precludes a convenient poisoning, so humour me and allow me to treat the break in your arm. If the Mother is kind, you'll heal completely.'

'What would it matter if you killed me anyway? My father must be dead, or you wouldn't have the courage to enter Tintagel. Do what you want.'

Morgan seemed drained of the anger that had fuelled her, listless and defeated. She drank like a small child, in large gulps, and a little water slid down her chin. Myrddion gently wiped the moisture away from the corners of her mouth with the edge of her blanket. While he waited for the drug to take effect, he found a pair of wooden hairpins in Morgan's jewel box in a clothes chest. When she made no protest, he searched the room for items that could be used as splints while the princess watched his efforts with dulling eyes.

'Tell me how my father was killed,' she whispered through swollen lips. 'And don't shake your head at me, Storm Crow. You owe me the truth, if only because you didn't attempt to defend me from Uther's dog. You let him humiliate me!'

Her voice was flat, almost matter-of-fact, but Myrddion dreaded the inevitable hysteria that would come when the numbness of shock wore off.

But he did owe her the truth, because he *had* cowered in the corridor like a craven dog while she was raped. Shame kept his voice at a whisper, but he managed to recount what he knew of Gorlois's assassination with uncompromising honesty. Because he had nothing else to offer in reparation other than exposure of his part in the assault of Tintagel, he told her about her father's decapitation and his excuses for complying with Uther's demands.

'I recited the holy prayers that were invoked during the ritual of beheading that was used after the death of my grandfather. I hope I didn't offend your noble father, because I attempted to carry out my task respectfully. I chose the lives of two girls who are neither noble nor important over the welfare of Queen Ygerne and yourself. Perhaps I did so for selfish reasons, so I can't beg your pardon. Such a sham would serve no purpose, because I'd still be forced to betray you if I had the chance to live the past week over again.'

'Honesty is refreshing, Myrddion.' A little colour had returned to Morgan's face and the first tears began to brim over her eyelashes. 'My father was too fine and decent to be killed from behind. I acquit you of any guilt in his murder, for I know where to lay the blame for that crime.'

She lay back against the cushions and closed her eyes, although she still wept soundlessly. When a little time had elapsed Myrddion gripped her wrist, and with as much speed and dexterity as he possessed he slid the broken bone back into place and bound the wrist firmly with bandages. Then, using the wooden hairpins to hold the joint rigidly in position, he wrapped the lower arm as tightly as circulation permitted. When he finished, Morgan released her breath in a little hiss of pain and opened her eyes.

'What about my mother? What has happened to the queen?'

'I don't know, my lady. While you are sleeping, I'll do my best to find out what has befallen her.'

Morgan closed her eyes and seemed to drowse, although she was obviously in considerable pain. As he began to rise from his knees on the wooden floor, she murmured a last message from the brink of unconsciousness.

'When I wake, we'll become implacable enemies, Myrddion Merlinus. But on this night, the truth should be spoken between people such as you and I. Tomorrow, I'll try to tear down everything you've planned and suffered for, I swear by my life, but my grudge is not against you. I was no maiden, so Ulfin stole nothing from me but my dignity . . . but I'm surprised at how dead I feel inside. Do you understand what I'm trying to say? I'm rambling . . . but anything I do to you over the rest of my life isn't aimed at you, but at your master. I'll not rest until all the heirs of Maximus are dead, root and branch, and Pendragon is only a fireside ogre to frighten small children.'

'Hush, Morgan. Nothing matters more than healing sleep, so close your eyes,' Myrddion crooned. She obeyed like a small child and slid into poppy-induced unconsciousness. While she slept, Myrddion prayed for both their souls.

When the winds had stilled a little and a glimmer of light greyed the eastern sky, Myrddion uncoiled his long body from his uncomfortable position guarding the doorway. In the corridor he discovered Botha leaning against one of the raw walls, so he begged the captain to find a woman to tend to Morgan's needs.

When he described what Ulfin had done, Botha bit his lip. 'That fool grows worse and worse. There'll be blood spilt and enemies made for years to come over this. Uther will be furious – he ordered us to spare Gorlois's daughter.'

'Sin has a very long shadow, Botha; we'll all pay for last night.'

The captain nodded and deserted his post to search for a serving woman. Before he returned, the door to Ygerne's apartment opened and Uther crossed the threshold, his face impassive and his hair tangled from sleep.

'You're here, Merlinus? Good! In the absence of her women, the queen needs your ministrations. But he careful what you touch, or what you see. Everything in that room is now my personal property for as long as I choose to keep it.'

'Morgan was raped by Ulfin, so I've had to set a broken wrist and give her a soporific to help her sleep,' Myrddion said baldly. 'Botha is finding a servant to tend to her needs.'

'That fucking idiot!' Uther snapped, his good humour moment-arily shattered. 'I thought my orders were explicit. Ulfin will be sorry that he disobeyed my instructions, especially as the Otadini tribe will be after *my* head, not his.'

Myrddion bowed his head to hide his satisfaction. No more fitting punishment could befall Ulfin than the displeasure of his master.

The room that Myrddion discovered behind the closed door was larger than Morgan's cell, but it was tiny compared with even the smallest apartment in Uther's hall at Venta Belgarum. Yet for all its cramped proportions, and even in the cold, dim light of another winter's dawn, Ygerne's hangings and her gentle spirit transformed the spartan space into a rosy nest. Lost in the large bed that had been her refuge since childhood, the queen was huddled like a damaged infant.

With sick revulsion, Myrddion followed her glazed, dry eyes to a clothes chest, where her husband's greenish head rested on a tangle of torn-down wall hangings. Only the sweet smile that Myrddion had placed on that livid face was vaguely familiar. Ygerne stared blankly at the ruined features.

Myrddion crossed the small room with two quick strides and threw the edge of a soft yellow weaving over the monstrosity. Uther has treated rape and seduction like a pre-emptive strike. How the Dragon understands extortion! In one stroke, he has deliberately crushed Ygerne's spirit, ensured her compliance and filled her mind with terror for her daughter, by giving her her husband's head.

'Uther's such a cold-blooded bastard,' he whispered. 'He had every eventuality covered before we departed from Anderida.'

He approached the huge bed and Ygerne responded by cowering as far from him as possible. Her eyes were wide and glazed, and she sucked pathetically on her thumb as she searched for comfort.

'Please, highness, it's only Myrddion, and you know I won't hurt you. Please permit me to satisfy myself that you're unhurt.'

As he examined Ygerne's empty eyes, Myrddion pondered that some hurts are more lasting than stab wounds or broken bones. Ygerne's spirit had vanished, leaving a husk to sleepwalk through her imprisonment. With careful treatment she might recover, but not while Uther was free to force himself on her as often as he wished. No one could protect her from the man who now owned her. Although the queen was naked beneath the covers, Myrddion knew better than to touch her.

'Please talk to me, highness. Gorlois wouldn't have wanted you to be harmed, so I must discover if you have any wounds.'

'No.' The monosyllable was so softly whispered that it was little more than an exhalation of breath.

Knuckles rapped on the door, and Ygerne's eyes swivelled towards it, the pupils dilated with panic.

'Don't be afraid, highness. No one will harm you while I am here.'

She seemed to recognise him then, so Myrddion hurried to open the door and deal with the interruption speedily.

Botha hovered awkwardly on the threshold. 'I've arranged for the cook to stay with Lady Morgan, as most of the younger female servants are . . . ill,' he whispered. 'Do you need anything further?'

The captain was acutely embarrassed, and obviously wished he was leagues away from Tintagel. Shame-faced, he refused to acknowledge the cowering figure of the queen in the large, tumbled bed, and seemed ready to run at the slightest provocation.

'Get rid of that head,' Myrddion hissed. 'Gorlois's head. Covered – on the clothes chest. Wrap it and take it away so the queen won't be distressed any further.'

A succession of painful emotions was clearly written on Botha's open face as his eyes flickered over Uther's instrument of mental cruelty. With obvious distaste, and using his body as a shield, he carefully bound the wrapped head before carrying it out of the queen's bedchamber.

'It's all true – Gorlois is dead, and all my bad dreams were portents of the future,' Ygerne whispered. 'I should never have gone to Venta Belgarum, or I should have killed myself before I permitted the High King to touch me. Too late! Too late!'

She sighed again and her flower-like face looked as if it would shatter at the slightest touch. 'Is my daughter alive? Is she safe?'

'Yes, highness. Her wrist has been broken, so I've drugged her to give her bruises a chance to heal – but she will be well again within a very short time.'

Ygerne mewed in distress, then her countenance smoothed as if a hand had wiped her crumpled face with a damp cloth. 'Such is the fate of women, I suppose. Men will always take what they desire, and will always suffer for their lusts. My father and my husband protected me all my life, so I didn't recognise how cruel men could be. You were right, Myrddion, for the sight is only insight, but I didn't understand the lengths that men could go to in their determination to satiate their desires. The visions I had in the past should have prepared me for my awakening to what other women learn in girlhood.'

Myrddion listened, and was relieved that the queen seemed to be rallying as her daughter's plight forced her to return from the empty space inside her head. Her words seemed lucid, although he regretted the blame that the queen placed on her own prior ignorance.

'What will become of me?' Ygerne asked in a voice so flat that Myrddion doubted she was speaking to him. But it gave him an opportunity to reassure her, so he answered as honestly as he could. At least he could offer her some frail shadow of hope.

'Uther won't harm you any more than he has already done, highness, because you are his property now – for a time. He will soon tire of you. He always does – and then he will permit you to return to Tintagel alone. I promised Gorlois that I would help you, and I swear to you that I will.'

Outside the shutters, a gust of wind hit the fortress and moaned through the cracks in the wood to stir the hair on Myrddion's neck. Within the small room, Gorlois's spirit seemed to be crying out to his beloved, and neither queen nor healer dared to break the low groan of sound.

So they waited in their separate miseries on the desires of Uther Pendragon, High King of the Britons. Both knew that their master would soon return and neither had any hope that the king would show them mercy.

Spring came at last with a flush of warmth and regeneration, and with it, Uther's army marched into the Dumnonii lands to rescue their master and escort him home to Venta Belgarum.

At Anderida, when he discovered that Gorlois's head had been removed and that the High King had ridden post-haste to Tintagel, King Bors had fumed over the betrayal and had sworn that the Dumnonii tribe would refuse to follow Uther Pendragon in the future. Leaving the fortress unsecured and driven by fears of treachery, the Dumnonii force had ridden fast and hard to Tintagel in an effort to protect Queen Ygerne. Failing, Bors had surrounded the fort in a visceral surge of fury and had refused to allow the High King and his troop to depart.

So, for the weeks that followed Uther's rape of Ygerne, matters of state remained in a precarious impasse. Even when Gorlois's body was laid on its funeral pyre on the cliffs above Tintagel, Bors refused to make any concessions to the High King, although Myrddion insisted that the head of the dead king should be lowered over the wall to the Dumnonii to ensure that it was cremated with the rest of the body.

High in the fortress tower overlooking the funeral pyre, and oblivious of Uther's demands for silence, Ygerne rent her clothing and keened with sorrow as the flames licked at the corpse of her dead husband. Through the opened shutters, and even over the gusting winds that sent smoke and flames billowing from the funeral fire as it twisted and guttered, Ygerne's grief could be heard by the waiting army. The Dumnonii warriors bowed their heads at such love, and swore that Uther Pendragon would pay for his betrayals.

This state of affairs would have endured until one side relented or retreated had the Mother not provided a new complication that would change everything. Although believing herself to be well past the age of child-bearing, Ygerne quickened. Myrddion himself sent the message to King Bors and the Dumnonii forces entrenched on the cliffs above Tintagel that the High King had chosen to honour the widow of Bors's uncle and would wed her in all pomp and ceremony within the fortress. Summoned from Glastonbury, Bishop Lucius agreed to officiate, for Ygerne had begun to take her erstwhile casual respect for Christianity seriously. Further, she had endured Uther's undiminished ardour and suffered her daughter's sullen fury and open desire for revenge with great dignity. Reluctantly, Bors agreed to the arrangement, and the sombre ceremony took place in the forecourt beside the gates. Then, as imperious as ever, Uther departed from Tintagel with his new wife, his step-daughter, his troop and Bishop Lucius, leaving Bors to fume at his arrogance.

Ygerne had begged the bishop to stay with her until the birth of the child. In her selfish grief, Morgan gave her mother no comfort, being wholly obsessed with the complete destruction of Uther Pendragon. Although Myrddion attended to the queen's physical needs and offered what companionship his nature permitted, Ygerne was wholly isolated for the first time in her life. Only the calm presence of Bishop Lucius offered any serenity.

'Please, Father Lucius. My thoughts turn constantly towards death, and I need your presence to remind me that suicide is a mortal sin.'

'I will stay,' Bishop Lucius promised unwillingly, for proximity to the High King was causing the prelate to suffer agonies of conscience. For the first time, Lucius understood why Myrddion had come to him months earlier seeking guidance concerning the sins he had been forced to commit in the king's name. With sympathy and a new comprehension, Lucius sought out Myrddion's company, and despite the gulf of religious differences and personal experiences between them, a strange mutual respect developed between the two men. In their separate ways, their common desire was to protect Queen Ygerne during the debilitating, sorrowful journey to Venta Belgarum and to encourage her to accept her lot as the new Mother of the Britons.

During the months that followed, the queen began to suffer all the physically exhausting symptoms of a late pregnancy, obliging healer and prelate to offer medical and spiritual solace to a woman beset with troubles on all sides. Indeed, many women would have been driven to madness by her husband's murder, her subsequent rape and the ironic aftermath that forced her to become the wife of the architect of all her miseries. Somehow, with skin so translucent that she seemed about to blow away in the wind, or to shatter at the sound of a harsh word, Ygerne stayed alive, sane and dignified through the continued attentions of the High King.

'I hate Venta Belgarum in high summer,' she murmured to Myrddion, as bees hummed in the small garden attached to Uther's palace. The king had gone to the borderlands outside Londinium, for the Saxons had taken liberties during his long winter absence and had extended their sphere of influence once the warmer weather began to thaw the frozen earth. No one was concerned at his absence, least of all his pregnant wife who was still summoned to his bed every night when he was in residence at Venta Belgarum.

'You're feeling the heat, my queen, which is oppressive for a woman in your condition. Drink as much chilled water as you need to keep cool, my lady, and put your feet in a basin of cold water as often as possible, for I've noticed your feet are swelling.'

The queen blushed and tucked her feet self-consciously under her gown.

Myrddion lifted her limp wrist and easily found her pulse, for Ygerne had become very slender. Only the swelling of her belly, which was unusually large for this stage of her pregnancy, gave any indication of vigour. Her marked loss of weight was a cause for concern and Myrddion had set the cooks to work in an attempt to stimulate her poor appetite.

The Mother of the Britons sat with her ladies in the rose garden, attended by her physician, Bishop Lucius and Andrewina Ruadh, who had become a virtual body-servant to the mournful queen. The two women had formed an instant bond, possibly because opposites attract and both were mothers, but also because Ruadh distrusted Morgan, who had begun to watch her mother with active dislike. Using a fan of woven reeds delicately painted with floral colours and bound with gold on the handle, Ruadh fanned her mistress to dissuade the persistent insects that showed no respect for dignity or rank.

Myrddion had recognised this antipathy in Morgan, and was worried because Ygerne could not endure any more loss. Therefore, before the king had departed with his usual speed for Londinium, Myrddion had begged him to allow Willa and Berwyn to act as the queen's body-servants and companions. Uther had agreed, recognising that the two girls had no ties to either the Dumnonii or Uther's Atrebates tribe and couldn't be coerced into treachery. Besides, his hostages may as well serve useful purposes. And so

Myrddion had ensured that Ygerne was surrounded by females who were unflinchingly loyal to him – and to the gentle queen.

'Father, is it wrong of me to hate this child?' Ygerne asked Bishop Lucius. 'I do – although I've tried to divorce it from the way it was conceived. But when I feel it move, I think of my other pregnancies, and how happy I was with my dead Gorlois.' She lowered her heavy, modestly covered head of braided hair and Myrddion saw tears running down her flushed cheeks. As always, he felt her suffering as if it were his own.

'Your child is without sin, daughter, so pray earnestly for the strength to love it. Any son of your body will inherit this vast land one day, so he will need to carry out the harsh duties that kingship demands. He will require your devotion to grow into a strong, true and just man of the people.'

'I will try, Father,' Ygerne whispered. 'Although life is sometimes very difficult.'

Lucius took her hand and stroked it with his work-hardened thumbs. Even in Venta Belgarum, the bishop contrived to keep himself busy and spent his free time tending the queen's garden with his own hands, thereby ensuring that many neglected plants flowered for the first time in years. Not surprisingly, Queen Ygerne spent hours in this small, verdant place.

'I wish Morgan would soften towards me,' she whispered, and her tears fell even faster. 'As you can attest, Myrddion, I had no choice but to submit to my husband, but Morgan believes I betrayed Gorlois when I married again. What must I do to heal her?'

'Humph!' Ruadh snorted. She had told her master forcibly that Morgan was quite capable of poisoning her own mother to kill a potential half-sibling. Ruadh had taken to tasting every morsel that Ygerne ate or drank, and she watched Morgan constantly with narrowed green eyes that reflected her dislike for the younger woman.

'Morgan has also suffered heinous crimes,' Myrddion explained carefully. 'Her wrist is only now returning to full mobility, and I worry about those wounds that can't be seen because they exist within her mind.'

'I pray for your daughter, Ygerne, because she is turning towards pagan darkness,' Lucius stated baldly. 'I apologise if I offend you, healer, but Morgan takes the Old Religion and distorts it into a tool that she can use for her obsessions. She risks her immortal soul.'

Lucius's proud Roman profile was lifted in disapproval until it resembled the face of an emperor on an old coin, but Myrddion also detected a tremor of superstition under the cleric's slightly raised, sardonic eyebrows.

Although the priest cloaks his concerns with religious disapproval, he fears for Ygerne's safety at the hands of her daughter as much as I do, Myrddion thought helplessly. Damn Uther! He causes chaos for everything and everyone he touches.

'My poor girl was raped,' Ygerne said. The ugly word fell into the quiet sweetness of the garden with all the force of a stone tossed into a pool of still water. 'Her dignity was stolen, and the only recourse she believes she has is contempt.'

'Uther issued direct orders that Ulfin was to be publicly whipped near to death for his stupidity. Worst of all for Ulfin, he was demoted from his post at the king's right hand and has been commanded to serve in the guard in a subordinate position. Morgan watched his punishment, but I fear it did little to assuage her need for revenge.'

Myrddion's voice was ambivalent, for he had enjoyed Ulfin's humiliation. Also, he had refused to treat the guardsman's flayed back, and had left his care in the less expert hands of an apprentice. Ulfin would carry the scars of his master's displeasure for all the days of his life, and Myrddion had taken pleasure in the warrior's shaming.

'Blood calls to blood from the earth,' Ygerne whispered. 'I have dreams of a blood-stained child who is under attack from night ravens. Perhaps Morgan sends the dreams to drive me mad.'

'No, mistress,' Myrddion tried to reassure her. 'Your inner self knows that no person can harm you in such a way unless you permit them to do so. Morgan's obsessions lead her to dabble in horrors such as her latest abomination.' He turned to Lucius to explain. 'Morgan has a bandage for her eyes that is made from the skin that lies along the spine of a dead child. She believes that such a horror will open the door to the sight, but her spells and portents are impotent because they are based on error. She only hurts herself, for such spells always demand payment from the person who seeks the power. The dark arts extract grim coin from those souls who would master them, and in the end they give the seeker nothing of use.'

'I've begged her to burn that filthy thing, but she laughs at me and then binds her eyes to force the visions to come,' Ygerne said. She rose, slowly but gracefully, and walked up the narrow bricked path between the flourishing rose bushes. An errant thorn plucked at her skirts, and Ruadh hastened to free the delicate fabric. 'I know that she sometimes sees things that frighten her.'

'I will try to speak to her,' Myrddion said. 'She listens to me sometimes when I offer advice because she believes I have some skills in these matters, although I can't promise that I can deflect her from her purpose.'

'She taunts Uther constantly,' Ygerne said sadly. 'But he is just as scathing with her. The two of them seem to enjoy baiting each other, and they drive me to distraction. Uther still keeps his soothsayer close at hand, but he turns to Morgan as well, although I can't believe he trusts her at all. And he shouldn't use her. She'd kill him without any regrets if she had the slightest chance to harm him with impunity.'

'Don't dwell on the relationship between Uther and Morgan,' Lucius advised her. His stern mouth twitched with dislike for the unspeakable practices that had been described.

'I agree with the bishop, highness. Come now, I will ask Ruadh to heat one of my herb teas to strengthen your blood. Your health is all that matters, so you must try to dwell on pleasant thoughts and surround yourself with beautiful things. I'll pluck some roses for you and Ruadh will put them in water so the perfume can help you to sleep.'

'I rarely rest in daylight, but I *am* very tired,' the queen responded, smiling tremulously. Both Myrddion and Lucius desired only to protect this vulnerable woman, and the bishop coaxed her to accept Myrddion's suggestion while the healer cut the huge red roses. The queen loved their heady perfume and took comfort from their velvety petals.

Finally, drooping with weariness and the weight of the vigorous child in her belly, the queen was taken away by Ruadh to recline on her great marital bed with the roses close to hand in a container of green glass. Myrddion's tea and the sweet smell of the huge, full-blown blooms lulled the exhausted woman into a fitful sleep. Prudent always, Ruadh sat beside her bed and stitched a piece of wool into a baby's robe.

In the rose garden, the bishop and the healer continued to converse in the midday heat. With Uther away on campaign, Myrddion discovered that the oppressive weight of suspicion had been lifted from the palace, so he spoke more freely than was his usual custom.

'Uther isn't enamoured with the idea of fatherhood, Lucius. Botha spoke to me before the army rode to the east, and confided that his master might choose to expose the child to inclement weather when it's born. The High King prefers that no questions concerning Gorlois's death should be prompted by the birth.'

'But why would he do that?' Lucius mused, his broad, tanned brow furrowed in confusion. 'Every king desires an heir.'

'Uther is not every king. He desires, more than all else, to eclipse the power of every other British king, even his beloved brother Ambrosius. Uther must be the cynosure of all eyes to fill an emptiness that lives within him, even if the mob should fear and hate him. He's not prepared to share the authority of the throne with *anyone*, not even a son from his own body.'

'That degree of egotism is lunacy,' Lucius protested.

'Then Uther Pendragon is a madman. He's often a monster, like the dragon after which he is named. And he now professes to doubt that this child is the product of his own loins.'

'Then his arithmetic is poor!' Lucius snapped. He rarely brooked any criticism of the queen, for he recognised in Ygerne a nature of unwavering gentleness and love like that of the Madonna whom the Christians revered. Where Myrddion was sometimes irritated by the queen's fragility, preferring women who were able to defend themselves, the Roman in Lucius was devoted to Ygerne as a symbol of the perfect wife – graceful, faithful, loving and fired by duty.

'Uther doesn't give a snap of his fingers whether the child is his or Gorlois's. He *knows* the child is his, but the possibility that it might not be is sufficient justification for killing it. If the infant is female, he may permit it to live. But the child will surely die if it is male.'

'No! He can't do this thing! Ygerne would suffer terribly and there would be no legitimate heir to the throne. I've heard that Uther fears the passage of the years and has even asked Morgan to concoct potions that will ease the developing aches in his bones. But even Uther must acknowledge that no man is immortal.'

Myrddion laughed sardonically. Sometimes Lucius's goodness made him naïve.

'True! He turns to Morgan because he trusts nothing from my

hands, despite my healer's oath which precludes me from treachery. Personally, I'd trust nothing that Morgan offered. I don't really understand her motives, although you can be sure she offers her potions for a reason.'

Suddenly, the veil of darkness was lifted from Myrddion's vision. 'So that's why she hasn't killed him!'

'What are you saying, Myrddion?'

'Morgan plans to destroy Uther slowly so she can feast on his suffering. But first, she plans to make him totally dependent on her. By the gods, I'm almost tempted to warn him. Women can be more fearsome than any warrior, even one maddened by bloodlust.'

Then he laughed. 'I'd rather be elsewhere than caught up in any battle between those two. Uther has brought Morgan's enmity on himself, just as every ache in his ageing bones is inevitable, given his years in the saddle. Likewise, Morgan has always been a law unto herself. I first met her at Deva, when she offered to enter into a sexual partnership with me – solely for the acquisition of power. Yes, she adored her father, but she hasn't risked her own skin to demand the blood guilt which is undoubtedly owed to her. Nor will it happen unless she is able to watch the results of her success in safety from somewhere close at hand.'

'How could such ugliness be born from the loins of Ygerne, who is such a good woman in every way?' Lucius asked thoughtfully. 'And Gorlois was noble and direct – not given to manipulation or sadism.'

'Why, bishop, it seems you're a little in love with the queen yourself, just like the rest of us. She weaves a magic about her that will outlast the skein of the years. But even her qualities have little chance against her poisonous daughter and a cruel, vindictive husband.'

'Doesn't your famed gift for prophesy tell you what will come to be?' Lucius's wariness of the dangers of the sight charged his voice with cynicism.

'The goddess has lifted that curse from me. Although I still dream, the waking fits of prophecy are gone and I will travel this life with only my two eyes and my wits to guide me. I am finally glad to be blind.'

'Then God has been merciful because you remained true to your vow to Ambrosius,' Lucius suggested, for he was genuinely curious about Myrddion's talent. Like all Romans, he had been raised to believe that prophecy was real, and separate from religious belief.

'No, my part in the betrayal of Ygerne was my fate. Sometimes, I wonder if I was born to preside over the birth of Ygerne's infant, but I suppose that notion is just a sick and selfish fancy. At any rate, my gift of prophecy appears to be dead and gone.'

Lucius glanced up at Myrddion with inquisitive brown eyes. 'Could you abandon Ygerne's son to the elements if your master demanded such an act?'

Myrddion toyed with a rose that was past its best. The flower petals fell to the chocolate-brown earth under his restless fingers. 'I don't know, Lucius. Given the tasks that Uther has forced upon me, I have no idea what I would do if he added infanticide to the list. I don't believe I could kill an infant, but how can we ever be sure what we would do if we were placed under pressure?'

'You're honest, as always, Myrddion. You make my decisions easier because of your candour.'

'I do?' Myrddion said, but he knew in his heart that both men had crossed some invisible line and that the blinded Fortuna no longer turned her great wheel.

They sat quietly amid the over-blown roses which sweetened the air with the scent of new days and fresh possibilities. Somewhere in Myrddion's tired, over-burdened heart, hope began to grow.

The horns blew, wild with victory and triumphant arrogance, as Uther returned to his city, laden with wagons that groaned with

Saxon booty. His restless boots trod the long corridors of his hall, driving out any serenity with the clash of his armour and the raucous celebrations of his guard. And in the soft lamplight of his private apartments, he dropped a pair of golden earrings, dully blinking with large garnets the precise colour of dried blood, into Ygerne's hands.

'Wear them out of love of me,' Uther ordered, and Ygerne obediently removed the golden hoops that Gorlois had given her and replaced the gifts of love with the bonds of lust. What the queen really thought was hidden by her downcast eyes.

'The child grows well,' Uther stated unnecessarily. His mouth twisted with disgust at the rounded swelling that marred the body he still desired.

'Aye, my lord, your son waits eagerly to be born. By my reckoning, only a month must elapse before he demands to be here. He will be strong.'

'Hmm.' Uther's noncommittal response caused Ygerne to frown in turn. 'The child is a confounded nuisance. He, she or it is making you ill, which I can't abide. I've been gone for months and what kind of welcome do I receive on my return? A warm wife who waits eagerly for my arrival? No. I have a woman barely able to move or eat for the brat she carries.'

Ygerne played with the spirals of his wild curls and tried to still the trembling of her fingers. Since childhood, she had understood that she had the power to soothe, and now she exerted this talent over the fractious, irritable man whom she had the misfortune to be tied to for the rest of her life.

'What are a few weeks, my lord? I will be well and healthy again very soon, and I'll be able to take care of you as you deserve.'

Mollified, Uther never heard the ambivalence in her careful words.

That night, he took his pleasure with a servant girl whom blind chance had given pale blue eyes much like those of Ygerne. The girl was terrified when he kicked her out of his bedchamber, bruised and bloodied, with a handful of coins and an order to keep her mouth shut. Like any sensible female, she fled the palace and the city, for Uther could always find other girls.

Week followed week, and the pleasant days in the rose garden became a memory of lost comfort and tranquillity. Uther went hunting, easing the violence in his nature by killing every unfortunate creature that crossed his path. The kitchens could not use all the deer, the rabbits, the plump pheasants and the pigeons that the king and his guard slaughtered. With the prudence of the poor, the peasantry became accustomed to following Uther's path through the forests and marshes, collecting the spoils of the hunt that Uther rejected for his table.

The night of the dream was memorable because the first real hint of cold chilled the autumn air. Fortunately, the harvest was almost over, and after such a warm summer the granaries and root cellars were filling with the earth's bounty. The frosts of the night crisped the apples still left upon the trees, leaving them to rot and blacken after the sudden freeze. Mists hung heavily over the fields like a breath of winter, while the furrows ploughed into the fields shivered under a rime of frost.

The High King had been drinking late into the night with a clutch of Parisi and Iceni warriors who had arrived with tidings of the new fortifications in the north. Tired and irritable, he had stumbled into bed with a vile headache from too much sour ale and Hispanic wine. When the screams began in the silent hours before the dawn, Botha was the first to break into Uther's room and was forced to strike his master across the face to release him from the control of the dream that was tormenting him. Trembling, Uther leapt out of his bed with an ashen face.

'Send for Sea Bright. Send for the wise woman,' he panted. 'I cannot endure these night terrors any longer.'

Botha read the panic in his master's eyes and quickly left the room, leaving the newly roused servants to minister to the High King's needs.

Huddled in a patched cloak to hold the chill of the dark morning at bay, Muirne arrived before Uther had been shaved by his manservant, so she waited patiently in a corner of the opulent room. During the year she had lived in the High King's house, she had saved every coin that came her way and told fortunes for profit whenever credulous women sought love potions or desired to know the future of a clandestine romance. Uther troubled her rarely, so Muirne had grown a little complacent, although she had heard rumours concerning how Ygerne came to wed Uther Pendragon. As Muirne awaited Uther's pleasure, she expected nothing more taxing than dreams similar to those he had described when she first came to the court. Unwisely, she was also anticipating the coin that Uther Pendragon would toss her way if she should please him.

'It's about time,' Uther grumbled as he pushed his servant away, careless of the sharp blade that had removed the reddish-blond hair from his chin. 'Come closer, Muirne, and tell your master what he needs to know.'

'The sight comes unbidden, your grace, so I can't control what it tells me.' Muirne's accent was still as broad as ever, and her matronly figure, coupled with her plain, no-nonsense features, encouraged confidences.

'Once again, I have had the dream of the spears that grow like wheat, the two women and the portents of a bloody child, but this time there were some added refinements that I require you to interpret for me.'

Muirne nodded, bowed her head and waited.

'This time, a dragon came out of the sun in a blaze of red and gold. I was engulfed in fire and I watched my skin blacken and curl away from my bones.'

Uther shuddered as he relived an agonising memory. Muirne raised her brows interrogatively and noticed that the whites of Uther's eyes were reddened with broken veins. Belatedly, a guarded look washed over her face.

'I saw a woman with white hair and another with black curls. They both pointed fingers at me, and they laughed before stepping aside so I could see a child covered in the bloody slime of childbirth. When I shaded my eyes, I could see that the child was crowned with the coronet of Maximus. Then I saw an old, old man with *my* eyes. He was shrunken and withered by illness, and I realised that the creature was *me*.' Uther shuddered. 'I woke when my captain roused me after hearing my cries,' he concluded with a flourish. 'What do you make of *that* vision, soothsayer?'

Muirne didn't need the sight to interpret Uther's dream. Gossip and rumour swirled around his palace like a swarm of wasps, and the antipathy of the witch, Morgan, was well known. Muirne had resented every instance when Uther had consulted his mortal enemy, the Dumnonii princess, because she lost prestige and profit by his defection. Perhaps Sea Bright should have been more careful.

'Your dream has changed very little, my lord,' she began cautiously. 'The dragon is, of course, an image of you, so you are burning yourself up through your actions. Remember, my lord, that you must not kill a child, especially one that has your bloodline. The powers that allow me to see into the future have warned you that even an attempt of this nature will bring all the worst horrors of old age down upon your head.'

As soon as she spoke, Muirne realised she had made a crucial error in judgement. Uther's face reddened along the cheekbones, and Botha shot a warning glance at her. When Uther was in a temper, even the truth could drive him to extremes of behaviour.

Muirne bit her tongue and dropped her eyes.

'If I wanted such unwelcome advice, I'd call on the Storm Crow or that bitch Morgan.'

Mention of Morgan brought Muirne's resentments to the surface, and she snapped back at the High King without thinking. 'I cannot control your dreams, my lord, and you are the only person who can know if there's any truth in what I say.'

You silly woman, Botha thought, as Uther rose smoothly to his feet. Being right won't help you if he breaks your neck.

Frightened by the feral gleam in the High King's eyes, Muirne frantically attempted to repair her gaffe. But in spite of her best intentions, her gift for prophecy sent her tongue wagging along paths she had not intended to travel. She wondered, as she spoke the dreaded, unbidden words, whether she had angered the goddess through her greed.

'Ah, macushla. Truly, the Great Ones send dreams to deter us from actions that would offend them. We mortals must listen when the gods speak so clearly to us. Kill no child, master, else you will wither and suffer.'

'But you'll be gone long before me, woman. Remove this crone, Botha, since her advice is so impudent. As of now, she can live as a beggar for all I care. Throw her out into the streets where she can reconsider her foolishness.'

Now the wise woman's face flushed with distress and anger at her own stupidity, but her temper would be her undoing. Her Hibernian brogue broadened, and then she spat on the floor near the king, completely disregarding Botha's bruising hand on her plump upper arm.

'Even dragons can perish, master,' Muirne retorted in her rough accent. 'Even the strongest and fiercest of beasts can be slain in their dotage. You cannot always kill your problems to remove them from your path.'

She never had the chance to protest or to cower. Uther took two quick steps, scooped up the blade that had so recently been used to shave his chin and slit the old woman's windpipe. She died in a welter of blood, her eyes wide with astonishment. As her senses dimmed, she knew she was being punished by the gods.

Although Botha had leapt away from the wise woman as soon as he divined his master's intentions, he was still drenched in gore that left him gasping ineffectually as he tried to clean his leather cuirasse with his sleeve.

'Damn! Your impetuosity will be the death of us all, my lord. What did the old woman do except tell you what you didn't want to hear? As far as I'm aware, she's been a faithful servant to you.'

'The woman has been reading the runes and telling fortunes like a fairground whore under my very nose. Keep your mouth shut, Botha, unless you have a desire to join Ulfin among the ranks of my foot soldiers. I am the High King, and I shall do as I choose.'

Uther waved the blood-covered blade in Botha's face and the captain drew away in ill-disguised disgust. Uther's eyes reddened further, and his expression hardened.

'Get rid of the woman's body by the time I return,' he hissed. 'I intend to go into the forest to hunt. Oh ... and you can warn my wife that I expect her in my bed tonight – pregnant or not.'

Then Uther stalked away, leaving Botha and the servants to dispose of Muirne's corpse, just another victim in a city filled with men and women who flinched away from Uther's touch.

And every night that followed, Uther entered the same frightening dream and played out the same ugly scene. But he was weary of soothsayers, so he asked for no more dreamspinners, and determined to trust to the power of the sword to save him from the wrath of the gods.

CHAPTER XXII

THE BLOODY CHILD

'I count him braver who overcomes his desires than him who overcomes his enemies.'

Aristotle, *Stobaeus, Florilegium*

The trees were almost bare of leaves in the fields beyond Ygerne's window, and although she had no solid reason for her terrors but the dreams that came nightly, she was convinced that she would not live to see another green spring. While she had no dread of imminent death, believing that her immortal soul would be reunited with her beloved, her daughter's descent into witchcraft and the fate of the child growing next to her heart demanded that she faced each day with courage. Although winter had yet to turn the weather bitter, grey skies threatened cold and freezing winds by morning and she sighed, remembering the previous winter and how her carefree happiness had fled so irrevocably.

As her confinement grew closer, she became convinced that she would die in childbirth, for over twenty years had passed since she had borne her youngest daughter. Like the season, she was producing her last fruit before the frosts of old age turned her into a barren old crone. She examined her huge belly, much larger than her other pregnancies, and feared that either the child would kill her, or her narrow hips would kill the child.

Then, as she contemplated the pale landscape that was so like her mood, an ache began in her lower back and spread around her sides, a familiar constriction as muscles rippled with strain. A low moan escaped her lips as she felt the spasm strike her, building in her muscles as the child clamoured to be born. Biting her lip to silence any further outcry, she clutched at her belly and tried to breathe through the pain.

No, she thought desperately. When the child is born, it may die, so it can't be born. I won't allow it. None of this was meant to be.

She stood so still and so rigid that Ruadh sensed something was seriously wrong. Deftly twitching the crumpled covers into place over the queen's bed, Ruadh decided to force her mistress to lie down, for Ygerne had been restless for days and had slept very little. By the time she reached Ygerne's side, the queen's shoulders had relaxed as the spasm passed, and she could catch her breath again. She turned to face her servant with a calm, untroubled face.

'Are you ailing, mistress? You're a little too pale for my liking.'

'I'm quite well, Ruadh, so don't fuss.' Ygerne smiled sweetly but Ruadh wasn't deceived. She noticed fine beads of sweat on the queen's forehead, so Ruadh took her closed hand and carefully prised the fingers open. Red crescents from Ygerne's nails marked her soft white palms.

'You've gone into labour, haven't you? Don't lie to me! I've borne children, highness, so you can't fool me easily. Have your waters broken yet?'

'No, it's just a twinge – and it's of no moment.' The queen wrapped both hands around her swollen belly as if to clutch the babe even closer to her heart. 'I'll rest and be strong again.'

'Liar!' Ruadh was incapable of tact. 'It's off to bed with you, madam. You will soon be a mother again, and then you'll need all your strength. I'll send word to the king and arrange for the midwife to come at once.'

Ygerne gripped Ruadh's hands in both of hers with a clasp so fierce that the servant winced in pain.

'I don't want a stranger caring for me, Ruadh! Whatever her ability, that midwife smells. You've been trained by Master Myrddion and you've carried children yourself, so I'd like you to deliver my child if you are prepared to do so. Berwyn and Willa can assist you, for I don't trust anyone else. Please?'

The queen was becoming agitated, so Ruadh appeased her by agreeing to serve as midwife, although she was fearful of what Uther Pendragon would make of his wife's decision.

'Let me talk to Captain Botha. He'll ensure that my master sends me herbs to relieve your labour pains. If you wish, I'll also ask Bishop Lucius to attend on you.'

'Yes, please, Ruadh, for I'd like to make my confession in case I should die during the confinement.'

Ruadh realised how dangerous the queen's agitation could be for both mother and child. She wanted Myrddion close to hand in case something went badly wrong with this birthing.

Having coerced Ygerne into resting on a comfortable, cushioned stool in the delivery room, Ruadh left her in the care of Berwyn and Willa and slipped out of the queen's apartments to run pell-mell in search of the captain of the guard. She found Botha at the back of the High King's hall, where he was guarding his master while Uther dispensed his own particular form of justice.

Nervously, she attracted Botha's attention, knowing that Uther Pendragon would be offended by the presence of a female servant within his hall of judgment. Glancing cautiously at the king's back, Botha beckoned to another guardsman to take his place and then slipped through the curtained doorway to join Ruadh in the long corridor that linked the hall with the living quarters of the palace.

'Why do you risk the skin on your back by venturing into the hall of judgment, woman? I hope you have a good excuse, for even your master won't be able to protect you from a whipping if Uther is informed of your presumption.'

'The queen has begun her labour and the king must be informed at once. He must also be advised that the queen has asked to be shriven by Bishop Lucius in case she should die during the birth. My lady has refused the services of the midwife and wishes me to bring the babe into the world, so I will require the tools of my trade from Master Myrddion, as well as soporifics, herbs to strengthen the blood, belly binders and clean bandages. My master will know what is needed.'

Acutely uncomfortable, Botha coughed with embarrassment, and swore to carry out Ruadh's requirements to the letter, including the task of informing the king. Confident that he wouldn't fail her, the Celtic woman hurried back to the queen's apartments.

As soon as she entered the disordered delivery room, she could see that neither Willa nor Berwyn was coping with the demands of midwifery. Willa was distressed and almost in tears, but she had sent for hot water, knowing that cleanliness was important in childbirth. The girl was now almost thirteen and a beauty, regardless of her scarred arm which, self-consciously, she always kept covered by long sleeves and high necklines. She had an abundance of softly curled black hair which was usually kept under control by neat plaits but, in the turmoil, loose tendrils of hair had escaped to fall over her pale face. As she fetched water for her mistress, she ran one hand through the escaping locks, tousling her braids still further. Willa was usually painfully shy, but she was comfortable in the queen's presence. She idolised Ygerne for her gentleness and grace, and was struggling to stay calm when Ruadh returned.

'The queen says her waters have broken, Ruadh, and she must

change into a shift for her travail, but she won't stand still long enough for us to assist her.'

'Hush, Willa, my darling. The hot water was a good idea, but we must insist that Ygerne undresses. Master Myrddion demands that the body of a woman in labour should be cleansed to prevent evil humours from entering the womb, so you must find a roomy shift that she uses for sleeping while Berwyn and I undress and bathe her. Don't be frightened, lass. Few women die when bearing children, else we'd never want to have them, would we?'

While Willa hurried to a carved clothes chest to find a pretty, loose shift that would make her mistress more comfortable, Berwyn and Ruadh bore down on Ygerne and forced her to stand still while they unlaced her gown of heavy rose wool. As they helped her out of her tightly bound inner garments and the delicate gauzy shift that she wore closest to her skin, the queen sighed with relief. Then Berwyn knelt before her mistress and sponged her loins and legs until Ygerne was clean and comfortable, although the process embarrassed her and caused her face to flush a becoming, girlish shade of pink.

Then, dressed in her loose shift but still unwilling to take to her bed, she was bullied into sitting while her long hair was carefully unbound, brushed and then plaited into two long braids that hung almost to her knees. Willa completed this task carefully, biting her lip with concentration, while Berwyn and Ruadh stripped the queen's bed of the luxurious covers and found pillows to support Ygerne's back. Ruadh remembered how her own russet hair had become wet with sweat and matted from her long hours of labour, so she understood how important it would be for her mistress to be tidy before the worst of the contractions began.

Although still restless, Ygerne was abed when Bishop Lucius arrived at her door. When he entered the bedchamber, she was tucked under a fine woven sheet like a small child, with only her face and clasped hands visible to comply with the rules of modesty. Unlike many prelates, Lucius was not intimidated or repulsed by the mysteries of childbirth, so he prayed with her easily, heard her confession and calmed her with his serenity. Before he rose to leave, she gripped his hand and whispered in his ear so that the other women couldn't hear.

'You must promise me that my child will be safe if I should die. My husband must have no part in the raising of it, for he would poison the poor little thing with his violence and suspicions. If I must die, my spirit will be at peace if you swear this oath to me.'

'You'll not die, highness. I predict that you will live to see your child grow strong and tall, but if it relieves your mind, I will vow to obey you. Your child will be safe, as the Lord High God is my witness.'

Ygerne sighed, smiled and then grimaced as another contraction began.

Lucius rose gracefully and bowed low before departing for the king's rooms. But his mind was in turmoil, for he had made a sacred oath to Ygerne that would be difficult to keep if Uther decided to expose the child. He decided to make his excuses and depart for Glastonbury at the earliest opportunity. Bishop Paulus would baptise the child, so nothing remained to keep Lucius here any longer.

'It seems we are all in the hands of God,' he whispered to Botha as they made their way to Uther's apartments, feeling like a coward and sympathising with Myrddion Merlinus who was, to all intents and purposes, the only effective conscience governing the behaviour of the High King.

'Yes, my lord, so I hope that your God is listening to your prayers.'

Uther had reluctantly cancelled his judgments to await the birth of his first child, and was enduring the proffered congratulations of nobles and servants alike with scarcely hidden irritability. The High King was no fool, and he could read curiosity and amusement in the sharp faces of his nobles as they enjoyed the whole scandal surrounding his marriage. 'Well, rot them and their title-tattle!' Uther swore vilely. 'The sooner the brat is dead, the better. And then all mention of Gorlois will be forgotten.'

As he knocked and entered the luxurious rooms, Lucius saw that Uther was in a vile temper, but he was sullenly enraged rather than displaying his customary ungoverned fury. From a sideways glance at Botha, who had become quite wooden and mute, the prelate deduced that a brooding Pendragon was far more dangerous than an openly furious one.

Within a few moments, Lucius had learned that the High King considered the child to be an unwanted and unwelcome intrusion into the normal patterns of his life. While most men would be excited at the birth of an heir, Uther was mindful of his night terrors and the prediction of his seer that he would suffer because of a blood-covered infant. His resentments were all too visible, and Lucius worried that he would act intemperately. Even the eventual arrival of Paulus, the timid bishop of Venta Belgarum, failed to calm him. This child was a potential disruption and Uther wanted no changes to his way of life.

When Myrddion arrived, burdened with supplies for Ruadh's use, he was forced to wait in the corridor until Uther deigned to see him. As he paced, Morgan passed by with a servant in tow. Her eyes were mocking and cruel, and Myrddion was immediately on his guard.

'Save your efforts, healer,' she said impassively, although the scum of gloating in the hard brown depths of her eyes belied her solemn face. 'The child may survive its birthing, but it's fated that no heir of Uther will live past a single day.'

'Do you plan infanticide, woman? Are there no depths of depravity you won't plumb to take your revenge for Gorlois? Your father would be ashamed if you killed an innocent babe.'

Myrddion knew he was making another enemy with his all too truthful attack, but Morgan's smug confidence had burrowed under his self-control.

'Why are you so scrupulous, Myrddion? I won't kill the child: Uther will do it for me. He has terrible dreams, you know. I simply congratulated him on the birth of a fine, strong son who would become the greatest man in the tribal lands. Uther's face was a picture of jealousy and chagrin. He is planning how his own child will die, even as we speak.'

'And if it's a girl? What then, Morgan? He'll not order a female to be exposed.' There were no words for the horror and disgust that Myrddion felt, for Morgan had played her games with Uther Pendragon to perfection. Her triumph turned her cold eyes the colour of warmed amber, for Myrddion had admitted, without words, that Uther intended to kill his own son. Now, Morgan smiled luxuriously, as if she tasted something sweet and delicious.

'Mother will be ill for a long time after the birth at her age, but Uther will still demand her absolute devotion and attention towards *him*. She will lack the necessary time to look after a babe while she warms Uther's bed and panders to his whims. I will raise any girl that is born, and may the king have pleasure in what I make of her.'

Myrddion lowered his gaze. Anything rather than be forced to watch Morgan's beautiful features twist into such ugliness of soul. The healer granted her the right to be angry at her father's murder, just as he acknowledged her bitterness over her rape and the queen's acceptance of Uther Pendragon as her new husband. But such cold fury! Perhaps the Christians who damned woman as the source of all sin had some truth on their side.

'You should be aware, highness, that the Greeks were very knowledgeable about sin. They described you exactly when they said: "Those whom the gods would destroy, they first make mad."'

'Is that your best insult, healer? If so, our conversations will be short in future. Farewell for now, for I wish to learn how my mother's confinement goes.'

Then Morgan moved away, swaying her womanly hips with conscious grace. But her attraction was lost on Myrddion, who saw the serpent in her willowy body and frigid eyes.

The hours stretched out like years, for Ygerne was too thin, frail and elderly to bear children safely. Ruadh refused permission for Morgan to enter the queen's chamber, so Willa and Berwyn shuddered under her acid insults. But Ygerne remained the focus of all their toil and passion. Her muscles had lost the elasticity of youth, and she suffered greatly as the child demanded to be born with a wilful, angry strength. Only Ruadh divined that her mistress was endeavouring to prevent the birth, fearing her husband's wrath and the constant anxiety that would become her lot once her child was born.

The queen's hair was soon drenched and dark with sweat, and her face pale with the effort she wasted in futile struggles. Her shift had been changed twice, while Berwyn and Willa sponged her body with cool water to relax her muscles and keep her as clean as possible. With a sick fear of her own inadequacies, Ruadh watched Ygerne's contractions ripple through her belly as the queen arched her back and moaned in agony. Then, before her courage deserted her, she gave her a single drop of one of Myrddion's soporifics diluted in water.

'Scream if it eases your pain, mistress. There are no rewards for being stoic and silent,' Ruadh urged. Willa stroked the queen's forehead with a soft, cool cloth while Berwyn gave her a little more water to moisten her dry lips.

'Thank you, Willa – that makes me feel much better. And thank you too, Berwyn. I cannot scream or make a spectacle of myself, Ruadh, for I'm not a peasant woman who drops her child in the fields. We noblewomen show our courage in our silence, and I'll not betray either my breeding or my status.'

But the contractions grew ever stronger until Ygerne bit her lips hard enough to taste blood in her mouth. Despite her determination to suffer in silence, a thin cry was eventually dragged from her lips. She longed to sleep, but the child was inexorable and tore at her womb in its eagerness to enter the world. When Myrddion's potion began to work Ruadh was both relieved and terrified, for the queen's eyes grew dull and distant, although she cried out more freely in her agony.

Down the corridor, Uther heard his wife's cries and was further irritated. Although Botha gave him heavy red wine, the drink merely fuelled his growing dislike of the whole disruptive and noisy process.

In vino veritas! Myrddion thought bitterly as he watched the High King begin to lose his composure. Finally, when the cries grew so loud that the priests began to pray in a corner of the room, Uther ordered Myrddion to walk with him to escape the tormented sounds.

Here it comes, Myrddion thought. The greatest test of my life is upon me. What am I going to do?

'Not you, Botha. Stay here and guard the priests. We can't have any harm befalling men of God,' Uther ordered briskly as the captain moved to follow his master. 'If I'm not secure in my own house in Venta Belgarum, then I'm never likely to be safe anywhere in these isles.'

Glumly, Myrddion followed the High King down the corridors, through courtyards and down dank steps into the foundations of the palace. Although the original building had risen straight from the packed sod, some enterprising builder had dug out a cellar and lined it with rough-hewn stones using the famed Roman mortar that made buildings so strong.

What king and healer entered was a small space, only fifteen feet square, that would be almost impregnable during an attack by enemies. Although the ceiling should have collapsed under the weight of stone and earth pressing down on it, the magic of the old Roman builders preserved the curved barrel-shaped vault that was taller than the whole room was wide. Carefully, Uther closed the iron-bound door behind them, latched it securely and lit a wall sconce with an oil-soaked torch he had picked up on the way.

'What are you thinking, healer? That you're like to go to your death in this place? No one would ever find you, it's true, and you could scream for hours without being heard. I found this bolt-hole with Ambrosius when I was a child, and we decided it was a place devoted to the worship of Mithras. See?'

Uther raised his torch and, above head-height, someone had painted the sacrifice of the soldier god in colours that were so life-like and rich that the artist might have finished his masterpiece only yesterday. The utilitarian, grim room was suddenly a tiny temple, right down to a single square stone that had obviously been a miniature altar.

What a place in which to starve to death, Myrddion thought despairingly. Uther has planned this strategy well. With unconscious blasphemy, Uther seated himself on the altar stone, swung one leg reflectively and ran his eyes analytically over his healer.

'We rarely see eye to eye, Myrddion, do we? But we both want the Saxons to be defeated for our people's sake. Correct? You endure me, for you are increasingly aware that no one else can fill the role of High King better than I can. I see you nod in agreement.' Uther laughed as if he had won some important and difficult test of strength. 'Therefore, you obey me even when to do so sickens you. What does that make you, Myrddion Merlinus? A coward? A pawn?'

'A hopeless fool!' Myrddion responded cynically. Uther ignored the interruption and continued with his prepared speech as if his healer had not spoken.

'A good servant of the tribes, I believe. You are a man for the times and that is *all* you are, Myrddion. Yes, I've coerced you, but you'd have regretted leaving me to my own devices if you had escaped from my clutches.'

'I doubt that, your highness. You can prove your faith in me by returning Willa and Berwyn to my care. I'll serve you anyway, as I swore to Ambrosius Imperator.'

'It's a sad but inevitable truth that no man remembers my brother any more. Ambrosius was a great tactician, but he was weak and trusting, and that's how he got himself killed. Pascent, or another of his ilk, would never burrow that close to me.'

Uther's face was so arrogant and proud that Myrddion felt a little ill, although he was well used to the High King's boasting. There was an element of truth in what Uther said that even Myrddion could not gainsay, so the healer remained silent and hoped that Ambrosius's shade would forgive him.

'If I must have an heir, it must not bear the tainted blood of Ygerne nor be contaminated by the memory of Gorlois. By Ygerne's own account, she dreamed about her husband's death decades ago through this sight nonsense she claims to have inherited from her father, Pridenow. I neither know nor care about family curses, but one excuse is as good as any other. Besides, you can see how such a child would remind the tribal kings of the Boar's unfortunate death and the rumours surrounding the brat's conception. Nor do I want a male version of Morgan snapping at my heels as I grow old. You can see, can't you, Myrddion, with all your famed clarity of thought, that such an heir would be disastrous?'

'Perhaps, but Fortuna has decreed that you *should* have such an heir. We cannot argue with the decisions of the gods and your son is likely to be much like you – or Ambrosius.'

Myrddion had chosen his words carefully, for he saw the way this conversation was heading. Was Uther truly mad enough to demand infanticide of him?

And how had Lucius deduced that Myrddion would be chosen by Uther to kill the unwanted child? Maybe it's because I've been a useful pawn and have acceded to his demands again and again, including closing my eyes to the murder of Carys. The answer echoed in Myrddion's head, reminding him of every concession, every time he had looked the other way, like Botha, and every stain on his honour that he had tried to pray away. Belatedly, a thousand years of Celt and Roman ancestors awoke in Myrddion's blood and he stood taller for their sudden appearance in his mind. The voices whispered encouragement to defy the High King's words of threat and promise, while Myrddion allowed his slow anger to rise.

'Rid me of this child, Myrddion. I'll give the order for its exposure, never fear, so the weight of its death won't be on your conscience. All you must do is take the brat into the woods and leave it there for the snows to work their mercy. Fortuna may yet save it – who knows? But I must be rid of this child if it isn't fortunate enough to perish at birth.'

'And then you'll have a good reason to be rid of me,' Myrddion answered evenly, his handsome face suddenly older and harsher beneath the fitful torchlight. 'You'd turn me into an infanticide and make me your creature forever. I'm not surprised that you've chosen me to carry out this dreadful task, because I have been weak and I have permitted you to commit such sins that my soul shivers at the judgment that will eventually come to us both from the gods.'

Uther nodded, confident that Myrddion would whine and complain, as he always did, and then, reluctantly, obey his king. 'I'll not kill you, Myrddion, for you are the only person who can run my spy network. Do this small thing for me, and you will be free of any more demands that might compromise you. To show my good intentions, your hostages will be returned. A newborn babe isn't worth a moment of tears.'

'True. Barely a moment. If I take the child, allow me one concession, Uther, one chance to provide you with my counsel without fear of reprisal. We are in the temple of your soldier god, and we are planning a murder. For once, I would like to have the last word – even if I'm just another weak-minded fool.'

'What are words to me? You may say what you like as long as the child vanishes.'

'I have lost the gift of prophecy, Uther, but the Mother has sent me dreams for years that warned me of my fate, so I'm not surprised. You won't ask this murder of Botha, because you trust him and you know he'd be sickened and likely to kill himself, even if he obliges you. You're clever, Uther, but not as intelligent as you think you are. I am the Demon Seed, and you cannot kill me because you need me far too much. Once I have done what you ask, I'll stay out of your way and I'll not cause you any humiliation – you'll do *that* to yourself. But all your murders, your plots and your vicious executions will do you no good, for their repercussions will accumulate despite your best efforts to control them. You are doomed, Uther, and your death will be as terrible as any I have ever predicted. Inevitably, you'll be supplanted by a man who is your master in every way, because he'll have to be, and though you try to kill him you will only make him stronger. I saw this portent years ago, although I struggled against my fate. You saw it too, in the dreams that cautioned you to kill no child. Muirne should have known you'd never listen, no matter what she said, or how she died. The bloody babe will live, no matter what we do today, and I will serve him in time, when you are in the cold, cold earth. No one will send your body to the pyre, out of fear and loathing of your person. They'll be afraid to touch your corpse.'

'Once I'm dead, I won't care.' Uther shrugged, but his face was very pale as Myrddion's verbal barb worked its way into his brain where it would lodge and fester for the rest of his long and painful life. 'As long as you are the one who kills the child, Storm Crow, I cannot be harmed by anything you say. Let the dreams come. I'll not listen to them, nor change my road because of them, so to hell with the gods!'

'Then I'll obey your command, highness. But ask nothing further of me, for I will refuse. I will give you nothing from this day forward other than what our people expect.'

Then Myrddion bowed to Mithras and kneeled to pray at the altar. Uther quickly grew tired of watching his healer's piety and thought to give his fool a taste of the darkness.

'Close the door when you've finished,' Uther hissed as he turned to make his exit. 'And don't bother reporting to me about the minor details of the child's death. To all intents and purposes, it died at birth.'

Uther took the torch to light his own way, but left the wall sconce burning. Once out of the chamber, Myrddion would have to retrace his steps in pitch darkness.

'Aye, master,' Myrddion whispered and then continued with his prayers. Out of the shades, Melvig came like the grizzled shadow of a wolfhound, his eyes bright and angry, and told his great-grandson what he must do. Olwyn, ever fearful for the common people she had always loved, whispered that he must trust to others in the ruse, because the High King was capable of killing every newborn infant in the land if he suspected Myrddion's perfidy. And Branwyn, whom Myrddion thought was safely abed in Tomen-y-mur, came on a wave of perfume composed of salt sea air, dune flowers, seaweed and new death to whisper in his ear. He would have flinched away from her shadow in the darkness, but he felt the unfamiliar touch of his mother's mind within his own and consented to listen to the warnings she brought from far away.

'I never loved you in life, my son. How could I, given your conception? But learn well from your childhood, Myrddion. You can have no part in the babe's upbringing, for you have been soiled by the will of the gods. This boy must travel to far-off places until Uther forgets that he ever existed. Even you, for the sake of your own soul, should not know his whereabouts until he is almost grown. I am newly dead, laid on my bier and waiting to be interred in the chilling earth, so I can never speak to you again, but remember our long enmity, and free the child of this torture – at least. Let him grow clean and strong, able to love and to be untroubled by his parentage and his dangerous future.'

The room became still. Myrddion knew that he had been dreaming of his beloved dead, but he wept anyway, for the hours ahead would tax his ingenuity. His only solace was that he could finally wound Uther fatally, although the blow would not be felt for many years. For a few moments, he wondered why he presumed that the child would be a boy.

Then, his decision finally made, he left his ghosts in the warm darkness and retraced his steps, stronger and more determined than he had ever been. As he extinguished the wall sconce, he swore that the lips of Mithras smiled at him.

When Myrddion returned, Lucius stared at him as if he had never seen him before. A newly born man had entered the room and bowed to the seated king, who was already drunk from the heavy red wine and his heavier sins and triumphs. Myrddion's face was as handsome and as aristocratic as ever, but the boy had been burned out of him, leaving a man whose face was as strong and cleanly defined as a good sword. On his forehead, the white stripe of prophesy seemed wider and more pronounced.

'How goes the queen?' Myrddion asked. 'Has there been any change in her condition?'

Even his voice had changed, becoming firmer and less harried than in the past, Lucius thought in amazement. He has seen his way clear to some decision. After Uther came back with such a self-satisfied smirk on his face, I expected the healer to return as a broken man. Instead, Myrddion has become the master rather than the fearful servant.

The bishop turned away from the grinning death's head of Uther Pendragon and surreptitiously crossed himself for protection. Although he was a man of God, the Roman in his blood still cringed away from the creatures of darkness.

'We've heard nothing, healer,' Botha said softly, but his eyes were wary and unsettled. 'Perhaps you should investigate.'

The captain sees the changes too, Lucius thought with relief. Good. I'm not being overly imaginative. 'I'll go with you, Myrddion. I promised I would pray with the queen if her condition worsened,' he murmured. 'Also, I must prepare for my departure from Venta Belgarum. Whatever happens, my duty to the queen is done and Glastonbury calls me home.' He turned to Bishop Paulus. 'Please excuse me, Paulus, if I leave you with our noble master. I'll send word as soon as the child is born.'

Together, Myrddion and Lucius quit the room, leaving the king behind, befuddled with drink, but still very pleased with the agreement he had wrung from his healer.

Outside the queen's apartments, the two men could hear Ygerne cry out and, for the first time, Myrddion considered the possibility that mother and child might both perish. Death in childbirth was common, and many more infants died within a few months of being born. Myrddion winced at the sound of Ygerne's agony and wished that men were sufficiently enlightened to permit healers, regardless of their sex, to assist struggling mothers. Too often, filthy

521

old hags earned their bread as midwives, killing as many women as they saved, through ignorance and dirty hands. At least Ygerne was spared the touch of a superstitious old woman. Ruadh would do everything possible to ensure the survival of both mother and child.

'Uther wants me to expose the child in the forest as soon as it's born, regardless of its sex,' Myrddion confided baldly as Ygerne's screams grew more insistent.

'Why would he expect you to agree?' Lucius asked, his forehead knitted in suspicion. Why would Myrddion bare his soul when the stakes were so high? 'You're a healer, and your oath precludes infanticide.'

Myrddion stared directly at the priest with eyes that said nothing. 'I promised to obey. I lied, of course, but Uther has always found me truthful so he never doubted my oath. What's a bare-faced lie after the sins I've committed for him? It's just one more blot on my conscience. As you can imagine, Uther thinks he has my measure. He took me to an underground cellar that was sacred to Mithras, and then threatened me, in his delicate way, with entombment if I didn't comply. The man's a fool! I intend to give the child to you, priest, and beg you to spirit him away to an unknown place of safety. I don't want to know where he is taken, for I don't trust myself to stay mute if I know where he is. Uther is too clever by far – and too ruthless. Sooner or later, I'd be forced to give the child up to him.'

'You presume the child will be male,' Lucius retorted. 'It could so easily be a girl.'

'But it'll still be a pawn in Uther's power game. The High King was correct in one detail when we spoke in that cold little cell under the earth. Any child of Uther Pendragon will suffer if it is raised in Venta Belgarum, or even if it's fostered in some far-off place, if anyone should become aware of its sire and dam. I understand this truth, for I was the Demon Seed during my childhood and I suffered the taunts of children and stoning by peasants. How much worse would it be for the child of the Dragon King? What would Uther create out of such a child? And what power would it give to any of the tribal kings if they should hold it to ransom?'

'I understand what you say, but why can't you spirit the child away yourself? Do you fear Uther so much?'

'Not at all, Lucius. I'm well past any personal fear of him, but if I knew where to find the child I'd be tempted to use it as a pawn at some future date. I know my nature, bishop, and I understand my weaknesses. I truly believe that a High King must control all the warring tribes of Britain and lead a concerted attack against the Saxons. I have spent my energy and my conscience towards this end and I would have no mercy on Uther's child when the High King begins to grow old and weak – as he surely will.'

Lucius eyed the young man who stood so comfortably before him as he exposed his weaknesses for the bishop's perusal. 'Uther may expect you to betray him,' he began slowly.

'Probably. He trusts nobody and nothing, save Botha, and then only to a limited degree,' Myrddion continued. 'But our ruse will only fail if you are caught, and I am confident that any man who was once a commander in the legions would be a better tactician than that. It is my intention to take the child into the woods, and then wait for you at the crossroads leading towards the north. There, if you have the stomach for it, I'll guide you to the child, or place it in the hands of any person in whom you have total trust. For your part, you must swear to me that you will never tell me where the infant is. I'll seek it out anyway, eventually, so it's best if you keep the infant hidden for as long as possible and as far away from Uther Pendragon as can be managed.'

Beyond the door, Ygerne screamed in a high, shrill voice as if her soul were being torn from her body. Then, while both men held their breath, they heard a strong and lusty wail from the lungs of an infant.

'The child is born,' Myrddion sighed. 'Give me your answer quickly, Lucius of Glastonbury, for we have very little time in which to decide what to do. I'll give you time to depart, but don't dally if you choose to save the child. As you've said, Uther cannot be trusted.'

Myrddion gripped the prelate by the forearm and the priest was amazed by the strength in the healer's fingers. Such hands were made for the sword, Lucius thought, but perhaps the scalpel has served his people better.

'Aye. I'll take the child, but Uther will also suspect me. I'm certain he'll order Botha to have you followed, because there's no way he'll trust you to keep your part in the bargain you've made. You can expect to be followed specifically to ensure the child is dead. I'll need to have a considerable start if I'm to avoid any retribution.'

'We'll cross that particular bridge when we come to it. Square your shoulders, bishop, for now we must view the object of so much hatred. And the child is but a few moments old.'

Considering the long hours of pain and labour, the queen's apartments seemed unnaturally tidy except for some blood-soaked cloth on the wooden floor. Exhausted, Ygerne was dozing in her great bed while Berwyn sponged her lower limbs free of blood. The queen was very pale and new creases marred the fine skin of her face from nose to jawline. The glamour and mystery that had surrounded her for all of her adult life had vanished during the terrible night of pain, leaving an ageing woman lying wanly on the heaped pillows with great purple bruises under her closed, blued eyelids.

'The poor woman,' Lucius whispered softly. 'One way or another, her child will be stolen from her, so her solace will be stolen as well. She will lose everything.'

He knelt beside the bed and began to pray quietly, while Myrddion approached Ygerne and laid his hand on her brow, ignoring the infant for the moment.

In a delirium of weariness, the queen stirred before opening her wonderful eyes. Myrddion smiled gently at her, but he knew from the lack of soul in her empty irises that she was wandering in dreams that were far more pleasant than the reality of Venta Belgarum.

'We have a son, Gorlois. At last, I have given you your heart's desire,' she whispered, and Myrddion discovered that a lump had formed in his throat while tears prickled at the back of his eyes. Impulsively, he kissed the careworn face and her dreaming lips smiled.

'Thank you, beloved,' Myrddion whispered. 'You have been very brave and strong, but now is the time to rest.'

'Yes, Gorlois, I'll sleep now.'

Myrddion left Ygerne reluctantly. Her innocence in this tragedy made his betrayal more poignant, but at least he could ensure that her child would live. The pity was that he could not tell her so.

'Show me the babe, Ruadh,' he ordered, and Ruadh picked up the well-wrapped infant, deftly unfurled the blanket that covered it and presented the child for the healer's examination.

'The son of Uther Pendragon's loins,' Myrddion whispered. 'Ave, little one, for so much rests on your tiny shoulders.'

The boy was very large, but not chubby like most newborns. Berwyn had washed away the blood and mucus that stained his vigorous, squirming limbs and cleaned out the questing mouth that already contained the swelling buds of several teeth that threatened to break through the gums. The boy was abnormally long and had no hair, except for a fine down of reddish-blond fuzz that was so like Uther's hair colour that Myrddion caught his breath. Then the child opened his eyes and Myrddion would have crossed himself had he followed the Christian faith.

The boy could not yet focus his vision, but his eyes were struggling already to pierce the fogs of birth and feed the brain that lay beneath the large skull. But the wonder of the baby was the colour of those eyes – clear, transparent and grey, like winter skies before a storm.

Lucius examined the child with disquiet from over Myrddion's arm. 'He has raptor's eyes, like the wolf or the sea shark. Will the Lord High God have mercy on us if we save the life of a danger more potent than Uther Pendragon?'

But the babe tried to smile, or grimace, and the sweetness of that unconscious expression softened the hearts of both men at a glance.

'His mother smiles thus, so perhaps she is born anew in the heart of this child,' Bishop Lucius whispered softly. 'I will pray that it proves to be so.'

The two men whispered together while Myrddion nursed the squirming child. Ruadh could tell from the set of her master's shoulders that he was tense and expectant by turn, and her heart sank.

As Myrddion rewrapped the babe's long body, the little creature gripped his hand tightly. The small fingers wrapped around his thumb with amazing strength and determination for one so newly born, and Myrddion wondered if the child held his heart in the same way. This strange little creature would never set him free until death took him.

'I must spirit him away to a safe place, Ruadh,' Myrddion hissed so that Willa and Berwyn couldn't hear him. 'Please tell Uther Pendragon that his son has been stillborn and that Myrddion Merlinus remembers the Temple of Mithras. The High King will understand.'

'You can't kill this child, master. He's too important – I know he is. If I must, I'll try to stop you, I swear it, although your strength is far greater than mine.' Ruadh was so desperate that her eyes were filled with tears and she clutched at her master's cloak with balled fists.

Gently, Bishop Lucius prised her fingers away from Myrddion's cloak and set him free of her grasp. With the babe in the crook of his arm, the healer moved swiftly across the room and out into the dark corridor.

'Be quiet, daughter, for Myrddion is saving the life of the boy with the fiction of exposure. I will take the babe from him at the crossroads on the Roman road, so do as the healer demands and then keep your mouth firmly shut. These little girls,' he indicated Willa and Berwyn with one hand, 'are not strong enough to carry such knowledge.'

As Ruadh hiccuped with distress, and the first tears in many years began to pour down her cheeks, Bishop Lucius raised her chin and kissed her forehead. 'Be brave, daughter, and tell the High King nothing but what your master told you to say. I have trusted you overmuch with the life of this child, but Myrddion's plan depends on your ability to lie to Uther Pendragon. Wait for a little and allow him time to depart safely, in case Uther tries to betray him. Can you withstand questioning by the High King?'

'Watch me, master! If it will save the babe, I'll convince Uther Pendragon that the sky is falling. And I'll wait. You'll also need time to leave the city, and I can use the queen's condition as an excuse. The poor thing! She is at peace now, but she'll soon begin to weep.'

'You must keep the girls safe by explaining that the child is sickly, and that Myrddion is trying to revive it. The fiction that it dies will then be believed, for many infants succumb to death during the first day. Willa and Berwyn will only remain alive if they know nothing of what is really happening. I must go now, or Myrddion will be waiting overlong.'

'God bless you, Bishop Lucius – and the Mother – for this child belongs to her more than to Uther or Ygerne. The little thing has a destiny, I know it.'

After Lucius had hurried away from the birthing room, Ruadh explained the fiction of the child's weakness to Willa and Berwyn, and all three waited patiently with the sleeping queen until the morning sun began to sink into afternoon. Then, with real repugnance and anxiety, Ruadh made her way to Uther's rooms. Botha admitted her to the king's bedchamber grudgingly, but reasoned that her message concerned the birth of Uther's heir.

The High King was drunk and belligerent, his whole length sprawled on his bed while he propped himself up on one elbow to stare owlishly at Ruadh. At first, he didn't recognise her, but then memory overcame the fumes of wine in his brain.

'You're the Pict bitch, right? Ambrosius's whore from beyond the wall? Yes, that's right, and now you serve the queen and bed my excellent healer, my hair-shirt of an adviser. I'll wager he didn't know I spied on *him*. Even spymasters can be spied upon if they begin to think they are too clever. Well, what do you want, or does Myrddion send you to my bed to replace my sick wife? Always sick! Damn all women! Crying and moaning and whining. They never give a man any peace.'

Ignoring his ramblings, Ruadh curtseyed as formally as she knew how and prayed that her message would sink into the High King's wine-sodden stupor.

'Your highness, I bring you tidings from Ygerne, Mother and Queen of the Britons, and from Master Myrddion, your healer.'

Uther fumbled with his pillows and hoisted himself into a seated position. 'Are you there, Botha?' he called. 'I want you to hear this.' He shook his tousled head like a huge, shaggy bear and a crafty expression crossed his drink-blurred features. 'There's someone else I need. I remember . . . yes, I want Ulfin. He's a disobedient dog, but even dumb curs can be useful. Fetch Ulfin before the bitch gives us her message. Hurry up, man. I don't have all day to wait for you to move your sorry arse.'

If Botha was offended by his master's insults, he didn't permit his anger to show. He slid out of the room and closed the heavy door behind him while Ruadh stood quietly and tried to remain as unobtrusive as possible.

'He thinks you might assassinate me in his absence,' Uther giggled, and Ruadh's blood ran cold. 'But we both know there's no chance of that, woman. I don't know what my brother saw in you, or that whining healer, for that matter, but perhaps I'll need to discover your appeal when I have time to spare.'

Ruadh swallowed convulsively. Uther's treatment of bed servants was well known in the Great Hall and sensible serving girls avoided his notice.

The High King mentally undressed her without any attempt to hide the lewdness of his thoughts, and it took all her courage to remain composed under that insulting, inhuman stare. She was relieved when Botha and Ulfin entered the room, for Uther's eyes turned away from her immediately and he set his basilisk stare on Ulfin, who grovelled at his master's feet.

'Now, woman, what is your message from the queen?' Uther suddenly seemed sober, and Ruadh felt a twinge of concern for her own safety.

'Queen Ygerne has given birth to a boy whose fuzz of hair is the same shade and texture as yours, my lord. He is your son.'

'So Gorlois didn't get the bitch pregnant! Damn!'

His listeners winced at the High King's crude disappointment, even Ulfin.

Then, before she could lose her nerve, Ruadh delivered the second part of the message. 'My master bade me to tell you that he remembers the Temple of Mithras. He informed me that your son was stillborn.'

'How sad,' Uther grunted. A moment, presumably of mourning, was permitted to stretch out, and then Uther was finished with the subject of his son. 'You've done your duty, woman, so get out. I'll deal with you later, after I've spoken to the queen. Is she aware that her son is dead?'

Ruadh shook her head. 'The labour was long and hard, and we feared that the queen might die. She sleeps, so we have permitted her to rebuild her strength.'

'Then return to your mistress and I'll speak to her myself when I decide to see her. Don't delay, woman. Get out of my sight before I change my mind.'

The king's hoarse voice warned Ruadh to retreat as quickly as possible, for the sheen of something unpleasant gleamed in those pale blue eyes.

Perhaps that was the reason she latched the door firmly and walked away loudly, then tiptoed back and placed her ear against the narrow gap in the timber of the door frame. She realised that she would die a swift and painful death if she was discovered, but the presence of Ulfin, Uther's dog, raised a host of questions and suspicions that Ruadh wanted answered. What she heard chilled her blood.

'Ulfin, follow Myrddion Merlinus and make sure he kills the brat. The healer is too obedient for my liking. If he's trying to hide the babe, kill him. He's ahead of you so you'll need to hurry!

'There's no need for you to look so disapproving, Botha, because I'm not asking you to get your precious hands dirty.'

Without waiting to hear more, Ruadh fled down the corridor, pausing only to snatch up a guard's cloak that had been left discarded on a bench. In her haste to escape, she missed the rest of the king's instructions.

'We obviously can't have witnesses talking about my business, Ulfin, so while you're obeying my orders, Botha will send a trustworthy servant to bring the Pict bitch and her two girls to my chambers. So far they've been useful as hostages, but they are unnecessary witnesses now since Myrddion is tied to me by the manacles of his own conscience. I want to clean up this mess.'

'But, master, they've done nothing,' Botha protested weakly. He wanted to shout aloud that *Uther* wasn't cleaning up anything. He expected his servants to get their hands dirty.

'So? Just carry out your instructions. What you think doesn't matter – just do what you're told until such time as they are in my hands. You can go and pray, or do whatever you wish. I don't care how you salve your conscience. Now get moving, both of you. And, Ulfin, this is your last chance with me, so don't fuck it up.'

Fear gave wings to Ruadh's feet as she hurried across the wide courtyard outside Uther's hall, down the broad avenues and up the crooked streets that led to the house of the healers. Barely stopping for breath, she asked a house servant for Myrddion's whereabouts, and learned that he was some hours ahead of her. So, avoiding questions as if she were deaf, she took her master's second best horse, mounted lithely and gave the beast its head. Muffled in her stolen cloak and cowl, she escaped detection as she passed through the city gates, which were still open to allow passage to and from the busy market place.

'Please let me be in time,' she prayed, forcing the grey-dappled horse into a reluctant gallop. She was familiar with the location of the crossroads, complete with a stone carved with Celtic interlace, nearly one hour's travel to the north of Venta Belgarum. From there, Myrddion could disappear with ease, but Ulfin wouldn't permit himself to be shaken off. He had been chafing at his demotion, and she knew that he would do anything to restore himself in the High King's favour.

Her horse was foundering, for she had driven it hard and had been careless of the hills that blew the animal's wind or the icy surfaces that made a headlong rush so dangerous. Although she fumed at the delay, she was forced to stop and rest briefly, or else the beast would have dropped dead from exhaustion. Finally, as the sun started to set and the light began to darken on the stone in the middle of the crossroads, Ruadh saw a vague shape, possibly the bishop, as he rode away on a donkey in a northerly direction. Then she spied her master sitting at his ease in the dry grasses beside the road. His horse cropped the dry stalks desultorily and stared at the passing traffic with long-lashed, incurious brown eyes.

'I'm in time. Thanks be to the Mother of all good things.'

She whipped her horse hard with the dangling reins and the beast summoned up one last spurt of effort as she dodged past a caravan of pilgrims who were heading afoot to Venta Belgarum.

Cursing in Pictish, she avoided the small cavalcade with difficulty and arrived at the crossroads, sweating and shaking with exertion.

'Where's the babe?' she gasped, as Myrddion's eyes widened with surprise. He realised that Ruadh would not have followed him so precipitously unless some imminent danger threatened, so he answered her immediately.

'The bishop has him. I'm just stalling for time to ensure he has some distance between himself and any possible pursuit. What's wrong?'

'Ulfin has been dispatched to check that you've not had a change of heart and contrived to spare the child. I came as quickly as I could, but he must be close at my heels. He'd have asked the gatekeepers what route you took when you left the city.'

'Shite!' Myrddion looked at Ruadh's horse. The grey's legs were shaking with distress and its chest and flanks were spotted with foam, underlining its exhaustion. His own mount had been rested, but any fool could tell that Ruadh needed a change of horse. 'You're far lighter than me, Ruadh, so take my mount and ride like the wind after Lucius. A donkey will never outpace Ulfin and the child must be saved at any cost. Perhaps it might be best if the bishop allows you to take the babe to its destination.'

Ruadh swiftly climbed into the saddle and Myrddion laid one hand comfortingly on her thigh. 'Take care of yourself, Andrewina Ruadh, and I will pray that we meet again when these afflictions have passed us by.' He took her hand and kissed her knuckles, wishing he had more to offer this great-hearted woman than respect.

'It's best that you return to Venta Belgarum while I chase after Bishop Lucius on your horse. But you must check on the whereabouts of Willa and Berwyn when you return,' Ruadh warned him from over her shoulder. 'I don't trust Uther, because he never leaves anyone alive to spread rumours or to undermine his position. That man is the very devil.'

Then, before she gave the horse its head and turned it away from the healer, her soft voice floated down to him. 'I love you, Myrddion Merlinus of Segontium.'

Then she kicked the horse's ribs and the animal moved smoothly into an easy canter. Some streak of common sense caused her to slow her breakneck pace through the skeletal landscape, for she would be of no use to the bishop if she killed her mount in the finding of him.

Meanwhile, back at the crossroads, Myrddion seated himself on a grassy bank and watched a desiccated corpse swing gently on a gibbet in the afternoon breeze. Felons were hanged at crossroads, and the long-dead man opened his bony jaws in a soundless scream of old agony as he searched for his earth-entrapped soul.

'Appropriate, my friend, that death presides over what we do. I hope we have won a little breathing space, but what will come, will come.'

In the western sky, the sun sank through the clouds and edged them with a smudge of blood red. Another weary day had ended with the promise of the first bitter frosts of winter.

CHAPTER XXIII

THE LONG ROAD TO NOWHERE

To see what is right and not to do it is want of courage.

Confucius, *Analects*

Bishop Lucius and his donkey had made surprisingly good speed by the time Ruadh overtook him on the long roadway leading to Sorviodunum. In the cool of the late afternoon, Lucius could feel the pleasant warmth of the child as it lay asleep beneath his cloak, and he began to worry that it would soon waken and be hungry, which would warn the woman that he had the infant in his keeping.

'What is amiss, my child, that you should desert your mistress and half kill your horse?' he asked, even before Ruadh had caught her breath. Her plaits had fallen and come undone so her red hair flamed in the setting sun like a beacon of hope.

In a minimum of words, the servant explained her mad dash and the role of Ulfin as Uther's hunting dog, including her belief that he was close behind her on the road leading out of Venta Belgarum.

In the pride of youth and as the scion of a noble house, Lucius had served on battlefields across the Roman world until his soul was eventually poisoned by the slaughter he witnessed. He had ordered men into battle as he learned the hard lessons of command, so he had become inured to making speedy decisions involving life and death.

His part in the child's salvation was done now that Uther was in hot pursuit, so Ruadh must become the protector of the babe and spirit him to a safe place where he could grow to manhood. With a soldier's practicality, Lucius understood that he lacked the speed and the youth required to evade a seasoned warrior, yet he was reluctant to send a woman on such a dangerous quest.

His decision made, he flipped back his cloak to expose the warmly wrapped infant, carried in a sling across his breast so he had the full use of both hands. He began to undo the length of cloth and the infant awoke and began to cry lustily. Carefully leading his donkey off the roadway, Lucius produced from his saddlebag a small leather bottle to which was attached a primitive cloth nipple which he thrust into the babe's mouth. As the child suckled noisily, Lucius ordered Ruadh to dismount and began to transfer the sling and the feeding child to her breast with a sigh of regret.

'Where can I take him that will ensure his safety?' Ruadh protested. 'I'm a stranger in the south, so I'll be travelling blind.'

'A woman with an infant in tow isn't as memorable as a priest and a babe. You have a far better chance of escaping notice than I do, so Ulfin would find me quickly. There is a ford at the bottom of this hill, and when you enter the shallows, ride upstream for about a mile before heading across country towards the northwest. Keep the sun on your right side during the mornings and on your left in the afternoons. That way, you will always be travelling in a northerly direction. Do you understand what you must do, Ruadh?'

Without waiting for a response, Lucius took the saddlebag down from his donkey and tied it into place over the withers of Ruadh's horse.

'With luck, Ulfin won't discover where you leave the road, even with all this mud, although you must travel in easy stages to spare the child. I've packed clothes for the babe and more breast milk, but I fear you will need to find some watered cows' milk before you arrive safely at your final destination. You also have dry rations and a tinderbox in the saddlebag, and you'd best take my water bottle.'

'I can't take all your supplies,' Ruadh protested. 'You'll be hungry and thirsty.'

'I'm a man of God and my Lord will provide for me. Your final destination is near Aquae Sulis, which is far off in the northwest. It is a famed Roman centre, so you will easily obtain directions to it.'

Lucius fished out two small leather bags from his robe. The leather was warm where it had rested over his heart and when Ruadh hefted them, she heard the clink of coins.

'This bag will purchase your supplies. I'd not have you go hungry on your journey, and you must pay for milk to nurse the child.'

'I understand, Bishop Lucius, but where do I go in Aquae Sulis?'

Ruadh was frowning with concentration and the bishop regretted the responsibility that was being placed on the woman's narrow shoulders.

'Don't enter the city itself, but take the eastern road that turns off before the city gates. Once away from the city, follow the stone markers – I recall there are three of them. Eventually, you will come to a track and a gate branching off the main road to the right that leads up a steep hill. At the very top, you will find the Villa Poppinidii and its master, Ector, who will take you in. If you travel too far, you'll reach a village which will set you on the correct route. Give Ector the coins in the second bag and ask him to foster the boy for my sake. One day, either I or another friend will contact him concerning the boy's future, but until then Ector should raise the infant with his own son. You must not explain to Ector, or any other person, the details of the babe's parentage, for it would amount to signing the boy's death warrant. Do you understand, Ruadh?'

'Yes, but are you sure that such subterfuge is necessary, Father?'

'Aye. Uther is trying to kill his son, so I am hiding him in one of the last Roman enclaves in Britain, where the High King cuts very little ice. Nor will he seek the child within a Roman family, believing that the boy will be used as a tool by the tribal kings to weaken his hold on power. His own selfish madness colours his expectations of the actions of others. Yes, Uther will search diligently for the boy, but he'll not find him where I am sending him.'

'Should he have a name?' Ruadh whispered, as she felt a tiny fist pull at her breast. She felt the ice of old losses melting, as if this child could bring back her own children.

'Aye, he should. I have thought carefully on this matter, and I believe we should give him the name Artorex, which is a combination of Roman and Celtic words and, therefore, belongs to neither. Perhaps the boy will grow into such a powerful name – but perhaps he will not. We can give him life, but the rest lies in the hands of others.'

'And what should I do after I deliver him to Ector, Father? Do I stay with the child, return to my master or head north into the land of the Picts to resume my old life? Tell me what to do, for I've not had a moment to consider what to make with the rest of my life.'

'You have many miles to travel before you can rest, Ruadh. During your journey, you will discover what God has planned for you, so be careful how you go, little one. But I have one warning for you. For the sake of the babe, and for the soul of Myrddion, don't tell your master where you take little Artorex. Meanwhile, I will remember you in my prayers.'

Then Lucius slapped her horse across the rump, causing it to plunge down the hill towards the streamlet. Pensively, the prelate stood watching as Ruadh guided the horse deftly into the slow-flowing ford where the setting sun was obscured by large willow trees. Straining, he watched her movements for as long as the dying light permitted, and when she had disappeared from sight, he mounted his donkey and applied a switch to its withers without causing the animal any hurt.

'It's time to go, faithful creature,' he whispered softly into its long ear. 'I wish I could protect Andrewina Ruadh, but she and Artorex must go where I dare not follow, lest Uther use me to murder his son. I cannot ensure the babe's safety, but, still, I wonder if I'll ever see him again?'

For a short time, Myrddion rested beside the crossroads before turning his horse towards Venta Belgarum in a leisurely walk. The animal would have to be nursed throughout the journey, for its legs still trembled and sweated. As the sun sank below the heavy cloud cover the afternoon dimmed around him, so Myrddion dismounted to walk in the fitful, failing light with the reins held loosely in one hand.

He was still some distance from Venta Belgarum, where the road was busy with carts, farmers and several priests bouncing along on fat donkeys, when something blotted out the last of the afternoon light. Raising his eyes from the stony roadway, Myrddion looked up into the cold face of Ulfin, mounted on one of Uther's favourite destriers. The guardsman's eyes were hooded with dislike as his gaze swept over Myrddion's person, his horse and the empty saddlebag that flapped against its flank.

'Well met, healer. So, where have you have been so late in the day?' Ulfin's voice had lost none of its sneering superiority during his months of banishment, and Myrddion shaded his eyes with one hand and answered in a like tone.

'It's none of your business, Ulfin. I travel on the orders of Uther Pendragon and only the High King has the right to demand an explanation of me.'

As fast as a striking snake, Ulfin whipped the ends of his reins directly at Myrddion's face. Only the healer's sharp reflexes saved him from a spiteful blow across the eyes.

'If you want me to tell you anything, then I can assure you that you're going about it in the worst possible way.' Myrddion's voice was silky as he examined his forearm, where the end of the leathers had raised a nasty welt.

'Where's your package? You know what I mean, so don't dissemble. The king has sent me to make sure that it's gone for good.'

'If you ride into the woods to the right of the standing stone, you will come to a small clearing. I left the *package* at the foot of a blasted oak.'

Myrddion had taken the precaution of finding such a landmark, for he was sure that someone would check on his movements. The tracks of his horse and his footprints would lead through the mud and fallen leaves to the foot of a riven tree, a landmark of note, just as Lucius's trail would lead away from it.

'How can I be sure that you're speaking the truth?' Ulfin demanded sullenly. His small, piggish eyes roved over Myrddion's face as if some answer lay in those handsome, ironic features.

'You can't, but only a madman would return to Venta Belgarum if he had disobeyed the High King's instructions. In case you haven't noticed, I'm not insane.'

Ulfin snorted with disgust and spurred his horse. As the beast plunged past him, the healer noticed that Ulfin carried provisions. Perhaps the guardsman was learning to plan ahead.

Ulfin rode through the foot traffic at a gallop, careless of the curses of travellers as they attempted to avoid him. As always, Ulfin approached his task aggressively, and once he reached the crossroads he searched the margins of the four verges for a trace of Myrddion's horse. Once he found what he was seeking, he followed the crushed grass stems and broken shrubbery to a small clearing where an oak tree was reeling drunkenly after being struck by lightning.

No child wailed in the exposed roots. Cursing Myrddion's perfidy, Ulfin threw himself from his horse and followed a set of prints in the mud to the foot of the tree.

No child. Another set of prints moved away to the western road, so Ulfin snatched up his reins and followed. 'Got you!' he whispered exultantly as he saw churned earth where someone had departed, using the firm roadway where no tracks could be followed. Kicking his horse savagely in the ribs, Ulfin set off in pursuit, cursing the failing light and the poor visibility that was certain to slow him down.

'I hope Uther flays the healer slowly. The bastard has attempted some trickery and is trying to save the child – I can feel it in my water.'

So Ulfin travelled westward, cursing as he was forced to pick his way down dangerous slopes on a long straight road that threatened a nasty fall for those who were less than competent riders. This wide track was empty of traffic, for all sensible travellers had sought shelter for the night from the cold wind that was blowing in from the east. But Ulfin was desperate. Only the corpse of a dead child would redeem him in his master's eyes, and Ulfin could not endure the humiliation of being barred from Uther's confidences any longer. Better to freeze on the road than to return empty-handed.

Ahead of him, Bishop Lucius drove his donkey towards a distant inn, conscious that his headlong rush to the safety of Glastonbury was suspicious in itself. But every mile travelled took him further from the ford and made Ulfin's task just a little more difficult. His donkey was plodding with effort, and Lucius knew that the poor animal could not be driven too much further.

The lights of the inn were tantalisingly close when Uther's servant caught up with the bishop. He rode around his quarry before halting his horse in the very middle of the roadway.

'By my oath, it's the bishop of Glastonbury. Why are you abroad so late, Father? For that matter, why have you left the High King's court in such unseemly haste? Surely the queen needs you at her side more than ever since her son has died.'

'Ulfin!' Lucius exclaimed and tried to lead his donkey round the guardsman, who moved his horse to bar the way again. 'Why I left Venta Belgarum is my concern, not yours, so I must ask you to allow me to pass. I don't answer to kings or to their servants – only to my God!'

Ulfin was tired and irritable. A simple task had been made difficult by his failure to locate the child, so, not surprisingly, he lost his volatile temper. The guardsman threw himself from his horse, drew his sword and advanced on the bishop of Glastonbury.

'Get off that flea-bitten ass and answer my question, or I'll cut its throat, closely followed by yours.'

Slowly, so as to gain the time to think, Lucius complied. Without knowing Ulfin very well, he was sure that he would be reasoning with a desperate thug, so he tried to look as inoffensive as possible.

'I have many outstanding duties at Glastonbury and I informed the High King that I would depart for my home after the birth of Ygerne's child. The High King is aware of my departure, and a donkey is hardly the mount for speedy travel if I intended an escape. I'm not hiding from anyone. The building you can see yonder with its lights ablaze is an inn owned by a man I know. He always seems able to spare a free bed and a cup of wine for a man of God.

Why have you intercepted a man of the cloth who is going about God's work?'

Ulfin thrust his face so close to Lucius's nose that the priest recoiled from the stink of unclean teeth. Roman to the core, he stood a little straighter and his still-dark brows rose with undisguised dislike.

'Where's the child?' Ulfin demanded, insulted. 'I am certain that you collected it and handed it over to someone else. And who would that person be, I wonder? Don't bother to shake your head, priest, for you're going to confess everything before I've done with you.'

Lucius drew himself up to his full height, barely five foot seven inches, but generations of senators stared out of his brown eyes with a look so laden with disdain that Ulfin was momentarily taken aback.

'Do you see a child? I'm a priest. What would I do with an infant?'

Ulfin picked Lucius up by the front of his priestly robes and shook him as a terrier shakes a rat. One hand slapped Lucius's face until the priest felt his lip split and blood began to trickle down his chin.

Praying for forbearance, the bishop of Glastonbury tried to remain true to his vows of non-violence, but a ringing punch to the cheekbone drove him back onto his haunches in the mud and filled his head with the red mists of blood lust. His resolve snapped and he launched himself at Ulfin with a scream of unpriestly rage.

The old patterns of training in unarmed combat, practised daily as a Roman officer, came instinctively to the fore, despite the many years Lucius had spent in the priesthood. Over-confident, Ulfin took too long to bring his sword to the ready, so Lucius had more than enough time to step inside his swinging blade and strike his neck a punishing blow with the base of his hand. As the blade suddenly gained weight in the guardsman's fist and his arm began to sag, Lucius brought his knee up into Ulfin's groin and the warrior fell to the ground before the priest's satisfied eyes.

Picking up the discarded sword, Lucius held the tip of the blade at Ulfin's throat.

'I've had enough of you and your accusations, servant of the king. If Uther Pendragon wishes to question me, then he can come to Glastonbury, but I fear he'll get the same answers. I don't know where his son is. Do you understand plain speaking, Ulfin? Anyway, isn't Uther's infant son supposed to be dead? I was told by Myrddion Merlinus that the babe was stillborn. Are you saying that the child still lives?'

Ulfin's face was a study of confusion, guilt and concern as he realised from his admissions that the priest was innocent of any collusion with the healer.

The guardsman used profanities that would have made a man of God quiver. A look of pure malevolence warned Lucius that the guardsman wasn't finished. 'You can't watch over me all night, priest. Sooner or later, you'll lower your guard and then I'll have you. By the gods, I'll make you scream before you tell me everything you know.'

Lucius grinned recklessly. 'I think not, servant!'

Then he raised his voice in a hoarse roar of pretended panic and pain. 'Thieves! Footpads! Sound the alarm! Awaken at the inn! I am under attack! Lucius of Glastonbury is under attack.'

Behind Ulfin, Lucius saw the doorway of the inn open, so he redoubled his screams as several men poured out onto the roadway and began to run in his direction. 'You'd best leave before they kill you out of hand,' the bishop warned, and threw Ulfin's sword onto the roadway.

Ulfin cursed again, rose to his feet, gripped his horse's mane with his left hand and leapt into the saddle, pausing only to collect his sword where it quivered, point down in the mud, on the weedy verge. Then he thundered off at a gallop in the direction from which he had come.

'I've done all I can, Andrewina Ruadh. The rest depends on you.'

After Ruadh's punishing ride, his steed was in such poor condition that Myrddion Merlinus led the horse on foot all the way to Venta Belgarum. Man and horse were exhausted, for the moon had almost completely risen by the time the closed gates of the city came into view. The night was so cold that his exhaled breath left little puffs of vapour in the air, and horse and rider were both shivering with cold when their journey ended.

After pounding with his clenched fist on the gate, Myrddion had to wait impatiently for some little time before the gatemaster roused himself, thrust on a pair of breeches and staggered out into the darkness to open the smaller door within the large, reinforced and barred gate. Thanking him, Myrddion threw him a coin for his trouble.

'The king's healer ain't so bad for all that men call him the Storm Crow,' the gatemaster told his sleepy wife. 'Look! He gave me a silver piece just to let him into Venta Belgarum.'

'Umm,' his wife murmured, and opened one eye. 'Why would anyone be abroad on a night like this? Mark my words, there's trouble ahead.'

'But we've still got the silver,' the gatemaster chortled, and bit on the soft metal for emphasis. He was a practical man.

Unaware that he was the topic of idle speculation, Myrddion strolled directly to Uther's hall after leaving his horse at the king's stables in the care of ostlers who were none too pleased to be wakened in the middle of the night. At least, Queen Ygerne would require an explanation from him, so he made his way directly to her door. There were no questions from the guard, although several warriors looked at him sideways from under their brows with expressions that Myrddion couldn't fathom. In the queen's apartments, he found two strange women sitting with Morgan and the Mother of the Britons.

'Tell me that it's all a lie, Myrddion Merlinus,' the queen begged when she recognised her visitor. 'You took my son to your house of healers because it was sickly, or so Willa told me before she was taken away. I don't understand, Myrddion. I saw the boy. I saw him with these two eyes and he was strong and lusty. He had Pridenow's eyes, as if my father had come back to me from out of the shadows. He can't be dead!'

Myrdion lowered his head to hide his lying eyes. 'Your child is lost to you, highness, where neither you with all your love, nor I with all my skill, can find him. I wish it were not so, for your sake.'

The queen sobbed as if her heart would break, while across the sumptuous gilded bed Morgan smiled enigmatically. Did she guess how carefully Myrddion had worded his reply to the queen? Even now, was she factoring a new possibility into her poisonous plans for her stepfather?

Myrddion shrugged. He didn't care what Morgan did to Uther. The High King had earned Morgan's interpretation of vengeance. First things first.

'Where are Willa, Ruadh and Berwyn?' he demanded, so that it became Morgan's turn to flinch and ponder a politic reply. As usual, the queen's daughter decided to enjoy the echo of another person's pain.

'They've gone, Myrddion Merlinus. Aye, you're the Storm Crow indeed, for those whom you love seem to vanish in a puff of smoke. Don't ask us. We were summoned to attend to my mother when she was left alone. You could ask Botha, I suppose, because he knows everything that my stepfather does.'

'Ruadh never came back from seeing my husband, or so Willa

told me. Those lovely girls!' Ygerne wept harder and turned her face into her pillow.

'Shite! Uther wouldn't dare!' Myrddion exploded, but he knew that any High King who had just won a dangerous game would wish to sweep the board clean of all the minor pieces.

'Wouldn't he just? Perhaps you know our master better than we do,' Morgan gloated.

'Please excuse me, highness,' Myrddion muttered, and rushed from the room. His booted heels struck the floor with the sound of bones breaking, and his hands clenched and unclenched against his will as he strode towards an explosive meeting with the High King.

Botha attempted to bar the door. 'Don't make me kill you, healer,' the captain begged, his honest hazel-brown eyes stark with distress. 'Your girls aren't within, I promise you.'

'Let me see him, though I go to the shades because of it.' Myrddion's temper, controlled for so long, now vomited forth like the waves of lava he had seen in the Middle Sea, sending cool waters to boiling as oozing sheets of liquid stone poured onto the black sands at the volcano's flanks. 'Let me see that son of a whore.'

'Let him in, Botha,' Uther called in a loud, unnaturally reasonable voice. 'Although I cannot see why I should be disturbed at such an early hour of the morning.'

Myrddion's palm hit the door with a thud and sent it crashing inward. Uther still lounged on his disordered bed, but his hair was unbound and cascaded in a wild tangle down his back. The odd glint of silver marred the blond lights in his hair, caught by the unkind, revealing light of the oil lamp.

Myrddion scanned the room and the one beyond it. Empty! Every item of furniture appeared to be in place, but Myrddion noticed a small smear of blood on the woollen blanket that was tangled around the king's long, bony feet.

'Where are the hostages, Uther, damn you?'

Slowly, Uther swung his legs over the edge of his pallet and stretched his long spine to sit at his ease on his disordered bed. 'You'd best ask Botha, for I have no idea. Of more moment to me – where is Ulfin? And have you done what you vowed to do?'

Myrddion moved forward impulsively, and Botha barred his way once again. His honest face was shadowed by distress and his big hands were ready to grasp the healer if he attempted to attack the king's person. But Botha's sword still rested in its scabbard, against all his warrior instincts.

'I have done what you asked of me, Uther Pendragon,' Myrddion hissed, spitting out the High King's name as if it were a curse. 'Your dragonlet is gone, but Queen Ygerne told me it had Pridenow's eyes. Do you plan to explain to Ygerne's father beyond the shades what you have done to his grandson? By the Mother, I can smell your dead as they wait for you where the shadows are darkest in the corners of this room.'

'And Ulfin?' Uther asked, but his calm was sufficiently shaken to send his eyes darting towards the darkness at the edges of his comfortable chamber.

'I met him at the crossroads outside the city several hours ago. He rode away after trying to blind me with his reins, but I've no doubt he'll turn up like the base coin he is. To Hades with Ulfin! I'm more concerned for the girls.'

Uther shrugged and Botha forced Myrddion out of the king's room by sheer force of muscle, although the burly warrior took care to spare the healer any hurt. Once the door was closed, he sighed deeply and patted Myrddion on the shoulder.

'Apparently we are brothers in sin,' he muttered under his breath, so that Myrddion was forced to strain to hear him.

'Where are they, Botha? I acquit you of any blame if they've come to harm, but I must know because they're my responsibility.'

Botha signed and Myrddion could almost feel the weight of the captain's honour pressing against his warrior heart. 'I was ordered to take all three women to Uther shortly after noon. Ruadh, the midwife, was gone, praise be to the Mother, so a little less guilt presses on my soul. But the girls ... I brought them to Uther's apartment and I waited outside this door. I'm afraid my lord took his pleasure with them. I heard what he did to them.'

Two tears leaked out of Myrddion's eyes. 'Neither had ever known a man.'

'So I supposed. Their innocence mocks my pretence at manhood.'

'So where are they now?' In his heart of hearts, Myrddion didn't really desire to see or hear the truth, but habits of clear thinking forced him to go on to the bitter, brutal end.

'Afterwards, Uther called for a member of the guard to take them away,' Botha replied, his broad, strong face creased with shame. 'The High King tried to spare my sensibilities, I suppose.'

'I don't envy you your duties, Botha. I hope you have the courage to endure what you must, but I have no ties left to Uther, other than those I choose to grant to him. Now, take me to the guardroom, if that is where the girls are being held.'

Botha led the healer out of the great building, into the stables and then to the barracks behind them. Half a day had passed since the girls had been taken from the queen's chamber, so Myrddion held only a frail hope that the girls were still alive.

'Stay here, healer, and permit me to discover what has happened,' Botha ordered. Myrddion obeyed reluctantly, although common sense told him that Botha would wring the truth out of the warriors faster than he could.

A very angry Botha soon returned in company with two shamefaced warriors. 'Follow me, Myrddion,' the captain hissed. 'As for you two, fetch bolts of cloth from the stores. I don't care where you find them – just make sure you do. And ensure those other whoresons complete the tasks I demanded of them. I don't care if it's the middle of the sodding night. I want six men equipped with sharp axes ready to chop down trees for a funeral pyre. If they aren't ready when I return, I'll take the skin off *your* backs.'

Myrddion tried to question Botha as the captain stalked away, but the warrior glared at him so ferociously that Myrddion's heart sank to his boots. At a fast trot, Botha led him through the gates of the city wall towards the open midden where the town's rubbish was thrown – and eventually buried.

'Not the midden!' Myrddion gasped, but Botha had already roused the gatemaster with oaths and fists to assist them in their search as they passed out from the dark skirts of the city. As Botha ploughed ahead, Myrddion snatched a torch from the gatemaster, who shivered away from the expression in the healer's eyes.

The rubbish dump was located in an eroded, narrow ravine that ran parallel to the city walls. Many enterprising citizens simply dumped offal, broken goods, the bodies of dogs and other pets, the contents of their night-soil containers and bowls of food scraps straight over the walls. Botha was already wading through accumulated filth towards two pale glimmers of white that were outlined by a heavy yellow moon.

Myrddion knew what they would find.

Holding his torch high and cursing as his robe and boots were fouled by soft, unspeakable sludge beneath his boots, Myrddion struggled to join the large warrior.

'Here are the little ones. Shite! Shite! Shite!' Botha shouted as, beyond the wall, dogs began to bark at the sudden noise.

Berwyn had been tossed face first, so Myrddion was spared the sight of her bloodied, birthmarked face, but Willa was sprawled half over the other girl's legs and her wide-open eyes and mouth shrieked soundlessly at uncaring gods.

Her body had been stripped bare and was swollen and livid with bruises, burns and cuts. Blood smeared her loins and legs, and

Myrddion turned away, unable to imagine their deaths.

'So Uther did exactly as he promised.'

'Aye. They were killed by his guardsmen. Raped to death, I suppose, unless their poor little hearts stopped from fear of what would befall them.'

Myrddion's mind rebelled from the nightmarish scene of waste and murder. Moonlight glinted on his straining knuckles and the rigid set of his jaw as his lips moved soundlessly in a prayer or a curse. Even the jaundiced moon seemed to recognise the wretchedness of the crime that had taken place below it, for it hid its face in a mass of cloud and concealed the pathetic, tumbled corpses.

'Look for me no further, Botha, except in those times when the news is too terrible for contemplation. I'll heal no more men who serve under Uther Pendragon's banner, nor live in this city of cowards and knaves. I wish you well, Botha, for all that you serve a monster, so I beg you to give my girls a clean burial, as I believe you plan to do.'

'Ah, healer, we who serve must sometimes suffer more than the dead. I regret I am a coward, hiding behind an ancient oath. Aye, I will ensure that the whoresons who killed them will sew them into shrouds, lop down trees and build their funeral pyres. I don't care if it takes the entire night. Then I'll send the little ones to the flames as if they were men and warriors.'

Botha wept soundlessly, but Myrddion could see the silver snail-tracks of tears on his cheeks. He understood the shame that Botha felt, but the healer had no words of mercy to offer. As he strode away, he heard the captain's final words, asked of the uncaring, dolorous night.

'What else can a man do?'

When Ruadh rode her horse into the stream that would eventually wind its way towards the small settlement of Spinis which lay to the north, the servant felt sick with worry. She was determined to travel as far as possible while the light lasted, so she drove her horse to splash through the shallows even when the sun had virtually set. Then, when she spied a shelf of rock protruding out into the streamlet, she forced her steed to climb out of the water in the concealing darkness. The task was completed with much complaint and splashing, a disturbance which set little Artorex into lusty crying.

'Damn you, horse, we can all rest when we reach the woods. I know it's dark but you and I are going onwards.'

Although the horse bridled in complaint, Ruadh's only concession was to dismount, put one finger in Artorex's questing mouth and then lead her steed through light cover until the streamlet was behind her and she could no longer hear the gentle swirl and burble of its waters.

She rested for several hours, wrapped in her stolen cloak to keep them both warm, although she decided to forgo the comfort of a fire. While exploring her meagre rations, she discovered that Lucius's saddlebags contained a further surprise: a worn eating knife with a narrow, razor-sharp blade. Its handle was made of polished wood that had been smoothed by generations of hands, and the blade had been sharpened with a whetstone so often that Ruadh decided that it was halved in width through many years of regular use.

'Look, Artorex,' she told the baby. 'Lucius has given us a sharp little stinger in case someone tries to hurt us. Now, who would want to do that to a fine and bonny babe like you?'

Tired, hungry and soiled as little Artorex was, he responded to Ruadh's crooning voice and sucked hard on her forefinger as she hunted for the leather bottle and Lucius's dwindling supply of milk.

'It's nearly all gone, sweetheart. And it's cold! We'll have to find a cow, a goat ... whatever ... by morning, or else little Artorex will be hungry.' As she crooned, she filled the bottle and put Lucius's makeshift nipple in the infant's mouth. He sucked vigorously.

Wise to the ways of newborns, she waited to change his loin cloth until after she had patted away his wind. Once he felt himself clean and dry, he sighed like a tiny old man and promptly fell asleep. Too weary to eat, Ruadh followed him into slumber after wrapping them both in her purloined cloak. As she drifted away, she could hear the faint tinkle of her horse's hobble bells as it searched for sweeter grass under the spreading elm trees.

She woke long before dawn and, mindful of Lucius's instructions, she gave little Artorex the last of the milk, chewed on a strip of dried meat herself, thrust an apple in her robe for later and sought out her horse. The sky was a sullen charcoal, but a rime of light illuminated the eastern horizon, so she knew it was time for them to go.

Day followed day in slow travel as she settled into the rhythms of the child and her horse. She managed to purchase milk and wash the child's loincloths at a crofter's cottage beyond Spinis, and found a woodcutter's wife in the forests outside Cunetio who was carrying a chubby, year-old child on one hip and had another, a little older, clinging to her skirts. For a few coppers, the woman fed the infant to satiation and replenished Ruadh's bottled supplies, accepting her tale that she was the child's aunt, and was trying to return the orphan to her parents in far off Glevum. The countrywoman smiled and nodded, accepting Ruadh's glib lies because of the red shades in her hair and the peach fuzz on Artorex's skull.

Although she had avoided all villages and towns, a woman alone, mounted on a valuable horse, must have excited some talk, even among the isolated peasantry who lived far from the network of roads that marked civilisation. When she rested for the night in vestigial forests south of the hamlet of Verlucio, she had almost relaxed in the knowledge that she had Lucius's knife and scabbard concealed in Artorex's little linen robe, which had become quite grubby from their travels.

She had risked a fire to cook a plump chicken she had purchased earlier from a dour elderly couple who had driven a hard bargain. But Ruadh hadn't begrudged them their small victory. While Artorex slept, she rode through the dense trees trying not to lose her sense of direction as she plucked the feathers from the poor bird on horseback. A small trail of brown and orange feathers marked her passage, while the smell of sodden fowl was a necessary evil. Fortunately, the elderly couple had agreed that she could dunk the fluffy, bronze-coloured bird in boiling water after she had wrung its neck with an efficiency born of long practice.

As the chicken cooked over an open fire, the mouth-watering aroma of crisping skin and bubbling chicken fat was as delicious as the white meat itself. As she gave a little chicken grease to the drowsy child on one finger, Ruadh discovered that although she was lonely, she felt an odd happiness. She fell asleep beside the dying fire with her arms wrapped around the sleeping child cuddled into the curve of her shoulder.

She woke with a knife blade against her throat, a male body pressed against her back and hot, foul breath on the nape of her neck. For a short moment, Ruadh was disoriented and confused but then, as her heart raced and a rough hand followed the contours of her body, the ice in her blood caused her brain to begin working.

The baby awoke as a rough hand gripped its leg and twisted. Artorex's scream of outrage was shocking in the quiet darkness under the trees and two horses whickered in alarm.

'You've got the king's brat! By the twisted sisters of war, you're a clever little bitch, aren't you?'

A rough hand jerked her head sideways and bared her face in the dim light, although the knife blade never wavered from the hollow of her throat. Within the enveloping cloak, and knowing she only had seconds to act, her right hand slid under the howling child and gripped the scabbard that was tangled in the hemline of his robe.

'The Pict bitch! Well, I'll be damned!'

In the last of the firelight, a pallid moon outlined a shaggy head, but obscured the features of the man who now kneeled above her, straddling her trapped hips under the cloak.

But she knew who it was. How could she not? 'You're Ulfin. Uther's dog.'

'Aye, bitch. Why weren't you killed with Myrddion's other whores? But I'll soon remedy that – and then I'll see to the child. But first I'd like to find out just what Ambrosius saw in you. What do you say, bitch?'

'Your breath reeks like a man ten days dead,' Ruadh gasped as she extracted the knife from the scabbard as gently as she could. Artorex provided a handy diversion by screaming even louder.

Ulfin struck her hard enough to jar her teeth in her head and make her senses swim. Stunned, she still managed to hold the knife tightly against her body.

A brutal hand tore the cloak away so Ruadh spat at him, hoping to keep him engrossed in his task.

'You've got yourself a filthy mouth, whore. Maybe I'll cut out your tongue before I kill you. Uther would appreciate such a gift and your fancy boy, the healer, would be touched to have a part of you to cherish, if Uther is stupid enough to let him escape with his life.'

Ulfin changed his knife from one hand to the other, but Ruadh knew that she gained nothing by the exchange, as an able warrior could use either hand with equal skill. With his stronger right hand, he dragged her robe open, tearing the wool where it laced together, so that her breasts were exposed. Ulfin bit them until they bled.

Just wait, Ruadh's mind told her. Remain patient. If he tries to rape you, he's the one who will be exposed and vulnerable. That's when you'll have your chance. Just wait!

He reared back from her, took off his belt and let it fall, scabbard and all, across her legs. Then, even as she winced, he pushed up her skirts to expose her lower body. His hand was rough and meant to hurt her, but Ruadh steeled herself and allowed no sound to escape her lips.

Artorex screamed on in the stillness of the oak trees.

As Ulfin fumbled with the lacing of his trews, he dropped his eyes for a moment. Ruadh acted without thought, even though she was pinned down. She suddenly reared her upper body towards him with a strength fuelled by panic and rage and plunged the slim knife deep into his bared lower belly. As her Pictish husband had taught her, she immediately twisted the blade to gut him.

'Bitch!' Ulfin howled, and clutching his belly with one hand he struck out at her with his knife. Even though she twisted and rolled her upper body away from him, she felt his blade graze her ribs with a sharp sting of fire. Before he could strike at her again, she wielded Lucius's knife like a scalpel and attacked his genitals.

Howling, screaming and clutching the ruins of his manhood while he tried to stem the rush of blood from his wound, he fell away from Ruadh's pinned legs. With the speed of youth and desperation, the Celtic woman rolled away from Artorex with one part of her mind trying to protect the infant whose clamour was loud, enraged and demanding.

But Ulfin was not quite done. As Ruadh clambered to her feet and crouched warily, seeking a firm foothold in the nest of leaves that had served as a sleeping pallet, Ulfin focused on the source of his pain with a malevolence that chilled her to the bone.

Slowly, slowly, he switched knife hands. 'If you've killed me, then you'll go to the shades with me, you dirty whore,' he whispered in a voice that was pregnant with menace. Then, through willpower alone, the warrior moved at a speed that would have been impossible for most wounded men. With a quick lunge that Ruadh almost evaded, he half buried his knife in her thigh.

But Ruadh knew that he had been forced to extend himself to reach her, and her own knife slashed at his groin again so that, finally, like a lightning-struck tree, he began to topple backwards until, panting, he lay supine on the earth.

Ruadh kicked his knife away into the darkness and threw his scabbard after it. Then, smiling, she retrieved Artorex and wrapped them both in her stained cloak. She crouched on the ground just out of Ulfin's reach, knife at the ready, and waited. A few pieces of discarded wood on the fire coaxed it back to life, and Ruadh warmed her cold hands and even chillier spirits while she waited for Ulfin to die in agony.

At first, the guardsman screamed obscenities until he heard Ruadh laugh at him. Then he begged for assistance, knowing that she had been Myrddion Merlinus's assistant. When that plea met with no success, Ulfin started to pray to every god he had ever known.

'Can't you even die like a man?' Ruadh snapped. 'You've raped and murdered for years, yet you've never understood what it's like to be a victim. I plan to leave you to consider your own death once I've repaired your little love tap in my leg.'

And so, although he begged and threatened by turn, Ruadh checked the wound in her thigh and used a little water from her bottle to clean the nasty puncture. Wishing she had any one of her master's unguents, she bound the wound with a strip of her robe taken from along the hem, placed Artorex in the sling around her neck and retrieved her horse.

'Farewell, Ulfin. With luck you'll die before the scavengers find you, but I wouldn't count on it. Look out into the shadows under the trees and try to remember the innocents that you killed on behalf of Uther Pendragon and your own lust. Gorlois is certainly waiting for you, since my master was sure that you killed the king by stealth. You might just pray to him, if you think it would help.'

And, although Ulfin howled and cursed, Ruadh rode away into the early morning towards Verlucio and the road that would lead her, eventually, to the Villa Poppinidii. The wind sighed through the flat green lands, and as the sun rose she marvelled at earth that bore man's touch so fruitfully. Because she had approached Aquae Sulis on the eastern road, her directions had been reversed and two weary days passed before the gates of the villa hove into view.

Ruadh was tired, her head ached insistently and she knew she had a slight fever, but nothing mattered except for the completion of the task. When she first saw the villa, neatly whitewashed in its cluster of well-kept outbuildings and surrounded by rows of fruit trees, vegetable patches and the ploughed fields that would bear grain in the spring, she felt as if she was finally home. Even Artorex was no longer squalling, although he announced his hunger as she rode her horse up to a crazily paved forecourt and eased herself out of the saddle. Her thigh ached with a sullen, nagging persistence, but she felt herself begin to smile, and Myrddion's ascetic face swam to her from her memory.

'We made it, little king. Artorex will live and thrive here. And, with Ulfin dead, he is safe from Uther and all of the tribal kings. We are home at last.'

POSTSCRIPT

Non omnis moriar.
[I shall not altogether die.]

Horace, *Odes* III, 2

Bemused by their strange visitor, Ector and Livinia, master and mistress of the Villa Poppinidii, agreed to foster the child, Artorex, out of respect for Bishop Lucius of Glastonbury. Although she was born in Aquae Sulis, Livinia was the last child of the wealthy Poppinidii gens and her father had but recently succumbed to death, leaving her tribal husband, the bluff, strong Ector, to run the villa with a devotion that was just as powerful as her own. Ruadh, the Celtic woman who was the bishop's messenger, refused a place in the household, pleading the plight of her children who lived north of the wall. Livinia eyed the girl's pallor with concern but, out of respect, said nothing.

Frith, the nurse of Livinia's son, was blunt and observant. She persistently demanded to know what ailed the girl until Ruadh admitted that she was suffering from a knife wound. Clever with woman's medicine, Frith stripped off the filthy bandage and eyed the suppurating wound with concern. Her sensitive nostrils told her that the wound was poisoned.

Andrewina Ruadh knew the signs better than Frith, having served in battlefield surgeries with her master for several years. She had feared as much when her temperature had begun to increase, but the safety of Artorex was far more important than her own life, so she had continued onward when she should have sought treatment.

Frith applied a drawing ointment and what poultices she had, but both women knew the meaning of the livid line heading up into the groin. Frith hugged the flame-haired girl who was so brave and forthright in her acceptance of impending death.

'What might I do for you, child? I can keep you comfortable with drugs, but you will die anyway.' The elderly woman's face was still and proud below her white-blond hair.

'We shall do nothing, Frith. I wish I'd seen my children one last time, or told my beloved master, Myrddion, that he is not responsible for my death. But these wishes are only foolish, girlish dreams. I knew what could happen when my leg began to swell, but I continued with my journey. The child is the important thing, so perhaps it would be better if I simply disappeared.'

Then Ruadh gripped Frith's work-worn hands passionately and her grass-green eyes were compelling and full of prescience, although her flesh was burning to the touch. 'Protect Artorex, Frith. Care for him fiercely and with all your heart for my sake. I have loved him as if he were my own child and he filled me with new hope and purpose.'

'I'd love any babe, regardless of his appearance or nature, but when I hug him I'll speak of you, so he will always know what was sacrificed for him.'

'No!' Ruadh's voice was sharp with a terrible urgency and her flushed cheeks and bright eyes were hot with feeling. 'You must promise me, Mother Frith, that you won't burden that little boy with any guilt about my death. I understand the deadly ties of obligation, so promise me that you'll not doom him so thoroughly before he becomes a man and learns what is his place in this world. I will disappear, as is fitting, having played my small part in his salvation. That's enough for me.'

'What will you do?' Frith asked with her strange, pale-blue eyes full of compassion.

'I will ride fast and hard, for I've a wish to see the sea before I die. Who can say? For now, a warm bed and good food is all I require. I'll be gone by sunrise.'

By the next day, Ruadh was far too sick to ride very far at all. Her leg was swollen and blackening and her temperature continued to increase. Frith would have told her master, Ector, how gravely ill the younger woman was, but Ruadh begged the luxury of choosing where she met her end. With Frith's assistance, she mounted at dawn and disappeared as swiftly as she had arrived.

The Old Forest beyond the Villa Poppinidii seemed so cool and inviting to the delirious woman that she forced her reluctant horse into its dripping green depths. Careless of lichen and moss that was treacherous underfoot, or the dangers of fallen, mouldering logs, she allowed the horse to pick its own way as she dreamed in a daze of pain and high temperature. With an animal's instincts, her horse forced its way into an inner glade where sweet, fresh grass grew under an insipid sun, even in winter. But Ruadh was almost finished. Scarcely knowing that she had fallen, she struck a long, low monolith of stone that lay in a weak ray of sunshine.

When she returned to painful consciousness, Ruadh lay partly across the slab of stone, practically touching a rudimentary cup and a series of lines and spirals that had been carved crudely onto the flattish top of the monument. She had split her head when she fell, and a spider-crawl of blood had run down the spiral pattern and into the tilted cup. Bemused, she stared at the bloody cavity for a long time.

She wished she had a fraction of her master's gift so she could know if the child, Artorex, was worth the sacrifice of her life. Ruadh loved the sunlight and the darkness; she revelled in the small joys of existence, even the miseries that came with every new day; she would miss the experience of growing old, and a part of her confused brain felt a momentary resentment for the years she was casting away for a baby with compelling eyes.

'Ah, Myrddion, he's such a little boy for such a great fuss and so much blood spilt. I will miss you, my last and best love. I hope you remember me . . . but I suppose you'll forget. Everyone does – as they should.'

Perhaps Myrddion's legendary kinswoman, Ceridwen, took pity on Andrewina Ruadh. Perhaps the poison in the wound and the delirium that could only end in death lifted briefly so that Ruadh's mind was swept clean of the confusing images that clouded it. With a clarity that turned the events of her last days into a shaded dream, she saw the small glade, the blood-stained stone and the shadows that danced with every stray breeze to reach the drying grasses without the filter of pain and fever.

'This forest is a good place to rest . . . a sweet place, Myrddion. I'm dying, but it's not so very bad, and the sun is shining . . .' she whispered softly to the empty glade. Her words were inadequate for the sudden outpouring of love that she felt for the land, her family and her friends, the baby and her dear Myrddion. She continued to whisper her thoughts to him as she rolled herself off the stone until her poisoned leg struck the ground and sparked an agony so intense that she almost fainted.

'I must go . . . not here . . . not now,' she whispered, and began to drag herself painfully across the sere grasses towards the cool shadows of the trees. In that painful, last burst of struggle, she slipped and slid over the detritus that covered the forest floor as, like a wounded animal, she sought the place of her final sleep.

Then she found a nest of roots, raised out of the leaf-shrouded loam to form a twisted roof of wrist-thick, curving shapes.

The mosses that covered the ancient wood beckoned with a promise of velvet softness that would cool her addled, over-heated mind. To rest her hot cheek against that cool green bower! Only a little more effort and she could drag her body into the womb of the tree and curl into the shape of that small, welcoming space. Then, with the last of her strength, she said her prayers like a little child and allowed her consciousness to soar away.

Myrddion Merlinus hunted for Ruadh for a long time, but he was eventually forced to accept that Andrewina Ruadh, his Celtic woman, had returned to her own children who lived north of the Vallum Antonini. He never discovered that her bones became a part of a twisted knot of roots in the Forest Sauvage, and he took pleasure in dreams of her life, healthy and happy, with her grandchildren by her side.

Although he returned to Venta Belgarum in times of need to serve an increasingly dangerous and erratic king, he steadfastly refused to give his healing skills to Uther Pendragon's war machine, preferring to train apprentices and oversee the spy network that had become central to the High King's defence of the realm. Myrddion became a traveller, using his significant skills of diplomacy and his understanding of science and weaponry to drag the tribal kings into the dangerous present. With Llanwith pen Bryn and Luka of the Brigante by his side, he scoured the north, building alliances and solving old blood feuds, but always searching for the child he had given away a decade before.

In Segontium, Myrddion's cadre of friends and healers prospered and, in the fullness of time, spread throughout the west. With an ageing woman's stoicism, Brangaine mourned for Willa, although Myrddion never told her the full and brutal story of the children's execution. Other little ones needed Brangaine's big heart, so she held her sorrow close to her breast and continued to live with a calm but pensive face.

One grey day, when the winds blew bitterly across the charcoal straits from Mona island, the companions gathered on the sea dunes near Myrddion's old home. Only a tragic set of circumstances could bring these rootless warriors against warfare, disease and accident together, all at once and in the same place. The gulls wailed mournfully, the skies were flinty grey with pregnant clouds and the sea was a mad, crashing beast under the dull, senile sun. The growing white stripe in Myrddion's greying hair streamed in the wind as he hugged Finn Truthteller to his breast, while Bridie, Brangaine and Rhedyn clustered around his tall, austere figure.

Cadoc had died, untimely, of a fever caught at Canovium as he treated a household of sufferers. In death, he would finally rest within a stone's throw of Olwyn, Myrddion's grandmother, and Myrddion realised that his youth had irrevocably fled, leaving him to accept a lonely middle age.

'Do not mourn for my dear Cadoc.' Myrddion's voice was sombre, but his face was illuminated from within. 'Our dear friend lived in joy and in service to others, long after a time when he believed that his usefulness was over. The goddess took him back to herself, overly jealous of the love and laughter that he carried with him throughout the world. We should weep for ourselves, for we will never see Cadoc smile again or feel his strength at our backs, as dependable and solid as the flint of these mountains. Such friends are rare and fleeting gifts from the gods and we should cherish them while they dwell among us.

'We must rejoice, for Cadoc cannot die while one of us remembers his pleasure in each day, his compassion for those unfortunates who bleed and suffer, and his practical ability to create order out of chaos. We'd have starved to death in Gaul without him, wouldn't we? Or we would have gone afoot at Châlons without his capacity for thievery.'

The companions of the road laughed then, remembering the scarred man's loyalty and practical common sense. And they wept too, but the tears were fleeting as they shared their memories as friends do after long separations. In joy, they consigned Cadoc's body to the earth.

In Venta Belgarum, Ygerne dwindled, her beauty fading to a transparent memory of a terrible curse. Never again did she bear a child for Uther Pendragon, although he remained in her thrall although loathing her for being the embodiment of his many weaknesses. He never discovered that she quickened three times and that, guessing at the fate of any child who resulted from her travesty of a marriage, she begged for Morgan's intervention. The spark of each new life in her womb was quickly extinguished.

Ygerne prayed until her knees were twisted with arthritis as she offered the God of the Christians an earnest penance for the children she believed were murdered in her name. The queen begged her cruel husband to release her from her long service, for she hungered to enter a nunnery close to Tintagel where she could hear the sea crashing against the cliffs and watch the hawks and gulls hunting on the wind. But Uther, although impotent and coldly vicious in his jealous old age, would not even release her to God. So, frail and distant, she sat in her ruined rose garden and waited for the mercy of death.

But fate had not quite finished with the fabled Ygerne. Nor had it forgotten the Dragon of the West and the Demon Seed.

Fortuna turned her wheel once again, and time clicked forward with a sound like thunder, or with the echo of distant, future battles. Ceridwen and the Mother answered Myrddion's fervent prayers and smiled upon their children at last.

The child, Artorex, was growing tall.

AUTHOR'S NOTES

This novel has been a labour of sweat and tears, and it proved to be far more difficult than I ever expected. From my point of view, the legend of Merlin has always had some gruesome contradictions at its heart, and interpreting these oddities became my hardest task. A wise and decent man could never betray Queen Ygerne as brutally as the legends suggest that Merlin did. I could never understand the flaw in Merlin's nature that made him Uther's collaborator, for some versions of the legend suggest that Uther tried, like Herod, to murder his son by killing all the infant boys in his city in an effort to destroy the seed of his loins.

No, no, and . . . no! My Merlin couldn't be such a monster without good cause.

So, as well as creating the plot line, weaving in the legends and devising a believable Uther, Ygerne, Gorlois and Morgan, I was challenged to make Merlin into a man who does his best with what he's stuck with, a mantra that I chanted mentally, day after day. How do I avoid the healer becoming a contemptible, annoying whiner who constantly complains that Uther made him do it?

My answer was simple, but I found it quite difficult to achieve. Coercion had to be used via the two elements that I had already made central to Merlin's character. First, he worshipped the goddess, Don, who is still immortalised in the name chosen for Aberdeen's river, and she remained a formidable Celtic deity. If Merlin believed that the goddess had chosen him to create the circumstances that brought Arthur into the world, then he might have felt impelled to assist the High King. Also, through the people he loved, and because family mattered so much to the man who was a rejected boy, his companions could be used as bargaining chips by an unscrupulous High King.

At least, I've tried to explain the contradictions in Merlin's character. The reader is the only person who can judge if I've been successful.

Another challenge for me was the fact that I wrote the Merlin trilogy out of order, after the publication of the novels on King Arthur, although they are actually a prequel to the Arthurian series. I can honestly state that when I started writing the first trilogy, I wrote my Arthurian books for fun and without any real thought of being published from a remote outpost such as Australia. But the Merlin books create the groundwork for *Dragon's Child*, *The Warrior of the West* and *The Bloody Cup*, so it became imperative that the third book of Merlin should flow seamlessly into *Dragon's Child*, the first book of Arthur.

Incidentally, if you want to learn what happens to Merlin, *Dragon's Child* will answer most of your questions.

Morgan and Ulfin were two particularly difficult characters to place within my version of the legend. Ulfin assisted Merlin to inveigle Uther into Tintagel for the specific purpose of the rape of Ygerne, so he becomes a person of importance. Yet anyone who served under Uther Pendragon when he was at his murderous worst could not be a benevolent character. Hence, Ulfin becomes very like the guards at Belsen or Auschwitz. He is not entirely monstrous, because he lacks the intelligence to be truly evil, but he is a born follower who gains all his status and respect by sheltering in a powerful man's shadow. If such a flawed character should lose the approval of Uther, it would be much like losing the ability to breathe, so Ulfin would have searched for Ruadh until he found both her and Artorex. Only death could stop him from completing this quest. I decided he should die appropriately, at the hands of a woman and during an attempted rape.

Morgan did not become wicked overnight. I hope I showed that her desire for power pre-dated her father's death. In many ways, she would have made an excellent man, but as the warrior's role was denied to her, she takes power in the only way she can. After all, she lacks the glamour and beauty of her mother while possessing Gorlois's strength and determination. Perhaps, out of love for her father, she would have rejected the role of fabled witch eventually if he had survived to old age, and might have chosen the more benevolent role of wise woman and herbmaster. Hence, Gorlois's death sent her into a dangerous new search for power and revenge that would ultimately poison her life.

Botha is another matter entirely. His terrible fate in *King Arthur: Dragon's Child* and the lessons that his loyalty to the High King teaches Artor makes him a pivotal figure in my version of the Arthuriad. Botha is the only person who actually loves Uther Pendragon, although he is aware of the dark side of his master's nature. To a certain extent, The High King protects Botha and his precious honour from Uther's excesses. I found it extremely difficult to create a character who serves with Ulfin, but who is as decent as Ulfin is vile. As with Myrddion's character, I had to analyse Botha's difficult situation, which rose to a crescendo with the murder of the little girls, and marked the end of Botha's more privileged position with his master.

Readers of *Dragon's Child* will see a notable difference in Uther's treatment of Botha. The High King no longer has a brute such as Ulfin to serve as a buffer between himself and his most loyal servant.

What can be said of Uther Pendragon? In modern times, his lack of conscience would mark him as a sociopath or a high-functioning psychopath whose excesses are kept in check by his obsessive love for his brother. But that love becomes a two-edged sword, and Uther would have considered it a weakness. An oath can be manipulated, so that he feeds his demons while, ostensibly, remaining true to his promises to his brother. His one saving grace as a monarch is his brilliance in warfare and his steadfast hatred of the Saxons. Ultimately, because of his childhood banishment and the travails in his youth, Uther becomes the man he is because he has grown stunted and angry.

Today, we recognise the damage done to children if security and love are taken from them at an early age. They never recover from this early loss. Uther is as he was made by Vortigern when he lost his mother and his brother at one fell swoop and was cast away from his home, left only with another brother to provide any sense of stability. The same could be said of Myrddion Merlinus, but the healer is loved passionately by his grandmother, Olwen, who is a grown person rather than the child Ambrosius is when he becomes Uther's sole support. Just as Myrddion grows to be assailable because he needs friends, so Uther turns more brutal as he actively rejects the need for a companion. Under his vices, Uther is an impotent figure, like Morgan, because he rejects love and beauty.

The problem of his hatred of any heir is another odd part of the legend, in that transference of power from father to son was of paramount importance in those dark and unpredictable ages. Uther seems to hate the very thought of being replaced by anyone, least of all a child who is a tangible reminder of his murder of Gorlois and his treatment of Ygerne. Even Uther was capable of shame, and the birth of such an heir at such an inopportune time would have opened him to suspicion and ridicule. Besides, my Uther is a megalomaniac who hates the idea of a son who is as capable and competent as he is. He aspires to being remembered as the greatest of the Celtic war chiefs, one who can rival the feats of his ancestors. No one, not even a child of his own blood, can be permitted to eclipse or weaken his reputation. Today, he would be diagnosed as a dangerous narcissist: but then he was a man of the times, ideally suited to keeping the Saxons at bay.

Andrewina Ruadh is a complete invention sparked by a woman I saw modelling nude for a room of painters at an artists' colony is Montville, Australia. I have rarely met anyone who embodies the Celtic look so accurately. This woman also radiated an aura of steadfast loyalty and strength of character. We met briefly and, if she should read this book, I hope she recognises something of herself in the character. Unfortunately, I can't remember her name.

Ultimately, Andrewina Ruadh, the ultimate tragic outsider and heroine, has her opposite: the fragile and sometimes irritating Ygerne.

Ygerne's beauty is a vital part of the legend, for Uther Pendragon becomes obsessed with possessing her. He risks his throne to murder her husband, and uses a disguise to breach her fortress, thereby also risking his life. I once knew a woman who was very beautiful, but utterly ignorant of the nature of her looks or the effect they had on others. I confess I used this woman as a starting point in my descriptions of Ygerne.

Ygerne is not totally weak and helpless. In fact, despite appearances, she has considerable fortitude, although her relatively charmed life becomes less so when she accompanies her husband to Venta Belgarum. After all, because she is certain that her new husband has killed her son, she aborts three other unborn children. This is a mortal sin that she knows will weigh heavily on her soul. Nor does she kill herself, although she longs for death.

Sometimes it takes more courage to live.

How such a pious woman could produce Morgan and Morgause

571

seems impossible, but the girls have certainly been spoiled by their parents. She also tries to accept her gift of the Sight, although she is appalled by it. Ygerne, in my Arthurian world, is a special innocent who is also a very tragic figure.

Men ruled the Dark Ages; women could only hack out a place for themselves if they were very beautiful or very skilled. But great, good or infamous, time washed over them and they vanished from the pages of history. Only the odd, old name remains to remind us of the faint perfume of their skins, or the sheen of their hair by torchlight.

Vale, brave hearts.

GLOSSARY OF PLACE NAMES

The following is a list of place names in post-Roman Britain with their present-day equivalents.

Anderida	Pevensey, East Sussex
Anderida Silva	A forest north of Anderida
Aquae Sulis	Bath, Avon
Bravoniacum	Kirkby Thore, Cumbria
Brocavum	Brougham, Cumbria
Caer Fyrddin	Carmarthen, Wales
Caer Gai	Llanuwchllyn, Gwynedd
Calcaria	Tadcaster, Yorkshire
Calleva Atrebatum	Silchester, Hampshire
Cataractonium	Catterick, Yorkshire
Corinium	Cirencester, Gloucestershire
Deva	Chester, Cheshire
Dinas Emrys	Ffestiniog, Snowdonia, Gwynedd
Dubris	Dover, Kent
Durnovaria	Dorchester, Dorset
Durobrivae	Water Newton, Cambridgeshire (Fort bridge)
Durobrivae, Cantii	Rochester, Kent (The walled town of bridges)
Durocobrivae	Dunstable, Bedfordshire
Durovernum	Canterbury, Kent
Eburacum	York, North Yorkshire

Forest of Dean	Forest of Dean, Gloucestershire
Gesoriacum	Boulogne, France
Glastonbury	Glastonbury, Somerset
Glevum	Gloucester, Gloucestershire
Isca	Caerleon, Gwent
Lactodorum	Towcester, Northamptonshire
Lagentium	Castleford, Yorkshire
Lavatrae	Bowes, Durham
Lindum	Lincoln, Lincolnshire
Londinium	London, Greater London
Magnus Portus	Portsmouth, England
Melandra	Glossop, Derbyshire
Mona island	Anglesea
Moridunum	Carmarthen, Dyfed
Nidum	Neath, West Glamorgan
Olicana	Ilkley, Yorkshire
Petrianae	Stanwix, Cumbria
Petuaria	Brough on Humber, Yorkshire
Portus Udurni	Portchester, Hampshire
Ratae	Leicester, Leicestershire
Segontium	Caernarfon, Gwynedd
Seteia Aest	Dee and Mersey Rivers
Tamesis River	River Thames
Templebrough	Templeborough
Tintagel	Tintagel, Cornwall
Tomen-y-Mur	Llyn Trawsfynydd, Gwynedd
Towy	Towy, Wales
Vallum Antonini	Antonine Wall
Vallum Hadriani	Hadrian's Wall
Vectis Island	The Isle of Wight
Venonae	High Cross, Leicestershire
Venta Belgarum	Winchester, Hampshire
Venta Silurum	Caerwent, Gwent
Verlucio	Sandy Lane, Wiltshire
Verterae	Brough, Cumbria
Verulamium	St Albans, Hertfordshire
Viroconium	Wroxeter, Shropshire